the Sword of Shakespeare

where stories and poetry wait in the wings

this book is dedicated to those readers that think there should be more to a novel than just temporaneous entertainment, that part of the human soul should reverberate loud enough that they hear it more clearly every day thereafter.

this book is also dedicated to the great musicians, some of whose work formed the backdrop for every scene you're about to read. There's a lot more to song than just singing along; sometimes it's the other way around.

but mostly, this book is dedicated to Breah, and the hope I have of her finding a way home.

This is a work of fiction. Characters and events portrayed in this book are fictional.

Beryl
©2012 Dean Michael Christian
Published by GreenDragon Publishing
199 Highland Dr.
Bloomfield Hills, Mi
48302
[www.SwordOfShakespeare.com]

GreenDragon Publishing

BERYL

a song of swords novel

DEAN MICHAEL
CHRISTIAN

Envelope

Dark Night of the Soul

A rising sun places delicate but worn fingertips in the way of advancing tidal strings, as if looking for music suitable for dawn. An inner rush of sound threatens to drown the palpable beat of blood, rising and coursing like piano notes in an effort to win free. And there's the firm mold of sand beneath it all as an endless swell of ocean mesmerizes time.

Time. It is all we have, it is all we know and when it's gone, sometimes, even the memories can't hold on.

The fierce commitment of lunar tides did nothing but boil the breath held so desperately in his lungs, as if holding it could bring him succor. Respite; born of endless cycles man is wont to mold into thin trellises. It's what he uses to decorate the white space surrounding his blackened story's text; nevertheless, it comes at last. So the man breathes, takes in sobbing lungfuls of air, sharpened with the tang of the sea...and mortality. Upon the verge of succumbing, life wrests free from the lattice of purpose once again. But why? He just wants to let go.

The pull all around him is intense, the sand beneath forming his new skin, the texture of myriad failures and disappointments. He knows them well. He is haunted by their sting, as if they are the pincers of crabs gathering around him, also glad that the water is receding. He'd struggle against them, would force the water further and curse it's endless cycle, but he's tried this before and still he's bound to the beach.

Beryl

The ripples cascade into riptides of essential clarity, their own paths seemingly fixed and yet not. Beneath their glamour, the sand burgeons stones more solid than even his pain, though it's hard to conceive. Still, he hears the notes in his head, the ripple of fingers across piano keys, or the deft strum and pic of chords from a mandolin...

These are the stray thoughts of the day, the surge of liquidity that taunts him in delusion, an insouciant dapple of breaking dawn that traipses the silver crests of morning tides. He's taken to seeing his world this way because all other thoughts have failed to release him. Only the sea is left to mock, and it never fails to do so.

The salt works on his skin as it frets at the leather binding wrists and ankles. He knows a new breath will break its creeping hold, for a while, until the ocean swells and surges unerringly toward high tide, hungering to swallow him whole once again. He sees this with a clarity that once was unnerving. Now, it is a welcome distraction to his memories. Only when the water rises high enough to fill the voids in his head does surcease come, though it brings with it a panoply of survival skills he didn't know he had. He will not succumb, this he vows, not until his broken heart is sure. Until then, he lies supine on the beach, headfirst, pointing toward the sea where all the depths he ever feared lie waiting. He has been staked here by his enemies, though even he has forgotten what they look like.

At night, beneath the water's surface with only an ever shifting sky field to embrace, he can let his mind rest even as his body strains to withstand the suffocating pressure of death. But sometimes, that's better than reliving failed moments.

The day is hardly better as with morning, the splash of crystalline brine hangs almost motionless, high above the breakers. The eddies close rank and suppress ripples until one clear mere of truth can be seen. Turning his head violently, this is now routine, his mantra and mission; to glimpse that one clear vision of how it all ends. But the leather binds and the sand recedes beneath his neck as he strains to turn. The sight still eludes him and even as the sun breaks the furthest horizon, netting the ocean's edge with orange fire, the breath he's held is released from the dark his soul harbors. Again. One more time...

Prologue

Borrowed Time

Another pus-oozing scrap of his skin hit the keyboard, reminding Rhey that he was sitting too close. Moving back, the three digits on his left hand deftly swept to the floor the piece of cancerous skin that had just deserted his left cheek. The rot continued there, no longer minded. Still, these pieces of him that were falling away were nonetheless missed. He was coming apart at the seams, as the humans would say. The gloss of the computer screen in front of him changed focus, and he saw in its salient reflection, the tatters of facial skin hanging precariously.

It was the same all over his body and if he moved too much, the attacking virus gleefully reminded him of the consequences. There wasn't really any pain, though parts of his skeleton ached sometimes. No, it was more a silent embattlement in which he found himself. Ironic, in a way, devious and surprising in another.

They'd done this to him, those outside the white mortared stone building in which he now felt confined. Oh, he could move beyond the lab's boundaries, but as already noted, the lesions and scabrous tentacles marking his body just mutated faster. Time wasn't something in abundance at the moment. It seems he'd made a mistake with the woman, the result then altering his chance for success. Humans were more surprising than he'd thought. In the end though, it was all borrowed time.

How many had he extinguished so far? Thousands, surely, maybe millions? They were adept at hiding once they understood the breadth of his power. Not that they hadn't shown some strong opposition—he'd expected that—but almost according to the manual, extermination had gone as planned.

Until now. Or rather, until the simplest of weapons had been used against him. Not that there hadn't been a contingency for biowarfare—the practice was not unknown in other parts of the galaxy, but for some unknown reason, this particular virus was proving difficult to stave off. Indeed, already the disease had progressed beyond normal confines, hence he found himself barely able to keep the bug at bay.

It was a simple pathogen, perhaps too simple. At least that's what he tried to tell himself. When he became aware of the virus' existence though, it was too late. By the time he took measures to stop its spread, every one of his shipmates had succumbed, and where once the eradication process had been almost formality, it now hung in a balance too precarious to ignore. Too late, oh yes, he'd been too late to save his brethren. The humans hid and crawled outside the stone walls he'd chosen as his base, attempting futile resistance, but their world was already in ruin, their military destroyed and technology thwarted like flies underfoot. All but this one fly, this one bug, and even now, he worked diligently and robotically toward a solution. If only the woman had lasted longer.

Smeared with a layer of soot and the dust of blasted concrete, the windows still let in the light of another day, showing in which direction this world's sun rose. He turned his head slightly, the stab of yellow light reflecting off his green irised eyes, pupils contracting as if to deflect an assault of another kind. It showed him the destruction outside, how charred his own weapons could make a landscape. It had been a good fight; a grim smile creased lips that showed clear signs of being the next casualty of the virus. Which only made him frown and redirect his gaze; a male human lay strapped tightly to a shiny metallic table amidst a plethora of half-filled test tubes.

So far, none of his efforts had purged the human of resistance long enough so that the extraction of the virus' DNA could be had. That's all he needed, that's all it would take, but as noted earlier, humans could be the most obstinate and surprising of creatures. Threatening the life of the woman should have worked.

Holding a glass phial containing a shimmering blue elixir, Rhey carefully injected it into a bag of colorless liquid. Without acknowledging the ensuing show of rarified bubbles, Rhey was precise in waiting for time to pass and the reaction to complete. His thoughts moved from the sounds of bitter insufficiency outside, to the rattle of breath emanating from the man's chest as earlier injections took their toll. Sometimes, there was partial movement toward a solution as the man's mind grew passive. Then, the signals being sent through probes attached to his skull recorded as blue phosphor graphs on the monitors to either side. There was a threshold to breach, wherein suggestion would be mere formality. The man *would* give up what he knew, and what he knew would lead to a cure. Already, on a stainless steel bench to the man's left, a beaker of aqueous solution brimmed in waiting. Rhey had the carrier prepared but needed specific data so the encoding would be accurate and complete.

But time was frittering away and even though his kind didn't show what the humans called 'emotions', nevertheless, he was acutely aware that if his skin continued to shed, that the virus would rout his mind soon thereafter. Then, no one would care about the last alien to conquer earth, nor the human who would die on the table next to him. Time would only record an end and Rhey knew he didn't want it to be his.

Tapping on the hypodermic, a thin stream of boiling blue fluid squirted from the needle's end. Irony, again, closed a smirking hand about a peeling alien wrist. Rhey approached the human, noting the lines of hair marking his face, the greasy nest of darkness sweeping back from his temple and behind the ears. The man's face was almost florid, the rise and fall of his chest erratic but persistent. Yes, mankind could be very surprising sometimes.

The clutter of laboratory paraphernalia didn't bother Rhey at all as he strode to the man's side, noting how veins popped and writhed, as if the torment were being manifested before him. Surely the human couldn't be awake, striving to escape by hiding beneath unconsciousness. But there were ways to reach Martin's thoughts that even the scientist knew nothing about.

Martin Hennessy, second grade genetic biochemical engineer and part of an obscure wing of the land's governing body, hadn't been easy to find. Eventually though, Rhey had traced the attacking virus to this nondescript white stone building in the heart of a city called St. David, in a nation called America. The man was just another soldier to Rhey though, and as such, was treated as someone to neutralize.

And ordinarily, with such technology as he had at his disposal, it would have been an easy operation—*had* been for too many other human soldiers—but not this time. No, he had to be more careful because unlike the others, this man held something he needed, something that couldn't be lost due to carelessness. This man held the key to the code and it was only time that Rhey feared now. The source of the DNA was locked inside the mind of Martin Hennessy, the man who gibbered and slobbered on the smooth metal table. What he dreamed about was of no concern, not now, and if anything intelligible ever came out of the human's mouth, it wouldn't matter. No, what mattered was being hidden in the intricacies of the human cortex. The data was there, he knew it, and so too did his prisoner. Victim was a much more accurate descriptor, however.

A clear tube dripped a viscous yellow liquid into the man's arm through a triple stint of needles that allowed Rhey to control the man, despite the leather straps. The man once would heave and struggle, summoning a depth of desperation that no doubt would have proved valuable in another instance but not this one. Still, procuring information wasn't anything new to Rhey.

The man didn't struggle anymore, not since the mistake with the woman, and though at first Rhey didn't think much about it, later, in retrospection, he did find it odd how quickly the scientist had lapsed into almost a comatose state, as if waiting. Odd.

Rhey pushed the new cocktail of chemicals into the holding bag, watched the colors merge and change, a kaleidoscope that lasted mere seconds before the blue surged into bubbling brilliance. Once the fluid hit the man's veins, he'd know how close he was to a cure. But time was not on his side and even through alien features, a frown couldn't be mistaken.

It had been a last minute consideration to hook the man's mind to his own computer, as if maybe through a familiar medium, Rhey could find the answers more quickly. With modifications, the wire leads had been input to Martin's laptop. Even as the signals were displayed across his own screens, Rhey watched to see where Martin's mind fled. And flee it did, ever since the accident. Up until that moment, the man's mind had been holding out, bracing against the different drugs being forced into his veins, as if this soldier had undergone terrorist training at some point in his life. Rhey considered this possibility but dismissed it upon remembering Martin's life; the human was just too much of a weak link to be anything other than a lab rat, someone who apparently did have a strong sense of loyalty but lacked the backbone to fully implement any sort of strategic plan. He was the type that was given orders and didn't operate on his own initiative. At least, that's what all the data told him.

Searching through the files and folders that spiderwebbed the magnetic drives within human technology, Rhey had found out all he needed to know about Martin Hennessy. Once the virus's path had been traced back to this man, the rest had been relatively easy. The focus narrowed to reveal what motivated this human; like dissecting a dead animal, the man's life had been laid bare, especially the fact that though the original lab containing the virus had been inadvertently destroyed in one of Rhey's first attacks, there was still the creator whose mind possessed its blueprint. It had taken time though to locate Martin because the man had never been considered part of the first strategic initiative, no doubt believing as most of the other humans did, that his small contribution to the conflict would be inconsequential. Like the others, no one expected that the minor bug Martin Hennessy had created would ever be valuable enough to deploy. The very fact the man had even let the virus loose in the first place still mystified Rhey; hadn't he and his kind shown enough to cow the humans into instant surrender? Apparently not, as another piece of alien skin slid on pus-filled tracks down his right ear.

A soft sound emanated from the blue screens on either side of the table, showing change was occurring. The frown began to lift on Rhey's face even as he watched the lines transform from graphic lines describing the man's vital signs into lines of text, tapping into the core of his brain. At last, readouts that found ways past superficial data and baseline defenses...

Rhey was focussed on the text, trying to make sense of the man's delirium brought on from too many chemicals and a growing lack of hope, too focussed to notice the man's hands clench spasmodically against his thighs, as if tightening his gut. He also missed seeing the man's eyelids move over eyeballs that now swerved and veered, as if they were frantic to find escape.

But Rhey did notice the man's chest halt in mid-rise, as if a breath was being held, and he wondered at this new development. Maybe it was the piece of eyelid that slipped and partially obscured alien snake eyes that caused Rhey to momentarily take his focus off the text and curse the man. But whereas a moment before the text was a tumble of words that only needed a pattern to be understood, now letters that wove humankind's language devolved into cryptic, cyrillic characters to which no pattern could ever be ascribed. The man's brain, once being decoded, suddenly merged and formed a mesh of stability which both surprised and perturbed the alien. The lines were no longer technical data being reported from within the man's mind, instead, they flowed like strings of well-ordered text, weaving an incongruity which Rhey found all too easy to understand. The data changed and morphed, but all too easily seen was that they formed wings upon which Martin Hennessy flew. The text transposed on the screens, their blatant expression of fantasy and anxiety only too obvious. What had the new drug done?

With his jaw dropping unheeded and the skin at the corners of his mouth cracking with the sudden pressure, Rhey began to read...

Chapter 1

It Was You

Precious small bones erupted amidst a trail of sticky saliva, staining the dark granite floor. In his hands, the lowest string of his mandolin still vibrated. Beyond the last sweet chord just played, and the reverberation of large stones striking the castle wall, an intruder broke his concentration. The two were intimately intertwined; Piper had thrown up...again.

An unfortunate mouse...did Jareth sense a growing irony in that fact? The black cat's fur was soft against his roughened hand as the small animal sought to gain attention. But the external sounds had come on the soft footfalls of yet another, one which sought to awaken him from his melancholy.

He realized maybe his luck was running out, or perhaps was coming due. He sighed, cursing the fact he could handle a sword *and* a bow, and glowered at his post, high up in the west tower. Sentry duty was tedious at best, especially when under siege. It wasn't his choice though and besides, everyone on the inside had a job to do. No more songs inside warm castle taverns, now there was only singing softly to himself as the days and nights dragged into a depression of time.

In the far corner of his post stood a wrought iron candelabra, bent and scraped, sending the glow of three guttering candles up and inside a bricked-up portico. There were precious few windows now available for he and his bow, and one less view of those outside surrounding the walls.

Heedless, Jareth thrust his head outside, dismissing the possibility of feathered shafts and anyone paying attention.

Overhead, the moon was in decline, sloughing into its last phase. Darkness gibbered on the horizon. Still enough light to limn tents and trebuchets stabbing up from the eastern plain.

East; he'd never been this far before and the experience was chafing at his skin, as if a beetle whose carapace was just a bit too tight. Was this the cause of his growing unease?

The stone beneath his scarred hands was cooling, signifying a change in the weather. As if the build of cloud that was swallowing the stars to the north wasn't warning enough. The moon's current brightness wouldn't matter soon as he suspected there'd be more than the collision of rock and wall to mar the night.

He longed for respite. But he imagined many wished for this. Not for a surcease to the fighting, just a brief moment in which to breathe and gather what inner strength still existed before the last stand. The last stand—something which even the slowest witted peasant knew was imminent. Indeed, it seemed a long time since the great stone gates had been closed and barred. Jareth knew this because he'd been part of the reinforcement detail.

But respite wouldn't be had with the sky's show of brewing anger to the north. It looked like those outside the wall would bear the brunt of the storm, though. So, why did he still feel this urge to escape? More than rain was being promised from the creeping horizon. He liked getting wet about as much as his cat did, so why the sudden urge to leave?

Piper growled low, a sound others liked to call purring, but something which Jareth knew meant more than close comfort. It was a warning, the sound of a watchdog.

Stretching his hand and swooping under the cat's belly, Jareth hoisted the expectant animal to his shoulders where despite the leather pauldrons, razor-like claws pierced his skin for stability. And the cat would need it because unlike a month of past nights, Jareth was emerging from a lethargy he hadn't fully understood was lurking. How long had he been in stasis, waiting, always waiting for something to happen? This wasn't part of a minstrel's life—to wait; he tended to go where and when he wished. Such ideals didn't matter though when something deep in the night of his soul stretched, and began stirring strings of the heart.

Strings defined the pattern of his life, actually. But not now; now there was only the unrelenting assault from those outside. And his song had echoed the dismal situation in which he found himself. It hadn't always been this way, though he tended more toward sad songs than not. The reasons for this escaped him at the moment. The moment...now, why was this so important? Time. Did he sense its movement or was he the one who'd been fully stalled? While such intricacies laced up his thought, he knew too that it was time to go.

To go was an idea formed from within a dream even before that last reverberation of the walls. The seed at this point had burst from its husk, breaking past dementia and trampling reality. Go. No, more like the urgent yet soft decree from the whores up the street, those that understood he had to leave as another was coming all too soon to take his place.

Jareth gave in and abandoned his post, keenly feeling the lateness of the hour. To stay would only serve sentiment's cause and there was little chance that a change of the castle's ownership would also bring a better audience. Besides, a minstrel's survival depended on looking out for number one. The walls shuddered again, the interval shorter than he'd expected.

There wasn't any doubt that another escalation was in progress. Looking around the tower's small room, Jareth didn't see it as a place of fortitude and strength anymore but rather, as a cell. The broken and bent bars from an earlier blow reminded; they'd been the only thing holding the stones up.

But that moment seemed long ago and many trebuchet scores since. The tower really wasn't as important as the main gate—it was there the demons outside had concentrated their fire, as was expected. He thought about alerting his captain but dismissed the idea as superfluous; this tower wasn't going to stop the invaders no matter how many he put on the spit of his arrows. The city was lost and most were braced with the sword or holed up in deep shadow. Maybe both.

There'd be no parlay, not with this enemy. When the heads of those cowards who'd tried to escape were flung back over the wall, the message was clear. And even as he gave consideration to the victims, he didn't for a moment ascribe that label to himself now. Everyone-for-himself time had come and gone; Jareth was just late in acknowledging that fact. He wasn't immune to the obvious signs of torture and mutilation and had foreseen this eventuality. Lately, the homeless ways of his kind lay heavy and he was growing tired. He dismissed the stirring misgivings and strode to the window again, assessing the distance between storm and wall. There was still time.

Flee.

The word was sinuous, like an exhalation too swiftly taken by the wind. It was like an echo though, and the resonation inside was a familiarity that surprised him. There was also confusion because behind the word, or perhaps enveloping it, was a voice that sounded like a single note echoing from his mandolin.

Flee...you're running out of time.

Jareth paused at the top step, trying to separate the voice from those that now rose in hysteria outside. It had begun. He disassociated from such sounds because only the unexpected ones were important. Just like Piper's growl.

Looking back, the window taunted him, calling him a coward and a liar, no better than a thief as this new course of action went against his vow to defend the castle. Not that anyone was going to care about him or his songs anymore. The city was lost and now there were only pieces waiting to let go. Which is why he knew there was more behind the urge to leave, and it was being mirrored by the faceless voice. It was then he realized that his purpose had changed. But to what was still unknown.

The fallen pile of wood that had kept him warm too many nights, lay strewn in a pattern that spoke in mysteries more often associated with his songs—simple and effortless, yet holding something beneath the surface of which few people really understood. But Piper did and that's all that mattered to Jareth, most of the time. He didn't play his music for them as much as for the cat...and himself. Sometimes, it was the only way he could safely hold the memories.

As the sky darkened and all light coming in through the mortised stone arch of a window was extinguished, Jareth stood frozen for one near-fatal second, his eyes closed, feeling his lids raked by the swiftness of movement beneath. The realization of what was happening was astonishing. When the huge boulder hit the outer rampart and crushed in his window, the force threw him backward and down the spiral stairs. If he'd been anywhere but in the entrance, the force of bursting rock would have embedded his bones deep into the opposite wall before they too crumbled under the force. There was a reason trebuchets were feared!

Having the wind knocked out of him battled with each bruise inflicted by stone steps. This kept his momentum harshly against the curving wall. Flesh scraped at each turn and tumble, but since he didn't know when his next breath would come, it was almost a relief he didn't have to hold it.

Still, the stairs eventually ended and four flights down, bleeding and battered, Jareth groaned with every new breath, rattling the ache in his back. His eyes quickly scanned the debris, looking for the cat. The welts on his shoulder comforted him more than he let on because they wouldn't be there unless the animal had launched itself free in time.

Scanning quickly, he saw his mandolin swinging rhythmically on a wall sconce. Jareth secured it once again before he heard the unhappy mewl indicating that indeed, the black cat had survived. A fleeting grin appeared as he saw a dusty and annoyed fluff of fur clinging to a cross beam one flight up.

"Time to go, Piper."

And as if absolving the man from any responsibility for its plight, the pupils of the black cat dilated, gold-green irises glowing in the shadows. Sometimes, it was the only way Jareth could spot the cat when the dark closed in.

With a deft leap and bound, the cat caught the stair edge and slipped down the remaining steps until at the man's feet, it bunched its muscles again and leaped back on his shoulders. As Jareth took stock, noting his short sword was still at his side, he flipped the red hood of his short jerkin over his head, as if to conceal himself within the growing shadows. Night wouldn't last forever and really, he had to go.

Grasping firmly but without drawing more blood, Piper settled into a sentient hump, just another shadow looking for its corner. With eyes growing wider by the minute, the animal looked comfortable and secure even as the man increased his pace, picking his way among the new debris, looking for egress.

The rush of cool night air hit him forcefully as he pushed open a heavy stone door, the tunnel behind it leading toward the outside. The guardroom was empty—as he'd expected. No reason to inform him that it was time to leave and they hadn't. But where the others had gone didn't concern him anymore, even as he passed to the lower levels. Soon, the force outside would flood beyond the gates and he had no intention of having to fight his way out. There were easier ways to die.

He heard muted voices but for the most part, the noise of lurking storm and invading force dominated to the north. How fortunate was it that the voice in his head had spoken when it did?

Jareth dismissed such thoughts because right now was not the time for questions.

The row of windows facing west ran at intervals down a long hall which was dimly lit from burning sconces. The shadows burned in their nakedness. Almost alive, they wormed their way ahead, stroked window arches and caressed stone tiles too cleverly laid. The fortress was old, more ancient than Jareth could reasonably guess. But he knew its foundations were rooted deep into the bedrock below, its history a stalwart stone framework even as it was being threatened. There's a soul here, Jareth thought, something which hints at stronger magic than I could ever understand. But, wasn't that as it usually came to be? Such mysteries always enthralled and delighted, but they also prompted thoughts that he should know these secrets, that he should take the time to understand their nature.

Forcing the timing of such idiocy away in disgust, he urged himself forward, taking time to stroke Piper once in assurance when the animal began to dig in.

"We're not caught yet, no, not yet. Have some faith."

The sound of his words surprised him as they sped off and echoed down the empty hall, their portent chiding mock confidence. The cat didn't notice.

And there, even as he neared the hall's end, visualizing the castle's layout, he saw one of the shadows move. But was it the darkness or the sliver of mirrored steel (where none should be) that first caught his attention? Nevertheless, his hand went to his side and he began to withdraw a shiny blade of his own.

"You're going to need more than that, methinks!"

The sound of the voice brought him up short. Piper's precariously balance slipped and caused new blood to trickle beneath his pauldrons.

In the dim light of torches, a thin line of darkness oozed down and seeped toward the ugly blackness of archaic letters emblazoned across the man's chest. The pain of his shoulder was nothing compared to his astonishment, though.

From the shadows, led by the ever increasing glow of a long, basket-hilted sword, a woman dressed in lacquered black leather armor and similarly clad heeled boots, stepped toward him. She approached as if she knew him, as if the familiarity Jareth was feeling was real. He knew her. Or did he?

The woman was tall, her face drawn in shadows and milky pale skin, cheekbones high and as deeply shadowed as her eyes, which were as sharp as her outstretched sword. This extension bothered him as he recognized it was being offered in supplication. Gold irises split dark pupils amid purple shadowed lids, while long dark eyebrows arched and disappeared beneath a lustrous weave of midnight tresses. But not totally, because Jareth could see the shimmer of white that curled through her long hair, beginning near her neck and furling like a sail beneath black waves. She was stunning in a way few women ever affected him, causing his tongue to tangle. She turned her head and he noticed pointed ears that were almost too delicate for such a perilous face.

And perilous is exactly the vibration that resonated from both her demeanor as well as countenance. But something else beside the look on her face and tone of her voice was dominating the moment; as if the true meaning of seduction were undergoing transformation, this woman exuded a sensuality that Jareth felt not only within his loins but as a tourniquet around his heart. He knew then that he knew her and yet, he did not. She was the very depths of the ocean in dreams so wet they belied existence. And yet, there she was.

And he knew something else, as well.

"It was you!"

Chapter 2

Not As We

The tremors emanating through the walls now spiderwebbed beneath his feet. He took in his unexpected guest. Surely she hadn't been in the fortress all this time—nine months of siege is too long not to know almost everyone. Especially her.

"It was?"

The woman's lips piqued with her eyes, a look of confusion mixing with her originally playful jibe.

Jareth nodded, understanding innately how much trouble he was in, and it didn't pertain to the attackers outside. And why was this hall so empty? Where was everyone?

"They're probably all too busy giving each other those strange marks even as the walls are coming down!"

The woman had an easy way about her, smoothly flowing past the niceties and etiquette detailing first meetings.

"I know you."

Jareth was sure he could have said something more pertinent, or at least less banal, but he couldn't get past the woman's beauty. As she turned her lithe body and emerged from the full shadows, the slim sliver of moonlight rained a blue radiance throughout her hair, and slipped wist-like around her eyes. Her golden-irised pupils didn't seem out of place, no more than her elfin beauty.

"You should—you brought me here!"

Jareth choked.

"I what?"

The stones of the west tower took that moment to finish caving in and behind him, Jareth felt the thunderous jar as tons of rock smote the floor, shearing stairs and darkening wall sconces once and for all. Truly, it was time to go.

"Not a lot of time for this, Jareth; shouldn't we be leaving?"

He slipped his blade back into its sheath, somehow confident that this woman meant him no harm, when the sudden thought that she'd been reading his mind blossomed.

"How...?"

"No time, Love, unless you want those outside to know the answers too."

Jareth started, still unsure.

"Here, take your sword; as I said, you're going to need it. That pig-sticker at your side is meant for squires."

Dumbly, the man looked from his own side-sword to the blade the woman proffered. When a foreboding flooded over him, he hastily pulled his hand back.

"No, I can't...I don't want to."

He couldn't have explained it but for some reason, he feared touching the weapon.

The woman eyed him speculatively, surprise spreading across her moonlit face.

"Oh? Are we doing this again?"

Jareth didn't even shake his head in denial because he didn't remember ever doing this the first time, let alone now. His confusion kept the words inside.

Near his ear, Piper rubbed against the stubble of a day-old beard. When the pinch of claws dug deeper, Jareth understood how quickly urgency was transforming into danger.

"Okay, we'll do it your way—for now; the cat's right; you're going to get us in so deep there may not be a way out this time. Follow me, I think I can get us to the front gate."

"The front gate? Are you insane? Where do you think the Tuskellions are going to push hardest?"

"Didn't you wonder why it was *your* tower that got hit first, Dear? And it's not the Tuskellions you need to worry about; there's something else prowling out there, something far more worrisome than a determined feudal lord looking to expand. Better move it—their aim is getting better!"

Indeed, the force of another far flung stone smashed into the remains of the western tower, bringing rocks down on top of rocks, as if trying to smother any remaining rats in the area.

And I'm one of the rats, Jareth thought.

He followed closely as she sprinted down the dimly lit hall, swinging the sword he refused to take over each torch they passed, darkening the hall even further. What the hell was she doing? He wasn't a cat, he'd have to slow down if it got much blacker, no matter that he knew this part of the castle well. The kitchens; that's where they needed to go, not toward the front gate!

And as a fork approached, Jareth sped left as the woman in black leather turned right.

"Jareth! They've already blocked that way, the one leading to the tunnel beneath the kitchens. Someone else must know you very well. Follow me; it's the way he'll least expect."

And though Jareth heard her in a voice loud enough that he'd have sworn she was right behind him, still he kept on, seeing the light of the kitchens ahead. But long before he approached the familiar portal, the eerie silence that loomed warned him that something was amiss. There should have been others, there should at least be panic and disorder, but nothing—only silence. Maybe she was right...

"I am, Jare; what's wrong with you? I've always been here to protect you and you know it! Why would I deceive you now?"

Looking into her widening black pupils, where he now noticed a golden fire growing inside, truly she looked hurt. And yet, there was something twisting her words, like the truth not fully told. Nevertheless, she hadn't shown to be a threat yet, so why not give her a chance?

"Aye, why not indeed? Another time, you'd have dared death for my kiss!"

Jareth looked at her, wondering what the hell she was talking about. And at the same time, a surge of heat inflamed his loins, taking him by surprise and forcing blood to his cheeks.

The laugh ensuing was both bold and wicked, laced with irony and chagrin, as once again she seemed to be reading his mind. After suddenly pinching the wick of lust she had ignited, this just darkened his mood.

Glaring, which stoked the fire of familiarity still more, Jareth motioned for her to lead the way; better to have her in front.

Which just brought more laughter. She turned, and pointing with the long sword, indicated the direction of the front gate. Damn; the front gate. All hell was going to break loose there. He stiffened his back, certain they were making a mistake.

But the woman flitted from shadow to shadow, taking what light there was with her and swallowing the night. Who *was* this woman?

And as they found the lower levels, working themselves northward and away from the broken tower, others imprisoned with Jareth began to appear, their hurried rushes and scampering demeanor telling him that perhaps the wall had already come down. Soon, the king's own soldiers could be seen passing in the opposite direction, some last minute strategy that was supposed to protect royalty. Jareth even saw a few mercenaries as they eyed him darkly when he passed; was it with envy?

Jareth didn't give them much thought as he'd already determined this battle was over. Nothing like a lost cause to alter a person's loyalty.

He bumped hard into the woman, suddenly halted. Turning to face him, there was no more playful banter, not as she'd first adopted. Now, there was grim concern in her eyes. Pursing full, dark lips, the shock of white running wildly through her long braided hair began to glow. Is that where the light was going?

"Something's happened—we are not as we were; I thought you were only jesting, but I see now that nothing is sure. We'll have to talk, and soon."

More cryptic words but she hushed any response from him and motioned to continue. The courtyard leading to the center of the castle should be right ahead...

"No, we can't be seen, not in the open. There's still some safety here, the stone is shielding us. You know, this would be easier if you'd just sing. Any chance of that happening?"

Jareth thought she was talking to herself until she pointedly waited for a response.

"Sing?" His words were less sure than he hoped and he felt like the storm had caught up, engulfing them.

"Thought not—we had this out before but I hoped maybe you might not remember that, either."

Which he didn't, and tried to tell her so.

She waved him to silence, pointing with the sword toward the outside.

"We'll talk—but later. They're coming."

Which made Jareth start to doubt because other than some frantic cries, there didn't seem to be the sound of anything but rocks hitting walls—much as had been happening for months now. The damage had always been minimal, until tonight. What had given the Tuskellions the idea they could end the siege now?

"Everything is changing, Jare—what you thought set in stone is now turning to sand. The seas are flowing again—why else do you think I'm here? Not like you typically call me when your life is on track and you're not writing. You *are* writing again, aren't you?"

She arched her brows, the look hinting at tales he should know.

And truth to tell, he *had* resumed with quill and ink, writing deeper verse than the usual song lyrics and chords that wanted to escape. It was while lost in thought, drifting in the words as he liked to say, that the urge to flee had come. It was then that being so near the tower's window had seemed like folly. How had *she* known?

Jareth looked closer at her, trying to ferret the answer from behind her eyes.

Laughter, low and melodious, spread like crystal being struck by a metal ewer. The pathways once so clear were now being clouded. But the sound still wasn't threatening, and if Jareth didn't know better, he'd have sworn he heard undertones of melancholy flowing. She turned her head, almost as if to keep *him* from reading *her* mind now.

She raced ahead, working her way steadily and stealthily, avoiding large groups of fleeing peasants and clusters of king's men as they tried to maintain the idea that all was going as planned. Hell, anyone could see it wasn't, but Jareth didn't want to call them fools, no more than he wanted to call himself that. Why had he sought refuge here in the castle in the first place? Had his life been so routine that he'd needed to force a change? To let out a breath and inhale something new?

"Knowing you, Bard, I doubt it's that simple."

Jareth started to retort but wasn't even sure what she was talking about. She obviously thought she knew more about himself than he did.

"Aye, it would seem so; we'll have to go down that rabbit hole in the very near future. Seems there's much to be gained even though much seems to be lost!"

The flicker of light on sword led the way as Jareth let her riddle slip into the darkness of their wake. What was she looking for? Halting to let another group of soldiers pass, Jareth reached up and scratched Piper behind the ear, more to reassure himself rather than the cat. The nagging thought that he should be careful with this woman, that she might have motives of her own, squirmed within the miasma of confusion in which he wallowed. It didn't seem she was going to betray him, but an uneasiness still persisted that demanded answers to questions for which they both didn't have time.

"This way; it won't be long before the hole in the west wall is large enough; that's when the real battle will begin."

Jareth wondered how she knew this, then dismissed the thought almost as soon as it was birthed because it didn't matter; the urge to flee was taking stronger breaths.

The steady thrum of rock hitting stone wall reminded Jareth of drums; the beat was steady, as if there was no more opposition...

"They've abandoned the wall, haven' they? That's why no one came to warn me."

The woman paused and turned, her face solemn and pinched. She nodded slowly, sweeping her hand through the air as if the fact wasn't germane anymore.

"It was your voice telling me to flee, wasn't it? It was you."

Jareth was reluctant to move, even though her body language ached forward motion. She nodded again, but this time added a small quick smile. Damn, but she was beautiful when she did that!

Which only brought a silver sheen to her laughter, oddly endearing her to him in a way he couldn't understand.

"Okay, let's get out of here; there's nothing good about to happen and it's time to move on. The people here are on their own, stuck with an inherent weirdness I still don't understand. I'm sure it will prove more trouble than if the Tuskellions would have just left them alone."

The woman put a long fingered hand on a brass handle, pushing lightly on a door Jareth knew should have been heavy.

And yet she easily opened the portal into a back alley. Jareth's eyes widened; better not underestimate her.

"Oh, I think you already learned that lesson long ago, my Jareth!"

She disappeared outside, her fluid form beckoning him into the crisp night. Outside, the storm clouds were gathering, their arms spreading to envelop the castle.

Damn, it was going to get wet.

Chapter 3

Set Fire to the Rain

"They're coming, Adelia."

"I know," said a wizened old woman whose cloak was more than holey, like shreds hanging by threads. She took the washcloth from the basin and draped it across the forehead of the girl lying before her, a bloody gash that blackness was trying to scab.

The first woman spoke, her voice low for no reason; no one could overhear anything they said, not with the horrific slamming of rocks hitting the wall.

"What are we going to do?" She too was dressed in peasant clothing, the skin of her arms covered in strange black and gold markings, some single words, others short sentences. And if one looked close, most of her body was like that, as was the older woman's. Though, she was more vain than the older woman and kept her skin covered.

"We're going to try and get out, that's what we're going to do. It's because of this child that Fate has decided to intervene tonight; it's as clear as any golden mark."

"It's all her fault," said the first woman, who then with hardly any forethought, touched the girl's hand lightly, her fingers leaving a single black symbol, as if her fingerprints on the girl were made manifest. And indeed, it was almost so.

"Stop that—she's got enough of those already, Ida. Go on now, get her things and follow me. If we're lucky, we'll slip past the brutes even as they slip in. There's a storm coming or I'm the Great Morgoth! No time for us, not now—but if we can get the girl outside the walls, maybe we can avoid the maelstrom. Just maybe there's a chance, if she's not found."

The younger woman busied herself by gathering the girl's things, stuffing everything into a deep green pack.

"Get it all, Ida; anything left behind will leave a trail. We don't want that!"

As the older woman bent and lifted the girl, a small groan escaped and the blood on her youthful forehead seeped anew.

"She'll bleed to death, Adelia! Can't you just take it from her and we'll take our chances with the dark?"

Even in the sputtering light of the candle on the table, the sag of old shoulder and wistful shake of whitened head was evident.

"Can't; it came to her, not us. I tried once to look at it and nearly burnt my fingers even through the cloth of her tunic. No, it's hers to bear, I reckon."

Ida looked on as the old woman hoisted the girl to a still sturdy shoulder, old age melting away for the moment.

"I remember when you used to carry me like that, Mom."

At that, the old woman turned and crooked a wistful smile at her daughter, a shimmer beginning in her eyes.

"You were younger, and it was only when you fell asleep near the fire. Someone had to take you to your bed. Still, I don't think you were ever this light—hard to believe the girl is almost grown. She would have been sixteen next year, if this hadn't happened."

Ida came and adjusted the pack on the unconscious girl, being careful not to touch any skin with her own.

"She seems both younger and older at the same time; did you ever figure that one out?"

Adelia shook her head, then shrugged her shoulders.

"I think it's because of the stone, but who really knows? Doesn't make sense, but there you have it. Still, glad for it now.

Not sure we'd make it past the walls if she was any heavier. Now then, don't forget her strings; not sure she'll ever play again, but we don't want a trail, remember? The last thing we need is to set fire to the rain."

And so saying, the two women exited the small stone and wood room to be enclosed by a night whose moon was a slivered claw of light. In the sky, clouds were racing to be pricked on the same moon, promising a deluge.

The fact that the heavy stone gate was set with pulleys was a godsend or else it would have been too massive to open. During times of war or siege, the pins were taken out to make opening the gate quickly impossible, should the enemy scale the walls and infiltrate the wheelhouse where the pulley gears were housed. Jareth cursed beneath his breath though, as he searched in vain for the pins.

"You shouldn't have hit them so hard; how are we going to find the pins now?"

The man's voice was petulant, pinning their current predicament on the woman.

"Really, Jareth? You think they'd have just opened their hearts to us and handed them over, just because you asked? Not like its going to do them much good if we open the gates on them, is it? I'm sure they'd have had other ideas."

And she waved off his accusation as if it were dew on clover. Jareth noticed how frustrating she could be.

"And I'm sure the pins have to be handy; not like men are that clever..."

Jareth scowled and continued searching the wheelhouse, wondering if there were some crafty secret door in which they'd been placed. Men could too be clever, he admonished beneath his breath.

"Nay, I don't think so." She also had terrific hearing.

"Why can't we just slip a rope over the top and slide down? If there's no one on the other side as you say, then there's no danger, right? Not that long of a drop, and I've found plenty of rope there in the other room."

The lacquered plates of leather constituting her armor moved softly, subtly, as if alive on her skin. In her hand a long dagger pried at loose stones in the floor, her eyes steadily tracing lines of dust, looking for disturbed ground. It was almost like she was retracing time, searching for the scene that showed the pins being hidden. Jareth went out the door again and onto the parapet, peering over the wall between cracks in the top, looking for shadows moving below that would tell him the woman was wrong. How could the enemy *not* be out there? Surely if *he* was besieging a castle, the front gate is the easiest for moving troops in and out, even if someone had to break in someplace else and make their way to the gatehouse.

"Maybe it's because they fear the storm, Dear."

More cryptic talk, another idiosyncrasy Jareth was loathe to dismiss. He played along.

"And why would they be afraid of a bit of thunder and rain? You think they haven't already been enduring such these past nine months? I've watched them from the tower—they have, trust me, and it didn't turn their feet in another direction."

The nights had passed over and over, whether rain or clear sky, whether frozen ground or swollen rivers as they washed the moat higher, and the Tuskellions hadn't budged. Nothing had made them move. They were determined and often, Jareth wondered at both sides' obstinacy; but minstrels weren't supposed to care one way or the other. Pay was pay. A gig was a gig. Simple as that, sometimes.

It was then that Jareth found himself with the urge to write— when his thoughts could not rationalize the situation, or he couldn't reconcile an emotion. Especially the latter; sometimes, songs wouldn't take away the ache and he spiraled down into a place where only true lyricism could save him. Sometimes, it required words that were almost poetic to bring him back and balance him out. Sometimes.

It was why, when the woman had called him 'Bard', that a tendril of unease had been released. He knew a bard was much more than a singer, more than a lyricist; a bard understood that there was magic in words. Worse, a bard used them.

It made him shudder even now to think about that. He glanced at the dark-eyed woman who stretched on her knees, teasing the slim light of the moon to traipse over her shapely shoulders and down her back. He saw it limn the creases of leather armor and ply at the texture of her long hair...stop; he shouldn't have such thoughts. How did she do that to him? Like some power he couldn't resist...

She turned and caught Jareth's stare, understanding the desire forming on pressed lips, twitching the skin along restless fingers and lining the lump forming in his throat. Like she knew what was happening, like she was creating it...

Quickly, he turned his gaze beyond the walls again, trying to tangle his thoughts in case she really could read his mind. Inside, still bent seductively on the floor, the woman took her knife and slipped it between two stones, the gleam of pointed teeth touching her beckoning lips. A small chuckle dripped like honey, slow and full, toward the floor and darker shadows.

The quiet whisper, in which they'd been moving like shadows, was broken as furious feet pounded on the steps below, alerting both Jareth and the woman that company approached.

"Dammit; what now? There's nowhere to hide and I don't think these new fellows are going to be understanding when they see what we did to their friends." Jareth gritted his teeth, accusingly.

The woman flowed to her feet more catlike than Jareth thought possible. Speaking of which, where *was* Piper, by the way?

"This wouldn't have happened if you'd have brought my familiar here with me. But as it is, we don't have any extra eyes, so this was a possibility. Guess we'll have to reason with them!"

Slipping the sword from its scabbard across her back, the sultry-eyed woman grew tense, her eyes belying her cavalier attitude. Jareth drew his own sword, understanding she was probably right.

The first soldier entering the room went down with little effort as Jareth whacked him hard with the flat of his sword. The man wasn't wearing any helmet and blood leaked from one ear. The second found himself with a broken nose, toppling back out of the room as the woman withdrew her fist, the basket hilt sporting a smear of darkness it hadn't had before.

"Swiftly now, there'll be others. Help me barricade the door. We just might have to use your idea after all."

"I told you..."

"I'm just not sure how you're going to get down the rope one handed, what with carrying the girl and all."

"The girl? What girl?"

Confusion raged and mixed with shouts toward the wheelhouse. For those barricaded inside, the fear that the Tuskellions had broken past their defenses took wing.

Chapter 4

Eclipse (All Yours)

"Sure would be a good time for a song!"

The woman smiled broadly, moving to the window even as she registered Jareth's blank look, as though he knew what she meant but didn't have any idea how to implement it. Or maybe it was just the look of exasperation? Nevertheless, she wasn't one to let an opportunity to needle pass her by.

"You might want to go get that rope you found."

She looked at him encouragingly until he didn't move, and then darkened her gaze accordingly.

"Now, Jareth—they're almost past the gate."

What the hell? Who? The Tuskellions? His impulse was to run to the parapet and see for himself, knowing they had precious little time before the soldiers outside battered the door down. And even though there weren't any of the enemy inside, explaining what he was doing here wouldn't be a better option. So far, he'd managed to avoid killing his besieged comrades but the time to get serious was fast approaching. It had been a close call to keep the woman from running the second guard through the heart. Somehow, he didn't think she had that much compassion in her, should she be let loose. Still, she'd surprised him by not using the business end of the longsword.

"Tie that end to the gear. Do it quick while I secure the door."

Working the thick rope as fast as he could, trying to manage a knot he knew would not come loose, he paid scant heed as the woman went to the door and laid her hand on the iron handle. Then a peculiar silence dampened around his ears and sound turned hazy, like fog on the river after a rain shower. He distinctly heard her voice, which had earlier urged him to flee, as soft tones now. The tune was familiar even if the lyrics were not, but something stopped Jareth from totally catching the song, as if it were a moth that danced before an erratic flame. Or was it the other way around?

"Aye, almost like that; you're remembering, maybe?"

But she made no sense and he didn't answer.

"The rope is ready. This may be our only chance."

The smear of darkness flowed from the door and her face grew as unfocussed as her song.

"Jareth!"

The snap in her voice pulled him back, or pushed him forward, through the veil, but whichever, he had his full senses back. What had just happened?

"Not now, no time. Quick, down the rope. We're going to have to open the gate another way."

She held the rope expectantly.

He grabbed the end and slipped over the side, the hemp tightening as his feet fought for minute footholds in mortared joints. Too late, he realized that she'd thrown the rope on the *inside* of the wall! What was she doing? They'd be trapped!

He ground his teeth and slid down.

Above him, the rope moved, swaying erratically as the long lithe legs of the woman curled around, the moonlight momentarily splaying through her hair, firing with molten blue. Then the vision was gone and shadow enveloped them both.

Having to drop the last ten feet, Jareth hit the hard packed earth, barely keeping his balance. And before he could warn the woman above him, she reached the end of the rope and let go, falling heavily but securely in Jareth's arms. Staggering with the unexpected weight, his arms nevertheless closed tightly about her.

There was an answering crush of strength in her arms as she pulled him close. Without warning, she placed her lips on his, and sucked in his breath like it was life.

Lacking the ability to breathe, the strength too soon went out of his arms and he buckled beneath her weight, her kiss still rooted and delving deeper. His mind muddled and confusion reigned before the woman disengaged and actually helped him up. His head spun as he tried to fathom what had happened. Then the thought to curse her for her folly rose.

"Sorry Love, but it's been a long time!"

And though he wanted to glare and raise his voice in protest, he found himself too tangled by sensations hovering just beneath the surface of his skin. It hadn't been just any kiss.

"There they are; it's about time. Come, help me head them off. Like you, they think it's safer to escape out the back way."

Dammit, who was she talking about? He watched as she moved toward the west wall. There, hardly visible in the shadows, it looked like a large hump-back was working its way with a smaller man toward the ruined west tower. But why were they hiding?

Running to keep up yet trying to remain silent, Jareth fell in behind the woman and as they quickly closed the distance.

"Wait, there's danger that way!"

Jareth cursed himself for calling out, surprised at the anger.

The raven haired woman just smiled and he could see her pointed teeth in the dark. Curious gold glints in her eyes shimmered in mirth. Was she mocking him?

The two forms stopped, afraid, thinking all was lost. Jareth could see them better now and knew they both were a breath's length from flight.

"We're not going to harm you...or stop you for that matter. The castle is lost, but trying to get out that way is a trap. The trebuchet deluge on the western tower was cover for the holes the Tuskellions are cutting below."

Hell, how did he know that? He was guessing, wasn't he? Didn't matter though, not now.

With his words, Jareth could see the shoulders sag on the large one and the face of the smaller fall. That's the thing about sieges; they were deadly for those inside if the walls ever gave way.

"Why are we here?"

Jareth aimed his words at the strange gold-eyed woman, trying to reclaim the place she'd wrested from him with all her confusing ways. Was that a smirk he saw growing on her face?

But she just gazed brazenly back, her voice carrying only far enough for him to hear.

"The girl. They have her."

At which point Jareth turned back to the two and looked even closer. Girl? And then he saw through the layers of fabric and cloth as the large one resolved into an old woman, whose burden hung limply over her shoulder. The other was also a woman, looking even more despondent than the first. And like all in this land, they bore gold and black ink upon their skin.

A mighty roar of sound broke, as if the approaching storm had released its lightning, smiting the earth with pent up fury. But Jareth also knew that at the same time, the Tuskellions had finally burst through the wall.

"Quick, follow me."

Not even looking, Jareth turned and hugged the wall, angling northward back toward the gate. Still, it seemed like folly as the cries of those trapped inside drowned before the invading horde.

Jareth's hard stare cut through the night as he crept along, feeling guilt rise up as the Vesparians, those that had taken him in, rushed to stop the attackers before they were unstoppable. Right now, the enemy was massed in one place—castle arrows couldn't help but find targets, but too soon, the enemy would spread and outflank the defenders. That's when the massacre would begin. If the Vesparians had had any sort of army, they'd have sent out sorties long before this, but the siege had taken its toll and the walls had been their best line of defense from then on. Winter had never had a chance to come and soften up the Tuskellions, either. Time had just run out.

"Not this time, Jare; you'll have another chance. Right now, it's imperative you run and live for another day. We need to get free of this trap; this fortress is no longer a sanctuary."

The woman was right, and he saw the other two nodding in pitiful agreement.

"Time to remind you who I am!"

And with that, Jareth watched as they returned to the gatehouse tower, the wheelhouse above abandoned once the Tuskellions true strategy was known. For a little while, they had the stage to themselves.

"How are we going to get the gate open? Back up the rope and find those damned pins?"

Jareth sounded petulant, even to his own ears, so he let his voice dribble away. The two women eyed him speculatively but didn't say anything. They were actually more concerned about the armored woman than he was. They could only hope she knew a way out, now that the attackers were inside.

Jareth turned to the darkly glowing woman, wanting an answer but not expecting to like what he was going to hear.

"No, not enough time, Love; I'll have to do this the old fashioned way. Better hold onto something—I don't have much time for finesse!"

And so saying, she held her arms skyward, her long limbs arcing toward the fast approaching darker sky. Jareth noted black fingernails, an oily sheen beneath the moon, which also shrank away from her growing presence. Then the orb was eclipsed!

The wind intensified further, as if the words she was singing added impetus. Its sound got louder until it drowned the sound of fighting behind them. Incredulous, Jareth began to feel the storm as it blew in, the wind and thunder mingling. It was like being beneath a waterfall. The sound was deafening and he clutched at a stone doorway as the wind's fury built. Keenly aware that his cat was still missing, he glanced at the other three, noting that the old woman had lowered her burden. With a gasp of surprise, he saw it was a young girl.

A sudden spasm of pain ripped through his body as if the lightning above had struck, eclipsing his emotions. Staggering, Jareth couldn't believe the pain and began to shriek along with the storm.

At that moment, despite the deluge of wind and spikes of lightning, behind them, the enemy was rushing toward the gate. They'd been seen.

Chapter 5

Runner

She held the storm between liquid arms of lightning spears while a song burst forth from dammed lips. She thrust out her hands, shifting the air to thrash the ground before the gate. Severed from stony roots, the two halves tore off rusty hinges and disintegrated like grains of sand. Stone slid like a river, foaming the road beyond like tatters of a dress worn too long.

"Quickly now, I can't hold it for long."

She looked then at Jareth, her gaze the sharp point of distant lightning brought to the fore, consternation on her face and anguish lurking in her voice.

"What have you done? Something's different..."

Jareth stared dumbly back, unsure what to say in his ignorance. He hadn't done anything.

Yet the urgency in her question surged forward—again, tumbling his soul like rocks down a hill. Time to go...must get away...time is leaking. They were her words, but they now sounded like song lyrics in his head, and their eerie tune laced through him like verdigris and rust.

Muscles ached to move, first one step then another, but even as momentum was gained, her voice slapped at the flesh of his cheeks, a force not unlike the captive wind writhing between her upraised arms.

"Not without the girl!"

The girl...the older women—what had happened to them?

Turning was anguish as he faced bared teeth. Forward wasn't an option. The Tuskellions gusted toward him, actually propelled like leaves in an autumn storm. It was then one of the women thrust the young girl into the maelstrom of air before turning to stand on eroding ground. The glitter of sharpened steel was a glaring crest on the advancing wave.

He wasn't fast enough and the first woman disappeared beneath the arc of a scimitar, whose tip ripped storm clouds in its descent. The dark of night groaned where she'd been. Lashed by sudden rain, Jareth's cheek bled in shadows as the other woman hardly sighed when she too succumbed. Swirling inside comprehension, his body slowed and lurched to a stop as the slaughter rose to meet him next. As if the choir, the wind screamed in concerto before the sound of his name buried itself dagger-like in his chest. Through the tumult, it was clear; he must get the girl.

As fire worked the lines of her hair, the elfin woman let her arms fall, releasing a malevolence that howled in its glee. As if burst from the womb of Spring, a thousand storms wailed in displeasure. But their path was clear and they beat mercilessly at anything in their way. As if sculpted from desert sand, those behind the gate found threads of life failing into iniquity. Surging forward, those not on the ground were stripped and scoured, hit with more anguish than that from thirty-nine strokes of a cat o'nine tails.

A torn thread that still held on, Jareth stretched to where the girl lay inert on the ground, her form like a flattened flame whose candle has been knocked to the floor. She still breathed but for how long, he did not know, nor dared to guess. Slipping an arm beneath her slight form, he raised her from the dissolving ground and noticed as he did, that she was one of 'those'. Like too many in this doomed city, she bore the imprint of all her failings on her skin, in the form of spider-wick black lines, too often linked with text.   Black ink spoke to him and verses tried to form but he dismissed their attempts.   Still, he felt a moment of compassion also try to claim him as he noted she bore only black and no gold. She was more than 'one of those', she was a pariah.

His eyes turned to stone; this was her culture—not his.   He folded her into his chest, the compassion leaching to earth as if a bolt of lightning.   It was her problem, not his.   He didn't know her.

Looking to the shining woman in jet black, the question of who she was would not dissipate.   The blood of the two older women dampened the cobbles beneath his feet and he knew he should care, but nothing came.

The sting of rain pelted his skin and he clutched the girl tighter, gritting his teeth as the storm rushed past in its ache to establish its will.   Moving beyond the gate was like grinding grain into flour and his skin took the brunt of the force.   The woman, whose skin glimmered wetly as if post-coitus, bent, her form seeming to shrink in on itself.   The loss of vitality could be clearly seen, yet she was trying to stay upright.   He noticed she was mute now and no siren song issued from darkly scorched lips.   Gaining her side, Jareth's other arm plucked her haggard shape from the moment of surrender, finding her surprisingly light as well.

With the seductive beauty of catastrophe, Jareth passed through the wall of the besieged city while behind him, those that remained fought with warriors of the wind, whose spears thrust far deeper than the physical world.   With his mandolin slung precariously on his back, the road took his feet and he staggered forward until strength returned and he could carry both women more easily, as if the wind was now grudgingly bestowing approval. Whatever force of might either Vesparian or Tuskellion wielded, somehow he felt relief at having escaped a far greater might, listening even against his better judgement at the sounds within the storm.   There were voices there, of this he was sure.   He didn't want to know what they whispered though, didn't want to understand the terror being inflicted; he just wanted to escape, to be the runner. He bent beneath his burden, feeling the rain welling inside his boots, wondering why the hell he was involved.

Falling to one knee, his short sword dug painfully into the ground, holding them all erect even as balance tried to betray him. Clutched tightly and near his head, the ornate swirl of white metal glimmered in long, delicate fingers whose nails he noticed were long, black, and sharp. Even as consciousness left her, still she would not let go. Jareth glowered, remembering she'd called it *his* sword.

On the other shoulder, youthful face close to his, the girl presented a similar alabaster skin, though her eyes were not dark nor dangerous. An innocence danced on lashes, and her immature beauty was just as clear. Dark bangs of hair plastered the girl's forehead, welling out in straight shifts beneath a dun colored hood. She breathed shallowly albeit regularly. A flicker of Healing flared but he didn't recognize it. Perhaps the witch could do something.

She must be a witch—this was his first thought. But why? And who *was* she. Who was the girl to her?

Such thoughts needed to wait as Jareth was ushered forth from the falling fortress like tumbling stones beneath the rushing stream. And as such, his thoughts became just as jumbled. A slight shadow, Piper burst from the clutter behind him.

He sighed, understanding that breath was leaving the stone walls of the castle; he knew few could withstand a gale like the one he'd just witnessed. Uncharacteristically, Jareth gave thanks for being one of the survivors.

Chapter 6

Angel of Mercy

The change was hardly noticeable at first. The road wound down and down, then turned and flowed out toward what looked like the city's edge. And though Jareth knew there should have been scorched earth and ravaged ground for miles, such details eluded him until he was in the middle of the change. It was a slow, thoughtful exchange of detail; where lines of the enemy should have been evident, only tendrils of familiarity existed as skeletal remains held a tapestry that hinted of once being stone. Yet, there *was* stone, only now its shape seemed at odds with his remembrance, as if each scene's core was being altered.

He rubbed tired eyes, looking again at the ruins that ran like streamers on either side. That there had once been an outer city wasn't in question—that its architecture was different, was. Ramparts of towers and crenelations where archers used to wait, merged into twists of corrugated wire, ravaged by huge slabs of flat stone, pebbles embedded by the gray cement of intention. There'd been an order to the ruins, this was all too clear; their straight surfaces were broken by portals lined with broken glass and molded metal, like nothing he'd seen before. Or had he? The memories bubbled, troubling him with doubt. And where there should have been no trees, scabs of twisted stunts dotted the plain ahead, obscuring a horizon which once hinted at mountains. At least, from the heights of his western station, they'd always been there. Perhaps the dawn would bring surety again. He hoped so.

The two women, one full-bodied and mature—whose dark eyes and gold-ringed pupils still haunted him—and the other whose youth was almost as grave as truth—and whose waif-like demeanor mocked him—grew to be a heavy load, but he kept moving. Though the storm had been left behind, its mystery had not. And as sure as he was that he had to escape the castle, an anxiety still pressed like never before. It wasn't the reasons for leaving that worried him, it was those that urged him not to. Perhaps that's why he'd not questioned the witch in the moment, perhaps it was why he hadn't just dropped both by the side of the road and gone about his business. Some riddles needed understanding, and he deemed this was one of them. That the dark-haired siren was a witch, could hardly be denied, nor that she belonged to a riddle in her own right. Or a mystery...

Ahead, looming like the side of a mountain, a large structure blotted out the scant sliver of moon which had emerged from the storm's wake. It let him see the strange terraforming with more clarity, while he put distance between himself and the besiegers. As he approached, more smooth, gray stone rose and arched toward the horizon. Gradually, he realized it was some sort of bridge, spanning the gurgle of water ahead. Had there been a river so near the city? For some reason, he couldn't recall.

Rounding a huge pillared entrance, Jareth ducked beneath and into the arch of shadows, the weight of his burden suddenly a concern. It was time to rest.

It was more than an hour before the pale skin of the witch warmed with the glow of a small fire, tendered from the scattered remnants of slaughtered trees littering the riverbank. The fact he didn't recognize the white wood was something he wouldn't admit aloud. Still, it burned like any other wood, and the warmth was welcome. He kept the flames low just the same; no need to let others know of his presence, especially when he wasn't sure where he was or where he was going.   He hoped the witch might illuminate the former for him, if she ever regained consciousness. Which was slow. So slow in fact that he had time to lean on the comfort only his music could bring. Idly, he wondered if it was the light notes of his mandolin that had finally awakened the woman. He let one particular note linger as he discovered her obsidian eyes watching him. How long had she been awake? No telling, and he wasn't sure he should ask.   He waited for her to make the first move. His fingers moved across the strings not without thought but automatically just the same.

"At least that hasn't changed, though I see you've switched from percussion to strings; I kind of like it."

Jareth eyed her with both interest and wariness; she still hadn't explained who she was, or where she'd come from.   Not to mention what happened at the gate.   How should he pose his questions so as not to break this new and budding relationship?

"Oh? Now you want to trust me? That's rich."

Jareth stopped playing and looked steadily at the woman, her face flushing with more than the fire's glow. So many emotions vied for attention that he knew he could get lost too easily. He decided to err on the side of caution. How she got into his head was only the first of his worries. No witch he'd ever heard of could do this.

"You were never this pensive before...do I need to worry more than usual? And stop calling me a witch...you know I'm not."

The woman rose to a sitting position, plying at her body as if looking for signs of abuse.

"I didn't touch you."

The liquid ebon of her eyes swirled, admitting the gold to flow more freely, and it took an effort for him to resist their silent calling.

"I see some things don't change. Still, at least I'm not locked completely outside; you know me even if you can't remember.

Perhaps I should let you know me all over again? And you *have* touched me—and me you, but you'll just have to take my word for that. I wonder..."

The look in her eye turned torrid, igniting a flush of color that rose to his face even as it fused southward as well, hardening more than his thought. She was the epitome of regret, the well of unimaginable ecstasy and the doorway to a prison. Each feeling rose to suffuse his confusion with a lust so keen he hurt. Damn, but he could feel himself knowing her, owning her, and wanting her.

She smiled a wicked grin and tilted her head back insolently, daring him to fulfill untold promises. *Did* he know her then? Why did he ache so unmercifully?

"Because, Darling, we belong to each other; me to you and you to me. Because, though the world seems to have changed, we have not. At least there's hope in that."

"Who *are* you?"

Rising tall above the campfire's flames and stretching into the pale moonlight, she pressed her hands against a leather-worked breastplate, hands enfolding more than a hint of yearning. The pout of her lips held more than mischief. When she smiled, small, sharp teeth jutted against a lower lip swelling with burgeoned desire. Sweat began to form on the minstrel's brow.

"Who am I? Shall I tell you, then? I wonder if it wouldn't be better for you to find out for yourself. But then, would the result be more to my liking? I wonder..."

She came to where he sat on the far side of the fire, his mandolin having slid to the ground and his hand too aware of how close the hilt of his sword lay. Could she read his anxiety and taste the fear welling?

But the dismay that overcame her features flooded as shame into his heart, and sorrow wriggled to the fore. He had no right to make her feel this way...did he?

The sultry look in her eyes melted, hidden now by a deep despair. And take upon himself. Why was he feeling this way?

"Because, Jareth, you're a bard; it's in your blood. Would you know any other way?"

And she laughed, though it was far more sad than mocking. Bending, she leaned close, her face almost touching his, noting his gaze pull abruptly from the shadow of her cleavage before locking on her own eyes.

"Some things don't change, as I said!" This time, the laughter held more than a hint of wickedness.

"Why do you call me a bard?"

He heard his voice and it sounded like it came from a great distance, as if a separation that needed to be closed.

"*A* bard? Oh, so maybe the idea isn't known here, wherever here is...that part is quite bothersome; always before, there were no restrictions. But, imagination is like that, isn't it? Sometimes, even the creator cannot define it. Still, can't say I like it—not yet, anyway. I hope you at least have a handle on its purpose. You do have an idea about that, right?"

There was more anxiety in her voice than either wished to hear.

"I'm not sure what you're getting at."

She lifted her hands to his face and he found resistance had fled; something about her strained his nerves in ways that he both loathed and desired. Which only made the ardor in his loins rise further.

"Maybe I shouldn't tell you who *I* am if you're going to deny who *you* are...maybe this is all part of the purpose? And exactly what is it this time? We aren't going to repeat history here and have to go through all your feelings of insecurity again, are we?"

But the way she said the words belied her excitement. He knew only too well that it was something she'd relish—to repeat whatever history they had between them.

"Oh, to find that initial magic—wouldn't that be interesting!"

The way she looked at him almost brought him to his metaphorical knees; he had to stand up, as if forcing the tightness lurking in his muscles to expel would also allow him to breathe normally.

For a moment, he felt the emptiness of her fingers leaving his skin. There was a hollow pang somewhere in his soul which called out for surcease. The longing only increased as she backed away and folded into the creases of night that hovered near the edge of the camp. He didn't want her to be that far but fought the urge to follow.

She turned toward him, moonlight racing down her cheekbones and limning her delicate jaw before disappearing into the milky softness of her neck. That she drew him to her was obvious; why was he resisting? Was there something more utterly dangerous about her than just passion? He tried to push the questions ahead of his feelings. He repeated his question.

"Why do you call me a bard?"

She gave him an appraising glance, undressing him almost in the same way he surely had done her.

"Because you are, of course. But not just *a* bard, *the* Bard. It is a notable inclusion to almost everything you are or create. It just is. Now, *what* you are? That's perhaps the real question needing an answer. But don't worry, I'm not going to address you by your title all the time—that would get pretentious and you know I'm anything but!"

Jareth tried not to let either her demeanor or candor get to him, but he found himself wallowing in delusion—or was it denial?

"Don't know what I am, but my name is Jareth Rhylan and I sing the songs. This you apparently already know. You also know my name but I don't know yours."

The woman had gone to the girl, her hands searching for something. As she did, a soft glow glimmered from between her long fingers, firing the gray of unconscious skin into pulsing pink.

It was strange that he hadn't noticed how sickly the girl looked before now. But then, the myriad black tattoos tended to get in the way. Already, he could see shallow breath becoming more hale and whole. The girl now looked to be in a deep sleep and not comatose. She also had a recent welt near one ear.

"So, you sing the songs? Well, that's certainly within the confines of your nature, Jareth, aye? Reminds me of when we first met—might be more to this than I thought. It was Jason, then, but I'm sure you don't remember. And too, there's the matter of your real sword."

With a nod toward the long rapier, she watched as he switched focus, noting the sudden swelling of the man's pupils. He did seem to know a connection existed but was visibly unaware of how to define it. But, she could.

Yet she also saw ignorance play behind sea-gray eyes—no, more silver-blue. There was a vastness there which she knew only too well, depths that haunted them both.

Jareth shook his head, wondering what kind of spell she was trying to pull over him.

"You're not paying attention, Dear; I've already told you I'm not a witch. Though you might not understand the distinction, Fae are much more than that. Better you get that straight right away— will be easier as we go along. And like you, I'm far from ordinary; my father is a god and to my people, I'm a queen."

Queen of the Fae; was this supposed to mean something to him?

"It should, but I guess you've forgotten that too? This is surely a strange time you've placed us, Love. Are there other surprises I should be aware of?"

But Jareth still felt like he was behind in the conversation, or she was trying to play him for a fool. Which only began to stir his anger.

"Ah, That hasn't changed; still haven't got that under control, I see. Well, I can use that to my advantage—angry love can hurt so good, methinks!"

Her laugh once again held a note of malicious wickedness he found hard to resist. She exuded a seductive quality that both excited and rang warning bells.

"Oh my yes, we've had plenty of both, I think!"

Jareth thought he'd force the conversation away from himself and with it, gain breathing space. He hadn't realized how much he was holding his breath when she spoke.

"What's wrong with the girl?"

"Her? Nothing that I can see, except for the bump on her head. I'm not the one singing these verses, it's not up to me. But, she's bound to your story in some way, that's for sure. You claim the title of minstrel, right? That would presuppose that you don't know how to use that sword."

Again, she'd turned the talk back to him.

"You don't live long if you can't fight."

She eyed him speculatively.

"You feel a need to fight? Is it strong?"

Jareth wondered where she was going. Surprised, he heard himself further the introspection.

"Not as much as I feel the urge to flee."

Now, why had he admitted his fear so readily to her? He didn't really know her motives yet, did he?

"I know—it's strong within you right now and I'm glad; saved your life, you know. Though I'd like to think I had a hand in that."

Jareth considered her comment.

"You're still full of unanswered questions. Who are you, Queen of the Fae? And what I especially want to know is why you helped me escape from the castle."

Her form seemed to grow as she stopped administering to the young girl, standing to look him full in the eyes; she had this way of holding his attention while part of him tried to hide from her gaze.

"But I have, Jareth; you just don't remember. You call me lover, but always, man and myth has called me the Dark Muse. Leanan is my name, given me by my father Mannanan. I am Sidhe."

Here she paused, as if that should mean something.

"As to why I helped, well, consider me your angel of mercy. If you look deep inside yourself, you'll know that you know me, though you don't seem to know why. That's because I'm the one you run to, Jare, when all the feelings inside you can't be contained. As I said; you belong to me."

She fell into the void of Jareth's silence as he tried to fight off mixed emotions surging at her words. She spoke truth and yet, something was missing, some elemental omission of which he should be aware. But the answer would not come in the moment and he fell back into her words, wondering how much to trust her.

"You know the answer to that one too, Jareth Rhylan; now go down to the river and fetch some water. I need to awaken the sleeping beauty here or else one of us is going to be carrying more than just a sword. You're not going to like who that one turns out to be, so don't dawdle."

She let her mischievous chuckle slither inside his head even as he found himself moving to follow her orders.

"The girl has a slight fever, something which you could easily dispel, but I doubt you're up to understanding that riddle just yet. For now, I'll have to do it the hard way. Hurry as we should be going; no telling how long until pursuit begins. I have little hope they'll think you died in the castle. I heard the Hounds, so don't think too hard."

She cast an eye first back toward the burning light of the castle, and then at the dark road winding beyond the river. They'd need to cross the bridge and only the man knew what awaited. But there'd be no thought of leaving him; that too was only his purview, an annoyance she too often chewed upon.

"This night won't last forever, Jare; we need to be moving before the new dawn. There's still a purpose to recover."

Dismissing his protestations before he could voice them, she turned her attention back to the girl, watching the man hesitantly disappear outside the protection of the stone arch. Placing one long nailed hand on the cold support column, she understood his reluctance; too much was not the same—even she felt it, but for now, her own doubts lay squirming in consternation. One problem at a time.

Jareth slipped down the bank, his canteen in hand, his thoughts on how easily the Dark Muse merged with the shadow of the overpass. Dark Muse indeed...Queen of the Fae...daughter of gods...all of which didn't shed much light on what was happening. Still, somehow, there was a link between them and he knew it. The water gurgled consolingly, its countenance hardly darker than his at the moment.

He glanced back one more time before the camp was shielded from view, noting she was as dark as night...maybe that's where she'd come from in the first place...

Chapter 7

Dream

As outriggers of the storm swept ragged tatters of their sail across the stone bridge, Jareth was busy beneath keeping the fire from going out.   When the girl's fever wouldn't break, he was surprised to see Leanan's anxiety rise. He'd decided not to call her by either of her titles as both seemed absurd and pretentious—though she assured him that she was neither.   For now, he'd just accept her story.

The night went on with little sleep to be had.   As if just wakened from dream that once held him securely, his mind would not conform to his body's need for rest.   He spent much of the time watching the women from across the fire, noting that once Leanan determined she could do nothing for the girl, that she then watched back. Which initially unnerved him. He wasn't sure of his thoughts to ask the questions that still needed answers, and wasn't going to play at the woman's game, whatever it was.   So he set about securing the fire and honing his blade. And when that was done, he found his sewing pack and began to mend the rips in his boots.

Still, when that was finished and the night seemed bent on prolonging itself forever, he found he could not keep his eyes off the woman with the gold-ringed eyes. Which of course made her smile even more wickedly. Finally conceding her persistence was greater than his, and with thoughts beginning to relax into emotions, he took his six string mandolin from its place by the fire and softly strummed a tune that would not be denied. It was always thus though, and he was only too aware of it. When song needed singing, it practically ripped at the seams of his soul to get out. Like nothing else, when he put his thoughts and heart into melodies, the cradle of peace could be had. And if ever a night needed such peace, this was certainly turning into one.

So he sang. Softly at first, something more like nonsense than any real verse. The notes of his instrument lifted off the flickering flames and once untethered, were swept into a river of wind, one that displayed much angst at not being able to get at the camp beneath the bridge.

"I don't remember your voice being so deep, Jare; it's nice, like a dream...I like it."

He didn't stop playing but his voice faded as he took in her huddled form, the dark leather looking far from warm to him.

"There's a goat's hair cloak in my pack; do you want it?"

Gold flecks suddenly swirled inside pupils of black, glimmering for a moment before dying back into slumbering shadows. She smiled and he couldn't mistake how honest she looked; maybe she wasn't more than she pretended to be. Maybe.

She nodded slightly and he set the mandolin down carefully, the last note still clearing the underpass.

He draped the cloak over her shoulders and noticed how difficult it was to resist sitting down beside her. He wondered why he resisted at all...

"It seems your voice hasn't lost its touch, even if there's a shallowness in what you sing, Jare."

Now, why did she have to be antagonistic?

"I'm not; I'm noting a fact. There's more inside you than you are admitting. Those songs you sing are the merest flicker of the candle that resides inside you, Jareth. You're only seeing the tip of the flame. I wish you'd serenade me as you used to..."

Jareth stared hard at her, but she avoided his eyes for once, which only made him wonder all the more. Like he used to? Well, she did say they belonged to each other. Could there be some truth to that? The undeniable urge to avoid this question was founded in wariness, something which he never ignored.

"Aye, I see how it is now, Jare; I hadn't realized how immersed you've become in this new guise. Can't say I like it any better, though; at least there was a sense of honesty between us before...not like it is now. But maybe that's part of this story's purpose? To find that thread of honesty?"

Jareth strummed lightly across the strings, wondering what she was talking about—again. There were truths only she seemed privy to and this bothered him.

"We need to leave before morning, rain or no rain, Jareth."

His fingers stopped as he contemplated her words.

"Says you? I didn't know our roads were twined."

Leanan arched her dark-lined brows, her eyes gaining luminance all their own. The set of her lips though was anything but sure.

"You want to be here when they come?"

Her tone was less petulant than it was calculating.

"You won't even take up your sword; how are you going to withstand that which comes?"

He lowered the mandolin, his anger beginning to bristle.

"The Tuskellions? I hardly think they'll be tracking one poor minstrel. They wanted the castle, they got it; war's over. As the wheel turns, so too does the new landlord over the Vesparians. And in time, the Tuskellions too will be vanquished. It's how it goes, over and over."

She glared at the man, as if unable to believe he was questioning her in the first place. The flush of color to her cheeks surprised both of them.

"Oh, they're surely coming; you can bet on it."

"And you know this how?" Though, Jareth conceded that she'd been right about the front gate. And she knew more about him than she should, which might mean she was telling the truth.

"The wind brings me many voices, Jareth love; once, you too could hear their words. Much has changed indeed."

He was about to scoff at her claim but the sudden image of her arms holding the storm's fury at bay until she needed it released, surged up and stopped him.

"You should see what I can do at sea; you might not be so quick to question, then!"

As if to underscore her words, the driving rain swept almost to the campfire's edge, its lash cold on his neck. Something told him he probably didn't want to see that at all.

"So why will pursuit come? What do they want with me?"

Seemed an honest question, if she could answer it.

"Oh, the Hounds are not Tuskellion, though no doubt we'll see their cloth as disguise. It is part of what's different this time; I can't see as far as usual. So, there's more choices than even I can fathom. I find it ironic; once, you tried to get *me* to understand mortal choices."

Her laugh was full of the irony of which she spoke.

"Mortal choices?"

She picked her gaze from the fire and placed it squarely on his even as he fingered the hilt of his sword, a sudden danger lurking too near. It was an instinct which he'd come to trust.

"But what you failed to understand even then is that I didn't need to understand; I'd already chosen. Didn't matter if that bent the rules."

Jareth's eyes began to widen as the depth of her words was beginning to penetrate, as if some of the hidden answers were becoming known.

"What is Sidhe?"

She repeated his question, surprised he was only now feeling the truth between them. The bond they shared was surely more fragile than she'd imagined. What had happened to him? Why all the amnesia?

"Sidhe belong to those tales your fathers call myth, folklore, and old-wives tales, Jare. The Fae are your fairies, and not the ones in the children's books, but those that haunt your adult mind. We're not bound to your world, not by you, but by our own whim. You see me because I want you to, not the other way around. The others see only my effect—what I do to them if I so desire. And if it weren't for your magics of religion and science, we'd still rule the heavens and all the land beneath. Still, don't begin to forget that you belong to me."

Jareth stared at her in disbelief. He'd heard about magic but even the rumors were rumors that never could be confirmed. The nearest magic had ever touched him might be said to be in the feelings certain songs evoked. But even then...

"That's the one constant I'm banking on, Jare; at least in that one area, you're the same."

She lowered her painted eyelids and long dark lashes detailed her high cheeks with textured shadow.

"Though your face is changed, you're still the boy with silver eyes; this is what makes me sure."

"Sure? Of what?"

"Of you, Love, of you! And of course, I heard your voice. You called and I came, as I always have and always will. Like I said; I belong to you. Don't forget that, either."

She grew silent as her words settled upon them both. The flames guttered but Jareth didn't notice.

"But I didn't. I don't even know how I know you, despite I understand this familiarity. I didn't even know your name..."

But another question nagged at him even as he was trying to couch all her words in a more practical context. The implications of what she was saying surely boded ill for him, and that was a worry. He was a loner, someone who took care of himself; he didn't need anyone else, and didn't want even the shackles of friendship. A minstrel had only one god—money. And the tool of his trade—the mandolin—was his lover. Everything else belonged to those living for something intangible, something swathed as love or caring, as family or promise. And the only promise he cared to honor was between himself and his cat. Who by the way, was even now curled happily asleep on his lap. But his music often had that effect on Piper; it didn't take many chords to entice the feline from wherever he was slinking at the moment. His earlier songs had brought more than emotional comfort, they'd summoned his only real friend.

"Still, you know you know me, even if this story has faulty lines. And your songs affect far more than just that damn cat, Jareth love; but you'll have to trust me about that. In time, maybe you'll even see the depths whose ends are hidden from me. In time."

"Why are you telling me all this? And stay out of my head! Fairy, muse, witch, whatever; I didn't ask you to help me, I didn't call you despite what you think, and in the morning, you and the girl will have to find your own way. I don't need any help and I don't want it! Whatever scheme you're working, you can just find someone else to extort!"

While the suddenness of his anger surprised the man, Leanan merely took in the tirade, absorbing his emotions as if she were a sea sponge. And though she felt a flash of anger herself, she stifled the urge because she understood it was what Jareth did. And it was why he needed her, despite his protests. When she spoke again, it was as if time had thickened, like a river of honey was moving before them both. Still, her voice, when it came again, was softer than she could remember in a long time.

"Sing Jareth, sing to the savior of your soul. It is in that truth that your true nature lies. So, sing, sing...sing of healing, something both you *and* the girl need right now."

But while he heard her admonition, and recognized the softness of her tone, he was already lost in the revelry of words that needed to come out. He sang but it was not at her bidding, not for her consideration, and not to ameliorate any of his harsh words. He sang because it set his soul free and right then, it was what he needed most.

Chapter 8

Jar of Hearts

From the square stone hillock, through his battered scope, Jareth swept the eastern horizon yet again, cursing the morning for being even more obstinate than the night. If he looked behind him, he just knew both women would still be standing where he'd left them, directly in the path of pursuit, pursuit he wasn't even sure had a name. He cursed again, remembering that hour after dawn...

The new day had come with little more than an hour's sleep before the woman was shaking him awake, an expectancy on her face that suffocated his implacability. And so he arose in an awful mood, the surety in his head matching Leanan's warning; pursuit had indeed come. Not with the sound of hunting dogs, but as the rumble of heavy machinery on the road. The tremor he felt through the ground had re-directed dreams long before she'd roused him. Piper hissed once at the sound and slid off into the underbrush.

Yes, even the girl was now awake, though far from coherent, judging from her rushed speech and crouching terror upon seeing them both. And whereas he was more than happy to ignore the girl's hysterics, Leanan dropped much of her haughtiness and assumptive air to try and comfort the waif. But each time the fae tried to touch the girl, whimpering and wailing was the result. Which made no sense to Leanan until Jareth took notice.

"She's afraid you'll mark her."

Leanan eyed the man in confusion.

"Mark her?"

"Aye; see her skin? All those marks aren't natural—that's part of her weird culture. When you fail, or are deemed one, they're quick to mark you in black. For each success or good thing, gold is your reward. They let you know what they think and they do it permanently—in symbols, lines of text, or just some damned mark. But whichever, you'll notice she doesn't have any gold on her. Means she's an outcast, someone who's never done anything right, not by Vesparian standards at least."

Dark eyes flamed amidst golden fields, as if the very thought brought on by Jareth's words were fiendish in ways even she couldn't fathom. But then, maybe she could. Jareth noted the grimace on Leanan's face turn suggestive, like a sneer.

"Like a jar of hearts."

Jareth caught the muse's words, even if the girl didn't.

"Like I said; weird. Never did understand that part of their society. They've even tried to mark me."

"Is that where you got the tattoo across your chest?"

The girl spoke, uncertainty in her trembling.

Jareth followed the girl's stare, her words indicating the strange amalgam of symbols on his chest. It wasn't that he didn't know it was there, but rather a sudden remembrance of why.

"No, your people didn't do this; mine's self inflicted."

And that's all he'd say about it despite Leanan's knowing look. Turning back to the young girl, eyes almost as dark as the fae's, the muse attempted to soothe the growing fear.

Jareth watched peripherally as he broke camp, preparing to hit the road again. The witch wasn't very good at comfort, and he wondered exactly how she'd been such to him, in another time, according to her. But it didn't take long to solve the riddle. Mothering wasn't Leanan's specialty, unlike seduction.

"Jare, we don't have time for this..."

"Nor are you good at it."

She ignored his comment and continued, haste lacing her words.

"They're coming—we need to go!"

"Aye, I hear something heading our way, though no war engine I've ever heard makes that kind of sound. But where I'm going, I'm not worried; it's hard to track a single man in the woods while making that much racket."

"You're leaving us?"

Though there was a note of incredulity in her voice, Jareth didn't hear any concern, as if she already knew the outcome of this debate.

"There's the road; it runs in two directions. I advise getting off it though, and staying parallel just inside the forest's edge."

"Jareth! You can't! You need me, and this girl has something to do with your purpose here!"

The man pulled the pack onto his back, the mandolin strapped tightly, and whistled sharply for Piper, who hadn't been seen since dawn.

"My only purpose is to find myself another tavern, someplace where the music is rare and the wine more so. There isn't any mystery to that, and hardly involves either of you. You say I need you but I don't; you say the girl's destiny is linked to mine, but I don't see it that way. Whatever you're trying to do, it'll be without me. There's only one purpose that I can see, and having escaped the siege, it would seem to be accomplished."

Leanan glared at him, her fist suspiciously near the pommel of her knife. In her other hand, she'd picked up the basket-hilted sword again, as if it was her only real possession. And indeed, as he surveyed the two women, they hadn't much between them. The beginning of a misgiving started and he squelched the emotion with the hardness of his heart. He didn't need either of them— they'd surely slow him down...

"Here; take the canteen and follow the river. I'm thinking that the approaching machine won't like water much. You should be safe near the banks."

And so saying, he unbuckled the water jug, pitching it unceremoniously at their feet, while the young girl leaned against Leanan unconsciously, understanding what the minstrel was doing; he was leaving them to fend for themselves.

"Jareth; what the hell happened to you? Are you forgetting who I am? Even if you don't know who you are, think about how I know so much about you. You think this is not fated, that this is all about moving from one hiding place to another, finding a new audience each time? Is your conceit so strong that you can make it through life alone? Is that the ultimate truth? Think about it...feel what is lurking in your heart, Jare!

You've been down this road before, you know where it leads...don't let history repeat itself! Though you don't believe me, indeed you've called me here, and this girl too, though I'm not sure how or why yet. Still, you did so with some dangerous limitations; I won't be able to save you this time unless you trust me. And there's the irony, no? You, having to trust me. As if such a thought hadn't entered your head a thousand times before. And in this moment, it's something you need, *I'm* someone you need. Don't harden your heart, Jareth Rhylan; there's more going on here than either of us can really explain."

So now he scanned the distant lines of his vision with a growing suspicion that maybe the witch was right; he didn't know the way as he should. It was as if the scene was changing before his eyes, that the fields and forests of his youth were being rearranged. The castle, a plume of dark smoke still rising above distant ramparts, looked the same, still clung to ground with which he was familiar. And yet, when he tried to recall the lands to the south, there was a void. The skies to the east were darker than he thought they should be, the vista in that direction pocked with holes of doubt; what really lay that way? He reached out a hand as if to nudge the offending landscape, to uncover paths he knew should be there but weren't.

And there to the west, two still figures waited, rooted to the hard gray slab connecting one side of the river to the other. The girl wasn't making any noise now, none at all—he had better than decent hearing and only the sound of advancing mechanical tracks could be heard. Even as he contemplated the girl's silence, as he scoped the face of the fairy woman whose head was still defiantly looking his way, the muted intrusion of baying hounds tickled at the back of his neck. As if that sudden urge to go—to find 'home'—had returned in earnest, Leanan's words came back like an echo and he knew what he had to do, even if he was loathe to admit it.

The road widened to the east and narrowed to the west but both ways were arrow straight and immutably sanitary. Both ways were shrouded in mist at both ends, thanks to dawn, which was still in the throes of lifting. But the bridge where the two women waited, went to nowhere; just an expanse that lifted its head and arched over a spillway filled with too many cobbles to count. Nevertheless, even as Jareth turned back and approached the junction, he couldn't help feeling a twinge scratching at his inner armor; it was a knowledge bound in fear—that he really didn't know the way, whether it be home or temporary sanctuary. The further he'd moved from the bridge and Leanan, the more doubt grew, and with it, an odd sense of displacement. Though he didn't really trust the witch, at least his thoughts were grounded around her, unlike how they flitted and fluttered now. In a way, he felt sorry for both of them, but covering all his emotions, he knew the two couldn't be left to face what advanced upon them from the road. Carrying both last night surely should have taught him that.

But what made him return he couldn't quite say, and he wasn't very happy when he saw Leanan's face break into a grin of I-told-you-so. He let her know his displeasure with a glare that would only permit silence.

"Don't say a word—either of you. There's naught but mist to the east and machinations I can't describe to the west. South is like a deep hole in the sky where stars go to die, so that just leaves north. I take it you agree? A nod will do..."

Leanan pulled the youth in front of her, nudging firmly in the direction of the bridge, all the while nodding at the man whose life was intricately entwined with hers. Whatever had brought them here, they would face together, and that thought sparked the wicked fires burning just behind her eyes.

Slinging the long sword across her back, she fell in front of Jareth and behind the girl, listening to the voices on the wind, keenly aware that the baying had changed its tone; there was more than a hint of frustration now. The three of them crossed the concrete causeway and were quickly engulfed in a flood of trees so dense, that when the iron tracks of the machine pursuing them came into view, neither party saw each other.

Chapter 9

One For Me

Too soon, Jareth found himself on the lookout for a defensible position. Judging from the sound, perhaps no more than four dogs, but the wind played tricks with the echoes and even the woman wasn't sure of their number. He cursed beneath his breath once again; their progress would be much greater if the girl wasn't with them. He had to admit that the witch wasn't as much a hinderance as he'd feared. Traversing hard, flat stone surfaces like inside the castle or road was one thing, but they were now floundering in the wild, searching for anything that resembled a path. Those that pursued wouldn't be hindered by a few trees, though. And yet, Jareth would rather have it this way; foreign and scraggly, the trees promised a deeper forest to come, and if they could just make it there, the situation would change. Tall trees would work against the dogs.

Unbroken, the line of the forest stretched east and west. They plunged randomly, crushing the undergrowth in ways that made him cringe. Along with his sword skill, woodcraft had saved him more than once, despite he knew they were leaving a track that almost anyone could find, let alone dogs.

"Hounds, Jare; there's a difference."

He shot Leanan another glare but kept moving; they had to find some sort of path or this tangle of burr and thistle would be their end. As it was, there was barely space now to swing a blade. And to make his anxiety even worse, Piper launched himself to the ground soon after entering the woods and became a shadow melting into the ground. With another, louder lunge of sound from behind, Jareth forgot about the cat because pursuit had just gained the trees. He gave Leanan another glance as she practically pushed the teen forward, trying to pick out the least amount of tangle. Was she any good with that knife? Could she use a sword? Too bad she couldn't use her persuasion over the wind here, beneath the boughs. But when he'd started to ask, her silent head shake eliminated that option.

"And stop calling me a witch."

To which he merely paused and nodded. She didn't need to know he felt relieved to know her position as goddess wasn't all encompassing. But then, if they did know each other already, he felt sure he'd never have taken up with her if such were the case. Still, a windstorm aimed in the right direction would surely help at the moment.

"Keep heading due north and try to get the girl to move faster—you can tell which..."

"Aye, the wind is always my guide; I know where true North lies."

His sentence unfinished, he noted that the girl had turned her head back toward him, a look of exasperation on her face, as if to say she was already moving as fast as she could.

Jareth chuckled; nice to know she wasn't a complete princess. The increased baying behind distracted him from any further thoughts about the girl. Hoping the women would keep a straight path, he slowed and began to hack at knee-high goose weed, heaping the sheaves overtop the trampled path, hoping to obscure their scent. Keeping the wind at his back, he set off in a different direction, not even trying to cover his track, making it obvious for the hounds. . The hounds would be using their noses close to the ground with no wind-born scent as guide. Jareth meant to draw the dogs off, all of them, hopefully. Still, he needed something at his back because once surrounded, it would be only a matter of time. Whistling softly, he caught sight of the black cat. Nodding in a forward direction, he knew the cat would understand and follow.

He searched for a perfect tree but they all looked the same, the largest trunk no more than six inches around. Not much, but it would do if he got pinched. Without the women to slow him down, his pace increased until more than a mile separated them. The soft leather of his boots made no sound as he ran, his lithe body wove a path through the trees, plain at first and then more cunningly; once sure the hounds had his scent, he wasn't going to make it easy for them.

Listening as he moved, he heard the sound of his pursuers change as they came to the junction point. Confusion reigned.

Come on, take the bait; this has to work.

Closing his eyes, he let the sounds around him amplify, the touch of wind and ground more acute to his senses. It was one reason he survived. Beneath his feet, time stalled and he swore he could hear the earth's song evolve. There were always patterns to nature, if one was patient enough to discover them. And as rhythm and cadence were naturals for Jareth, this one was no different. He heard, and more importantly, noted the change when the pattern was disrupted. As the new rhythm established, he knew the chase had resumed, and in his direction! When the dogs howled with his scent, he was sure. Dropping his head, he bent to put more distance between them, all the while looking for someplace to make his stand. There was no hope of outrunning them, and once he accepted this, all that was left was the fighting. Patting the hilt of his sword, a grim smile fixed itself.

Each time the girl wanted to slow down, Leanan ruthlessly pushed her forward; she knew more about their pursuit than Jareth did. These weren't just any dogs, they were hounds. She recognized early on that their sound wasn't earthly. And despite understanding that her own world of the Fae was being used against her, it didn't make her witless. Knowing the enemy was the first step in defeating him. But like Jareth, she knew they needed something at their back if fighting through was to be an option. A cave would be better but there seemed scant chance of that. Oh, if only she had open sky or sea to parlay—those baying behind would understand Sidhe fury then!

The girl looked tall for her age, which Leanan pegged at mid-teen. Or perhaps younger, judging by the girl's behavior. The youth's hair was long and dark, not unlike her own, and framed round, brown eyes which always appeared a bit too wide. Pretty in a way, Leanan still thought she was too skinny and a bit haggard. What was it Jareth had said? She was a pariah? Someone the others picked upon and kicked to the street. It was a wonder the girl looked as healthy as she did, though the bruise on her temple was a reminder that there was no fairness in life.

But pity and compassion were not Leanan's better traits and so the girl was pushed hard. Flashing the long steel blade of her knife had stopped an endless flow of distress that only made escape that much harder. Run, girl, run; those behind won't discriminate should they catch up.

And indeed, the surety of this fact propelled the girl far more than the woman in black leather ever could. She ran, fearing the woman's touch more than the dogs, despite the fact no new ink flowed. But each time she was, the tattoos flowed as they always did, damning her in ways the woman behind her could never know. Only when she was alone and held her guitar could the pain be assuaged as the music lingered. It was a temporary reprieve that kept her alive. But there was no time now for that.

The hounds had closed the distance by half before Jareth's senses noted a wrongness; their sound had changed, and once he realized this, the prickle of a dilemma stabbed hard, much harder than he would have thought possible. Behind him now, there were only three. Which meant the fourth had not followed. Jareth didn't think these dogs were smart enough to guard the back trail, so that must mean he hadn't covered the women's scent well enough. And the dilemma was clear; what should he do? One small part of him urged a course change—maybe he could head off the fourth dog. Maybe not, though. And what about these three? The distance between his track and the girls' had not been meant to be great, but it would still be substantial. Damn! Isn't this why he traveled alone in the first place? Isn't this why other than Piper, he wasn't tied to anyone or anything? This all started with an urge to flee, underlaid with the purpose of finding home. Hell, he didn't have one, and that was the irony of it all. It was why the call had been so confusing in the first place—he and Piper had wandered for as long as he could remember. Hadn't they?

Home...even as he unconsciously altered his path southward, the idea swirled in his mind, causing him to lose focus. He didn't have a home...or did he? And the more he thought about it, the more he realized that Leanan hinted at that probability. Raising his fingers to his lips and letting out a shrill whistle, Jareth cut purposefully southward, a new urgency added to his flight. He'd damn any hound that followed.

The trees bristled as he swept between their tightly packed branches, but could not dissuade his passage. And behind, bounding over the thistles, a black shadow quickly followed. Neither needed another burst of baying as encouragement to hurry. One last backward glance was enough; through a glimpse between the trees, three hulking gray shapes, mottled with black, closed the distance. Now, there was only picking the thickest set of trees to make his stand. Selecting a copse of five, Jareth drew his sword and waited. Wouldn't be long now.

Silent, the fourth Hound had trailed the women flawlessly, coming upon their hot spoor despite the goose weed. It needed nothing else; the hunt would soon be over.

Leanan pushed the girl deeper into a copse of gorse berries, the trees having thinned. She knew something was wrong as the baying of the Hounds diverted further east. But unlike Jareth, she knew their song—had grown up with the forebears of these offspring. She knew not all the dogs had followed the man. It was the wind which brought her confirmation of their silent stalker and as it did, determination flamed in pupils flamed leaching gold. Her aura was mythic, a force few would dare face. The Hunt approached her threshold and was about to knock on the door. And behind it, the daughter of Mannanan simmered, the edge of her knife slicing thinly across her arm and releasing blood so black that the girl almost blanched. Who was this woman?

They came side by side, dodging the trees like water flowing between rocks. Their tongues slavered, firing the ground. In their eyes, all light was stifled. It was then that Jareth knew these were no ordinary dogs. Leanan had called them Hounds; hounds from Hell? Damn.

Still, he raised his sword to his ear, looking for vulnerable places on the hounds to stab. He hoped they could die.

Leanan's snarl was vicious.

"One for me."

Despite the girl's whimper beside her, Leanan heard the beast's dry, cracked voice as it hurled epithets in response while her own three words resonated on the breeze. The hulk hovered just beyond sword's reach, eyeing the wicked blade. This is why dogs hunted in packs. Alone, indecision kept hunter from prey.

The words flowed from between ruby-black lips, her sharp teeth bared, mimicking the Hound. The girl didn't understand the

Celtic tirade and merely clung tighter to the Leanan's shadow, as if hiding within would save her. With the sword stretched out before her, the muse baited the animal, hoping it would carelessly enter the limit of her reach, just once.

Circling the two, the hulking beast snapped its jaws and growled deep in its throat, eyes black as the abyss. A snarl of hate lined its lips and each drop of saliva sizzled on the bracken beneath. Lines of darkness cloaked a shaggy gray body which swelled at the shoulders. Massive in front, its hindquarters would be much weaker, but that did little if the Hound never turned. Its jaws were lined with yellowed teeth, the stink of its breath the cause of more anger from the woman. One lunge is all it needed...but it had to avoid the prey's sticker...

The three brutes bore down on Jareth with no thought of lunging and crushing his neck, but rather, to overwhelm and destroy. The man realized this and contemplated where his first stroke should fall. If he got another one, no further planning would be necessary. He had to take advantage of the trees around him, hoping their closeness hindered the pack's rush. But there wasn't a lot of hope in that and he knew it.

From his left, the sound of wind being split snared his ear, and just as quickly, it was followed by another. Distracted, he forced himself to maintain focus on his attackers. Shocked, he saw two dogs fall, their legs kicking even as they lay thrashing on the ground. The third monster kept charging, hardly aware that its mates had gone down. As Jareth saw the eyes of the remaining Hound narrow and its haunches bunch tightly, preparatory to a final leap, the animal opened a hideous mouth.

As the animal soared through the air, its paws thrust forward and its mouth wide, Jareth lunged forward too and twisting in mid-air, stabbed upward with his sword. The force of the animal's body grabbing at his arm nearly wrenched his arm out of its socket.

Jareth hit the ground, sliding up and hitting his head on one of the trees. The pain in his arm and head competed for crucial seconds, but it didn't stop him from rising to his feet, his only purpose that of locating the Hound. Weaponless, this wouldn't last long...

But nothing moved, or at least, nothing but the heaving of his chest. He sucked at air as lungs beneath the belts and buckles of his harness, strove to keep pace. The strange tattoo of symbols expanded on his chest as if they too were trying to breathe. Nothing moved and yet, the area was more alive in that stall of time than ever Jareth could remember. He'd had clashes near Death before and knew the adrenaline rush, but this was different. There was more to this moment and he struggled mightily to grasp it's secret.

Then like a wisp of wind, it was gone. Taking a deep breath, Jareth started forward to retrieve his blade, noting long dark shafted arrows lodged deep in the skulls of the first two Hounds. Placing his foot on the last dog, he yanked his sword from the thick hide, cursing as the ensuing flood of blood bathed his boot. It would be hell cleaning that later.

He whistled once for Piper's benefit and broke into a run.

The fourth hound bled in three places, but none vital. The drip of dark ooze formed yet another stripe on the animal. Behind her, the girl had gone deathly quiet and it took a quick glance from Leanan to assure herself she wasn't now alone. The leather scales of her boots slid sinuously as she balanced on the balls of her feet, the sword streaming darkly halfway down its length. She'd been aiming for its eyes but the Hound was faster than she'd thought, and only an ear lay on the ground. Two other superficial cuts marked the flank of the beast, curtesy of a sudden unexpected lunge on her part. That time, she'd been out to rip the heart, but for her efforts, the Hound had raked its fangs across her arm, taking only leather in its stead. The shock of white that wound itself through her long braid, gleamed against the oily darkness of the rest of her hair; this animal didn't understand it had chosen the wrong prey.

The two combatants stood still in the moment as time stalled and everything crept in magnified slowness. Her eyes blazed cold fury, matching the Hound's. Air rushed into exhausted lungs and lifted her mail corset, much like the heave of mottled fur on the animal's chest. She bared her own fangs in defiance of the creature, and her words sizzled like the dog's slavering.

The moment ended and with a snarl, the hound lunged, ignoring the blade this time. Leanan pivoted to get inside one of the Hound's paws, her blade arcing in the same movement. In her other hand, the long knife waited.

A cusp of sound rifled the space between hunter and prey, and Leanan witnessed a breaking of the voices on the wind. The sudden cessation was like the blink of an eye, a golden eye shot with the blackest ink. And then it was done. Leanan raised to her full height, the sword in her hand slimed all the way to the hilt, its basket-cage a swirl of black and silver. At her feet, the muzzle of the Hound exhaled one last time, further defiling her boots and half her leg with bloody spittle. The eyes flickered open once more before finally dying out, watching the Dark Muse and her charge leave the thicket. As darkness claimed the great hound, Leanan muttered to the wind.

"Now, that was different."

The red-feathered shaft that split the animal's skull aimed skyward, it's point buried amidst slow oozing.

Chapter 10

Bouncing off Clouds

Ice had formed complex patterns between the window's mullions, evidence that the season was entrenched. The change of weather had caught Rhey by surprise because on his world, there was little variation. Two suns and three moons guaranteed that. With the edge of a pencil's eraser, he dialed the thermostat five degrees higher, anticipating further detrimental changes outside. Human habitation had its downside, he decided.

Behind him, the monitors pinged again, alerting him to the fact that more text poured. He'd been reading for a while now, and had even tried to interject some code of his own, just on the off chance it could be that simple. But alas, his first attempt had gone awry and it would now take some analysis to determine why. Somewhere behind the crystalline pane, a mongrel dog bayed again, a deep, soulful sound that said much about cold and loneliness. Idly, he wondered if the man strapped on the table could relate.

It had been this same dog that had inspired Rhey when it was time to form up his character, or rather, his hunters. As another howl bubbled miserably from outside the snow-washed building, the alien adjusted miscellaneous dials and knobs as he monitored the outside world as well as the man. Almost all human resistance had been eradicated, though pocket cells still existed. His own hunters, mechanized and deadly efficient, were still out there, and unlike the dogs, they had not been stopped. There was no escape anymore; it would be like bouncing off clouds.

Beryl

The intrusion of both women meant more data to decrypt and proved to be variables that demanded accountability. He was getting a clearer picture of the one called Dark Muse but the younger one's importance hadn't been determined—yet. The idea Martin might be using her as a decoy occurred to him but there wasn't enough evidence yet to support that theory, so he had to continue to track all three. And too, there was now an archer involved. With a morbid fascination, he limped back to the stainless steel chair with the torn headrest, back to the monitor where the cyrillic threatened to become the lead wave of a tsunami. Back to work, and while part of his mind deciphered for meaning, another part was already working up a more effective characterization to use, now that he'd put a foot in the doorway...

Chapter 11

A Sorta Fairy Tale

Jareth still wasn't buying Leanan's explanation, though he would acknowledge the coincidental luck of it all. Their second encampment allowed for a larger, warmer fire and for that, he was glad.

The scrub forest seemed endless, and while the three had reunited amidst some discerning looks on each side, it didn't dispel the fact that that all they could see was trees. And though Leanan anxiously speculated that more pursuit would come, Jareth wanted only to bask in the moment. For now, danger, like water, slept.

"You don't seriously think the Hounds were acting of their own accord, do you?"

She stopped administering to the girl so she could give her full attention to Jareth, her displeasure showing. She didn't seem to like the way he was leading their escape. But that was part of the problem; escape from what? From who? And to where?

"Could be a roving pack."

Her eyes blazed momentarily and the hue of her hair burned darker.

"Would a pack separate like that? And have you ever seen animals that size?"

Granted, she had a point about the latter; even bears didn't get that large. Despite knowing he should get back, he'd still spent some time examining the dying hounds, just so he'd know his enemy better the next time they met.

Upon coming to the place where the fourth dog had perished, curiosity slowed his pace. Understanding that the muse and girl had survived only caused more thoughts to swirl. By nightfall, all three were united and once again heading north, even though something nudged him to curve eastward, as the cooling air spit out promises. He hated snow.

As they prepared to make camp, he cursed the land, albeit under his breath in frustration, thinking that it sure would be a bit of good fortune to stumble upon rocky ground; something which would break up the monotony as well as provide cover. He was loathe to start a fire that could be seen so easily, small trees or not. Piper mewed plaintively, as if reading his mind. Leanan was again nagging at him.

"Can't you sing or write one in?"

The annoyance in her voice rankled and he swept past the confusion in her words.

"I don't know these lands; not many from the north ever venture as far south as Vespar, so you'll forgive me if I can't find you a lodge or something quaint. Damn!"

He was reacting to the smooth surface of rock showing at least three dark openings, that had just opened up before them. Inside was the promise of shelter, and maybe more. He glanced suspiciously toward Leanan, wonder vying with confusion.

"Not me, so it must have been you; I should have asked sooner."

The explanation made even less sense. Wishing didn't make something true, no matter what she thought, though asking wasn't exactly the same. This wasn't a sort of fairy tale. He dropped the matter as coincidence and laying his mandolin down, began searching for firewood. The cold was beginning to go through him, the dark thought that because the wind flowed even inside the cave, it meant there was another entrance, somewhere. Well, he'd worry about that, later.

It was while Jareth was taking stock of their hurriedly packed rations that he discovered the girl's guitar. Not to mention a much more thoughtful supply of food in her pack. Someone had been anticipating a long journey, apparently. His discovery caused the girl to act out, imploring him not to touch it, as if he would leave black lines. He gave the girl a thoughtful moment and though he dismissed her misgivings, nevertheless leaving the strings untouched. It meant she understood music, and some part of him warmed.

Leanan's agitation bubbled over and her words were strained.

"The Hounds belong to those of the Hunt, Jare; you know this."

Whether he did or not, didn't matter at the moment.

"They are part of the it, not the whole. Those that command them will be following, of this you can be sure."

But he glared back at her.

"We need to rest; the girl isn't going to make it if we force her to move as we have."

It was simple logic, something he'd have thought obvious to the witch, too.

"Have you become obtuse? How many times do you need to be told that I'm not a witch? A witch is part of *your* mythology, not mine. Why can't you accept that I'm a muse?"

And truth be told, he wasn't sure why he was having trouble with that concept. Maybe he didn't want to face what acknowledgment would mean—that he needed help when he wrote his songs.

"You think the words in your heart just tumble out in a coherent stream all by themselves? Just the fact they're there should be proof enough. How many do you know that have such a love for music and verse, and no muse? None of the better ones,

I'll warrant. But this is annoying; a muse isn't a witch and vice versa. Accept it and be done; we've more important things to do."

That last hung pregnant in the moment. What important things? A spark shot toward his lap, leaving him wondering if he'd even feel the burning ember, while he waited for her to continue. Which she didn't. His words poured then more harshly than he intended.

"Oh, so *now* you don't want to be in my head? Why so silent? Do I need to ask?"

She glared imperiously at him but her face softened as his hardened.

"Well, I've no clear sight yet, but there's too much that's happened in the last twenty-four hours to deny something's abroad. You've never been that forthcoming with me, Dear; it's your fault...something about not wanting me that close, though eventually, it's a place to which we always come."

Why did she always have to speak in riddles?

"I am Fae, Jare; you shouldn't have to ask."

"And that means you need to be inscrutable?"

His demeanor was becoming just as defensive as hers.

"It means Love, that I see events, time, and people in a different way, that's all. You see the moon as half empty, and I see it as half full. It's precious few that are aware of a sky flowing beneath. And even less that understand which moment is real."

He went back to eating dried figs and sticks of smoked meat. That last claim sounded true but struggled as if restrained. He chewed then in silence, overcome by foreboding.

Across the fire, the girl devoured her rations and looked plaintively at Leanan for more. As their words grew loud enough for him to hear, he distinctly heard her utter that she just wanted to go home.

Home; perhaps the only reason he'd come back to the women in the first place. He saw the witch—muse—shake her head not in denial but in ignorance, as if confused by the girl's request.

"She's part of your purpose, Jareth, that's for sure."

The man turned his gaze from Leanan's dark beauty, and looked long at the younger woman, whose face flustered in confusion at being caught in the middle of something she didn't understand.

"And who exactly *is* she?"

The look on the muse's face stunned him; whereas he was expecting another riddling explanation, he received only a blankness more mystifying yet.

"I don't know."

Jareth's brow furrowed tighter, if that were possible. Leanan continued, trying to placate him...or explain her ignorance, he thought.

"She's an answer, Jareth, that's all I know. That, and that you're supposed to help her."

He continued to lock his eyes with Leanan's, but curiosity finally got to him and he switched his focus back to the girl.

"An answer to what?"

The young girl pulled back, keenly aware of being the center of attention, anguish festering because this was just the type of moment in which someone ultimately proclaimed her a failure. The despair inside her soul welled, and tears squeezed silently from tightening eyes while her face pinched tighter. She seemed to shrink.

"What kind of help do you need?"

But the girl was too wrapped in her anxiety to respond. Leanan's gaze upon the man grew rigid, demanding he stop being so pushy. She began to put two well-meaning hands on the girl's shoulders only to find empty air.

"Hold still."

To which the girl squirmed still more, uttering small sounds of torment.

"She's afraid."

Leanan's glare smote Jareth.

"Really? I can see that; but why? What is it with her?"

"You needed to be there, back at the castle. It's just the way they are. It's like they wear their heart on their sleeves; everyone knows their faults, and their graces, too. Seems this one doesn't have any of the latter."

Leanan forced her fingers to relax but kept their grip on the girl, whose eyes searched through tracks of tears. There was a weakness inherent in the waif that was bothersome. The force of her nature didn't admit such weakness, and to see it now, made her gag. Yes, who *is* this girl?

"Maybe we should find out why that is, Jareth."

He didn't like the idea of forcing information. For him, there was always the choice of walking away, if what he needed couldn't be had. Not much had a hold on him and as long as he kept his wits, he could continue that path. Still, basic information was needed. Absently, he stroked Piper while uttering a soft crooning sound.

"Do you have a name, girl?"

He found it better to lessen the tension by making the confrontation more personal; you learned more quickly about the situation, more surely, this way.

The girl held her knees to her chin, her long gangly arms wound tight. The tears were slowing but she showed no real signs of emotional stability.

"What do they call you, girl? Until we decide what we're going to do, we have to call you something."

She opened her eyes and cast a doubtful glance at the muse before considering the man. Her voice was low, barely more than the crackle of burning embers.

"They call me Beryl."

Her name didn't change the look on Leanan's face, but a slight twinge gripped Jareth's right eye. Like a nervous tic, or flushing an irritation, the name meant something, but he didn't know what.

"Beryl then, okay, that'll do."

Leanan's voice softened now that they were getting somewhere.

"You can stop crying—we're not here to hurt you. Quite the opposite, we're going to help."

But Jareth wasn't as sure of Leanan's statement. He didn't even know if he was signing on yet. A traveling minstrel was more like a one-man-band, and he was happy with that fact.

The girl continued to tremble, trying to shrug off the older woman's grip, though with less effort.

"Leanan, let her go. It has to run its course, or you'll waste a lot of time twisting her mind until nothing she says makes sense."

Leanan glanced at Jareth, noting he'd used her true name for the first time. The fleeting familiarity on his face made her pause. Intrigued, she relaxed her grip, half fearing she'd leave black marks behind as she let go.

The girl named Beryl rocked back and forth, the words slipping between her lips barely coherent, undeniably like a nightmare made manifest. The lines of text and symbols of black ink on her skin spasmed, rolling like ocean waves to crash against each other. The two watched as the girl braced for a mental onslaught, the like of which they could not understand because this was not their way. From her whispered gasps, Leanan began to understand how years of detrimental words aimed at the young girl had twisted her. It was as if her skin absorbed each and every mock, each insult and negative comment. She was a lost soul, someone who could never do anything right, and those around her let her know it. To an extreme. The words were not momentary, they were not temporary—they were not to be held in the psyche or imprisoned only in her heart, they were to be made public for all to see. These were the moments in her life where failure was posted for all, including herself.

Regret creeped on the edge of Leanan's heart. Somewhere in her dark soul, Leanan gleaned a vision that Beryl's life was like a fairytale gone wrong, and she shuddered; as such a force of confidence, the muse would never have given even the wisp of thought to such an outcome. For her, the power that lay within was stronger than any mortal perspective, and it was this which threatened to strike the earth for glory. The deepest hurt within Beryl was contrasted by Leanan's lust for recognition.

For Jareth, what the girl went through was not something he could hold, and so he didn't. He only knew it too would pass, if he gave it time. He'd seen this before and gone numb to the process. He'd no more scoff as doff his hat either. That the girl suffered was only too obvious, but how did that affect him?

As Piper lay curled in his lap, the fire glowered back and he pondered the implications of being on the road with a muse and a pariah.

Chapter 12

2 - 1

"Dammit, we have to do something."

But Jareth didn't say anything because he knew there wasn't a cure. Leanan's anguish surprised him, though he didn't know why.

"I've seen body painting before; when did they become more than self expression?"

"You mean, when did it become more than 'all about me'? I dare to say this is the eventual outcome. The Vesparians are all about letting you know when they approve and when they don't. As I said; it's the girl's culture, her society. She's grown up with this all her life. What is there *to* do?"

Jareth seemed genuinely nonplussed with Leanan's growing concern, though he noted it held a hard edge, and nothing in her voice indicated the soft landing of compassion. Strange; he'd not met too many women like this. It seemed the hard seductive edge the woman presented, ran rife throughout her persona. He supposed she would be harsh in bed, too.

Lifting black-lined brows, Leanan pursed her lips while the dark slits of her pupils closed tighter within the churning gold.

"Oh, you might be surprised at how untrue that last is, Jare. Aye, you might."

The retort set his mind on trajectories he wasn't sure he wanted to be on.

"They're all like this; some with gold ink running over their skin, others with black. Most have both though. There's very few with her condition. But there's nothing we can do about it."

He stood and giving both women a long look, went to the cave mouth and pried the night for answers. Why hadn't he just kept going east?

From behind him though, he was surprised to hear the girl's exhaled whisper above the crackle of the fire.

"Not all of us...there was one who was different."

Turning his back on the cool air, Jareth eyed the girl, wondering.

"What do you mean?"

Leanan's curiosity was also piqued and the girl realized she'd been heard. It wasn't something she'd meant to say aloud.

"What do you mean, girl?"

His voice was tinged with a growing anticipation, as if whatever she might say could explain his own misgivings. Never before had he been saddled with such an unexpected burden; traveling light was all he could remember. Or was it? A drift of sensation tickled at a memory, as if someone had scratched at a barrow mound. And this thought made him frown.

The girl saw his face and shrank back, as if fearing he was displeased and would tell her she was being weak, inflicting pain merely by stirring the echoes.

Leanan saw too and her face clouded with the riddle he was presenting. This wasn't as she always knew him. But then, Jareth's character had morphed before she'd arrived. There were still questions she was loathe to ask.

"Answer him, girl; what are you talking about?" She too wondered at what secret lay with Beryl; there was something, or else why had she been placed before them in the first place. The girl had a role here, they just had to find out what it was.

Beginning to fear that maybe there was another threat to Jareth, Leanan's form seemed to grow, her shadowy complexion adding to the girl's anxiety, but demanding answers nonetheless.

"There was another...he talked of someone called Eli."

Leanan turned, looking quizzically at Jareth, who didn't even shrug his ignorance. He was waiting for the girl to go on, as if her words were living within an echo deep inside.

"What about this other? Who are we talking about?"

"He said he was called Puchinello. And he had no marks."

Leanan heard Jareth snort in derision, his voice low but not beyond her hearing.

"And he had clear skin?"

The girl nodded, brushing back tears.

"Like you."

Leanan looked at the girl, incomprehension on her face.

"No, not like me. Neither one of us belongs to your land, girl, neither of us is from your world."

Now, why had she stated it like that? Though for sure, he didn't feel any kinship to the Vesparians. Perhaps that's why he'd never fit in? But then, minstrels generally didn't. Momentary distractions, that's what we are...

He was keenly aware now of the strange glyphs adorning his own chest, and their cryptic meaning. With his cloak draped about his shoulders since they'd met, the girl would see only the skin he allowed to be seen. But wasn't that so very human nature—to keep the sins and lies hidden from others?

Leanan took Jareth's words further. Did he remember more than that for which she was giving him credit? The look in his eyes receded, and she couldn't help but feel that the shade of the Jareth she knew, had peeked beyond this facade.

As if he thought his whisper would never be heard, nevertheless, both women took in his words.

"Our sins are just hidden."

With his eyes downcast and his mind wandering, the flicker of recognition was fully disguised from both women, though Leanan forced the confines of her intuition, trying to find to what depths he'd fallen. It was important if she were to find him...and protect him. The black cat stretched his chin and the man absently scratched, a reflex that sought to bring both comfort.

The muse redirected the conversation back to the girl.

"Why didn't this Puchinello have any tattoos?"

For some reason, Leanan needed to understand this strange girl and her unusual social ways. Her voice softened just a little with encouragement. Jareth stared at the ground, or into the heart of the flames; lines of focus were blurring.

"He did, once. He was like the rest of us. Like them...none are like me."

The girl was filled with a rue that tugged at Leanan's mercurial heart, and she felt something stir that others might call real compassion. The feeling bothered her and she scowled, though averted her face so as not to interrupt the girl's lessening reticence.

"How are you not like the others, Beryl?"

But the young girl's tongue became tied and her eyes widened in growing apprehension.

As Leanan's brows knit tighter and her dark lips formed a grim line of persistence, Jareth's voice interceded.

"She doesn't have any gold marks on her, that's why."

Leanan looked first at him and then back at her, his revelation already having been explained but obviously not its importance.

"Aye. So? She only has black lines. And?"

"Means the others don't think much of her, to say the least."

Leanan wondered why this was so important.

"So they brand her with their opinions? Is that it?"

Jareth's voice became softer still, as if aware his words were like blows to the girl's body. And indeed, Beryl was doubled over, her hands over her ears, as if blocking the sound of his voice would give her protection.

"Not quite; some get gold marks just because they're tall, or talented, while others get black ones because they're small, inept, foolish, or even because they're considered not as good as the rest. It's in their blood, Leanan; it's what they do. Because she has no gold ink adorning her skin, it means her life's been very hard."

"So what's with this other, then? If he didn't have any marks at all, that makes him like her—a pariah, though of a different kind."

The girl's next words came out in a sob.

"No, it wasn't that he wasn't given the marks, both black and gold, the others tried; it's just that the marks didn't stick."

Leanan let the girl's words sink in, wondering exactly what was going on. Was this a different kind of magic? Jareth heard her too but didn't fathom the importance. It didn't matter to him, just like the girl having only black tattoos didn't matter either.

"That's why I need to go home."

The knell of sound was translated into a rush of feeling that nearly choked the man as Beryl's whisper rasped free. Leanan saw astonishment but only briefly. Surely the girl's last words had meaning for him.

"Home? The city we just left?"

"No, home—to Eli; Puchinello says that if I want to understand why the marks won't cling to his skin, I'm to ask Eli. He knows.

"Who is this Eli?"

"He lives in the place where all my people come from, at the top of a hill, behind the green door, on a great chair where he carves all of us from the boll of the Tree of Life."

Leanan let all sound seep into the wind, its voice spinning their own meanings. There was much more behind what the girl was saying than she was letting on.

Jareth heard the word 'home' and the longing inside him intensified; he was vitally aware of how much of an echo he'd become. Maybe Leanan was right; this girl could be the answer to his own question. But he was unsure and his confusion was there for Leanan's penetrating stare. Two to one odds that both women would yet be his bane.

The muse's own perception of the girl was rapidly altering. She *was* important, yes, but why? Was this the secret she'd sensed?

The fire had died down and was smoldering, but only the girl noticed. She felt the enclosing night air as it crept along the cave walls and curled ravenously about the shadows, lending strength to growing fears. Who *were* these two? The strange-eyed woman's dark countenance called as sickly as a tattoo. She had a source of strength Beryl envied, though wouldn't have expressed that way. In thinking this, she cringed, fearing someone would mark her yet again. Cruelty morphed, drawing more pain.

Across the flames, she thought the cat was looking at her.

And there was the man—the one who looked almost as lost as she. Perhaps even more so, though outwardly there was a calm confidence. But Beryl didn't fear him as much as her—there wasn't enough life on the man's face for her to feel much threat, whereas the woman practically burned with a potent venom. Burned and yet not for her—Beryl was intimately aware of how such feelings were being routed around her misery, a dark river of malevolence that formed a wall of protection. And with a keen sense she never knew she had, Beryl also saw that Leanan's flow of power was the offshoot of a larger fountain within which the man drowned. Was she the only one who could see this?

"This must be why the girl's here, Jare; it's how we're to help. I think we're to get Beryl home."

Leanan's voice stirred the fire's embers with their passion and growing conviction. But though she looked at Jareth, he didn't return her gaze. For him, the idea of finding home had solidified;

independent of the girl's story and Leanan's proclamation, he felt the grip of melancholy, a bittersweet feeling he didn't want. The urge to ask the muse was strangling breath in his efforts to speak.

"I think it's time you got some rest, girl; we can talk more in the morning."

Leanan began to protest.

"Jareth; we can't. There's something to her story that needs investigating. The morning might be too late."

He eyed her blankly, not fully understanding her sudden anxiety.

"The Hunters, remember?"

Ah, yes; the ones who'd sent the dogs. Supposedly.

"In the morning; I doubt pursuit could be as fast as their dogs. We have time. We've entered an unknown country and I don't want to wander in the dark. Besides, this cave is the first place we've found where defense is possible."

"Are you going to let me go home?"

Fearing she'd been forgotten, the girl spoke, her lower lip quivering in her hesitation to interrupt.

"Let you?"

The words sounded odd to Jareth's ears; did the girl think his permission a necessity?

"I don't think it's like that, girl. The winds are whispering of roads you're already on, and allowing you to do anything isn't part of the riddle, neither yours nor mine."

Leanan gave him a purposefully look, her hair cascading around her face and drawing his eyes as he stifled the urge to be drawn a different way. The woman was asking questions and providing answers at the same time, if only he cared enough to read between the lines. The look he projected was a facade of apathy, even though a spark of unrest mimicked the burning embers before him. The muse spoke into his reverie.

"Rest now, Beryl; be ready to travel hard tomorrow. Our road lies north and you're going with us."

Jareth gave Leanan a surprised look of his own as she tried to placate the girl. Us? But the muse just gave him a lascivious smile in return, daring him to gainsay her.

Putting another branch on the fire, Leanan stood and moved to the cave mouth, following Jareth. As the girl huddled miserably by the flame, wondering what these people meant to do with her, she could hear Leanan's curt whisper in the dark, its undercurrent evident.

The wind moved uneasily on his face, its source still steady from the west. Northward; aye, he knew that was the right direction, though not why. Certainly not because the muse had said so.

"The wind tell you that?"

His tone was tinged with curiosity, yet implacable; he'd go his own way, no matter what. It was only to be seen if either of the others went with him.

"You're going to need me, Jare, that's certain."

He turned and looked into the pale face of the muse—*his* muse. So she said.

"And the girl's going with us, of that much I'm sure."

Still he said nothing and just looked at her, measuring in ways she couldn't possibly know. Again, she skipped through his mind.

"Oh, but I do, Love, that's another thing free of doubt."

And as she let her earlier flirtation infiltrate, a small smile creased his face.

"I know the Hunters will follow, Jareth; it's only a matter of time before they strike. We would do well not to ignore them."

She leaned closer, her darkness not nearly as cold as he perceived it would be. As she intertwined his arm with hers, creating an intimacy he both thrilled at and feared, the sound of her voice lowered.

"I'm more concerned about the *other;* something else is on this journey with us."

He turned his face from hers, the moment passing. He knew her trepidation but for some strange reason, didn't share her unease; after all, those arrows could have killed either of them, instead of the Hounds.

Chapter 13

With This Ship

Beryl bolted from the road, her long hair trailing like a cape, her voice wailing in despair. Jareth called it a road, but it was more a deer path.

"There she goes, Jare—I'll get her!"

Leanan leaped the path's edge and she sped away after the fleeing girl. Jareth stared at both of them, caught between surprise and annoyance. The whole bloody sky was dropping behind them in more shades of purple than he'd ever seen. What had started as merely a sunless dawn had now turned moody and malcontent. Indeed, Leanan had been right; pursuit had been swift.

Hell, where did the girl think she could go? The path at least gave them room to swing a sword—not that that was much help. By the sounds of them, there'd be riders too. Why hadn't he at least checked the ground last night when there was still time? Horses made a bloody damn racket, even moving between trees. Idly, Jareth wondered if maybe they'd have been better off staying away from the path now that they'd found it. Apparently Beryl thought so.

And where had Piper gotten off to? Maybe the animal knew better than to sink with this ship.

He watched as the deep violet nimbus that had been trailing them ever since the cave, bore a startling resemblance to the growing glow surrounding the muse's form. Surely she must be a witch...

She'd no doubt be in a foul mood upon her return, if she could pick up his thoughts so far away. For some reason, the man didn't put it past her.

There wasn't time for this nonsense! The day was rapidly worsening, Jareth grumbled, remembering.

"They're coming, Jare."

"Just let me sleep, woman, it was a long night."

She poked him with the toe of her leather boot, the point surprisingly sharp. Or maybe it was just the muse adding her own anxiousness to the motion. Rolling over and opening one eye, he noted the fire was out and the sky darker than it should be. Lifting his head, a line of drool was curtailed. No wonder his lips felt so dry.

"Want me to help you with that, too?"

Leanan's grin altered wickedly and her gaze sharpened.

The girl was already up and fretting, hands rubbing at arms, trying to keep warm. Or was she trying to ward off more ink? He was hardly concerned either way. What was that throbbing thrum in his ears, anyway?

"I told you; they're coming. Did you expect they'd be walking?"

And then he bolted upright, the real meaning of her warning like a lash across his backside. Riders!

They hadn't been able to break camp soon enough and he cast more than a few glares at the two women for not waking him sooner. Didn't anyone understand how vulnerable they were? Abandoning the cave wasn't an easy choice but he hadn't wanted to be trapped inside, either.

"You tell me when you want your sword."

Again she was trying to foist off the long, icy-blue blade on him. And knowing what he'd say, she slapped at him with her words, her displeasure obvious. But he *had* a sword...and judging by the way the last of the Hounds had been skewered by the muse, it was obvious she could wield a blade. Almost as well as himself...

"I'm more comfortable up close though, Jareth, as you should know!"

The teasing glint in her eye sliced at his closed demeanor like a scythe, drawing more than figurative blood. She knew where his weak points were, and she slipped the tip of her weapon inside deftly. Dammit; it was like she really *did* know him.

"Knife work can be so very intimate, you know..."

Her words trailed off as she bent her attention toward a recalcitrant teenager who was wallowing petulantly. The woman could move when haste required it though, Jareth noted.

Slinging his mandolin over his shoulder and tightening the straps across his chest, he quickly took up his red-hooded cloak, which did double duty as his bedroll—minstrels had a need to travel light. Time to go.

"Wait! You're going that way?"

Jareth could hear Leanan's confusion and saw the girl wondering too.

"Aye; told you last night—this cave has another end, another entrance, and I hope its one too small for yon riders. It's probably too much to hope it's a shortcut through this infernal woods. I'd like to see what those riders would do with a really steep incline just now..."

"No, you don't want to know that, Jare; when you can fly, why worry about falling?"

He fervently hoped she was not being literal, but pressed a grim smile on his face just the same.

"Why indeed."

That was the last of his witticisms this day.

*

"You can delay them with the Guth, if you dare."

He looked at her as the rear exit came into sight. The hastily conceived torch they had, had been sputtering for a while now, and as it was getting too hot to hold, the light of overcast day reached out to them like a lance. And dimly, emerging from the cave's shadows, Piper was silhouetted against the wan light.

"The what?"

His words seemed inordinately loud in the encroaching darkness, alerting them all that the cave had broadened and arched into a cavern of some sort. No time now to ponder if it were tenanted. He could feel the earth rumbling, muted by being underground.

"It translates to 'the Voice'; it's one of your better traits, Jare."

Damn, what was she talking about now?

"There's more to your songs than you know; it's actually one of your skills...that and another particular to beneath the sheets..."

Her laugh echoed brazenly, sleeping in words and mirrored in eyes.

His face was emotionless as he pointed with his sword toward the distant light.

"Maybe you can come to understand how much power there is in silence, hey? I'm sure that last made its way all the way back to last night's fire."

He was more confused than upset with her, but he wasn't going to let her know that. The two women fell in ahead and picked up the pace.

The far exit appeared and with a look of grim satisfaction, he could see how narrow and small it actually was. Only enough room to admit one at a time. At least if pursuit followed them this far, they'd be hard pressed to get any horses through at the same time. Made the odds much more palatable.

Leanan went first, the long-bladed knife in one hand and dragging the girl with the other. The guitar sticking out of Beryl's pack got caught on the rock and she squealed in distress, thinking it was being damaged. She feared she might be required to leave it behind. And indeed, Leanan started to throw the instrument aside, but relented when Jareth surprised her with a shake of his head. Leanan showed her displeasure.

"Keep it then, girl, but get going. Not sure what good it's going to do when the Hunt catches up, but I see you're like Jareth—a stubborn troubadour and proud of it."

He had to bend in ways he hadn't in a while, but Jareth squirmed and wriggled until they were all standing in the fresh air of midday. He started forward, preparing to take the lead when the woman's long nails raked at his pauldron, jerking him back. Off balance, he toppled into her, noting that not even her leather armor could hide the firm softness beneath her chest plate.

"Hold up there, Cap'n; might want to check out that first step."

Quizzically, Jareth turned from her taunting form to see Beryl perched on the very edge of a drop. And coming to her side, his expression turned grim as he noted all the loose shale and rock below, kept in place only by the endless scraggly trees. At the bottom, the dark ribbon of a snake wove. The water below looked cold and he shivered involuntarily.

"You can thank me later, Dear."

She cast him a lascivious smile and winked as she passed, helping the girl begin the descent.

The path paralleled the river and for that, all three were thankful, even though Jareth bent his sight to finding a way across. Piper is going to hate this, he thought. The expanse wasn't great but by the water's very motion, he could tell it was deep. Too deep for horses, and that would be a good thing. Looking up as they navigated from the cliff's head above to the deer trail below, Jareth could see the welling sky whose colors contorted fantastically. The clouds gyrated, racing up the valley.

"Advance riders, Jare. At night, they're hardly visible, lying on the black field of stars, but during the day, the dark somnolence breeds fear and failure."

He noted that the trees were changing with the terrain; more and more, the lushness whittled away the scrub trees and real arboreal candidates took their place.

"You sound like you know these hunters."

To the east, the slopes of the other side of the valley could be seen. Long lines of briars and vines formed an impossible network of tangles, as if the vegetation spiderwebbed with purpose. Fleetingly, Jareth wondered what purpose it might be.

"Aye, I do. They aren't the ones you want on your trail."

"And how do you know them?"

His curiosity was more than piqued, it was saturated; there was too much about this woman which he didn't know.

"They belong to my world, Jare. On occasion, I've called upon them myself!"

What? What did she say?

She eyed him speculatively while pushing the girl further in front as the whining was beginning to get on her nerves.

"Aye, you heard me, I didn't stutter."

Damn.

"So is there a way to stop them? I don't even know why they're tracking me in the first place."

He had his hand on his sword, the comfort there less than it usually was.

"Magic can stop them, or at least magic as you know it. Short of that, few have the physical power to withstand their onslaught. Of course, they have to find their prey first, and in that we have hope. Both the cave exit and the steep slope should cause them issues. Without their dogs, they'll have to listen to the wind, and I've been working that since we awoke. Already, other guth are weaving a lattice of deceit that should distract them."

"Now, why doesn't that surprise me?"

Her laugh merely echoed the uneasiness in his soul.

"Not a lot surprises you anymore, I notice; I'll have to see about changing that!"

It was then that the girl shrieked and shot off into the woods, followed by the cat. At the same time, like a roaring hurricane, the thickening sky fell.

Chapter 14

Darkness

Unreal, he thought, even as he turned to face the rushing darkness bound by cloud and wind. Whereas the trees had hindered the gathering sky, down in the valley the river was spreading like an avenue before the force of their pursuit. Like nothing he'd ever seen, the forms and faces of those Leanan called the Hunters, became cruelly clear. And whereas he and the two women had to flee over the game path, the rush of warriors, and their misshapen steeds, ground their passage on the soil of the wind.

Jareth's hand hesitated momentarily as he cringed before the sound of their rising horns and the stampede of hooves, though how the air could manufacture such sound was beyond him. It was magic of a type that seemed familiar and yet, alien. It was as if he should know these hunters, or rather, Hunters, as Leanan liked to delineate.

"Can't you do anything? Like you did at the gate?"

His words were rank with doubt as he acknowledged her return, the girl limp by her side. He cast an inquiring glance at Leanan.

"She wasn't being cooperative."

He nodded absently, his attention fully on the maelstrom heading their way. Maybe Piper was smartest of them all as he remained missing in the thick brambles of the encroaching trees.

As the lead riders struck their lances against iron shod shields and sent up a roar of discovery, Leanan stepped forward on the path, her black-cloaked form invisible but for the blue that limned her limbs. Like blue fire, Jareth thought.

Against his back, he felt the wind stumble and realign, pulling an equally cold draught of air from the river's grasp. Rushing past him, the gale force lanced out toward the coming charge. Dimly, Jareth thought he heard the sinuous voice of Leanan rising, mixing with the wind and strengthening its resolve.

The earth started to tremble, as if the pounding hooves of the wide-eyed steeds were too much for it to bear. The point of his sword wavered and dipped. Jareth stared aghast as he saw many of the horses bore six legs, some more. And they had a tangle of sharp horn protruding from their heads while lightning streamed as manes. Red fire blazed where tails should be. And the warriors—each large and heavily muscled, bore their breath to the earth.

Jareth felt the coming of battle and he could see these were bent like berserkers, their faces wild and fey, their eyes protruding and teeth gnashing. Even as they clashed their weapons together, the clamor was deafening amidst the endless blowing of horns, so loud that the clouds of storm were envious.

All this bore down on the two standing on the path and the one lying limp at their side. One stood with upraised arms, fury shrieking from her lips, the sense of which was torn from her breath by the heart of all winds. Another held firm with a pretense none were sure could be sustained. Skies roiled like the current of the river rushing past, in a clash of opposing storms.

"Go back, Sons of the Asgardsreien; there is no satisfaction here!"

Leanan's song rolled like thunder, piercing like lightning when she hit high notes. And in return, streaks arced toward them like living flame. Arrows of blue fire burst and scattered like fireflies against the ward of her hands even as Jareth blanched involuntarily, raising his sword as if it would help.

One great steed that looked like a dragon-headed horse, pushed to the fore, carrying a warrior whose helm sported living wings. The man's visage was dark and his eyes shone, while the battle cry from his throat was a guttural blow. He raised his arm and swung a long pole to its highest point; Jareth waited for its arc to find its zenith.

"Nay, Gwydion, turn away! Find another to hunt this day. Dawn's behind, sun rakes your back, shredding nighttime and foe's attack!"

The air shimmered then shivered as the mighty Huntsman swung his spear toward the man, trying to evade the woman's glowing form. Jareth let the sword fall limply from his hand, held in thrall by the sight of hooves and steel falling upon him. From the back, he felt his lungs being crushed as the force of the Hunt found them. He felt pinned to the ground even as he saw Leanan's figure grow, slowly at first then ever faster, until she was as colossal as the mythical figure who smote the air.

Steel clashed and screams grew strident, the thunder roared and rain sluiced the ground, muddying Jareth's hair and face as it poured in a fierce deluge. He felt his strength ebbing before the all consuming blows of the winged-helmed warrior as he swung his blade against Leanan's flashing knife.

Gripped in the storm accompanying the Hunt, the river rose and smashed at its shores, ripping tree, rock, and root in its mad haste to get free, for it too was embroiled in a bitter fight for survival.

The blaze of his chest burned and Jareth cried out, ridiculed by the irony of the proclamation across his skin. Survivor of the World, indeed; if only he didn't feel so mocked in the moment, he might have found time to sneer at such insolence. But he'd been younger then, when the characters had been inked.

The day was morphing into night, despite Leanan's furious attempts to stop it. The air before her resonated, shaking like flames, erratic and yet dangerous just the same. Jareth felt consciousness ebbing, his mind fracturing as the Huntsman's spear pierced further and further beyond her protective shield. If only he could do something...

"Dammit man, you can! Use the Verse! Bridge the worlds and fill the void!"

But her words were like water over cobbles, each a voice unto its own but blending nonsensically to his ears. Her form began to bend.

"What have you done, Jareth? Why have you dammed the ocean's mouth? I can't release it...I can't form a hold on it...the Spear of the Hunt smells fresh blood!"

Jareth's lips moved, mouthing a smatter of words that struggled to break loose from his reticence, trying to answer her call.

"Break the blade, shiver the lance...shear the wind and rain, stand tall in the path and bare the fangs of blood and pain!"

Leanan howled at the tremor of his barely uttered words.

"By the teats of Fand! Sing it, you fool!"

In concert, the river overflowed its banks and lent their music to his own, repeated but this time, as if born of strings.

Chapter 15

Shadow of the Moon

He remembered the smell of fur, of rank, coarse, unbridled wildness filling the air above him and flashing past as he lay pressed to the earth, the beat of his heart bubbling painfully. Where had they come from?

As prelude to infusion, the power of their tongue filled the voids between bursts of thunder. Mixed with a depth of soul, howls were filled with growls and gnashing of teeth. When the snapping of jaws cut across the sound of the storm, that's when Jareth's vision fully blacked out. Much of the fight was irrevocably lost to his sight but not to his ears. Like Banshees at a funeral, the sound of battle scored heaven's veil.

"You mean O'Ban Sidhe; I always hate it when you mortals contort the old language like that."

Leanan leaned over, giving him a generous view of her breasts and perspiring skin, bound by scales of leather and studs of silver. He lived, or maybe he didn't and was now in Heaven...

"The former, and you're welcome. I'm not sure if it was you or me, this time. Certainly, I have no influence over wolves."

The road was wet and he dripped water from his shoulder-length brown hair and onto muddy blue pauldrons. His white kirtle with the dragon imprint was also darkened. He had an urge to throw up but swallowed hard, not wishing to look weak in front of the woman.

Who just laughed with glee, her face sweeping close to his and showing sharp teeth. He longed to stroke the pale white skin of her throat as she threw her voice to the air.

Above them, the sky was breaking. As Jareth sat up, rubbing at his eyes, he thought he saw the remnant of a pack of wolves, large black and white beasts, chasing the last of the Hunt's riders. What had happened?

Leanan turned her attention and helped him upright even as she eyed the sobbing girl at their side, who was hysterical and would need some time. But Jareth didn't see Leanan as the mothering type and felt a surge of confusion swarm his first thoughts of how to comfort Beryl. Why did compassion feel so awkward in his hands?

"Near as I can determine, you sang up a wolf pack, and in the nick of time, I might add. That and the river warriors that heard me. Though, there's still something wrong, as if you're not letting me have my full powers."

Her words fell on Jareth nonsensically; how did he have anything to do with her magic?

"No, it's not magic, you should know that. Now, what *you* just did, well, we might have to label it such. Indeed, just might."

"What? Are you saying I did that? Hardly. I'm no more magical than a turnip. You're the one that controls the wind and rain—I've seen it twice now. Witch, just as I said."

But even as he called her that, denying the woman's words, he knew something didn't sound right.

"Oh? Jareth, let me ask you something..."

She was helping the girl up, her hands forcefully yanking the cringing teen to her feet and eyes daring defiance. Beryl bit her lip and shrank away from the woman's hands, but she too was more than aware of how the winds and river moved at Leanan's bidding.

As the low clouds shredded yet further to let in streamers of sunlight, the three gathered their strength and forced themselves northward.

"When you sing your songs, when you play your strings, do you not think the sound magical?"

Jareth started to protest but stopped; he did think that. Indeed, it was what he hoped he conveyed every time he performed. He noticed when time seemed to hang while the tune took control of his tongue, of his mind and heart. The feelings that would come over him urged only to be shared. Gladly, he'd oblige and usually, when the collection pot had been passed, it was confirmed that he'd done just that. But, he'd never thought of it as magic before...it was just something he did and from which others found peace.

"You're not being fair with yourself, Love; they feel much more than just that and you know it. If you're honest with yourself, you know many fair maidens swoon beneath your words, and men find that soft spot in their hearts, that children are taken on roads of whim and wonder. Often, your songs can bring a madman to his knees and a whoring wench to repentance—*if* you're so inclined."

And she gave him a sly look while pressing her dark lips into a pout. Her lids lowered and the liquid gold gleam of her eyes was like last night's embers, warming him all over again.

"What does that have to do with wolves and swiftly-flushed storms? What does my music have to do with the Hunt and its Hounds?"

She looked at him, her face contemplating a response.

"Far more than you remember, that's obvious. But at its core, your music is your source of power. I couldn't have held off Gwydion without you, though that's your fault too."

Say what you mean, woman, stop the riddling. Jareth's head hurt and he was tired of not understanding. It was as if she knew something he didn't, and this worried him far beyond reason.

"I *am* saying what I mean; you're just being obtuse!"

In a moment's sympathetic confusion, Beryl's wide eyes fixed on him. He wasn't the only one who didn't understand.

"Jareth; the Hunt is from my world, and I should have been able to control it. Mannanan knows, I've used it often enough over the years, and yet, there was something definitely wrong, because it was like strangers making love; there was nothing but elemental powers colliding. There was no recognition in the warriors that rode upon the wind, there was no light of familiarity in their steeds' eyes. It was like they didn't know my name…a surreal possibility I have to ponder. Their power was great this time, as if Midsummer were upon us and yet, it is not. If you hadn't summoned the pack, if you hadn't added your own guth to mine, we'd not be here to talk about such mysteries."

And she went quiet. But that was fine with Jareth because he had enough thoughts scurrying around in his own head to wonder further about hers. When Piper slipped from the roadside and fell in behind him, he didn't give the animal even a glance.

He hadn't meant to take his voice down such paths, but he did. He hadn't wanted to revisit such feelings, despite how weary he was of being without them. But as Leanan lowered her voice to match the night's, her song brought out the pain of his soul.

Jareth had been strumming lightly on the mandolin while Beryl huddled to one side, attempting to coax Piper nearer, and Leanan sat cross-legged by the fire, her gaze on him. He felt a need to release the feelings building inside, some of which he couldn't define. The usual suspects though, ached to be let loose, and he knew if he wanted some answers, such feelings and emotions needed to be bled. It was always this way, and lately more so, beginning with the tension of the siege followed by the frenzy of escape and then strange pursuit. He'd hoped the feelings would be assuaged, but once free of the castle, they'd only morphed. What to do though, was not a mystery and so, he sang quietly, urging the night to listen.

Deciding the man needed more than his own introspection, Leanan fished for her silver comb, lifting it from a hidden place beneath her leather armor. She then unbuckled the two top stays, knowing it exposed her throat and skin below more fully. The fire meant to warm them from a long day of traveling and being chased, did more than push fears away, it pulled earthly desires. Deftly, she began to unbraid her hair.

Beneath the slow rise and fall of her chest, a rising hunger stirred from fitful rest. Above their heads, filtering between tangled fingers of a deepening forest, the moon sent purposed light, muting the effect of the fire.

Jareth watched the girl watch him, her fascination with his own instrument lulling her into a moment where she forgot how the ink in her skin wanted to writhe in protest. The girl was relaxing but even as her eyes rounded in envy and her mouth in awe, his gaze was gone, taken by the night and left to wander over the thoughts that surged in his head. There, gleaming like flowing ink and blue-shadow mountain snow, Leanan pulled his eyes until he didn't even recognize he was drowning in lust. Her body called to him and he felt himself respond.

The song changed and his tone grew more fluid. The words took what they needed from the night and fashioned a silver net so that he might catch the necessary words. As he wrote in his mind, the words flowed out to the rhythm of his fingers. Notes practically wept from his mandolin. And as he closed his eyes, he felt her hands on his, felt her breath warm against his neck, and knew the desire of her skin on his. He succumbed to the tilt of her face and the deep shadow of the moon swallowing her eyes. He knew he sang but he didn't hear the words audibly anymore. And when she added her own voice to the chorus, her rich vibrant dulcet tone merged and twisted, making it impossible to know where one voice started and the other stopped. Somewhere, somehow, he know the girl was deep in sleep.

The night hung a cloak about them both as he felt her hands on his arms, releasing the buckles and catches of his short tunic. Her breath became his kiss and he merged the feel of the night with the feel of her skin, sinking far deeper than he had in a long, long time.

He felt the touch of the moon slip, its hold on him more tenuous and brittle. Still, he tried to hold on because the dreams were so very powerful and real. He didn't want to wake and yet, a voice urged just that, the same as the one in his dreams, which made waking that much more confusing. But opening his eyes soon brought clarity.

"Awake, Jare—there's no time to lose. Beryl's gone."

He lurched upright, his red hooded cloak dropping to his lap and exposing the bare skin of his chest.

He felt her fingers brush across and lingering, dig in sharply before leaving.

"Sometime soon, you're going to have to tell me the story of this tattoo; I'm beginning to think I need to know more about these changes you've made. I think it might be important."

He glanced down at the glyphs, staring without reading because he already knew what they meant. Changes?

"No time—they're probably already deep into the woods and you know I'm more potent on the open water. I'll get Piper and you get dressed."

Numbly, he muttered in response.

"Don't bother—he's not going to let you touch him; you know that."

She paused and eyed the man, a brow arched.

"Oh? What else do you remember?"

But the glazed look on his face didn't answer either her question or his own inquiry. How *did* he know that? And why not?

"Maybe because he doesn't like my crow, aye?"

Her laughter was short and clipped, instilling her urgency. Then her words penetrated.

"Who's already in the woods?"

"The ones who took Beryl."

More confusion as his eyes swept to where the girl had slept last night. Her bedroll was there, as was her pack and guitar, but no girl. She was gone? Why? Where?

"Aye, she's gone but against her will. Or I think so as there's signs of struggle."

Struggle? What was the witch talking about?

Leanan glared and continued, offering her hand so that he might hoist himself to his feet, while fumbling at belt buckles and adjusting straps.

"My boots?"

She tossed a worn leather pair toward him, then hastily slipped into hers. The way they hugged her calves caused Jareth's blood to surge momentarily.

That's when Jareth wakened fully and stopped in his tracks, wondering exactly what he was doing.

"So, she's gone?"

"Aye, my bard, I told you that already. We need to pick up their trail and get her back."

Jareth brought his arms up and slowly folded them, his mouth hardening.

"Do we now...ah, and why is that?"

Leanan stopped breaking camp and placed her slim but firm arms on her hips, her brows bending over darkening eyes.

"Do we have to go over this again? I told you already; she's important to finding your purpose here."

Jareth had been considering this idea since the other night, and if it hadn't been for the Hunt, would already have had this out with the witch.

"I don't see it that clearly. Up until you showed up, I didn't even know the girl existed. Why is she so damned important?"

He glared back at her, cowed by her fierce look but unwilling to admit it. Why had she changed from his dream of last night? Then, there'd been nothing but deep-throated kisses and melding flesh...

"Stop it, Jareth—we don't have time. If you want answers to where *your* home is, you're going to need the girl. Helping her helps us. You do want to go home, right?"

His words choked in his throat even as he thought to voice them. He realized he did, or rather, that his heart was calling for just that.

"You don't know the way, do you?"

She said it not as a question but rather, as an accusation, which surprisingly stung.

He faced her in silence though thoughts whirled in the gales of his mind. Then he shook his head, aware that she'd been more aware all along. And seemed to at least have the beginnings of an answer. Still...

"Still what?"

Imperious, she bore down on him like a flock of ravens circling a battlefield.

"I don't need the girl. I can find home without her."

There, he said it, believing that the uncertainty both women brought to his life had inexplicably complicated matters far more than he liked. Breaking her gaze, he bent to scoop up Piper. Stroking with a fervor that belied his confidence, he placed the cat on his shoulder where it nuzzled the side of his face, asking for more.

"Can you do without your sword?"

He slapped at the rigid steel at his side, looking for confirmation that it was still there. Relief flooded over him.

"Not that one—the Sword of Pain; the one I was carrying. Your real sword, not that dandy's affectation."

And the truth was, he hadn't forgotten her earlier assertion that the rapier she'd been lugging around, was really his. There was an affinity he couldn't deny but also, couldn't explain.

"Sword of Pain?"

"I didn't name it."

She said this last accusingly, as if it were his fault. His fault? Though he couldn't deny the sword's allure, he also was loathe to grasp any truth in her claim.

"When they took the girl, apparently, they also grabbed your sword. It has no power for them, so I'm not sure why they took it, but there you have it; your sword's gone, too."

He tried to digest his feelings about this secondary development, wondering about the nagging tug at his heart. He switched the focus off the missing blade.

"So the Hunt came back? Thought they'd been chased off."

Leanan took a breath, her exhalation speaking volumes.

"No, it wasn't them—there's no feeling anywhere that any of the Fae were here last night. Someone else crept in while you were dreaming and stole them both."

Jareth arched an eyebrow at Leanan's description; stole the girl, dreaming? She didn't belong to him or Leanan. Still, Beryl didn't belong to her captors, either. And, now they had his sword. Or at least the witch said so.

"Muse," she corrected.

"Aye, right; muse. I find it hard to believe though, that they left us alive, risking pursuit. Especially with their efforts yesterday."

"We're alive because they couldn't find us last night."

"What? What do you mean? We were all sleeping around the fire."

"Oh? Do you forget so easily, then? Did you sleep the whole time?"

Her eyes flashed wickedly and he felt his loins clinch.

Blushing, he was aware that not only could she read his mind, but obviously involve herself in his dreams. And what a dream it had been..."

"Well, thank you, Love; at least you're still honest it seems. There's hope, yet."

"So why didn't they see us?"

He couldn't believe he was even talking about this, and was annoyed she was taking his embarrassment so lightly. She'd been there too...

"That's part of the power of my song, Jareth, though for some reason, you're making that part more difficult than it usually is. Others can see me only if I wish them to, and yet, those attacking at the castle—and your girl Beryl—seem not to have had any problem. How, I don't understand, but at least last night, you allowed me to be who I am, fully. When we made the words come alive, there was only you and I. For that moment, you were in the land of the Fae. Be glad we were; I can't say what the Bone Warriors would have done to us otherwise."

"Bone Warriors?"

Leanan looked surprised herself at naming those who'd taken the girl. She nodded, not trusting herself to explain further.

"Never heard of them. They're not part of the Hunt?"

Again, Leanan shook her head.

"Did the Tuskellions send them?"

The muse looked hard at him, her eyes touching his face as if physically working the skin of his temple. He could literally feel their weight as he had her hands...

"No. There is a crease of night that opened and set loose something that crawls in your mind, Jareth."

"Who or what are Bone Warriors?"

She started to say something then thought better.

"They belong to the enemy; it sent them beneath the guise of the Hunt in case the Hounds failed."

Jareth stroked the thoughts in his head. It seemed she knew things he did not, and it was about time they were on the same page.

"The same enemy who sent the Hunt, sent the Bone Warriors?"

"Aye, same indeed. The same that has flung you to this world, or perhaps, has forced you here. I'll know the enemy's name when you tell me, but it's clear already that it's not from your world. It comes from afar and has done great evil, Jareth."

Her words didn't make much sense. She'd tell him when he told her? What the hell was she playing at now?

"It's hard to explain, Jare—trust me. Just know you're not out of danger but the opposite. I fear this river of time is being dammed. Without the girl, we may never get home."

The muse's words penetrated like the sting of a needle filled with black ink, coursing its story on his mind. For a brief moment, he thought he understood how the girl must feel.

"And these Bone Warriors have Beryl...and the sword?"

He realized he was repeating what he already knew, but his grasp of the situation was growing tenuous.

Leanan nodded.

"And we need both, right?"

The growing dawn light played over the muse's high cheekbones, the pale skin contrasting with the color of her hair, hastily braided, its shock of white lacing the knots.

Piper dug his claws into the man's shoulders, bracing before an imminent decision.

"And what are Bone Warriors?"

She looked into his eyes, the silver a mercurial flow of clouds all his own. Maybe the memories weren't as lost as she feared.

"They're the shades of the dead, Jareth, those who have died at your hand."

Damn...is that all?

Chapter 16

Destroyed

"I hate this."

The words were louder than he wished, his body tensing against the hard-scratch ground on which he lay, eyes staring unseeing at the night sky. The stars would have been familiar, if he'd looked for them, but at the moment, butterflies of apprehension flitted in his gut as he prepared for the fight ahead. There didn't seem to be a choice and that bothered him.

"Doesn't have to be this way, Darling; you could use your voice, you know."

The woman had been on him all day, cajoling him, coaxing him, even berating him, and all because he refused to capitulate to her demands. Not that she didn't send mixed messages though...

"Oh? And now *you're* feeling fire lacing your thighs? Maybe later, Dear. We have work to do, now."

Why the hell couldn't she just stay out of his head? And the gall she possessed was infuriating...

"You like me that way—don't deny it, Jare."

She sat cross-legged beside him on the hill overlooking the enemy's camp. She called it that, refusing to put a name to the entity behind this sudden aberration of his life. There must surely be a village in the near distance, one with a cosy tavern where the wenches would keep his mug filled for less than a chorus' worth. At least, he liked to think so.

They'd tracked the bandits for miles along the forest path, noting that their speed did not waver. Perhaps because they feared pursuit?

"Nay, more that the Hunter has reason for their haste. It'll be calling them, urging them to bring the girl home. Now, isn't that ironic after what she's told us?"

Hunter? Hadn't they already defeated such?

"Nay, Jareth love; those were from my world, they are the ones who are bound to midsummer nights and lanes of night-blooming mothan, the rare moon-flower. The Hunter who sent *these* warriors is your doing. There's irony in that, too."

For much of the day he'd pondered why Beryl had been taken at all. What part did she play? The muse had given him the idea that it was he they wanted. Still, Jareth didn't like it when another took something of his without asking.

"Great; another hunter. Just what I needed."

He'd pushed hard along the well worn path, feeling the earth and woods changing as they went. Whereas the scrub forest had seemed flat to him, a prairie of stunted sticks, they'd now entered a true forest, and its change was already working its own kind of magic. For some reason he couldn't define, breathing grew easier. Or maybe it was because now, *he* was the hunter.

Leanan had been unwavering, keeping pace and showing more fortitude than he'd expected. Not that she appeared soft—though he speculated how soft some parts of her might be—no, though well proportioned, her arms were firm and steady. The way she'd beaten at the forest as it crowded the path convinced him of that. He was surprised though that she could move so silently on such high heeled boots; his own feet made only slightly less sound, and he considered himself a woodsman.

Which was surprising because most of the time, he'd trade a bed on the lawn for the soft yet lumpy mattresses of more than a few inns in his past. And the memories of waking up in such pillowed luxury made him wistful.

"No time for dreaming now, Bard; the last one looks like he's about to drift off. From the looks of them, I didn't expect they'd need such a human necessity. More to them than first glance, I deem."

Indeed, the Bone Warriors for all their gauntness, looked anything but human. She was right; why would such need to sleep?

"Maybe it's you who needs them to need sleep..."

He heard her but didn't give her comment any validation because she was making her usual nonsense remarks. Nevertheless, he listened to the night as the rustling sounds below in the warrior's encampment grew subdued. One soft choke of sound caused his eyes to widen. Seems the girl at least was still alive.

The trees had bunched before opening into periodic glades, wherein the path would stretch sinuously beneath the shortening day's sun. It was then that he could actually see Beryl, trussed and hanging like a sack from the shoulder of a large, black-cloaked fighter, whose face was pocked and marked, showing little flesh and exposed, scarred bones. Before disappearing beneath the further shadows of the trees, the true nature of these raiders was made known. Bones with swords indeed, he thought.

"I never heard of Bone Warriors, and no song I know tells tales of them either. They aren't part of your world, are they? They don't feel like fae to me..." which made him frown; how did he know that?

She looked at him as they spied the group, their progress having put them high up the slope while below, Beryl was hustled away. Still, they were gaining.

"Nay, none of my folk, to be sure. These are mortal scions, bereft of underworld magic but full of bloodless emotion. There seems to be six, though I'd be careful; hard to imagine you've so little blood on your hands.

Her words bothered him, much as they had when she'd first explained how the Bone Warriors were manifest from those whose lives he'd destroyed. Why did she make wearing and using a sword seem like such an offense? He didn't like to think of those times when after a long set of songs, complete with more than a few tankards of ale and his purse half full, that the town's brigands had wanted him to share. And of course, he wasn't often inclined toward that weakness, which necessitated whetting his blade. There were others, and though he couldn't easily pull their names from memory, he intuitively knew he didn't want to, either.

As night fell and the track thinned, causing the raiders to slow while allowing them to gain, it was just a matter of when to engage. He'd rather have done it their way—sneak in and quietly slip away with what they'd stolen, but the Bone Warriors didn't look like the type to sleep that deeply. Still, he might yet try...

It was then she'd suggested he lull them into just such a deep sleep.

"You're the one who seems versed in that kind of thing; why are you looking to me?"

The question begged to be asked.

She padded silently behind him, her eyes curious and smiling, as if she was privy to a secret insight. She was infuriating, sometimes.

"Keeps you from becoming bored, don't you know that?"

Her chuckle was deep in her throat.

"For some reason, you've limited my abilities here, and until you release the binds, there's only so much I can do. I suppose we'll just have to fight our way in and take her, aye?"

Her eyes glinted lustily, confusing him. He turned his gaze back to the trail, all the while shaking his head in regret. What had he gotten himself into? Already the girl was proving more trouble than he could ever remember having. And why was he so keen to recover a sword? Familiarity aside, he didn't need it. Or did he?

"You do—you're just not aware of it yet. I think it's the blade we most need to recover, though don't ask me why. The girl is less of a secret and yet, might prove more important. We'll see."

He didn't like the idea of fighting any of the Warriors, and didn't think they'd even bleed if he *should* stick them.

"Not a lot of places to poke, at least places that might do some good."

She laughed lightly, a sound that was surprisingly at odds with the deepening atmosphere. Just as his breath was becoming more earthy and hale, so too did he notice the rising resonance in the muse's words. As if the woods held a growing power of which he was only now becoming aware. Damn, what was going on? How had he come to be mixed up in such intricacies? The only magic he appreciated was that which came from the strings of his mandolin.

"Exactly; maybe there's hope for you yet."

She was irritatingly smug too, sometimes.

"You lead for awhile, I need to think." He let her pass and noticed she made no effort not to brush against his arm, a firm softness radiating even beneath the leather cuirass. The fact she had it half unbuckled wasn't lost on him, either.

She took to the trail, melting into the deepening gloom with their quarry almost within reach. With his ear to the ground, he confirmed Leanan's startling but acute hearing.

Some liken us to elves, Jare, so don't be so surprised.

He grunted, as if that explained a lot.

And so he lay, wondering how he might avoid the conflict he expected, while Leanan swept her long bladed knife against a sharpening stone, the soft hiss merging with the night. It wasn't fully dark as the moon rode over the trees, it's half-dressed silhouette lingering in mid-step as night's dance began. Enough light to see the camp below where four of the Bone Warriors readied for sleep. Did they truly expect no resistance? Then again, two were missing. Probably sentries to either side of the path that lay within sight of the camp. Well, two meant only four were guarding the sword...

"And the girl," Leanan chirped, her long fingered hand shaping itself almost erotically around the dirk's pommel. He glanced quickly at her face in the dark, seeing her eyes glimmer, as if a smolder of lust longed to be free. Her pointed teeth gleamed, contrasting against blood-red lips, a promise he didn't miss. Pale rivers of her neck ran to deeper clefts wherein a man might get lost...

"And the girl," she repeated, her eyes forcing recognition from his eyes.

"Yeah, right; and the girl."

"There's still time to do it the easy way."

His quizzical look changed to irritation as he lowered his voice.

"I told you; no song of mine is going to put anyone to sleep—that's not why I sing. If I put folks to sleep, they'd miss the melody and the story behind it."

"Aye, Jareth, you're right, but there's more to your Voice than you suspect. If you could trust me, I'd show you."

For a moment, the temptation almost consumed him as he fought with the duality of what she was saying. That she meant something entirely different couldn't be denied, though physical proof was scarce. Trust her...now, why did that thought both delight and scare him?

She saw his struggle and her face softened, surprisingly; from a deep recess within her heart, a whimper of compassion and concern clung dearly for life. If she wasn't careful, she might lose him...

"Jareth, do you know any lullabies?"

What?

"A song to lull children to sleep. The Fae have many of these."

"I know what a lullaby is. This is no time for such innocence—a damn kid's song isn't going to do aught but get us killed the quicker as they harken to my voice."

"Ah, you'd be surprised, Jare, if you really knew. Well, at least think of one in your head—if the wind hasn't already gotten in and swept away your mind."

And truth to tell, the breeze had been surreptitiously flitting about his cheeks, causing him to brush it away as if alive. He waved her to silence, motioning to the left.

"Ready?" His voice lowered beyond a whisper.

Leanan nodded, her knife poised at her waist. As the shadows took her, Jareth marveled at how easily it happened. Then he lowered further and just as quietly, approached the camp from the south, listening for the first sentry.

As the moon shone through a tangle of boughs, stripes were painted on the trunks, chasing the texture with fissures of darkness. It was within this pattern that Leanan drove her long blade, the thrust piercing between moonlight ribs. But there was no living organ for her to penetrate. Her balance was thrown off as the thrust swept in to the hilt, jarring her cruelly against the giant Bone Warrior.

With a sweep of his left arm and a twist of his barrel-chest, a crude hook-edged blade flashed toward her, utterly soundless and just as deadly.

Ducking beneath her hand, Leanan felt the air above her head grow chill, as if death was being released from its coffin. The effect momentarily paralyzed her as she felt lungs stiffen and stall. Then the blade struck the trunk with a thud, burying itself deep in the bark while the muse rolled beneath the warrior's sword arm and twisted to the right, her knife flashing free. With a feral snarl, she bared her fangs and fire blazed in her eyes as she closed the distance between them.

It had to be here somewhere—didn't make sense to post a guard too far off the road. Almost anyone approaching from the woods would make far too much noise not to be heard, so any danger would come from there. But neither he nor Leanan were anyone. They'd been off the path for the last few hours leading up to dusk. When night had poured in and the Bone Warriors had begun camp, it was from a nearby hillock and far off the road, that they'd been watching. From the deep of the forest, they were in essence already inside the guard, though the Warriors didn't know it. This is why he'd thought there was a chance to get in and out without any fuss. But he'd have to neutralize the sentries first.

He placed each foot as if he were stepping on a gossamer web, and he did so without really trying. This was the woodsman in his soul, this was a part of him he didn't have to make an effort to draw; like his music, the chords of stealth were natural. As he thought of this, an image of his wooden mandolin sprang to mind, and with it, the scent of song.

He could describe his music many ways and though he didn't write most songs down, still his melodies were like poppies sprouting in the field of his mind. They just 'were'. It was why the strings came alive beneath his touch. It was like stretching a line of gut from heart to mind. And though he didn't acknowledge it to others, sometimes he felt his soul complete the triad. That link though, was harder to reach and pluck, but when he did, it created a depth of song he couldn't qualify; it just was.

A lullaby...that's what she'd asked and he'd dismissed out of hand. Why a lullaby? To put these raiders to sleep? Wasn't possible—although, he mused, he'd heard of bards affecting village children that way. But that was only in the old stories, he admonished, and that from one of the bards.

Still, she'd called him that, hadn't she? But he was just a mere minstrel, a vagabond player who sang for food and lodging, and enough coin to get him to the next town. Not a sad singer you rushed back into the wild, but still only one who could entertain, sometimes. That was who he was, wasn't it? At least, it's all he recalled being.

A lullaby...something a gammy or nurse would use to sooth the ravages of night, something that placated the tendrils of uneasiness, that liquified the hard lumps when facing the dark.

Shadows moved now as clouds scudded over the half-moon, deepening the undergrowth his eyes were surgically taking apart. Where was the sentry? As apprehension rose to its knees, the sweat beaded from his hand and slid down his exposed sword.

The tune was banal, it was naive and full of an innocence he hadn't known for a long time. The soft threnody of sound played in his head as subconsciously, his footsteps kept time. Soon, he could hear the percussion of his heart accompanying the humming that leached from his throat. It took a moment to realize that the sound in his head was now audible!

At the base of the spine and up—it was the kill stroke she'd been looking for. There was no heart—as she'd almost fatally found out, but something drove these creatures, something as sure as the vastness of the sea that accosted the shore. As wind drove water, something drove these bones, these bones thrown together as soldiers of guilt and shame. She knew of Bone Warriors, but their stature was much less in the world of the Fae; not that such sins weren't accounted for but rather, that they were claimed righteously and therefore pitied and not enabled. Still, these weren't her Bone Warriors, they belonged to Jareth. As such, they held a power strange enough to be respected. She hoped his memory remained dormant for the moment else there'd be more than sentient irony with which to deal.

The bones suddenly separated, their sound a hollow tumble she found soothing. It surprised her, this sound of Jareth's fear folding. If she hadn't known him as well as she did, there was doubt such a formidable creature could be defeated. And though her pride swelled unreasonably, it wasn't because of the piling bones that were bleaching whiter beneath the chaos moon. Aye, it truly was such; a chaos moon was one whose coming and going was mired in indecision, whose path waited to be determined. Of course, it had to be, else how would the Hunt ever had found them yestereve?

She swept the sickly yellow ochre pus from her blade, the streams oozing down bent and broken fronds that even now were trying to devour the remnant bones. How curious, she thought, that what she wiped from her dirk resembled the marrow of bones...

It wasn't a tree because it wasn't bark into which he bumped. It wasn't the rasp of a bough of shadow-darkened leaves, be they Night's or more earthly designs, that brushed his cheek as he stumbled. It wasn't the gnarl of roots, having heaved viciously from the earth because the soil was hardened with rock, that he tripped over. It was a sentry, and only as he fell, extending his sword defensibly, that he grasped this fact. And yet, no blow came from the hooked blade in the warrior's brittle hand. There against the swelter of shadow, beneath an old oak bough, he held his sword rigidly, point squarely aimed at the toothless mouth of a skeletal face. The pitted eyeholes glowered back but absently, as if stricken by time, by a verdigris of rusted moments. Or maybe it was just what the maggots had left intact.

The Bone Warrior was still, hunched in repose, arm clutching the lowest branch for support. Jareth dared not move until his opponent did; that's when he would strike and hope to escape that first punishing blow.

But nothing moved and minutes passed, minutes in which Jareth saw the lines of shadow lighten as the half moon emerged.

Then the cloud cover came and it was veiled again. When moonlight came a second time, still there was only silence.

Jareth could feel the sweat on his brow beginning to track uncomfortably close, the trickle threatening to race down his neck and into his short tunic. It was then he realized he had stopped singing. And almost too late, he rushed to continue.

The verse tumbled, croaked and then smoothed as he imagined pressing his fingers down lightly on strings, a tune lifting within the sound of his voice. It was the damn lullaby!

Jareth turned slowly, his blade never altering its aim, just in case. He daren't even think of what was happening, of what he was doing. She couldn't have been right...could she?

As he urged the song and strengthened its spine with a familiar resonance, another thought simultaneously took flight; why hadn't he seen the warrior? Why had it been so invisible to his eyes? Surely he'd been in the woods enough to trust in his craft. And yet this time, he'd been surprised, almost fatally so. This doubt started to creep faster and gain momentum when he felt a cool touch on his temples. It was a subtle yet growing sensation, as if a woman's hands were softly tracing the lines in his forehead. He fought its influence for only a moment before closing his eyes and capitulating, drowning before an utter depth of feeling.

He heard his voice, heard it in ways that resided deep inside as palpitations of his heart. He knew he was singing, crooning the age-old melody of a song sung to him when he was young. It was the lullaby that had first lodged in his head, but whereas it began as a notion, now it surged into chords and a phalanx of notes whose wings were sweeping to enfold him in its center. He sang as only he knew he could.

Get the sword.

The words were flutterings, fragile feathers of time as he stretched out his voice, raising its tenor until the whole woods seemed likely to hear. The trees seemed to swell and the shadows shrank, as if the half moon was waxing full, having now decided it would live. The branches swayed as a wind sprang up in accompaniment, and their leaves rustled to fill in the gaps between chorus and refrain. He heard the voice and it was familiar.

And don't forget the girl.

Opening his eyes, he made his way from the sleeping Bone Warrior sentry and down into the small glade where the center of the camp barely breathed. Every sound he made was like an echo of the verse, holding notes of song. His footfall became fluid, rising and falling as if he was one with the earth. The shadows fell away and he entered the glade, his sword strangely forgotten in his hand. Across from him, he saw the shadows part and Leanan's form slip into the moonlight, her armor as blued as her long hair. The white shock was muted, flooded by the color of Night as She wove her fingers among the muse's long tresses.

The look on Leanan's face was full of mystery as well as an unholy pleasure. And he saw too, how her smile exposed her hunger.

He felt the wind swerve and lightly slap at his cheek, chiding him for his indulgence. And like the fading of a string just plucked, his voice drifted off, to be absorbed by the always-moving crenelations of Night's hems.

"Not always, Jare, not always. I could tell you of moments you've stalled time longer than is healthy, of timeless seconds you've smoothed out such creases. But, maybe you remember too, aye?"

But he didn't and just stared at her, uncomprehending.

"That's okay; it's a start. Now, help me get Beryl's things. Silly girl. Your song got her too and I dare say, she's going to be a load on your shoulders—again. Nothing for it, not this time. Be quick about it now, I don't know how long your magic lasts here in this world and I'm thinking it's best not to find out the hard way."

Jareth felt the flush of night and his body tightening, as if spirit had rejoined flesh and bone. Mechanically, he cut the leather binds around the girl's wrists and bent to hoist her over his shoulder. Without catching Leanan's eye, he began to make his way toward the path.

"Did you get the sword?"

He paused and turned but just stood staring at the woman, his lips tightening the longer the moment lasted.

"Never mind, I'll get it. I might need it before you do. Still, I wonder what's holding you back."

Leanan carefully scrounged about the four stone-steady forms, her hands flashing in the moonlight as her black-lacquered nails stemmed from shadows.

'Aha!"

He could hear her quick footfalls behind him even as he struggled to gain the higher ground of the path. Once there, he stopped to catch his breath; the girl was slim but no child. Why did he seem so lethargic? The distance hadn't been that great.

"Part of the effect of using the Guth, my love, that's all. Why do you think I'm careful when I harness the wind? It's all the same and yet not. What *you* do is less elemental and more spiritual. Part of your own mystery, methinks. Though that's not the definition you usually favor. Here now, wait a moment; something I forgot..."

Leanan dropped the girl's pack and guitar to the night sward and smoothly slipped back down toward the glade. Jareth watched as she moved, black amongst dark, shade amidst shadow, until he could see her emerge beneath the moon again. That's when he almost dropped Beryl.

The blue steel flare of light that erupted in Leanan's hand swept the night as if cutting molasses. Four times her arm swept up and four times it came down, and with each stroke there was a clatter of dullness that could only be falling bones. She sliced and cut at each warrior, the light slashing at the base of each skull. As she finished, Jareth finally managed to turn away. He wasn't sure if it was the way the silence filled the place where his song had lain, or the utterly emotionless face of the muse that stuck in his craw, daring him to vomit.

Chapter 17

In the Air Tonight

He felt her wince at his touch, but overall, she was getting better. And as Beryl turned from him to hand the plate to Leanan, Jareth chewed slowly, considering the girl. He'd seen her type before, just not this abject. Many in the castle had been marked with black ink, but they'd also had at least some gold lines running on their skin. Apparently, Beryl did not. At least, he didn't see any evidence of it. Which made her an enigma. Still, when the day had passed with no further pursuit, it gave him time to study the reason he was on this road. It was a path he was not sure he still wanted to travel, though. Questions remained and if not for the press of time, he'd probably have already parted ways. His teeth moved mechanically while his mind sorted through the pattern in which he found himself. There had to be a reason.

"Oh, you have one too! I thought I was the only one and..."

"That we were different? Nay, girl, we're more alike than you imagine."

Beryl was pointing to a spill of black ink that stained the small of the older woman's back; Leanan had been shrugging out of her beaten leathers and exposed a satin shift beneath, complete with open back and laced corset top. Such hadn't gone unnoticed by Jareth, either, but he'd said nothing.

"Still, it's a small one, something for Jareth."

He raised his eyes, wondering how his name had come up in the quiet conversation between the muse and the girl, noting the dark beauty of the muse's features glowing with her words. But he didn't take the bait. Leanan could keep her gibes to herself; she'd get no satisfaction from him.

"It's a bird, though like none I've seen."

"Aye; its called a badb, or crow, and it is my familiar. Or..." and here she cast a puzzled glance at the man who sat in silence—one he'd hung around himself since last night's rescue—while the trees around him crowded in, keeping the fire's flames from touching. It wasn't a harsh darkness but one that fit him comfortably. Too comfortably, Leanan thought. *He belongs to my darkness, not the forest's version. What was going on inside his head?*

"...at least it used to be; now, I don't know where it flies. The boughs surrounding were dull, devoid of all life, as if a great pestilence has been released and only the trees survived. I doubt my familiar would like the air here. Okay now, help me off with these boots; my legs ache after wearing them so long."

The girl did her best to tug the leather wrapped knee boots down slender, strong legs.

"Inside the castle, the air was the same—and it closed in on us the longer the siege went on."

Leanan thought she understood.

"The feeling of being trapped..."

But the young woman interrupted, shaking her head.

"No, not trapped, much worse; it felt like the walls were being pushed in on us, that every day, there was less and less ground to walk. I don't feel that. And here, it's also easier to breathe."

Leanan draped a shimmering burgundy cloak over her body, the weave alive with its own light. Something was in the air tonight. Above, the moon rode steadily but the dense boughs did not let any light sneak past. Across the fire, Jareth stabbed another piece of blackened meat.

"Aye, Beryl, I know that feeling, but for me, its only the ocean's great sigh that can really free me. Here, the wind has too many obstacles for it to flow cleanly, has too many intricate paths to navigate. Here, there is dilution, and the familiar breezes are bereft of much of their power. The ocean has no hold here, though currents still surge deeply beneath our feet."

Leanan leaned and placed her palm to the soil, long fingers splayed weblike. She sniffed and turned her nose up.

"Earth like dust, having drifted here long ago. But at its heart, the ocean knows its birth because She was here first."

Jareth's silence pervaded, turning time into grains of sand to be counted.

"Lady?"

Beryl swept bangs from her face, plying the strands behind her ears and fully exposing widening eyes. Leanan noted how rich and deep brown they were, filled with the vast promise of youth and shallowness of inexperience. She held a hidden yearning to know the mysteries, yet Leanan sensed the girl was only just awakening. The seam of her hem though, was woven with trouble. Leanan felt a tremor of memory lace her mood; it had been a while since she'd been called Lady.

"Yes, child?"

Idly, she took her silver comb from within her tunic and turning the girl around, began to sweep tangles free. The girl's hair was rich, with deep furrows that harbored a night all of its own.

"Why is it you don't mark me, as the others do?"

Beneath her graceful hands, Leanan felt the girl stiffen, knowing it must have taken much for her to voice this dread. If everything Jare had told her were true, this child was perpetually being demeaned, was always the butt of other's jokes. She wondered if mercy was a commodity in short supply in this world. Not that she had much use for such weakness, but she'd often noted this affectation when around mortals. Good thing the girl wasn't facing her to see the mockery that lingered just beneath the surface of her reply.

"And why should I do that?"

The girl's tangles melted before the muse's touch, the comb sending each shrieking away in terror, followed by a hand which melded each strand unto the others as if separate currents being realigned with the sea.

Jareth watched and saw Beryl's hair transform, the luster a liquid beauty he knew lay behind Leanan's own. It was as if elvish magic was loose, the kind he could sing about, if he were so inclined.

Leanan cocked an eye in his direction, an impish grin forming on her pale face. Her lids lowered, the long black lashes feathering the simmer of gold beneath. But the muse's pupils were dilated wide, consuming the night's continual flow of dark. When Beryl spoke, it was in a very sad voice.

"It's what everyone does."

Leanan resumed her manipulations, releasing Jareth's gaze from hers. She knew he was paying attention, though.

"I'm not everyone, Dear."

Beryl was quiet, having no answer to that. She held her guitar tighter, seeking comfort. She didn't suffer from the memory of the previous night because for her, all had been a dream, and one which was hard to refute. Even now, she didn't know if she should believe the story Leanan told her upon waking, bouncing along on the man's shoulders. She'd squirmed and beat at his back in misery though when she'd gained consciousness. The feel of being touched caused her to writhe in pain, despite Leanan's assurance. As Jareth had put her down, she'd fretted with her hands over her body, looking for further signs she'd been marked.

"Can I touch it?"

Leanan started. She turned the girl around, appraising. The girl's dark eyes poured into her own and something within the nature of a woman struck a chord she hadn't experienced before. It was strange, to say the least.

"Whatever for, Beryl? It's just a tattoo, an expression of art, though others might think I did it as a sign of vanity."

"My people don't do this to themselves, not like you do. I want to feel it's life, to understand why there's no fire."

Leanan was surprised at the girl's request; for her, the mark was born of whim. Unsure why, the muse turned and exposed her back.

Jareth, from where he sat watching and listening, grunted at a second sighting, noting the flow of pale skin that glowed. And as he looked closer and longer, then deeper, as Beryl took her slim hand and traced the black ink outline of what the muse called a crow, he couldn't help but notice the fine cracks, like minute fractures in a porcelain vase. As the girl's fingers touched the design, the lines wavered and shifted, not quite moving but close. When the young woman lingered on the wings, Jareth was sure they began a slow flapping motion, and he feared that there might be something more to Beryl's skin than he suspected. Damn, how did she do that? He paused in petting Piper, who lay curled asleep next to him.

For Leanan, the girl's touch was too soft to know when it began or ended, or if the tingling sensation was an echo of a memory. But when the girl's skin was in contact with hers, there could be no denying an underlying surge, as if the ocean's undertow had just been found. It rolled deep and coursed in harmony with the movement of air on her cheek. As Beryl traced the tattoo, the muscles of her back melted and she closed her eyes in response. Unnervingly, a connection between herself and the girl was made. And then, gone too soon, Beryl's touch faded.

"The bird wants to fly."

Leanan looked hard at the girl who desperately looked like a young woman, perhaps seeing more of herself than she was wont, but understanding that something was missing. And with a bitter sigh, she turned her head and glared darkly at Jareth, who'd seen everything while understanding nothing. He was still a man after all, though she knew he was the answer. She looked at Jareth but her words were for the girl.

"Aye, it has always been so. But not now, he won't let it."

Beryl looked up at Leanan with soft kitten eyes, no small wonder being reflected.

"He won't?"

Leanan shook her head slowly but without rancor. She knew this was just Jareth's way, and sometimes his way took time to unravel. She'd been here before.

For his part, Jareth scowled, understanding he was being blamed for something, something of which he had no knowledge. Just like a woman...

Leanan's laugh was rich and resonant, rippling like a river winds between rocks in a shallow shoal, a sound that shred a deepening despair that had been lurking.

"Oh, he shall, my dear girl, oh he shall; it's only a matter of time! He's still writing my part in this and he's usually slower to accept his life than I am. The babd will fly, Beryl, just you wait."

Jareth broke his gaze and concentrated on mending one of his boots. The needle caught his thumb and a pin prick of blood welled, but he continued nonetheless.

"Lady?"

Leanan turned to look full into the girl's face; both of them unaware of how tenderly the long black nails gripped youthful shoulders. The muse smiled slowly, one eyebrow raised. But beneath those nails, black ink was chafing.

"Are you really going to take me to Eli?"

Leanan's lips tightened as she formed her response.

"Are you sure you want to find him?"

A long moment passed before the girl nodded, tears welling.

"I want to know what it's like to be unmarked, Lady, that's all."

The muse held the girl's gaze, daring her to cry yet silently urging her to be strong.

"Don't we all, child, don't we all."

*

"I'm just hoping there's an inn up ahead; I've had enough of sleeping on the ground."

Leanan had been berating him again, wishing he would make their path easier.

"And what would you have me do? Beat on the stone hillside and whistle up a team of dwarves to pave the road? This land's not familiar to me, no matter what you say."

He fell into curses beneath his breath as he slowed to put some distance between the women and himself. What did she want from him? Was it his doing that the forest had grown wayward and lumpy, that what used to be a fairly well worn game path, had become a rutted mess of mud and loose shale? At least the strange wire and metal structures, which had beset their path outside the castle, had not returned. There should be some comfort in that, he reasoned. But the more she insisted this was all his fault, the more stubborn he became in his belief she'd come to torture him. Or at least haunt him. But that thought was predicated on another, one which he was successfully ignoring.

Jareth's response caused Leanan to raise a brow; just the fact he mentioned dwarves meant he at least wasn't averse to the idea that magic was a living thing. Not that there was much chance of the elder races intervening—it had been too long that they'd been quiet, and with Jareth's state of mind, she was just glad he wasn't completely dismissing her own abilities and questioning his sanity. Mortals did that a lot, she noticed.

Even when he'd disbelievingly hoisted Beryl to his shoulder upon finding that he couldn't wake her the other night, there was still hope. She smiled, remembering.

"She's not going to wake up? Why not?"

Leanan had smiled, the hint of seduction always lurking.

"Because she got caught in your song; tis your fault, so don't complain to me."

"What? I had nothing to do with that."

Leanan had eyed him despairingly.

"Really, Jare? You aren't going to believe anything your eyes see? You think those Bone Warriors just let you walk up and dismember them? They were under a spell—your spell. Just suck it up and admit it."

But the man was recalcitrant, the words of denial too close to his lips.

"You're just saying that because you want to forget, Jare; you've always wanted that. And for some reason, here in this place, you have. For good or ill is still to be determined, but there you have it."

"I haven't forgotten anything. I know who I am and I know where I'm going..."

"Oh, do you now? And where is that, exactly?"

She'd closed her eyes dangerously, demanding he face the fact he was rudderless in the moment.

Jareth trudged along, the girl still asleep on his shoulder. The moon rode low behind him but it wouldn't last long. Ahead, the forest was closing in on the path once again. The spectacle of what the muse had done with the sword hadn't sat well; where there should have been blood, light had poured. For a man who'd striven to avoid such entanglements, a lot of unexplained events were occurring.

"Best not to keep fighting it, Jareth. I may not know all the answers, but I know you well enough that your choices are going to demand a lot from you this time."

This time? The repercussions of such contemplation made him grit his teeth and wonder where Piper had gone. Sometimes, he envied the cat; to come and go without anyone to answer to, was tempting.

"You'd hate it and you know it, Love."

Get out of my head, dammit!

Only laughter ensued, long, slow and deep within his mind. Was there no escape?

"Is that what this is all about? Escape? Haven't we played this scene before, Jare?"

He said nothing and just kept walking. And when dawn came and went, at least the girl had finally awoken, giving his back some respite.

Now, she was demanding he make their road easier, as if this road was his personally. He didn't even know if it was actually the right road in the first place. Wasn't she the one who was supposed to know? Or the girl; where was this mysterious Eli? Vespar was the furthest north he'd ever come, was the coldest place he'd ever known. Up until now, that is. With every step north, the season grasped him with its turning. Soon, he figured snow would be inevitable. Shivering at the thought, he dawdled until the two crested the next ridge, his mind a gnashing grind of ideas that sought to make his head cornmeal. Why was he continuing? Why didn't he just turn around now? Let the muse take the girl home, let *her* find Eli. If he even existed.

But as Jareth stopped and leaned on a slim aspen, whose willowy line arched skyward and drew his eyes, he realized that when he'd first heard Leanan's voice there in the tower, that there had been one certainty; in his soul, the urge to go home had been as strong as her voice. But was this the way? Leanan certainly seemed to think so, going as far as insisting he listen to her. And she was telling him that he needed to help Beryl. She was telling him he had to follow this path to its end. Dammit; did he?

Glancing back down the trail, its downward slope evidence that they'd been climbing steadily, he wistfully wondered at his life which lay slumbering to the south. Where it was warm. Where it was known. He had dim recollections of memories there, but when he tried to pinpoint even one, they slipped from his grasp as if grains of sand. As the roar of the tide swept in, he was reminded of a huge sucking sound that also lurked to the south. Why had he holed up in Vespar in the first place? Why had be been swept up in the siege? Surely there must have been warning signs and yet, he couldn't remember any. The castle had been a refuge, a respite all its own and deep down, he knew this. Leanan knew this too and repeated the notion unceasingly whenever he tried to protest. He noticed she was good at deflecting his arguments, almost as good as she was at getting inside his head. And heart. Despite he thought he heard her mocking laughter at such a thought, he wasn't sure he wanted to test her. No matter how hard his body reacted.

More laughter reminded him that he was falling behind. Far behind. A sigh built and despite the fact he tried holding his breath, it leached forth from between clenched teeth and his mind relented—for now. There was still time, of this he was sure. The sudden thought that he knew this, and that Leanan probably did not, gladdened him.

He hoisted his pack higher, feeling the mandolin's head against his neck, the eight metal keys cool on his skin. His sword hung at his side, giving him a sense of security. At least he had that. And his music.

"Piper! C'mon; guess we better keep up."

He gave a low whistle, knowing the cat would hear because he was never that far away. Piper wouldn't desert him, and that was another comfort, too.

Chapter 18

April Rain

The town of Terra was not large, boasting only two inns, a smithy, a cluster of central stores where the largely agricultural citizens could barter their way into materialism, and a dentist who doubled as a doctor. That last was almost as strange as the crowd that literally poured into the great room of the Black Boar, whose motto included 'never a good time wasted', carved on the swinging wooden doors. Well, it was a place to start, at least.

Jareth's voice rose wave upon wave, a crescendo of vibrato that unerringly reinforced each word of every verse, each syllable of every word. The room filled until it overflowed, a steady cascade of mulling voices. On the far left, near the cozy hearth, Leanan smiled like a cat that just found the cream. At her side, Beryl sat mesmerized.

The scents of ale and wine perforated the haze of smoke that clung like lichen to the ceiling rafters, mixed with the pungent aroma of sausage cooking on a grill. As he brought his song to conclusion, Jareth felt hunger gnawing. One more tune, maybe, and the cook would offer up his wares as sacrifice—he hoped.

The mandolin's resonation continued for more than a few moments after his voice drifted into the ambiance of the evening. He'd always had a way with music, ever since he was young. An uncle, or maybe it was his grandfather—strange how the memories were so elusive, lately—had been the first to show him how to place his fingers on the strings to create a chord with new notes which he could parlay into a whole sequence. From there, it only took the forever days of a youth's summer to hone a skill into real magic. Even Leanan said so...

"It's like magic, isn't it?" the girl murmured.

Beryl's eyes were wide, deep pools that eagerly savored the minstrel's offering, in turn making her the acolyte. The others in the room were mirrors of the same, their lips on mugs—they worshipped at the altar of ale and it was probably the only interruption that could pierce the spell. And when Jareth finished, even Beryl could not help but wonder at the melody's effect. Or rather, the singer's, because surely she'd heard these songs as a youth, but never this way. It was as if Jareth's fingers found places on the fretboard that produced notes between notes, an otherworld transition that plucked at more than just mandolin strings. There are twists of gut more profound between the heart and mind, between the heart and soul, than any mortal understands.

At least, this is how Leanan rationalized Jareth's ability. She'd been the subject of intense scrutiny since entering, but once the music had begun, all eyes had been pulled to center stage where between flaring tallow candles half as high as the girl, Leanan's artist performed. He was every bit one too, and far from those she disdainfully alluded to as crafters. She sipped Commandaria from a crystal glass, this particular version an amber color that began as honeyed raisins on the lips, only to end up tasting like coffee.

"His song is almost as sweet as this Mana."

Leanan preferred to remember the drink's original name; mankind liked to alter identities too much for her liking. Everything deserved to be remembered. Like myself, she thought, and that idea brought a small chuckle from between sips, her eyes flashing dangerously, though no one was looking.

"Mana?"

The girl's healthy curiosity was no doubt the reason she had so many marks on her skin.

"Aye girl, from a time long before you were birthed. One of the best vintages of this elixir poured the day the Lion-hearted consecrated his nuptials. Now, that was a celebration!"

Beryl sat quietly, pulling into herself as much as she could, even as the mostly men-filled tavern crowded beyond reason. She'd seen the way the older woman had played the looks and earnest whispers containing her name though; it was as if she were the cat and not the mouse as they'd intended. Even as the game stretched the boundaries of etiquette, the girl knew it was folly to get involved with Leanan.

Then why am I, she wondered. Would either Leanan or the man really take her to Eli? He's a moody remote vagabond who has a surprising talent with strings, and she's like the devil incarnate. The fact she's looking at me so strangely right now confirms that, as if she can read my mind.

Leanan licked impulsively, the amber liquid a dew on her lips. The girl couldn't help but notice, once again, how pointed the woman's teeth were. She shuddered as the music's spell sputtered yet did not die. Even as her attention was drawn back to the man who sat easily on a high wooden stool by the candles, she was aware of how much she wanted to hear more. They all did; it was a desire which only a minstrel could create.

"Not just any minstrel though, girl; Jareth is far more than that."

The notes welled up in his head, aching for release even as the lyrics sat poised, ready to wing into the hearts of the audience. This is how he thought of his playing; that every song deserved to be heard, by someone. But he'd be the first to admit that the very best songs were reserved for himself, or for someone he loved. Problem was—and the thought altered the tenor of his music with the mandolin delving into sadness and loss—he couldn't recall such a love, couldn't aim his verses at anyone in particular. This melancholy that was rising to claim him, articulated his words and strangled his tune, pulling chords of misery from those that listened. The mood was changing and he was professional enough to catch it. Now was not the time for this...

"He's opening up, but not in a healthy way, I deem."

Leanan pursed her lips, as though the crystal's contents had suddenly soured.

"What?"

The girl was listening after all.

But the muse did not explain, her thoughts growing darker even as Jareth attempted to rescue the song. And he would, of this she had no doubt—she'd seen him do it before, much to her chagrin. Her emotions grew conflicted as she herself tried to battle against the spell Jareth was weaving, understanding him better than anyone in the room. Indeed, she understood because she was naive enough to believe his inspiration came only from her.

He lingered on one note in particular, drawing out both the last word of the verse as well as the end chord, his mind battling viciously with his heart. Changing a song midstream was not an easy task, and the sweat began to pour as he fought to regain the music's direction. He needed to move the emotional trough into which he'd plunged them, to something far more shallow, more stream-like and less like the sea. He caught the eyes of Leanan flashing momentarily as that last crossed his mind. She knows...of course she does...

"How does he do it, Lady?"

The girl was getting on Leanan's nerves but only because she was a distraction. Beryl had no way of knowing how it was between a muse and her artist, between inspiration and passion...

"He does what he does, girl, that's all. *You* play—*you* should know."

The muse knew this was true; long after Jareth had fallen into his own thoughts while playing sentry, the girl released notes of her own, thinking she was the only one still awake. The girl had talent, though the muse would never admit that to her face. Still, it was a new variable to the situation, one Leanan knew needed investigating. If they had time. As if fearing being caught in the wilderness would be their ruin, Jareth had pushed to reach civilization—any conclave of humans would do—so he might lose his inner turmoil amongst that of others. She sighed; hadn't he learned yet that postponing the inevitable meant even more trouble later? The man could be so stubborn at times.

Like a master, Jareth swept one song into another, blending choruses and emerging stronger for the effort. It was his skill, it was his talent, and it was his fate, Leanan mused sourly. She caught the barmaid's eye and raised her empty glass.

"But how? I know the notes, I know the verses he sings, but how does he make me feel so much?"

Beryl's eyes had taken on the luster of rising panic and this caused Leanan to raise a brow in response. She knew the girl meant 'hurt so much'. Just in time though, she heard the melody change as Jareth got his song under control again. Hmm, the girl was so new, so raw around the edges. Was it because of the marks? What had the ink done to her? In sudden revelation, Leanan turned her head swiftly back toward Jareth, a glimmer of deeper truth having just been revealed.

"Oh, you have no idea, girl, really. He's as necessary though as April rain. If you knew what he was capable of, you'd tremble with soul-wrenching fear or tear-wringing joy; that's what he can do with his song. And even Mannanan would void his bowels if Jareth's Guth met his Verse. Even the most unholiest of gales of this earth break upon the rocks of that shore."

Beryl eyed the older woman suspiciously, wanting to believe her but not understanding why. Was it because for once, the mocking challenge the muse typically presented, had dissolved into something like respect? She found the courage to whisper a question, despite Leanan's countenance.

"I heard you call him a bard once, while I was still with fever. I heard your voice and felt your touch on my head, and too, soft music that urged me to rest. I thought it was a dream but now, after your words..."

Leanan, a full decanter of precious Commandaria on the table again, turned toward the girl, taking pride in the sudden cowering, as if Beryl was vaguely aware of whom she was addressing. Mortals could so easily be manipulated, she thought.

"He's *the* Bard, girl, because *I* say so."

She broke her intense stare but not her gaze, allowing the girl to wriggle back into the corner of her insecurity. A mist filled the muse's eyes, like clouds hurrying to cover a clear sky.

"He just doesn't like to remember that."

The music didn't stop, just as Jareth planned; the annoying departure into grim reverie was past and now he plowed the fertile night air with vestiges of great conquests and impassioned glories of war. He painted each of the men as a tribute to their manhood, and the women as dire and utterly devastating vessels of beauty, the like of which no man has seen before. He sang and played as every minstrel before him, enrapturing the audience into the most believable of human escapes.

And for all this, he received the coldest ale and the hottest sausage on the grill. It was enough, for one night.

Chapter 19

Feel for You

"Jare—move! Dammit, I should have known you didn't kill him. 'Ware the trouble you've brought on us now!"

He hit his head on the bedpost as she kicked him hard. Didn't the woman know how much mead he had in him? She was going to regret this in the morning.

The darkness was complete because with Leanan's motion of waking the befuddled minstrel, she'd knocked over the only candle in the room. Somewhere from the floor, he thought he also heard the girl cry out. What was happening?

"Grab your clothes and sword—no time to get dressed now; they've reached the main gate and nothing is going to slow them down."

Like hell he was; his head hurt like an iron in the fire and his backside now flared like his anger. But his mad needed a better focus because even besotted as he was, the note of concern in Leanan's voice was still clear. Something was definitely wrong.

"Out, get out, girl; there's no time for chafing at your skin. We need to get out of this place and now. The only thing stalling them is the fact we're not the only mind he can sense. The others are causing him confusion; seems you bought us some time, Jare. At least your instincts are intact."

The words were shrill yet urgent, demanding acquiescence, but only the cat had enough sense not to object as it already waited in the hall. To add a sharp note to her impatience, she began to whack them both with the flat of her sword. When she touched the man with it though, his grunt of annoyance turned to pain. He flashed a look of confusion at the shadowy face of the muse, noting how her eyes were aflame.

"Sorry; forgot. Time to go, Love, there's still a way out of this frying pan. Into the hall—we need to make for the hill path."

The hill path? And then he remembered—dimly. Something Leanan had told him last night, something the locals had told her. Apparently, Beryl's maker lived in a land beyond the woods to the east, past a meadow where gold was said to run, living in a thatched hut on the last hill beyond the bridge. Behind the green door, of course. Supposedly. But to enter the woods was said to be fraught with danger all its own. No wonder no one sought Eli; who'd want all that trouble?

"I'm not leaving here naked; you'll just have to wait or go on ahead. I don't care if all the Hounds of your Hunt have come back, I'm not going to run with swords and other things dangling."

He put on his best hangover glare and stood, hands curling into balls of defiance. He realized the cat must have been sleeping on his chest again as a fresh rake of blood oozed just beneath the black stain of his tattoo. Damn cat; should have sensed Leanan's kick coming and moved sooner.

Leanan rolled her eyes and shoved the girl out of the room, the latter having only had just enough time to grab her guitar. She was a disheveled mess, mewing her protestations to the dark hallway while those in adjoining rooms stirred at the ruckus.

"Who the hell is coming, anyway?"

He managed to shout after her even as he stooped to grab at his pack and weapons harness, and a thought as to where he'd stashed his own blade. He moved quickly nonetheless; this wouldn't be the first time he'd had to leave quickly after a performance...

Leanan jerked to a halt at the doorway, the long sword in her hand burning with blue flame, as if whatever coursed through the muse's blood stemmed from the metal.

"You remember the bones you left alive in the glade?"

He hesitated before nodding. Sure, what about him? Oh, he'd left him alive...

"Yeah, well, he's come back to thank you."

And she disappeared into the shadows of the hall, her footfall as silent as a wraith.

Dammit, she was too good at that, Jareth thought, pulling on his belt and buckling leather straps, his sword's sheath poking him brutally as he quickly swung his gear into place. If only he hadn't drunk so much...

The others in the inn were almost all awake, even as he found the back door and encountered the brisk spring air. It caused him to gasp, too loudly for Leanan's comfort and she let him know it. In the distance, a strange dragging sound could be heard approaching. He looked first in the sound's direction then toward Leanan, whose face was grim but glimmering wickedly, as if the trouble approaching just reinforced how much the man needed her. Like hell; I can take care of myself, the thought dragging even as he fumbled trying to unsheathe his sword.

"No, not this time; we're going to try and lose our trail and not be entertained. We've more important things to do and time is still a commodity."

That last hit Jareth like a knell, causing his legs to buckle. Or was it last night's mead? Time...he did indeed feel its surging presence and heard its anxious voice.

"We're actually going into the woods?"

His voice was a bit petulant, as if whatever was chasing them seemed the better choice.

"Have to; Beryl's quest is at the heart of this, I'm sure of it. Why else are they so relentless? You think it's your song they're really after?"

Her laughter echoed in the night, the setting moon chasing its echoes.

"Aren't there supposed to be ghosts in there? I'm sure I remember you saying that. Must be a reason the locals stay out; I'm inclined to heed them."

Jareth felt as if his feet had grown roots, as if the winding path he eyed going up the hill were giving him one last chance. But, for what?

"It's just the drink, Jare; you've forgotten how it is when you combine two formidable powers. I feel for you, I really do, it's not going to be easy. Trust me though, tomorrow, you'll be glad your back aches with the pain of purpose and not with the spine-softening that comes with feather mattresses. There's no time now to remind you that no good comes to a rolling stone when it's covered with moss. Away, we must slip away now while we can. Not sure if bears pulling a chariot can manage between the trees."

Jareth arched an eyebrow, though it made his headache worse.

"Bears?"

Leanan nodded, already turning and pushing the recalcitrant girl forward. Like the man, the story of ghosts haunting the woods did not sit well. She itched at the skin of her palm, wishing nails were longer so she might dig and feel pain all the better.

"Bears?"

Beryl's voice was like the short squeak a mouse makes just as the owl's talons pierce.

Leanan rolled black pupils while a tight-lipped sigh escaped her lips.

The nimbus of blue that was Leanan moved off, leaving both the man and girl behind. Almost absently, she sheathed the long blade and began to pick her way up the hill, merging with the shadows.

"Let me know how it goes with the bears."

The sound of dragging grew louder, definitely coming their way. Moonlight scattered on a late spring frost as he scanned the road beyond. Something *was* moving, and if his eyes weren't playing tricks on him, it sure looked like animals pulling something. Bears? If so, they were dark and large, imbued with the shadows of night, dragging what looked like a sleigh behind them. The glint of moon off polished harness convinced him maybe the muse was right.

"Move girl, Leanan seems prone to understatement. Right now, she's probably less dangerous than any bear."

Laughter rang through the upper boughs, cascading like cruel rain back on those down lower. The two hurried to catch up, their passage far from silent.

Dawn came and went and with it, the illusion of security. Though truthfully, for Jareth, there was also a huge feeling of sanctuary. He felt the rising fear as hairs on his arm and yet, it was a wave of dark benevolence in the form of eyes. Eyes, everywhere, and as long as the night lasted, they glimmered and glowed, their presence unnerving. Until the morning when he had enough light to see their source. It was the girl who first said anything, though both he and Leanan had been aware for over an hour.

"They're frogs!"

"Yes, Dear, they are. Keep moving; no telling if they'll travel by day as well as night."

"The frogs?"

Leanan shook her head.

"No, the bears."

Beryl looked quickly back down the hill, eyes desperate and heart quickening.

"I don't see anything."

"You won't; they've stopped for now, perhaps stalled by the trees. We can only hope. Still, there are others he can call, if we give him the opportunity. For now, keep moving. Oh, and don't touch the frogs."

Jareth had pondered the source of the eyes from the moment he'd seen them, their soft greenish glow limning the boughs of trees and dotting the trail on both sides. Whereas at first they'd been merely beacons, after awhile, their continual stare began to weigh heavily. As the day grew stronger and the light of the eyes dimmed, he could see indeed that the source was myriad frogs, most no larger than his finger, clinging to the trees all around. They were everywhere but on the path. He couldn't fathom the reason, though. He was going to ask Leanan but when he raised his head to catch her attention, she was already shaking her head. Nothing to be gained there, though she sure seemed to know more about the situation than he did.

And it was not a lot of comfort that there were those in the audience last night that knew of Eli. He noticed some had gold and black tattoos on their skin as well. Beryl had cringed further into Leanan's shadow whenever any got too close. But most were enamored with the woman's unearthly beauty, of which the muse was only too aware. Did she smile seductively at him from her table knowing he was affected? Still, such was flung to the wind when he struck that first chord on his mandolin, all thoughts of those around him funneled into the very tangible touch of the muse. He closed his eyes and felt her with him, inside him, intimately bound to him. She said it had always been thus, so when the music started, the very texture of his sinews changed, the muscle of his heart transforming blood into adrenaline-laced emotion, liquid promise that could stall time.

Chapter 20

No Second Chance

They camped as midmorning ranged freely, sending errant shafts of sunlight down between newly burst leaves. The season was sprung and despite the presence of the frogs, Jareth felt his heart gladden. Being watched turned into being watched over, and even the girl started to feel less animosity from the woods.

"Frogmoss Forest; now I see why it's called that."

Leanan perused the thickets to either side; trees arched tall and trunks thickened the further she looked.

"Not exactly what I expected."

Jareth had to concur; when one is told of ghosts and haunted woods, the aspect of creepy bare tree trunks and leafless boughs comes to mind. Certainly much of the night had seemed like that, but now in the shimmer of day, the place took on the look and feel of a cozy armchair nestled next to the fire, footrest within reach. But all green and fuzzy. Strange that light could change perception so much and so quickly.

Loathe to cut any living tree, Jareth gathered old, fallen pieces for a small fire, which he prudently constructed on the path itself. There was a presence surrounding them for all the perceived safety day was providing. They were not the only living things within a stone's throw of their camp, and both Jareth and Leanan knew it.

After a warm meal, last night's efforts caught up to them all and one by one, each dozed in a haze of delirium. When Jareth awoke first, he made sure the fire was out and then went in search of the frogs. Despite Leanan's warning, he didn't think the muse meant him.

He found the ground immediately off the trail to be soggy and unspoiled, though firm enough to support his weight without sinking. Still, he could feel the moisture already trying to penetrate the skin of his boots. The vegetation rose and consumed his passage, as if trying to cover his way from one world to the next. And a different world it seemed to be, with much more vibrancy just waiting to be set loose. Jareth moved quietly, his woodcraft an extension of himself. There were those who'd told him he could move as silently as the night, an ability he took for granted. Unless he needed money, he liked to stay submerged beneath civilization, fleshing out his passion in solitary ways. Especially with music, and sometimes, when he pretended he wrote true verse.

True verse was what Leanan had teased back in the cave, when he'd wanted to deny he had any bardic ability at all. Still, he knew there was more truth to her words than not. He did have the urge, sometimes, to put down the lyrics in such a way that the music was inherent and not filled by his mandolin. Then, whether he let the words loose in his head or actually wrote them down, the music came from the inflections of the words themselves, and meaning transcended time. It was then that he found himself within the folds of night, even if others saw only a crease.

The moss was everywhere, just like the frogs, though the latter seemed restricted to the trees, their skin blending in with the striations of the bark. One had to look sharply to even see their forms, especially during the day when their eyes were closed. He studied one rutted husk of a hoary maple, the finger-like leaves splaying down all around him like a canopy. The ground near the tree was firmer so Jareth crept under and folding his legs, sat near the old tree's bole. To the north lay the shorn part, still being consumed by the living green of the forest as it took back its own.

The words came then, more easily than usual, no less pervasive though, and cunningly sculpted what was in his head. The frogs were whispering to him, telling of new skin and yet, the echo was firmly set with no second chance.

There once were poems of frogs and moss like holes,
and Sarah told me; 'Don't just fade away,
just keep the same name when you feel the mole
in you. The shame is, she's the one who strayed.
I contemplate the words of unknown faces,
look for reasons why my time's displaced.
The moss had eyes and bark was well aware;
how is it friends have changed the way they care?
Did evolution come and touch a time
where all emotions came to meet the dare?
The feel that time is slipping, redefines.

I read a chant royale that failed the goal—
to use the rhyme and watch while meaning plays
upon an errant mind, a digging soul.
There's stories, now, and prose in stalking sprays;
so very far from Shakespeare, talk's replaced
the frogs and moss whose movement nurtured space.
She also painted, poet-artist, heir
to wind's creation, put in us to share.
I saw them once—a still life of design
where static came to life like doubts we wear;
the feel that time is slipping, redefines.

I thumb back through the 'skin' of poems I know;
each word seems wrought with pain and fear today,
but thoughts are working hard like frogs to grow
beyond what meanings meant, what words would say.

Beryl

It seemed important then, but now that brace
seems stilted, tilted, hardly worth the grace
I once bestowed, the angst I used to wear.
That's then and this is now despite the stare
that haunts me from the white space I've assigned,
expressing fear that changes made despair;
the feel that time is slipping, redefines.

They're hardly held—no standard's worth, they stole
my meanings even as the ink was fey.
No matter answered-verse showed truth its toll,
I reached a depth and saw that few purveyed
just what the moss was showing, frogs were chasing;
these were still-lives propped in sentient's vase.
Some core of lives that frothed poetic air,
became entangled, found a passion's scare
and grabbed the fletching arrow, realigned
their bursting seams which minds had sewn in squares;
the feel that time is slipping, redefines.

She told me 'don't you lose yourself but roll
as if the moss could be upturned, and pray
that all this verse we pour can keep you whole.'
But she was wrong, and she has gone; betrayer.
The frogs continue, yet their sound's disgraced,
it's buried as the rules are bent and traced
beyond convention—where's the mind that cared
to marry heart and soul as if prepared
like lovers, rose and thorn upon the vine,
to see past shadow, past a running tear?
The feel that time is slipping, redefines.

I kept my name and promise, this I swear;

she lost her own in moss her frogs would wear.
They changed the way that ink and white were twined;
where nothing stays the same then life declares
'the feel that time has slipped is redefined'.

The tenuous silence that ensued enthralled Jareth. Within his soul, he felt another story lived and breathed, fought to string memories like notes from his mandolin. He hadn't brought it from the camp and still he heard it playing. It was strange that he could so easily slip into this place where his words lay like a womb, that it could also become his tomb. Who the hell was Sarah? Shakespeare?

"I told you not to touch the frogs."

Chapter 21

Let it Go

Behind him, Leanan stood ankle deep in creeping green water as the lichens struggled beneath her heels. He looked at his hand and saw it pressed on the back of the largest frog he'd seen yet. Gasping, he quickly pulled his hand back. The glow of pale green eyes shut down almost as fast.

"You seem to be good at denial, Jare, except when you need something. Why is that?"

She wasn't exactly angry with him but her question still seemed out of place. What was he supposed to be denying?

"I heard you—your song even woke the girl. You might want to pick a better place to use the Guth. He's tracking us somehow and I'm beginning to think it's because you won't embrace who you are."

Jareth stared uncomprehendingly at Leanan, feeling that the space between the tree and himself was far too close. Why had he wanted to touch the frog in the first place?

"Another good question. Seems you get these fits of remembrance and then nod off into total ignorance the moment I try and ferret answers. Used to be we made a good team, Jare, but you're beginning to try my patience."

The emotion flared before he could stop it, surprising both of them.

"Trying? Whenever is it not so?"

She smirked once the familiarity of what he'd revealed was securely put away.

"Whenever? Guess you need me more than I thought."

She slipped the sheath containing the longsword off her shoulder and extended it to him.

But he just shook his head, the momentary hesitation gone.

"Thought not, but I had to ask."

"Not yet."

She lifted a dark-lined brow at him, her pupils dilating until fully encompassing her eyes.

"Oh? Not yet? Does that mean you remember what it is?"

"No, but I know I don't want to touch it. Not now."

"Still, you at least understand you will; there's a bit of hope in that. Maybe you're beginning to understand where you are, hey? What we're doing here?"

Jareth just shook his head, the mask of forgetfulness shrouding his mind, sure only that he didn't want to touch the blade. On some level though, he knew it was his.

"Like I said; that's progress." She turned to go back to camp.

"Leanan?"

Turning her lithe form toward him, taking a deep breath so as to show off her assets as much as she could, her face held a criminal smile as she met his gaze.

"What was I singing? I mean, I heard the lyrics, heard the music, but where did both come from?"

The woman's hands plied at her hair, raising it into a arch above her head then deftly cording it with silver twine. Her breasts rose as she did.

"You don't remember but it's part of your past—long past, I might add. Must be something about these trees and the frogs which prompted a memory to wiggle loose. I remember that time, though; it was a sad place tinged with both regret and defiance, even then."

"Even then?"

"Aye, Jare; once, you liked to live in the place your words dwell. Quite a struggle getting you past that, but maybe you never fully escaped. I'll have to see about that. Not sure how this is going to help, though. This world is being bent with more than the mind of a bard, no matter how talented he may be."

Most of Leanan's words were incomprehensible to Jareth and it showed. The muse sighed heavily.

"Oh fine. Sarah was one of those that wrote with you, a long time ago, during your disillusionment. Actually, preceding, if I remember correctly. She was a poet too—an artist of words who also had a talent for watercolor. It was she that warned you not to lose yourself, but to be true to your craft, even though she knew little about which she spoke. You were never a crafter, Jare, of that be assured."

He hadn't realized how far off the path he'd come and as they trudged over the soft ground, he noticed that the trees seemed to move, allowing passage. His fingers touched the bark of each as he made his way among them, secretly hoping he might put his hand on another frog.

"Haven't you had enough of that for a while, Love?"

Always in his head, always.

She snorted in derision.

"Oh, I'm more than that, trust me."

Then she turned and placed her lips full on his, taking him by surprise and whisking away all breath.

Gasping in both confusion and sudden desire, Jareth took his arms from around the muse's waist, feeling the way his body molded to hers as more than natural...more like unnatural.

"I miss you, Jare. There, I said it, now, no more questions."

But he hadn't even begun to address the whirl of confusion in his head, brought to a precipice by her kiss.

"Just tell me what you meant by 'poet like me'. What did you mean by that?"

She shook her head, a sly smile enveloping her face, the arching pony tail on top of her head dangling just above the teasing white shock running through the back of her hair.

"You know what a bard is, right?"

Jareth nodded, fearing where her words were going.

"Well, bards and poets are one and the same except that the former uses music to dress their words. Poets don't need that. They're the ones who write true verse."

His head felt like spinning.

"Aye, Jare; like Sarah, you can write your lyrics without need of strumming or plucking or plinking or stroking of strings. Helps, I'm sure, but totally unnecessary."

"I've never heard of..."

"Oh yes you have—you just don't remember, remember?"

And here she had to laugh, pulling him into another soft embrace, her face close to his, her eyes flashing.

"Shakespeare—the other name in your song; he was once a master, too."

"Once? Too?"

She eyed him keenly, and broke her hold on his shoulders, though even that action seemed to hurt.

"One of the best, Jare, one of the best. Lived a lot longer ago than Sarah did, though. You drew inspiration from him—when I let you—sometimes, though his style can't match yours. Once," she grew wistful, a faraway look cloaking her face, "I had high hopes for him, too."

Damn! The woman had been involved with him, too? A dread feeling glimmered at recognition of who Shakespeare had been, and it shook him to his core. He did know the name...now. And he knew Leanan spoke the truth. William Shakespeare had been a poet from the Elizabethan era...from the isle of England. Now, how did he know that?

"Because you studied him—along with others. Don't you remember? Petrarch was your favorite. Surprised you didn't mention his name."

The names she was dropping were like stones to an eleven year old boy, stones found on the creek's edge, just flat and perfect enough for skipping...

"Oh please, don't rehash that particular story now, that one doesn't end as well."

The mist of confusion was lowering and he felt it keenly.

"Who the hell am I, Leanan?"

His voice was strained and he struggled to get the question out, fearing why he really wanted to know.

"That, my Jareth, is what we're going to find out. Much has changed here, but at its core, you must be the same. I feel it will either be your succor or your bane. Time will tell. But not before I have a say, at least!"

He was following her lead and in the distance, could see the girl and the camp. Why was Beryl's despair so evident, even from such a distance? Did she ever get any respite from the flowing marks on her skin? Then again, why did the question echo his way as well?

"Just let it go, Jare, for now at least. There'll be time for reconciliation later. At least, I hope so!"

Her low chortle was far from alarming and he wondered why.

Chapter 22

Black Sheep

Once the girl accepted the fact that neither Jareth nor Leanan would mark her, she more often than not would quietly strum her guitar, lifting a particularly lovely voice to the forest canopy. Jareth would hear her from afar as he scouted the undergrowth for edibles, absently noting that the girl didn't do much else. Maybe that's partially why she has so many tattoos, he thought.

Clustered like eggs in a nest, golden brown-caps clung to the base of a fallen tree, the stump showing it had only recently been felled by an axe. So, where was the chopper? Why had the wood been left to rot? He took care where he placed his feet as avoiding the frogs had turned into a full time occupation whenever he had to forage in the forest. He absolutely hated feeling their squirmy, slimy bodies under his skin, even through the leather of his boots. Didn't seem to hurt the critters, he mused, but nonetheless...

Many of the songs the girl crooned were ones he knew himself, and their familiarity often caught him smiling, as if a memory were being tickled. And he found that when both he and Leanan were absent, that Beryl would lift her real voice to accompany her deft playing of the strings. As if alone, she could pour her whole being into the music. Jareth smiled at that too—it was another point they had in common. Was he her age when he gave his first performance for others? Just family, sure, but the terror and secret thrill of setting his passion free that day still remained with him.

His shoulder brushed too close to another tree and whenever he also touched one of the many clinging frogs, strange emanations were the result.   Sometimes memories he didn't know he'd forgotten awoke, sometimes a heightened affinity for the life forces that lay hidden niggled at his conscious.   And this despite his woodcraft.   If such affected the muse, she didn't say, but Jareth wondered if it were because she was more acutely aware of where she placed her feet and hands.   Jareth found he could get lost too easily here, but that was because he had lost much of the fear that entering the woods had originally fostered.   Not that it didn't still exist—he could reach out and touch it, if he tried, but rather, that it seemed to be in abeyance, as if the woods had absolved him of his immediate sins.   No sentence coming, at least not yet.

Lovely, really, he thought, listening to the girl's singing.   His mind was divided and he found himself paying more attention to her now and bypassing another heaping of mushrooms...

Trees loomed high like living trolls,
standing Trail Guard;
I held back at World's Edge.
Sun bounced hill to hill,
held in check by leafy veil;
Forest hides her own.

Green beard hung in caricature,
Old Man Withered Larch,
with pockets full of darkness,
waiting Night's release.
Nearby is the broken path,
centaurs used to use.

Crossing over Wizard's brook,
touched with frozen breath,

there I found on shore rune stones,
stories carved by dwarves.

Sweet dew-laden bleeding-heart
tree sprites carry off.
Knobby-eye trees, cheeks of gall,
branching fingers grasp.
Beetles crawled from logs of holes,
goblins slept in late.

Moist and dark where fern leaves grow,
blankets for the elves.
Trillium swords hewn out of Spring,
night eyes for the hart.
Black squirrels stopped by to snack,
pixie caps were left,
acorn hearts were stored away,
unicorns found many.

Spongy ground that smelled alive;
scoffed at all the lies
of those passing Forest's edge,
warned to stay away,
of all lost little girls that
under leaves lay rotting.

Least, that's how I remember it,
back when I was nine

The very same sword ferns of Beryl's song shimmered before
Jareth, forming a sea of textured green, their saw-tooth edges
softened by sheer quantity.   Along with the moss, the fern
ostensibly ruled the forest floor.   He couldn't help but smile

because the song's images were those which had fueled his own childhood. It was as if he could see his grandmother's cottage as it hunched on the forest's edge, mushroom-like in its alignment. Perhaps that's why Leanan didn't seem so out of place, though truth be told, he didn't remember her type of fairy in any of his childhood stories.

The fact he accepted the magic that occasionally crept from shadows and campfire stories, was mainly due to his own abilities; growing up, it took time for him to see how his songs could affect people, and not always for the good. It was also why he'd had to leave home. The others soon realized he could affect their lives, and their fear grew larger than their memory that he was one of them. But then, he didn't know of many minstrels that stayed in any one place that long. We're bound to travel, his grandfather would say, and with a sage nod too. It was quite the surprise the day he'd actually figured out what that said about his grandfather, and how upon being cornered, the old man had winked before answering.

"Why don't *I* travel then? Well, you'll find that a woman has magic all her own!"

Did he mean grandmother? Is that why he no longer roamed, playing the strings?

His grandfather had been a willowy man, the gray struck more with blue than white, giving him an odd appearance. Not that his round, often too-bright eyes helped that perception. But his hands—oh, his hands; they showed the years of use having tamed the same strings which Jareth currently used. When his grandfather died, his strings bypassed the son and went to him, though Dad wouldn't have known what to do with the instrument anyhow.

"It's for us black sheep, Jareth. What we know isn't for the many, it's for the few. And someday, I deem this is your fate, because all the black sheep eventually leave the fold. It comes with the territory."

His grandfather's words still lay close to his heart...or had they now come alive because of the nearness of the frogs? What was it about this forest that brought back a heritage he'd somehow forgotten? Leanan said it was another form of magic, but a type she could not affect. Which actually made the him feel more secure; seems she wasn't as invincible as she liked to portray. *Mortals are too often preoccupied with their own security, have you noticed?*

The wind had wrapped itself around him as he stooped to pluck at an edible plant called arrowroot. Actually, it would provide a seasoning, if used properly. The fact he heard Leanan's words as if she stood right behind him, had lost its element of surprise, and now, he just clamped down harder in his mind, as if to shield his thoughts from her. He was sure of his effectiveness when he didn't hear any ensuing laughter...

Magic; the woods surrounding him oozed its presence, even if of the variety only a woodsman could appreciate. It bore itself out in the strange way his song was woven, it harbored in the vibration of strings and within the hollows of reed pipes and flutes. That he believed there actually were dwarves and elves, wizards and goblins, just gave him latitude to explain what he couldn't. Otherwise, he'd have probably gone crazy trying to explain how the muse Leanan could manipulate the sky. The fact she had, wasn't in question, though her story wasn't one he could recall ever hearing.

Maybe it was because he had lost much of his memory. Bits and pieces would come and go, each a result of another stimulus from the world around him. What bothered him more was that he didn't have a firm grasp of the ordinary magic—like remembering this forest even existed. The land they were traveling through, the placement of immovable objects like mountains, lakes, trees and roads; why couldn't he recall where they were headed?

Leanan hinted that it was because he hadn't written it yet, as if that explained much. He knew many songs but none spoke of Frogmoss Forest, nor had he any bogey-man tales involving Bone Warriors, and what about the chariot bears? He'd have been more at ease with a troop of dwarves than what the afore mentioned 'magics' might mean for him. And the girl. And the muse Leanan.

Dark Muse, as he recalled her saying, though it was not a title she'd given herself. Who then? Other men? What kind of tales existed in her world? She said it was his fault she was crippled here, as if they were from another place...or time. So, where was 'here', then? Too many questions and no one to answer. Leanan was feeding him driblets of information and he felt a growing need to know more, all that he *should* know.

How can someone tell you what you should know, though?

He stopped cold, his hand sliding automatically to his side, the metal hilt a chill next to his skin. He felt sweat forming.

The voice in his head did not belong to Leanan.

It was deeper, one he might ascribe to the dull rumble of thunder. No, it was more, and as he tried to wrap his mind around describing the voice, he saw images of trees, drawing his eye lower and lower, funneling his vision between the folds of corrugation formed by the bark. Down and through, winding until the earth was pierced and he thought he breathed soil, filling his lungs and pouring into his veins to mingle with the red of his blood.

It was a momentary drowning that soon passed and he knew then; the voice spoke like the movement of roots digging deep into the earth, their grip so strong and real that he saw the wind for the frail creature it was. A force, no doubt, but without substance to last. Not so this voice, not so the vibrancy he tasted even as the words echoed and faded. And the oddest feeling of all was that he knew he'd heard it before.

You hear whatever you want to hear, Jareth Rhylan, everyone does.

He swung his head fully around, thoughts of drawing his blade forgotten. There was no threat with this voice, with the words in his head. There was only the subtle hint of welcome, welcoming him home.

"And you are?"

His voice sounded small in comparison to the deep drone of resonation he could still touch. Not with his fingers, but rather, with the beating of his heart. There was a connection he knew how to tap, had known all along and yet, had forgotten.

It's all about choice; you can decide to accept me or let me go, Jareth, that's how it works.

The voice made it seem it had been his fault that any connection was lost. And yet, he had no memory of such a thing ever happening.

Because there's poison in your blood. You're dying.

The feeling of his skin shedding to the moss-covered ground was strong, as if the desire to spill himself was his only option.

It's not, but you already know that.

"I already know that," Jareth repeated dumbly.

The anchors in your life are evolving, re-deploying, but time is running out and the poison must either be removed or transformed.

What the hell does that mean?

It means what it means, just like all life does, if you have the true sight.

True sight? Is that like True verse? But he already heard the echo of sympathy welling, understanding that indeed, there was a link. Who *was* this talking in his head?

I'm your guide, Jareth, your father.

My father? But, he's dead, more than a decade now. And this voice spoke nothing like his Dad ever had. But there was more than a hint of his grandfather there, he noticed.

I knew your grandfather, he knew me. In the end, we were one.

His grandfather had been a minstrel, too. Dammit, the confusion has to stop; what is happening to me? Am I delirious?

Is it the mushrooms? And he dropped the bag at his side, seeing the caps spill haphazardly even though he looked hard at them for a sign, for a pattern.

"Who are you?"

I told you; I'm your guide.

Another one? He thought hard, thinking that these words were similar to the ones Leanan had used.

No, not like her, but we share a commonality. She is not like me, but she'll say I am. Once, you understood the difference.

Well, he sure didn't now—even the muse's presence had been mystifying, especially the fact he had agreed to accompany her and the girl. As if getting Beryl to Eli would actually help solve his problem...

The problem is time, Jareth, and what you do with it.

Hell, now there were two who could listen in on his thoughts, hear what he was thinking. Could this voice also know what lay in his heart, too?

Further than that, Jareth; the contents of your soul are mine to peruse.

Damn—could that be true? But how? And especially, why would anyone be interested in him?

Right now, you're the most important person beneath the sun, Jare.

"Really? How so?"

The strangeness of talking to the air, to someone he couldn't even see, would hit him later.

Time is running out. In this respect, she's right. The enemy is cunning and you're not strong enough to do anything by yourself.

The words rang in his head even though there was no condemnation, just a bizarre sense of affection. From someone he didn't know?

You belong to me, Jare. Of my sons, you are the one who holds hope.

"Hope for what?"

Hope for the survival of the world.

Damn. He brushed his left hand against the smear of black adorning his chest, remembering what it meant. The words were ancient Chinese, but the meaning far older; it meant survivor of the world. How could he be the hope of something he'd survived? What did that really mean?

It means you have something to do, you have a purpose.

Well, even the muse had intimated that, Jareth thought.

"Won't you show yourself? How am I to know if your words are true?"

The sound he imagined tunneling roots might make flickered between his ears, reminding him that he stood on that very same ground. Did he hear the voice chuckling?

I've been with you always—it's how you know me. And that the words I speak are not false.

And to be sure, there was no sense of darkness shrouding the voice, no hint within Jareth's being that everything he was hearing was corrupt. As one able to sing using the true voice, the similarity was there. Still...

Trust your instincts, Jareth. You know me even if your eyes are still blind. In time, your memory will clear and all will be made known. There is much for you to do. Just be careful and mind the roots of whatever it is you choose to hear.

"What does that mean?"

The forest peered back at him as he waited for an answer, unsure if he was even asking the right question. The frogs clinging to the trees hadn't changed position—they were still there, their camouflaged bodies molding to the bark, but more than a few now had their eyes wide open. Jareth shrank back, a momentary dread overcoming him. And he had no idea why.

The voice had gone, with no evidence other than a familiar stirring in Jareth's soul to tell him it wasn't imagination. Hell; he sure had a story for the evening meal tonight...

Chapter 23

Archangel

The detonation's flash surged and hit the dirty white concrete walls like a wave, bathing the building in orange light while the foundation rocked precariously. The remaining panes of glass shattered and their fall became the blast's echo. But Rhey had been expecting this and had already moved deeper into the building's bowels, knowing the structure would withstand his latest salvo into the heart of a growing resistance. How many still remained? It seemed impossible that their number could cause him so much annoyance. Across most of the planet and especially this portion, the only buildings still left standing were his. The feeble attempts by those that crawled amid the charred and twisted monuments of mankind wouldn't be enough, of this he was sure. Still, he didn't need the distraction.

Amid the whirring sounds and blinking lights, he moved slowly, his body peeling faster now. Soon, he'd be bound to the chair by the man's side, and almost as helpless. But not quite; at least *he'd* still be able to move his head. The man bound to the table though, could not. More wires had been attached to the man's head, more probes whose needles penetrated the skull almost half an inch into gray matter now. He was determined. If only inputting the data wasn't so slow, he mused, idly absorbing the running story before him on the new monitor he'd only just initialized. The lines were growing more complex and he needed to track them all as he looked for short-cuts inside. He'd been about to pinch the DNA sequence from its encryption when more variables had suddenly sprung from previously inert pixels. And whereas the first had been a surprise, one he could counter, this last held a familiarity that caused him to hesitate. It was as if Martin Hennessy was calling out for help and was suddenly getting it. But how? Or was it simply a matter now of using the rules against the story's creator?

Surely trying to manipulate manifestations of the scientist's fears didn't seem to be working, though he thought maybe there was another chance at intervention, a moment coming very soon— if the graphical representation of the data in front of him was accurate. The shifts in topography, and landscape in general, had been expected, especially when his presence had obviously been revealed. With the element of surprise gone, brute force was an option, but instead, he'd build his forces from an emotional base mainly because Martin Hennessy wasn't leaving him anything else with which to work.

And it had almost worked. The code was almost out of the computer's circuitry when the processor stalled, a spinning beach ball he'd not understood as a hanging computer cycle. By the time he'd resolved the conflict, all his hard work had been undone. Well, not all—one insertion was still operating and this is what he was using for another attempt. But those outside the lab's walls had demanded some attention. With that matter attended, it would be a while now before his cyberbots needed any further help from him; their programming would pick up the slack he needed, allowing him time to break the man's mind once and for all.

A finger of chill air wormed itself inside the pockets of dead skin hanging on his face, and its touch went right to the bone, reminding him why he'd chosen that substrate for his warriors in the first place. The winter was penetrating the upper levels and working its way down abandoned blasted steps until it found his lab. He hated the cold and stumped his way on one good leg to the wall, where he meticulously moved an archaic dial on the side of a box, having learned that it would increase the level of heat to this part of the building.

The latest element introduced to the story wasn't a surprise to Rhey, though exactly what form Martin would choose to give it wasn't yet known. Countering this aspect of the man's mind would require further study, time he didn't know if he dared take, because he depended on understanding all mankind's foibles in order to manipulate as needed. But faith wasn't as easy to understand as the more tangible lust and pain, or hunger and fear. He supposed the latter was still his best option though. Dragging a bloody digit against the touch screen, he proceeded to deal with this new entity, whom human history liked to call an Archangel. Names didn't mean anything to him, but he had to categorize all the components if he were to get a handle on the maze being built before him.

The many windows on his screen overlapped and created a plethora of scenes in which he could interact, making it a nightmare for a human to coordinate. But Rhey was no human and used this fact ruthlessly. Choosing a particular page, he pulled the flowing text to the fore, watching in amazement as even before he could key in his changes, the other windows inexplicably closed and exposed a desktop showing a computerized rendition of a galaxy—Andromeda in all it's purple glory, even though such a presentation couldn't compare to actually flying through it. Which he'd done more than once...

The text spilled faster, as if the subsequent windows being open had been a drain on the story's resources. Why Martin had chosen a minstrel to defend his code though, was still puzzling. Didn't seem like more than an unnecessary burden, especially when more could be gained using a character like a mercenary, even if reduced to using an archaic weapon like the sword. Still, Martin had given his characters some ability to that end...

In the distance, he heard an animal growl, remembering that there had once been an enclosure humans liked to call a zoological park. The former inhabitants had been on the loose only recently, one of his missiles having gone awry. That last sound reminded him of something called a bear...

The words were whirling and he bent his mind to contain them all, moving his fingers over the keys that would curtail this futile attempt at escape.

Chapter 24

Ashes

The girl didn't whine as much when their pace slowed nor as her pack's burden grew (they'd had to forage for food and when they found something edible, he was wont to collect all he could find) while they navigated the frogs, moss, and forest. Though the path seemed to be made by animals, it wandered far straighter than was usual. Deer did not have such foraging areas and he knew the path must be manmade. He noted this to Leanan but she merely shrugged her shoulders and labored onward. Secretly, he suspected the muse was bored with the endless trees.

He didn't think there could be so many frogs and yet, their number didn't diminish, though certain trees seemed devoid of the little amphibians, especially the evergreens. Maybe it was just too difficult for them to navigate past the needles. And just as peculiarly, the birches had the most. It was a revelation to see that there were frogs which could mimic black and white banding and thus meld to their host even more invisibly.

"They're the worst because they're poisonous."

Leanan's pointed remark zeroed in on the girl, as she could see Jareth already understood this.

Beryl though was oblivious, the pack on her back slumped to one side, her fatigue more feigned than real. A little time on the road would do her good, Jareth thought; toughens a body up so the world can't hurt you as much. Memories of his grandfather taking him out into the woods behind the cottage, rippled like waves a skipping stone makes, their effect lapping time until something solid was encountered.. The view from the top of the hill as the path crested, was one such.

Below, the forest stretched out to the north and south but east, there was a wide area of meadowland which looked like a pastoral sea, its newly sprung sheaths of golden wheat-like stalks arching precipitously toward the sun, like fingers reaching for mother's milk.

Beyond the open meadow the trees crouched again, as if this wide expanse was a mote of time arboreal sentience couldn't repossess. Cutting off the trees from the meadow, a dark ribbon of water zig-zagged north to south, trees strangely absent on the further side. And looking closely, Jareth saw that the type of trees ringing the meadow were ginkgoes, surprisingly with soft, purple leaves.

"As if the meadow won't let them in," Leanan voiced the thought in both their minds.

He just grunted, understanding the demarcation but his attention centered more on the reason. Could they go around? The small voice of survival inside was suggesting they should...

"Look; hawks. Now, I wonder what they're hunting. Frogs? Haven't seen anything else in these woods since we entered."

Leanan had her eyes often to the sky and Jareth thought he knew why; she was looking for her familiar.

"Aye, I do feel a bit lost without it, Jare, but I'm still waiting on you."

These words just continued the nonsense he often heard when she talked. The fact he was beginning to understand her more didn't mean he could fathom many of her gibes and her needling gaze was testament. Either he'd have to get over it, or she would.

"Here, let me help you with that."

As Jareth hurried to unsnag the girl from a leaning thicket of holly, he spied a brief flash of red as something slipped from within the girl's laced jerkin. And just as quickly, her slim hand caught up the light and stowed it out of sight again, black ink crawling with the movement. What was that? It looked to be a gemstone...he was still pondering as he rejoined the muse.

"It is; a very rare one at that, Jare. I know it as beryllos, which is what the Greeks call it. Translated, it means 'precious blue-green color-of-the-sea stone'. Vaidurya, from Sanskrit, though you would know it as 'brille' or 'shine' in French, or 'brilliance' in Old English. I've not seen one that color, though I've heard they exist."

Jareth looked at Leanan in surprise, her depth of knowledge surprising him.

She just gave him a baleful glare that turned into a sly smile as her lids lowered and her lips stretched out salaciously.

"Oh, there's more to me than you can know, let alone remember, Love; don't take me for granted."

The echo of her words stirred up an uneasy feeling of truth, like something he should already have known.

"But you said 'color of the sea'; what I saw was red as blood."

Leanan stared hard at the girl as she carefully made her way down the slope, heading toward the meadow in the distance. With her guitar whipping wildly, both were surprised the young woman could navigate and maintain balance. A little hardening on the road, Jareth reminded himself, is a good thing.

They stood at the top of the hill, Jareth still unsure they should be going in this direction, while Leanan had far-off echoes of the sea in her eyes.

"Aye, it is; rare—as I said."

"But how would someone like her come to possess such a gem?"

Leanan focussed her attention then on the girl, the moment of wistfulness passing.

"I think it's an heirloom, but I'm not certain. If the old women hadn't gone down beneath the blades of the Tuskellions, they might have told us. As it is, the girl doesn't know, or isn't telling—I've asked already."

Jareth remained in his thoughts, the path meandering down, the trees on either side thinning; the wood was receding before the sleeping power of the meadow ahead. Now, why did he think that? Another thought struck him.

"Wait a minute; beryllos—you mean beryl, don't you? That's the girl's name!"

Leanan laughed merrily, her hair flowing back into the wind as she took a step down into the valley beneath them, her voice riding the current and chiding him all the more.

"Aye, Dear; nice of you to be paying attention. 'Ware now; this path is not as firm further down—see how the girl is slithering practically all the way? We need to catch up."

And off she went, her battle-leathered form flowing blithely into the path, creating as little resistance as she could. It was like water flowing over its shoals, Jareth murmured, though a river that moved more like oil than water. He watched a few seconds longer, Leanan's shock of white hair wound into the blackness of a long braid. A fine filigree of silver netted the top of her head and enclosed the braid halfway down. Her slim shoulders moved beneath the leather, teasing him...

Now, what kind of coincidence was this? Was the girl named after the stone she wore around her neck, or vice versa? Jareth was thinking he didn't like too many mysteries and this one had just been deepened. The story behind this girl hinted at more than strangeness.

No more than your own stories, Jareth, no more than your own.

Damn muse; why couldn't she stay out of his mind, already? And he glared at her back, knowing she felt his gaze but feeling better just the same.

The trees thickened as if providing a last refuge before the meadow took control of the land and the familiarity of night eyes returned. But now, all three drew comfort from the watching and the renewed presence of the frogs didn't bother them.

"I've been wondering..." Jareth began, their evening meal finished and Leanan lounging insolently on a tree, whose legend must have fallen only recently as shown by the bark's still firm grip. Stretched out as she was and out of her leather-plated boots, the slim legs of the muse glowed beneath the filtered moonlight, each shaft evading the encroaching shadow of the boughs that touched her skin, becoming a river of moonlight flowing to the sky. The dappling became her, and forced Jareth's thoughts to trip. He cursed himself for becoming lax and continued with his query.

"...why did the townspeople speak of this forest with such dread? Surely the frogs and moss can get a little creepy, but I haven't as much as seen the wisp of a ghost since we entered."

"Hsst, Jare! Now why would you want to be stirring up shadows and their wraiths when there's no reason to?"

Her vexation was quite surprising, as if maybe she too had wondered but feared their good luck would eventually end.

"Maybe such stories are to scare everyone from entering and getting lost?"

The girl touched on one of the possibilities for the wood's reputation, though he was thinking others were more likely.

Maybe the only ghosts are those you bring with you.

This time, it wasn't the muse whose voice he was hearing. The resonation was deep and Jareth wondered if it wasn't just his own doubts rising to be heard, though it sounded suspiciously like the voice in the Forest again.

"Possibly," he intoned, not repeating what he was thinking or what the voice had said.

"Maybe it's because the road seems to disappear and fade in wraith-like manner."

He'd noticed this from the beginning, but since they weren't going back, it hadn't made much difference. Leanan though, seemed surprised.

"Oh, does it?"

Leanan turned her dark pupils toward Jareth, noting deft fingers roved over his mandolin, tightening the tuning screws, small trifles of melody escaping whenever he sought to perfect the pitch. His mind was fragmented though, of this she was sure. When he didn't have one whole song contained, this was the result; dribbles and pieces, fragments of melody which he might eventually string together to actually form something singable. But it also meant he was not collected in his head, that a doubt was lingering. She'd have to watch him more closely.

"And how do you know that it's moving? You don't have any memory of this way. We can see the path before us, plain in the light of day. I daresay, I could even see the track as it winds down to that meadow, were the trees lessen and the moon widens."

Jareth hesitated, a string laying between two fingers, its resilient nature at odds with the course texture of his hands. Maybe not though, because each had the ability to release what was held inside, if properly touched.

"I've seen it. Not before us—that way seems fixed, founded in a purpose that leads us through the frogs and moss, beneath a panoply of green—but behind; now, that's another matter. Look."

And turning his head, a stray shaft of moonlight hit his face, turning his skin as pale as the muse's, while dusting his hair with fallen stars. Leanan noticed this first and almost didn't follow his gaze along the path behind them. When she did, her gasp was audible. Beryl heard her and looked in consternation.

The darkness behind, and that which was flowing up the hill, was like a ribbon of river, its waters darker than overhanging banks.

The trees did not grow over the path and as the night sky blanketed them all, the trees waved slowly, restlessly. The eye followed the ribbon and as it did, gaps appeared until to either side, the inky ribbon found itself again, but further away. Following the slope up, it appeared the path didn't originate from the top of the hill but across the southernmost shelf. And if you tried to follow that, it too would disappear and reappear moments later, but either higher or lower.

"What is happening?"

The girl voiced what the man and muse were thinking but dared not say.

"Maybe that's the ghost they talk about?"

Leanan's whisper showed obvious disbelief.

"I don't know, but it looks like any thought of going back won't be an option...I wonder how the bears will deal with that?"

They had an unsettled night, sleeping fitfully while ribbons of road beneath their feet curled into circles of confusion. The feeling of being lost was most disquieting.

Jareth woke in the middle of the night, the moon having slipped to the south, its rays blocked now and thrusting the encampment into blue shadow. The small fire had long since burned out but that made him feel more secure, not less. Calling attention to themselves was something he innately knew needed to be avoided. He just couldn't say why.

As his eyes adjusted to the darkness, the moon's pale influence allowed him to see the two sleeping women, one curled in a ball, the other stretched out luxuriously, a dim blue nimbus of light outlining her form. Even when she slept, her beauty shone, Jareth thought, hastily dragging his mind from a path he couldn't dictate.

Carefully, he untangled himself from Piper, who'd been curled as well between his arm and chest. Jareth had long ago modified his movements while sleeping so as not to crush the animal.

Quietly, so as not to disturb them, Jareth got up and approached the girl, dreaming just like the cat but breathing much louder. She slept well lately, the day's exertion thoroughly wearing her out. He knelt and slipped his fingers to Beryl's neck, drawing out the plain silver chain upon which hung the gemstone. There was no light and yet it glimmered, as if his touch had wakened something. What the hell?

Releasing the stone, the light faded until he lost the gem's outline in shadow. The glow had pulsed, as if in concert with the girl's heartbeat. Or was it his? Now, how strange was that? And it was vividly crimson, a fusion of red embers that flared with the color of the blood coursing through his fingers. It hadn't seemed more than it was though, a round bauble the size of his fingernail. How rare was it? Something valuable enough that others would chase them across the country trying to get it? Perhaps it wasn't he the nameless enemy was chasing?

No, the world's growing enmity he'd felt since Leanan had shown up was still there. The urgency that he should flee and find home, had not abated; instead, it had grown stronger. Was this the effect of the forest? Did the frogs have anything to do with this feeling? Certainly, something was going on, but what?

From the corner of his eye, a flicker of movement caught his attention and he froze, the shape solidifying while his over-wrought senses keyed in on the intruder. It looked like a woman—and not any woman, but one made of stray moonlight, her figure disjointed and as fragmentary as the road. Dammit; was he caught now in the legend of the forest? Had giving voice to his doubts created the very thing they'd so far avoided?

The form flickered and reappeared, further away, no doubt wishing to lure him. A part of his mind rationalized while another was heavy into denial. The woman of light couldn't be real, she had to be made from the merging light of frog eyes which...

With a start, he noticed the light of the watching eyes had been snuffed out, as if their presence was gone. But it couldn't be so, could it?

He reached out beyond the lines of their camp, the first tree within reach a slender birch, an intensity of black lines scarifying the trunk. He felt flakes of paper beneath his hand and then, he touched one; a frog. Then another as his hand slipped over the first. No, they were still there, still poisonous but darkened. He carefully felt the other trees, noting the familiar and slightly unsettling feel of frog skin beneath his hand, their light having dimmed, increasing the creepiness of the night. It was a wonder now that the light of their eyes had ever seemed threatening, surely not as much as having their eyes closed.

He moved further into the woods, the solitude disturbed as the girl turned in her sleep. He froze in response until patterned breathing was re-established. He looked quickly at Leanan; she hadn't moved, the blue limning her body still a burning shimmer. He idly wondered which world she was currently in; his or hers? He had the sudden impulse to touch her skin and with it, the fear that if he did, he would be lost in her world for sure.

The flicker of nebulous light flashed to his left, cutting through his distractions. Careful in placing his feet, he melted into the woods, its shadow hungrily devouring his. But at the moment, there was no sense of danger, no confusion as to what he should do; the ghostly form of a woman beckoned, and he could only follow.

As if prelude to the golden meadow he'd seen from the top of the hill, a large expanse of open woodland appeared, saplings no higher than his knee dotting the moon-swept glade. As if the hem of Night had been lifted, the leaves of grass and stems of night-blooming jasmine glimmered before his eyes, their silvery-blue outlines mesmerizing. There was a single line of bent grass that went straight through and as if called, he followed, the moonlight lashing at his skin, angry at his gall. Yet, it was all he could do because in the distance, he could see the apparition moving off, her arms lifting and swirling, perhaps dancing to a tune only she could hear. But never once did she look back at him, though his heart strangely yearned for her to do so.

As he traversed the glade, soaking up the exposed moonlight, the track approached a stand of dense trees, their odd fan shaped leaves suffocating deeper shadows that struggled to get free. And as he approached, he saw too that another waited, but it was not the woman of light. The figure was dark, basking in shadows, though strange stray reflections glimmered back. The figure didn't move, patiently waiting as if Jareth's arrival had been preordained.

The form grew less nebulous and more solid until Jareth could make out the gleam of large eyes. Could this be the grandaddy of all frogs? Certainly the luminous glow suggested this but as the shadows receded, Jareth could see a muzzle, long and strongly cut, large dark nostrils flaring as if scenting the wind. Velvet-blue ears were turned toward him, wide and alert. The head resolved into that of a buck, a many tined rack of intricate spokes atop its head, like a crown. The limning he'd mistaken for moonlit branches, was clearly illuminated as antlers, their mien majestic in the creature's patience. But this was no buck as Jareth's eyes could clearly see; the form of a large-chested man, clothed in glinting blue-green armor formed a resonation of the night, the shadows enclosing its frame having been finally chased away. The creature wore an inner breastplate of softly glowing red scales, as if coals fresh from their ashes had been pressed into service on its skin. A blue-black leather kilt lay crumpled over dark green leggings, high enough to visibly show Jareth the creature's hooves, finishing dark textured furry legs. Two limbs hung at its side, forearms corded and sinuous, molding into dark half-gloves. The furred fingers were intertwined on its lap, the creature leaning forward, and its eyes now seen as pools of liquid shadow from which came a green glow.

The white blaze on its muzzle blued in the light, and the belt slung across the creature's shoulders kept a quiver of red-shafted arrows safe. With a start, Jareth's breath stalled; he knew this archer!

Chapter 25

Mummer's Dance

The track through the glade split at the purple-leafed ginkgoes, each half merging to either side and disappearing beneath the leaves once again. And at the epicenter of it all, the creature sat; huge, hulking and brooding. Behind the long red-feathered shafts, a dark bow of unknown resinous wood lurked. Jareth could see it peeking from the shadows, its mettle and purpose clearly calling out.

"Is this the path you've chosen, Estel? Is this where you wish to go?"

But Jareth was confused because both voice and naming were familiar. Another memory was roused, something from a book he'd read long ago...as a young man, when he could navigate the words of adults. But where? When? Which story was it? He eyed the impossibility before him.

"You're the archer."

Jareth said it flatly, not able to run toward denial.

The creature nodded slowly, turning the corners of its mouth up in what might have been a grin. Still, the eyes did not relent as they formed a living pool of unknown fathoms. They were the mirror to the voice, the one he'd heard before, in his head, out in the forest.

"You've chosen to show yourself."

His words hung, understanding that this creature was both the archer who'd killed the Hounds, as well as the voice whispering to him in his head—the one telling him to go home, nay, urging him to find the *way* home.

"Aye, there is a distinct difference, isn't there?"

Was the creature chuckling? Did eyes flicker in amusement? Did ears cup forward as if to better hear his confusion?

"You killed the Hounds."

The other regarded him with solemn eyes, deep green and penetrating.

"It seemed expedient in the moment."

Jareth wasn't getting anywhere with his poorly crafted statements so he tried to be more blunt.

"What do you want?"

The dark form moved then, albeit slightly, telling the man that at least it wasn't rooted to the ground, despite the reverberation of stretching roots in its voice.

"You're looking for something, Jareth; as I've told you, I'm here to guide you."

Guide me? The question didn't have any context in the moment and he wrestled with what possible meaning could be had...

"You're chasing phantoms, my child, that which could destroy you should you catch it."

And the reality of the moment burst in on Jareth like the dawn.

"The woman of light?"

The creature nodded, its eyes flickering in unison.

Jareth licked his lips and sweat formed on his brow. There was an anxiety he couldn't define trying to attach itself. Ruthlessly, he tore away from the feeling's grip. The other's voice rose in his head, again.

I see your defenses are as strong as ever.

Nonsense, and he didn't disguise his disdain. Get out of my head! Which promptly occurred.

"Maybe not now, but in time, you'll remember where the door is."

Even more, what was this creature doing here? What kind of being is this? Surely not a magic that belonged to this world...

"Not magic at all, Jareth."

The man opened his eyes wider, taking the creature in, wondering at the situation into which he'd stumbled.

"Why is my name known to you but I have no memory of who you are?"

The question had been there, even as he'd retold his tale to the women, later that night, after his first encounter with this voice. At least now he had a form to cloak it in, though he doubted either Leanan or Beryl would believe him. Though, the muse had been unusually quiet upon hearing of his encounter.

"Because she knows there's always been another Jareth, though it is not her way to share, unfortunately."

Share?

"What are you doing here, Jareth?"

The directness of the question caught the man by surprise, though he supposed he should have expected it. Did he sense impatience, too?

"As you say; I was following the light."

The creature chuckled, long and slow, but without malice.

"Interesting way you put that."

As Jareth stared back into the buck's eyes, he realized he was beginning to doubt his sanity; this was a stag with the torso of a man. Who could reconcile such a thing?

"*You* can, Jareth; you just need but remember. You know me, else how could you have perceived color from the folds of night where to all others, there is only shades of gray? It is because you are the one doing the painting, and it is you who chooses what raiment I don in this moment. In time, perhaps you will recall that

I am the Lord of the Forest, the Protector and Creator of life; the hand that wields both the hammer and anvil."

Riddles, again. Titles so provocative and brash that its mere abstraction hit Jareth hard. Abstraction could be defined as almost anything...

"Aye, it can. I'm sure you're glad then that you're aware of the true voice, and in time, you'll remember true sight as well. For now, this is how you'll see me."

Jareth had no reply.

The silence grew with moonlit deepened shadows surrounding; man half-naked with cords of wiry muscle and the other clothed in coarse animal fur. One with black ink striping his chest, the other unblemished but for one lone scar in its side. A man with a week's worth of hair framing mouth and chin, the other an animal in man's frame, hammered steel gorget rigged for war. One holding the flame of song in his mind, the other sequestering the rhythm of stars. Man with a blade, creature with a bow and arrows, but each with a weapon dipped in death. A halo of confusion ringed one, a crown of thorns the other.

Man and creature stalled in stalemate, one unsure of which piece to move, the other having already done so and waiting.

Jareth felt the moment and wondered why this was happening. What was this before him; creature or madness? Something which only his dreams or song magic could conjure?

"Legend calls me the Cervine. But for you Jareth, I'm the one whose voice you hear when your heart and mind and soul all agree. For now, eschew all night enchantments, be they women of light or dark—and don't deny both exist. All else must be lost before you can find your way home again. Start with the girl."

And as if the moon was eclipsed, the night crashed in and he lost the creature's form to shadow. When his vision cleared, it was gone. Of course.

He looked once, long and hard, in the direction which the woman of light had gone, her memory beginning to fade. Then he looked the other way, where the path showed a grim hard emptiness that needed to be explained. And last, he looked at the lone trunk of tree, toward where the image of the Cervine had manifested. Between the riddles and choices, there was confusion. It was then he thought he felt the ground tremble like a mummer's dance, reminding him that everything returned; ashes to ashes and dust to dust.

Chapter 26

Storms

"You mean they really exist?"

Beryl was opening up to the muse and Jareth idly wondered why. Had the Leanan's ice sufficiently cracked enough to let the cold water flow? Did the girl's growing adaptation to self-sufficiency endear her to the muse in ways only too obvious? Perhaps the girl just feared more black marks, despite their assurance none would be forthcoming, and relaxed into a pocket of security she'd never known? Maybe it was just the fact that someone cared enough for her to make her fears their own. Maybe.

They came to the fork of last night's encounter and Jareth half feared the Cervine creature would be sitting there waiting. The story of his last meeting he decided to keep to himself; hard to think either would believe a stag-headed man-thing could exist, let alone be riddling about their journey. And that such a journey included all three of them was more sure than ever. The Cervine had mentioned the muse obliquely and the girl quite directly. But what he made of his instruction still needed shape. Start with the girl...ah, how? He had to lose everything before this intense urge to go home would abate...start with the girl. Somehow, he didn't think it meant to lose Beryl but rather, to fulfill Leanan's promise.

Because of last night though, his mind had been turning over the tales and magics he'd been told when a child. Beryl's own memories confirmed his and at the mere mention of spells, Leanan had launched into mysteries which made the girl's eyes go wide. And surprised himself, if he were honest.

"Aye, girl; the bloody Mabinogion even records some events and tales correctly, though of course mortals like to slant the truth their own way."

She cast an eye toward Jareth whose brow was raised, questioning her disapproval, as if she blamed him for any errors.

Her laugh though took away the tension as they neared the fork. Why he felt a growing unease couldn't be answered. Perhaps *she'd* choose their path.

"And are there the little people, the dwarves, in the book?"

With more surprise, Jareth noted that Piper was following close to the girl now, occasionally rubbing the side of his jaw along her exposed leg, the edge of his teeth scoring the skin, though the girl didn't seem to mind. Hmm, what had she done to get all this attention, anyway?

"Not in that book but they do appear in the Voluspa, from the Poetic Edda poem. There's more than some truth to the rumor that humans are their fault, that Ask and Embla were the first from those out of Brimir's blood and the legs of Blain."

Leanan walked in front of Beryl while Jareth brought up the rear, her apprehension beginning to grow with the burst of wind the morning had brought. Conceding the lead, this alleviated him from any immediate course decision, knowing the fork was coming.

She lapsed into a silence that Beryl found frustrating. But Jareth was proud because the girl waited instead of badgering the muse; the girl's whining was her least favorite attribute. She was even learning to keep up whatever pace the muse forced, and with only the briefest of comment.

Then, as if appealing to both the man and girl, the muse began to sing, her voice much less contralto, falling into soprano territory, her voice fully lush and captivating. Why this surprised him, he wasn't sure.

"Then sought the gods, their assembly seats,
The holy ones, and council held,
To find who should raise, the race of dwarfs
Out of Brimnir's blood, and the legs of Blain.

There was Motsognir, the mightiest made
Of all the dwarfs, and Durin next;
Many a likeness, of men they made,
The dwarfs in the earth, as Durin said.

There's more, but that's the gist of it, though I could give you my interpretation through the years of dwarf obstinance and greed. Too many tales, actually..."

Her voice trailed off and it became obvious that she'd rather not talk about the 'folk of the mountains' as Beryl likened their race. Not that Jareth had ever seen any, but he also wasn't going to dismiss the possibility. Magic was a hard concept to keep in a bottle, as he was finding out.

"And what about the Elves? Have you any songs about them?"

Jareth realized how much this girl was smitten then with the stories of her youth and wondered why. Was there a reason she opened the window of escapism so wide?

The girl had practically dropped back to walk besides the older woman, the light in her eyes brilliant beneath the arching sun of afternoon. The clouds of the past few days were diminished and upon each rise, the golden fields of the meadow drew nearer. Jareth knew that if Leanan chose the northward track, it would provide a way around the lake of open grass that loomed, heading toward distant storms of mountains. The south track headed around the patch where trees refused to grow as well but what would that path's end look like? The distance was too great and the forest brooded. Weren't there cities and lands to the south which he should know about? Certainly it was where he'd come from...didn't that mean home should lay that way as well? But then, the stories out of Terra pointed them squarely due east, straight and through, to the last hill beyond the bridge. Didn't that mean that neither path at the fork was theirs? Why then had the Cervine not indicated that choice? Was there more to the riddles than Jareth assumed?

Dammit, can't assume anything, he mused, understanding what such a practice did to a person. Better to know than to assume, any day of the week. He breathed out a bit too loudly and both women turned questioningly.

He just shook his head and pointed forward, the open glade of last night emerging from beyond the tree line. There wasn't anything he wanted to explain, especially to them.

"The elves belong to many cultures, Beryl, much as the word 'fairy' has been used to mean any magical creature, including goblins or gnomes, leprechauns, jinn, and even wights. There's many more to be sure, but that's what the stories are for, that and bards."

Leanan shot Jareth a smirk and winked when he lowered his brow threateningly. He didn't like her categorization.

"Aye, did you know, Beryl, that one of the greatest magicians of legend is the bard? Minstrels are kit and kin, though some pretension exists there...you have the gift as well, though your aim is as unfocussed as a shooting star's."

Her laugh was at Jareth's expense and he knew it, glowering as she tried to skewer him with his passion.

"Ach no, dear Jareth; no disrespect at all. More like a nudge that gets the stone to rolling again. A minstrel relays history, a bard makes it..."

Her voice drifted off, as if meanings could not be defined so precisely. Something in her tone though made the condescension fade, and he knew there was much more behind what she was saying. The damnable part was he thought he should know what it was.

"Seems we have a choice; any ideas?"

Leanan tossed the question back to Jareth who had fallen even further back as the fork was reached. He loathed hearing her voice in that moment, as if she was forcing him to face a well-honed fear.

She noticed the lines in his face tighten and the gray of storm in his eye fall more distant. Dropping her pack to the ground near the girl—who was thankful for the rest—Leanan strode back to the man, his step having faltered.

"There a problem?"

She drew near, the open plunge of her neckline exposing the pale white skin of her breasts, her own heat rising along with the valley's. She parted crimson lips and Jareth noticed how her breath came out like mist, like exhaling on a cold winter morning. That didn't seem right and he felt the tension in his head pinch tighter, as if her nearness was turning his world upside down—again.

"At least I'm not boring, Love, you have to admit it."

He nodded woodenly but didn't know why; how should he know that?

"It's part of our story, that's all. One day, remind me to fill in the details—might hurry this particular portion a bit, and it would be nice to get past all these trees...speaking of which, those in Terra said we needed to travel past the Meadow of Gold and yet, the path splits to either side. So, which is it to be?"

Damn, he'd run out of time and there didn't seem any place to hide either.

"There never is, Jareth; there's only places to be."

Damn, the sound of the Cervine creature crashed through his reverie and shattered the circle of confusion in which he'd lost himself. Looking quickly beyond the muse, the fallen log was empty, and nowhere did he spy either green penetrating eyes or the creature's mighty rack of horn. Just the voice, and it too waited on him.

Leanan's brow lifted and he could see her moment of confusion, which surprisingly made him feel better. She might be able to read his mind, but certainly seemed not to hear the other voices in there...

"There something I should know, Jareth?"

Her own penetrating look shook the certainty out of him and he hurriedly shook his head, averting his eyes as if they would betray him sooner than his tongue.

"Nay, just not sure this way is one I own."

She crossed her arms, the edges of her eyes hardening.

"Again, Jare? Let me ask you something."

She paused, taking a moment to adjust the longsword sheathed on her back. Looking south, her voice was low but pointed, a brusque whisper that would not accept ignorance as an answer.

"There are many like those in Terra, those that wake up every morning, put on their clothes, take their meal and head out to harness the land. They work the day and toil beneath the sun until it sets and the evening meal is served. Partaking of that, there is perhaps an hour of time for recollection, introspection or typically, releasing the ague of the day—for those lucky enough to find such solace. For those, there is only the job at hand, and that's surviving what the world gives them."

She turned finely molded features back toward Jareth, long almond shaped eyes widening into vast pools of night. Her lips pursed and faint color in her cheeks dissipated until skin was almost alabaster white. The colors around her eyes flared, relentless promise for the unwary male, lashes merging spidery lines into her skin, framing the look flowing to him. In every respect, she was holding his attention.

"Jareth; you, don't do that. You don't see each day as the same, your tools are not the hoe and spade, your hours are not described by routine. You speak to currents of both wind and rain, with the flow of sand kissing the ever changing contours of the sea. You know the truth of the Word, you sing the song of the strings you play. Does this sound like an accurate description of the man called Jareth Rhylan? Or is he the one that can remain bound and happy with endless routine? See, the latter can be found to the south, in the soft cities mortals erect and tear down daily. The former doesn't belong and knows it. Where do you belong, Jareth? Which houses your soul?"

The pathos in her voice was like singing notes he'd never sung before and yet knew intimately. It was like she had shown him a part of himself he denied. As he forced his eyes from hers, the road south looked wide and used, tired and staid. He thought he could see the gates at its nether end; they'd be wide and golden, decked out with all the pomp and circumstance mankind could muster. It would be contrived and shallow, like a stream too close to the ocean.

To the north, a mystery lay, one that whispered for him, hungered for him, and he felt the touch of ice and snow. That way lay the comfort of sleep and giving up, though he did not know why. Something about the mountains and their distant menace warned him that their heights would be fatal. Did that mean he was not to take such risks, to avoid heights where a man could slip? Did it mean he was too afraid find the unknown in a world where risk-takers were renowned when they succeeded, and forgotten when they failed? A gust of freedom beckoned, calling him to find out.

And then there was the other road, the one which eschewed both the tame and the wild path. It spoke of purpose, that there was a narrower way by which he could travel, if he had the strength to believe.

"But what am I to believe in, I wonder?"

His words were spoken aloud, forgetting all about the woman and girl who waited on his decision. Leanan cocked her head and felt a moment of confusion, this third way not one of which she was sure. What was going on in his head?

Beryl sat and waited, her fingernails digging into her palms, worrying at the ink stains on her arms and legs, an anguish she translated to Jareth. There wasn't much doubt that she feared the way south, and was oblivious to the way north.

Ignorance is bliss, Jareth sighed, upon seeing the girl fidgeting with her tattoos. His sigh also signaled resignation; if he couldn't find his way home, at least he could help Beryl find hers. And up until that moment, the girl's fate had been less than important to him. But something about her innocence and victimization ached for a justice he just couldn't deny.

"Fine; we'll take the path forward—neither north nor south. We'll seek the meadow's gold and cross the bridge. If we happen upon the last house on the last hill, Eli better be behind that green door, that's all I can say..."

His voice trailed off and as if in response, the wind picked up, its strength forcing itself between the stand of trees bearing purple leaves, separating their branches to either side and opening a way forward; the other path was revealed.

Leanan tried to catch Jareth's attention and failing this, grabbed his arm. Leading him to where the girl watched with wide eyes, she urged them all into the lane between the ginkgoes, the wind sweeping their feet along as if they were already tardy.

Chapter 27

Running Through the Garden

The sound of rushing water grew, from the whisper of warm currents lofting toward the valley's heights, to a winding trickle of music neither Jareth nor Beryl could ignore. Its melodious churning over cobblestone became a lure, a promise of surcease from the road, and even Leanan found new heart at the prospect of soothing water on her tired feet.

The path beyond the ginkgoes forced its way between misshapen trees that seemed stunted from infection. What once was a proud old forest had turned into a cancer that bordered the river and ensuing meadow. Some force held the surrounding trees at bay, and those too close looked blasted and war-torn, though there was no evidence that such a conflict had taken place. The purple leaves tangled amongst each other, forming a fence of vine; perhaps as hedge against the meadow?

Despite much of the day was still unused, Leanan called a halt to their journey. Even Jareth could see that they could use the refresher. That, and his mind was muddled with the events of the other night. The woman-of-light had become his own personal haunt, and he didn't know why.

The water was deeper than it looked and though clear, a darkness clung to its bottom, obscuring the cobbles that must to be there. The river's banks were high enough to handle the swollen seasonal current of ice and snow, a melt far to the north where the line of mountains glowered at them unceasingly Jareth felt doubt lingering in that direction, as if time itself was reluctant to head that way. He turned his eyes in time to catch Leanan gazing in that direction also. He traced the subdued glimmer bounding the muse's head, noting the fluctuation of dark hollows beneath her eyes. Pupils were narrowing, giving her a serpentine look. She pursed her lips and lowered her lids in contemplation. What the hell was she thinking about? Beckoning, the river murmured louder.

As he expected, the water was both deep and cold. Still, there was soothing, at least initially, until the numbness grew too much to handle. Scrounging for his boots, he noted that Leanan still dangled her feet in the water, while her lips moved as if whispering her secrets to the fast moving flow. What did she say? What evocations did she impart? Was there reason and logic in the way the stream moved? Did she hear news from the north, as if talking to the wind? Without a breeze, is this the way news of the world came to her? Surely then she was kin to the elementals...

"The currents are strange here, Jare; I cannot separate their voices. But I do feel knots tightening the land and water feels this strain like moles running through the garden."

She turned gold-ring eyes his way, addressing him even as he yanked his boots back on, fumbling with the antique buckles and mold-tinged leather; he'd need some oil or wax soon if he wished to keep this pair. The path had been soggy—too soggy—and the constant moisture had stretched the leather until the bottoms were balding in multiple places.

He watched the light burnish her usually lustrous night-imbued hair with a golden glow that chafed at having to penetrate such forbidden depths. Forbidden indeed, he ruminated. The white linen of her shift beneath the armor gathered about her creamy neck as a constant invitation, while she slowly strapped a vambrace about each forearm. Long dextrous fingers plied at the burnished blue-black leather. The knife she most favored gleamed at him from the back of her calf. She was a woman of war, and was more dangerous than he could fully describe because her true power lay not in the sharpness of her weapons, but in her voice.

"I wish you hadn't bound my familiar to my skin...I feel blind operating this way."

Jare shook his head, once again not understanding.

"I know you always were suspicious of it, but at least then we had some warning of danger. Can you feel the meadow's building resentment? Something is alive there, Jareth, of this I'm sure."

He followed her gaze when she turned toward the golden field across the water. He felt it, most assuredly he did.

"What familiar are we talking about? The bird?"

The image of the way the woman's skin swept from pale white shoulders and into the small of her back where the tattoo lurked, rushed to his mind. It had seemed like a strange way to mark oneself.

"I figure you did that so I'd not wander off."

Wander off?

"Aye, though more often than not, it has been you with the need to be alone. Still, my skin crawls with anxiety at not being able to feel the wind, or see the land from afar. Would come in handy right now, aye?"

She'd taken some dried strips of meat from their packs, running her teeth and tongue over the coarse texture, savoring its flavor.

"Can we stay here awhile?"

Both Leanan and Jareth turned to the girl who'd been unusually quiet, despite her initial glee at seeing open sky for a change. Perhaps though, she too was feeling exposed now that the trees were barely against their backs.

Whereas the forest had intensified the moment one left the path, here, the sudden openness to the east left all three feeling exposed and naked, as if the wood's eerie veil, which had initially seemed strange and stark, was now being ripped aside, exposing their position.   Whereas fear had come with the forest, now it lurked in all the open expanse, whose fields of flowing gold belied its beauty. The few trees dotting the meadow were dead or twisted and this left them with a feeling of foreboding.

"Eyes in the sky could have told us what yon golden fields are hiding."

Leanan had lowered her voice so only Jareth could hear, before turning and addressing the girl.

"We'll rest a bit but the road to Eli lies that way, across the amber fold."

Jareth noted that though Leanan was filled with doubt, she'd put more confidence in her words to Beryl. Not that it helped as he saw her looking apprehensively at the further bank.

"Never thought I'd say I'd rather face a forest of frogs."

Jareth mumbled quietly, not wishing to make the girl more nervous either. Which surprised him; was he beginning to feel that much concern for the teen? And had he placed more importance on Beryl's request for song the past few nights? She claimed notes from his mandolin helped ease her into the cradle of sleep, but he didn't regret her interest. He recalled watching the girl curl up near the muse, his song guiding the two women along Dream's wistful road. He'd been as surprised as delighted.

He'd tried to catch Leanan's eye, but she was deep within a world all her own and wasn't even aware of drawing the girl to her. And yet, he knew she was with him in his, feeling her hand on his, her soft lips near his ear, and the wind of her breath a sigh on his cheek. As his voice fed the night breeze, the echo coming back to him was accompanied by a distinct feminine chorus.

The river snaked from far distant heights, past the border of trees and meadow where each fought for a greater hold. It was broader and the faint trail met rickety wooden planks suspended over the water. The bridge must normally have been dozens of feet above the churning waves, but now it clipped the rushing crests. The span of wood and twisted fiber wasn't long, but the way it was tethered to the meadow created a tunnel effect which was daunting. Part of their reluctance was the further shore's strangeness, as if the encroaching stalks balked at anyone going past.

"Like fields of corn on the edge of a farm," Jareth thought.

"Aye, just like that. There's something about not being able to see the path ahead that is just plain unnerving."

Leanan was echoing his thoughts. Still sprawled on the bank, he reached for his other boot, shooing the cat from under his legs. It was then that pursuit caught up.

Hidden by the swell of water, the sound of iron wheels gnashing at the ground went unheard. When trees moved in an effort to block the way, the rusted chariot began bouncing from side to side, shearing off those branches that sought to slap and stab. It wasn't until the bear pulling the chariot growled low that the three realized they were not alone.

One boot on and one dangling in his hands, Jareth jumped up quickly, turning to face the chariot's rasp, which tore at the forest's stifling aura and swatted at the rising wind. Behind him, he could swear the water's roar swelled toward crescendo. Piper bounded into the long grass and disappeared.

Leanan was quicker still, the thin whist of her knife sliding out of its sheath and into her hand. The longsword lay in the grass while Jareth's own blade was also too far out of reach. They'd had no warning and yet their movements to establish a defense was like a classic dance step, each sure of where the other would be.

A thin whine that sought to be a wail, emanated from the chariot's driver, attenuated by the air racing into a maw of a skeletal mouth and out any number of facial orifices. Hung by thin strings of flesh, an orange ooze pulsed, giving the illusion that the creature had eyes. The bone of misshapen teeth rattled against hollow jaws, resonating with the wind as the Bone Warrior rushed out of the trees from the slope behind. How it had gotten down without alerting them was a thought for another time, as Jareth dove to his left to avoid the deadly sweep of a mace, its iron core bristling with yellowed bone spikes. The earth was torn a foot deep where Jareth had just vacated, the weapon yanked back and arcing high for yet another blow.

Leanan had leapt the other way, her knife stabbing within close quarters at the massive bear. Movement in the grass behind indicated that the girl was just as quick. As the Warrior and bear swept past, almost toppling over the bank, Jareth lunged for his sword and rolled into a crouching stance, blade drawn and waiting. Peripherally, he was aware of Leanan pulling the girl further into the underbrush, their forms rolling and slipping beyond the bank's edge.

Jareth's eyes narrowed, a snarl searing his soul as the immediacy of the attack swept his emotions into a maelstrom of anger. The fear he'd been harboring from the meadow was now unleashed and his impatience churned like a cauldron. The earth near the river felt chill beneath his one unshod foot, tiny pebbles burrowing into his skin, heightening his focus and tightening his aim. As the bear twisted past Leanan and bent its body to turn, the chariot and Warrior beat the river rushes down, their lengths plowed under the massive iron wheels of the chariot.

While he'd seen enough of the Bone Warrior in the dark that first night, in the light of day the creature looked even more like a half-eaten drumstick, meat flaking and sinew worming in gristle-like manner. A fetid odor followed their rush, and Jareth wasn't sure if it was coming from the animal or the mace-armed nightmare. His sword thrust forward and cut wickedly as the Bone Warrior raced forward to crush him. If the bear didn't get him, the great spiked wheels or whistling mace might.

And then, he wasn't alone, though the strangeness of the entity emerging from behind him didn't immediately register. The shadow cast was too long for the woman to make. It grew and Jareth was swallowed within it. There was no time to worry at its odd familiarity. The bear opened its foul mouth and yellowed teeth arced skyward, emerging from drooling blackened gums.

Jareth avoided the sweep of a mighty paw and once inside its reach, lunged with his blade toward the bear's hamstring, hoping to cripple the animal. He felt a satisfying tightness trip his blade as he swung with all his might, the tendon a tremendously thick cord in such a massive creature. But his blade was sharp and he felt the tension release, along with the muscle behind the bear's back leg.

Beside him, a sweep of dark wood met the downward stroke of the Bone Warrior's battle mace, its arc curtailed and ripped away. Avoiding the iron wheels, Jareth leaped into the high grass and away from the river's edge. The shadow though, still stood, and its thrust made the chariot lurch precariously.

Gaining his feet and with sword ready, Jareth was shielded by the passage of the bear and Bone Warrior and it wasn't until both had cleared, that he saw the creator of the shadow; it was the one called the Cervine. Clutched firmly in two massive furred hands, a mighty bow of dark resined wood completed its follow-through. The rack of tines on its head glittered with the sun, tips bleached white like the bones of a beached whale, or a mouth of shark teeth. The creature's lips were pressed tight and its large black nostrils flared amidst white fur. Where at their first meeting the creature's ears had been extended, alert and attentive, now they were laid back in a purpose far more profound. The Cervine was taller than Jareth first supposed, nearing fourteen feet from heavy, sullen black hoof to sun-rippling antler tip, and as wide as two men. The emerald green and crimson red of its chest armor, shone as the sun flared full upon it. The Bone Warrior had regained control of his chariot and was ruthlessly tearing at the bit in the bear's mouth, turning the animal around to face the two who sought to stand against it.

Behind him, Jareth thought he could hear the girl crying, but couldn't be sure. No time now for that—he had to hope Leanan's stroke hadn't been her last. The bear growled in anguish as it tried to put more weight on its injured leg but couldn't. The chariot was beginning to slow even before the first of two massive arrows pierced the bear's body, the first severing the carotid, the next deep into its chest, the brilliant red feather of the shaft contrasting with black fur. As Jareth shifted his concentration fully to the warrior, he saw the bear stumble and fall full into an eruption of its own blood, the force of its lunge toppling the chariot.

Jareth raised his blade defensively, only too aware of the huge mace. Another arrow brushed past him, the wind of its passage whipping the red cowl of his short cape. The Cervine's shot hit the Bone Warrior flush in the chest, breaking its crude copper armor, the plate separating and pinching the dark shaft. Slowed, the Warrior did not stop and it began to swing the mace, winding up for a killing stroke. Trampling the reeds of the bank, its face twisted into a grin; the walking skeleton of death raised itself up, almost as tall as the Cervine, the orange ooze of its eyes dripping down a mottled bony cheek.

Jareth felt the distance between himself and the Cervine close like two lungs contracting, the air inside compressed and then exhaled out again. The Cervine caught the mace as it descended, the creature's huge palms taking the brunt of the spikes. Jareth ducked low and stabbing at the Bone Warrior's knee, slit leather-like tendons and splattered cartilage, severing the bones from one another. As the Cervine clutched the mace and yanked it toward him, combined with Jareth's disabling thrust, the warrior of bone lost its balance and fell to the ground. Jareth wasn't sure the sound it made was of pain or surprise.

A flash of his blade severed the other knee and Jareth sprang to the side, out of reach, while the Cervine ripped the spikes of bone from flesh and taking up the rotted chain, flung the warrior's mace back at its own skull, shattering the cranium and causing a black gruel-like substance to pour. Still, the demon of bone struggled to rise, to get at its prey.

From behind, the bright flash of steel flared, separating the space between the giant stag-man and Jareth even as both coiled and braced for another lunge from the Bone Warrior. The cold light of fury sparked and bled from the junction of spine and skull, scattering the fragments of bone and attached rotted skin that made up most of the Warrior. Between the Cervine and the man, Leanan's fury was like the absence of breath as she brought the longsword through its arc, the length of steel looking curiously black now. The guts of the bone monster smoked and smoldered as it slid toward the muse. Jareth watched in wonder as bits of what remained of the Warrior burned before ever reaching Leanan's pale hand.

As the cradle of day swarmed around them in the form of a sun-drenched river bank, three unlikely warriors stood watching as bones that should have died a long time ago, fractured, shattered, and spilled into a pile.

Chapter 28

Only Got One

Jareth realized an awkwardness as he considered his part of each relationship being thrust upon him. He couldn't say he knew any of the three that well. Leanan broke the silence, though not as he'd have done, addressing the creature with a fixed eye.

"And who or what are you?"

She held the longsword with a firm grip, its sharp end pointed at the Cervine, whom she scrutinized with dark eyes full of suspicion.

But the tall creature merely folded its arms across a barrel chest and tilted head and antlers against the sky, sunlight licking across impressive tines. It was difficult to tell, but Jareth thought the Cervine was grinning. Difficult, because he wasn't sure what a grin on a deer looked like. Quickly though, he moved between the blade tip and the Cervine, even if something told him it was utterly unnecessary.

"Stop, Leanan; I know him—we've met already. And he fought against the Bone Warrior too."

She looked at the stag unblinking, keeping the sword right where it was.

"You the one who's been following us? The one lurking just beyond the campfire's reach each night?"

The Cervine didn't say anything as he studied the woman, noting her teeth were slightly bared, pointed and contrasting against dark red lips. Then he nodded, just a slight dip of his chin that rippled with the movement of his antlers.

Jareth wasn't watching the Cervine, visibly startled to see the level of protectiveness Leanan was showing.

"Jareth?"

She practically hissed the words at the man, the urge to pull him from her sword's path growing.

The man turned toward the Cervine, realizing the he hadn't known they'd had a stalker. Or had he? Wasn't there something behind the light of frog eyes that hinted at a watchfulness, something that went beyond the frogs' intent?

"You've been watching us?"

His voice wasn't as demanding as the woman's, holding a curiosity that needed quenching.

The Cervine hadn't moved, standing still as if he was one of the trees and the rack of horn on his head a leafless bough. The slow swirl of moss-green eddied in brown eyes, a knowing contemplation already resolved into faint amusement. Was he laughing at them?

"Not at you, Jareth Rhylan, but with you. Though you probably can't see the distinction at the moment. Nor you, Lady."

While Jareth's eyes narrowed in consternation, Leanan's opened wider, as if suddenly aware the ground beneath her was not as solid as she'd thought.

"Who *are* you?"

Her voice grew less pointed and more confused, more curious.

"He's the Cervine."

Jareth answered, wondering what the muse would make of that.

She lapsed into silent memory, searching.

"Cernunnos? *The* Cernunnos?"

She was outwardly skeptical and yet Jareth could see the tip of the sword drop, as if on the precipice of being forgotten. Now, how did he know what *that* feeling was like?

Jareth turned to face the muse again.

"You know him?"

Leanan let the blade go slack but her eyes were once again calculating, new information forcing her to reconsider. She kept her eyes on the stag-man, directing her words toward Jareth.

"I know *of* him."

But curiosity wouldn't hold her tongue any further and she cast her aspersion toward the Cervine.

"Why have you been following us?"

Her question stalled in the moment while she decided if the blade needed to be raised again.

"It was your arrows that brought down the Hounds, wasn't it?"

She'd seen the quiver the moment she'd split the distance between her bard and the beast, and struck the Bone Warrior its death blow. The arrows couldn't be coincidence.

"You've naught to fear, Leanan Sidhe, Widow-maker of the Green Isle; like you, Jareth brought me here. Circumstance dictated that he needed some help."

Leanan's dark mane still held its braid, though the white shock running its length shimmered briefly in unison with her eyes, darkening at his words.

"That can't be; I would have known of you before this."

"There's much of Jareth that still lies hidden to you, Fae, be assured of this. But I would not be here unless he called. As he knows, I am always with him."

Her pupils constricted and the dark shadows about her eyes deepened, bringing a frown to usually sensuous lips. The sword wavered but did not rise.

"Stay your hand, Muse; we both have Jareth's welfare at heart."

But Leanan wouldn't pinch the wick of her suspicion and growing anger. Jareth could see this clearly even as he tried to make sense of the Cervine's words. Surely the creature hadn't harmed them, and killing the Hounds certainly made him an ally, didn't it?

"Or maybe he has an agenda of his own, Jare. There are legends and tales lost in myth that paint this being as something other than a god, though."

The surge beneath their feet was momentarily sharp before it petered out, almost too quick to grasp that it had happened at all. Jareth could only liken the sensation to turning the soil...or like the voice in the forest.

Indeed, the stag-headed man, who called himself the Protector of the Forest, was chuckling quietly, his ears relaxed and his posture sliding into ease.

"And shall I tell him your resumé, my dear? Seems he's lost some memories. Shall I enlighten him as to the machinations of the Dark Muse? Might that not be more illuminating insofar as agendas?"

The water gurgled past them as the sky worked to bring clouds to veil the sun. The Cervine raised his hand and gently swept a fur covered palm in a short arc to dispel the attempt.

Leanan's eyes momentarily widened before she regained her composure.

Jareth, watching the two sparring with more than words, had seen the muse wringing her hands; had she been trying to call up the wind?

"Severing the spine where you did shows you know how to protect Jareth, and that's bodes well."

The meaning of the Cervine's words didn't immediately penetrate Jareth's conscious, but Leanan understood; it meant that like her, this creature knew the true nature of the Bone Warriors. Did he understand the Hunt then, as well?

The soft brown fur of the buck-head was ringed beneath with a russet mantle of much coarser hair protruding from the green and red body armor. Nostrils flared once and the Cervine's lips moved again, his eyes deepening still further as he answered. Jareth noted the swell of muscle in the creature's arms as he stooped to pick up the great yew bow, slinging it on his back even as his words rumbled the air about them.

"Aye, that I do, and this is no ordinary hunt, as you've quickly found. There's an enemy seeking Jareth, one whose power you'll not easily be able to withstand, Sidhe; you're going to need my help. Ask Jareth if you don't believe me. The truth is inside him."

Leanan broke her gaze from the Cervine and placed it on Jareth, her eyes asking the silent question, concern trying to strangle confusion.

But Jareth just stood there while Leanan waited, braced by the longsword, her face a pale mask of apprehension. The one called the Cervine, confident and sure, went to retrieve his arrows from the bear's carcass. The death grin of yellowed fangs still faced them even as the animal bled its life to the trampled ground, reminding Jareth of how close he'd come to being crushed. The Cervine had slain this beast, had taken care of the Hounds, and had protected him when the Bone Warrior's aim seemed horribly true. The Cervine was right; the truth *was* inside, and though he couldn't say how, he knew it.

Leanan saw the boundaries melting, felt the bond of trust snap shut tightly, as if it had only momentarily come loose. It was much as she'd always fancied their own bond to be...

The man turned to face the muse, the sudden urge to move once again rampant in his head. They had to go; there must be others on the path behind...once again, the Cervine heard his thoughts.

"There are, Jareth; though you might have forgotten who you really are, your instincts are not impaired. Come, your path lies that way," and he pointed across the field of gold.

Casting an eye east, he felt a foreboding at the thought of treading that way.

Leanan, acquiescing for the moment and standing with the sword yet unsheathed, picked up on Jareth's reluctance; she even understood it. Her eyes locked with his, the dark iris breaching a silver field, and they supported him in ways he couldn't describe. Familiar, yes, and comforting, actually. The Cervine's voice broke in on his reverie.

"The Meadow is as dangerous as you make it, Jare, but you already know that. Just think how much danger then, that yon hunters behind us will find themselves in, aye?"

With such twisted logic, Jareth wondered if Leanan's reasoning didn't seem juvenile by comparison.

The muse snorted and glared at him, his mind only too open. He shut the window tight, surprise coming upon Leanan's face, which shocked him as well; he hadn't thought it would be that easy.

Choice; it's always been about choice, Jare. We've talked about this...

The Cervine's presence rolled through his mind as if the barrier he'd erected didn't exist.

If you don't want me to hear you, Jareth, such walls aren't necessary; all you need do is ask...

The harshness of that truth was so sharp that its mere presentation in such a gentle way dissuaded Jareth from even considering the idea.

Leanan's voice stabbed accusingly at him, her petulance only too obvious.

"If we have to cut across this field, let's get to it, shall we?"

Grudgingly, she was accepting their new traveling companion. She began to move off, the great blade still dangling at her side and her black nails curling tightly over the hilt.

"Don't forget the girl."

But Jareth was already at Beryl's side, his calloused hand bringing the young woman to her feet while a low whistle escaped from his lips. The Cervine cleaned the arrows on river reed before adding them back to his quiver, and moved off after the woman, his strong hind legs making less of an imprint in the bank's mud than did the muse. Jareth marveled because he knew how unobtrusive the woman could be, when it was her wont.

"Come on, girl, seems we're the weak links of this chain. Onward to find your Eli, hey?"

He tried to put a smile on his words to allay any doubt. Or maybe it was to hide his. Either way, there was no time to understand this newest riddle.

"Mr. Rhylan?"

He stopped in his tracks and felt something awkward and cool touch his heart, something that needed straightening.

"Jareth; call me Jareth."

The girl gave him a weak smile in return, surprised that the man's typical aloofness wasn't all consuming.

"I'm afraid of him...whatever he is."

She pointed guardedly at the retreating form of the Cervine as both watched the bridge sag under the creature's weight. Strangely, his hooves made hardly a sound. Uncanny, Jareth thought.

"The closest I can say is that he belongs to magic; what kind, I'm not yet sure."

Her eyes widened, the gleam of curiosity lit.

"Magic?"

He nodded, knowing he'd taken the coward's way out but not understanding why. There was more to the Cervine and he knew it.

"Is he a stag, or is he a man?"

Beryl's voice had sunk low. Jareth thought he understood the girl's trepidation; the Cervine's rack of horn was daunting to say the least.

"Says he's the Lord Protector, the Forest King, so I'd lean toward stag. But, what that means exactly, I don't know."

"Do you trust him?"

The man eyed the girl for a moment longer before casting a look at the retreating back of the giant cervine. He let out a breath, something which was half a sigh and half the release of captive winds.

"He seems trustworthy, doesn't he?"

The way he returned her question surprised him, as if he knew it was the right way to bridge the fact he might know but couldn't explain it.

The girl nodded, wiping the remains of a tear from her cheek. As he helped her to her feet and rooted for the scattered pack, he almost tripped over Piper, who'd slunk back from wherever he'd been hiding. The cat launched itself and in one silent leap, took his place once again on the man's shoulders, claws digging into pauldrons.

"There you are. Well, that should settle it, aye? Piper thinks we're in good company, so you shouldn't worry."

The girl reached up tentatively to stroke the cat before falling in beside the man. Jareth noted how far she'd come as the threat of her skin touching his lingered, but did not dissuade. And yet, mesmerizing him still, the black ink flowed down her arm twitched, squirming reflexively. It didn't matter; she was at least allowing him to help her up, and the feeling was a warmth not easily dispelled.

The muse crossed the wooden bridge easily and quickly, her eyes cast skyward, as if reading the clouds or hearing the quirky breeze, which started and stopped in fits.

The Cervine's hooves pressed the bridge down, an immensity of girth that surely belied his ability to move silently. The same wind which Leanan tried to scry, scuttled itself unmercifully on the creature's horn, impaling itself as if ordered to do so. Maybe Leanan was casting barbs at the newcomer in her own way?

When Jareth and Beryl touched the wood of the bridge, he could feel both the life of the water flowing closely beneath as well as the hidden meaning of the Meadow approaching. Crossing over, he held a moment when his hand lingered on the post supporting the bridge. Its massive cord was rigidly tied and the ground seemed bitter at its post, as if it were a reluctant sentinel. The urge to stop was strong, so strong that he almost gave in, the reason why a whirlwind of thought.

Purpose is like that, Jare; sometimes its the first steps we take that are the hardest, though.

And though Jareth was sure the muse hadn't heard the Cervine's words in his head, as if an echo, he felt Leanan's presence too, her words laced with more seduction than should be possible for a woman. He heard her plea in an arcane construction, as if Shakespeare were composing for her.

"Come to me, Jareth; worry not—these arms will hold thee."

With both voices harrowing the interstices of his resolve, he considered for a moment. With Beryl watching and the cat holding on tight, he deftly swept his sword through both cords holding the bridge to this side of the river. He turned his back then and motioned for the girl to get moving. They had no time to worry about where they'd been; there were too many paths that way.

"And now, we've only got one."

Chapter 29

Heartlines

Still early in the spring, the field through which they passed was waist high and Jareth wondered what it was like when full summer arrived.

"I deem summer *has* arrived, at least here, Jare."

Leanan voiced his growing dread, that the Meadow was anything but ordinary.

"Did you expect it to be anything else?"

She hadn't turned and he continued to watch her from behind as she used the longsword to push a way through the myriad stems. The plant looked like wheat, but didn't taste like it when he chewed on a short piece.

"There's magic here; make no mistake. But then, looks like we're armed to the teeth with some of our own. I wonder if we're the source, as if we're attracting those elements which usually are nicely shy and hidden."

The muse's voice carried to the girl, who pulled bangs of dark hair back and glanced around, her initial look of apprehension quickly replaced by curiosity.

Too quickly, Jareth noted, reminding the girl to look where she was going—there was no path before them, not yet at least. The Cervine had riddled them the promise of many paths to come and just as many choices, which seemed more annoying than promising, the more he considered it.

Beryl

As the sound of the river began to fade, Jareth noted that the meadow wasn't as it appeared. Once past the bent and gnarly trees, they were swept into a flow of golden fields. Looking back, the shape of the trees seemed different, less lonely and desolate, as if perception had changed. And whereas he thought the meadow stretched open and empty, once inside the meadow's borders, he saw it much differently; more than just the tall stalks filled the meadow as other plants and even animals could be seen if one was patient. All the land's attention was now trained on themselves, though. They were interlopers, he realized, wondering what that might mean. An unlike Frogmoss Forest, wherein the feeling of being watched turned into a good thing, here, the scrutiny grew to be oppressive.

Leanan walked in front, her sword turning aside the baffling ocean of wheat-like stems, her blue nimbus faint but resolute. Behind her, the girl struggled to keep in the muse's shadow, knowing the wheat wished nothing more than to resume its chosen pattern. They resented being bent. That meant Jareth had to also use his blade to fend off the stalks, muttering beneath his breath before eventually shifting into an old farmhand's tune, one that kept perfect time with the swing of his arm. Behind, with no visible effort, the Cervine wove himself through the meadow, his antlers easily mistaken for swaying branches. Jareth often had to look twice before the creature's outline unfolded from its surroundings. It was simply uncanny. Of Piper, there was no evidence but with infinite mousing opportunities, it might be a while before the cat returned.

Unconscious of the fact the golden grain was now moving on its own, Jareth kept swinging, his heart wrapped in the memory of his song and his mind pondering the strangeness of each traveling with him. When questions of why continued, he tried to quell his voice, changing the song to allay doubt. Beryl turned when he did this but didn't say anything, listening intently.

Eve's sentries fold within the velvet glow, withdrawn,
as promise spills from golden cups distance weans;
the foxes hesitate, unsure with morning yawns
that dreams of day won't follow those that night has seen.
I stand on edges, holding close my sutured seams
as roads are rushing toward me fearing what I'll find
when straight and narrow soon collides with curving screams,
before imagination cradled heartlines' time.

Unaware, his voice crested before forming troughs. Leanan though, understood fully because even as she threaded their way forward, making for what looked like a large willow in the distance, she felt Jareth draw energy from her, felt it as if it were his hands molding her curves. The light surrounding intensified, and her heart beat faster knowing Jareth was doing more than just singing; he was creating. Though the girl might think the song familiar, Leanan knew only the melody could be replicated, on errant winds and probably lurking at the edge of dusk...or perhaps dawn. Sometimes, it was hard to tell with Jareth.

Because no one could see her, she smiled, realizing that though the meadow held danger beneath its facade of gold, it was also bringing Jareth's guth to the fore. Her hope grew.

The song was a deceptive tune, one which seemed eerily familiar to Beryl. She counted chords, fixing them to memory so that later she could reproduce the same notes on her guitar. Indeed, though the field wanted to hold her back—as it did all of them—there was an ease to their track now, as if unwillingly, the meadow was letting them pass. This allowed her to relax, to catch the stealthy look of a fox as it passed, and the quick flutter of a mother quail followed by half a dozen chicks. The larkspur were scolding good-naturedly and she even flirted with a smile as a cloud of Painted Lady butterflies burst in front of them. Their herky-jerky flight confounded any predators long enough for them to settle back among the flowering thistles. Soon, Beryl forgot she was tired, forgot her anxiety regarding the Cervine, and for the first time, noticed the blue nimbus that clung like a shadow to the muse. Even the ink staining her skin slowed. Jareth's song had changed the road of her thoughts, at least temporarily.

The Cervine didn't look right or left and still he saw everything; the fox had a mate—a smaller female that was more cautious than the vibrant male. The quail mother actually had twelve chicks, but they clustered so close to each other that it was an easy mistake to make. Of the blue glow, he was well aware of who Leanan was and her outward disdain for him was of no consequence; if Jareth wished to change the rules, it didn't mean there wasn't a reason.

Without taking his large eyes from the women and the man in front of him, the Cervine looked further, wider, taking in all movement and interpreting what news the wind brought to his flared nostrils. Much was afoot, though he didn't think Leanan was aware of it yet. Whether their road crossed contingencies, was yet to be seen. His large hand slid to the pommel of a bone-handled knife stuck in his kirtle, the blade bound by a plain black sheath. He wondered if his great bow would be enough—this time.

The tree was huge, and revered, according to the Cervine.

"Oh? And how can you tell that?"

Jareth heard the distrust in Leanan's voice, though he too was curious.

"The voice of the Meadow tells me so."

Leanan leaned to one side, her normally pale face now sporting a bronze cast from the campfire. Her hands were restless and though she said nothing, Jareth knew there was something else on the her mind. What?

"Are you interpreting the heartlines, then?"

The Cervine gazed at Leanan, considering her query.

"Sometimes it's called that, aye. For me though, I know only the sound of its voice."

Leanan shook her head slightly, an unexplained frustration showing.

"The heartline of this area is muddled, tangled up in a sea of patterns that hide beneath the soil. The wind has only bits and scraps to tell; there is no way to distinguish a single line. Unless you are a god, of course. But you've not exactly confirmed my earlier guess."

She was challenging him, and Jareth wondered why. Surely since joining them, the beast had been nothing but helpful. Earlier, he'd dragged to the fire the husk of a large tree, and with child-like ease, snapped off enough dead wood for several days of fires.

"The willow speaks, if you would listen."

The Cervine's voice continued with his same sonorous timbre, and Jareth glanced at the muse to see if she'd take the dare. They were like two dancers on the same floor but each performing their own step, in their own space, flitting about but never crossing paths. Jareth smiled in spite of himself.

"I'd like to hear."

Beryl's voice was surprisingly bold.

The Cervine broke his gaze with the muse. With a slight nod, he invited the girl to approach. From the edge of the fire, both muse and man watched as the inked flesh of the girl's hand was place on the soft fur of the Cervine's palm. She was trembling, but whether with fear or anticipation was unclear.

The fire crackled as the dead wood burned golden, sending a small shower of sparks into the air, mimicking the glow-beetles that had been attracted. It really did feel like summer, Jareth thought, his hand scratching behind Piper's ears, feeling the animal's purr as a resonation beneath his touch. As he watched, he saw the swirl of black ink lacing Beryl's arm slow, as if being willed to do so. The lines were almost sensible now...

"Close your eyes and concentrate on the sound of your heart; it will be hidden at first but once isolated, you'll be surprised at its tenor."

The Cervine had taken the girl's other hand and put it on the bark of the willow, her fingers slipping almost naturally into the furrows in the bark. Above, the canopy of thin hanging branches wove another golden glow as it competed with the fire. And beyond that, Jareth could see the new moon rising. As if by magic, the stars were waking, yet he had to clear his sight of flickering flames in order to see them.

Leanan watched with suspicion as the girl's eyes closed and her trembling subsided. She knew the beast kept watch on them all, not just the girl, no matter that his eyes too were now closing. She could feel his presence in the soil beneath her feet and more especially, whenever the breeze swept his presence into her. He was not familiar—not in a normal way—and yet, he reminded her of the bond between the ocean and the beach; it was a reciprocal relationship that defined time. Perhaps that is what she felt most keenly. His voice belied normal passage, as if when he spoke, time didn't exist...or matter. There was more to this creature than simple magic, despite what he claimed. But how was he connected to Jare? This fact was undeniable; the man's mind was open to hers more often than was his wont, and though Jare seemed to have forgotten much, his sureness of this creature bothered her. If there was a threat, she needed to find it and quickly.

"I hear it!"

Beryl's whispered gush was like that of a child—a bright shiny moment of discovery too astonishing to keep inside.

The Cervine merely nodded, his eyes still closed, his ears and great nostrils tuned to the world while he looked deeper with the girl. There was something about her, something the others did not know...

"Now, beneath the sound of your heartbeat, there's another vibration; it is the willow's voice. You can hear its words as it moves the soil with aggressive roots. Can you hear this parting? Can you hear the deference of the worms?"

Silently, absorbed as never before, Beryl nodded, her mind painting pictures of the voices, of the feeling working itself from the earth and through the Cervine's hand.

It seemed like time stalled until reluctantly, she felt the connection fade as her fingers were released. On cue, the black ink spun and coursed, finding its place again, though all she saw upon opening her eyes was the same familiar black marks on her skin. Her smile vanished, despite the Cervine's efforts to make it reappear.

A shower of fireflies swept across the camp, glittering the spear-shaped leaves of the willow, mesmerizing in a swirling pattern. Rising, the swarm flowed toward the sky, their light filling the empty spaces between stars.

Leanan gave the Cervine a stony stare but said nothing. Then she turned toward Jareth and fixed him with an even darker glare. Stiffening her back, she marched out of the campfire, retreating to the far side of the willow, as if to distance herself from the tree's influence. Not that she believed it had any.

Jareth watched with some amusement, realizing that the muse was perplexed by the creature, as if everything she knew was in flux. The Cervine seemed to have that ability, he thought, remembering his conversation at the crossroads. And as he watched the woman fold her cloak about her, behind, out among the meadow grass, the woman of light glimmered, her face like the pale moon above, watching him in return. Intruding on his sudden reverie, Beryl's awe was apparent.

"How did you know?"

The Cervine's voice inveigled its way into Jareth's conscious, answering the question posed by the girl, momentarily distracting him.

"It *is* your story, is it not?"

The girl nodded, soft fur once again cradling her palm.

"The moving ink explains it all, as it was intended."

At these words, the girl's youth seemed to diminish and she looked as old as time. The shadows dancing around her eyes and mouth deepened even as the fire surged higher. In the light, Jareth could see the Cervine looking intently, the expression on his face typically buck-like; unless you looked into the eyes, there was no outward expression. Jareth wondered if deer could move their mouths into anything like a grin. He supposed not.

"But the story isn't done, is it? There is more for you to know and do."

Round and wide, the girl's eyes glistened darkly with traces of flame, a new strength rising. It didn't touch her mouth and make her smile, but Jareth knew Beryl had been renewed with hope. As *all* should be.

As all should be, aye.

The resonation that came from the Cervine, whenever the beast sought to mind-speak, was a strange confirmation just the same.

On the far side of the camp, Leanan was ignoring them, as if such mortal convention was beneath her. Turning his gaze, Jareth took a longer look at the stag-man called the Cervine. Why not 'a' cervine, he wondered.

Because before there was anyone, I am.

And this was supposed to mollify, Jareth thought, knowing it only deepened the question instead.

Will you sing for me, Jare? It's a cold night despite this phony summer, and I'm slipping into a gloomy place.

Leanan's sudden intrusion startled him, and he wondered if the woman had overheard his thoughts. But glancing gave no evidence of that; it was only his own reflection he saw, despite Leanan was gazing into the fire.

Sing for her, Jareth, sing for us all; it will do much good. But don't just take from her what she gives, take what's already there.

Which made him pause as he slipped the six-stringed mandolin from its shoulder harness. What?

He looked sharply at the muse and then at the Cervine. She, was lost inside her burgundy wrap, the fire warming the pale skin of her hands and turning long nails copper, while he, was still talking quietly to the girl—who was the only one looking back at him, expectantly. Damn, this was just too weird, sometimes.

Chapter 30

Awake My Soul

"Did you notice the gemstone around the girl's neck?"

The voice of the Cervine was audible only to Jareth as they made their way through the trackless meadow for a second day. There was more of the same as they paralleled the tree lines both north and south, heading toward still more woods in the far distance. It was their next journey marker and beyond lay the hills and last green door. Something like that.

They walked in pairs now with the women in front and the men in back. Calling the Cervine a man didn't sit right with either him or Leanan, though the girl had no trouble doing so; maybe in the actual presence of magic, she was overwhelmed. The Cervine was certainly strange, not because of its appearance or ability, but because it gave the impression that all the rules didn't apply.

Not all, Jareth; I'm held here by the rules you set. I disregard the ones I deem silly, though.

The rules *I* set?

The second statement only then penetrated Jareth's mind.

"I don't set silly rules."

It was a reflex, and the fact he said it audibly was a mistake soon noticed.

Leanan turned and gave him a sly look before lifting her lips in a smirk. Did she laugh as she turned away?

"Well? *Did* you notice the stone?"

The Cervine was back on topic.

Jareth cleared his head of all confusion and slashed at the wheat field more aggressively.

"I've seen it; Leanan says its a rare beryl stone, red instead of typically blue-green. Still, what's it supposed to mean?"

The Cervine brought a hand to the base of his antlers with a distinct scratching motion.

"You know, they say one of the gates of Heaven is made of beryllium."

Jareth felt the prick of 'I knew that' but it was fleet and he was left wondering what the girl was hiding.

"The girl doesn't seem to want anyone to know and I'm okay with that; we all deserve our secrets."

The Cervine turned his muzzle toward the man, the longbow in his left hand stabbing the ground like a walking stick. Once again, there was no expression, and this fact was beginning to annoy Jareth; how was one to read another without facial expressions to help with the unsaid words?

"There's more to reading a person than outward signs, Jareth; even the muse could tell you that."

If the woman heard the Cervine, she gave no notice, but the man wasn't so sure; the echo in his head sure seemed like laughter...

"So? What's the girl's secret then? I can see from her inking what she is."

"Can you? And you know what the symbols and marks mean then?"

Jareth started to retort but realized he didn't really; he just knew they were significant.

"Which is sometimes a good barometer but doesn't tell the whole tale. Your own history bears that out, aye?"

But did it? There were only a few times when the memories he knew were there, could actually be accessed. The majority of time, he found himself wondering why he was moving with such veils covering his confidence. He was acting out of instinct, not information, and the further he went, the more he could sense danger in that fact. But what to do about it? Both the muse and Cervine seemed more attuned to him than he was to himself. At least the girl had the decency to keep to herself, and wasn't harboring things only he should know.

"So why can't I remember things? What *is* my history?"

Why had the question been so hard to frame?

"Because you're protecting yourself, Jareth; you and the girl."

Now, that was a strange thought. I am?

"From who?"

There's a great enemy abroad, Jareth, and one of his agents is looking your way.

The man turned toward fathomless eyes, questioning. The meadow was thinning as they neared its midsection and around him, the trees were more numerous, especially northward.

"And you and Leanan are here because I called you, right?"

"Something like that."

They lapsed into silence and Jareth turned his eyes once again to the ripple of movement all around him. He found one became accustomed to the flocks of butterflies that shifted and moved seemingly at the wind's will. Occasionally, a daring bird would dart close, trying for one of the stragglers. Often, there was a flash of light upon collision and only a continuation of erratic butterfly wings to mark that anything had happened. The sun was high overhead, sending light and heat as if it were midsummer, though it was hardly April and the weather should have been damp and dreary.

Ahead, Jareth could hear Beryl humming a walking song and see the thin blue contour of light about Leanan's form pulse in time to the tune. He let his eyes linger overlong on the muse's waist, noting the fine curvature...

Deep water knows dark currents, Jare; beware of them.

The notion of a sigh thought to escape his lips, but Jareth stifled it in time.

"Do you know why I'm on this journey?"

Not that he expected an answer that made sense, but Jareth at least hoped to get more illumination than the muse ever showed.

"We're all driven forward, my son, and those that do so without purpose are often lost from the herd. Doing your part keeps you in the game, so to speak. But beyond that, don't you feel it? A subtle palpitating resonation that underlies the voice of the world around you, a sound that calls you?"

Like Beryl, you are called to meet your Maker; the sound you feel, the current you ride upon whenever you sing, this exists to awaken your soul.

Awake my soul? The Cervine's last assertion was felt rather than heard, and he felt connections being made of which he hadn't been aware were loose. What had he gotten himself into?

"Now, your history…well, some you are still hiding from me— and it amuses me to let you recover it on your own. Sometimes, lessons are better learned that way."

Jareth's shoulder came to the stag-man's chest and playfully, the Cervine bumped into him with what sounded like a snorted chuckle, almost causing the man to lose his balance. Jareth's arm flew up along with a leg as he precariously leaned into the wheat field's sea of gold. Alarmingly, the sheaves leaned away.

Both women turned at the sound of Jareth's yelp, with the older's sudden anxiety changing to mirth while the younger giggled from the beginning. Jareth heard them both and glared.

Damn Cervine, he'd get his…

"Both the stone and girl are more than they seem, Jare, so don't let them out of your sight."

The man turned, his sword arm once again moving to bar the encroaching field, looking to avoid the prickly thorns of the numerous purple thistles which attracted the butterflies. His voice leaked sarcasm.

"The muse thinks so too; glad to know you're both on the same page. Now if anyone would like to tell me why, the rest of the day can be brightened immeasurably."

But as if his words were hijacked by the flurry of errant wings enveloping him, no answer was forthcoming. He shooed the insects away with his short sword, trying not to hurt them. Not like they were a swarm of mosquitoes.

The land had been steadily rising and the ground became less fertile, allowing other types of plants to crowd in, along with clusters of large toadstools. Their colors were many, but most looked like just-baked bread, reticulated with the color of honey. Such fantastic shapes caught all their attention. With their appearance, the cat finally revealed himself too.

"And did you have much success?"

Jareth swept the black cat up into his arms, holding the animal affectionately while stroking him with one free hand. A distinct rumble of sound grew until it became purring. With its eyes closed, Piper extended his chin so the man could concentrate his ministrations there.

What had been flatland now seemed like rows of soil with defined ridges and gullies. The wheat-like stems still grew, but not as thick, and soon they could all see why; dead spaces erupted between thriving clumps, forming areas where nothing grew at all. Suspecting that stones had floated up from below, allowing nothing to grow, Jareth was surprised when they encountered their first earthen skylight.

Each was round with many panes, pieces of glass bound by what looked like lead vines, twisted and pounded into a framework. And all was fastened to the ground by the weight of more mushrooms, short, squat, and almost as hard as stone. The sun reflected back brilliantly into their eyes off the faceted glass. Beryl looked curiously inside.

And an inside there definitely appeared to be, as sand-colored walls stared back at them, bricks mortared with dried golden stems. That there was a passage beneath their feet was obvious by the shadows encroaching where no walls could be seen. That and the fact that as they stood above looking down and in, Jareth saw two winged forms fly past.

Chapter 31

Voice of Rushing Waters

Upon entering, the sound of rushing waters could be heard, accompanied by a the grind of a small motor and a splash of revolving light. On the wall directly in front of him, a mirrored piece of art showed him to be what looked like a waterfall amidst trees and rocks. The sound was coming from there.

Not far from the lab, Rhey was surprised he hadn't discovered the room sooner. Although, how was he supposed to understand humans that well that quickly? If he'd been that smart, he'd have foreseen the biological attack on his race sooner. Nonetheless, he was here now.

The room was small with no windows. This deep inside the building though, that wasn't surprising. Some humans were able to live and work without any physical attachment to sunlight, and apparently Martin Hennessy was one of them. A worn beige leather couch showed signs of recent use, though the whole place looked used in general. He supposed the scientist had often spent time here and was far from organized. At least on a personal basis. Whereas the data he'd already gleaned about Martin suggested an anal retentive mind was behind the creation of the super virus, the human's alternate living quarters did not, as old newspapers and half empty food boxes littered most of the flat surfaces not called a floor. Empty glasses and bottles were stacked patiently by the sink, a sign that the scientist wasn't a total slob. Electronics were in abundance and Rhey took a moment to touch a slender device with a multitude of buttons.

Beryl

When a flat screen mounted to the wall flickered to life, he watched the pictures move and form a sequence resembling a stream of frames. But that was impossible, wasn't it? First thing he'd done was take out the satellites. Then he noticed another electronic box beneath the screen; the lit markings indicated that a disc was revolving, over and over and over.

These must be from a personal collection, Rhey mused, noting the resemblance of one of the persons on the screen to the dead woman he'd interrogated too long. Old footage of Martin's wife...?

The images changed but Rhey's interest was drawn to the far wall where a myriad of books rested; some old, some new, and some unread, stacked to one side on dark wood shelves. A bar was mounted above each and flicking a switch, warm yellowish light illuminated the titles. Rhey read:

Nineteen Eighty-Four by George Orwell
Crime and Punishment by Fyodor Dostoyevsky
Lord of the Flies by William Golding
A Tale of Two Cities by Charles Dickens
Of Mice and Men by John Steinbeck
Animal Farm by George Orwell
The Chronicles of Narnia by C.S. Lewis

Intrigued, he read on, running his spongey finger along each spine, noting the thin trail of pus left behind.

Catcher in the Rye by JD Salinger
The Road by Cormac McCarthy
HMS Ulysses by Alistair MacLean
The Bourne Identity by Robert Ludlum
The Little Prince by Antoine De Saint-Exupery
Hamlet by Shakespeare
Adventures of Sherlock Holmes by Sir Arthur Conan Doyle

Lord of the Rings by J.R.R. Tolkien
The Bible, NIV translation

These were the titles he read just perusing the first few shelves. They looked to be old books though, their paper more than just yellowed. There were volumes by Ray Bradbury, Poul Anderson, Robert Heinlein, Frank Herbert, Jules Verne, and H.G. Wells. In another grouping, he came across authors such as Moorcock, Carter, De Lint, and Howard. He saw titles by Brooks, Rowling, Wagner, Asimov, and others by Burroughs, Donaldson, Cook, and Orson Scott Card. Shelves and shelves of what looked like ordinary reading books, although even he could see they were not typical at all, but rather, encapsulated a divergent niche taken as a whole.

Though the movement hurt, he turned his head down, looking at still more shelves of books, noting they seemed different. It was a smaller selection, and being near the bottom, had more dust.

Norton Anthology of Poetry
Collected Works of Robert Frost
Poetic Forms by Lewis Turco, Third Ed.

There were poems by Emily Dickinson, Walt Whitman and Shel Silverstein, and volumes on collected works by Edgar Allan Poe, E.E. Cummings and William Butler Yeats.

As Rhey placed the last tome back in its place on the shelf, he caught a movement at the corner of his eye, thinking it just another scrap of his skin flaking loose but it wasn't; there where he'd disturbed the neatly ordered books, an insect scuttled fervently, trying to avoid the light. With a quickness that belied his failing condition, Rhey swept the bug into his hand, pinching the carapace between two fingers and holding the book shelves' resident up to the light, noting how the jointed legs arched outward, as if trying to ward off a blow. The pincers were grasping at air, too far from his necrotic skin to do any damage, but trying just the same. Rhey admired the insect's tenacity and will to inflict damage, despite its vulnerable position. He imagined how much more lethal it might be if it could fly. And if it was larger.

That reminded him of another in a vulnerable position, and with some regret, he decided it was time to try again—but he'd be back. There was much he still needed to learn about Martin Hennessy, much within this sound of rushing waters. Inside the human's dwelling, there were plenty of clues. But now, he thought he had an idea that might replace ignorant first attempts. First though, he had to find them...where are you my little flies? Where shall I place my web?

Chapter 32

No Light, No Light

He could see it now that he knew where to look. As they peered ahead, the furrows on either side marked the tunnels which lay beneath. It didn't take long before they came across another skylight and after that, a regular pattern of about a hundred feet between one and the next. Each were marked by clusters of fungus in strange exotic shapes.

"I wonder whose tunnels these are," Jareth pondered aloud, while he was bent to the earth trying to see further into each passage, trying to glimpse more clues.

"Nothing I've ever heard sung, that's for sure," Leanan harrumphed, her rush to judgement not surprising him. The Cervine caught his gaze but just shrugged in response.

"I don't remember any of Terra's stories including what we just saw. Looked like two small women with wings holding candles or torches. Looked to be in a hurry, too."

The niggle of doubt had sprung in him and he was loath to dispel it. Such had kept him alive in the past.

Leanan's brow furrowed and her dark lashes half-closed, the makings of a frown growing.

"You *would* notice that."

He looked quizzically at the muse but didn't get an answer.

"So, what do you think? Friend or foe?"

Leanan was already turning, preparing to cut northward to avoid the mystery. The Cervine's attention was focussed east though, and the green fire spark in his eyes was dancing

"It might be best to follow the muse this time, Jareth."

The man stroked the short dark hair of his goatee, thinking just the opposite.

"But we're supposed to head due east, past this endless meadow and on to the hill country beyond. Something's spooked her—and now you, too? What am I missing?"

The Cervine's nostrils flared, rippling the white fur of his muzzle, almost as if he was chuckling. And yet, Jareth didn't catch the humor.

"Something comes, Jareth; I think the Sidhe feels it as well. She's closer to the wind than any of us and can understand its song far easier. Though, you've been known to lie among those spirits, once upon a time. Do you feel nothing then? Have you not considered how quiet it's been since the river?"

Jareth *had* noticed but the meadow seemed outside the world from which he'd come. The soil beneath his feet and the unity within the fields had indeed spoken volumes, and with more than a hint that it could protect itself.

"Perhaps that's what comes, aye? There's more to fear from the world than just the great Hunter, Jare."

Damn.

"Well then, maybe we should find the entrance to these tunnels below, maybe take to earth and avoid the fighting altogether?"

Jareth wasn't keen on the idea that pursuit always had to mean a personal battle; three times already was more than enough. Running was a good defense, too.

"I'm sure it is, but that's only if we have someplace to run. We don't even know where the tunnel entrance is."

"Hell, I can just tap out a pane and slip down; instant entrance."

The Cervine's gaze turned from following the line of the tunnel toward Jareth, seeing a growing apprehension.

"Why so quick to flee, Jareth? You don't know what waits below. And besides, breaking the glass might not be as easy as you think."

The last of the Cervine's words halted Jareth's argument against facing more conflict. Oh? And that's because...?

"Look."

Taking a step forward, the stag-man tapped lightly on the topmost pane, emitting a small shower of sparks where his longbow touched.

Jareth extended his sword and the amount of glittering light beneath his attempt was twice as bright. Worse, it was accompanied by a strange tingling which surged upward, into the blade, working through the pommel and into his hand. The buzz of power didn't bode well. Damn. Damn, damn, damn.

"I see what you mean. More magic. Why is the world suddenly overflowing with such strangeness?"

And this time Jareth was sure the Cervine chortled, the sound like water rippling past a dammed creek.

"Feeling less special, are we?"

"What's that supposed to mean?"

Jareth glared at the intimidating figure.

"When you sing, do you not feel like all the magic in the world is flowing from your lips? Like it's sucked from the air as you pick at the strings of your mandolin? It's a very nice feeling, isn't it, to be the one in the spotlight, as if you were the special one."

The man started to object but wisely pressed his lips tightly, knowing the Cervine spoke closer to the truth than he cared to admit.

"It's not magic, not like what I've seen lately, you included."

"Ah, but Jareth, you're denying the obvious. Oh well, be that as you want it. In time, you'll have to reassess your definition of magic!"

The minstrel didn't like the smirk growing on the beast's face, no matter how comical a grinning deer might actually be.

"So we follow the girls?"

Already the two were crossing over the next rowlock of soil, having plunged down and out of the shallow ravine to the north. As he looked, the lines merged and he couldn't say how many more remained.

"We follow the girls, aye."

Still wondering at what traversed the tunnels but mindful of the Cervine's discovery concerning the skylights, Jareth whistled for Piper and started to clamber down the slope, once again disappearing inside the golden wheat. The cat was going to hate that the ground was so much wetter at the bottom.

The sun followed their progress as one by one, the lines of tunnels faded into the southern landscape and the edge of the woods to the north grew closer. The trees, while kin to those of the Frogmoss Forest, did not seem as wholesome and Jareth began to fidget with this growing feeling. Hell, strange winged creatures in tunnels to the south, probably more Bone Warriors to the west, and now, a line of dark trees that seemed anything but welcome. Should have turned south, he mused. The Cervine's deep resonance interrupted him.

"The Cities lie that way, Jareth; there is no refuge there. There, there is no light, no light."

Pausing at the top of yet another tunnel line, the stalks grew shorter and less dense, allowing for rest. Beryl was especially struggling now; Jareth could see the girl's skin was an activity of frenzied movement, all script on the move and symbols shifting as if alive. Jareth looked down at his own tattoos, the string of characters across his chest that glared balefully back at him, solid and impenetrable. As they should be, he grunted. To see the one on his wrist meant taking off his leather glove, and if he did, he felt confident that that one too would be fixed. A sudden thought occurred and his confidence weakened; what if the moving text on the girl's skin actually illustrated her life? And what did that mean about his? Was Beryl more alive than he? Was he the one who was to be pitied? Scowling, he hacked at the wheat more forcibly, leading the way down into the next furrow, annoyed that his thoughts seemed to be fragmenting more and more.

"The Cities?" He heard his voice in dull repetition.

"There's a reason you chose to head into the wild country, Jare; unknown to you means unknown to the enemy, too. Levels the playing field, aye?"

"Not what I'd have chosen though, Love."

That was the first time Leanan had addressed him in one of her now familiar affectations since the Cervine had joined them. Was she growing more comfortable with the situation?

"I suppose you'd have had us deck-side with canopied sail billowing above, and a chorus of seagulls at hand?"

There was a distinct flicker of light in the Cervine's eyes, a confirmation of his jest, though only Jareth caught it.

"And the deep song of the ocean to sustain us too, aye, but how did you know?"

Leanan leaned tiredly on the pommel of the longsword, her hair now swept back into a long, lustrous braid, except for the stray strands Jareth felt sure she let hang to seductively frame her face. As dusk was approaching, her blue limning was more noticeable and its sheen imbued the shock of white in her hair that much more. Still, the sensuous smile on her lips was only for Jareth, and eyeing the Cervine changed her facial expression to more lurking suspicion. He eyed her mischievously.

"Oh? Well, Jareth told me, of course; who else?"

Leanan swung her obsidian pupils toward the man, a hand curling into a fist on a leather-armored hip, the line of her pose now grown prickly.

"Is that so? Telling stories out of school again, bard?"

Her laughter was unnerving in the deepening of the day. He tried to concentrate on the fact that they'd have to find a place to make camp soon. Jareth had hoped to be done with the rows of tunnels before that inevitability, though.

"Perhaps that means your memory is returning?"

Jareth just faced the woman, unsure where any of this was leading.

"You'll have to return the favor; I know hardly anything about our tall antlered friend. Be sure to come see me after you get the fire started tonight. Seems we have more to talk about than usual."

Again her laughter rippled across the dark gold of the meadow, its sound lower and more husky this time.

Jareth shook his head, wishing that the Cervine would just keep his mouth shut.

Beryl allowed herself a small grin as she watched the 'grownups' play, thinking that maybe there was hope for them after all.

The first warning that they weren't alone in the Meadow came from Leanan. Leading them to the peak of what looked like the last row of wheat-tunnels—as Beryl had proclaimed them—thoughts of making camp was welcome to them all, including the indefatigable Cervine, whose shaggy shoulders drooped with a full day's exertion of climbing. Of course, it could also have been from the numerous times the stag-man had carried Beryl.

"Ware! Something is moving from the south. See how the wheat shimmers?"

But to Jareth, such had been the norm from the moment they'd entered the Meadow, though as he looked back in the direction from which they'd come, the pattern *did* look askew. Usually, he could put a melody to the Meadow, but what he was seeing bordered on chaos, and he had no song for that.

Only the Hunter could sing this one, Jareth!

The Cervine's voice pounded at his temple, surprising him not by the meaning of his words but rather, by the strength of power rising within. What was happening?

The sun was setting and their vision was hampered, freezing movement. Realizing this, Leanan scathed the air, admonishing.

"Flee—whatever that is, wants us to stop. I can feel the malevolence—I can hear their voices on the wind, which struggles mightily to reach me! We must fly!"

But they were tired and the light was fading. Throwing themselves down the last slope, only a jungle of trackless wheat awaited and Jareth felt his will to flee this possible end in such a way, stall. He started and stopped, yanking the girl back with him, almost wrenching her arm from its socket.

"No, we're more exposed here on the tunnel's top, but so too the enemy. I'm not going to make my stand where I can't at least swing my sword!"

Leanan, halfway down already, heard Jareth's voice and the murmur of annoyance. Her grimace turned to wicked grin as she assessed his words.

"I think Jareth's right; the hill gives us high ground. We'll stand here."

And so saying, the great stag-man turned to face the sloughing wheat, his eyes flickering with a dangerous light. Leanan's fury was rising.

"Ah, the heart of a warrior, now this, I can understand! The vagaries of the clouds might finally be dissipating! It shall be as it was in the days of Oisin—I deem the Bard is back!"

And with a shriek, she called to the sky and its darkening countenance.

The first of the fell creatures emerged from the bottom of the ravine, its legs grabbing at the stems of wheat which the gathering wind was laying flat. They came as if following a scent, but Jareth couldn't be sure. Looking similar to a large cicada with clutching claws, they were about the size of a raccoon, but longer bodied. Six legs were multi-jointed and a dull blue carapace glimmered with red streaks. In the dimming light, they appeared like crawlers of night, released upon an innocent dream to swiftly turn it into nightmare. And once they broached the last slope, they groped forward, looking for their prey.

Behind him, holding a hurriedly kindled torch, Beryl gasped and let out a shrill squeal before the force of the wind tore away all sound. Leanan was standing in the middle, her lithe form glowing with a movement of its own as the blue tinge now grew into an unholy fire. Her arms were raised and her long black nails looked like blood. As did her lips, which were open and mouthing a chorus of Gaelic invectives at the unseen threat. About them, the wind swirled, building strength and threatening to explode.

Jareth felt the force gathering—much more powerful than what he'd witnessed at the castle's main gate. Though perhaps that time had been diluted, due to unexpectedness. Waiting to meet the foe on the top of the rowlock had also served to give the muse time to summon her magic, and magic it surely was. If Jareth had any lingering doubts, they were ripped away like the wheat stalks being blown flat. And he saw now why she was working the air in such a way; not only did it provide a potent barricade against the scuttling insect-like creatures, it also prevented the danger from coming unseen until the last moment. He just hoped he could move his arm without hitting either of the others.

As the first attacker hit the slope, using pincers to grip the beaten stalks, Jareth felt Leanan slip past him and armed with both the longsword and knife, slash at the antennae extending from the insectoid's head. Immediately, Jareth understood why; the stroke brought blindness and chaos to the creature's motion, making it a danger to its own kind as well. Taking his cue from the Sidhe, Jareth struck at the emerging chitinous bodies, noting that instead of thin bony shells, that the crawlers skin was more leather-like and pliable. This made his first stroke into an abdomen almost his last as the beast pulled his arm brutally, almost taking his sword.

The Cervine wielded his longbow with deadly force. Where the dark resinous wood made contact with crawler flesh, a crunching sound accompanied the breaking of pus-colored organs as they burst and spread, making the slope that much harder to gain.

Keeping the girl now inside their guard, Leanan and Jareth raised their flashing steel with deadly results. The Cervine strode forward and swept the crawlers with his bow until there were too many coming too fast. Then, his own knife flicked in unison with the longer blades. The bottom of the ravine began to fill with the dying struggle of crawlers, hindering the advance of those still coming from growing wheat shadows. If not for the single-minded purpose of their attackers, Jareth knew they'd have been overrun, as nothing prevented the insects from flanking them. But it was then he understood what Leanan had also done; with her storm winds building behind them, its force kept the attackers from doing just what he feared. But could it last? There didn't seem any end to the thrusting pincers, each as large as his forearm. Still, they could be cut easily enough when within reach.

But night was chastising dusk and as the darkness grew, so too did their danger. It was getting harder to see the insects, despite the guttering torch, shielded from the wind by the girl's slim body. They started to come from three sides now, keeping swords and knives busy, hacking and slicing at sharp, hooked mandibles. When the Beryl dropped the torch, it went out with a hiss as a crawler gutted by the Cervine rolled over it.

Night had fully come with the dark of the moon and now, there'd be no light.

Chapter 33

Blinding

The monster cicadas broke through at last and Jareth felt himself thrust backwards, knocking the girl down as he did. His sword went flying as he landed heavily, the breath in his lungs crushed. Beside him, he could hear the muse screaming Gaelic epithets at their attackers, her voice cracking the night like clutching barbed wire. He thought he could hear thunder too, but realized it was the deep throb of anger in the voice of the Cervine as he lent passion to the wind. A patch of the sky went fully black above him, compressing the air. Struggling to breathe, the feeling seemed oddly peaceful, but another voice was urging him to move. To move?

The form of the Cervine shattered the daze into which he'd fallen, illuminated by the eerie flare of blue light emanating from the Sidhe. Her face looked horrific, the hollows around her eyes sunken, the fire inside ebony orbs blazing, and her dagger-like teeth cutting at the crimson shadow forming her mouth. With another shout, she grabbed him by the arm and unmercifully hauled him upright, thrusting the hilt of his sword back into his hand. If only his head would stop spinning and he could breath again...

Holding the longsword, Leanan thumped him with the back of her hand, forcing what little breath he'd recovered back into the vacancy of night. She shrieked his name and more, but her words were not intelligible and he leaned heavily on the pommel of his blade, momentarily oblivious to the press of bodies all around.

"Damn you Jareth Rhylan—untie my hands! Restore my full power and bring me my familiar—it'll be our doom otherwise!"

Damn, even hurting as he was, the damn woman was relentless in her nagging. And that's when his anger blossomed as he saw in Leanan's unholy light, two of the crawlers lunging at Beryl where she lay in a heap behind him.

As the moment of clarity took hold, Jareth sprang, a reflex action that surprised him, slicing the pincers of the nearest monster. Ducking under its maw, rolling and stabbing upward and into the insect's carapace, he sought the place right below where the brain should be. He drove his blade deep and twisted, dragging the steel back just as quickly, the impetus of his roll taking him to the girl's feet. Lurching backward, he knocked Beryl over again, but this time down the slope and away from the battle, away from the chittering horde.

Seeing Jareth's anger segue into deadly force, Leanan's face lit up with a smile that was darkly joyful, and she burned even brighter, understanding that whatever lethargy had clung to the man was now gone. For the moment, she knew the poet-warrior she claimed as hers, was back. Renewed, she called on the sky for more rain to wash the insects back down the slope, and for more lightning to strike at their many feet. In her hands, both blades were dark with dripping blood and guts, testimony to the viciousness of the fight.

The Cervine closed the gap which had opened between them, breaking through carapace after carapace, the bow's thick wood a bludgeon he wielded with efficient strokes, shoving those that were too fast back down the hill, and ending the lives of those who weren't. He didn't smile though, when the man's anger bubbled over, adding vengeance to each stroke.

Control it, Jareth; if you lose your mind to this, the enemy wins. There are too many for the three of us, we must retreat and find a better place to defend.

Jareth heard the words as they slipped past his mind, maelstrom of confusion that it was. But he heard, and though slow, he did understand. There *were* too many; they had to get the girl out of here, even if it meant chancing the wheat field in the dark.

Or did it? There was yet another way...

You sure? We have no way of knowing how well we'll be received...

Again, the Cervine was cautioning control.

"Jare! For the love of Mannanan; free me!"

Leanan again, her voice shattering his deliberation. He didn't have time for this. His arm rose and fell, his body darting inside the cicada's thrust, slicing off limbs and mangling eye stems, bringing a malaise of blindness to them all; vision for them and sanity for himself. If not for the Cervine's voice grounding him...

"Free your own self, Witch! I don't hold you from anything. Take whatever you need and let me be!"

The sky hesitated, as if Time hiccupped.   Then the torrent really began as the wind tore past the four of them on top of the hill, the fury of the Sidhe fully released. Leanan's howl of pleasure rang against the splinters of night as forks of light stabbed all around them, smoking the earth and anything else too near. The longsword rose and coursed with trapped lightning.

The Dark Muse is now loose, Jareth; I hope you don't regret this.

But whatever doubt he may have had, coinciding with the deep murmur of the Cervine, Jareth had no time to consider as he clung to the hill, trying to escape the choices before him, weighing which would prove less tragic.

"Follow your heart, Love—it is ever what I most cherish about you!"

The water sloughed from Leanan's leather, the silver of her chain mail beneath sparkling with lightning fire as she alternately swung her blade and swept her hand, as if directing where the bolts should land.

Hell, I don't even know what she's talking about; if we get out of this, you'll have to educate me.

His thoughts brought a curious silence in return and it caused Jareth to lose his concentration for one almost fatal moment. But the long muscular arm of the stag-man punched forward and butt-ended Jareth's doom back into the slippery night, the clash and gnash of pincers an echo of just how close calamity had come.

Maybe you're right to release her now—you may not get another chance later.

These words only brought more confusion to the man as he swept his blade against another set of pincers reaching for them. The girl behind him had been far too quiet; was she still alive?

Follow my heart...those words had a familiarity that he was both loathe and excited to remember. Why was that?

"If you've decided, best give it a try, Jareth; we're not going to hold out much longer."

The Cervine was right; the crawlers were massing quicker, getting further past their guard, despite the numerous smoking bodies at the bottom of the hill, gaping proof of Leanan's fury.

"Give what a try?"

The muse had overheard, the look on her face a blend of curiosity and apprehension. Did she glare then at the Cervine?

"We can hold them until my familiar gets here, Jareth."

The Cervine's head shake was imperceptible; he disagreed. Jareth shut them both out.

"Don't have time to debate this, woman; whatever's coming isn't going to make it in time—we need to find a way out now. Guard my back, I'm going to see just how strong the tunnel glass really is..."

His voice trailed off as he bounded back to the rowlock's top, looking for that next skylight. As he did so, a section of the horde shifted direction with him, as if he was the primary target. Now, why was that? What was it they wanted?

Behind, the Cervine scooped the trembling girl, hoisting her over his shoulder so his knife hand would be free to keep Jareth's back clear. Leanan was not slow to follow, her blade singing death to those that gained the top of the slope. The storm, as if having lost its guidance, swirled and randomly raked the meadow, its malevolence anything but thwarted. The muse hissed in reproof of this new tactic, her anger and fury still cogent on her face.

It wasn't far, as he knew it wouldn't be; the skylight looked like a placid mere of water, a dark pool reflecting the night. But even as he found it, he saw that placid wasn't accurate. The flare of lightning radiated across its width, stroking mullions with the storm's light. He brought his blade down hard and as he expected, felt the energy repulsed back along the length of steel, absorbed by his arm and running through his body to ground. His scream put Leanan's to shame. Too much like a lightning bolt for his taste. His arm still tingled as he lifted it again.

His next strike came down on the clustered toadstools ringing the perimeter, and the solid thunk of living flesh was his reward. Whatever protected the glass did not extend to the anchors. Ferocious and frenzied, he sliced at the mushroom's base, sending larger pieces flying until he had a small hole started. As he released the glass from its frame, the others reached where he knelt, their breath ragged from sprinting.

"They're coming, Dear; you got a plan yet?"

The muse's voice was husky, as if she were playing at seductive and coy, as if this were all a game to her.

He grunted once, still busy digging. He had a hole large enough to squeeze through, but only if you were Beryl's size.

"Here, let me."

The stag-man filled Jareth's place and lifting a massive cloven hoof, brought it down on the earth near Jareth's hole. The power of the Cervine drove clear through the soil and into the tunnel below. As he drew his leg forth and touched the edge of the exposed glass, sparks raked at his fur and a faint burning smell rose.

"You going to be able to fit and not touch the glass?"

Jareth didn't think he or the women would have any problem but the Cervine was much larger in girth.

"We'll see, aye? Now, in you go; the crawlers are closing in."

And without any argument, Jareth slipped into the hole, mindful to stay away from the glass. The tunnel hadn't looked too deep and luckily, he was a good judge of distance. Still, he fell heavily and knew his knee would hurt for a while. Turning to face the hole with only the light of the storm to guide him, he saw Leanan's form blot out the light and before he knew it, she landed heavily in his arms, bending him to the earth. Oh, his knee was going to hurt all right.

Ignoring the muse's lips on his cheek as she slipped out of his arms, he turned again to face the hole. Already, the Cervine was lowering the girl through. This time, he was ready and caught Beryl easily, thankful she was still young-girl thin. As he turned to hand her off to the muse, he couldn't help but feel a sense of nostalgia creep as the moment reminded him of another. Had he done this before?

"Get out of the way, son; you're not going to like catching my weight, I deem."

It was a tight fit, but the stag-man lowered himself slowly down, a line of glittering light grating against the beaten plates of armor on his chest, the smell of brazed metal mixing with moldering fur. The large man-animal only grunted as the exposed glass grazed his body. Lowering down until he was standing on the tunnel's floor, the Cervine bent his head to keep his antlers from scraping the ceiling.

"This isn't going to be comfortable running, I'll wager."

Jareth smiled in spite of himself and Leanan snorted in derision, figuring it served the stag-man right, being so tall in the first place.

"Which way? No telling what we're going to encounter down here but I daresay we'll make better time. East takes us toward the hill country, West takes us back."

Leanan looked into Jareth's face, the dim light of the tunnel barely enough by which to see. It appeared that the source was more mushrooms, their amber glow a slow, steady pulse.

"There is no going back now, Jareth; forward into the unknown, but better than going back and facing more bugs."

The Cervine nodded his assent.

"She's right, and we need to move now; no telling if the crawlers will follow. I'd rather not wait around to find out. Follow me; if we encounter anything or anyone, they may just leave us alone if they think we're all my size. Being large can have its advantages!"

And so saying, the stag-man slung his great bow over his shoulder and holding his knife in his hand, pushed into the veiled tunnel.

"You all right, Beryl?"

Leanan, glad to have the Cervine lead so she could stick closer to Jareth, was taking a tangle of hair from the girl's face, using her long, slim fingers to caress Beryl's skin, lessening her fear. Jareth could see the girl's trembling visibly diminish beneath the muse's ministrations and he was glad. Seems the woman *could* mother when she had to.

Leanan laughed as she read that thought in his head.

"Of course, I've had a lot of practice; you artists are notoriously the biggest babies! That is, when you're not being impossibly talented. Nurturing isn't just for the young, Jareth; the human heart never really fully abandons childhood, you know!"

Jareth shook his head in annoyance as Leanan bundled the girl up in her cloak, drawing them together, sharing body heat, of which he was actually jealous. Her laughter just provided more echoes that too soon were muffled by the walls of the earth around them.

"Okay, we need to get going..."

"Piper! You forgot him!"

Beryl had spoken for the first time since the battle had begun. Her dark eyes were wide and flushed red, though in the gloom of the tunnel, purple would have been closer. Her face was streaked and her hands had cuts, attesting to the fact some of the crawlers had come too near. She clutched at Leanan's leather armor, a sudden courage abounding.

From above, the sound of rushing wind was growing exponentially; the bugs were almost on top of them.

"Well, not quite, girl."

And turning around, he flipped the flap of his pack away, exposing two glowing amber eyes.

Leanan snorted.

"I've always wondered why they're not green, as most cat eyes are."

Beryl freed herself from the muse and raising a hand to Jareth's pack, began to stroke the animal behind its ears.

"Ach, have we time for his now?"

Leanan's face contorted, her disdain so plainly evident that Jareth had to suppress a smile of amusement. No reason to give the satisfaction of always being right. After all, wasn't that the title he liked to claim for himself?

Leanan turned and winked at the man, pulling the girl back and urging her forward where the Cervine's huge figure was already far ahead, a fuzzy blob of lightless tunnel in the distance, until another cluster of the luminescent toadstools was passed.

"Indeed, it is one of your titles, Love, and claim it well you do. But, I'll forgive you for now—after all, you did remove the binds!"

"We better go—he's already far down the tunnel."

He just *had* to find a way to keep her out of his head on a more permanent basis. And this last he clamped shut in the deepest reaches of his mind, layering impatience and apprehension on top of his thoughts, like branches covering his tracks in the forest.

"Aye, we should. Can you hold this a moment?"

And without any consideration for his response, Leanan thrust the longsword into his hand, the intricate basket hilt warm on his skin, the fine silver wire braid melding to the lines of his palm. It was really strange how well it fit in his grasp; it was also breath-robbing as he felt the air sucked from his lungs. What the hell?

She'd taken a critical moment to tie back her hair, the braid having come undone.

"There, done."

And without another word, she took the blade back, thrusting it into the long sheath across her back. Jareth was left wondering why she hadn't just done that in the first place...

"Coming, Jare?"

The muse's voice lofted back to him, breaking through the sudden sizzling sound of coruscating fire above his head. The insects were attempting to get in, having found the hole too small to admit them readily. But it wouldn't take much if digging was in any way one of their skills.

Jareth secured the pack's flap, leaving a small window where the cat could peer out should he be inclined.

"I don't know which I hate more, Piper; her ability to get in my head, or her persistent mocking. Ah well, be glad you're just a cat."

The amber eyes were mere rings of blinding light as the cat's pupils dilated to their utmost, large and luminous and peeking back at the tunnel behind them. The animal curled tighter inside the pack, content, knowing he was more than just a cat.

Chapter 34

Foundations

"You used to know more than a fair share of fire songs; Lyr's stones, but you surely know *many* mentioning candles!"

Leanan's voice was beyond petulant, it was showing irk, and if Jareth didn't know better, embarrassment. And why was that?

"Anything would help, Jare. Not being able to see the path in front of me is quite intolerable!"

He understood even if her allusion to his singing prowess was flying right past. Truly, knowing what lay before them was becoming paramount, but what could he do? The crawlers had breached the tunnel and were gaining, if he was any judge of sound through the ground. The Cervine though, was even more adept and standing with his wide hooves on the dirt floor, took stock of their situation—again.

Only the girl gave any expression to their predicament, and that with a low keen. She'd been trying to keep up but didn't have the endurance of the others. From the near constant whining, he would have been surprised if she'd ever been pushed at anything before joining up with them.

"Didn't your parents teach you anything about persistence?"

His words came out more harshly than he'd planned, mainly because he too was feeling the pressure of the chase. It had already been a long day—he couldn't fault the girl for dragging down their speed, but there wasn't any good to come from stroking her esteem. As a matter of fact, he found that trait wasn't one in which he was that familiar. Shit happens; get on with it and keep from getting too messy. What memories he could recall seemed to support this stance, even if the Cervine *was* looking curiously at him and the muse *was* openly frowning. Though, he didn't think it was disapproval of his words as much as how much time was being wasted. This is what happened when parents didn't hand down the proper lessons to their kids; now just wasn't the time to melt into a puddle.

"Mother never told me the dangers of being chased by gigantic insects, no..."

In spite of himself, Jareth acknowledged his surprise at the girl's spine stiffening. Maybe there was hope yet. Sarcasm—now, *that* he could understand...

"We don't have time for this—which way?"

The luminous toadstools had disappeared a while ago and they'd been moving in the dark for too long. The nimbus of blue light surrounding the Sidhe wasn't even enough to forestall their abrupt contact with a cross passage. So, east was no longer an option. And yet, had they noticed any furrows in the wheat fields that went in a perpendicular direction?

"I think we're further underground, Jareth; from the surface, cross tunnels wouldn't be noticeable. I suggest we head north as any exit will lead us to the perimeter of the tunnels, and to the south, we know there are many more rows we'd have to cross back over."

Leanan liked that suggestion immediately and turned left, the blue-black shimmer of her hair a beacon for those behind. Curiously enough, the white shank of her hair also burned blue.

Carrying the girl wasn't a possibility because the ceiling height varied randomly, beside being already low to the floor. Perfect height for the bugs behind us, Jareth thought, while feeing sorry for the Cervine, whose spiked antlers too frequently rasped against the packed earth, scraping loose a mini-shower of dirt and stones. At least *he* didn't have to worry about that.

The new tunnel zig-zagged more than the previous one, and it was a challenge not to hit a tunnel corner and be knocked off balance. A torch would indeed be welcome, he thought, or more of the glowing toadstools. The wonder of such light below the earth's surface turned to regret at its loss.

The Cervine began talking to the girl, aware she was close to shutting down, her inability to handle pressure situations more than evident.

He didn't hear the question, but Beryl's voice was audible enough, as if amplified instead of damped by the walls. Now, how did he know that? Acoustics...aye, that's what it was, but for the life of him, he didn't know why he knew this. His songs were innate, but the science behind them seemed kin to book learning. Which books? He didn't have any in his pack and didn't recall any back at the castle in Vespar.

"There was only mother—dad wasn't around much."

The floor was angling downward still, and this worried Jareth as they needed to be near the surface.

"Memories of him? Some, I guess, but now that you ask, I can't recall many. It seems like a long time ago."

Ahead, Leanan was slowing, as if the side tunnels were choices she should continue making. Which one would lead them out?

"Mother taught me what I needed to know, though."

Did he hear some defiance in the girl's voice? And why didn't the Cervine's words carry back as Beryl's did?

"I do have one memory I like; Mother says dad used to sing me to sleep when I was a baby, a song Irish moms would sing to their children."

Leanan was moving faster now, more sure, it seemed. The walls of packed earth were colder than previously. There was also a faint smell of damp earth, though from which direction it was coming couldn't be determined. Jareth bet the Cervine could pinpoint it, though. Were they nearing an underground river?

"No, just him; guess that means he loved me, then."

The man cringed as he felt the sudden lowering of the ceiling, wondering how the stag-man had evaded it in time.

"Maybe that's where I got my love for music...I hadn't thought of it before you asked."

The cat squirmed, changing positions, pressing on the small of Jareth's back in the process. Soon, Piper, soon; then you can stretch your legs. It would be a nightmare if the cat decided now was the time to be aloof.

"Sometimes. I know Mother still misses him...missed him"

The girl's voice choked and grew inaudible, causing Jareth to glance and see what was happening ahead. But the Cervine's huge form blocked any possible wisp of sight he might have had of the two. Even the muse's outline was dimming as he realized the pace had slowed. Something happened to Beryl's mother?

The sounds of his footfall began to mirror his heartbeat, and he began to subconsciously keep time. As had been, he heard neither the Cervine nor the muse, but only the girl's sputtering step, aided no doubt by the stag-man, as it rose and fell depending on the twists and turns of the tunnel. Stopping, he let the others go on a bit, wishing the girl's footsteps into silence so he could listen for pursuit. Did he hear something within the foundations?

Unsure of how to read the tremors, he turned and following the sound of the girl, hurried to catch up.

"Oh yes, she was very beautiful."

"I see you got her eyes, aye?"

Closer now, he could hear both parts of the conversation, the Cervine's words reminding him of a creek flowing through a hollowed log, ruminating and baritone, like the lowest octave he'd ever heard.

He tried to imagine what Beryl's mother looked like, taking her words and stitching an image from their depth. As a song writer, he found his ability to form such images came easily, while his talent for singing rested more in his passion. If anything could be said to be his magic, this was it—the foundation of who he knew he was. Foundation. It seemed to be a place he hadn't visited in a very long time. Now, why was that?

Jareth felt a nudge in his head, a subtle whisper that at first he thought came from the darkness behind. But it persisted. He brought up the rear, with Leanan leading; she'd said something about having the best night vision. And looking into her strange eyes, he didn't want to doubt her. He picked up the pace and put more distance between the dirt showers and himself. The nudge turned into a strange inspiration whose migration transformed from idle to pacing, an ache to be brought to life. In his head, the idea he needed to sing the song 'Bright Blades' bullied itself loose. And so, he began.

It was an old song, birthed in Celtic lore, something he'd picked up while once in Ireland. Ireland? So familiar and yet, he was having trouble placing it geographically. It was a song of long odds and desperation, of rousing courage and an honorable death. That last didn't sit well, even as he heard his voice grow beyond a tune-filled mumble. Holding one hand against the wall, he kept pace, but also noticed how much easier the task had become. Glancing ahead, he could see Leanan with the longsword aloft, the blue nimbus glowing from the metal too, acting like the wick of a candle. If he didn't know better, he'd swear the light was pulsing to the rhythm of his song. And did he hear Leanan's voice, lush with undertones of dark joy, completing the melody?

Jareth held up his own weapon, seeing a brightness clinging to the blade. Or was it emanating? Hell! What kind of new magic was this? His worry spun back on itself, preparing to whirl out of control.

Beryl

The Cervine's voice slipped into his head, each word filling in the dead space where only the resonation of the melody lived, waiting for the next piece of verse, and like an echo, soothed Jareth's anxiety. There was no danger here, the magic was natural, and being used in a protective manner.

It is a magic I know well, having used it myriad times protecting my children of the woods, Jareth; be at peace. The way is illuminated before us, hastening our step. Careful not to tread on my hooves though, aye? Wouldn't want to clip you in the knee.

How could the massive creature be so casual in such a moment? Wasn't he on edge, just waiting for the tunnel to end or the crawlers behind to catch up?

All things in their time, I deem, Jareth; you're seeing the glass as half empty right now, and you need to see that it's also half full.

Well, yeah, but that kind of thinking doesn't solve problems, it didn't avoid trouble.

No, it doesn't, but it does give you a glimpse of possibilities, aye?

Jareth was quiet in his head with no retort to the Cervine's words. Holding his blade higher, he heeded the stag-man's words and dropped back, unaware while he sang that he'd almost closed upon the silent hooves.

The tunnel went straight for a long time, giving them a chance to quicken their pace. Like blind mice, they had their hands out, feeling for a passage that headed east again. Idly, Jareth wondered how the woman was doing. She was so quick to laud the idea she'd practically been nursed at the bosom of the sea. Even *he* felt the claustrophobia as the walls narrowed. But every time, they widened again and took the darkest shadow with them.

It was then he felt the burst of warning in his head, preceding the oral admonishment of the Cervine.

"Run! They've reached the cross-tunnel!"

The blue light of the Sidhe surged aggressively ahead and the girl gave a gasp as the Cervine crouched lower and scooped her up, then seemed to disappear. A curse on his lips, Jareth let go of the wall and quickened his pace, gripping his sword tighter.

The crawlers made straight for the fleeing forms, their ability to move unhindered by the lack of light. Or was it because they were drawn easily by the luminosity cast by the muse and the swords? It didn't matter as the rush of many feet grew into the sound of one, a lone wave breaking on shore and rushing up the beach, looking to be the highest of the tide. Jareth kept casting glances over his shoulder, the sound building in his ear and in his imagination; he wouldn't be taken from behind—this he vowed.

When they struck though, it did surprise him and he pitched forward with a grunt, hanging on for dear life to the sword, its light smothered by dirt from the floor. Rolling immediately, he just missed the jaws of two terrible pincers as they struck where he'd been. He tried to warn the others but his voice was covered by the hiss of the beast that had missed its quarry. If not for the blade, Jareth was certain he'd have gone down immediately because the darkness cloaked the crawlers too well, it was as if they were children of the night.

He cut swiftly in front of his face, sheering any appendage in the sword's path, gaining valuable breathing room. Another hiss, this time of pain, burst from the chitinous maw just on the edge of his vision. The blade in his hand was thrust forward, not in readiness for his next stroke, but simply to stretch the light.

Jareth lunged forward, trying to beat the unseen cicada bodies he knew were trying to cut him off from the others. And where were the others? He didn't see Leanan's blue halo, or her shining blade either. There was no sound of the Cervine, neither in his head nor audibly. The girl's whining would have been welcome in that moment but instead, worry rushed at him faster than the insects.

One step, two, then three and he was running blindly, no time now to hug the wall. He hoped the path kept straight or he'd run himself into disaster.

It sounded like the rush of wind at first, and not until after Jareth had been tripped up, did the Cervine ascertain that danger was upon them. Barking for Leanan to swing into the looming passage to their right, he felt pain drag at his temple as the tips of his antlers dug deeply at the lowering ceiling, scoring furrows in the earth above and raining down more debris than before. It made footing treacherous, especially bent as he was with the girl in his arms. Leanan's blue flame shimmered and changed shape, diverting like the point of an arrow as she slipped into the side tunnel. Could they make it before the insect horde overwhelmed them? By the look of it, the new tunnel was smaller, almost human sized, and that would prove to be advantageous as it would mean the bugs could enter only singly. With the bleat of a wounded buck, the Cervine pushed his legs harder, thrusting forward.

"Cut right, Jareth—before they catch up!"

And with a final lunge that tore at his arms because the tunnel was even narrower than he'd thought, the Cervine and Beryl darted inside, Leanan's familiar blue light still moving but slower now, as she glanced back, searching for the others.

The girl could move within the tighter confines but the Cervine found he had to turn sideways; at least the ceiling was once again far enough above his head to allow standing. What a close call that had been.

"Jareth? You back there?"

It was Leanan, doubt in her voice.

Beryl looked beyond the form of the stag-man, the cords of muscle in his arms still a vivid memory.

The Cervine turned his head, antlers scraping against the back wall, the emerald glow in his eyes flaming brighter as he saw nothing but shadow, heard nothing but the bugs' advancing chitter-hiss, and smelled only their noxious reek.

As the cicada crawlers surged toward the narrow side passage, there was only a feeling of dread as they realized that Jareth was missing.

Chapter 35

Beautiful Dream, Unbound

The ground sloped so suddenly that combined with his momentum, Jareth stumbled and slid forward, the ground scraping at his flesh as he tried to stop. And then, there was no ground to provide any friction at all, just a yawning expanse of darkness swallowing his grunt of surprise and Piper's long wailing howl as they both plunged over a precipice.

It was like every nightmare he'd ever had, that sick sense of falling and no amount of writhing found any purchase at all. But this was far worse—besides hating heights, the other form his nightmares would sometimes take, was of being caught in water both deep and dark. Both happened in the matter of seconds as he hit the unseen lake below, the impact on his legs buckling his spirit and crumpling the air in his lungs. If he hadn't twisted in midair, he dreaded what such a shock could have done.

The water wasn't only invisible it was cold too, though that may have been the slap on the face he needed to pull out of his panic. He went under and immediately spread his legs and arms, hoping to slow his descent. The air he'd taken with him bubbled all around, the sound harassing his ears as he fought to hold his breath. But more than that, he knew Piper was trapped in his backpack with even less realization of what was happening. The animal's frenzied movement was counter productive to his upward movement and Jareth despaired at the amount of time it was taking to reach the surface. Still, he struck upward using both arms even though one was still encumbered by his sword.

A great rasp of air was released and he hungrily inhaled while trying to stay afloat. He fought at the wet straps and metal buckles, trying to work the pack off his back, all the while managing to keep it above the water, a pitiful mewling emanating amid more rasping claws as the animal struggled to get free. The cat's tone turned to a full yowl and Jareth absently noted the cavernous quality to the sound. And blessedly, he also noticed that he could once again see.

The faint illumination came from walls where clusters of luminous mushrooms clung, their shape manifestly pale and translucent. Jareth wasn't sure he wanted to know exactly what they were devouring, here in the underground cavern. He was sure it wasn't wholesome...

Shrugging out of the straps, Jareth helped the cat climb on top, its dimly glowing iris a bright amber ring, its pupils totally dilated and black. The cat looked half as large with its fur soaking wet and slicked to its body, pitiful in every way.

There was no consoling the animal and so, Jareth swam for the light, hoping the walls were not sheer. He swam and was suffused in his nightmare, that of imagining beyond belief, of what might lurk below him in the deep, dark water. If nothing bumped into him in the next few minutes, he just might keep his sanity...

Where the mushrooms grew wasn't far, nor was the water that deep for long, and Jareth rose dripping, exhaling in thankfulness. The cat's sight was better than the man's and as the shore was reached, Jareth felt the animal gather and leap, its claws leaving a reminder that this wasn't his idea of fun. Lunging forward as his nightmare fear began to manifest, Jareth dragged himself from the lake, his breath coming in precious gasps while streams of water puddled. But he couldn't rest, not yet.

Smartly grabbing Piper by the scruff, he slid hands down the length of its body, squeezing out extra water, noting that the animal was shivering.

"Yeah, I know, I'm cold too. Hang in there, the worst is past."

Sweeping the animal into his arms, Jareth nuzzled Piper, his face against the animal's jaw, his fingers scratching all the right places, trying to alter the note in the cat's throat, which sounded so forlorn that the man berated himself for something he couldn't have foreseen. Which was foolish; how was he to know the main tunnel turned even as he plunged forward through a side passage? And up until now, there'd been fairly smooth, level floors. The slope above must be an abandoned pathway, and perhaps if a horde of cicadas hadn't been occupying his attention, this fact would have been recognized sooner.

Still, telling all this to the cat didn't change the situation. The animal continued to howl, albeit with much less volume now, confirmation that the worst was probably over.

Everything was wet, soaking or otherwise, and as Jareth gently stowed the cat inside his tunic and against his chest where any heat could be maximized, he grimaced to think of what the water might have done to his mandolin and writing tools. Any extra food was spoiled, that was for sure, and so he emptied the pack of anything that was no longer useful. It didn't take long, but Jareth needed these moments to gather his wits; how was he to get back to the unseen tunnel mouth above?

The muse wanted to rush past the girl and Cervine but the tunnel was so restricting that all she did was pinch them all with her attempt. Her fury turned to anxiety, realizing Jareth was caught behind with the insects.

"We can't."

"Don't tell me what to do, Buckskin, I'm not leaving him."

The Cervine's eyes hardened and the green flicker compacted into a very small ball of fire.

"We're not, but the way is blocked. He's still alive—take a moment to confirm it...I know you can feel him like I can."

And it was true, she'd always known this; once linked as muse and artist, it was like his heart beat in hers. If he were dead, she'd know it.

"Doesn't mean he's not fighting for his life even now!"

Her snarl made Beryl cower deeper into the Cervine's shadow, her hands wrung together, the lines of ink moving in a frenzy on her skin, mirroring the look in her eyes.

"Have some faith, Sidhe, he *is* the Bard, you know."

Leanan started to protest, pulling her lips back and baring her sharp teeth, but thought better of a retort. Instead, her countenance contorted into a tight grimace, though her eyes still blazed wildly. The crawlers were like water and the puddle would soon spill into their side passage.

"*I* know that and apparently, *you* know that, but by Mannanan and Lyr! *He* doesn't!"

The Cervine forced his lips to form what could be called a smirk and the fire in his eyes brightened.

"He's the master storyteller, trust him to know what he's doing even when it appears he doesn't. We're here because he needs us, not the other way around. At this particular time, apparently he needs something else. Give him the breath to exhale, Muse; even you know how long a final breath can take. And his hasn't even started yet."

Beryl gibbered into her frock, her hands beginning to scratch bloody trails into her palm.

"Here now girl, we'll have none of that. All's not lost, not while we know Jareth Rhylan still lives."

And so saying, he placed hard agate eyes on the muse and nodded for her to move ahead, down the narrow passage. With luck, they could find a connector back and flank the crawlers even as they tried to follow.

Leanan's golden-ringed eyes flared but for just a moment; the Cervine was right in that they couldn't get to Jareth this way, not with a whole swarm of bugs stopping up their exit. They had to find another way—and swiftly. She placed baleful eyes on the shaking Beryl.

"Come with me girl, and keep up; don't expect me to wait if you're inclined to wallow in a misery that hasn't even touched you yet. There'll be a chance for that later, and hopefully by then, you'll prove that helping wasn't Jareth's biggest mistake."

So saying, she turned, blue flame raging about her as she took out her frustration on the path ahead, the longsword tight in her hand.

Jareth could see the pale mushrooms weren't the only source of illumination; there were lines of glittering light, sometimes brilliant and other times dull, that coursed through the cavern's wall. He was sure now that he'd fallen into a large cathedral, probably carved by the very same lake into which he'd fallen. The ground at his feet was more stony than dirt-filled now, making movement easier. The cat continued to shiver against his chest, though he could feel their body heat pressing back at the drying cold.

"There has to be another way up, we just need to find it."

Jareth's voice, though audible only to the cat, sent shimmering echoes to all parts of the cavern, and it made him clench his teeth tightly—no telling what else might live down here, though he didn't expect any of the cicada crawlers to suddenly show.

He proceeded to follow the shoreline, often sweeping his sword out in front of him as wisps of shadow taunted, urging him to stop, to stay a while. Innately, Jareth knew this feel, understood the music behind it and wisely, sidestepped the temptation. He must have hit his head when the crawlers tripped him. Reaching his hand up, the bruise was there, the welt obvious, but no blood or scab met his probing touch. Didn't mean he didn't have a concussion, just meant he hadn't split his head open. At least Piper's yowl kept his mind from drifting too much.

The minutes began to seem like hours and he lost track of time. The cavern went on for quite a while though narrowed until the mild rush of a current could be heard. He had some idea that he could follow this underground stream and eventually, it might pour into open sky and grassy ground. But didn't water flow down? How then could the water reach the open sky? It didn't make sense but he continued anyway because there wasn't any other choice. The walls of the lake cavern were indeed sheer and there had been no obvious way up.

There was some thought about the others but he didn't fear for them—both muse and cervine were adequately able to fend for themselves, but what about the girl? An unsettling feeling churned in his gut, surprising him. They'd protect her in his absence, wouldn't they?

It was as if a great injury was massaging Jareth's guilt and he suffered from a mix of shame and grief, from absolution and responsibility, but he couldn't understand why. There were flags waving inside his head, memories trying to be noticed, but his head hurt, his body felt feverish, and the cat just wouldn't stop making noise. Just keep going, he urged himself, it will all end soon enough.

But unlike his nightmares, which brought him drunkenly from sleep, soaked in sweat and with a heart racing from the seeming reality of it all, this moment stretched on far longer than he wanted; he couldn't wake himself up if he tried.

The light alternated but gradually his vision grew more keen, using the veins of glittering rock in the wall to augment the numerous clusters of toadstools. What manner of dead organics did these fungi feed upon? And to grow this deep? Maybe they were magic, he speculated, growing and gnawing at the stones themselves, taking nutrients so small they couldn't be determined, like the impossibly small components of matter itself. Now, that was an odd thought, he mused.

If the toadstools were magical, then surely the faintly luminous form that he kept seeing in front of him, was also. It looked like smoke, or mist kneaded together in the form of solid light, though it wasn't, because the longer he looked, the more he could see the walls behind, could see right through the light, if he tried. Was he imagining that it moved, that it floated or danced? After awhile, he tried to reach out with one hand and it seemed to stop, as if his motion was like his voice, calling out to it. But then it would swirl and coalesce, firming and then dissipating, moving again, leading him on. Leading him on?

The idea seemed preposterous; leading him where? He had nowhere to go...and then he felt a nudge, and he knew; there were others, they would be looking for him...they would, right? And as he tried to coax their images to form in his mind, he found he couldn't, as if memory was slipping faster. He held on to the one strong feeling though, that he needed to keep moving, to not stop...

It was a long night, or day, depending on how many hours he'd been wandering, and the will to rest was a rampant beat in his temple, mirroring the pulse of blood in his veins. He stopped and felt the cat squirm, shifting its weight. Though they both were a lot drier, the air was chill this far beneath the earth, and Jareth feared they'd both die from pneumonia. Did cats get pneumonia? The thought seemed odd at first and then comical. A wisp of a chuckle escaped trembling lips.

He noticed that the dancing light was closer now, drawing in on him, even as he thought he could stay here forever.

Jare.

The sound of his name was like morning dew on the leaves, having formed silently and without weight, emerging from the air around him. It was a soft touch nonetheless, and one he thought he recognized.

Jare.

Again, he was named.

He opened eyes he hadn't known he'd closed, feeling the cat squirming again. The amber eyes looked up at him and he thought that of the two, the animal seemed far more lucid. Ineffectually, his hand tried to quiet the cat's struggles, and it was with the faint acknowledgment of sharp claws digging in that he let the cat down. Dazed, Jareth couldn't understand why...what had he done? He could protect the animal, couldn't he? But he couldn't do that if the cat left him...

"Don't leave me," Jareth murmured, his mind as thick as fog rolling in from a seaside dawn.

You must keep moving, Jare.

There it was again, the voice, and yet, it seemed to come from the light. From the light?

He pried his eyes open, forcing his mind to follow. It *was* the light...and now, up close, he could see it was in the form of a woman...a woman of light...

How often have you thought of me and wished I'd come, Jare? And now that I'm here, you have nothing to say?

His mind felt thick, like sap leaking from a maple. Of course he had something to say.

"Candace."

The light swirled, as if the clothing she wore were a skirt, a long, lace-edged dress that exposed her bare feet, as if the glimmer of darker shadow streaking up her thigh was a slit that showed what dreams were really made of. He was dreaming...again.

Did you miss me?

A feeling of reluctance was replaced by a yearning and then slapped hard by remorse. A great feeling of failure pervaded.

Don't, my love, there isn't time to weep over what has gone before.

"I can't help it, I can't control how I feel."

Always a truism I understood better than you; odd that now you seem aware of it.

Piper, who'd been clinging close to the man's legs despite not wanting to be held, mewed inquiringly. Jareth unconsciously bent and stroked behind the cat's ears, trailing down to scratch beneath his chin too. Then the animal lifted its tail, the end curling in an inquiring way, and walked into the spilling light of the woman, who also reached down and stroked the cat.

He always was your cat though, Jare; he just tolerated me. But then, it was you who picked him out from a litter of others at the pet store.

The sparkle in the woman's eyes darkened and for a moment, she seemed troubled.

He was our first Jare...why have you held on to his memory this way? You hold him so tightly, even though he's been gone for many years.

Jareth just looked at her, the throbbing in his head more pronounced. He had no answer, her words alien to his ears.

"I saw you in the Forest."

Her eyes lifted with a shower of sparkling light, a small smile on her face, glad to be leaving a darkness that threatened to capture them both.

Jareth steadied his gaze, noting her features despite the languid glowing light draping over. He knew her hair was an autumn brown, deep rivers of red where fingers were wont to drown. He knew the pronounced cheekbones and pert nose between. The smooth extravagance of her full lips, pouting now as they were, as if she were rueing the fact he was here.

Not at all, it has just been a long time.

She wore her hair down, flowing tresses that met at the small of her back.

I never understood why you liked it so long, not then, Jare. But perceptions change, if you allow them.

He ran his eyes over the burgundy satin choker about her neck, past her broad shoulders and down willowy arms, the gown of light obscuring much of her skin, though he knew a birthmark in the shape of a cross rested beneath the shadow of her left breast.

But it was her eyes that memory most coveted—a piercing blue with a hint of ocean-gray. These were eyes he knew he could not forget...or dare remember.

The light moved and swirled, giving him the impression she stood within, bound and yet unbound. He realized he was having a really beautiful dream unbound, and sighed.

You must keep moving, Jare.

It seemed like an echo, but Jareth wasn't sure.

Come, follow me. I will lead you out.

The cat walked through where the woman's legs should be and Jareth never saw him disappear. Curling back around, Piper sauntered to the man, arching his back to be scratched. When the man ignored him for the eyes of the woman, he reached up with both front paws and dug in with his claws.

The start of pain brought a gasp of dismay before it turned to despair, as he saw the form of the woman shift and move away, still in the image of a woman he used to know, and yet different. He didn't want her to leave.

Then come, follow, and I will stay.

Woodenly, he felt his body lurch, the throb in his head intensifying. Reaching down so as not to trip over Piper, Jareth hoisted the cat up, tucking him back beneath his jerkin, paying no attention as the animal secured itself once more. Jareth wanted only for the woman of light to stay. So, he had to follow, it seemed, and did so, his heart aching for reasons he didn't remember.

Chapter 36

Hollow Reed

"Manannan! The light is moving!"

From behind, the Cervine could see what the muse was talking about; in the distance, what had looked like daylight and their desired destination, a point of brightness had turned into flickering torches, fast approaching. With the cicadas still working their way into the narrow confines of the tunnel behind them, this turn of events only muddled things more. They had to find Jareth!

The Cervine grunted, acknowledging the advancing light, picking out details that the Sidhe had missed, like the glimmer of reflected light, as if off wings.

"I think the inhabitants of these tunnels have heard of our arrival."

Leanan stared first at the Cervine and then in the direction of the moving light, its ball of billowy orange bright in the near darkness.

"You think so?"

Again, the Cervine grunted, there being not much room to nod his head.

"So, which is it to be; giant insect horde or the unknown flyers? Not that I think such an ability will give us an edge but I'm not sure how much sword room we'll have, either. Think you can fit an arrow down the thin corridor and knock out the light? Might at least give them something to think about before we meet up."

The Cervine's ears pointed forward curiously and his nostrils flared, as if defining the world through such senses.

"We don't know they mean us harm yet. I'd advise not shutting down our options for escape."

Leanan brought the longsword up to her face, blue limning the steel just as it did her fluid form. The muse's face was a ghostly palette of colors, her eyes of gold shadowy green now. The look on her face was stubborn, resentful and impatient. Still, there'd always be time to fight, she supposed. Hell, Jareth—why did you have to get yourself lost?

"Aye, I can see your point. Well, won't be long to learn which it is. Yonder light is moving faster toward us than we are to it."

Beryl peeked out from her hood, the dark eyes spooling in the mesmerizing orange light as it came nearer. Her mouth dropped open, awe spreading as she saw faces swirling inside the orange.

"Look! Faces!"

But both cervine and muse already were aware and tightening their lips, pressed forward again, picking up the pace. There was no going back, not with the nasty, dark-clawed creatures scuttling ever closer.

We must go up, Jare; you fell into the lower levels and the girl is above.

The girl. Beryl! Of course. But, what happened to her?

Don't worry, she's safe for now—the large deer-man and the other still protect her.

Other? Jareth had to force his mind to conjure up the muse's face to understand who Candace meant. Candace...he was still having difficulty acknowledging her presence.

Yes, her—the other. You know I never approved.

It seemed a long time since he could easily understand when those that knew him, talked of the past. And yet, he hadn't had to look far to identify his wife. How was it that her memory was so strong when the others had seemed nebulous at best?

I don't know, Jare, maybe that makes me special? Still, it doesn't seem so special that we're here now.

Jareth looked around, once again taking in the striations of crystals that winked and blinked at him, their light forming a thin line of demarcation. Sometimes, this line on his left fell away, as if another great cavern and precipice were being traversed, while the right held true and solid. He often placed his hand on the line of light, feeling the smooth facets of myriad fused stones. At Candace's insistence, he'd sheathed the sword, trusting in her words that for now, it was an unnecessary burden.

There'll be more than time enough for that later, I suppose.

He'd noted her sadness, could almost see her eyes darken, forming small motes of shadow in a face of dazzling white.

"I saw you in the Forest."

He repeated his earlier statement, a curiosity while stumbling behind her, growing.

"You were there, you danced among the shadows beneath the trees...but you went away."

I am always near you, Jareth; it has always been your choice to receive me or not. Though true, there were times I never wished to see you again...all those late nights working, all those missed moments when our daughter was growing up...

The chimera's light flickered, as if resonating to her own words. The play of luminance on the walls was a fascination, augmenting the line of crystals and outcrops of mushrooms. The path was slowly rising and his cloudy mind was at last keying in on his surroundings. The ache in his head was slowly diminishing, especially after she'd touched his temple and sung those words.

But what words were those? Why couldn't he remember?

You're still hurting, Jareth, that's why. Maybe in time, you'll remember it all, maybe in time you'll listen like the hollow reed.

For some reason, Jareth sensed a much greater depth behind what she'd said than could be imagined. A small shudder went involuntarily through him.

"Where are we?"

He knew it was a stupid question because 'in the tunnels' would be the obvious answer, but still he asked, a growing trepidation working it's fingers into his psyche.

Beneath the earth, Jare, still in the dark, but following the light on the narrow path.

Not quite as he'd expected and just as confusing, like what he might hear from the Cervine.

He has your heart too, Jare; trust in him the most.

For no reason? Why did her impassioned plea rankle?

For more reasons than you can handle right now. I know our separation has formed the spear of distrust, but understand I never meant you harm.

This last was like a jagged-edge knife cutting at the skin of his wrist. Involuntarily, he glanced down, fearfully expecting a crimson seam and welling wetness. But the skin was clean, it was bare of any wound at all. Then he looked at his other hand, a foreboding darkening his vision. His other tattoo was stitched neatly, precisely, etched permanently into his skin as much as Beryl's were. But looking closer, he now saw the white of scar tissue, as if the black ink had been an attempt to cover up an earlier insanity...

I never knew about your attempt, Jareth; I didn't think you could fall so far nor feel that much. I'm sorry if my action drove you there.

And he knew, knew as if it was yesterday, though the details were still cloudy. The image of a slim surgical blade flashed in his head...in his hand...the glimmer of a desk light throwing more shadows around a small room than he'd ever known possible. Didn't light crush their spirit and send them packing?

Not that time, I suppose, not that time. Hopefully, the words you burned there later will not prove shallow.

He heard the woman of light, his Candace, but her voice seemed far away, as if the second coming of an echo, and he strained to catch every nuance, but failed. He still wasn't right in his head and he knew it. A grimace of new agony penetrated, mixing with confusion upon realizing he didn't know what the verse meant. Shouldn't he? He'd burned it there, hadn't he? But that time would not unfold and he had a distinct feeling that it belonged to the Night, and this was just one of the creases in which he was lost.

There's hope yet, Jare, but first you must protect the girl.

Protect the girl...

"You mean from the crawlers?"

Candace turned her beauteous face toward him, her light somehow overcoming the ghostliness and becoming something more natural, as if the sun was trying to shine through the clouds.

From the enemy, Jare.

From the enemy. Did she too know who this was? Why did they all know but him? Though, it didn't seem the girl knew either. Which was strange, when he thought about it.

He hasn't caught her yet...

The fear that clutched at her words hit Jareth like a hammer and his knees buckled, as if he suddenly understood its full weightiness. The resonation of anguish lurked, aching to become despair.

...and you mustn't let her be found, Jare; he'll do to her what he did to me.

To you? What was she saying? But of course—this wasn't really her, it was an apparition. His wife was solid flesh and blood, was beyond his sight but not his memory, apparently.

She turned her pale face toward him, the light dimming, her eyes wide with pain, her lips quivering. He forced the courage to come, to say what he didn't want to say.

"What did he do to you, Candace?"

The leading crawler thrust one giant pincer toward the Cervine's back, a signature hiss escaping in the shifting dark. But before it found the corded muscles of the stag-man, the stout end of a dark wood bow smashed into its face, crushing mandibles and breaking into the shell of its skull, releasing life forever. Behind, the others rasped louder and insolently climbed over their expiring brother.

"Faster, Sidhe; we got bugs at our back!"

The muse didn't need further encouragement and simply gripped the girl's wrist tighter as she increased her pace, trying to fan the blue flame surrounding her into a bonfire. The way was still arrow straight and the winged creatures with the orange torchlight were almost on them as well. What happened then, well, she didn't want to guess.

Beryl whimpered, her legs cut and past scabs ripped free as their pace caused her to stumble often. Each time though, the muse would reach down and yank her back up, most of the time ignoring the girl's cry. Too much softness in the child, Leanan muttered, worried that her own attention was divided; she needed to assess those that were closing in. They had the appearance of her people but were smaller. Elves with wings, faces too angelic to belong to the dark, though in this new world, could she be sure? Jareth could help but he wasn't here...and beside, seems he wasn't telling her much. The Cervine monstrosity had been a surprise— where had he found him?

Such were the muse's thoughts as she prepared to meet the people of the tunnels.

The Cervine halted abruptly and stabbed back into the encroaching horde three times, each lunge causing havoc. Trying to buy them time, he dropped his bow and bending his head, forced his body between the thin confines of the tunnel and shredded more chitinous carapace with the bone of his antlers, the tines filled, runnels now flowing with dark ichor. The stench was filling up the space and he stifled the urge to vomit, before sweeping his head back up and dragging it across the soil roof, knowing a shower of dirt would ensue, and hopefully, dropping the whole ceiling.

It had surprised him, the level of persistence to which the Hunter was willing to go; there was more determination and strength than was typical. The Cervine wondered if drugs were behind this new resolve. Then again, even Jareth was surprising him, both with the forced amnesia and with the stubborn refusal to share his plan. At least, there had better be a plan—certainly so far, there wasn't a lot to like about how it was playing out.

The presence of the muse had not surprised him, only the fact Jareth had taken away some of her power—that was anything but typical, and it had brought a small smile to normally staid stag lips. And though the man didn't seem to really understand what he'd freed, the timing was fortuitous. Still, here in the tunnels, the Cervine figured it was going to be all on him. *If* he could find room to fight, that is; this close knife-work was hazardous at best but hardly taking advantage of everything he offered. Right now, there wasn't much use in killing a score of bugs with arrows; there were far too many and their number would swarm both his and Leanan's efforts, Dark Muse though that she may be.

And yet, neither mattered compared to Jareth and the girl. Only in them did hope lie.

The Cervine felt the oozing remains dripping off his antlers and hitting his fine, tawny fur, grunting that he'd need to wash soon.

Before Leanan, the orange ball of light grew still brighter until the tunnel walls were flooded with its luminance, showing her the path that much better. She began to sprint, the girl's yelp of protest lost in the sound of whatever the Cervine was doing behind them. He'd better keep up, she grumbled.

As the muse was thinking it a good time to raise her longsword against the orange ball, a new sound began, seeming to come from the walls themselves. And then ahead, the tunnel people stopped, their light touching the wall to her left, and amazingly, disappearing within!

The Cervine grunted curses as he squirmed his body between the narrowing walls of the tunnel, his fur scraped and his knees cut. Raising his brows in surprise, he watched as Leanan's blue nimbus swelled and then slipped to his left, as if absorbed by the rock. The girl's dim figure followed, pulled against its will, or so it seemed. The sound of trickling water caught him by surprise until he realized it wasn't water, but molten stone and earth—the tunnel people were carving out a new passage. Wondering what this portended, the Cervine still held his great bow near.

As Leanan was about to hail the winged folk, she heard their building voice rise in song, in a tongue that sounded familiar and yet wasn't. It seemed similar to her native Gaelic but she couldn't make out what they were singing. But what they were singing was impressively apparent as before her, the side wall of earthen stone was melting into the floor. She couldn't be sure if it was the ball of orange light or their voices, but she didn't have time for further contemplation. A huge gush of air was released and if nothing else was clear, it was that the tunnel elves were providing a way out. She didn't hesitate and yanking hard on Beryl, ducked hard left and into the new passage.

The Cervine saw the small figures with cherubic faces clustered, waiting, their voices uplifted, small replicas of the huge orange ball of light gripped in their hands. Like Leanan, he didn't have any time to contemplate their intentions and figured they'd sort out alliances later. Jareth's whereabouts were still unknown. Ahead of him, he saw the orange light driving dirt and rock to either side as it receded into the distance. Its speed was shocking. And though he welcomed the fact that it also carved a ceiling that would admit his antlers more freely, he wondered if the orange fire couldn't be turned on them. Narrowing his eyes and tightening his lips still more, the Cervine increased his pace to catch up to the muse and girl, only slightly pensive as the cherubs behind began to close the gap they'd just made. Afraid if he stopped too long that the new tunnel would close on him too, he surged forward, hooves tearing up new-formed ground, and raced toward the orange light.

They'd come to a place where the earth and stone had spilled, an avalanche that formed a slope almost too steep to climb. Jareth feared for Candace. But she just laughed, the sound of her voice tinkling and melodic, a happy sound. Why did its tenor cause him so much grief as well as joy? Her earlier statement and his subsequent question that had gone unanswered, and still lay between them. What has he done to you, Candace?

For now, I'm beyond your concern, Jare. Maybe as your story has come unraveled, that the nuances of lost choices have been realized? If so, that makes me glad.

He was listening even as he was trying to navigate the spill of earth. Her words made some sense, but he couldn't contextualize it, not in a way that would explain why she'd come to him in the first place.

He slipped sideways and slid backwards at the same time, Piper's yowl of protest near his ear.

"Why have you come, Candace? I recognize the separation that lay between us, and yet, here you are."

The woman's light shifted, moving as she danced. She already stood at the slope's top, a darker opening behind evincing that a new path lay within reach.

A more apt question would be why you've called, Jare. For my part, I would always have come. I still believe in your song.

More of that? And yet, he heard her words ring true, they lay inside him, and nestled cozy and secure in his soul. He felt the warmth of her words and smiled, even as he gained the top to stand next to her.

"I'm glad you're here, Candace, but only God knows why."

Oh, you know too, but it's going to take breaking through the rest of your song before you begin to understand the whole refrain. Right now, you're just going along with the chorus!

She riddled just as the Cervine might. Such a thought was not disconcerting, even if it was frustrating.

In time, Jare, in time; unfold the story, prove out the plot and remember to sing your songs. In the end, its all we ever have.

And saying this, Jareth watched her fade, as if the light was being washed out by a greater one.

Ahead, Jareth, you'll see the exit; go straight, and when you enter the next cavern, sit and wait. Your friends will find you. Beware whose magic you imbibe, though!

And then, she was gone.

Chapter 37

Strangeness and Charm

Upon closer inspection, Beryl saw that their rescuers were like the muse. The girl was absently digging with her fingernails at the winding ink upon her face, feeling relief because it looked like they'd escaped the horrible crawling bugs at last. And yet, she was still apprehensive. Standing within the protective shadow of both muse and cervine, she couldn't help but wonder how their rescuers would treat them.

"They seem to be your kind, Muse, all strangeness and charm."

The Cervine's grunt was low without any hint of echo, though it would have been natural within the large antechamber. Leaving the frustrated horde behind, the three had continued on until the orange ball of light had halted, dissipating as they drew near. Still, the Cervine was advising caution.

"I can see that, Stag-man; too near my kind to believe they aren't false. Still, they've curtailed any pursuit."

"Aye, for now. What agenda do they put forth though, I wonder."

As the cavern reared up above them, showing the remains of dangling roots, a small host of winged creatures shorter than the girl, appeared to be hovering in place, their movement like the ripple of cotton in the wind.

They stood; the massive girth and height of the Cervine, the willowy and liquid demeanor of the muse, and the apprehensive girl. It was a pregnant moment waiting to be born.

He saw wings, bright, translucent, and filigreed in such a way that a different subset of words was needed to describe their nature. Jareth knew intimately exactly which words to use, and his imagination soared with possibilities. In the same moment though, the feeling was lost, as if he'd opened a window only to hear a knock at the door. His head hurt and he didn't know why.

Their touch was cool, surprisingly, as they sought to get him upright. The toadstools gripping the walls were more numerous and the light emitted was profuse. He could see again, the shadows having been flung back. Off in the distance, he thought he could hear falling water whispering their secrets. Nearby, Piper's plaintive mewling indicated there might be a problem?

They had this rapport between them, that of sound and tone, much as the rest of the world used but different. A closeness existed that allowed each to understand the other. Jareth heard confusion and caution. But what was there to be cautious about? What needed to be understood?

The buzz of sound before him mitigated thought, and he tried to sharpen focus to get a handle on the winged beings in front of him. Standing up didn't make the task any easier, though.

They seemed cast in feathers of green, or was it shreds of cloth? Woven about their bodies and limbs, threads undulated to unseen and unfelt subterranean winds. Their faces were child-like with rosy cheeks and dark, bright eyes, while smiles were hypnotic. What was causing the cat's mistrust?

The lead figure made a following motion and pointed toward the dark, away from the edge of the lake upon which Jareth found himself. The thought dredged up surprise; hadn't he already left the lake and climbed high into the tunnels? Memories of Candace dancing in pure light prickled at his senses, telling him it was true and yet, there the water lay, dark and malevolent, as if still waiting to swallow him. He shook his head. Had his struggle consisted only of making the shore? Dazed, he eyed the cat who was now licking its fur, luminous eyes emanating from a dark spot near the wall. The winged people motioned again, trying to get his attention. Nodding dumbly, he unconsciously fingered the hilt of his sword, the cold metal bringing awareness. Where have you gone, Candace? But the words in his head did not return with an answer.

There were three of them and they led Jareth from the water's edge, their wings vibrating haphazardly, as if communicating. Jareth tried to concentrate on the pattern, on the rhythm, but his head throbbed too much. Worried about the cat, he looked yet again to the shadowy path behind. Piper followed but at a distance, his amber eyes glowing omnisciently.

It seemed like a short time, but he knew better, as finally the path upward opened into a larger tunnel, more like the ones above whose ceiling housed the pain-inducing skylights. The walls were less rocky and laced with red clay, the rooftop once again showing the futile reach of abandoned roots. The mushrooms receded and if it weren't for the orange light one of the wingers held, Jareth would have had to rely on touch to navigate. The way began to wind and he had to stoop to avoid hard projections from the roof as the tunnels shrank and widened randomly. At least it kept his mind active; it didn't seem wise to dwell on Candace's words overmuch. Maybe it had only been a dream...

And unsure if he re-entered the mist of his thought, he heard voices, voices he recognized.

Time hadn't been long but had already exceeded the muse's patience. As her brows furrowed and the dark lines of her eyes pinched tight, preparatory to losing her temper, the girl laid a hand on her wrist. The touch was unnerving and it induced a confusion Leanan didn't know if she liked. Glancing down sharply she saw the strange writhings in black, moving one after the other, as if a story was being read aloud but through tactile means.

Not that the muse could understand though, but in the same manner she could immerse herself in Jareth's creative hunger, so too did this invasion of ink affect her. It was as if Jareth's words, so smooth and sinuous upon the winds she controlled, were being mirrored in the confines of the girl's flesh. The parallel was uncanny, and she brought her questing eyes to bear on the girl, seeing Beryl recoil visibly, dark pupils further receding.

And then, the touch was gone, the hand withdrawn and hidden beneath long sleeves of linen. But the moment was not something the muse could forget, and this fact troubled her; almost everything about mortals was forgettable. Well, almost everything, as thoughts of how Jareth could touch her, welled up intensely.

"Can you feel it? He's come."

The Cervine's deep threnody of words bullied up against her reverie and Leanan's mind snapped back to the present, confusion rapidly expanding into cognizance. Jareth was indeed near!

"Jareth!"

Beryl's voice punctuated the cavernous aura surrounding them, quick on the heels of the Cervine's words. The muse couldn't help herself and she gasped with relief. Muttering his name beneath her breath, in so large a place, the acoustics betrayed her and he heard.

A larger group of the wingers parted and revealed his friends, the girl's face growing luminous with a deepening smile. Her eyes widened in both surprise and relief. Leanan stood as she always did; hands on hips and a defiant look on her face. The muse's eyes were strict and straight, no deviation from a purpose too dark for most to consider. The Cervine's mouth moved and Jareth recognized it for a grin, prompting him to return the same. The large beast's eyes sparkled with a deep well of nutrient green flowing in a sea of molten earth. With only the slightest of nods, the Cervine acknowledged his gladness.

The feeling was strangely similar and Jareth felt humbled, as if unaware that this is how comrades felt upon being reunited. Had he been on his own so long that this feeling had lost all its charm, had been rendered strange? The idea wound itself about his mind even as the wingers were opening a lane for them to reunite.

The girl was most expressive and Jareth wondered why. The Cervine clapped him on the back while noting the bruise on his temple. Leanan glowered at him though, wearing her exasperation on her sleeve.

"You had to get yourself lost, didn't you?"

But surprisingly, she hugged him mightily and he felt his mind whirl with too many emotions to track.

"I think they want us to follow."

The Cervine's voice seeped beneath the aura Leanan had created and he reluctantly released his grip, feeling a similarity leaching back toward the muse as well. He was right; the wingers were surging in a different direction, their orange fire sticks ringing the quartet and lining both sides of the path.

"This is a strange song you're singing, Bard."

Leanan's voice drifted to his ears, low and guttural, meant only for him.

His voice was ambivalent, his head fighting the dull pounding.

"I don't think it's me who's singing."

"If not you than someone, that's for sure. It wasn't I that called these people."

And for the first time, he noticed that the features of the wingers did seem familiar, like the images of fairies he'd seen in books as a child. But they don't exist...

"No more than *I* do, Jareth, and yet, here I am."

Giving his cheek a pinch, Jareth felt Leanan's nails bite, probably to sharpen his senses and less out of spite. Then again, maybe he had that backwards.

"Whoever they are, they've got us surrounded, and if you notice, they're carrying knives and the same sort of orange light that melts granite and soil; it might be well to play along for the moment."

Even Leanan glanced sharply at their guides, noticing for the first time that what the Cervine said was true.

"Besides, we need to have a look at your head; the worst kind of magic happens when you try to sing and your head isn't right."

The Cervine nodded with Leanan's words while the girl just looked distressed; were these just more crawlers in fairy guise?

Only the stag-man saw the girl wring her hands in consternation.

Chapter 38

I'm Not Calling You a Liar

Jareth listened and shook his head in disbelief, even though he knew what he was hearing. The girl strummed her guitar from the dimly lit room next to his own hollow of a cave. He shook his head because her action mirrored his own desire—to pull on music and find succor from the world. She was only following her heart, and *that* he understood intimately. If his mind wasn't also engaged in assessing their situation, he too would have had his fingers on frets, and inclined toward strings. But he didn't have time, not now.

As he thought and listened to Leanan prattle on about how they needed to reach the surface, he absorbed the girl's tune, noting the subtle urgency to her melody, aware of its searching, reaching, anxious need for comfort. It was something he needed too. Candace's appearance had proven that.

Candace; he hadn't thought of her in a while, too lost in his own world to feel what he needed to feel. It was always so, when thinking about his estranged wife. How long had it been? The memories, though quite close to his waking mind, were still laughing indulgently on the periphery, waiting for something—but what? He had a need to know, now, so why did some memories still hide in the darkness?

"It's a self-defense mechanism, Jareth, we all have them."

The Cervine had joined him at the cave mouth, though he'd chosen not to remain stooped beneath its ledge, the full length of his antlers rearing high. Here, the ceiling vaulted into glowing heights, the outline of its vastness able to be ascertained only because of the multitude of mushrooms. Jareth knew that above them, the Meadow lay, that their path waited, if they could find a their way. Beryl called their host 'tunnel fairies'; would they be willing to let them pass through? Once they'd been shown their quarters though, the throng had moved away, leaving only a handful with orange light balls standing sentry. Jareth wondered what would happen if he and the others chose to leave the cavern.

"Without knowledge of these tunnels, we're at their mercy, Jareth. Going about blindly won't get us to the surface. For now, it might be best to see what manner of people these are, and what they want of us. They didn't collapse that tunnel without a reason."

The Cervine had a point, but Leanan just snorted in derision.

"When my familiar gets here, we won't need these doppelgangers."

Leanan had fumed to any that would listen that these winged tunnel fairies weren't anything like those of Gaelic myth.

"My people would recognize me, Jare, we wouldn't be held prisoner."

But were they being held prisoner? Jareth could walk past the two female wingers and they'd not even blink; he'd tried already. Perhaps because he noted their elfin beauty, Leanan was more than annoyed, maybe feeling mocked?

A grunt of disdain sounded from within the tunnel, causing the man to smile as he knew the muse at the moment was overly-tuned into everything flowing in the river of his mind. He supposed this meant he was getting better because she was less solicitous and more and more peevish.

When the Cervine winked, Jareth couldn't help but grin back.

What caused Jareth to dwell on Beryl's song wasn't the tune or how well she played, but the fact that as she did, the mushrooms surrounding her area of the cave were swelling with light, as if she were feeding them. There was something in the girl, something he'd missed and was only now seeing.

"Candace would be proud to hear you say that."

Jareth started, the reverie of Beryl's music dispelled as he brought his gaze to the giant man-beast, whose eyes were the deepest he'd ever seen.

"You know about her?"

The shadows against the cavern wall moved as antlers slowly bent in acknowledgment. But the eyes of the Cervine remained, poised with hidden anticipation.

"But how? I haven't spoken of her to anyone, let alone since you've shown up. And even then, I'd almost forgotten about her."

The Cervine turned his muzzle toward the light of the winged throng below. There were hints of a feast gathering, of a community event that was coming together. The sound of wings vibrating rose to their ears and resounded against the walls.

"The woman of light, remember? We spoke of her that night in the Forest. I warned you not to follow."

And Jareth did remember, but hadn't put two and two together.

"You knew it was my wife?"

The majestic head nodded.

"Why didn't you tell me?"

A chuckle escaped and lifted along with the tune Beryl was wrapping up.

"It wasn't time; you set the course of events, Jareth, not I, at least, not here."

Which of course, sounded too much like a riddle. He started to protest and then thought better of it, taking his curiosity down a different track instead.

"Do you know what happened to her?"

Again, a nod.

"I do, but don't ask; I can't tell you. It is between her and you, as it always has been."

That answer definitely didn't satisfy and the man grew petulant, pursing his lips in disgust.

"Better disgust than regret, I deem."

Which of course, sounded like another riddle.

"If you knew all the answers, would we even be here, Jareth? And once you know all the answers, what purpose would you have then?"

"I think if I had all the answers, my head wouldn't hurt as much."

The Cervine laughed and sliding to the ground, his back against the cool earthen wall, rested his hands on his great knobbed knees, the dark sheen of his hooves reflecting mushroom light. Jareth joined him, taking his knife and idly drawing in the dirt. At least the wingers hadn't taken their weapons.

"Haven't you ever noticed that when you come out of a dream, that there's confusion, and if you try to piece all the parts together too fast, that you get a headache?"

Jareth nodded, not knowing if the Cervine was looking at him or not.

"The same thing is happening here, now, Jareth; you're having to both sustain as well as put parts of the dream together so you can move forward. Of this I'm sure. If you don't, we all perish."

The stag-man's words sounded far worse than ominous and the man shivered in spite of himself. This was only bad if he could be held responsible and cared. A thought came unbidden, and though he didn't know how to form the question, he still couldn't not say the words that bubbled loose.

"I'm not calling you a liar, but don't lie to me."

The Cervine's expression never changed and he didn't say a word. For a while, they both sat and watched the lights as they moved below, without even whispers to dare the silence between them.

It turned out to be a feast, and famished as they were, only the girl couldn't understand why caution ruled. But they couldn't stop her from tasting the strange dishes, whose aroma was both spicy as well as mesmerizing. Finally, Jareth couldn't contain his hunger anymore and upon seeing that nothing untoward was happening to Beryl, helped himself to the next course. There was murmurs of what sounded like laughter as he did, their amusement due more to the way he ravished the plate than to his earlier reluctance. As there seemed no intention of harming them, gradually, even Leanan let her guard down and they indulged in one of the best meals they'd ever had.

The plates were heaped with odd assortments of mushrooms, toadstools, and truffles, often glazed with sweet or sour sauces, some sprinkled with dried herbs that Jareth found familiar, though he couldn't place them individually. And when the liquid refreshment came around, he eagerly drowned himself in rich golden wines and vessels filled with burgundy brandy, the rise of warmth reaching his sinus and beyond. The days upon the road were washed away, gratefully. The ache in his head was diluted until any remnant drowned blissfully in sleep.

Around him, music of a different nature rose, its effect hypnotic and lulling. The Cervine felt it and tried to dig his hooves deeper into the soil. Being underground, the force of the earth was strangely electric.

Beryl, assuaged by the warm light and sweet drink, fell into a drowse that had her humming along with the tunnel fairy's tune, her inability to add verse perplexing. Her head sagged and her body touched against the muse.

The girl's weight was strangely light, even as Beryl leaned. Leanan took the press and noted how the girl's ink was moving more slowly than she'd ever seen. She grumbled that though spicy and delicious, she still missed the green ales of home. It had been too long since she'd last quaffed her thirst this way, though the mushroom honey in her mug wasn't unpleasant. It filled her in ways she liked, coated her throat and swirled in her stomach until she felt her head lighten. No, it wasn't unpleasant in any way and the more she drank, the more she liked. The truffle cakes were also quite appetizing...

The orange glow of the fairy torches grew brighter, mirrored by the surrounding mushrooms, and while the voices of the singers didn't relent, a new undertone infiltrated, altering the music much as the food and drink overwhelmed senses. The room filled brightly and cast the four into golden shrouds as they one by one, slipped into fairy dream.

Remember when you used to sing me to sleep, Jare?

The mist around her face receded, exposing sanguine skin and burgundy highlighted hair, framing eyes in which latent storms waited. Was this a premonition?

I remember singing to you, yes.

He put his hand out, trying to feel her skin, trying to sense how real she was...or wasn't. This was yet another dream, the type he'd banished from his repertoire, as if he could do such a thing. But the miracle had been had, and he'd not dreamed about her for a long time. It had given him a respite from sleepless nights but forced him into a time where rest hadn't come either. He'd plunged himself willingly into a void where all emotional ties had been cut. It was as he'd wanted.

Do you remember the one about Miss Muffet?

The child's tune? Older than he could remember, and without any idea of how it had come to be in the first place, at least not to him.

Yes, that one; it was a cute melody, had whimsical verse; could you sing it to me now?

The absurdity of the request was just another aspect of his dream, he supposed, and being able to exert some control over his dream-scaping, he let that thought pass as curious but inconsequential. What did it matter? It was just a song.

But is it, Jare? Do we sing to the children out of innocence, or is there some subliminal message being sent, something to which only the mind of a child can respond? These are the basic lessons, the ideas that stem from a purity of truth.

Not all the time, trust me.

Why had his thoughts turned dark and skeptical?

Most of the time, though, most of the time. There's still hearts that would find the light and eschew the dark.

He heard her voice, a coarseness that belied the lightness he knew was also there. She was speaking from a wound, maybe from one whose scar was already set; he couldn't be sure, but the similarity to those he held close to his own soul was too coincidental to be dismissed. He understood himself too well to misunderstand that.

Some would use the voice for dark devices, Candace.

Had he ever said her name while in dreamscape? This thought worried him, as if that tainted the truth of what he was going through right now. There was always a thread of truth in his dreams and upon waking, he could find it, if not always agree with it. What truths were being bandied about now?

Sing me the song, Jare; I need to hear your sweet voice.

His voice; it was something which he knew was more than just superficial, it was something that could pull at the fabric of reality, if he tried. But no, he'd let all that go...he'd purposefully relegated such notions to the fantasies of his mind. Leanan was one of these.

But she isn't me, is she?

It was a question he hadn't expected and yet, knew had already been asked—a dozen times or more, if such faulty memories could be believed.

No, she isn't. But she keeps me well enough.

Still, one can turn a page and see writing on both sides without understanding the paper between is what gives voice the life it has.

Oh, the Cervine must be behind this sequence, Jareth's muddled mind mused, waiting to hear the low resonation that marked the other being he liked to pull from imagination. It was why both he and the muse butted heads—both were drawn from the same source, but clothed with different abilities to fulfill their purpose. And just what was their purpose?

They keep you whole, Jare, of course; it's why I never tried to take them away from you.

Candace wasn't as much talking to him as she was singing, and he heard her verse sprinkled with notes that sounded oddly like Miss Muffet.

I had to start without you, Jare. You seem to be ignoring your own voice right now, but there's need. And if you can't hear your voice, I pray you're hearing mine. Don't let him get you as he took me, Jareth.

The sweat was dripping off his brow and he felt the warm uneasiness saturating his clothes, despite the coolness of the air. He'd heard something, had felt the flick of a dagger's tip on his skin and the first true sensation of danger leapt from brain cell to brain cell.

He woke to find Leanan hovering over him, an odd look on her face upon seeing his expression, concern morphing into confusion. But that too passed and she once again shook him by the shoulder. Her hand felt warm, and firm in its unknown resolve. There was need and he felt it keenly.

From the shadows behind the muse, he saw something move. At the same time, he heard a hiss to his right and behind him, a low, angry, and fearful sound which pinpointed where Piper crouched, his tail flared. The light in the cavern was subdued, as if the mushrooms were recharging.

The shadows behind moved again. The Cervine? But no, he felt his other arm being gripped by the beast's fur covered hands, the strength inside the man of antlers more tangible than he thought possible. A great brooding base of power lay waiting, and it eddied only a portion of its reservoir now to lift him up. The Cervine stood beside him, the great bow protruding from over shaggy-mantled shoulders. Once again expressionless, only the eyes flickered intent.

And it wasn't the girl—she was laying beside him with Leanan's other hand on her face, gently caressing skin, chasing dozing tattoos as much as Beryl's mind. Both clung to the shadows of the dream, to a stall of time in which imminent danger lurked cunningly, working its way toward them.

Jareth could feel it now, as if whatever underground force existed had lifted, showing him that the surface still remained, that there was more to the world than dark, delving caves and tunnels.

The shadow though was moving, slowly, sinuously, ominously.

"Snap out of it Jareth, we haven't time for your indulgences right now; we need to get out of here. Soon, they'll return and it won't be in the guise of fairies this time."

Leanan's voice grew hard and the sound slapped at his psyche, whipping the webs of foggy refrains from his head. They were in danger.

"Manannan! Yes, we're in danger; can't you sense it?"

"What happened?"

He heard his voice even as he scrounged around for his sword, the shadow moving behind Leanan prickling the hair on his neck, a disbelief growing in him thinking that the others didn't see it too.

"Take your hand away, Jare—that's my familiar you're worried about. If you'd listened to me earlier, we might never have been drugged in the first place."

Drugged?

"Still under it?"

She looked Jareth full in the eyes, searching.

"Nay, just loose brain cells from waking up. I'm surprised; the Cervine took all I had to awaken, and Beryl is *still* asleep. Have you been singing in your sleep again?"

He was about to retort when he considered the haunting dream and what Candace had said. Then, another thought occurred to him.

"How is it you're the one doing the waking?"

The scowl on Leanan's face turned to a smirk, though there was still some rancor about her voice. She jerked her head behind, toward the shadow he'd been fearing.

"Not exactly the form I'd have chosen, nor as beneficial, but time will tell. Told you he'd get here."

And as Jareth peered harder into the dark, the shadow moved yet again and a face peered back at him, a face dominated by glowing yellow eyes—feline eyes!

The hiss at his side was repeated in empathy for the man, and Jareth had an inkling of what Leanan was talking about. The huge head of a tiger emerged from the mist of his head, his eyes noting that this beast must be as large as a small elephant, its shoulder the same height as the Cervine's waist. The cat must be at least fifteen feet in length, and judging by the prominent toes, have claws at least as long as his own fingers. In the dark, the tiger's tongue lolled in a mouth of wicked fangs, drool oozing down black-lined jowls. The striping across the animal's face reminded him of prison bars.

"My thoughts exactly, Jare."

Leanan was working at the skin of Beryl's temple, massaging and smoothing every crease she could see.   There was an impatience in both her movement and words as the lines of ink tried to tangle her fingers. She began to get surly, her anxiety to leave paramount.

"We don't know the way, though."

Jareth heard his voice even as he concentrated on why the girl wasn't waking.

"She's easily influenced, Jare—she doesn't have your experience yet to combat such a circuitous assault. Even I didn't sense what the fairies put in the wine. If it wasn't for him," the muse cocked her head in the tiger's direction, "we'd all still be deep under the drug's influence. Though, *you* seem to be abnormally cognizant considering I've only tapped you once."

I'd not let her know Candace is back, Jareth, not unless you want the muse to have a hissy fit right now. Time for such amusement later, I deem.

The Cervine's voice was in Jareth's head again and the advice seemed highly apt. He clamped his mind to thoughts of the woman of light. Still, he couldn't help but wonder if it hadn't been Candy's song which had woken him...

"Be glad I'm awake—means you don't have to carry the girl now."

And saying this, he thrust his arms under the still sleeping Beryl and hoisted her to his back. This was getting to be a habit, he thought.

"Grab her gear though; not a lot of places I can stow her guitar. And what about finding our way out? You didn't answer that."

Leanan Sidhe gave him an accusing look but quickly let it drop.

"I don't have to; the tiger got here, didn't he? He'll lead us out by the same path. If you're ready, that is; been wasting time with all this chatter while the tunnel fairies could return at any moment. I don't understand what they're waiting for as it must be hours we've been lying here under their spell. Are they waiting for someone? I'd really rather not have to face their light—or their song, for that matter. Unless you're ready to take them on?"

She tightened her gaze, Jareth dropped his.

"I thought not. Should we be going then?"

He didn't have anything else to say so he didn't. He just screwed his eyes tighter and motioned for her and her pet to lead the way.

She smirked and smiled with glee, knowing a point had been made at his expense. With a swirl of her cloak and unbound hair, she grabbed the tiger by its nape and nudging it forward with a low word, stepped into the surrounding dark, the distinct clack of her heeled boots practically shouting her defiance.

The Cervine motioned that Jareth should go next with Beryl, and bringing up the rear, nearly brought a huge hoof down on the black cat who was still hissing petulantly at the newcomer. Leaping, Piper pushed between Jareth's legs and with its tail lifted, cast a luminous gaze forward, keeping the giant cat and muse in sight.

Jareth smiled and silently promised the cat some personal attention later. He grimaced to think what the tiger had done with the sentries.

Chapter 39

Where No One Knows

He could insert characters but control was still an issue. Perhaps a modification of the drug dripping from the clear tube and into Martin's bloodstream would help. Not yet—there were still lab results he needed before he could attack from that angle. This latest intervention surprised him; it was as if Martin had attacked himself but then thought better of it in the last chapter.

Rhey had read as part of the audience, his attention rapt in the drama as it unfolded. The woman of light, whom he'd thought of as part of Martin's delusion made manifest through the drugs, had become another enigma. It wasn't hard to see that the scientist was creating his fictional comrades from the shades of his life—one apparently rich in fantasy and science fiction—but this latter confounded logic.

Martin Hennessy seemed to be invoking the ghost of his dead wife, and in doing so, was drawing a strength that was unexpected. It was quite the surprise when he'd found Martin's journal wedged between the last volume of Lord of the Rings and De Lint's 'GreenMantle'. An interesting read, and a valuable tool that might enable him to hone in on Martin's exact location. Or rather, Jareth Rhylan's. It was a mild shock to find such literary creativity in a man of science, but more so his amazement at finding Martin's emotions manifest so starkly in ink.

The man was far more complicated emotionally than he was intellectually, and that might prove a more difficult problem to solve. It was as if he was trying to lose himself in a place where no one knows him, perhaps even himself.

But all the math and science of this world couldn't compare to Rhey's own, as evidenced by the devastation outside the lab. This thought reminded him—he needed to increase the frequency of his electronic sweeps. Somehow, one rebel force had actually gained the outer perimeter and almost secured access via the front door. The pieces of human flesh still sticking to the asphalt roof though, still far outnumbered the flakings of his own, virus-ridden skin.

He moved from one beaker of glowing fluid to another, taking samples and projecting their progress beneath what the humans called a microscope. An ancient bit of technology, but useful in a pinch, he'd found. The chemical chains forming before his eye told him he was on the right track; soon, very soon.

Moving to his left, his foot crunched another of the crawling pests he'd used in his last contextual foray. His idea to swarm Martin's protective cavalcade hadn't worked, but it had shown that his improvisation could be effective. Now he had to slow the prose down, had to make Martin's mind work harder, overload it with so many details that the man would slip, and when he did...

The software routine he'd written to monitor Martin's unscheduled story changes sounded, wresting his attention from the swirling, bubbling liquids. His one good brow lifted, causing another bit of skin to separate from his face. Limping with interest and purpose, he went to his console and watched as an associated timeline began to plot all Martin's variables even as they were created. In this way, he used predictive focus techniques to show him probable outcomes, one of which could be the insertion point of a trap he was still formulating. He thought about introducing his own virus, just to hamper Martin's ability to create, but felt it was a last resort. Monitoring the man's vital signs, he knew the last drug had almost brought the scientist down, had caused massive cranial disruptions that barely escaped becoming permanently etched neurons. Only what looked like a brief flash of light on his monitor had jolted the man back onto his chosen path. But if he could duplicate the dosage and administer it to the center of Martin's cortex, then such a chemical event could be suppressed. The solution was even now cooking on one of his burners.

A light began flashing, slowly, noiselessly, and almost unobtrusively. He cocked an eye and wondered at its timing. Cautious by nature, he'd left a new sensor array in Martin's secret hideaway. The man was a reader and as such, it meant he had a thirst for knowledge. And this was a key they both understood only too well.

The light blinked, and blinked, and blinked.

He knew what it meant, but should he investigate now? Martin's character was moving again, the script being wrung out in similar waves, though with more complexity, as if the last 'close call' had been Martin's own sensor array alerting him to unseen variables. Like the one indicated by the blinking light overhead. Someone was in Martin's anteroom, someone his security force had missed in the initial sweep. Or it could be another of the rabid dogs that lurked outside? Sometimes, they crept past his electronic sentinels, their breed filtered from the parameters describing humanity. And too, there were force fields to stop even those. Still, like humans, these mongrels moved in a pack, and he found that the defensive magnetic coils killed most but not all. Sometimes, a stray got past. More a nuisance, still he should probably check it out. Hmm, had he left the door open, the one to the room filled with Martin's books?

The text began to spiral in front of Rhey, its pattern splitting, its pace transcending typical mathematical predictions. The story's main character was moving again, synchronized to whatever lay in Martin's mind.

Going to the shackled scientist on the table, he took a pus-edged palm and gently brushed the man's sweat-filled hair back.

Too many constricted throes had made the man disheveled and unkempt. The human's skin was filled with swelling lines—veins which were being amplified by alien drugs so he might more easily understand what drove this man. A slight sheen coated most of Martin's face, and so he withdrew his ragged finger, tasting the secretion with a pustule-crusted tongue. It was slightly sweet and definitely salty. Humans; they did so much damage to their body and all in the name of culinary pleasure. If only they knew the ill effects of animal proteins on their systems...

The light was still blinking, the beaker still bubbling, and the text still spilling; one would get his immediate attention while the other two would have to wait. Which one? The brewing drug would only get stronger if he let it steep, and the anteroom had increased surveillance. He decided to see what Martin was up to, now that the tunnel elves had failed to hold his captives long enough. Maybe it was time he inserted his will, personally...

Behind Rhey, shivering with sweat, Martin Hennessy's mouth contorted in a grimace before it went back to patterned nervousness. Where his alien torturer had touched him, a sticky trail coursed, moving down from his forehead and toward his ear. From the pus leaching from Rhey's skin, a squirming host of amoeba-like creatures had erupted, and the last of them was even then disappearing into the man's inner ear. Martin's shudder was but a futile, involuntary rejection of their passage. Once inside, they could no longer be retrieved. Moving through cell membranes, they began to attack...

Chapter 40

Go Your Own Way

The dawn brought sweat and fatigue, failure and success, though the latter was short lived. Behind them, erupting from the ravines between rows of hillock tunnels, slimy, slug-like appendages of something much larger, broke the surface and homed in on the fleeing travelers. The first wave had nearly drowned the four of them with sheer numbers. But with the awesome ferocity of the tiger and the intense defensive discipline of the Cervine, Jareth and the women had at last made it to the edge of the Forest. Finally. While the trees might hamper their progress and harbor more shadows, the Cervine surmised that anything was better than the Golden Meadow.

After the horror of the crawlers and the sedition of the tunnel fairies, clutching, sucking death proffered itself in the form of ground slugs with legs. Jareth exhaled and his spirit damped into despair. Beryl's weight was killing him and he ached to drop her to the ground, to begin flaying sickly, pus-filled flesh in an effort to slay his misery. In truth, he was beginning to sicken of running away all the time, much as when he'd turned to face the cicada crawlers. So much had happened that it was hard to believe so few days had passed. He felt the ague of his flesh and the building buzz of frustration in his mind, the effect of the tunnel-fairies' elixir still leaching from his blood.

"Quick—aim for the large beech."

The Cervine's voice rumbled and rolled, its sound resonating among the savior trees which were now so close.

"Mannanan! What's a beech?"

The muse's voice grumped back at the battling cervine, her eyes stirring with volcanic temper.

But Jareth knew which tree was which, and leaping the stream marking the last tunnel row defining the last ravine, forced his lungs to keep pace.

Leanan was at the Cervine's side, hacking at oozing flesh, while the huge white tiger was wrecking havoc on its own. Even Jareth could see that it needed to be truly freed if the familiar was going to be of any help. The animal's snarl of anger and hate billowed the threshing stands of golden wheat as the leech-like creatures wriggled over the damp ground. With great slashing claws and ripping fangs, the fading night had set lurid shadows on the animal's skin to blazing. The last shard of moonlight stabbed down upon the battlefield with fingers of illumination as dawn breached.

Jareth was glad for that; without it, the monsters would have overwhelmed them the moment they set off from the tunnels. If only he hadn't been so keen on collapsing the tunnel mouth, they might have already made it to safety. But that's not how it had gone and so, their only warning was the piercing blow to his temple. It had been so harsh that he'd dropped the girl to the ground and rolled in agony, the streaks of lightning from behind his eyes searing every strand of muscle. It had been the Cervine's hand on his head which had freed him from the initial pain. Upon doing so, a hissing, slithering sound had come from the surrounding ravines. They'd barely escaped.

Now as he felt the first purple ginkgo leaf brush his hand, a new vitality surged through him and his heart lightened. Whatever magic lay within the woods could be felt and he relished its touch. More, now he could use it. Quickly, as if his seed of an idea had taken root, he laid Beryl against a large sycamore. He gently lifted the girl's face and peered intensely, all the while hearing the fighting escalate amid Leanan's randy curses and the unearthly silence of the Cervine's driving fists. The muse seemed to dance, the wind swirling around her even as she sang snatches of a war cry, lifting her arm skyward and calling down the very heavens to squelch this new threat. Meanwhile, the Cervine mechanically used his sledge hammer hooves to smash and crush wriggling slug bodies, some that measured as long as Jareth's arm.

Though sightless, they knew just where the man and girl were, despite an initial zig zag escape route.

Gritting his teeth, Jareth shut out the battle behind him, put aside rising anxiety, and focussed on the girl's eyes. Unaware, his lips moved, a bare wisp of sound escaping. He still had one hand on the sycamore and the other on Beryl's forehead. As his tune supplanted breath, Jareth closed his eyes and really concentrated. He recognized what he was doing—he was going to the place where all his words met their music; it was a place where his creative soul was set free. And once there, whatever magic he summoned when he sang, could be set free. Behind him, dim but firm, he felt Leanan's presence, as if their minds were now connected. The raging blue fire that typically engulfed the muse, spread and claimed him as well. And within this joining, he felt the power of the forest surge through the sycamore. It careered inside his body before he could gain control and funnel it by using his mind, into the still form of the girl.

The leeches moved fast on their stubby legs and were relentless. And they were many, spilling from gaping darkness between the ravines, multiplying as if by rapid cell division. On the edge of the Meadow, there was an evil abroad that the Cervine felt keenly. He slammed his hooves down over and over, all while stabbing with the end of his bow, skewering the soft flesh and severing one slug part from another. But he too soon found that that only doubled the attack as now parts were also on the move, their nature of division obvious. But, if you carved the leeches into smaller bits, then the will to attack subsided, as if so fragmented, the mind of the monster couldn't replicate that much cellular material. In a similar way, the tiger was a wrecking crew all its own. The large cat swept in and scattered the denser groupings. Muse and myth, armed with bitterly sharp steel and massive hammer hooves, were furious in their defense of Jareth and the girl.

Leanan fought like the tiger, as ferocious as anything the Cervine had ever seen in the forest, as mad and angry as the King Boar and the Flaming Badger together, both myths to anyone but himself. She was the tiger personified. Even when the skin on her leg had been rasped raw by tiny but sharp whorls of leech-teeth, the muse didn't stop swinging the longsword. Over and over she hacked, just keeping ahead of the slithering host as it crawled over itself and dead brothers, mucus staining the ground. It had been Dawn when the second attack started but now, full day was about to break, and the Cervine wondered if the new light would make any difference.

With a gasp, Beryl opened her eyes and started to scream. But Jareth had been ready and his hand clamped forcefully down. His eyes seared through her waking daze and firmly pulled her out. He pressed his lips tight and her body close to the tree, watching to see the last effects of the elixir in the girl's blood neutralize. She began to sob as he let his hand loosen, but he didn't have time to comfort her, not then.

"Stay here."

He waited only for her eyes to show cognizance of his words and then whirled, heading back toward the battle. It had to be enough; sometimes a child just has to grow up.

The flashing of his own blade added silver to the shower of sparks and tempest of color the other two were creating. As the sun shot ruddy rays toward them, summoning dawn proper, he set his back to Leanan's and the Cervine's, and they began to whittle their attackers down, three by three. Letting the leeches too near could be lethal, as the corrugation of Leanan's skin showed. They dared not let that happen again, and so they fought, swords and hooves and the brunt of bow and knife. Leanan lifted her voice, a spectacular joy surging within the blue corona surrounding them, her slashes and thrusts slaying leeches as they approached. The white shock of hair winding through the Sidhe's braided hair, contrasted against the deep black lacquer of her leather armor. And like the Cervine, she lashed out with her long legs too, the heels almost as deadly as the stag-man's cloven hooves.

And still they came, multiplying faster than arms could swing. Jareth began to despair, casting backward glances toward the girl. He wasn't sure they could hold the forest's southern embankment. Still he swung, the side sword greased with black entrails and rotting, falling vestiges of slimy flesh.

It was then that he heard the sound of trilling start at the far reaches of his mind. It welled up and like the wind, blew past him in a wave.

Struck with awe, Jareth saw the trees move and a mythical creature, about which he sometimes sang, emerged from the woods. It was a troll, and it stood almost as tall as the Cervine, plastered in green, its massive legs moving slowly but smoothly toward them. Its face was utterly innocent except for two large teeth curving up from his bottom lip. In its open hands, a white substance sifted slowly to the ground, lining the earth on either side.

The Cervine had seen the newcomer as well and drew the three of them close, his eyes narrowing and his great ears pitched forward. With the Sidhe agonizing the wind as she was, it was impossible to catch scents normally, but his ears gave him what he needed.

"Quick, pull back—that creature is an ally! See? Even now, he is laying out the path to freedom. Swiftly, fall back behind and watch."

Leanan and Jareth gave the Cervine an incredulous look, their blades momentarily poised. And even as they did, they sensed the leeches gathering. Steeling his muscles, Jareth turned to face the horde of four-footed slugs, their advance released like the tides of the sea.

The Cervine leaned forward and grasping the woman and man by their collars, ignored their yelps of protest as he hoisted each and slipped behind the passing troll, whose expression was almost childlike. If not for the bestial tusks protruding from its mouth, it could be one. It crossed the mere of water pooling from a ravine's trickling creek and clumsily advanced on the milling four-legged leeches.

In stunned silence, Jareth stopped wriggling and turned to watch the hairless green troll drop the white powder, forming a line. He first ambled slowly and then running, created an arc over which the legged leeches had to cross. And when they did, the most horrible of sounds escaped, like a great oozing of air from a punctured lung. As the creatures tried to cross the line of white, they touched the powder and within seconds, fell writhing to the ground, which only forced more of the powder on their skin.

The sounds of their death throes became nauseous and Jareth was forced to turn away. The great white tiger had stopped its slaughter too and crouched to one side, no longer held by the muse's focus. She and the Cervine stood transfixed, watching as the deadly programming forcing the leeches, became their end. Each came and broke the plane of white powder, or touched one of their brethren, spreading white death even faster.

But Jareth didn't see the leeches' end because he was looking in some consternation back where Beryl should be. The sycamore was right where he'd left it, but the girl? She was nowhere to be seen.

Chapter 41

A Man of a Thousand Faces

His initial concern faded as the taste of salt spread across his tongue. The line of white seemed erratic because the ground was threshed, as if beaten into submission. The wind picked up behind him and a sodden coolness pervaded, adding irony to his reverie. With curious awe, Rhey looked down at the small islet of water, the day's setting sun illuminating the birth of a reflection. Ah, but it was good to feel whole again, to be released from the physical restraints of the virus' strange leprosy. He eyed his smooth skin—human, with thin hairs on his arm and five fingers on each hand. Quite different and yet, familiar. The strangeness of humanity had lapsed into oddity, allowing him to take on their guise. It was a necessity this guise, allowing him to traverse an unusual canvas with storybook elements. And in remembering the bits and pieces he'd read in Martin's anteroom, he began to see similarities. It might give him an advantage.

Rhey wiped his hand on the dull red woolen shirt that adorned his upper body, the smear of white inconsequential, the fact he'd marked himself—even if subtly—was meaningless. All the characters of this world had marks, why not he? All the easier to exploit.

The remnants of his first serious creation to the story were now just puddles of melted skin, salt being their nemesis. Even as he'd read, the leech army's pain had come through, louder to his eyes than he'd have thought probable. He would have to investigate that, later.

Beryl

The mere of water was dark except where his image stared back. His legs sturdy once again, the feel of movement only just halted, gave a pleasing resonance in the moment. Like time was eddying and pooling just for him...

His hands now whole and capable, reached to touch the face in the mirror of water, the texture of his skin different than he first imagined. It was one thing to see it on one species, and another to actually wear it. There was a certain stifling but once he learned to work his lungs, that too passed. Claustrophobia came and went like nausea until it became tolerable. His body was smaller than that to which he was accustomed, and it was also smellier. But then, it was a great improvement over the stench of reality, that of rotting, peeling skin.

His face wasn't as smooth as his hands; it was pasty and streaked with dark markings, like deep furrowed shadows dug into the folds of his skin. The hollow of his eye sockets were dark as well, and from within, luminous white eyes with dark black pupils looked back in contemplation. His lips looked widened beyond normal human lines, as if his lips were painted and animated. The skin of his forehead receded back into a half-wild mane of oily, tangled burgundy hair, the length falling over his ears and onto his collar. A thought was caught by surprise and he throttled it; could this be how the scientist saw him? Who exactly had control of this character? But no, this was drug-induced by his own hand and Martin would just have to add another act to his little play...

As he took stock of himself, he noticed there was another piece of clothing beneath a dull brown suit; a muted print shirt with open collar framed by an open striped tie. Such were the images he'd retained from the first delegation of humans that had mistakenly approached his kind in hope of arbitration. The meeting hadn't lasted that long and they never needed their suits, not ever again.

Rhey touched his temple, feeling the ripple of growing lines, symptomatic of consciously plotting what to do next. Wringing his hand in his hair and pulling it back from his eyes, the white chalky skin flared dusky as the sun finally set and night closed in. The battle had been over since early that morning—the man had a head start, but he knew which way they'd gone—and the text had given him vital data even before he'd arrived.

Still, he'd be more dependent now on the physical properties of this world. He looked around, sizing up the scene. The forest crouched on the edge of the meadow and threw quiet voices at him, whispers within the trees. Or was it from them? Another mystery he would investigate, when the chapter neared its end. The new moon was rising and its sickle heckled all assumptions. His voice was a croak, as though also affected by the virus, and he called out to the recesses of the wheat stalks. Bits and parts of flesh flowed together, an ooze that became a globule. Soon it began to build and then alter, forming the body of leeches once again. He frowned, noting the alterations that included coarse bristles where spongy flesh had once been. As the legs plumped out and snarling snouts were conceived, Rhey clucked his approval and turned to lead a multitude of stunted wild pigs against the forest.

The path had been easy, once Jareth's surprise and dismay had faded. Casting about for signs of Beryl, the first pang of anxiety surprised him before he quelled it's voice. She couldn't be far.

The Cervine reached the tree and bending, re-examined the ground just as the man had. Leanan, her breath laboring noticeably, merely leaned on the longsword, her black nails enclosing the pommel as if she would crush it beneath her palm. The metal glowed as much as she did at the moment. Her black leather armor hung like dragon scales, bound with rivets and splashed with the stink of fetid flesh. A frenzied mess, her ribbon-white serpentine stripe drowned amidst the dark sea of her hair.

"Where is she?"

Jareth didn't answer as he concentrated, looking for the girl's prints. Finding these almost immediately, he was struggling to understand why she'd left, and the direction she'd taken.

"The large one with the teeth is coming back, Jare."

At Leanan's words, he spared a moment to scan the battlefield where the insidious leeches were still writhing, albeit less severely, their flesh and blood congealing like cooling globs of fat. He could see the troll staggering in its patterned way, crossing back over the trickling streamlet. The look on its face would have been comically innocent if not for the protruding tusks. The white powder was gone from its hands and he could see over-thick appendages passing for fingers and toes.

"I'd hate to have to stick a pin in someone who's practically saved us."

The Muse's words came out more as a musing, an idleness which came with a lot of questions.

"Where's Beryl, Jareth?"

Leanan didn't like being ignored and fatigue was giving her impatience new meaning.

"That way."

He pointed with the tip of his sword toward the eastern forest. At least she'd run in the right direction. The cold to the north did not feel right, nor did the seduction of the south. East is where they'd told Beryl her Maker made home...

"What are we going to do about *him?*"

The troll was rolling forward in its odd, angular gait, its arms hanging to its knees, a rough bit of cloth about its waist tied by an oddment of string and gut. The creature's green tint contrasted with the rising gold color of the wheat as the sun began its race toward the well of sky.

"Maybe we should wait and find out what it wants?"

Somehow, Jareth didn't get the idea from the Cervine's words that it was really a question. Leanan voiced his growing concern.

"We need to find her, Jare, she's what this is all about."

Jareth looked into the fire emberring within the muse's eyes, her pupils darkly black except for that deep golden flame. Her face was still flushed from battle, and the rosy glow of her cheeks struck an odd collaboration of color with normally pale white skin. Her brow set as she tried desperately to maintain composure. The fire of the warrior flowed in her blood too hotly at times.

I'm glad you remember that, Jare; don't make a mistake and cross me when I have my mind made up.

Chagrin veered toward his face but he quickly rebuffed it when he felt the Cervine's eyes upon him.

Another of the Dark Muse's delightful attributes, I gather, aye Jareth?

With the Cervine's sardonic mocking still ringing in his head, Jareth shut down his thoughts and ears; that both of his companions could enter at will was really irritating.

As he paused in indecision, the giant white tiger softly padded up to the muse and flared its nostrils, much as the Cervine was doing. When he looked toward the animal, it turned its head and locked eyes with his. Large, round black orbs gazed back at the him, an appraising look on its face, as if they'd done this before.

The familiarity of the moment struck Jareth deeply, as if he'd seen those eyes before. They reminded him of raven eyes; black, glassy, and unfathomable. Damn, it was as if he knew this beast.

That's not gratitude you're seeing, Jare; like me, he misses his wings.

He?

Yes, he. He'll miss the sky but at least you didn't minimize him into an ordinary cat.

Jareth glanced sidelong at the waist-high weeds growing near the beech, half expecting Piper to be sitting there, admonishing him for adding another feline to the plot. As if there was room for another...

But the black cat wasn't there. Without thinking, Jareth placed two fingers to his mouth and closing his lips, sent a shrill whistle back out over the Meadow. The sound carried surprisingly well. The shrill pitch caused the troll to hesitate in its stride, its face contorting into confusion, but only for a moment, then it continued toward them.

Seems the Cervine is going to get his way, Jareth thought, as the four of them stood waiting, the errant wind lifting from the ground and hurried by dawn's departure. Day was properly come now.

They watched as the green hulk of man-shape plodded to where they stood; Jareth with his hand on the hilt of his sword, and Leanan with a thick fold of the tiger's nape firm in her grasp. She was ready to release the giant cat should things go bad. Only the Cervine stood with any sort of calm, as if the result of their impending meeting with the troll was already known. The great yew bow was slung comfortably over his shoulder again, nestled near the quiver of yard-length, red-fletched arrows.

The troll's mouth was lopsided, as was one of its eyes, which hung obscenely from its socket. The two yellowed tusks were mismatched, and between, a dark tongue rolled. The creature's nose was large and flat, its brow overhung to create shadowy pockets where the one lazy eye hung, and the other glittered as if struck by a nameless madness. When it spoke, only the Cervine wasn't surprised.

It turned its punch-drunk face toward the great white tiger, and Jareth thought he saw it smile.

"Like kitty."

The Cervine chuckled quietly while the man and muse merely exchanged glances.

"Good kitty, good kitty," the troll said, raising one massive arm and opening a large paw to lay atop the tiger's head.

Leanan spoke sharply in a language Jareth didn't understand but knew to be Gaelic. The blood in her hand fled, turning her knuckles even whiter. She tightened her grip on the tiger while pulling the animal back a step, out of reach.

Sensing that perception might be misleading, the Cervine intervened and placed his own hand within the opening palm of the troll, twining his large furred fingers with the troll's, securing their hands.

The troll's face fell and a look of disappointment threatened to become a pout as the Cervine strode between the tiger and the troll. His voice all the while droned in a low rumble of gentleness and his words fell inaudibly to man and muse, while his eyes captured the troll's. The tension which had flared now leached back toward forest's edge.

"Take us to Word, my friend, won't you?"

Jareth's brows raised and his mouth began to open in surprise as he realized the Cervine was talking to the troll.

The sun was rising and shading the creature's skin a lighter shade of green, murmuring like the Cervine, that time would not delay.

A quizzical look came across the broad face and the mouth moved unconsciously like a tic. One eye gazed deeply into the depthless pools of the Cervine.

God help him now, Jareth thought, remembering what that was like, how such a look brought windows of souls to shame.

"I like kitty."

The troll repeated the words again, but now there was a question woven within.

"Yes, I know; kitty is good...just like you. My friends are sad about the girl. She's gone but you know where he's taken her, don't you?"

Jareth and Leanan watched and listened, uncomprehending. They saw the troll pause again, turn his one good eye toward his hand, the one which the Cervine was holding. The stag-man's grip was gentle. A bit of drool escaped and rolled down a green jaw to fall on large hairy toes below.

"I take you to the girl?"

"You'll take us to the girl."

"I take you to the girl."

This time, more confident, more sure, more jolly. It *had* to be a smile Jareth saw on the long-armed creature.

"You'll take us to Word."

"I'll take you to Word...I'll take you to the girl, and the Word...I'll take you...you follow Tusk."

The troll broke the Cervine's grip, turned and began to walk past the beech and into the forest, taking two steps before turning awkwardly.

"You follow Tusk?"

While Jareth and Leanan stood with their mouth agape, something had passed between the troll and the Cervine, something they'd missed entirely.

"We follow Tusk, aye."

The Cervine stood, and lifting Jareth's pack for the man to take, turned to Leanan.

"We follow Tusk, aye?"

Then he speared Jareth with a look, his large eyes widening and his ears upright. When he chose to talk, his lips barely moved and often, Jareth wasn't sure he was audibly hearing the words or if they came to him as mindsong, as words in his head.

"He knows where Beryl went?"

It seemed obvious but Jareth was still trying to make sense of what had just happened.

"She's with the Word."

"The Word?"

344

It was Leanan's turn to forge some clarity as she stubbornly refused to move, even as the urge to let the tiger loose was growing.

"Aye, Word. Beryl is with him."

"Him? Him who?"

Jareth felt the Cervine's nudge to get moving but his mind was still in a fog. Leanan was hardly better, even though she was sheathing her sword and had released the tiger with another Gaelic command that could have meant 'follow'.

"Word. He is the One. Beryl is with him."

Jareth shook his head, a sense of frustration working to hold him.

"Beryl is with him, the One...Word. Is she safe?"

The Cervine paused, turning to look with more than usual scrutiny at the man, a strange flicker in his eyes. Was the creature laughing at him? Well? Was she or wasn't she?

"I'll ask."

Turning his head back toward the retreating form of the one called Tusk, a sound like a buck's grunt caused the troll to halt and turn, a look of expectation on its face.

"Is the girl safe, Tusk?"

The large green one thought about the Cervine's words and then nodded its large head, the small pig-like ears flapping in unison.

"Girl is safe...always safe with him."

The troll turned again and took another step into the woods, where the shadows of trees began to camouflage him in ways that surprised even Jareth. In little time, they'd lose all sight of the two-legged giant.

"You heard him, Jare, so should we go find her?"

Damn, we're going to lose sight of the big, dumb brute; of course we should go find her...but Jareth didn't say this aloud and just nodded. By the look on the Cervine's face, he was pretty sure the stag-man hadn't a clue as to his real feelings.

You trust him, Jareth?

It was Leanan, doubting this course of action and yet already falling in line behind the Cervine as they entered the wood's shadow. Alongside her, the great white tiger swung its massive head, eyes half closed and tail swinging absently. The low growl escaping its sharp fanged mouth sounded more like a scolding yowl to Jareth.

"Well, the troll did take care of the leeches...and the Cervine trusts him...guess we can play along and be alert just the same. The troll knows the way though—Beryl's prints go off in the same direction. And it explains the part of this mystery I was most worried about."

Leanan's boots broke sticks and crushed debris underfoot until a path appeared out of nowhere, hidden by the edge of the forest.

"Oh? And what was that?"

Jareth hoisted his mandolin higher and swung his sheath back. Piper slipped out from the surrounding vegetation and rubbed against the man's legs as they walked.

Bending down, he scooped the cat up and placing it on his shoulder, felt the animal settle down behind his neck, wedged between the fretboard and the back of his head. Piper's claws retracted because he knew his master would not drop him. Half closing its eyes, a low purr began that even Leanan could hear.

"It explains the other set of prints I found with Beryl's. Someone made this trail; I'm guessing it's either Tusk or this Word fellow. Either way, it's the way we'd be going anyway. If the Cervine believes the girl is safe, then she must be safe."

Leanan gave a small smile listening to Jareth while watching Piper settle in for the ride. Then her mouth tightened.

"She better be, Jare, she better be. I don't think it's wise to have her out of our sight."

Jareth nodded, understanding perfectly; feelings he'd had when lost in the tunnels, came back with a force that surprised him.

"I know. Haven't known her that long and already I feel the wrongness of being separated."

Then it was Leanan's turn to give Jareth a strange look.

"I've heard you say that before, Jare; maybe we'll get through this yet."

He looked sharply at her, unsure of her meaning.

"Before?"

Leanan broke their gaze and nodded, one slim fingered hand pulling a long strand of black hair from her face and twisting it back into the semblance of a braid again. The luminous blue glow had all but faded now, perhaps from fatigue. Or was it a small sense of safety?

"You wrote more than a few songs about it back then, and even dabbled with your *guth* too. Once, you were a man of a thousand faces. But, that was before, as I said."

"Before what?"

But she would say no more and lapsed into silence, one in which Jareth heard their passage that much louder. The trees which were thin at the Meadow's edge—as they were wherever the golden land met the Forest—changed swiftly into massive trunks whose heights rose exponentially. With the troll leading, the Cervine followed next, his antlers forming tangles of branches like those bending down from above. Next, the tiger's body rippled with black stripes which seemed to move on their own. Sort of like the trees, Jareth mused. Though he couldn't prove it. When he asked the muse, she glanced and changed the subject.

"I never thanked you for returning my familiar Jare. Though, he's not exactly in the form we're used to seeing."

Leanan was eying the tiger, its powerful hindquarters and deceptively casual padding pace. As bursts of sun made it through the canopy and turned the striping into living shadows, Jareth was mesmerized by how quickly the large predator could disappear into the surroundings.

"Hmm, and what form is he usually?"

Leanan looked quickly at him and then parting her lips seductively, clucked her tongue.

"Oh, he usually finds the sky his domain, the trees his resting places. Only during war did he seek the ground and then, it was only to steal the eyes of the dead, taking a soul back to the wind."

Jareth shuddered, wondering why he'd been compelled to ask.

"What do you call him?"

Leanan was silent, thinking.

"Well, Odin called him Munin. I always mixed him up with his brother Hugin, though."

"Munin? Odin knew your familiar?"

She laughed again as though at a silent joke.

"He was always worried neither would ever fly back to him."

Jareth strode lightly, Piper asleep on his shoulders, stretched out and ignoring the tiger.

"So says the *Poetic Edda*. The skalds wrote of them too."

"And did they?"

She turned, not understanding.

"Did they what?"

"Did they always return to Odin?"

The gold flicker of light stirred in Leanan's dark eyes, swirling with what Jareth could only guess was speculation.

"For a while; until *I* demanded their fealty."

Jareth waited for her to fill in the gap.

"I had a need for his 'eyes' and 'ears'; I really wish he would have believed me."

Jareth had visions of the old Norse god Odin, the Germanic deity called the Raven God; he'd totally forgotten that particular ballad of long ago...

"That's why I only have 'eyes' now, Jare, and it's probably for the best; if I had 'ears', I would probably not hear you as I do. And how much poorer would I be then, aye?"

The ballad told of two ravens, Hugin and Munin, Odin's eyes and ears, bringing him knowledge of the world. Jareth glanced at the tiger, trying to see a bird with jet black feathers, heavy bill and large wings. Then he recalled the tiger's eyes and understood now where he'd seen them. Indeed, the large cat had the eyes of a raven. The song told the tale and Jareth began to recall subtle details, such as Hugin meant 'thought' in old Norse.

His gaze went from stripes of black and white to the woman beside him, the one with jet black hair. Her tresses were imbued with night, except for one lone shock of white, interwoven now as part of her braid. She was like an anti-tiger, yet still the predator.

He pictured the muse, the body of a limp raven in her hands, its neck broken.

"I needed them, but he just wouldn't see reason, Jare."

Jareth remembered too that in old Norse, 'Munin' means 'memory'. How ironic.

Chapter 42

Fireflies

Whether it was a trick of the light, or the result of how slowly Tusk was moving, the fact it took all day to finally find Beryl, surprised Jareth. The idea he felt any anxiety was also disquieting, but he didn't know why. It seemed like years since he'd cared this much, and though he couldn't pinpoint the memory, he still felt the undertow of regret welling.

The northern forest was like a continuation of that which he'd traveled through prior to the meadow, except for one distinct difference; there were no frogs, even if the moss was still plentiful. When he noted this to Leanan, she merely shrugged her shoulders and nodded toward the Cervine, as if he had that answer. And if the curious beast had not been deep in conversation with the troll, perhaps he'd have asked. Though conversation was a misnomer, as only Tusk's voice could be heard, and in patched answers at that.

"She be okay...you'll see, Tusk knows."

Jareth wondered how the plodding giant could be sure. He'd kept an eye on where he'd left Beryl and at no time had he seen anything amiss, though fighting the leeches hadn't been without moments of complete concentration. Still, wouldn't the girl have cried out when this mysterious being named Word had taken her? And taken is all he could assume; it wasn't like Beryl to trust explicitly, nor to make it easy on her traveling companions.

"The One bandaged my thumb. Want to see?"

The troll held out a leaf-wrapped palm that was still covered with salt dust. The man watched as the Cervine's own furry palm enclosed the huge fatty fingers of the troll, dark eyes fully on the other. The eyeball hanging askew never seemed to focus, though it tried, while the other held an innocence which Jareth found puzzling. It was clear the creature didn't have enough sense to survive in the wild by itself—not that any tale or song he'd ever heard had proclaimed trolls as any different—and yet, Tusk looked healthy, and almost happy.

Happy, aye, that would be a good observation, Jareth. I think you'll find your answers when we find Beryl.

Jareth continued on beside the muse, his thoughts pulling back as he pondered when that might be. Already it seemed that forest had sucked them all deep into its patterned shadows, and the walking sun overhead grew frustrated trying to pierce the floor.

The soprano octaves slid deliciously from the gathering mists of dusk, as the ground dropped and the trees swelled in the bowl of a valley, one which smelled as fertile as it felt beneath Jareth's feet. Though the moss was still prevalent, many other forms of leafy green now paraded their textures onto the canvas, forming a richness he hadn't experienced in a long time. With each step that took them further into the heart of the forest, Jareth and Leanan felt the depths deepen, the confines widen, and their own awareness sharpen. It was like examining the intricacies of a really layered song.

"Yes it is, isn't it?"

Leanan had been noticing much the same as Jareth, and though she felt the sky's lessened power here beneath the forest's eaves, the touch of the tiger's fur beneath her hand was reassuring. The glitter of mischief danced more visibly once the threat and fight of those pursuing had been left behind. For a while, she hoped.

"Oh! Can you hear? It is a song to welcome Night! You know it's my favorite time!"

Her voice had risen, so they all heard her words. Jareth in the same instant, had caught the silken sound even as the muse had spoken, whereas the Cervine nodded back knowingly, as if he'd been aware of its presence for a while now. Tusk nodded his head in an animated bob, the lanky hair on its head slapping against pale green skin, and its pig-like eye widening along with its smile. The song flushed out the lingering interstices of Day, unwinding the stays of Eve as she woke and plied at the creases in her dress. A lilting song and a haunting melody that hinted at secrets hidden within the forest walls. Looking up, Jareth could see brief patches of sky as it turned sullen with sunset. There were too many branches in the canopy above for him to get an exact determination of time, but he knew the better part of a day was almost passed. Soon, the dark would hem them in. What then? Somehow, he didn't think it would be wise to burn any living wood, much as he'd felt since leaving Terra and entering the wooded realms.

But his fear was unfounded because though there were no frogs with glowing eyes, the still plentiful moss held a luminance he likened to the toadstools of the tunnels. But this light was less localized and more omnipresent, as if the furrows of bark wherein the moss grew, now ran with a green effervescent light, streams of glowing liquid that illuminated their path. They would not stumble, of this he was sure. Trying to probe the trees further off the track though, he didn't think the same light was reflected, but rather, something more nebulous. As if further away from the worn track, the trees and their shadows held more danger than could be seen.

Looking into the surrounding depths also showed him another; he could see *she* was following. The ghostly glow of Candace flickered on his periphery, following just within the realm of his reality. He was surprised at Leanan's snort of contempt when he tried to point out the dancing light.

"There's nothing there but swamp gas and moldy moonlight, Jareth. Whatever fuels the light of the trees on either side of the path is not the same as that further away. There's a power here, of that I'm sure, and though it is not known to me, still, I don't get the idea the troll is leading us into a trap. And if I'm not mistaken, that's Beryl's voice we're hearing, and she doesn't sound like one under duress."

But Jareth knew better. Or perhaps he saw differently. That it was Candace, he had no doubt. That she came to him only in the darkness though, was a riddle to be solved. He too was moved by the power he felt living in each tree his hand brushed against, in the supple feel of the earth beneath his boots, even as the air became more tangy. It was as if the wellspring of life was just up ahead.

Jareth tried to catch the flicker of dancing light one more time before the music trilling in his ears took over his senses. Deft notes and the subtle nuances of each verse's meaning infiltrated his mind in a way he truly understood. And Leanan knew it as well, as her free hand found itself on his exposed forearm, the heat of her skin co-mingling. Like the backbeat of percussion, she filled in the gaps of Jareth's reflective song, forming from the forest's echoes. Reaching out with strong, long-nailed fingers, she was removing the obstacles to Jareth's creativity with her touch.

A swell of mortuary gray swells in,
a silent shadow of another time;
alone, you stand too near where time begins
and letting faded orchids fall, consign
a fairy tale's heart to beckoning seas,
the same which bear this ship I'm on from thee.

Forgotten, love will not be stolen,
night comes and goes just like the ocean;
just like the ocean, I'll come back to you,
and broken now, fill sail unfurling two.

The jaded tears that felled your cheek lie deep,

a porcelain moist and shearing color's rein;
I still remember morning soft asleep
in eyes that swept my soul and found my name.
Forgotten at the inkwell's bottom, rhyme
has found that emptiness is eddied time.

Forgotten, love will not be stolen,
night comes and goes just like the ocean;
just like the ocean, I'll come back to you,
and broken now, a heart will beat for two.

I left you on a virgin pier while songs
were echoes telling me I had to go;
if choices fall between our fingers' wrongs,
deny me destiny whose winds will blow
me far from rest within your arms—I pray
this song finds setting suns come late today.

Forgotten, love will not be stolen,
night comes and goes just like the ocean;
just like the ocean, I'll come back to you,
and broken now, find love still blowing through.

Tell sailor's moon we reached for rents of sky,
tell storms at morn how love awakens tides;
there's nothing left to say when night won't lie
and nothing's left except tomorrow's sigh.
The pattern lace makes as your skin breathes fire
lives on when seas kiss rock with lips' desire.

Forgotten, love will not be stolen,
night comes and goes just like the ocean;
we're broken, facing oceans time has stolen,

crashing like waves, in constant motion,
back to you, I'm coming back to you,
I'm coming back to you,
no longer broken,
but new.

Perhaps it was the unconscious influence of the muse striding beside him, perhaps it was of thoughts of Candace, her haunting reminder just out of reach, or maybe it was just a piggyback of tunes, Beryl's voice overtop his, but such were the words in Jareth's verse, and they shimmered once before enfolding them all as they walked. Even the troll turned to listen more fully, his one good eye twinkling with a subdued light, as though he could understand what the minstrel sang. And while the twin melodies intertwined with each other like the branches and wind around them, all other sound faded into a hush so profound that it was as if they all awoke from a dream, once Jareth's voice ended. But within each, a resonance was still ringing, still shaping sinew and bone, still touching nerves and veins in a personal way. But if anyone had asked, none would have wanted the music to end.

And if not for the girl's voice continuing, there might have been enough sadness to stop them indefinitely, so hard did the words pull on their hearts. Opening his eyes as if he hadn't realized he'd had them closed, Jareth welcomed the night and didn't miss the others' glances, wondering though, just what such music did to each. For him, only another song would be able to approximate his feelings and at the moment, he was too afraid to set such loose.

But it is your nature, Love, it is your destiny, too. Be not afraid of who you are.

The muse's voice was sinuous and startling, despite he'd almost gotten accustomed to her mental intrusions. And yet, this time, there was a softness, a companionable trust he knew wasn't unfamiliar—he'd been here before, done this at will, but something held him with a wariness he found prudent though couldn't explain.

Remember, Jare, remember and immerse; there is no awkwardness nor hesitation—you felt it, you know it, you own it.

He heard her plea, heard the heart breaking in her muse's chest, and he could feel her lingering touch, another paralytic of the night. It was indeed familiar, like a dream achieved. But there was more, and he was aware of how Leanan skirted its existence.

There's also danger, Leanan; there's the real possibility of being lost inside the music, too.

At first, he thought perhaps she wasn't listening as he thought this, that maybe she'd reached out to tag the wind with her own mysterious soul. But as he thought this last, her laughter gurgled up to squelch such a thought.

Is life worth living if you don't immerse until you lose the last vestiges of mankind's trappings and see what lies beyond? Isn't it more dangerous to die in ignorance?

Her words rattled the sabers of his soul, once again bringing admonishment of a gentler kind, as her fingers dug in and he imagined the black of her nails tattooing new stains on his skin.

But one word she was ignoring, blatantly, was that this danger, this risk of being lost and which she supported, would encapsulate more than she could fathom. It wasn't his heart—nor the inclusion of his mind—that made Jareth ambivalent, nay, it was when he considered how it might catch his soul.

As if he'd reached out and placed a firm but heavy hand on tired shoulders, the Cervine's voice smoothly overlaid both his and Leanan's thoughts.

And of that, the Dark Muse has little knowledge, Jareth. There are only a precious few who truly understand what immersing a soul can do to a person. Most find out only after it is too late. I think for you though, time still is playing catchup, and that gives you a chance.

A chance? For what?

But the Cervine's somber voice faded, leaving only the sound of Beryl's song still floating on the night air, its invitation tangible only to him, it seemed.

A swarm of fireflies provided a profusion of light that danced into oblivion as they emerged from the forest and entered a cleared space. Here, a dome of trees had seen fit to arc their limbs, and intertwining, netted the stars and moon, while still allowing their light to pass. A great, round mirror of water, ringed with flat stones, lay in the center of the clearing. In the middle of the small pond, a fountain erupted man-high, and arched gracefully back to transform the otherwise placid surface into gleaming, rain-danced turbulence. And yet, along all edges, the water was still, smooth and utterly reflective. Tusk didn't even pause as he passed the reflecting pond and kept along the path, his head moving with the sound of the girl's breezy song, which was now closer. Or was it only magnified here beneath the dome of trees?

Jareth approached, consumed with curiosity. Behind him, the Cervine and Dark Muse watched, their perception of the living fountain far different than his.

The Cervine saw each drop of water that fell as moments of time, and each disappeared beneath a dark surface never to return, while those hanging in midair, glimmered with promise and an innocent joy. The base of the fount was in the form of a large turtle which spit a stream of pond water into the air. Upon their gazes crossing, vision and sight was exchanged, causing the Cervine to exhale softly, reflexively, in a knowing sigh. For him, the rocks surrounding the pool were sharp, stained and veined with color that either flared with fire or oozed cooly with the dark of night. For him, the peace and turmoil of a lifetime collided.

Leanan put her hands on her hips, almost unconsciously, her mind bending her will toward the water, whose call was strong. She was put off by the absence of any wind, of any air movement at all, but her heart was doing most of the sensing at the moment. She felt its crush of blood and muscle mechanically delving away at everything she'd never experienced. This was a moment in which she felt the hollowness of her immortality, of her two dimensional existence, and she bristled in response, not seeing the fountain's beauty as much as its continued pour of resources that could never be regained. The droplets that splattered the surface were harsh and condemning, mocking all her achievements, while their dance seemed more the frenzied rush of what she'd come to see in humankind; a madness that eventuality would claim them all once every secret was unlocked. Did she sense this was her chosen path? Did she feel the ambiguity of her reasoning when it came to choosing a new lover?

This last caused her eyes to flow over the ringing rocks without seeing them at all. To her, the pool was bordered with a grassy edge, long tendrils of green stretching out but just unable to break the mere's reflective surface. Instead, she was caught looking at Jareth, who was after all, her latest choice. It was strange that she'd doubt him now, in this place, while all around them the swirling fireflies were tracers of a greater purpose yet unnamed.

For Jareth, the water was like notes from his mandolin, each shining and sparkling, each catching the light and turning it into something different, before releasing what it caught, returning to the music's birthplace. He not only saw, he heard. And though the tune enraptured, he was keenly aware of how peaceful the pool of water had become since he'd approached, as if changing to become what he wanted it to be, what he needed it to be.

There's a dichotomy here, one that grasps how fleeting life on Earth can be.

This was the echo Jareth heard within the Cervine's mind, as if for once, it was he who could eavesdrop.

359

Beryl

It's ever changing and nothing we can do will stop that. The droplets come, the droplets go, and all we can do is get wet.

Leanan's wave of thought washed over the Cervine's, unconsciously trying to drown Jareth. But he tread water of his own, and it was warm where it should have been cold. Again, it was as if he overheard without getting caught, but a quick glance at the muse showed she was deep in her own thought with no time to pay him any attention. What was this strange mere of water, this silvery reflection framing his sight?

"There are more mysteries than man can fully know, Jareth; here lies the water of life, the place from where all time flows."

The Cervine's words intruded on their forced silence. Beside him, the muse stirred and her hand resumed caressing the tiger which had padded up to the fountain as if on wings of air. Jareth felt the water's spell fading and he sighed for no reason. Or perhaps there was one, but he didn't realize it.

A touch on his leg grounded thoughts that had been scattered, as tangled as shifting firefly light. It was the cat, and as a purr reached the man's ears, he let the heaviness of the moment drop away to be replaced with the throb of urgency. There was no time now to rest, there was a job to do. Now, where was Beryl?

Jareth was the last to leave the pool, the cat following at his heels, black tail upright and amber eyes mimicking the fireflies. Now, he followed the girl's song as much as anything. The Cervine had rejoined the troll and was walking abreast, as if he too knew the way, while Leanan stalked behind, more lost in thought than was her wont. As the fountain was left behind and the trees channeled them into a natural hall, they could see the furtive glances of wildflowers as spring's influence was still being felt. To his eyes, Jareth recognized the three-lobed trillium whose burst of light green mixed jovially with the many spreading ferns. He also saw yellow trout lilies with their eyes staring earthward and the creamy pantaloons of Dutchman's breeches. Blueberry-color radiated beneath arching dogwoods, showing him where the Hepatica grew.

On both sides of the path, the overhanging trees moved back, widening the way, providing a greening sward of grass which promised red clover blossoms later. There were trees and shrubs that grew in particular shapes, forming natural places to sit or climb, though what one would view in the great hall of trees wasn't immediately obvious.

There were more birds than they'd previously seen, and Jareth had to place a restraining hand on Piper, while gently advising the cat that this was not the time nor place to exert his predatory instincts. Just like burning the wood, there existed a sense of living, a presence that transcended the woods surrounding them.

As the hall narrowed into moss-covered steps that led further down into a hollow in the earth, they could see bridges and ladders made of rope slung tree to tree, and overlaying the hollow beneath which a trickle of a stream wound, trying to find its course. Jareth suspected that this is where the mere above would drain, when the storms of spring came.

The troll came to the first rope bridge and Jareth quailed to think it could ever hold its weight let alone all of them, but the creature just plodded along, its weight inducing a sway but surprisingly, without making a sag. Even as they neared the midpoint, still the evergreen vining of the rails and plank binding held tight with no hint of collapse. Jareth marveled and even Leanan put aside her skepticism to wonder at the craftsmanship.

From one tree to the next, they made their way with only Jareth showing signs of uneasiness; he really hated heights. When he saw that the tiger took no notice, he braced and shook off his misgivings, no matter that he could feel sweat forming beneath his tunic. And as they rose higher and the light breached the tangle of branches easier, he could see that night had retreated, though there'd been no obvious cessation of time. Still, it looked like day had come nonetheless.

"There is no darkness here, Jareth, only light. That is what you sense."

The Cervine had dropped back to his side and let the muse and tiger take a position behind the troll. Jareth looked at the stag-man quizzically.

"She feels better taking the point; she's not had any reason to suspend her doubt, not yet."

Jareth saw the muse was indeed uptight as he watched her fidget at the sword's hilt, nails paling in the blossoming light.

"And you feel differently?"

He didn't fear imminent danger but there was something here that would not be ignored.

"Me? Nay, there is naught for me to fear, not here; this part of the world is kit and kin to where I come from, this is a place where I can actually rest, for a while at least."

"Oh? Why is that?"

Jareth was pleasantly surprised he wasn't being riddled. Was this because the Cervine did indeed feel comfortable?

"I think Word is someone you need to see for yourself, Jareth, and not someone I can do justice with my inadequate vocabulary. Perhaps someone like you, a bard, can come close, but with this one, I think you'll only create an echo."

Well, that didn't last long, Jareth thought to himself, rubbing at the stubble on his jaw. Still, the Cervine's words stirred a curiosity he hadn't expected.

Jareth noticed that the volume of the girl's song had remained as steady as a held note, and he marveled. Was it a trick of the forest, that the acoustics perpetrated the original and just kept it flowing until it ultimately dissipated against the unliving, or faded into the desert of no audience? So it was with some surprise that

Jareth could see two figures sitting together on a bench which looked to have been woven from branches. It was from there the music lifted. He saw the girl, her hands cradling the guitar, her fingers smoothly flowing across the strings, the source of gentle chiming echoing throughout the forest. She was accompanied by a voice so soft and melodious that Jareth just stopped, his breath taken away as Beryl set loose the chords and notes which only hinted at heaven's itinerary. He hadn't really appreciated her voice until then and part of him chastised his penchant to hurry. As a musician, he should know better.

She had her eyes closed, as if plumbing the depths of verse, allowing her song to be lifted and snatched by the breeze, faint though it was. Her bangs were hanging loosely in front of her face and as Jareth listened, he thought the ink tattoos halted too, as if they could once and for all, be contained. Is this why the girl chose to sing? Or was she born to it, just the same, and the ink stains were only a society's way of expressing itself?

Next to Beryl, sitting cross-legged on the bench was a boy who looked to be no older than seven. He was smiling broadly, his eyes bright and soaring with every note. As the girl finished one song and began another, he clapped animatedly, and his face flushed, as if the wind's filter.

"Seems Beryl has acquired an appreciative audience."

Leanan relaxed her grip on the tiger, allowing the big cat to wander over and after taking an exploratory sniff, to settle with its head on its paws at the girl's feet. The gold in the muse's eyes swirled in exasperation.

The troll clapped and giggled.

"She sing good!"

Tusk, his behavior and innocence mirrored by the boy, ambled over to sit against the tree, his head nodding in time to the girl's tune, his fingers drumming against green knees.

"Who's the boy?"

Jareth figured someone should ask.

The Cervine, walking slowly with Jareth, came to a stop and bending on one knee, turned to the man.

The boy had been watching every step of the way, his brilliant blue eyes filled with a mist of stars, as if heaven's nets had been laid for all to see. His sandy hair was cropped short, his smooth skinned face filled with an explosion of freckles, and his ears stuck out almost comically.

"Jareth Rhylan, let me introduce Word, he who is called 'the One'.

Jareth halted and felt the Cervine nudge his mind while addressing the words aloud. He felt the urge to kneel as well but resisted, not understanding why he felt he should show fealty, or why he resisted. There was obviously more to the boy than could be seen, but Jareth held to a stubbornness he couldn't explain and remained standing.

"Did you send the troll?"

He found his voice even as Beryl opened her eyes and smiled at seeing them again. She rushed to encircle the muse, much to Leanan's consternation, though all anyone saw was an answering smile. The tiger lifted its head and gave a low peeved yowl before getting to its feet and nuzzling at the muse's hand.

The boy remained sitting, his face thoughtful and glowing still, as Beryl's melody hadn't yet been extinguished. Faint echoes were still returning from heights unseen. Jareth marveled at how well sound carried here.

"I hope you didn't mind. I'm sure you could have coped with the Hirudi but I sensed time was not on your side and so, sent Tusk to help. Such a simple compound, salt, and thus a simple solution."

The boy's words sounded like any other seven-year-old's but Jareth could hear the depth of voices from which they sprang. There was an undercurrent of impenetrable age and fathomless experience, as if this boy knew every answer to every question ever asked.

"Hirudi? The four-legged leeches?"

Word nodded, his demeanor playful as he sized up the man. Jareth wasn't sure he needed to be sized up however, and a frown took root. The boy put the burden of explanation back on the man.

"Isn't that what humans do? Size each other up and make judgements?"

When the man didn't respond, the boy unfolded his legs and hopped to the broad branch whose leading edge secured the bridge across which they'd just walked. He came to stand next to the kneeling Cervine, to the standing man and woman. Unlike Jareth though, Leanan was keeping quiet, too aware she could feel the breeze blowing right through the boy.

Take care, Jareth; nothing seems able to touch this Word. There is more to him than should rightly be.

Jareth heard the words but was trying not to pay any attention to the muse. He felt invisible probes working at every sinew and corpuscle of his body. Much more indeed...

"Thanks for the help...Word."

The boy had released the man from his gaze and was now pouring his scrutiny into the depths of the Cervine's eyes, a smile reaching out as well. The boy raised his hand and slid it up the stag-man's muzzle until he scratched affectionately between the mighty rack of antler. A high pitched trill began but neither Jareth nor Leanan could place its source, though it looked to be coming from the boy. Beryl looked in awe as the huge deer-faced man remained kneeling, lost in a silence that was anything but.

"Can you hear it? He's singing...no! They're both singing!"

But whatever the girl heard was lost to both Jareth and Leanan; only the soft caress of the wind left any audible mark.

A sudden burst of sound, as if time had hiccuped, released the stasis momentarily binding them all. The birds in the trees clicked and chirped, warbled and crooned to each other while the newly formed buds of spring could be heard breaking loose from their hard shell, giving a hint of green to come.

In the distance, Jareth thought he could hear the fountain, and his mind nagged to go back, but he squelched that urge as unreasonable. Somehow, he knew there wasn't time right now.

"Come break bread with me, won't you? It has been a long fast and I'm hungry. Aren't you?"

And as the depths of the boy's eyes burst with new star-mist, he motioned for them to continue along the broad and smooth branch, leading toward a large opening in the mighty tree.

Jareth looked at Leanan who still showed her doubt, but felt the Cervine's gentle prodding and understood that there was no danger.

"The only danger is what you bring, Jareth, that's all. Word will guide us, just trust him and you'll not fall."

The Cervine's words were loud enough for all to hear and despite the dizzying height to which they'd climbed, the usual feelings of falling faded for Jareth, to be replace by a sense of quiet security. As he thought about it, his stomach rumbled. Indeed yes, he *was* hungry.

Chapter 43

Riders of the Storm, Come Undone

The resonation of a single string finds its life tenuous, riding on the intricacies of a musician's insight; if the note is to move, it has to have faith in what comes next. For a moment of time, Jareth didn't know what to believe. The events that had delivered him to the mindless heights of an ancient forest, surrounded by more magical beings than he'd deemed possible, had begun to gnaw at his foundation. And if an artist has no foundation, there can only be chaos. Art can exist inside chaos but not the other way around.

From the first, when it seemed a lethargy was being dispelled, Leanan's presence had changed the definition of his song, of his verse, and though there was resentment, there was also a grudging acceptance of what the muse did for him. Still, he didn't like the idea he needed any help. And yet, her touch could redefine the next lyric or chord.

So the note hung, and in the instant the world wanted to throttle its life, the will of the artist cut arteries open to bleed into the sound, giving sustenance where once there was only silence and emptiness.

Fingers moved slowly at first, mirroring the minstrel's barely audible voice, the wind louder at the moment. Though if the audience listened with purpose, that too held promise. This is when he first felt the muse's touch, and once understanding he'd been waiting for it, he inhaled deeply as one verse ended and the mandolin's persona languidly eased to the fore. While his fingers moved effortlessly, his mind and heart were infiltrated by the spirit of the muse—nay, much more than that, by her passion and fire. As if she had placed her hands on him, Leanan stroked the artist's embers, adding length and breadth and especially, depth. The verse followed, building and pulling, transforming the music into something unearthly. For those listening, this was the process; for the minstrel, it was like coming home.

Tusk cracked his knuckles to Jareth's beat, the troll's face sanguine and indisposed, as if small minds were being kept awake by sound alone.

The child Word sat facing the west, the sun having just set. Rays stroked the sky with a brilliance few painters could have reproduced. Painters though, work with pigment, whereas Jareth was manipulating light and sound. It seemed that darkness could come to this part of the forest but no one doubted it was only because Word willed it so. Much as with the man's melodious crooning, there was more going on than eyes alone could know. The same wind which Leanan harnessed and fed to Jareth, was softly blowing against the child's skin, increasing sensitivity. The boy's white linen shrift was open at the neck, and though the air was chill, he seemed unaffected, sitting and gazing toward a horizon steeped with purple and orange. It was enough to make Picasso jealous.

Leanan had her eyes closed, feeling the wind keenly, her arms and hands outstretched, dusk's light playing about the shadows of her face as if unsure where to settle. She too knew these shades were atypical here.

Her lips were full and parted, as if nurturing seduction, and her breath was coming faster, shallower, as if her whole body were being absorbed by the music. Wild hair shimmered beneath its customary penumbra of blue, the muse's white shock streaming silver in the gloaming light. Like a river of unknown depths, looking upon Leanan now was akin to leaning too far over the edge and falling in, falling down and falling deep.

Beryl sat cross-legged beneath a branch whose bark had been glowing since the boy had first placed his hand upon it. She marveled at yet another outward display of magic, thinking she was in a dream. It was kin to the retreat forced upon her by the other kids when gibes grew too much to handle. It's where she went when they touched her and stirred the ink.

But they couldn't know that she thirsted for such wells of magic. When they'd repeatedly touched, adding their disdain with voice as well as black, did they think she'd die and wither, not to be seen or heard from again? Inside, a need had nurtured itself in the songs she heard, while staying hidden in the shadows, out of their bullying sight.

The music rose and infiltrated the budding leaves, some of which were opening early in response to the music. Beryl understood because this was how she felt; and yet, how could she ever call herself a musician anymore? Never in her short life had the songs seemed more alive, not even when she sang and believed.

"He's so good...the music seems impossible."

Her voice had been an exhalation, and yet the words were audible. The cat in her lap lifted its head, ears pointed with question, eyes wide and pupils voluminous. She absently resumed scratching the feline's jawbone, working her fingers up from the throat until it's sharp teeth grazed her fingertips. Piper's purr was restored and his eyes half closed. Leaning into her hand even further, the cat extended his head and neck.

"He's beginning to find himself, perhaps. He's more than good, girl, he's genuine."

The Cervine sat next to her while the light cast shadows that changed position as often as the black on her skin. But these lines were formed from a rack of ten tines that arched over the creature's head, antlers that formed a wickedly pointed cradle. Like a crown, because he *was* the Lord Protector of the Forest.

Beryl wasn't sure she understood but tried to wrap her mind around the idea that music could be genuine, as if there was song which wasn't.

"There's much of that in your own life, Beryl. You see it in the others' teasing comments and sing-song ridiculing. What you're hearing, what you're seeing, is a man on the edge of surrender; but which way will he fall? Into the oblivion of denial, or into the sharpened light of responsibility?"

The Cervine's words hung, pregnant with possibility.

"Who is he surrendering to?"

The Cervine chuckled, the question so full of answers he didn't know where to start.

"Some would say it's 'what' rather than 'whom' but your question is just as apt. He's had to erect a fence around himself just to survive, and now, he's found there's rot in the wood. There's a first tentative step forward for inspection, and doing so, he's also noted that he can see between the slats. What he sees isn't something desirable, so he's tip-toeing, trying to find a way around, or determining if he must take apart his fence and face what lies beyond."

Jareth had muttered more than once about the Cervine's riddling way, and now, Beryl understood. She let her attention wander from the Protector, back to the man who gave a first impression painted with apathy. Certainly until lately, he'd avoided her, despite his professed understanding of her plight. Still, what could he know about having sins in plain sight, etched in black for all to see, moving, writhing, proclaiming wrongness? Even if he too held such tattoos, what did he know about such shame? Leanan had said the marks were self-effaced, were actually desired, as if wearing such a mantle could give him status.

"Some want the attention without having to openly, audibly, proclaim it, girl; once, Jareth thought this was the way."

Beryl eyed the shadows merging on the man's face the way night developed—like silver halide on film emulsion. She watched, charting the way his dark facial hair flowed from dark creases underlying eyes and cheekbones. As his voice careered against the trees, his head tipped back and long hair escaped from the red hood, forming a silken wave that brushed shoulders and neck, where one of Jareth's three tattoos was burned.

"What does that one mean?"

The Cervine twisted his head, following Beryl's line of sight, noting that the minstrel's head was thrown back as his notes arched higher. Peripherally, he saw how Leanan's posture mirrored the man's and it caused him to pause, as if what hadn't been a problem might now be one.

"That one is an artist's deceit, Beryl; it means 'harmony', though Cyrillic is known for being ambiguous. Some think it also is a portent, one of danger. But then, harmony is the condition wherein two opposing forces are balanced. That could mean good and evil, peace and danger. I wasn't there the day he got that one."

Beryl's interest was piqued even as the soaring in her heart braved new heights when Jareth brought his song to its crescendo. It was as if the Cervine's words were pulling from the fabric of the minstrel's song.

"Were you there for the other markings?"

The mighty tangle of dark antler shifted with a nod.

"Why didn't you stop him?"

"Stop him? Whatever for?"

"The ink marks you as a loser, someone who can't do anything right. Only the gold lines can stop the black ones. But I don't have any of those..."

Her voice trailed off, the intense nature of Jareth's song flushing her very guarded secrets, from which she usually fled.

Beryl

"There's a difference between his marks and yours, Beryl; his don't move, his are dead. It is only because yours are alive that you feel the pain. Though, I bet Jareth would beg to differ with me on my assessment. He'd tell you—if he remembered—his marks are self-inflicted because he wanted such pain to live. But his type of artist is like that—they usually wear their heart on their sleeve and thus live out a mostly messy life. And where there's mess, there's pain."

Beryl thought she understood but looked deeper, suspecting more riddling was going on than that of which she was aware.

"So you didn't stop him because he wanted to hurt?"

The Cervine started, as though the way the girl had taken his words was a view few considered.

"At the time, it seemed prudent; the alternative wasn't any better."

"But how could you let him mark himself that way? How could you want him to hurt so much? It's as if his black ink is as alive as mine."

"Maybe more, Beryl, maybe more. You didn't want your marks, but he actively sought his. For you, the lies of your life are to be escaped, for him, they are to be embraced."

"Leanan says the words across his chest mean 'survivor of the world'; isn't that really a good thing?"

The girl's words were like water; pouring and looking for banks between which they could be held.

"It could be—would be, Beryl, but for him, it was a mockery of himself. See, he didn't want to survive...not then, and sometimes, not now. I shudder to think if his tattoo were alive like yours. He'd self-destruct in an instant."

The girl hugged her thin legs together, wrapping her equally slim arms around, the cat having left as Jareth's voice had risen higher, summoned perhaps to a different place. Above them, silhouetted against a birth of stars, the white tiger lounged precariously, hardly the sentinel of which Leanan had hinted. But even as she looked up, the tiger moved its head and looked down, its black obsidian bird eyes strangely morphing a feline face into one resembling a crow. One of the large animal's paws overhung the great branch and Beryl pulled back instinctively as massive, hooked claws extended in reflex action. When the tiger opened its mouth and yawned to the risen moon, she saw dark sabers of teeth blacken in the shadow of the branch.

"But it's the tattoo on his wrist that is most to be watched; that's the one to which he is most vulnerable."

Beryl had seen that one too, more glyphs that looked dead to her, covering threads of white skin, which reminded her of tiger striping...

She glanced swiftly above them again, but the tiger had lost interest and it stoically faced east, its nose flared to catch any scents.

"Why?"

"Because he did that one with shame, a deep hurt and regret of which he isn't sure. The one on his neck is a conceit, the one on his chest is a mock, and the one on his wrist a reminder."

"And that's bad?"

Somehow, she wasn't sure she wanted an answer.

The Cervine nodded, his hands busy in his lap, re-fletching an arrow, the red feathers glowing with the branch-light. The mighty yew bow was across his lap, the way the cat had once been in hers.

"The ink on his wrist was not put there by needle, nor by those that can touch you; it was put there to stop the blood."

"But how can ink stop blood?"

The Cervine lifted his head and nodded toward Jareth, whose mandolin was cradled to his chest and whose fingers moved in dizzying fashion across the strings. The man's face was taut but his skin alive. Both could see his hood was thrown back, the corded muscle of his arms constricting as tendons pulled the strings of his bones, urging fingers and hands to move still faster. Jareth's voice rose and yet faded, the song distilling the night air and weaving itself between, layering and folding, creasing with stories that he both pulled and put there. The silver light of his eyes was a mirror of the emerging star field above.

The Cervine nodded toward the minstrel who sang with all his might.

"He's doing it now."

The ground felt strangely spongey, as if the earth's life-force were filling capillaries beneath, surging and spreading out. When Rhey looked at the herd of wild pigs surrounding him though, he didn't sense the same proliferation. Out beyond his touch, the world was as described in pixels on a screen, strange though the images might be or become. He reached up to touch his temple, wondering for a moment why he didn't feel the electrodes. Back in the lab, it hadn't been much effort to attach the same setup used on Martin. It had taken some creativity though for him to ensure his own presence could be disconnected at will, unlike Martin's circumstance. There had been the thought to also put a stronger drug in his own drip bag, but only so his clarity of the story could be the same as the human's. In the end, Rhey had opted against that choice, putting his faith in his vastly superior science. This was only a test; if it worked, he'd find a way to maintain the connection longer next time. For now, it was enough to be able to physically affect the retrieval process. Knowing he was on the clock, Rhey forced the pace, feeling a strange vertigo on his character's body. Was this also the reason for such strange emanations in the soil?

The forest stippled the land all around him and Rhey cursed this fact; why couldn't he have done this when Martin had had his character in the Meadow? Movement would have been facilitated. The sound of the herd was haphazard, grunts and squeals punctuating the silence which hung among the trees. And large, dark trees at that. He'd have thought Martin drawn more toward light and day, not shadow. If this experiment ended without profit, he'd have to look more closely at Martin's library. There had to be secrets there that would help him reassemble Martin's mind more accurately. Books were the x-ray of human life; what you read is what you are. Of this Rhey was sure.

The other nuisance detail to which Rhey was having to adapt, was the dancing light in the distance. The fact it looked strangely like a human woman didn't bother him as much as that the face was so familiar.

Leanan hadn't been happy but already Jareth was more than aware of how often his actions incited this reaction from her. After his voice had given way before a wash of emotional waves and his last note had at last died into the night, the Cervine had asked if Beryl would sing next. As her face beamed at the request, which the child Word heartily endorsed, Jareth faded into himself. He heard the girl's song and appreciated its nuances with variable heights, but it ultimately was unable to hold him long. The building doubt and scars of his soul were throbbing, forcing him to withdraw; hadn't it ever been so?

From her position across the circle, Leanan sensed when the disconnect happened and frowned, her face darkening and her eyes pools of thoughtfulness. She understood and yet disapproved. The way to healing wasn't to fall back, it was to embrace the hurt. She wondered though if their history was holding the process back, that the man feared repeating what had nearly drowned him so long ago. Leanan looked with both concern and an undercurrent of fury; this wasn't the way an artist was supposed to treat his muse...

As Beryl lit the eyrie with music and enthralled the others in her way, Jareth released his hold on the mandolin and wandered aimlessly beyond where the others sat. Part of him wanted to stay and fall into the girl's song—as the others had his—but emotions bubbled with turmoil, the source of which he wasn't sure. Times like this would often find him alone, searching to work through the conflicting feelings that never seemed fully under control—especially when he sang. If there'd been a friendly tankard of ale handy, that would have been his first port of call. As it was, he just sat and withdrew his presence from the others.

"Where did your music go, bard?"

The words were comically childish, though the boy's meaning was laden with a depth that shocked Jareth. He pulled from his daze and eyed the boy, noting a gaze that didn't blink. The boy might look seven but Jareth doubted it was his true age. Again, he found himself being labeled.

"The others have called me that...why do you do it?"

A smile slipped quickly beneath the freckles and Word's eyes sparkled with mirth. In the light, it was difficult to even say if they were still blue.

Jareth had pulled back from the main branch and into the shadows. He saw now though, that where Word went, the bark beneath his bare feet glowed, much as he'd provided the overhead lighting. And more strangely, the light was seeping toward him like a puddle, emanating from the boy and working into a tight circle. And yet, the light did not reach the Word's face. He looked at his hand and noted it was only dimly lit, but enough by which to see.

"We're all given gifts, Jareth Rhylan, even you."

"But bards are not just minstrels, they are workers of verse magic. They have the ability to make their songs real."

He paused, as if that was explanation enough.

The boy shook his head slowly, then impishly, as if for even a split second the thought of dismissing such a title could be an option.

"More than real, sometimes, Jareth Rhylan; often, the bard can take his magic between worlds and change time's fabric."

Jareth scratched at his mustache, wondering why the boy was telling him this and more, what kind of authority was he in the first place? They only had the Cervine's word that this youth could be trusted, that they were really safe here. Taking a moment to eye the distance to the forest floor, Jareth sagged back toward the trunk, sorry he'd given in to the urge.

"Ever hear of Jim Morrison?"

Word's question surprised him.

"Who?"

"Jim Morrison—lead singer for a band called the Doors. Long time ago, in another age—or story, if you want to split hairs—he did just the opposite of what you've done."

"Then why are you telling me about him? Am I suppose to emulate his life? Be who he was?"

Some bit of pride had crept back in and the man felt his defenses rise.

The boy walked around him, his footprints glowing like a line of spotlights until they merged with each other, forming a molten trail of light.

"No, Jareth Rhylan, I don't think that would be the best way. You know, he thought he was a poet, too."

"I never claimed any such thing."

The boy chuckled and stooping, brought himself to his hands, his body rising vertically until his toes pointed skyward. Then he began to walk on his hands, all the while continuing the conversation.

"Difference is, you actually are; it's just part of what you've forgotten, is all."

Jareth began asking himself how this kid could know anything about him, let alone tagging him as a poet. A poet was truly a rare breed, and was said to be extinct in the world. Though some fancied themselves such, he'd heard them; each and every one had been merely a poser. Their voice had been so weak as to barely move the smoke from a slow burning candle. That wasn't as he'd heard it, and certainly didn't come close to the stories he could recite, or the songs he knew. He decided to force the issue.

"Why would I forget something like that? Magic of that kind could do an awful lot for a guy like me."

Word continued his hand stand, the prints of light forming in the bark now sporting finger lengths. Sensing Jareth was looking to distract from the main question, he flipped back to his feet and drawing near the man, placed a small hand on the man's arm, right above the tattoo on his wrist.

Jareth was shocked at how hot the boy's touch was, then how cold as he felt his skin merge with the boy's. He tried to step back and withdraw, but Word was quicker.

"Be at peace, Jareth Rhylan, there's no one here that wants to hurt you, especially me. I'm just trying to get a gauge on how far you're prepared to take this deceit."

Jareth was flustered at first, still trying to withstand the intense fluctuations of temperature and take the boy's last word to heart. Deceit?

"Well, maybe not by choice, but then...yeah, maybe this is the best plan after all. Must be hard on you though, denial can be a hard place from which to recover."

"What am I denying? That I'm a bard and can bind magic? Even if I did think I had that power, I surely don't know how to use it. Wouldn't a bard know how to do that?"

Still, the boy was only repeating what Leanan, the Cervine, and even the ghost of his wife had told him; that he'd forgotten how to sing. Hell! He knew well enough—hadn't his earlier song been proof of that? But he asked a question that had always come when he considered maybe the others were right.

"Why would I forget? The only hint I have is that I'm protecting something. How is forgetfulness a benefit in that regard?"

The boy's hand was still on his skin but now, the hot-cold pulses were balanced and no longer burning. He did note however, that the scars on his wrist looked molten and the tattoo that covered, was writhing. What the hell?

"These are dead words, Jareth Rhylan, but you knew this when you burned them in, or rather, filled them up."

Jareth forced his wrist down and away, breaking the boy's touch, anger flaring for reasons he thought he didn't want to know.

"Do you remember Jim Morrison, Jareth Rhylan? He too lost the music, but in his case, he was absorbed by it, whereas you have given it up freely."

But the man was still caught between glaring at the boy's impudence and averting his eyes for fear some truth might be transferred. Did he know this Morrison? The name *did* sound familiar, now that he gave it some thought.

"He was still a young man, Jareth Rhylan, younger than yourself, but he didn't see his music, or his verse, as sacred enough to keep pure. You on the other hand, believe you've tainted any such notion you could ever be that pure. In a way, the music has lost you, not the other way around. I'm sure it helps you hide."

Jareth gave himself over to glaring outright.

"Who am I hiding from?"

And even before the boy said the words, Jareth heard Leanan's and the Cervine's voice rise up from memory.

"The Hunter, of course."

Of course. A person or something that didn't seem to have a name or shape, just a purpose.

"Jim Morrison thought he was invincible, thought he'd never sell out, and when he did, found it had been by his own hand."

"How'd he do that?"

Despite his growing feeling of uneasiness, Jareth found he wanted to hear the story. But then, wouldn't all minstrels worth their salt? A story was like silver coin to one such as himself. And to a bard? Even more...but Jareth dismissed that thought as though it were an insect crossing his path.

"He imploded, Jareth Rhylan, he put stimulants and sedatives into his blood as if the music would save him. But no man can hold what was born to be free."

What was born to be free...well, such thoughts about his own music had come often to him. He knew well that he never could keep inside any song he ever wrote. One of his earliest memories was that this force was undeniably inside him. And even when his voice was new to the world, it had always held an element of rhythm deep down.

"You know the kind I'm talking about, don't you, Bard? The kind that have the ability to sing, but no notion of when to stop? They have no idea when they've taken something beautiful and twisted it into something hideously mocking in nature. That's why they run to drink and drugs; it's too late to escape then, isn't it?"

Why was the boy telling him this? There hadn't been *that* many moments he'd sang himself into wet oblivion...

"That's not me...I know better."

The boy nodded slowly, sadly.

"Yes, you do, perhaps too much so. Jim Morrison ran into the music and drowned, but you've run away because you're scared."

Jareth snorted, the impulse raw and lurking too near emotional stability.

"What is there to be scared of? I haven't run from anything."

The declaration was flat, devoid of any feeling whatsoever. Word's brows raised and his eyes widened.

"You're scared of making the same mistake, Jareth Rhylan, that's all. And you've run so far that you don't even remember where you've been, though pieces of your memory bubble up at the strangest of times."

The man started to rise in protest, the words hanging back in his throat, on the edge of strangulation.

"Can you tell me where you were a year ago, Bard?"

Disregarding the boy's label, he started to blurt out a place but bit his tongue; no, it hadn't been there. It had been...but the name and any faces associated danced as if far away, their identities suddenly secret. Why was it so hard to answer the boy? Why did he struggle to find pieces of information that he knew lay within his mind but remained elusive?

"I was at the Vesparian castle, that's where. The siege held me for a long time."

But not that long, surely not a year ago and before that? Not for any length of many years. How old *was* he, by the way? Thirty? Forty? The reflection seen in the silver mere suggested somewhere in that range.

"The landscape is changing, Jareth Rhylan, believe me—I've seen it. The shapes you wrought are undergoing change, though for now, I'm able to keep them inconsequential. But beyond this forest, where you must go, there will be no such protection."

Jareth looked bewildered as it seemed Word was changing the subject.

"The castle was on the edge of your refuge, Bard, and when you left—when you had to leave—the chase to end all chases began. Your purpose was born and the beginnings of a last journey begun. Do you remember the broken wasteland surrounding the fortress?"

Jareth nodded after a moment, picturing the twists of steel and concrete, of the broken and burning wrecks of strange vehicles. The road had been about the only thing untouched by the destruction.

"The woods are being assaulted even as you progress forward. What you created to cover your tracks has been breached, and even *I'm* not sure you planned this. Granite and fieldstone is morphing into sharp cut brick and mortared block, vast roots of trees churning beneath the Hunter's touch as they are thinned and carry the lightning's charge. Great rafts of trees are altering to form storied buildings whose glassy windows are mostly dark inside.

He's taken quill to your words and is learning your way. If you don't reclaim the text, he's going to do more than leave you bereft of options. The only weapon you'll have left then is yourself; not even the Cervine will be able to reach you then, and the wild mysteries of the Dark Muse will comfort you naught. He's come himself, Jareth Rhylan, and the level of his desperation is approaching yours."

The man couldn't deny a sinking feeling growing inside, nor could he explain it.

"Who exactly are you?"

The freckle-faced boy grinned, hoping to disarm Jareth's rising wariness.

"I'm the One, Jareth Rhylan, the Word; like you, I have written deep and layered the verse. My song went before yours and in mine, yours echoes. As the Cervine told you; the only danger here is what you bring yourself."

So, like the stag-man, the boy's riddling ran counter to what the man wanted to hear. Was the boy a minstrel too? He hadn't seen any instrument...

"Can you remember a family, Jareth?"

The boy's voice had softened and for the first time, he'd dropped the sir name and been more familiar. The sudden shift in focus caught him off guard, as he was still contemplating Word's nature for what it really was.

"Family? Sure, I had a wife...once."

Why did that last bring a pressure behind his eyes, lancing like the beginning of a migraine.

"Yes, you did. You lost her. Do you remember how?"

But he couldn't; hadn't he already begun to face up to this ghost there in the tunnel of the underground elves? Isn't that the first time he'd actually admitted that fact? Surely her ghost hadn't caused him surprise as much as sadness. He shook his head, not really sure he wanted Word to go on. Grimly, he then heard the boy echo the whispers of his ghostly wife.

"The Hunter got to her first, Jareth, and he's looking for your daughter, too!"

The moon gave enough light for the herd to avoid most obstacles as Rhey's merciless will drove them forward. The lattice of branches above were sluiced by pale light which upon touching his face, held a faint tingling sensation, as if he could feel its presence as it strode in the sky of the real world. Though, this one seemed concrete enough.

As the wild pigs crossed from pickets of trees and onto the open sward of grass, he could hear the distant gurgle of water. Rhey directed the herd in that direction. He was getting close, as if the longer he immersed himself mentally into this world, the easier it was to find Martin's loose canon of a spirit.

And better, he could feel the encryption unwinding, as if its presence was more tangible. His face cracked into a smile of mirth, the caricature paint of his face mocking all from which this story was being wrought. He limped along after the pigs, his hair flowing back from a shiny, pasty scalp, but his eyes were burning coals of purpose and he bent his body to follow his mind. What he saw as he passed the silver mere of water, was inconsequential, and the border surrounding even less important. As a matter of fact, he sullied the reservoir altogether by running his herd of pigs through it and stomping great muddy boots down hard, splashing with an insolence that the trees surrounding frowned upon.

"If I didn't know better, I'd say that Beryl has a future in some girl band. But with all her inadequacies and non-existent self image, I doubt even I could help one such as her."

Leanan wasn't being harsh as much as re-evaluating, but her voice wasn't as soft as she'd thought and the Cervine heard.

"She's better than either of us know, Sidhe."

The muse shut her lips, not in concern for what the antlered being thought as much as because she didn't. What Jareth saw in the stag-man to keep its company was still unexplained, and until she could ferret what the connection was, she was loath to open herself to another's scrutiny.

"I know she's good—but who taught her?"

The muzzle of the Cervine lifted and large nostrils flared because even as the muse spoke, so too had the night. His ears pricked and widened to their fullest, pulling in sound from far away. Something was amiss.

Leanan caught the Cervine's distraction and summoned the tiger to her side. At the same time, she let a low tune loose from between pinched lips, knowing the wind needed very little to hear her call. Like the Cervine, she was gathering information, trying to discover the source of the disturbance.

The graceful neck of the guitar cradled in her left hand, Beryl sang on, oblivious to how the night was changing. For her, there was only the sound of her voice in that moment.

Word was approaching from the other side, his face lost in thought, the light of his steps still following. But the puddle engulfing the bark where he'd been sitting talking to Jareth, had receded, had almost been totally absorbed.

Jareth! Where had he gone? The Cervine swept the far side of the wide branch, raking the smooth-barked spoke back to its hub, then upward, as if expecting to see the man where the tiger used to be. Rising quickly, his hand pulled the bow close and his other hand itched to remove a dark-red feathered shaft.

"Where's Jareth?"

His words were directed at the approaching boy but Leanan thought he'd addressed her.

Dean Michael Christian

"He's right there, with the...boy." She saw the youngster approaching and her voice faded. She too rose and her palm clenched the hilt of her long dagger tightly.

"Word?"

The Cervine's voice rumbled the boy's name, a deep, earthly tone that felt as if the beast was trying to communicate more with the tree upon which he stood than the boy.

"He's okay. We talked and he had a need to be alone."

"Alone?"

Leanan's voice was a tight, hardly suppressed stab of sound that pierced the night air like a dart.

"A need to be alone?"

The Cervine showed concern too, though not the growing hostility he could see in the muse. Leanan's face was taut, her cheeks flush with rising blood, and her eyes narrowed to slits, the gold fire barely held in check.

"We must go inside; he comes, and my presence is strong enough to be felt. Now is not the time for a showdown."

"He? He the Hunter? What are you saying?"

Leanan's voice grew strangled, as if she was as angry at herself for being lulled while danger had not slept. Fool! She cursed herself but once, reserving then the next invectives for the Cervine and the boy.

"He's here, and it didn't take him long to figure out how to put a hand in the mixing pot, did it?"

Both muse and cervine shook their head, as incredulous as the boy's words seemed.

"It's Jareth; I can only hope he knows what he's doing or else we're going to have to be extremely blessed. He barely knows who he is and what's at stake, though I tried to tell him."

"What did you tell him, boy?"

Leanan's snarl brought an echoing response from the huge tiger who padded restlessly at her side.

385

Word looked at the muse, his face as innocent as dawn.

"I told him the truth."

Both the Cervine and Leanan bit back a gasp which laughed maniacally to be free.

To the west, the sound of thunder rolled impossibly slow, a rumble which did not crest or ebb. The ground beneath the tree trembled, the soil between its roots gripped ever tighter. As Beryl finally keyed into the change coming and her song crumbled in doubt, the boy looked east and saw the sun. The girl came and slid fearfully into the protective embrace of the muse, her face falling as fast as her song.

"We need to find Jareth."

"You'll take the girl?"

The Cervine's question was propped in hope even as he nocked an arrow in his black bow. The muse shot the boy a sharp glance too, understanding that the girl would be no good in a fight anyway, but still hesitant to let her out of sight.

The boy just grinned in affirmation.

"Which way did Jareth go?"

Leanan's voice held a mixture of concern and wrath, as if she was appalled that once again he'd opted to avoid her company.

The boy pointed west, out along the branch to where a distant rope ladder was tied. It was one of many ways to get about the eyrie.

"He needed to touch ground, in more ways than one, I fear."

"He did?"

The boy nodded at Leanan's query, already turning and untangling the girl from the muse's grip.

"I think he's gone to look for the light, the dancing light."

The Cervine perked up his head, a dancing green light of his own eddying.

"Is he ready?"

The boy shrugged and gave the two one last glance, as he herded the girl toward the massive trunk and a connecting rope bridge.

"He may not have enough time to do this his way; the Hunter is forcing the issue."

"Damn it to Lyr!"

Leanan bit her lip, drawing blood with her exclamation.

The boy smiled and the Cervine's lips attempted to do the same.

"For a bard, he's almost as much trouble as a muse, aye?"

The wind snatched away both the Cervine's amusement and the muse's snort of derision.

Chapter 44

Just Call My Name

The rope ladder led Jareth down to where branches radiated like city roads, but these stretched out toward the sky. Whereas Word lit the darkness with his touch above, here there was only moonlight to show him where he stepped. But it didn't matter, because as before in Frogmoss Forest, the trees were with him, lending their voice and giving him sight. He moved easily, not sure exactly of his direction, but knowing he needed to be alone nonetheless.

He just needed to think. And as if his need was being cradled, Beryl's voice muted and his thoughts were no longer beguiled by the beauty above. He was grateful without acknowledging that fact. Staying close to the trunk, Jareth worked his way down until he once again was standing on fertile earth. Moist with the unfurling season, the trees brushed against his hand and he found a desire to be grounded. He marveled to understand how the trees accomplished such a feat so easily. Right then, his mind was ragged and torn, something he hadn't noticed before.

As if recurring thoughts of Candace summoned her, prompted by the boy's words, there at the tree's base, her form flowed like liquid light, her nebulous cloak was stirred by hidden winds. The night was still. And nothing touched his cheek. Still, there was no cause for doubt. She moved to unseen forces, much as he was, ironically. His heart tensed, then his hands, words shifted in his mind. Which for such as he, was a true danger.

"How, Candace? How?"

Beryl

His heart had been prepared but be couldn't keep his feelings from showing, as anguish ripped at his lips and from corners of his eyes. The smooth darkness rippled, and his sight was tinged with a wetness he disdained nonetheless.

"You weren't there."

The accusation pierced him as he feared it would, even though her face was full of pity. She answered truthfully as only spirits can, but it would not have been her first choice.

"I wasn't there...then where was I?"

But did it matter? He felt a major rampart of his defenses buckle. Feverishly though, his psyche worked to bolster the walls.

"As always, Jare, you were working...always working."

His immediate response was pure reflex but she held up a slim, glowing hand, her face a mirror.

"That's not the cross you think it is—the government always did overplay the patriot card. And too, even when you were home you weren't really there; you always had a book to read or a song to write. Carving out time together became necessity, but you didn't hear me, not then. In many ways, I'm surprised you hear me now. There used to be a time when I prayed that you'd just call my name."

Her words settled into his skin and if he dared look, was afraid he resembled Beryl, with her lines of flowing black derision. But he didn't dare and just stared at the ground in front of him, the familiarity of his position a slap of irony. It was a place he'd put himself, and then from which he'd fled. The many disassembled memories he sought to avoid, were scrambling to re-invent themselves, wringing pain from guilt.

Candace loomed closer and placed a blue-white hand on his head. He'd fallen to his knees when the memories began to exert their power over him. The wet lines of horizons that threatened before, were now fully risen suns of tracks down his cheeks. He felt her touch though, and the warmth fleeing his body grew confused. Her loving touch had the same magical quality that he'd always hoped his songs possessed, but different; hers was a feeling that grew from within him and not without. His music pervaded from the surrounding air, coalesced and manifested itself with the intent of changing another, while pouring from his minstrel's soul. No; if he could believe the others, from his bardic soul, though it was still an idea he was loath to embrace.

"It's too late then."

His voice was the utterance of a man on the brink of death, the last rights having been said and an awkward silence ensuing, because no one could foretell their moment of leaving.

"But all is not lost, Jare, not if you're willing to live and learn, to love and persevere. You still have a purpose in living to accomplish, though death may have claimed some you didn't know you loved."

But he had, and he tried fiercely to implant that idea overtop the truth she was laying out. He *had* loved her, had since they'd first met at the college bookstore so long ago. An english class had first brought them together, and then two years of courtship. These memories flooded and threatened to drown him.

"Even now you harbor in memories of beginning Jare, but the river of time does not stop, not even for you, though I think you've tried."

The uplift in her voice, the small grain of impish delight he heard, confused him in his anguish. Was she trying to make him feel better?

Taking his hand, she pulled him upright and looked deep into his silver eyes, the moon a haunting echo of what she saw.

"Walk with me, Jare, for it is only while the dark reigns that I can manifest, and being with you now weighs heavily on all the times when I could not. I truly wish you could stall time, for I'd ask it of you now..."

The flow of the river was in the distance and its emerald sound churned at Jareth's emotions, wishing to carry him away. He felt the tug inside that wished the same, but a part of his mind would not relinquish complete control. He'd need his mandolin for that...or the muse.

"You know she doesn't like me, right?"

Candace's voice was small and petulant, though Jareth was at a loss for the reason.

"She has a part of you I never did, Jare, and you always did deny that fact."

Where had he left his strings? And his sword—it was missing from its sheath...had he actually left them both with the others? Word's startling revelation had caused that much confusion that he'd gone off without either? How unlike him...

"Not as much as you think, Jareth; that grain of selfishness you like to nurture always had this tendency, and much of life around you is forfeit. Its how we came to be."

"No one's perfect, Candace."

He felt as if his reply was a broken record, playing over and over in its groove, the same message repeated until he actually believed it.

"You're right, no one is. It's something you couldn't see in me, though, was it?"

Was that the truth of the matter? Had he come to need her as perfect and when she'd failed this test, he'd dismissed everything else?

There was a vibration now underfoot and as they walked off the path with Candace leading, he realized it was a sound that was growing. What was happening?

He picked his head up and as he attempted to swing his gaze past the ghost of his wife, her eyes caught him. Held tight, slowly he realized that her face was not as smooth as he remembered, not as young or beautiful. Held in thrall, he saw the lines of distress form, saw the opening of wounds break the porcelain of her skin and with a surge, rush upon her fragility with a vengeance.

The touch of her hand pulsed as if each was fracturing, and he feared for a moment that he'd lose her. Gripping tighter, he cried out that she should stop it, as if it were all her fault...all her fault.

But truth has a habit of sneaking up quite silently, and this time, Jareth was unprepared as the surge of memory lashed at his consciousness, full blown remembrance assaulting him viciously.

He saw images, flickering like an old world slide show on the silver beaded screen, and each picture twisted an unseen knife deeper.

He saw Candace lying on a metal table...much like the one he lay upon...and a dark shadow whose limb was uplifted, arching against an artificial ceiling of light where something in its hand gleamed. A sharpness accompanied both the reflection as well as his thoughts because at the same time, Candace cried out at his side when the shiny object descended. Again and again, each time his ears refused to close, the shadow railed at him to relent and forfeit his secrets...his secrets?

"You lived in a world of secrets, Jare; it was your world. More than anything you've ever known with your music and your fantasies, these were all too real and in the end, doomed us."

What was she talking about? As his confusion reared, he saw the cracks in her face spreading, felt her image beginning to loosen and fracture upon itself, as if the part were separating from the whole.

"That's what he wanted, Jareth, and when you refused to relent, he murdered me, Jare...he murdered me!"

The ground moved as if the skin of the earth was wrinkling. Leanan lifted her sword and bared her dagger, the Cervine stepped forward with a challenging bark to the moon, his antlers thrust back and then brought forward viciously. Tusk had a long broken branch in his hand that was twice as thick as his leg, and he raised it with a howl, inspired by the Cervine. While one good eye glittered pig-like at the horde before them, his other eye hung slack and listless, like always.

"In Mannanan's name, how are we to keep them from crossing?"

As the three ran toward the First Bridge, they saw the wild pig herd was already at the far bank.

"Can they swim?"

The Cervine's voice rumbled low like the crack of distant thunder. He rushed toward the stays, his own knife bared.

"I don't know, but it wouldn't hurt to find out."

"I'll attend to this side, you grab the other."

But even as they began to cut at the massive twists of hemp holding the bridge, the pigs rushed madly toward them, released to do what they'd been created to do.

"Can you call on the river? We could use its help!"

Leanan let her focus divide, one part still on the dagger and knot, the other on the song she needed to sing.

As her voice strung itself out, her fury mounted and the great tiger screamed the chorus. Still the pigs rushed forward, their number milling on the far side, pushing those in front with their ramped anxiety to cross.

The sound of fierce grunting was gradually overwhelmed by the rising wind and more—in the distance, a new chorus threatened to roll over them all. It was the river, clutched and grabbed as if by the nape of its neck. Leanan was throwing its full force at the bridge! It charged forward like stampeding cattle.

Almost too late, the Cervine reached forward and swept the muse off her feet, knocking the breath out of her. She hit the ground hard where he'd thrown her. The water came and raged until it hit the bridge with the force of a thousand hammers, taking any still upon it downstream. But many had gotten across and they didn't even flinch at the fate of their comrades, as if a sterner will directed their actions.

"There, on the other side, one who wears the paint of clowns, face marked with blood lines and mocking contempt. Do you see?"

Leanan gasped and refocused her gaze. And truly, there did seem to be a white nebulousness that her eyes could not define.

"Is that him?"

The Cervine nodded slowly even as his right hand swept back for one of the long, red feathered arrows. The pack of pigs that had gained their side gathered together, and suddenly filled with direction, turned bony-tusked mouths toward the trio. The tiger was nowhere in sight.

"Watch it—they've got our scent!"

But the Cervine was oblivious to the muse as he adjusted his aim.

Leanan swept her sword down nearly at his feet, the head of a wild pig bouncing against him as its still struggling body careered past. And then, the rest of the herd crashed into them. But not before the Cervine had freed his arrow.

The restless feeling beneath his feet grew more intense and Jareth knew it was getting nearer. He recoiled with distaste when his hand brushed the tree's bark, echoing his guess; something evil was heading toward them.

Candace had been murdered...but he already knew that, had suppressed the memory so far down inside him that even now upon her confirmation, he wouldn't receive its resonation and only nodded as the fact whimpered to life. Then mercilessly, he mentally stomped on its life, as if that would once and for all take care of it.

"You can't, Jare; to do so means you'll separate any link that still remains between us."

And she was right, as he was bracing himself to do what he had to do—again, her form was pulsing fainter and the touch of her hand less solid. It was then he realized it wasn't something he wanted to do without.

"Then hold onto me, Jare, hold on."

Her words summoned action and he pulled her diaphanous form into his arms, her pale light flickering stronger as more of his skin touched her veil of light. Embraced as if the dream had never been broken, Jareth began to weep, but in a way he hadn't ever done before. In a way he'd been incapable of.

"Come back to me, Jare, shadows are growing. The Hunter comes; can't you feel him? He's looking for you, trying to get to you, having failed with me. Jareth, if ever you needed to sing, it is now!"

It was like a dam, huge, solid, sturdy and structurally sound, and yet, he could feel its flaw. But he recoiled from reconciling with that fact and in doing so, heard Candace's voice grow more anxious. Why?

"They're coming and he's controlling them, Jareth. He comes with more knives and hurt, he's coming to claim you as he did me."

Something sharp and solid thumped hard at his heart, then at his mind, causing a searing lance of pain across his temple. He wanted to vomit and withdrew his spirit from Candace in an effort to thwart that idea.

"He's coming, Jareth. I need you...please, can you hear me? I'm calling your name!"

He heard her but she made no sense. He knew his name...and he was here; what else was she talking about?

"Jare—sing to me, as you once used to, as you once wanted to...sing me that song that likens us to two trees in the garden...please, Jareth, sing!"

The dam was so old and thick that the flaw was almost invisible but still, he located it. Funny, he'd never known of its existence before. Or did he, and had only been ignoring its place? It's place? Why would a flaw have a place? That would mean it had a purpose, too...

A song? Like he used to sing? Well, yes, he *had* sung to her—once. He'd been younger then, perhaps still in his early twenties, and it had been before they'd been married. Hadn't it? Had he sung afterward? Surely he had...but not often was a niggling thought that crept, suddenly noticed. He knew the bitter taste of that memory. Oh, why had he begun to remember at all? There was a peace in his ignorance...

He heard her voice, her plea, he also heard the rumbling sound of small hooves striking the ground, their din audible even though the forest floor tried to swallow it up in its anger at being so spoiled. The sound was growing louder, too...

"The song, Jare, the one about the two trees...please!"

He knew many songs, some were older than the written histories of men, having been passed down by the minstrels. By those called bards, masters of musical stories, their magic more powerful than the pen. So it was said, at least.

Yet, he knew the song. As her grip on him tightened, he reflexively returned it, feeling her curves beneath her robe, the light no longer an impediment to absorbing her presence. It was as if she were once again flesh and blood...

The mighty bow swept around and slammed against the pigs, brain matter spraying over the ground and the next wave of attackers. The Cervine hadn't seen his arrow's end flight as the muse had screamed his name in frustration. Almost too late, he realized that the pigs were morphing into wild boar, their teeth rasping against upper lips. Agonized grunts of hate bore witness of pain and delusion, when the bow was brought to bear. Far more than he'd thought had crossed the bridge and a sudden fear leapt to his throat.

"He's changed them—these are not what Jareth put here!"

Leanan hacked and swung with all her might, her golden eyes afire and her voice silenced; there was no time for her fury to manifest audibly. As the river beyond calmed, she could still see the rest of the herd, lost and grunting their confusion. What was the buck-head talking about?

"But did you get him?"

She forced the words out from between clenched teeth, the line of her dark lips like blood from a knife cut. She brought her sharp sword around and sliced the legs from three more boar that had surged too close. And then she understood; the pigs on the other side were smaller, different. These were full grown wild boar whose tusks were infinitely more dangerous.

"I didn't see, but since the change has stopped, it can be hoped he's at least not able to raise his voice against us."

The Cervine smashed a boar in the face with his bow and backhanded another with his massive fist, pig flesh turning to putty beneath his onslaught.

"Where's that tiger of yours?"

Leanan felt her blade bite solidly against the thrust of boar tusk. The jarring impact sent her sprawling as she was not about to lose the blade. As she slid, two boar lunged.

The Cervine was quicker and impaled one boar on the end of his bow, slinging the carcass away even as he rolled and kicked upward with pylons for feet, his hooves as dense as concrete. The second boar was sent skyward, its whole right side crushed in.

"I sent him to find Jareth."

The boar encircled the two, more wary now of the flashing blade in the woman's hand and the dark-as-night wood of the bow. Sight was not their strength—scent was—and within the crease of night in which they fought, their own fear was beginning to overpower their senses. It became more difficult to separate scents as neither the woman nor antlered creature exuded fear of any kind.

From behind the boar, there arose a bellow ludicrous in both its ferocity and tenor as the troll battered its way back to the muse and cervine. It's meaty stick was so splattered and blunt from pig brains, that Leanan wondered how it wasn't broken.

"Let's get to Tusk. Better to have three backs than two!"

And so saying, her voice rose to smite the sky, the beginning of a war song on her lips, something from which even those of the Hunt would shrink. As the moon arced toward the horizon, signaling dawn's imminence, the boar rushed again.

It was a song he hadn't sung for anyone, not in a long while, and he remembered it wasn't the type that audiences liked; it was a song laden with what he called layers of meaning, a song which told a tale on the surface, but relayed some profound truth beneath. One had to be listening to catch it the first time, much like reading a good poem...a good poem, aye, just like that...it was a song about two trees that grew so close to each other that they wound their growth around the other, their branches clinging and vining until it was hard to distinguish one tree from the other. It was a tale of love, of two that were one.

His voice arched up as if a seedling having found good light, shedding its husk and extending an arm toward the sun. At the same time, his words threw down tendrils of intersection, a lattice forming of fingered meaning, gripping the substrate much as tree roots, but more—these roots could move. He sent them deep with each note emanating from his throat, the feel of Candace's skin cool on his, her breath which had once been trembling and rapid, now easing, now slowing, as if in cadence to his melody.

He sang of two seeds, sprung from a rich garden soil, their combined purpose to reach the canopy above, and life. Only in the light could they live, and as seedlings of the earth, it was an inheritance. Jareth sang of sapling strength, of willowy and flexible stems, of the capillary flow of sap running from root to leaf tip. He sung of expansion, a living growth that thrust them together...

Two stems that wind and kissed the glade,
their limbs and leaves a living glow;
one reaches out and twines the same,
the other bends and tendrils flow.

Two spent in soil, two reached for sun,
two bound with toil, when there was none

one branch is hers, the other his
one leaf to bud another furling true,
embracing interleaving trysts
that which spoke when days were through.

Two spent in soil, two reached for sun;
two bound with toil, when there was none.

Two spent in soil, two reached for sun,
two bound with toil, when there was none.

In gardens they began rebirth,
they tapped the river of the earth.

The glow of blue white light about Candace flared around them both as Jareth sang. His voice was like the cradle of the stars, the music alone challenging the beauty of the stream nearby, so melodic and fluid were the chords. He was telling a story, and the music came only from his words, hesitant at first, but growing stronger as he continued. Candace pressed herself tightly against

Jareth as if trying to imbue him with her light. Or absorb the beauty of his voice.

Either way, when the horde of pigs broke through the underbrush and swept toward them, there was only two twining trees, their limbs wrapped more tightly than vines on a fence, their bark electric with light and trunks stretching skyward toward an invisible sun. Or perhaps it was the moon—a lover's moon. The grunts and squeals added to the herd's crescendo of noise until finally they passed, working their way mindlessly deeper into the forest. Long after they passed, all that could be seen was churned earth, except for one place where the wan moonlight showed something living had been. But of Jareth and Candace, nothing could be seen.

Like the minstrel and muse, Word's touch did not cause Beryl's tattoos to move when he held her hand, as if there was an innate trust between the other's fingers and the ink. It was as if such could not touch the boy called Word.

"Where are we going?"

She looked down at the youngster, the moonlight dappling them both with patterns formed by the trees overhead. Much to Beryl's delight, the black cat snuggled on her shoulder with claws dug into her cloak for support. They'd left the place of song (or so Word had called it for lack of a better name) and were slowly descending toward the forest's floor by connecting rope and plank bridges. Each was smaller than the next, like streams feeding a larger river until it reached the ocean. She thought they made a strange pair—her height and long dark hair against his short stature and frenzy of freckles. The surreality of it all was acute.

"I'm taking you to the heart of the forest; you'll be safe there. At least for a while. I sense though that everything is changing and not even the trees will go untouched. The Hunter is getting a grip on Jareth's mind. That means he's going to be able to create scenarios even the Bard hasn't seen before."

"Are the others going to meet us?"

"They've gone to find Jareth first. Tusk will show them the way back."

The bark beneath their feet was just as smooth as the back of her hand, and looking at her palm in conjunction with the broad branch they were traversing, she saw more similarities.

"They're alive, aren't they? And I don't mean in a living plant type way."

The boy turned his face toward the girl, the meager light by which they steered emanating from his skin, in contrast to how the ink upon hers was wont to gather shadows. It was as if the boy were her opposite.

"You live in the woods?"

The thought was alien to her; people lived in houses, in towns and cities, in communities where they could support each other...she caught the thread of her thought and stopped, the irony slow to engulf. Not everyone supported everyone else, and it was indeed like she lived alone.

The boy ignored her queries, preferring to let Beryl work out the riddle for herself.

"Can I see it?"

His question caught her off guard. See what?

"Why, the jewel of course; it's the reason your people sent you away, isn't it?"

Beryl was confounded. She hadn't spoken of it to anyone, not Leanan nor Jareth even, and they'd been the ones who'd taken her in and promised help. The Cervine had seen it, though he hadn't said anything, just a quick wink when it had inadvertently escaped from beneath her blouse. Even among her own, the others had only thought it a trinket, worthless—just like herself. When one boy named Herzekel had palmed it when trying to take it from her, he'd been given a nasty shock. She still remembered that day, and the fact that he and the others had marked her all the more for possessing such a horrid stone.

But she liked it well enough; its deep crimson color and smooth surface reminded her of a heart, as if something inside flared and beat. She liked to think that's what had shocked Herzekel. Against her skin though, it lay peacefully, dormant even. In times of stress, she'd finger the jewel and its touch sometimes lessened her anxiety.

The fact the boy knew of it lowered her guard, and before she knew, she was pulling the small round stone out from beneath her clothing, the dull chain wrapped about her neck.

With small but nimble fingers, Word rolled the stone in his palm, then between forefinger and thumb, his eyes intent on the way the stone glimmered beneath his touch. When Beryl saw this, she gasped in surprise, half expecting the boy to feel the sting of its shock. The fact the gem wasn't solidly opaque hadn't ever been known to her. It had always been red but now, it pulsed with light, in the way she imagined a heart did.

"You better keep that hidden; now is not the time to waken it."

Word's words did not mean much to the girl and she returned the stone in confusion.

"It is very valuable, you know."

Surprised to think the boy thought the same as she, Beryl turned and looked appraisingly. Could he also know the reason?

"Because you and it are one, it's your namesake."

The boy's explanation was as stunning as the fact she just realized she hadn't spoken aloud. And still, he'd heard!

"Shhh, it will be our secret, okay?"

The boy grinned with mirth and taking her hand, propelled them off one branch and onto a another. They were nearing the ground now.

As he hustled them forward, the girl was still reappraising the youngster, while stowing down deep the real reason she thought the stone so valuable; while it was true, she was named after the stone, it was the fact it had been given to her by her father that mattered most, a father about whom she hardly remembered anything.

The carnage was all about them, the boar intent on either getting to their prey or dying while trying. Leanan's leather armor was saturated in pig blood and the smell repulsed her. Catching her breath as they waited for another rush, the Cervine was busy wiping his knife against the ground, several gashes on his legs and arms still oozing. Still, they'd given a good account of themselves and working together, had fended off each brutal attack. Leanan was keenly aware she was within the trees and very far from water.

"Then we'd see how long this brood of devil swine would last; I'd pull the very sky down on them, if these damn trees weren't in the way!"

"Be at peace with the forest, Sidhe. If you haven't noticed, unlike the four-legged leeches that chased us this way initially, these boar when slain don't get back up. You can thank the trees for that!"

And when she looked beyond the circle of boar, the flesh of the dead was gone, and all that was left were white stick-like bones that might have been roots gone wild. Come to think of it, there *had* seemed more on this side of the bridge than she'd thought; had they been replicating like the leeches? As if someone were manipulating death by either whim or scene.

"The trees did that?"

She still looked dubious, but when Tusk bobbed his head in affirmation, she gave the hulking troll a swift smile. Perhaps she'd been too hasty.

"Always was a flaw of your kind."

Leanan bristled at the Cervine's comment.

"Keep quiet, Buckface; it's my kind that gives meaning to the night, and to life! There isn't any flaw to immortality!"

The Cervine just chuckled and shook his mighty antlers.

"I see the Bard isn't the only one who's forgetful. I think Jareth's already taught you that one, if I remember correctly!"

Leanan shot him a venomous glance, wondering what he knew that he shouldn't.

The boar sounded their grunting squeal that signified another charge, diverting the squabble. The bow swung high and crashed down low, a mirror to the muse's flashing longsword and a shadow of the troll's big stick.

Sometimes the speed at which everything happened in this world caught Rhey by surprise; the bridge episode was one of these, leaving him with more than half his pig army on the wrong side. That said, he knew enough now that he could reassemble props as he may, providing the physical aspects allowed him. Upon seeing the two giants—the stag with a man's torso and the green skinned troll, he altered his antagonists and made them more lethal, their stubby legs more muscular and their jaws more fierce. Pigs turned into warthogs. From the far side of the bridge, Rhey threw those that had crossed against the combatants.

His focus was suddenly shattered as the force of an arrow pierced his left breast, exactly where a human heart would have been. But Rhey was not human, and though it caused a burning pain, he staggered back out of sight and continued his assault, trying to work out exactly where Jareth was in the melee.

The man was missing, and the moment he was sure of this, he sent a regiment of pigs to scour the woods, sure that some clue at least would be found. When they returned with only hints of his scent, Rhey's countenance darkened in annoyance; how could something so simple be this complex? He had the basic pattern of his prey, it was only a matter of correlating the data. The pigs should have sent the man to ground, or up the proverbial tree. Still, there was a trail to follow, and affixing the idea of keeping Martin's protectors busy on the boar across the river, Rhey faded into the underbrush, pushing the pigs ahead of him. He was intent on finishing this once and for all. Time wasn't exactly on his side and he was fooling himself to stay within the man's confines.

The snuffling, grunting, and shuffling of pigs stretched in a line to the north, their track easy to follow. Persistent and annoying, the trees leaned, lowering branches that slowed his progress. He had to belligerently force a path whereas the pigs scurried easily beneath the limbs. He crested a rise, and with the river gurgling behind him, heard the sound of battle behind like a distant storm. The man had to be close, his familiarity becoming as tangible as the smells of bubbling beakers over a flame, just on the horizon of his consciousness.

It was then that two events happened simultaneously, timed so exquisitely precise as to not allow him any choice. The first was the strange unraveling feeling of soil beneath his feet, as if a coil was being unwound and with it, vibrations were being sent in its wake. The second was no less surprising but much more visceral as the breath was viciously knocked out of him. His whole body was thrust hard to the resonating earth. In the split second consciousness was still allotted to him, he heard the angry scream of the predator which had borne him earthward, and with even less time, he saw the long saber-like teeth of a huge white tiger as it lunged for his neck, tongue tight against drooling black gums!

Leanan backhanded yet another boar, its heart bursting, sliming her blade even more. But she was slowing and her arm strength was failing. This time, the boar almost made it to her heeled boots before it died. With her left hand, she stabbed with her blade at an angle, missing the second boar as it leaped toward her back.

In a single thrust, the Cervine drove an arrow through the leaping boar and continuing his line of force, whipped the dying porcine into the river's grasp where the body began to steam and sear, so heated had the water become. Such was the muse's fury that even the stream was infused with scorching battle.

Grunting her thanks as an afterthought, Leanan twisted and once again, faced the reckless horde as another regroup began. The troll was limping and she could see it had multiple wounds, though if what oozed was blood, it was a color she hadn't seen before.

"You all right?"

The Cervine was breathing heavily, and leaning on his bow more often between rushes. His knife was whetted so much that the metal could hardly be seen for all the gore attached. He reached out and pulled the troll closer so their circle was tight and the gaps small. He looked to the east and wondered if the dawn would arrive before more pigs did.

The muse didn't answer, figuring her upright posture said it all. They were alive and that was enough.

"Did you feel it?"

This time she turned and glanced quickly at the Cervine.

"The song?"

Her eyes glazed over a moment as if she'd gone inside herself, a vision of a different kind being accessed.

"I know he's still alive, if that's what you mean."

"No, I mean more; he's sung."

And at these words, her eyes widened to show great opals ringed with fiery halos, her brows rising in accompaniment.

"I would have heard it."

"Not this time, he wasn't singing for you."

Leanan's face was stony for a moment before a flush of color rose that she ruthlessly killed the moment it reached her cheeks. A grim smile showed her sharp teeth.

"That's impossible; she's dead."

The Cervine's lips spread in a mock grin.

"Seems you still have some things to learn about mortals, Sidhe."

Then the sound of consternation rose from the boar still alive on their side of the river. In the distance, doubt and confusion was spreading, as if the mind of the pig herd was linked.

"Something is happening. Look!"

"Jareth?"

Leanan's query was more whisper than anything, and it was fraught with an unusual fear.

The Cervine shook his head.

"I don't think so...the herd, it's no longer united. The link between them has been severed. I felt something similar but not so sure, right after I released my earlier arrow. If I'm not mistaken, I think the Hunter has left."

"Left? Without being dead? Can that be?"

But even as she voiced her concern, she too saw the herd milling in growing confusion, some even beginning to wander away. With the bridge out though, Leanan wondered where they'd end up. She glanced across the water and saw much the same; many had already left, and those still there looked back at her with an absence of malice, as if they too questioned what they were doing.

"Come, help me with Tusk; seems his leg will need some mending. Know the right song? Never mind, I'll do it."

And placing a calming hand on the troll, with eyes conveying nothing but trust, the Cervine's lips quivered. A deep rolling rumble of sound began to reverberate against the nearby trunks, the echo cascading back upon itself and doubling in potency. With a soft touch, both the hands and music of the Cervine brought much healing to the battlefield and its victors.

"We better find Jareth and get to Word and the girl. No telling how long this luck will last."

The muse was wiping her blade in the lapping water of the stream, her hair askew and just beginning to glow golden as dawn peeped over the horizon.

"Aye; it would seem we have a reprieve but it won't be long before the Hunter takes up the trail again."

"You think this was Jareth's doing."

It was more statement than question, but the Cervine shook his head at Leanan's words.

"Nay, he surely sang, but the chorus I heard within the soil was one of protection and defense, a tune that was as utterly innocent of purpose as the girl. Nay, if he'd truly sung and been heard, the boar would be no more."

And realizing how right the Cervine was, Leanan folded back into introspection, wondering what this new development might mean.

"I think it means Jareth is waking, but to what and for what, well, we'll just have to watch as the scene unfolds. I just hope he's the one in charge of turning the pages and not the other. If not him, I fear not all of us will see the end of this journey."

The Cervine's troubling words fell on the first fingers of morning gleefully, as they scattered the shadows which night had left behind to fend for themselves.

How ironic, Leanan thought.

Chapter 45

All Along the Watchtower

'There must be some way out of here, said the joker to the thief...'

The tinny sound of music rattled from a small box sitting next to an old radio system. The voice was both deep and gravely, and the sound particularly annoyed Rhey, so he touched the small box again and another song began playing. So, silencing the device wouldn't be easy either...at least this next song was less grating.

And yet, as his sunken eyes retraced the lines of Martin's anteroom for the third time, that first lyric stuck in his head, running over itself again and again. There was irony in what he was hearing, though his labeling would conflict with the artist's, perhaps even Martin's. He did not think of himself as the thief for breaking into humanity's house, and if others saw him as a joker, well, the last laugh would be his.

He'd been so close, so tantalizingly close, until the muse's tiger had triggered his failsafe. The dim glow of the laboratory was harsh as his mind readjusted, having just come from a night of moon and little starlight. Ripping the wires from his temple, the streaks of blood that oozed onto the floor would be a grim reminder of how lethal Martin's pseudo world could be. The very fact his body could be touched physically both surprised and intrigued him; it was a facet of world-building that might be exploited, if he was better prepared next time.

The sound of singing emanated from two smaller boxes attached to the ceiling, the air in front exhorted into making the prescribed melodies. Rhey gave the two speaker cubes a thoughtful glance before lifting up an emaciated arm, and ripping one from its mooring. That halved the problem, at least.

And after the other box was similarly disabled, Rhey pondered more than the tiger's attack, able to do so now that the rents and punctures in his skin had closed. Not that much flesh was still covering him, but enough to still move around. Soon though, too soon, he'd be bound to the chair as the virus was doing what such entities did; spread and eat the host until it died due to lack of food. Currently, he was the food, but his near success in getting at Jareth, at Martin's alter ego, had shown him it could be done. He'd only been experimenting before...but not next time.

He read the sides of clear cases enclosing silver discs; more music he supposed. The titles meant nothing to him, though he noted a similarity with Dylan the author and Dylan the singer. Maybe there was a meaning here...

There *were* clues—all he needed to do was put them together. The fact someone else had been in the room since he was here last, wasn't forgotten either. As he prowled about the small room, he noticed crumbs on the floor. He'd need to realign the cameras as nothing had been recorded from this angle. Another detail to take care of...

The thin slivers of bone making up his three fingered hand gripped a large handle on the man-high white box against the wall. His initial pull encountered resistance. What?

Pulling harder though, the large door opened toward him and cool air rushed to fill the voids made by the tiger and virus; he couldn't keep it open long; the air's touch was like that of a serrated knife. But he'd seen enough; there was food inside, boxes and glass jars, green and red colors, though overall, the inside looked more empty than full. With all the destruction he'd wrought outside the government building, with all the remnants of humanity crawling and scrounging to survive both hunger and his bots, here was a feast that seemed incongruous at best. He let the door go and it was pulled magically back upon itself, the sound of contact surprisingly firm. The same sort of hold I have on you, Martin. He mused while moving back into the larger room where the scientist's books still hugged one entire wall. A small electric chiming began as he noticed that the book order seemed different from the last time he was here.

But the alert was what he'd been waiting for, and casting a swift glance about the room, as if his intuition could scatter more than just shadows, he exited the anteroom, taking care to lock it this time. Whatever was eating the food and rearranging the books, wasn't going to get out this time.

He reached the sliding door of an elevator, and pressing the smooth metal button, staggered into the small box. Then he touched a similar button inside. There wasn't time now for dealing with intruders, not with Martin's ability to avoid him demanding his attention. Whereas the tiger's attack had had a greater immediate effect on the situation, it was the other event which preoccupied his mind; the feel of unraveling soil beneath his feet. There was something about it that nagged at him, something familiar...eating at him.

And was that the problem? That his mind was being eaten along with his body? Hadn't he taken enough drugs to stave off that final effect? At least temporarily? At moments of doubt like this, he immediately began reciting mathematical formulae in his head, working to swift theoretical ends and confirming that he still was in possession of his mind. For now.

The unraveling surge was something that needed analyzing, and he hoped to feed the log of events into a specific program already prepared. But it would take precious cycles away from cracking the DNA code, even if up to this point, Martin

Hennessy's creation resisted. Brute force would find him the answer, but time wasn't going to help him, hence he really needed to re-enter Martin's world and finally corner the minstrel-warrior. He knew about the tiger now—there'd be no more surprises from that corner.

That Martin had created a protection program hadn't surprised him, it was only the means by which he was operating it; there were some expected characterizations in the muse, in the creature called the Cervine, even with the troll. The boy character 'Word' though, was a wild card.

On the surface, the boy posed no threat whatsoever, but even as he had tried to locate Jareth within the trees near the pulsing fountain, a subtle interference had commenced, like low-level noise in a digital photograph. It was there, could be identified—not from what it was, but from what it wasn't; unlike pattern noise from a sensor, this manifested from something similar to black-frame subtraction.

The boy was there, but it took a mathematical calculation to prove it, as opposed to the pixels that never ceased to run rampant on the monitors. Whereas Martin was running the story lines together—with basic elements lining up according to some humanistic standard—with Word, that was a physical impossibility. It was as if that character was an insertion by another user.

Another user...the memory of the anteroom intruder crossed his mind again.

So, two variables that still needed to be accounted for, and this time he'd be prepared. Re-attaching the wires to his head, Rhey took a somber glass of oily liquid off the lab bench where it had been cooling. The other possible variants still warmed slowly, their progress monitored by probes and sensors. He did have a stronger version cooking but he didn't want to wait...

Without taste buds, the elixir slid down his throat easily, soothing it. He opened his mouth to call out to an external sensor-monitor, but found he could only croak; seems the tiger had done more than just send him back, it had also altered his vocal cords. No matter, he wasn't going to do much talking anyhow.

The words of text, which had been coming in a steady stream, now doubled their speed as Rhey flowed back into the story to reclaim his joker-like appearance. A fleeting thought that maybe the Dylan character's line about thieves and jokers might be a foreshadowing, lingered on the edge of his ingress. But that would be too much like human-thought, he surmised, and let the moment go. There was too much to do...

The lines and dots of fluorescence blinked mechanically, their range of color and pattern of light pre-determined. The monitors overhead were mostly devoid of movement and all were in black and white, their silent electronic eyes faithfully recording whatever passed before them. Those on the exterior showed a hanging cloud of darkness, signaling the earth's evolving destruction.

But the cameras inside were just the opposite as each room and hall was still lit by the building's backup power plant in the basement. The lights flickered sometimes, as fluorescent fixtures often will, but the shadows were brief; all except in one room, where the lanky form of a young girl could be plainly seen slipping from a hidden passageway near a bookshelf, flitting just out of the light, and cloaking her identity in enough shadow such that even if anyone *had* been paying attention, no detail was exposed. Then once again, the cameras showed only stillness.

Chapter 46

Nobody's Home

The trees were like those ringing the Meadow, the same fan-tail purple leaflets that here, were in full bloom. The glade was filled and if Jareth hadn't been preoccupied, he'd have seen that for a while now, the path had been lined with the strange ginkgoes. But he hadn't paid attention, had merely thanked the Cervine for keeping good care of his sword and mandolin, and fallen in with the others as Tusk padded barefoot between the trees, his clumsy touch hardly so between the trunks. The forest was swallowing them with a magic all its own.

"I heard you, Jareth; have you reclaimed what is yours?"

But the Cervine's words didn't mean much to the minstrel and he merely shrugged, conveying only that he didn't want to talk. When Leanan tried to slip alongside and accidentally on purpose let her skin touch his in secret places, he withdrew further, not trusting his emotions any more than his mind.

"Did you uncover your guth, my love? Is it time yet?"

His eyes weren't focussed and as he looked toward the muse, her words a muddle to his mind, she saw he wasn't going to let her in. She relented, which for her was an unusual occurrence. She'd taken the time to pull her long hair into a pony tail and its bobbing was accentuated by the white shock running through it. When Jareth wouldn't treat with her, she crooned softly for the tiger and it silently fell in beside her.

Leanan's black nails dug into the weave of black striped fur as if the two were one.

Tusk was talking to himself, counting.

"We're meeting up with Word?"

The Cervine's words nudged gently into the troll's mind, disrupting concentration. Tusk had to start again.

"The One will be there, yes, he'll be there. Must count—many trees and they all look the same. Look for purple, look for its glow—that's what he says. Guideposts for the One. Follow, you follow Tusk; he'll see you safe—that's what master says, yes, Tusk brings you safe."

The Cervine left the troll alone now that their destination was confirmed. He still held his bow even as his large ears and nose combed through the various markers the wind and air brought him. His antlers deftly slipped through the low-hanging boughs as the troll led the way; both were being shown deference by the Forest.

Leanan, on the other hand, was constantly irritated by the branches that swept her way. If the Cervine hadn't warned her against taking steel to limb, she'd already have been hacking joyfully at their impudence. As it was, she tried to keep close to Jareth because without any visible sign, the man wasn't touched by anything.

He might not even be in contact with earth at the moment, she pondered, understanding the look on his face even if she didn't like it. It wasn't right; she was his muse, it was she who gave him his inspiration, it was she that fueled his flame...

Well, she and the other. Glancing sharply around, she wondered if the light of day filtering beneath the canopy was enough to keep the dancing light from forming. It seemed so.

Jareth's mind was whirling as he tried to make sense of last night, for all that had happened, and that which hadn't.

I cannot come into the light, Jareth.

Candace had impressed the depth of this truth upon him, even as the night waned. The wild pigs had passed by as if the two of them hadn't existed.

Nay, Jare; we still exist, but to them, we are not the same. I daresay, you should know what your song can do, how it can warp the very air.

And he did know, but not like that; before, he'd always been a central point, woven within the seduction of his song. He knew the music moved hearts and nudged minds.

When you weave your soul into the music, transformation happens.

It was a concept he could understand, even if he'd suspended belief. A song could do wondrous things for an audience, but other than move the emotions, any lasting effect was dependent on a soul's emptiness. Then, and only then, did it seem his song could be more than it was.

And some minstrels can't even do that, dear. What you just did was to change the fabric of the world around you; you needed to be invisible and using your voice, you created that.

Truth to tell, he *had* felt the song on a more personal note, had known its melody as different, more intimate. But he'd associated the new feeling with Candace's presence. It had been their song, once, and maybe the memories hiding inside the chords had been allowed to live again? Briefly?

"The boy mentioned our daughter..."

Yes, I did too, but you weren't being receptive at the time; have things changed?

There was the hint of stain in his cup, as if the wine had been sullied by water droplets.

"Have I lost her, too?"

Candace's face was glowing dimly, her form beginning to fray about the edges as dawn moved on slippered feet.

He felt her drawing breath, as if his hand was still around her back, wrapping and melding their beings. He thought he could feel it, and a sigh escaped.

Time will tell, Jareth, but I can say only that for now, she is lost. I fear though that if you find her too soon, she'll lose her hiding spot and be destroyed.

Destroyed like you?

Candace nodded solemnly.

The light about her feet was dimming and it was hard to distinguish toes from the tree roots around him. His heart lurched and he blurted the words before he could stop them.

"You can't come with me?"

It was a plea he'd been wishing to utter ever since their first meeting beneath the ground. The small boy in him felt so very lost.

I am always with you, Jareth; but in the daylight, a shade cannot walk. Only at night is your memory strong enough to clad me thus. But be warned; we're not supposed to seek the darkness voluntarily.

He looked at the glimmer-glow of her face, the long lashes and deep eyes, her full cheeks and slightly parted lips...and night faded faster than he desired.

Be at peace with this; there once was a time you didn't think of me at all...

He felt only an emptiness, and that she was lost inside it, that peace was more elusive than anything he'd ever known.

Lost in his thoughts, he didn't even realize that the boy and the girl were in the center of the glade, waiting.

Chapter 47

Lowlands

"It's begun."

Word uttered the words even as they emerged from the protection of the forest where once again, the strange purple-leafed ginkgo stood guard. For someone that claimed neither home nor permanence, Jareth felt an odd disquiet overcome him, and he choked back a sigh, keenly feeling it would be better to stay. Leanan stood next to him, her bare arm brushing his, darkening the tattoo adorning his wrist, as if blood was once again oozing forth. Her countenance was starkly defiant as they gazed upon a land that should have been rolling hills, and beyond, a last house where Eli was supposed to dwell. But that's not what any of them saw at the moment, as trailing twists of re-rod and wasted steel merged with chunks of fallen concrete, mixed with shards of brick. It was as if a great modern city had fallen forward and scattered itself over the countryside.

The boy's prophetic words came back to the man and he shuddered, not expecting this at all.

"Where are the hills?"

Beryl's voice was tentative and wary, as if the small bit of trust she'd since found was now being proved wrong. There were supposed to be hills past the Forest and Meadow.

What looked like the beginnings of a road peeked out from the shifting red sands. They'd emerged from the forest world with the landscape and weather having changed drastically. They were forced to shield their faces from the flying debris and the setting sun; more than sand lurked ahead, cloaked in red.

Jareth tried to penetrate the broken ruins, trying to see past the immediate obstacle. And when he did, the sward of green grass and half-erupted hillsides merged with what had been fractured buildings. Even the road now seemed less flat and straight; rocks poked up like nubs of teeth. What the hell?

"Are you looking for the world you conceived, Jareth?"

The last stretch of forest passed beneath their feet, and as they strode forward, Jareth saw the boy's face wrinkle, as if the freckles were shifting along with the landscape. And gone too was any hint of life, giving way to a flatness that scared him.

He nodded absently, hearing the words, but the changes demanded his attention.

Word turned widened eyes toward the man, and reaching forward, took both of Jareth's hands. Leanan wondered what the boy was about, her suspicious nature waxing. The Cervine stood tall against the shadow of the forest, the setting sun limning his antlers. He stood as if encased by fire. Beryl's indrawn breath was evidence that she saw it too.

Tusk stood sullen and silent, both eyes out of sorts, as if someone had just powered him down. Sitting woodenly on its haunches, the tiger gazed at the muse, knowing instinctively that it was to rise and protect. And yet, it was as if the giant cat was caught beneath a huge umbrella of lethargy.

"A clash of wills, the struggle for imagination."

It was an ominous statement from the boy and Jareth wondered if everyone with which he surrounded himself, were always so cryptic.

"It looks like a war was fought."

Jareth amended his query as Beryl spoke. She at least spoke plainly; it looked precisely like she said. But the damage was far surpassing anything done by mechanical wizardry such as trebuchets. It simply looked like the sky had fallen and taken everything standing with it. Surely the hills and trees must still exist beyond his sight. Jareth felt the boy's hand slip into his.

"Unless they've been clear cut and the land turned to pasture, Jareth."

The Cervine had finally spoken, pursuing the man's thoughts.

"The Hunter has learned how to manipulate what you've created, Jareth Rhylan, and will lean harder on you as you go forward. So far, you've seen the world as you imagined, but now, the crossroad comes and you'll have to navigate against what he wills to be."

The boy's face regained much of its youthfulness the longer their hands touched. Word, boy of the woods, was solid, was the same who lived high among the trees and yet kept watch over the forest floor as well. He was kin to the Cervine and their purposes intertwined.

All this flooded in as Jareth forced the scene to align with what he remembered. And even in that, there was irony.

What you chose to forget, and what is forced to be forgotten, Jareth, are two very different things.

Why the Cervine chose to speak only to his mind was a question Jareth longed to ask, but dared not. Still, when the great stag of a man spoke in this way, it meant he should pay attention.

"Can't we go around?"

Jareth heard Leanan and wholeheartedly supported her suggestion.

"I dare to think the Hunter can shorten the boundaries, Jareth; I fear no matter which way you go, you'll be opposed. Even a bard has limits."

They all peered east where the landscape was nothing but torn and cluttered.

Leanan turned to Jareth, her eyes mere slits of simmering golden flame.

"So we'll fight fire with fire, aye?"

If her smile hadn't been so hackneyed and her visage so glowering, Jareth would have merely rolled his eyes; did the muse always think walking into conflict was the best solution?

You know I'm right—don't dare deny it!

He shut his mind down before she could eavesdrop further.

You know, Jareth, she's not always wrong despite her impetuous nature...

He closed off the Cervine too, not even wishing to catch the other's eyes for what he might read there. There was a growing pressure and he felt the inclination to back away.

"If we're going to do this, let's get on with it; we need to get to Eli, and if it means we have to go through this, we will. Haven't come all this way to be thwarted now."

Surprised at his words, Jareth lapsed into an uneasy acceptance. Against his back, snug inside the pack, Piper's purr was deeper than usual. The mandolin's bowl rubbed against the skin of his bare back, the strings silent with promise. With regret lurking around every broken column and busted railing, his thoughts kept returning to the boy, and the fact he wouldn't be going with them. He could leave the girl in the youth's hands—Word would keep Beryl safe and he felt embarrassed to think he could do the job half as well. The fact he considered this a job was actually an improvement from how the adventure had begun. At least, the muse liked to remind him of that.

But no, as the road cobbles swiftly turned into slabs of canted gray stone and then to concrete, they left Tusk and the boy at the edge of the ruins, knowing they were leaving safety. Now, they had to depend on each other. Jareth glanced sideways and traced the form of the muse, her lustrous hair pulled back and bound by silver filigree, braided once again as if for war. The white shock wound throughout and muted the faint blue glow Leanan liked to affect. She strode beside him, lips pressed tight and eyes ranging skyward, as if seeing something he couldn't.

The tiger prowled to her left, taking time to occasionally sniff at the broken remains, as if a scent lingered to tell a history they would be better off knowing. In the failing light, the large cat's coat glimmered like a wraith, while its stripes hovered like shadow cracks, both a lure and a warning to stay away. It's eyes burned brightly, more so since the sun had set. Why were they doing this at night again?

The Hunter won't expect this, Jareth; his knowledge of humans tells him that you'd rest, that you'd wait till day, and then work a way around his trap, for a trap this surely is; still think this is the best way?

Like a hand on his shoulder, he felt the muse's words, understood her doubt and shared her misgivings. But the inner voice telling him to use the night hadn't ceased; perhaps it would provide a cloak of invisibility he surely missed. Invisibility? Now, when had he ever had that talent? And why had he needed it?

Not invisibility as much as the ability to hide, Jare; not your best artistic trait and if you'll remember, it shows up a lot in your songs, and more so in the lines between your poetry.

My poetry? I can write that?

Oh, more than you remember, obviously. Believe it or not, that's where your bardic voice works best and strongest. I am still waiting for you to rediscover that fact. And then? Well, I wouldn't want to be the enemy at that moment...

Leanan's voice trailed off as he turned the words over in his mind, beginning the process of getting lost. At the moment, he didn't have a lot of faith in his music doing anymore than it always did; sharpen the points of his pain so he could release them and move past. Songs were like shallows of the pond and poems its undercurrent; however he threw his stone, it had better ripple true or else they were all lost.

The muse glanced sharply at her artist, a smile glimmering. But as she felt him withdraw, she too understood the resonance of what she'd said and how its effect might not turn out as she hoped. The tiger opened its mouth and exposed long, starkly white fangs with a huge yawn that wasn't. If silence hadn't been pressed upon it, she knew the huge cat would have sent a challenge into the night. And the irony was, she'd have done it first if she'd been able. With the brooding artist on her right, she nudged the tiger out front to scout their way; night wouldn't bother such a hunter. Also, it would allow her to fall into the melancholy Jareth was stirring.

Night fell and the voices of the Cervine and Beryl behind, muted with the growing mist.

"But why do we have to travel at night? Aren't you afraid we're going to get lost? I heard Jareth say he didn't know this land—that it was changed, despite memories of how it should be."

The girl walked in front of the tall Cervidae, but had eyes for the man and woman who'd somehow been assigned as her guardians, though neither seemed to originally want the job.

And is that what she'd become? A duty?

She saw how Leanan's height only enhanced the way she held her body poised, more regal than any queen she'd ever seen.

"Jareth says it will be to our advantage and I think he's correct. The Hunter is stronger now after failing to keep his hold on Jareth's creative lattice, though I fear it was merely a first attempt. How Jareth remembers it should be, that is key. If he can recall and recreate, the enemy will have more than one focus. It's said there can only be one cook in the kitchen..."

Beryl looked back and caught a flicker of warm green in the stag-man's eyes as his gaze locked on hers, his nostrils flared for what might lie ahead. The thought tickled her fancy and she giggled, which snapped the Cervine's attention back. She placed a slim hand to her mouth and turned around.

They walked for a while in silence, letting the moon light their way, avoiding the dark places on the road. When a bed of stars opened before them, they hesitated before Leanan announced it safe. Ahead, the remains of broken glass from one of the shattered structures shadowing their path glittered. Navigating around was more complicated because at odd intervals, the ruins were interrupted by misshapen trees. A waterfall that looked to be coming from the window of a fallen building, pooled across the road. It wasn't deep however, and they passed easily. Sometimes, there was a normally shaped tree, as if the forest was trying to re-establish itself despite the destruction and perversion.

The Cervine shook his head when this happened because even he could see that the damaged city was far younger than the upstart tree; a wild mix of two worlds, or two imaginations, was loose. If there was an end to this war though, he couldn't imagine what form it would take. The girl was droning on, asking her questions again; was this one of the reasons her people defiled her with marks of ink? She could be intensely curious sometimes...

"She's awfully pretty, isn't she?"

The Cervine's thoughts were jarred back as he couldn't place her question in the right context.

"Who's awfully pretty?"

She turned and gave him a smirk of amusement, the twinkle of precociousness lighting her face.

"Why the Lady, of course."

The Lady? Had Jareth been telling tales again? No one called her that except him, and that because he'd not known her name the first time they'd met.

"I heard Jareth call her that and thought it fit most appropriately. Well?"

The Cervine faced the back of the girl's head, noting how the long tresses were exposed now, as opposed to her usual habit of piling her hair up on her head and beneath a hood. For some reason, Beryl was loosening up.

"Well what?"

The girl did have a way of making your skin itch.

"Isn't she pretty?"

The Cervine grunted first before figuring she wasn't going to let the night have its silent way.

"I think the word you want is exotic."

Beryl slipped around a long dark shadow in the road that turned out to be a lamp post, the glass housing littering the concrete like diamonds. It wasn't something of which she knew personally, only from the stories those from the South brought; there, all manner of magical things existed, if one could believe even half the tales.

"Exotic...I like that; you're right. She reminds me of the fabled sirens that lured Odysseus."

The Cervine nodded his head, wondering how much of the truth she knew.

"She does have their voice, but she belongs to a different kind of Fae."

"Fey? You mean she knows the moment of her death? I have heard of those people, again from the Old Stories."

But here the buck head shook slowly and eyes darkened.

"Nay, not fey but Fae, as in those of the Faerie; her kind are part of a mystery few dredge from history. She belongs to another time; it's only she who denies this fact."

"And Jareth too, I'd guess." Beryl's voice lowered as she contemplated the couple walking in front of her.

The Cervine reluctantly nodded affirmation, as if mere hesitation could change the facts.

"They seem to fight a lot, don't they; are they married?"

A snort caused them to turn and stare at the Cervine, Jareth and Leanan silently questioning while the girl wondered at the sudden attention. As all eyes resumed their forward track, Beryl pressed the issue.

"I mean, *she* seems to be in love with him, at least; I'm not sure about *him*, though. Why does he seem so distant at times? Even I can tell she cares."

The Cervine collected his thoughts, wondering again how much the girl knew.

"Do you know who the Sidhe are, girl? Have you heard of the Dark Muse?"

Beryl turned and seeing the seriousness on the Cervine's face, kept her amusement and ignorance in check. She wanted him to go on, and as life had cruelly taught her, answers were the only way to get ahead. She shook her head.

"The Sidhe belong to the Celts, to the Gaelic world, and the Faerie abiding there are a different kind, using a special magic. They dwell in the hills, in barrows of the dead, and their world is open only to those with a death wish. It is said the Sidhe turn the unlucky wanderer of their realm loose on the Mothan track that leads to the Great Hunt. None of those that come back, come back unchanged. And of those that come back, there are few."

Beryl listened in wonder, as if the Traveling Man of her youth had shown up again to tell tales to the children. It was like listening to a bard without the music. Fascinated, she took her eye off the road and nearly tripped trying to avoid a length of rusted cable, its twists invisible in the moonlight.

"Leanan belongs to those people, Beryl; she is a Queen among the Fae, so don't underestimate her; Jareth did, and it almost killed him."

Her eyes flicked from the back of the woman to Jareth's squared shoulders. Leanan's cryptic glow had leached over, and beginning where her hand was laid on the man's arm, it oozed and spread to engulf them both. An odd couple, Beryl still couldn't understand their connection, not at its core at least. She acknowledged that though a bit severe in nature, Jareth still had the smooth look of a man in his twenties, even though everything else about the man pegged him as much older. He had the suspicious air of a father figure though, and this was surprising because the man hadn't shown enough concern for anyone yet to justify that label.

"How did he almost die?"

The Cervine's eyes misted, almost as thickly as the fog which dogged their trail. It rose up occasionally to engulf their vision despite they kept to within ten paces of each other, and other times, it faded away, exposing vast tracts of landscape to either side. It was then that strange lettering on billboards and across slumped storefronts could be read. But this language was alien to the girl, and her eyes only traced the various fonts, imagining what color might be splashed there in the light of day. If not for the brightness of the moon though, even this would have remained a mystery.

"It's not my right to tell another man's tale, Beryl; suffice it to say he learned the muse's true nature in the nick of time, as though sailing a ship on the high seas for the very first time. Few do; Jareth has learned to balance, a trait woefully lacking on this trek."

Beryl let her imagination loose, creating a scene where mighty waves washed over deck planks and lashed at sail, while a rigid keel reached deep to keep the vessel upright. The flash of sword and the crash of thunder echoed in her mind, the lightning striking at her periphery. The sounds of the ocean merged and tangled with those of the storm and for a moment, she couldn't imagine which might prevail.

"But who is she, then? I know she's magic—anyone can see that, but why isn't she more scary?"

The Cervine chuckled quietly, the irony of the girl's words gripping his words too tightly for him to do anything about it.

"Oh, she's scary, no doubt; you've already seen that. How many women do you know who can slay a monster hound?"

Memory of the fight in the scrub forest came back to the girl and her eyes lifted in growing respect for what the muse had done for her.

"She's so scary you would not even be alive, were it not for Jareth. For that matter, she wouldn't be here. In reality, shouldn't be. But I'm not the one telling the story, not the one singing the song; Jareth is, and we're all here to do something important. In time, our purpose will be revealed, and in that moment, the truth of our actions will determine if the story goes on."

Beryl became lost in the Cervine's words as he lapsed into concepts that were alien to her. Realizing this, he couched his next words more simply.

"The Hunter has his minions and in a way, so too does Jareth. The muse, myself—even the awkward and misshapen Tusk—play a part. It's what good stories are made of, Beryl."

And though she thought the Cervine was trying to be less cryptic, she could only wonder exactly what his last words really meant.

"Do I have a part, then?"

A furry muzzle compressed and nostrils tightened while deep green iris expanded into molten pools, swirling as consideration was exhumed.

"I can only say that you're here because Jareth's purpose demands it. That may be your only part, but well, the story isn't over yet, is it?"

Beryl chewed on that thought, both figuratively and by working at a lock of hair that had slipped between her teeth. It wasn't a thought she'd ever found herself bumping up against; she hadn't ever considered herself valuable enough to be considered part of any endeavor, let alone a quest. But maybe, just maybe, her answer would come with Eli. She decided to switch the subject back to her initial inquiry and probe what the Cervine knew about Jareth and the muse.

"Not 'the' muse, girl, *his* muse. There's a difference."

She was put off by that explanation.

"What's the difference?"

"Leanan would take great offense, if she heard that characterization. See, muses exist for many, but the Dark Muse is an independent; it's *she* that chooses whom she inspires."

Beryl's eyes widened, the width and breadth of her query exposed.

"Of course, with Jareth, she found an even greater mystery, an even deeper well; whereas she normally would choose an artist and when he invariably succumbed to mortal self deceits, would devour him. With Jareth, she found her vampiric ways abrogated."

"You mean she eats her artists?"

Beryl was shrinking back from the two shifting forms in front of her, afraid the night winds carried her words and fear too far. But the reassuring palm of the Cervine gently held her upright and she did not stumble.

"Leanan isn't called the Dark Muse for nothing, girl. And whereas another kind of muse would be two dimensional and secondary, with her, there is only stark reality. She draws her power from the artists she loves, and the greater the artist, the greater the love they consume. It is a symbiotic winding of two hearts and minds when it comes to dancing with this Sidhe, Beryl. And history is littered with the shattered remains of artists. Some painters, sculptors, dancers and writers are lost to their craft, believing that their talent can be learned and worked. And it can, to a degree."

The road began to swerve and more attempts by the forest to reclaim it could be seen, as the blasted stump of a white pine evidenced. Where the top half had gone, none of the four could see. As the moon disappeared when they strode beneath the remains of a felled bridge, the shadows capered and pranced, trying to induce fear, as if the brokenness of the city wasn't enough.

"But there are others, Beryl, those that can take their talents to unimaginable levels, those that we call masters. The great names of historical art are there, you've been taught them as a child."

The girl felt the protective bulk of the Cervine hover near as they emerged from the shadowy tunnel remains of the bridge and back beneath clean moonlight. It was strange how she thought of the light that way, as if all around her was dirt and grime. Did she feel the way she did because she took on her surroundings? Was this part of her curse?

"I remember; they taught us in school...when I went."

Such memories did not sustain her and she rapidly set them free to play with the bickering night shadows.

"Then you know how lasting their works can be. These are the true artists, and it is those that a muse seeks; within such fragile spheres of vision, muse and artist become one. Rare, but not unheard of. With Leanan, this became her obsession until finally, she was lost inside her own passion, her own relentless drive to feel something more. But with her love, there comes a cost."

The Cervine's voice stopped abruptly, almost as if he were afraid to continue. Beryl heard the odd note of hesitation and glanced upward, trying to read the shallow green glow in the creature's large eyes. But all she saw was a slow stirring of an emotion too strange to understand.

"What cost?"

The wind swept up suddenly and lifted her hair as if a cape, the fresh brusqueness like a slap to her senses and she recoiled, wrapping her hair back inside the hood's protective boundaries. In front of her, she saw blue light waver and rise like a bonfire, or solitary flame of a candle; both images pervaded and Beryl was surprised she was captivated by the inclusiveness of the thought. Were they one and the same?

Leanan tilted her head back and opened her face to the air, its touch on her skin hardly as cold as she spread her arms unconsciously, enfolding the elemental as much as it engulfed her.

Jareth just pulled his cloak tighter and grasped the pommel of his sword, as if bracing himself against the ground, fearing the force might tip him over to fall endlessly.

Beryl asked again when the breeze died. Two amber eyes flickered intently; Piper had stirred in the pack and pushing his black head out from under the flap, had pierced her gaze with his. Uncanny, Beryl thought, as if the cat too was cognizant of what was happening.

"Leanan tried to seduce Jareth's soul away, thinking him much the same as all the others, but when pushed to choice, Jareth found the balance between lust and love, and in the end, was no longer bound to her. Instead, she became bound to him."

That explained a lot, the girl thought; it was as if the honeymoon were over and the real marriage begun.

"Is he married to her?"

The Cervine rubbed his jaw, thinking, the question full of layers which he wasn't sure he should expose.

"Not in the way you understand, though in light of them sharing a mutual need, aye, they are. Beryl, whereas Leanan has in the past made great masters out of credible talented fools, when she tried the same with Jareth Rhylan, she found he already touched the rarified earth of creativity. It's like he wrote the sonata before she taught him the cantata. And that changed everything."

"Everything?"

Not sure why, Beryl asked the question; everything was so large a concept that she didn't even know how to define it.

"Everything."

And the Cervine didn't define it for her, either.

The girl looked anew at the man trudging in front of her, so obviously fighting an inner turmoil that one would have to be blind to miss it. Even when the muse tried to use her seductive presence on him, the girl watched as frustration mounted and anxiety breeched.

"She can't reach him, not now, can she?"

It was a bit of insight she hadn't realized before.

The Cervine shook his head but grunted in agreement.

"She can, but he isn't letting her; that's the difference. See, he *is* beginning to remember. But the muse still has her place and before long, Jareth will admit it freely. He's going to need her as much as he needs me."

"Why doesn't he give into Leanan? If he's learned to control her, what's the harm?"

Though she didn't expect a chuckle, the grin trying to spread across the beast's muzzle momentarily horrified her.

"I didn't say he learned to control her, girl; no one can do that, not even though Jareth is *the* Bard himself. And perhaps that's his key, that's the trick."

"What is? What key, what trick?"

"That he knows better than to try."

In the waning moon, the shadows were growing larger if more fuzzy. They'd soon have to stop and let dawn fully dance her way into day; sharp shadows cast by moonlight was one thing, but hazy, nondescript outlines of broken power lines laced across the blasted street was another. They could do with a rest anyhow.

"If he has such insight, why is he so persecuted?"

It was the Cervine's turn to start, surprised at the agility of the girl's mind. But, should he have been so surprised?

"Sometimes it's easier to fight the devil outside than the one within, Beryl. As powerful as Jareth can be, he's still got to face something even greater and this journey is showing him that there's more to life than verse and chords. It is another choice that waits for him to fully engage."

Of the few mutterings Beryl had overheard from Jareth, she'd decided the man was right in one thing; the Cervine could be so frustratingly cryptic at times.

Chapter 48

Must Be Dreaming

It wasn't that his kind didn't have their stories, it was that his mode of communication rarely involved writing anything down. So while the man's ruse was a rarity regarding its form, it was the intricacies of imagination which was confounding Rhey. He could manipulate much with his chemicals and drugs, but too often he saw his effort as lagging. How did the man write both so fast and fluidly?

He tapped the hand held monitor, watching as pages reversed themselves and earlier chapters were displayed. He read again, trying to ferret out Martin's technique, understanding that within such crudities, a key might lie. Or it might not—certainly nothing so far had jumped out and demanded attention. The fact he'd found precious little, except one volume by De Lint that shed light on the scientist's characters, had begun to irritate him.

And though there was some similarity to the GreenMantle character, Martin had let the creature evolve and devolve, in the same instant. How could such a power be so effective if under constraint? Why was the entity even being used? Wasn't there enough real life portraits from which the man could choose? Why hang so much mystery on the likes of a cross-breed, a myth, and something so nebulous as a word?

Then there was the character called Leanan; from his research, he could understand her inclusion, even if he had very few resources from which to document her existence. She was also a myth, the one mentioned in tatters of articles on this world's information highway, the internet. But since he'd disabled all the satellites upon entry, much of what he had was from computer caches. Martin's own personal computer had been the most comprehensive, and even that was sketchy at best. Dark Muse; a title that evoked horror movie aficionados everywhere to pony up hard earned cash. She represented what was missing in the man's life—a deep need for both sensuality and intrigue, for risk and high reward. And no wonder; what he'd learned about how the land's government classified its employees, made for the most droll of reading.

But Martin had escaped that trap, or at least found a way to balance the two worlds. That he'd chosen to hide the DNA code within the framework of his story was nothing short of brilliant and yet, the ruse had been discovered. Undeniably though, the human's intellect paled in comparison to his. Too bad this game had a clock on it though, else he'd be tempted to see how long he could play out the scenes.

Upon his abrupt exit at the hands—or should he say teeth—of the tiger, he realized that more contextual control was needed, something that would distract the man from merely fleeing and force him to broaden his energies, effectively slowing down the pace at which text flowed upon the screen. Up until now, the landscape had been Martin's choosing, with subtle tweaks to the source code; now, that possibility was open to himself as well.

The camera monitors beeped again, reminding him that his as yet unknown intruder had triggered another sensor. Glancing up and digitally zooming with a light sweep of his emaciated forefinger, the image cracked under the enhancement pressure. His need to accurately identify this unknown variable had grown acute. He knew the shadow form was thin and fluid of movement, indicating a youthful age perhaps, and that it was extremely cautious, barely glimpsed and then, only briefly, as if it were aware of being watched. But hadn't he taken care of that problem by adding another camera to the original installed by the government? Perhaps he should alter its angle of view still lower...

The landscape Martin had created for his story was working against finding the character named Jareth, so he'd begun to change attributes, preferring to use what he could see from the library's window; the torn and twisted skeletal remains of humanity as it stretched outside the lab. There was no dearth of material from which he could draw, though he was not as nimble with each description. Surely Martin had the upper hand, but hopefully that would change. He only had to immerse himself further into the tomes upon the scientist's bookshelves, passages he could lift and plagiarize; what concern was it to him if he borrowed from what humanity considered masterful creation? If it brought an end to this chase, all the better.

Pulling up an archive of world news still trapped on a device Martin must have used often—if finger prints told any tales at all—images both in color and black and white flitted before his eyes. Rhey absorbed them all, timelines unimportant compared to the details of construction. He'd implant those in hope of overwhelming the human's drug-controlled mind and maybe, just maybe, a trap could be sprung.

Glancing from the tablet to the monitor, the shadow was gone and what frowned back at him was the anteroom in all its fluorescent glory. Soon, he'd have to find the mouse which skittered in his house, but now, he had more creating to do...

Behind him, the mechanical sounds of the lab were broken as he was reminded that he'd found another way of understanding this human, that of investigating the man's amusements in the form of music. An odd construct, he understood the effect of vibrating air against a sensitive pick-up device and making such a pattern, but the practice wasn't something into which his kind had deeply delved. The cosmos made enough 'music' for a lifetime's study and after eons, such minor niches seemed trivial. Still, Martin and his kind doted on the entity. If he wasn't mistaken, the next 'song' in the queue should be by an individual named Dylan. It seemed appropriate since there was also a book of poems by someone of the same name. *Were* they the same? He hoped to learn this by listening to the specific cadences and decrypt the lyrics against what he'd read. Just more research to end this chase once and for all.

Outside, against a sullen sunset which showed the still toxic clouds in shades of virulent red and blue, a penumbra of light cascaded down, forming a perfect crystal dome of radiation as it descended.

Now that, Rhey mused, was an idea that could be exploited...

Chapter 49

Let Go, Glittering Cloud

The light of day was oddly suffused with swirls of burning clouds, red and blue veins shooting through coruscating orange and bulbous pinks, as if day was only just being brewed. It didn't take long for the girl to ponder the portent of what awaited them as they advanced further into the twisted scenery, their sight now fully capable as they saw the eclectic mix of hillside forest and demolished city interior. All around them, eerily empty of humanity, the brokenness lay, and to a person, their hearts sank. Nothing of the path in front of them showed anything but despair and futility.

"It's *his* doing."

The words were quiet but heartfelt. And all understood what the Cervine meant. The Hunter had flanked them and instead of pursuit, he lay in wait.

"We should find a way around."

"Already been considered, discussed, and abandoned."

Leanan didn't like the Cervine's brusqueness and clearly let him see her displeasure as a hard line edging her eyes and mouth.

"Doesn't mean we have to accept this as our only means to the end."

"I fear it does."

Still, the muse was setting up her defiance, bracing herself as if the ground would understand. She crossed her arms and glowered at the creature with the head of a buck and the torso of a man.

Beryl

The soft brown in the Cervine's eyes did not harden; it was not easy to get a rise from him, as Jareth had already guessed. Leanan was just a bit more stubborn and obstinate, though.

"Turn to the south, Sidhe; start off in that direction and tell me what you see."

Determined, the muse ramped up her rigidity and then without preamble, threw her arms down and with hand on hilt, began striding purposely in a southerly direction. It may not have been the girl who saw it first, but she was the one first to voice dismay.

"It's changing! Oh, look—the trees are falling!"

But what she didn't say is what convinced the muse to halt after a dozen long strides. Willing her mouth to shut, she stared in frustration as the distant tree line was melting before her, replaced with a rising veil of blasted structures that looked too much like those on all sides to not be the same.

"He's changing the land, creating the chaos from which he came, Sidhe; no matter which way we go, we're headed into his world."

The Cervine's words were both ominous and final; not even the muse had a way to refute his assertion. But that didn't stop her from looking for a way out of the trap.

"Jareth can change it back."

The Cervine looked at her, brows lifting.

"Can he?"

They both looked at the man who stared southward, watching as the trees reformed when the muse retraced her steps. He wasn't sure what was happening let alone what they wanted of him.

"I can't control that."

"Not in a way you understand, but as with all such stories, it depends on the teller. We don't refer to you as the Bard for nothing; that's a capital B, by the way. There are those that think they can sing—the modern world, which you're pointedly ignoring though the evidence surrounds you, is full of those willing to sell

442

their souls for an infamous fifteen minutes of fame—and those that actually can. The media is all over the former, and promotion is what feeds such machinations. Humanity has fallen into some crazy schemes; that one there is an original, based as all such schemes are, on pride. Few will tell you they sing for someone else's cause, Jareth. But you know all this."

The Cervine's words rang harshly even though his tone rumbled beneath their feet, as if the current his words floated upon lay just beneath the surface of their hearts. Beryl looked back at him with open dismay even if understanding eluded her. Wasn't it a good thing to be able to sing? Wasn't there an innate joy when song was set loose?

With his nostrils flaring, the Cervine leveled his gaze at her, the faintest hint of sarcasm infiltrating his words.

"You've learned more than that girl, if you would get past yourself that is. You can't always hide behind your excuses, that it's someone else's fault what you think and what you do. The world can be harsher than my words and usually is. Don't let the niceties of music and its presentation suck you into false worship. At least that's not Jareth's problem."

Leanan felt the surge of anger as she took in the Cervine's words, an explosion aching to escape her lips, but too much rang true, especially when she considered her own history and the lovers she'd taken. Hadn't that been the failure of every one of them?

She glanced sideways at Jareth, seeing his face contorted with his attempt to unravel exactly what the Cervine was getting at. Every one of her lovers that is, except him.

"This journey is being redirected and our path points straight into the enemy's camp, no matter how circuitous we might try to make it."

Jareth spoke, and it was from a deeply held memory, and loath was he to expose it.

"But stalling time was part of the strategy; we are here because we have."

The Cervine regarded the man's appraisal, nodding slowly.

"Up until now."

"Up until now." Jareth repeated. "How close is he?" Though he didn't want to know, he still had to ask. The stir in his breast was like a heart attack.

"He knows there's another but not their identity."

Not their identity.

"Do you?"

The words burst forth from the muse, though they came out as a hiss, accusing.

The Cervine shook his head, though some might have mistaken the sudden glimmer of his green eyes as contradictory.

"I haven't been told—he's still holding a lot of secrets very closely."

"The Hunter?"

Beryl's voice was like a squeak and ignored was the fact she had spoken at all. When trouble awoke, she invariably chose to hide from it, to avoid conflict. It was a trait she'd inherited from her mother. The Cervine's answer was almost beneath his breath.

"Nay, from Jareth."

Only Beryl was surprised; both muse and cervine merely took a breath and with it, signaled their acceptance.

The girl rounded on the man who wasn't as confounded by all this talk as the girl supposed he should be.

"You?"

"Don't push, Beryl; there's a reason for everything he does, and I would hazard a guess that all he'll say is he doesn't remember."

Jareth had wanted to speak exactly those words, though why he didn't just deny involvement in the first place also squirmed in its primordial ooze of possibility. The Cervine still knew more than he should, but shouldering him with all the responsibility was far from fair.

"You think this all revolves around me, don't you?"

His words were full of bitterness, more than he'd imagined.

"Not in the least, Jareth, but only you can turn that final page."

The return to such an idiotic metaphor broke his reticence to be polite, and Jareth began to spew invectives not entirely aimed at the Cervine or the unseen enemy.

"Not unseen, Jare, just elusive."

What? What did the muse just say?

"She's right, Jareth; but I daresay he's chosen to draw us in with the intent of changing that last fact."

Leanan looked east toward the center of the city and where unexplained reflections were teeming. Though the risen day had shown them their existence, none had any explanation. Heat mirage was the tentative theory of the moment but the muse wasn't betting her immortal life on that. And the very idea that here, such an attribute might be proven false, had already crossed her mind. She was glad her blades were sharp.

"Shit."

It was all Jareth could say because acceptance of a different kind just couldn't be ignored. It was like a dream from which he couldn't wake, and yet, was trying his damnedest to avoid. He *did* want to move on, didn't he? There wasn't any comfort here, certainly.

"It's like looking for peace, Jareth Rhylan; it begins inside a person. Everything you see though, is like reflections of yourself in the funhouse; hard to know which to believe in, aye?"

The Cervine's words lingered.

"Let's not keep the Hunter waiting, though do take the doorway out should you see one. I doubt he's as gifted as you, though from this recent development, he's learning fast."

Damned creature, riddling all the time, Jareth grumbled, hoisting his pack onto a shoulder before reclaiming the mandolin. Piper had jumped out as they'd gnashed about details and with a bored look, had sat patiently waiting. Every now and then he'd spit at the tiger, who seemed intent on agitating its smaller counterpart. Just watching and imaging what was on the cat's mind, brought a bit of levity to the moment, and like a breeze, Jareth felt lighter of spirit.

"*You* watch for exits—I have a feeling I'll be too busy pointing my sword to see them anyway."

The Cervine grunted to second that thought while the muse just narrowed her gaze. Giving up, she rolled her eyes once before turning on her heels, her quick shushing of the girl and subsequent poke to move ahead keeping her from murderous thoughts. Sometimes, the men in her life could be so tedious.

The closer they got, the more unreal the scene before them became. The hard gray surface of the road, which had seen drifts of dust and sand upon occasion, was now so thick they were hard pressed to pass through. Staying on top of the drifts was impossible and invariably, they pushed waves of the dirty gray matter with tiring legs. The Cervine was especially affected, though he gave no indication he was having more problem than any of the others. His massive hooves spread the loose sand to either side and he bent his shoulders while lowering his antlers, as if he were challenging another buck during the rutting season.

Jareth found it easier to just go with the flow of the path and almost swimming, he kept pace until the reflections they'd seen from a distance, had solidified into glass domes. There were dozens of them, some connected, some not, but beneath each, the city through which they'd been passing, was intact, as if whatever destruction had befallen the outer perimeter had touched nothing inside. It resembled glass but as they neared, Jareth wasn't so sure;

it reflected objects and yet, they could see inside like a two-way mirror. The drifts of sand ended only because they were banked against the dome's perimeter. And now so too did their path. The road went on but what they saw from their side didn't resemble what their feet had been traveling upon for the past day.

Glad at least to see that there was no sand on the inside, Jareth approached the dome's outer surface, eyeing the movement beyond and wondering why their own presence hadn't evoked a similar curiosity from those inside.

"I don't think they can see us."

Leanan put forth the same thought crossing his mind, even if neither could explain why. Maybe it was a two-way mirror after all.

"Where do we go now?"

The girl was attached to Leanan's side and Jareth noted with amusement that the muse seemed oblivious. The fact she could empathize wasn't his first thought as to the reason, though. More like Leanan was distracted. By what?

He looked at the milling people and strange moving boxes that flickered past at speed. Their familiarity was tantalizing. It made being on horseback seem ineffectual.

"What are those people doing?"

Beryl's curiosity was piqued.

"They're crossing a road."

From behind them, his massive frame overhanging, the Cervine's voice rumbled.

Beryl shrank back.

"All of them? At once? And so many?"

"It's not like your world, girl; here, there are many, and all with the ant's purpose to provide. They're going about their trade as you might set up singing at a family gathering, or the tinker at his anvil with hammer and nails. They go about their business like the smithy forges his weapons and farm tack, like the merchant setting out wares for unsuspecting customers. I daresay, many are probably doing exactly the same, though I don't think any of them are bakers."

They all watched the various faces come and go, crowds that waited and upon a light color change, merge into a flowing river and go from one side to the other, their faces usually stolid and blank, some animated with their hands to their ears.

"Those boxes on the other side, those that wait for the herd of people to reach the far bank, I think those are called cars."

It was Jareth's voice, more sure than he wanted his words to be.

The Cervine and muse just locked gazes and didn't say a word.

"They're machines of the masses, the way most get around, though as you can see, many still use their feet."

Beryl looked first at the moving four-wheeled machines that swept past her visage, just as the people who waited patiently for the light to change.

"But where *is* this?"

Jareth didn't answer at first but just kept gazing ahead, taking in the scene as if remembering why it was familiar.

"Not where, but when, and I can't tell you more than that. It's magic though, that's for sure."

Beryl bobbed her head as it was exactly the thought she'd had since approaching the dome.

"Ready?"

The girl started, not understanding the man.

"Now?"

It was Leanan, who hadn't any problem with Jareth's line of thought.

"Why not?"

The Cervine interjected, taking Jareth's words from his head.

"It's getting dark."

The muse glanced up at the turbulent sky, the red streaks having turned purple. The sun was almost set and its frantic stab of rays limned the profusion of connected domes with a fiery sheen.

"It's not night there."

And Jareth had to concede that point to the Cervine.

Damn.

He surely wished both muse and cervine would stay out of his head.

"But how? There doesn't seem to be any obvious way inside."

"We're going inside?"

Beryl had finally glommed onto the meaning of the others' conversation. What she saw terrified her, as if seeing it for the first time.

"It's in Jareth's way, Beryl, and you can't always avoid obstacles. Sometimes, the only way past is through."

Leanan's voice resonated far too strongly in Jareth's soul for his comfort. He grimaced while acknowledging her spoken truth.

"But again; how?"

Jareth reached down and unsheathed his sword, the steel tip a lurid color with the falling of day into night. Tentatively, he touched the glass surface.

Surprising all of them, the blade penetrated easily and from their side, they could see its end brighter in the light of the dome's artificial sky. It had to be artificial else the alternative was too unnerving to contemplate.

Jareth moved his arm further forward and the sword went in up to its hilt. Then he stopped, not sure he wanted to continue with the obvious. He hadn't felt any change in the way the sword felt, though.

Withdrawing the sword, they looked for any change to the metal but saw none.

"Doesn't mean flesh won't be affected."

Leanan was only voicing a possibility, not holding up a reason to not make the attempt.

Beryl

Jareth knew their eyes were all on him and sighing heavily, pushed his blade once again toward the dome, watching the same silvery line of light outline its entry point. Hesitating for a second, he thrust the rest of his sword, including his hand, into the liquid glass.

With a yelp of surprise, felt himself sucked off the ground and into the dome.

Chapter 50

Rangers, Swimming

The skyscraper reared up to one side with another half as high on the other. He could feel the seep of blood from knees and elbows, even if his sight was clearing. The corner with all its people and vehicle traffic was still there, and the ground was a rough profusion of decaying blacktop, the passing of seasons having broken its spine for a while now. He felt the warm trickle of blood more than the pins of pain, and it helped to bring him around quicker. He was in an alley.

As he got to his knees, he looked around swiftly and reclaimed his sword where it had been flung. Turning, he saw nothing of the dome, nothing of the muse or the Cervine, or the girl. Distant though, he thought he caught the sound of a large cat growling; the tiger?

Turning again, nothing but the alley and all its debris could be seen. What had happened? The dome should be at his back...

But there was just more alley, its dead-end marked by a large dirty green box filled with debris. And behind that, a graffiti filled surface that had seen better days. The smell of garbage made him gag. Realizing that his clothes didn't match those he saw on the street-crossers ahead, he pulled his pack off and letting the cat loose, slipped into a dark red cloak; at least it would hide some of his differences. Where was everyone? Could they see him even if he could not see them? In a half gesture, he waved at the dead-end.

As Jareth disappeared, Leanan's startled gasp brought a snarl from the tiger and a cry from the girl. The Cervine merely looked thoughtful and approached the glass of the dome, eying the substrate speculatively. Leanan's voice rose.

"Damned to the desert, we have to get him out of there!"

"Not necessarily, Sidhe; the path leads through the domes, not around it, remember? Somehow, I think this is the way it has to be."

"Then we have to go help him!"

The Cervine turned with an expression on his face that caught both the girl and muse by surprise; he seemed genuinely mystified by the girl's reaction, as if he was expecting something different. His retort was soft.

"Do we? And, can we?"

Leanan stepped up to the glass herself, defiance growing by the minute.

"Mannanan! Yes, we can; you know that's why we're here in the first place, Deerman."

Her face bore a scowl much the same as the tiger's. Beryl noticed for the first time that they shared the same eye color. As the muse wound her anger tighter, the blue flame was amplified. She unsheathed her blade and started forward.

The Cervine put out an arm. The muse stopped.

"I think I speak for both of us, muse, when I say that trying to work outside Jareth's constraints might play right into the enemy's hand, and disarm Jareth in the process. Do you want to risk that?"

Leanan looked hard into the Cervine's eyes, watching as the green iris boundary moved languidly. She was so sure she was right and yet, what if she wasn't? Did she dare break a bond that once had been her choice alone?

Beryl listened and her anxiety for Jareth grew as she watched him from her side of the glass. He fumbled with the pack and saw the black cat bound loose. Immediately, Piper went to check what lay behind large garbage containers. She saw Jareth look right at them and never find a focus. It was as if he couldn't see them.

And that feeling was one she knew only too well. Once upon a time, her father had done this, though not in a forever way, just one that prolonged her pain. He'd left by not being around, and though she'd tried not to live within that identity, she'd failed. Sometimes, she blamed him for what she'd become. That feeling of being lost and alone, was something very close to her heart...

The tiger growled too late as the girl flung herself into the glass. As when Jareth went through, a fluid stitching of light limed the breach and a sucking sound was heard.

Leanan watched the girl's momentum cause her to stumble into Jareth as he surveyed the street. She saw him stumble with her. She and the Cervine stood side by side, one with arms folded and a fury building, while the other reposed in thought, eyes deliberate. Around them the wind kicked up and whipped sand toward their feet. The Cervine wondered if this was Leanan's doing or just a mischief of the world.

The wind was howling by the time the man and girl edged their way out of the alley and turned the corner, disappearing. And with that, the streetlights turned yellow to red and back to green again.

We look like homeless people, Jareth thought, understanding both he and the girl were in long cloaks while everyone else looked dressed for the office. The office...as each term came to him, it was as if a key to the lock on his memory was being turned. But with each new term and visual oddity, he had to acknowledge there was more than a hint of building pain, too. This feeling had come with the realization his knees were skinned. Looking past the initial scabbing, he realized that the real hurt was coming from within, from a place he thought hidden...inaccessible. When the girl had run him to the ground, it wasn't the renewed bruises on knees and elbows which resonated loudest.

He stifled any distracting musings. They walked too quickly until he sensed they were drawing more attention by doing so, and exhaling a deep breath, slowed their pace. He tried not to let the girl's anxiety distract him either. He needed to think. Beryl's fear rose, and he heard its reflection in her words.

"They're looking at us...at me, just like they used to."

The streams of people would part as they saw the glowering countenance of the man and the fantastically painted face of the girl; tattoos were not uncommon—Jareth knew this, and banked on it to a degree, but none had so many on their face. This made Beryl extraordinary. As he walked and thought, he took in their surroundings while memories flooded back so quickly that he knew his actions must be instinctual.

Ducking between two shops where more garbage containers dominated, he quickly lowered Beryl's hood. Taking a section of his shoulder harness, that which held weapon and pack tight, he fashioned a wrap, twisting the soft metal in his hands and then working it around the girl's long hair, jacking it higher into the air. Then he took some dark cooking grease from a jar hidden in his pack, and touched his fingers above and below the girl's eyes, creating a haunted look. Lastly, he removed some silver chain that hooked around his waist, and dressed up the girl's arm, letting the coil work its way up to her elbow. Not completely satisfied, it would have to do.

"What are you doing?"

Beryl was confused, shifting her gaze from those approaching to what he was doing. Her natural inclination toward fear was feverishly working to reclaim her.

"Making you look more punk."

"Punk?"

Jareth nodded and continued, taking his sword and cutting a length of the girl's robe and wrapping her other arm. Not the same but close enough to another he'd glimpsed gathered with a group of similarly 'punk' youths. Despite her protestations, he caught the fabric of her top and ripped downward, exposing skin which was also marked, curiously sharing her embarrassment. That would take care of the girl, now his own transformation...

They needed to ditch the cleric look and he needed to conceal the sword; of these he'd seen none and wondered if there were other weapons carried instead. Images of hand held devices in silver and blued black crystalized in his head. Another term bumped to the fore of his mind; such weapons were called guns, and their lethalness was a memory that came just as swift.

"Where are we going? What are we going to do? The others are still back there..."

Beryl tried pointing vaguely in the direction from which they'd come, all the while aware that they were the target of blatant voyeurism. After her gaze was trapped by one such witness, she averted her eyes; as if she could feel their mind in her head, the images and thoughts they projected were so unwholesome that it made her want to vomit.

"I don't know, not yet. First, we have to blend in better. For now, this will do, but I need to do one more thing."

He moved to place his hands on the girl's face, intercepting her inclination toward withdrawal, a habit too ingrained for his taste. He closed his eyes so he could focus, shutting out the sound of cars and scattered conversation, his mind demanding quiet. He began to sing softly.

Beryl felt his fingers and wanted to pull away, but he thwarted her by moving closer. As she felt the panic leap in her heart, she began to hear a secondary sound, one which was barely audible above the great din of street noise. She writhed and squirmed but it seemed her ability to fight was draining away, flowing from her body and into Jareth's own. Her eyes widened and she clutched at her mouth to stave off a stabbing wail as she saw how Jareth's hands were filling with black lines, inky text and dark marks that lifted from her face and into his skin. She had an irrational thought that this wasn't words escaping but just being transferred, one prison to another.

Jareth's voice lessened and he broke his connection, staggering back against the cold brick of the shop. He hadn't been expecting such depths of remorse and pity that had been attached to what he'd taken. He'd only hoped to transfer the physical patterns, the visual outlay of the girl's malady, but the currents he plumbed were so enormous that he choked. There was no understanding of how to do this, no conception of exactly why. He felt as if he'd been hit from behind and sagged toward the ground...what had he done?

But the girl knew, she could feel it, and even though she saw Jareth drop with fists clenching and unclenching, in obvious turmoil, she flitted out of the alley and searched the shop's mirror-like glass for an image she hadn't allowed herself to see in a very long time. There, despite the flash of color from the movement behind her, she found the contours of a young girl's face—nay, the face of a young woman, eyes still a bit too round and skin child-like soft, but woman nonetheless. She saw beyond the grease Jareth had painted around her eyes, saw past the wild look to her hair; there was a person there, a girl becoming a woman, and if nothing else, the glitter of a life not lived. She appraised her slim but budding body, her breasts impatient and her body undiluted.

And her visage didn't fall, not even as she saw there were still lines and marks of black scarifying her arms beneath the mock jewelry and impromptu arm wrap. He'd taken her cloak and cut a short skirt which barely covered her thighs, the tight black leggings she typically wore beneath for warmth now starkly exposed. With just a hint of hostility, she saw the winding of tattoos that laced her feet beneath worn leather sandals. It was one of the least marked places of her body because few liked to stoop that low.

Jareth finally emerged from the alley and found the girl staring at herself in the shop window, noting the changes wrought. Now, he wore the cloak like a jacket. The white kirtle was covered by the jacket's length and much of his own scars were covered, though arms were open. The dead glyphs on his wrist were shockingly evident and then he saw what the girl saw; his bare arms were now laced with new tattoos, lines of living ink that flared once and then became silent. Both their eyes widened even more as both witnessed his skin absorbing the new lines. Five minutes later, there was only scars left.

Beryl stifled a cry and looked closer at the man. She noticed how his arms were the echo of the Cervine's but proportionately smaller. Stiffened by the scars, he exuded a tough streetwise tenacity that even she recognized. Was this the real Jareth?

But the man seemed oblivious to everything he did, doing so with an unconscious need and programmed purpose. Intuitively, he knew they couldn't be plain enough, so he made them oddly normal. She'd be the streetwise addict that no doubt gave sex for drugs, while he'd be the muscle, the pimp.

This sudden thought caused him to gag. Those that dared to stop and watch were immediately sorry when he raised his face and glared back. It was not what he felt but his role demanded it. Inside, he felt like he walked on soft ground, and drunkenly too. Maybe it was the shock of having the world change so quickly, but he doubted that; whatever memories he'd repressed filled in holes to the questions he should have been asking. It was the fact the girl hadn't been more hysterical that had surprised him; it would be hard to pull off their disguise if she decided to resist.

He'd given her a persona which he surprisingly found abhorrent, though necessary. The ambivalence of such a thought bothered him too; was it the way some of the dark-eyed watchers around them followed her? He'd tried to disguise her to be like them, so shouldn't that give a sense of familiarity? But perhaps there really was no honor among thieves after all...

They hadn't walked far before Jareth was reminded that they had another problem. At the very next street corner, as they waited with a few dozen well-dressed suits, off to one side a street singer plied his trade, authentically phony right down to the eyepatch.

Beryl saw the gaunt man who couldn't be much older than herself, even if his face showed decades. When he saw her notice him, his smile grew. She was repelled as he took stock, appraising. It hadn't bothered her when he'd done this to the others, only when his methodical gaze fell on her. And when he found her watching him, a gleam deep inside his eyes flamed around the edges, wariness reaching up like a cobra being charmed. And yet, it was *she* that felt summoned by his flute.

Jareth saw the vagabond musician first, well before they even reached the corner, and his thoughts were a swirl of images being matched, like a puzzle. And though he was aware of the black skinned guitarist probing the assembled crowd that waited at the light for their potential charity, the tune in his throat was there long before the other's gaze fell on them.

Unconsciously, Jareth hummed a song of summer, a melody filled with cattails so dense that even a red-winged blackbird would be hard pressed to find a place to nest. His song spoke of shutting out shore from pond, of separation and isolation, the bird representing a creature that had found a way from one world to the other.

And it was through these eyes that Jareth looked, seeing it all. With his hedge of invisibility in the form of the cattails in place, he took in the whole scene and was not surprised. Whereas those waiting were being sung into being robbed, Jareth skirted the street music's net and stood outside, watching with intense curiosity.

He'd never seen music used this way before, and was glad he was aware enough to witness its execution.

That is, he was glad until he sensed the gangly black's gaze fall on the girl; then the song in his throat faltered and the rise of emotions rose to claim him.

The street singer saw Beryl's guitar first, slung negligently off one shoulder, it's neck stabbing toward the ground insolently, playing off the girl's rushed disguise. He followed the line of her instrument and though he got tangled by the odd affectations about her arm and neck, he found her face an empty gothic howl. He saw her fraudulent pose, registered her alien demeanor, and pursed his lips at the way she'd slung her ink. He'd met many a woman who'd turned her body over to needles, but not like this. The others had been reflections of a persona, whereas this one was the real deal. It was as if she defined her tattoos instead of the other way around...he lifted his guitar.

"Touch a string and you'll be doing it with one less finger. Doubt me, and lose a hand, too."

The voice came to the gaunt street musician as a fog and having arrived, turned into a storm. As if he hadn't always been there, a hard-faced man materialized. His dark goatee bristled from within a dark red hoody, as much as his threatening small smile. And the air surrounding him, that which he could usually read, dulled and blurred, the details and nuances held at arm's length, an arm holding a glittering sword. What the fuck?

"We'll be going now. When that light changes, you'll not remember we were even here. I'm even going to take some money from your pot. You won't remember that, either."

The strange goateed-man had brilliant silver eyes and his voice braised the air like a welder's torch, his sound akin to the light. The wiry black street singer knew he shouldn't look, knew he risked irrevocable blindness, but he couldn't help himself.

"This way, girl; this isn't Kansas anymore."

Beryl didn't understand but let herself be nudged forward, into the flow of pedestrian traffic that had once again resumed with the change of the light.

Hell, Jareth wasn't even sure what he meant by that either; he was running on memory surges now, just trusting what his mind wanted his body to do. The fact he'd seen the snake at the corner first, had shocked him into admitting there was more to what he knew, what he *was* in this new reality. It didn't feel wrong, just alien. But he'd known that the scrawny black minstrel being left behind would surely have blown their cover, *after* taking what he could from them, if allowed. Instinctively, Jareth had known this adversary, someone who understood the power of music too. They both felt it as it lay beneath the fabric of society here in this iteration of the world. And if that were true, what did that say for the world he'd just left?

"Come on, Beryl; what he's doing might be heinous to the art but I don't think he'd line up as anything but a crafter anyhow. A smart, wicked, and criminal crafter, but surely not an artist. What he does we do better, and now, we'll need that skill to navigate this world. A world full of teeming people and busy-ness, where one needs money to survive. Hold up; don't want to get hit by that—not like getting kicked by a horse; here, you don't get back up."

He hauled back on the girl's collar as she'd been too immersed in his words to see the people surrounding her had stopped and the next light had changed. She turned and surveyed those around her, the vast majority ignoring them both after the merest glance of disdain. There were no dark-minded people in this group and for that, she was glad. Her gaze settled on Jareth's face. Whereas the others looked away in disinterest—or never made any kind of eye contact at all, as if they were dead inside—he looked back. She knew then that she was not alone after all.

Chapter 51

Stranger With the Melodies

The streets were full of classic urban excess, and extreme poverty as well. Jareth soon found that he and Beryl were part of the latter. They wouldn't be able to sustain themselves with what little was left in their packs.

"Are we going to be here that long that money is a problem?"

The girl was keeping close to his heels, ever since the incident at the corner, when she realized later just how close she'd come to succumbing to the street musician's wiles. Not that he'd have taken much, but when Jareth reminded her that any musician wouldn't blink to hock an instrument for some meal money, she'd taken to clutching her guitar that much tighter. The girl was now more silent than usual. Which was good for Jareth as he was scratching together a means by which to stay alive in this new world, as well as preparing for the Hunter. Between all the lines the muse and cervine had detailed, he'd finally come to accept his position among them. And as if breaking through the dome had ignited a fuse, he felt an explosion was imminent.

"Long enough, unless the enemy acts immediately. But right now, it behooves us to keep moving forward; he can't continue to encapsulate this world forever. Sooner or later, he'll have to intervene himself. We'll want to meet him on our terms, not his. According to the Cervine, my walls concealing identities and masking scenery have been breeched."

The girl looked at him through contemplative eyes, her mouth pursed. She wasn't sure the man's change was any better than his typical aloofness. But she also couldn't not see him as different in a good way; taking the marks from her face was like witnessing the birth of a second sun, miraculous and awe-inspiring. That he'd taken something so malevolent from her just could not be ignored. Like waking from a restful sleep, or falling face forward into an oasis, she knew another side of life.

"You've been concealing us? Seems more like we've been running away."

Jareth nodded, the argument a matter of semantics.

"How have you been doing that?"

The day was getting on and night would be falling soon; he needed to get them a place to stay, or at least a hole into which they could crawl. He didn't like the idea of being out in the open though, so he was formulating a plan that included money; after all, it was what their kind did.

"I'm a minstrel...and you can sing; it's what we do."

The girl was becoming more comfortable in her skin and her questions began to pour forth.

"But you've not been hiding that fact at all."

Secretly, she smiled when he included her in his statement; it was but a gentle stroke of her insecurity and her ache to have others hear her songs, to hear her voice.

"I think I have—if Leanan were here, she'd confirm that fact—but seems I also have forgotten much. Being on the streets—these streets—is nudging more and more memories from their confinement."

"Confinement?"

Jareth nodded.

"Aye; but I fear the Hunter is close to where they're hidden as well. That's why we need to find our feet here in this world and prepare."

A sudden thought occurred to the girl.

"Are you and the Lord and Lady still going to take me to my Eli?"

Jareth heard the tremor in her voice and turning, softened his silver blue eyes as he held her gaze, nodding slowly in answer to her plea. Even as he spoke though, he too marveled at how the girl's face had cleared, and in doing so had exposed her elfin beauty. Beryl's skin held the smoothness of youth which was accented by her dark, framing features—brow, lash, and hair. Even her lips were full of life, blushing in the fullness of beginning.

"Lord?"

Beryl's gaze dropped, afraid everyone around her was staring as they stopped. The evening rush of people split and flowed around them though, oblivious. This too, the girl noticed.

"Well, I heard you call Leanan 'Lady' once, and surely the Cervine is Lord Protector of the Forest, right?"

Jareth paused a moment.

"Right."

"Then they become the Lord and Lady; I don't know yet what to call the tiger, and I've not heard her speak his name yet. Jareth?"

Anxiety crept swiftly into her voice, where it had been conspicuously absent since the alley.

"What?"

"Where are they? The Lord and Lady, I mean; have they lost us? I thought they would have followed me into the dome. Then again, maybe their caution was more prudent than my impulsive behavior. Oh, Jareth, what have I done? Where are we and is there a way out? I feel like someone is looking for us with eyes we can't see."

Jareth placed a calming hand on the girl, altering the pitch of the song he'd been humming, becoming more serious as he saw the eyes of the crowd flowing about them begin to bend the wrong way...

"Don't worry about them, Beryl; they're not as far as you think. The rules have changed, and until I get a handle on this world's exact nature, I can't change them back. But the memory is there— I can feel it. See, I've been here before..."

He took the girl's hand and began moving once again, his words lingering in the air until he hit the refrain of his song and a sudden burst of wind scattered the unwanted echoes. New rules indeed, he thought.

There was only a door, and the single pane of glass it held was darkened, as though those inside wanted to keep the light at bay, be it sun or moon. The former was only now setting, and in the eastern sky a sickle shape was gradually firming. There'd be stars tonight, Jareth thought, noting how clear blue the day had been.

Inside, the dark reached out and pawed at their clothes, the shadows warming to the blood pulsing in new veins. Like the regulars at the bar, such darkness was mired in routine's boredom.

Jareth motioned the girl to a table nearby and approached the bartender, whose Hollywood looks identified him more than his position did.

Beryl sat on the edge of the wooden seat, laying her guitar on the table and parting the darkness. She made out those that called such a place home. For the most part, she knew the type; back home, she'd had to serve them and her most virulent marks had come from this kind of patron. But when you're least of the least, no one cares how you feel, no one at all. Beryl sensed the clutch of a familiar rush of anxiety and instinctually she tightened her grip on the guitar.

The forms around her were all dressed as if they hadn't changed clothes in days, and their exhalations became everyone's next breath. It was like an endless loop; each drunken sigh begat an inhalation of another's miseries and broken dreams. As each absorbed the others disillusionment, it became a seed for more.

They were all lost, though the girl knew if she asked, there'd be only denial. It was a pervasive attitude she'd run from back in Vespar, but different. Here, there was no obvious siege each patron was asked to withstand. Here, such conflicts and struggles were happening on the inside. And with that last ironic thought, Beryl understood just why Jareth had led them here. In too many ways, this was the epitome of both their souls.

As her panic mounted, she unconsciously began to fret at the strings of her guitar. Soon, without any obvious intent, a sad song rose and engulfed her part of the bar, as if what was going on inside had been freed. Still, she sang softly, in a voice hardly audible; her youthful vision had recoiled and sunken.

She sang so quietly that the music lulled her fears enough so she didn't even hear Jareth return, nor did she know how long he stood waiting, listening. It was like she could see again and her awareness of their surroundings returned apologetically. His voice though, was surprisingly reassuring.

"That's just what I needed."

Her confusion was like waking from a dream and she stuttered in a low voice.

"What was it you needed?"

"Why, influence of course; seems yon barkeep wasn't going to take us in, not at first, but then he heard your voice and it was easy to slip my words between your tune. I suggested he might get more mileage out of employing us rather than putting us out on the street. Good thing he agreed as I didn't like the look of his bouncer."

And with this last, he cocked his head toward a dark, muscular man at the end of the bar, beer malevolence lingering on his lips.

Beryl looked quickly and then shut her eyes; she knew his type as well, and her skin writhed in memory. Unlike Tusk, this giant of a man would not be kind hearted, even if he would be similarly slow witted. As a servant, she'd been forced to endure this type of man, to submit to curiosities and cruelties until avoidance became her only haven. It was his kind that finally forced her to the streets and into the hands of Adelia and her mother Ida. More than the taunts and depredations of those her age, it was the ingrained prejudices of the adults which had hurt her most. She shivered despite the bar being dankly warm.

Jareth saw this and wondered whether to ask the question before deciding it wasn't necessary.

"Don't worry, girl; no one's going to hurt you as long as I'm around."

The words came before he realized their importance, but once loose, he shrugged and returned to posturing as her pimp and protector. The thought of being her protector didn't immediately repel him so he sank into its raw depths, touching on emotions long at rest. The warmth rising surprised him.

As he tried to calm the girl, a rushed and sweaty servant came and dropped a basket of bread on the table, along with a small dish of spiced butter. Jareth dragged a wooden chair out and plopped heavily down, steeling himself to find a way out of this trap. And trap is what he surely feared.

"Eat up; he's not paying but is willing to feed us, and if you're as good as he heard, I think he'll put us up for the night. Maybe longer, if we play this right. Though not sure if we should stay in one place too long."

Beryl's fingers slipped under the tantalizing muffin, cradling its goodness and hesitating just long enough to satiate her nose before indulging her palate.

"Did you see where Piper went?"

Her words came from between mouthfuls of bread as she licked her fingers greedily.

"He slipped in behind us and is crouched up on the near ceiling beam. Don't look though, his eyes are closed and your concentrated search will alert the others that he's there."

Despite Jareth's words, she couldn't help at least taking a peek toward the rafters, running her gaze along the dark wood's length and searching for the cat's shape. She didn't see him but knew the animal would be near; he always was. Perhaps he was patiently waiting for mice...

"I told you not to look..."

She glanced back at the man and his scowl, the sight humorous enough to get her to grin.

"I know, but I had to. You know he likes me, don't you?"

Jareth just grunted, or was it a harumph? Beryl dismissed the thought and reached out for another muffin, surprised at how hungry she had become. Too quickly, the basket was empty. As the same hurried server came and replenished the appetizer, Jareth cast an eye toward Hollywood and wondered if the misgivings he felt were reliable. The man was staring at them too long, and even as he realized it wasn't him but the girl getting the scrutiny, he felt an unusual flush of anger. But why? He'd been in taverns and inns most of his life and this is what the male patrons did; they ogled the women and made their dreams. Sometimes, their dreams even turned into plans. So what was so different now that this man's growing obsession was a bother?

With an unexplained grunt, he turned to face the basket, reaching for a muffin even as Beryl did. They touched hand to hand and the girl's face turned cherubic, her embarrassment unfounded. But then, maybe it was only that she feared what his touch might do to her. Or her touch to him; didn't matter, there were more important things to keep a minstrel's mind busy.

He watched as the girl ate like a bird—small pecks at the roll, small but fastidious, purposeful and swift, as if truly needing seven times her weight to stay alive. He watched as her eyes roamed, furtively at first, until she relaxed again and began to linger longer on the faces of those around them. Jareth knew their type too; hell, he use to be one of them—sometimes felt he still was—but time and excuses had finally numbed him until the reasons for running away had been lost. Or forgotten; sometimes, he couldn't explain the difference.

He watched her face, scowling because he'd decided he'd put too much black around her eyes; it made her look too much like a street walker, too much like a skank. The term surprised and bothered him, or was it merely because the terms were characterizing Beryl? She wore it well; was this part of her history then? She didn't seem to mind, at least.

He watched as she bit her nails after the bread was gone, but not in a nervous way as much as contemplative assuaging, a means to keep her hands busy. Then he understood; it was a nervous trait he knew very well, one that was only really placated when fingers found musical strings...

He saw as she placed her fingers on each tooth, forming a D chord, then moved intricately to get the G, or strain to form an E minor. When the A chord rolled back around to D, he warmed to her deftness, surprised she could do more than just sing. But now he knew better and a part of him was looking forward to later, when they needed to perform.

"I want you to consider what you're going to sing tonight; I want you to separate yourself from how you feel and not let the emotions overwhelm your music, okay?"

The girl flinched, realizing her anxiety was being noticed. The fact she'd been working to stay calm, suppressing her anxiety, lent an eerie echo to Jareth's words.

"I'm not singing by myself...am I?"

Jareth softened his gaze and lessened her heightening anxiety.

"I'll be there, don't worry, but you're the headliner tonight."

"But why me?"

"But why not?"

His gaze sharpened not unlike a glare.

"I didn't ask to sing."

"I didn't ask to protect you, either."

But he saw her face tighten and tried to undo his rash words.

"No, our benefactor did, Hollywood; but you're worrying too much. Remember; I've heard you—I remember that night in the eyrie, too. Sing even half as well as that and you'll have these miserable sots putting Jacksons in our hat."

"Jacksons?"

"Ah, I forgot; you're probably not familiar with this world's currency. Think silver piece or tokens of copper; though Hollywood isn't the one who'll pay us—it's those around you, and any that come tonight."

The bar had three spotlights that illuminated a corner where the piano sat, but only one was still in working order. It's thin blue light bathed Beryl securely though.

Don't leave the light, he'd told her.

I'll try not to, she'd exhaled.

Conspicuously, she pulled her foot back into the center of the beam. Her skin looked even more alien with the colored light, but so too did those looking at her from the brooding shadows of the bar. The yellow dots of lights that lit up the racks of liquor behind the bartender faded to mere fireflies, their glow ineffectual and indifferent. The spotlight though weak, was made then more powerful simply by its omnipresence.

Stay in the light, he told her.

Off to the side but well within easy reach, Jareth had positioned himself so he could watch the whole room, with every distance measured twice. Beryl would be the lure on the end of his fishing line; tied but let out to do her job. She had to impress, had to influence, had to initiate the sodden minds as they stirred themselves in every drink. She would sing, would be the lure, but would anyone bite and expose their position? While the others watched her, he watched them, contemplating more than the distance between. Jareth measured hearts and minds, taking in details with eyes and ears, absorbing the scents and resonant touches each patron exuded. It was like fingerprints, and he played them to the beat...

Beryl did as he asked, playing songs that were not tied to her feelings of the moment. She refrained from singing those songs harbored close in her heart, those aching to be free from her mind. He had empathy for what he was asking of her—the music had always assuaged his pain, too. Still, he knew she could do this. But her talent was drawing music from the heart. He listened and nodded approval. Some tunes he knew intimately, and some were completely alien. To those listening though, she sang songs they'd never heard before, even if the tunes were vaguely familiar. She sang songs that reached out and teased, flaunted and poked. She hit notes that dragged the hidden toward the light, and chided uncertainty to dance with assurance. She sang. And she was good.

"She's very good."

Startled, he turned to see that a dark haired-woman had joined him at his table, even though he'd left no extra chairs open, just empty shadows. He looked at her pinking cheeks and long brown hair that shimmered in the dark. He looked at her profile and traced his gaze over full, pouting lips, over a delicate nose. He noticed the velvet choker around her neck and the softly burning shoulders of bare skin exposed by a familiar sleeveless black cocktail dress. She'd pulled a chair next to him and sitting cross-legged, exposed long legs and stiletto heels of silver. He took in her form, noting the curve of breast and firmness of her arms, despite their repose, which began and ended with delicate French-manicured fingers.

"Candace."

She turned then to look at him, a smile growing on both their faces.

"Jare."

They looked at each other and whatever Beryl sang only served to deepen the strains of their own music, flowing between. As the silence filled and it no longer could sustain itself, Jareth let out a sigh, something from another time and place.

"She's better than I thought."

Candace nodded, her eyes holding Jareth's gaze the whole time. Despite the murky air of the bar, he still found familiar curves, remembered nuances like the lie of her hair, the perch of her lips, and the cascade of lashes when she blinked. He saw echoes of the subtle shape of her ears as they peeked from beneath long hair. She glowed, and it was a light only he could see...

"She was always this good, Jare; you just had to take the time to listen."

He reached out a hand, palm upward, tentative in his approach.

The chimera of light coalesced and flowed from her face, down her arms and finally illuminated fingers reaching out to take his.

"I've missed this, Jareth."

He had no words, only a profusion of tears trying to untangle. The girl's song was changing, the mood becoming more intimate. He turned his gaze toward Beryl, as if to ensure she kept to the light.

"She heard you...she understands; no need to worry that much, though it does bring me surprise. It's a part of you too often kept hidden, Jare."

He heard her words much as he perceived the halo of hovering light; it wasn't so much tangible to his touch as to his mind...and heart.

"I like that; mind and heart. Did you sing me a song like that once? Seems very familiar, though long ago."

He didn't know what to say because there were many songs flooding his memory, and all kissed and lashed at his soul because ultimately, it was there he'd missed the mark.

"Not now, Jare, okay? Let's just enjoy this night?"

He nodded, taking her form into his conscience, letting the better memories remain free while restraining the darker, guilt-ridden ones.

"How...?"

She laughed lightly, a sweet smiling sound that felt like she'd skipped a rock on the pond of his heart.

"I told you, Jare; I can find you at night when the darkness comes and builds its walls of shadow."

"What do you mean, Candace? Don't talk in riddles."

She arched an eyebrow, her smile imbued with a beguiling undercurrent. Did he see pain?

"Isn't riddling what *you* do when you write your verse, Jareth? Don't you layer your meaning just beneath the surface? Didn't you tell me once that it was only for those that saw with their hearts and minds to find, that those who chose to be superficial needed to understand there was really more to life? Isn't that what you do when you sing?"

Her voice both chided as well as yearned, which only confused him more. He understood as well as tried to deny ever being that obtuse.

"I only ever wanted a voice, Candace; I just wanted to be heard."

She sighed and leaned closer to him, her forehead lightly touching his, her breath lifting like a rain-laden rose, a bud searching for a hidden sun. She tightened her grip on his hand, not to inflict pain, but to infuse more closeness, as if trying to make his skin hers.

Jareth felt her like he did the strings of his mandolin, and the urge to strum her built. But he forestalled himself and instead let her glimmer glow, she was a faint warmth further penetrating his skin. It was almost as if he could feel her...

"I know, Jare, I know; it took a while, but I grew to understand I needed to learn about you as much as you did me. Time is a relentless teacher, you know?"

Beryl lifted her voice higher, sending it out over the crowd even as they drew closer to the mock stage, the pale blue light lapping at worn shoes and even more worn feet. If any eyes had not felt the pull of her music before, now they capitulated and found themselves entranced. No longer was she the painted girl on stage singing songs, now she was an elven legend from Gaelic folklore, come on blue beams of moonlight, plucking at a glass harp. Beryl's fingers caressed the strings as she became entangled in the music herself. The title to a song she hadn't been able to recall earlier, came back with a flourish. As she played and forgot what Jareth had warned against, the notes and lyrics lined up as if they were one, and once they began moving, there was no stopping them...

The music claimed an old story, one in which notes and chords defined the length and breadth of each lyric, in ways the bards of yesterday might. In strokes too broad for most to comprehend, the subtleties still remained...

I only needed sleep,
having just come from the road
pursued by exhaustion
day turning to midnight gold.

When from the room next door,
a simple tune was struck
and a single song was played...
and wouldn't you know my luck

it played over and over,
the same few simple chords,

Beryl

the same scattered notes,
just some tune without some words.

And for a time, I was glad
to fall into repetition,
imagining myself a moment
a crystal cymbal collision.

I heard the tune as it was whistled,
when it was laughed and then hummed,
I heard it cried before it was pleaded,
and I heard it softly strummed.

But after a while,
when sleep began to beat
the same few chords I heard
became a song of wet defeat.

Listening made me tired,
became a void to hear my thoughts,
the last thing that I needed,
the last place to be caught.

So I sit up in my bed,
and didn't really understand
I placed a purposeful fist
on the wall by my bed stand.

I started a new beat
one that pleaded please to stop...
there's someone who needs some sleep,
and I heard the notes just drop.

The wall's between us lingered
in the eddy silence brought
until even the pulse of Time
understood what hearts had sought.

Then an old cracked voice began
with inner pain and woe,
spoke from between the rooms,
in a voice I used to know.

It carried tides of time
and flowed sobriety's way,
"You know, it wasn't long ago dear boy,
they paid me to play..."

My thoughts began to whirl,
plied at my own mistakes,
harangued me as a hypocrite
forcing me awake.

My heart began to soften,
my mind to cringe and crease,
afraid I'd not be understood,
I opened my mouth to speak

"It's three a.m., dear sir,
and it's kinda late at night,
for music of any kind
that doesn't make it right."

The old voice crackled soft ini reply;
"That's when I need my music most
in the cradle of the night,

when dreams are but a ghost.
I tried to drown in bottles,
but it's an endless river's game,
and though I sing I know I'm still
drowning all the same."

I knew the silence wouldn't last
as I imagined paper-thin hands,
pursuing the strings of music
that flowed like tears on sand.

"Won't you let me continue,
and I'll be in your debt;
you see, I'm not singing to remember,
I'm singing to forget..."

Without waiting for an answer,
I heard the song resume,
the same song over and over,
that wouldn't leave my room.

It wasn't that he played so bad,
it wasn't that he didn't sing,
it was only that it never changed
and yet covered everything.

"If I'm supposed to listen,
you got to tell me then,
why you only sing one song
over and over again?"

If violins are strings with angels,
then piano keys are echoed souls,

his next words were deafening,
for the likes of those not whole.

"We used to fight like cats and dogs,
no one's perfect, that I know;
I don't know if she left me or I left her,
I just know she's here no more.

She used to be my lyrics,
and I was became her tune;
and a song without nothing to say
is not a song at all too soon."

I heard his voice start breaking,
telling of timeless melodies,
songs I know we have come to know
in the dark when Hell agrees.

I listened then and recognized,
the voice from behind the wall,
"You sound just like Harry..."
but he cut me off and took the fall.

"You're right—that's who I am,
just a man who's left with chords;
but a name means nothing
when the music has lost its words..."

Jareth felt disembodied from the bar and his place at the table, from the vision of his wife whose translucence wafted in and out of his sight. He'd found a thread in the girl's music, and pulled, been taken for a ride, just as music can do. But in this case, the song's story forced open the rusty hinges of his own trunk of bad memories, and too much escaped, overwhelming him with emotions that he thought he'd buried forever. It was a fool's hope, but one he'd banked upon.

And even as Beryl's voice pulled at the fabric of his psyche and grabbed at his heart, it was his mind that held out longest, until he finally succumbed. Or did he merely drown? He wasn't aware then of even Candace's fervent efforts to revive him. To those in the room, it was as if a junkie had just reached nirvana, but the drug of choice in this case was remorse, and Jareth wasn't rising higher but instead, falling deeper.

It was even more doubtful that when the band of bikers, who'd slipped in just prior to Beryl taking the stage, came up behind him that he even knew they were there. When their balding tattooed leader clamped a hand over his mouth and two others pinned his arms back, he didn't struggle but instead, slipped between layers of dream, one which was being exposed as a nightmare. They quietly parted the front door and as night shut it once again, the only witness bore two amber eyes, glowing near the ceiling.

Chapter 52

Rabbit Heart

Leanan sat with her back against a tree, which had wormed itself up through the remains of a ravaged automobile. Rotted rubber hung from upturned wheels, a skeleton to mark where civilization had once been. The wind skirted around the dome and sloughed in from the north, bringing a brittleness to the day. She brought her black cloak up more snugly to her neck, begrudging her need for the wind. Rumors of the world came all the more swiftly when prodded by impatience.

"How is it I know so little about you, Stag-man?"

The Cervine was reposing as well, but purposefully; he sat cross-legged, arms slightly extended, attention focussed within the meditation of silence. At least until the muse deigned to speak. He opened one large fluid eye, the mist of a green pupil barely stirring; he would not give her the satisfaction of thinking he was put out.

"And yet, I know much about you, Sidhe."

She arched her eyebrows and glared at him, her lips doing their best to form a pout, but without a pliable audience, the ploy was dead at birth. The Cervine had not proven very easy to crack, which did give her a challenge in which she could pass the time.

"You know nothing about me, Horn-lord, though I suppose your mysteries are just as unfathomable as mine. Still, Jareth hasn't spoken of you before now and I wonder why."

The Cervine turned away from her, his face as expressionless as the broken stone to either side. He spent a moment perusing the shattered remains of the city, stirring some long lost memory. Leanan watched him and thought he looked like someone who'd been here before. This thought didn't bother her at first because after all, the city was dead—what did its history matter when the future hung so precariously?

The creature rose to his hooves, flexing the muscles of his legs and working out the last bit of tension. Turning toward her, the crown of bone above his head shimmered oddly with the day's last rays; sunset was come, and a whole day of separation.

"Jareth is more complicated than you realize, Muse. Perhaps he has hinted of my presence even as you were working your game of seduction?"

A flush of anger coursed across her elven face, color congealing in the depths of shadows that swallowed her eyes. In the moment, her paleness was accentuated and the wine of her lips deepened, so much so that the Cervine wondered if biting her lip with her sharp teeth wouldn't go unnoticed.

"I assure you; when Jareth is with me, he is *only* with me; there's no room for another."

The way she said it confirmed for the Cervine that she truly believed her words. But sometimes, that's all they were; words.

"I have no doubt of your abilities, Sidhe, but you'd be a fool to forget he's not truly all your own."

She started, not with more anger but surprise.

"What are you saying?"

The Cervine knew she understood exactly what he was saying. Still, a little humility was good for a person, even if they were Fae.

"He's the only one, isn't he?"

Leanan's stare remained fixed though her body was tense. Her hand ached for her sword. Actually, Jareth's sword.

"No one else has been able to walk such a fine line, not with their artistry, and certainly not with you. They all failed before him, and each in the same way."

"They were all weak, even the strong ones. Eventually, they either forgot or turned stupid."

Leanan's voice wasn't meant for him though he heard it; it was more like she was muttering beneath her breath, exhaling words that formed the core of a foundational truth.

"Aye, that's what mortals do. Did it take you so long to figure that one out, Fae?"

His voice remained neutral yet sombre, like the great rush of water curling into currents, forming an undertow. And yet, the image which formed in Leanan's mind was her way of clothing what his tone implied. She couldn't grasp the real nature of digging roots, of delving through fertile soil, past the rich but viscous clay and further, until boring through rock of Earth. She was not of the soil but of the water, the daughter of Lyr and proud of it.

The Cervine regarded the woman as she tensed, hinting that a fight was imminent. He knew her litheness belied a feral strength and fury many regretted. She was the child of elementals and mystery, but ultimately tied to her emotions. It's what was most attractive to Jareth, even if the man would not admit it.

"I'm true to my nature, Beast; can the same be said of you? There is no lie about me, and with those I choose to love, there is only the bared skin of vulnerability to protect."

"And they say *I* talk in riddles!"

The Cervine made a sound that was like a grunting chuckle, causing the woman's brow to rise again. Was he mocking her?

"Oh, I know what Jareth Rhylan sees in you—and thinks he needs for that matter—but there's more to him than has been counted so far. Even you'll admit that he's stronger than he looks."

Leanan started to retort but quickly pressed her lips, afraid her words would only substantiate the creature's claim. Jareth *was* stronger, had *proven* it, and was more of an enigma than she. Whereas lovers of the past had slipped and fallen, only to be devoured by her wrath, this mortal man had found a way to walk between both worlds. Infuriatingly so, she thought, remembering how he'd turned her anger back on herself without ever giving into his humanity. She hated him for this...and loved him too.

"You're not going to get in the Woman of Light's way, are you?"

His question came out of nowhere but she was just as quick-witted, enough to not show how close the Cervine's dart had landed.

"You know I'm only here to protect him, to free him emotionally so he can breathe."

Her words danced around the question, not exactly forming an answer and not quite destroying it either.

"Aye, he needs to do that every now and again; still, you have to realize you're not like him and never will be. The Woman of Light still reaches him in ways you cannot, despite her passing."

The Cervine watched the muse's face closely, wondering if he'd see what he expected; gleeful jealousy at the circumstance. Whereas the muse stroked the man's id, it was he who nursed the ego, while another laid claim to his super-ego. The sudden thought caused him to choke back a chuckle which even the muse couldn't miss. He held his furry hand up, palm open, and forestalled the expected furious retort.

"That was not meant for you, but for me; sometimes, a cigar is just a cigar, you know? But perhaps that field isn't filled with the type of artists you prefer...nevertheless, I beg your pardon."

Leanan wondered again just what Jareth saw in the beast. Good in a fight, no doubt, but really, where was the creative spark that linked life to purpose? So far, there didn't seem to be any...

"She's already done what neither of us was able, Leanan Sidhe; bear that in mind."

Leanan didn't let the fact this was the first time he'd called her by name derail her thought, instead, it deepened it. Still, her petulance couldn't be restrained.

"Only because he wouldn't let me."

The Cervine stared hard at her, his eyes setting up a repository for the muse's burning gaze.

"Could you have convinced him if he had? Somehow, I think even you would have considered his emotional fragility at the time, and thought better. He's too close to the fire as it is, even now."

Leanan thought to nod her head but didn't want to give the Cervine reason to believe she agreed. Convincing Jareth would have been tough, no doubt. She spoke her next query softly.

"You know then, don't you?"

It was a suspicion she'd had since they'd first joined forces. If Jare hadn't been so obviously comfortable with the stag-man, she'd have summoned gale and blade gladly to rid this world of another undocumented surprise.

"You know I do; you are like Jareth's yin to my yang. We're each here to bring him home, Leanan."

The way he said her name this time rattled her core, sending shivers that she could feel in her teeth. Did he know more than she thought? Did he know more than she? The creature called cervine would bear watching...

"Your tiger isn't right."

What? She twisted her head, eyes flashing in alarm and confusion. And then she knew; something was happening.

The great white tiger had been restless since Jareth first disappeared and finally, she'd had to admonish it to settle down. Fearing her, the animal had obediently lowered to its haunches but steadfastly faced the shimmering dome, its gaze locked on the scene inside. All day it had remained vigilant, hardly moving. But now it was up again, and with hardly any space between its nose and the glass, was woofing shallowly, not sure a growl wouldn't be more appropriate. Something had caught its attention.

"Like a hound before the chase."

The Cervine's words held expectancy too.

She nodded, drawing closer to her familiar, her hand and crooning trying to soothe the animal.

Inside the dome, they could see it was night, the street lights and glaring great eyes of cars rushing past, like animals looking for the river, all on a single minded mission. It was a kind of magic that made her leery.

Then they heard a single crystal note of song coming from within.

The tiger jumped, white shot with black merging with the coruscating surface of the dome.

Then it was gone, bounding into the alley where Jareth and the girl had first landed.

"It's time."

She nodded, knowing exactly what the Cervine meant.

Chapter 53

Drumming Song—the Instrumental

"This isn't going to be like it is in the lab, Martin; here, I *can* affect you."

Jareth heard the voice like an echo as he fought against the moonlight spilling inside his cell. Like bars, the light striped his skin, like chains, the words sought to hold him tight. The straps on his arms and legs cut severely every time he struggled, providing another jarring memory to surface.

He had no idea how long his torment had lasted but was adamant he didn't want it to continue. He knew he'd been cut, possibly maimed, but denial raged at the pain as he sought solace in oblivion. He was afraid to open his eyes for fear nothing had changed. And this was *with* the threat of losing his sight.

"What need do you have for eyes anymore, Martin? It's almost over, and really, what's there for you to see? Your precious world is laying in so many pieces that it would take another million years of evolution just to remind the monkeys they do have opposable thumbs. I'll give you credit though; I'd never have suspected humans could be this creative."

And then the voice uttered the words, the echo which had forced him to pull back into his mind and hide his heart.

"...here, I *can* affect you."

The name Martin threw him at first, but whatever this joker-faced being wanted, it wasn't confusion. The mad-eyed clown with the pocked eyes drooled over him as he lay bound, skin burning from whatever had been inside the last injection.

"Your plan almost worked, yes it did, but as you can see, human minds are no match for my race, scientist or not. There's more to you than first appears though, so we're going to find out just how much there is."

And that's when he knew the sting of razors, and pain radiating from nerve bundles he never knew he had. It was so intense, he'd passed out. Waking hadn't been much better. He withstood another injection, watching the man in the seersucker suit whose hair was highly greased and swept back in broken curls. But it was a hairline that was in recession. When the joker smiled, that's when fear began to penetrate. Jareth heard his own voice but denied the agony within its depth. The pain was more intense than that which he'd experienced once upon a time, when he'd burned the glyphs into his chest...

He knew shame, he knew betrayal, he felt the cut of failure and worldliness because he hadn't been there. And when he had, it was too late...he'd tried to drown out the shrieks of the woman on the table next to him, but the effort had been titanic. Some sounds invade and repose forever in the mind, some lay seeds of hopeless in the depths of the heart, but for those that reach the soul, then there is only an end of days.

All this was the echo of a mad-eyed torturer, whose voice was relentless, feeding words and lines that bordered on fiction, a never ending litany of pressure points to which his body jerked and pitched, writhing in the black ink of writing; a pool with nowhere to go, a welling of darkness from which all evil formed its letters.

He heard the woman's screams, calling out a name that couldn't be him. He was Jareth, a singer, the minstrel, the man who fantasized about a world where swords and song ruled. Even now, he felt the urge to feel the metal

*winding of his sword's hilt, to feel it beneath his hands. Alternately, he ached
to have his fingers gracefully stroking fine steel strings, to raise notes that would
save the day.*

*But he heard threats and curses, cajoling and begging. He listened while
the voice torturing him aimed his venom at the woman, finally making silence
strangle time and unmaking song...*

*It was all about secrets, about information that would solve a problem, as
if this knowledge held the power to save the world...which of course it didn't,
but no matter the words croaking from his mouth, the torturer wouldn't listen,
wouldn't understand. Too many words and questions about sequences, about
chains. And the only thing he could feel was the cold chain of guilt that held
him powerless on the metal table. He felt binds that cut his wrists each time he
tried to get loose. Still, he needed to overpower his captor and free the hurting
song maker...it felt like he was killing the only real music that existed...*

*He hadn't been there. This memory stabbed at his breast, but he had his
armor, and it had become very thick. Years had gone by, and each lay like
another scale of metal across his heart, mistakenly protecting him. Too late, he
knew he'd done the wrong thing, and too late, he learned that loyalty was
secondary to covenant. It was far too late when he tried to pick up the dying
song. When breath was at last released, it found him already far away, trying
to outrun what he'd done.*

*The alien had killed his wife...had murdered her before his eyes, and he
hadn't been able to do a damn thing to stop it...*

*The song was lost...it was broken like a crystal goblet, the wine once held
so securely now a rolling, streaming river on the tile floor. There was nothing
left but sterile metal tables. He'd gone and lost the song, and for this, there
could be no mercy. The ultimate sin demanded the ultimate sacrifice.*

But it was night now, thankfully, and though the joker's words
filled his brain and rattled against sanity, still he could isolate a part
of his mind, putting distance between memory and reality. The
comfort that lay there was immense and he wallowed, afraid to
leave

The moonlight streamed in and his eyes tried to adjust but couldn't, so he closed them again and felt wetness well at the corners. Parts of his body felt numb and he hurriedly forced such thoughts away, fearful of what truth such images might prove. He felt a huge imbalance and at the heart of this feeling, another truth lay, one that promised an end to the pain. All he had to do was reach it...

But isn't that what his jailor wanted? For him to succumb and spill memories in return for cessation of the pain? For surely that's what this was. Like no other time in his life, he felt powerless, helpless and frail, like hope itself wasn't real.

We all need hope, don't we?

The question felt like the echo of the painted-man's words, haunting and revealing, as if probing at the very fabric of his mind. Yet, it wasn't, because why would the devil ever admit such a basic idea? What was to be gained? Only in hopelessness could a demon be succored.

He heard the voice again, beneath a layer of pain-induced echoes from the day, as if all the words uttered by his tormentor had been inside the syringe, flowing through the needle and into his body. He choked and blurted softly, because the thought that this is how Beryl must feel, overwhelmed him. Words insinuating and withering, marks on skin resonating derision and desolation, within the boundaries of heart and soul.

No, not the soul...he can't touch you there, only the Word can do that.

It was a woman's voice, tinged with silver bells, as if each syllable floated in sound. The voice was lyrical, imbued with a great light; magical. Like a song, the words permeated the haze of numbing pain wracking his body. Turning his head again toward the impetuous moonlight, he opened his eyes and saw how the streaming rays formed a familiar shape. Even silhouetted, he couldn't mistake Candace's brilliance, and she was singing.

"Candy."

The shadows were fervently working to re-establish their domain, throwing wasted scraps of darkness back at him, working monsters from the blackness of sinful night, of folded night.

It's just a crease, Jare, just a wrinkle of Night's fabric. I've brought you her light; can you see it?

And he could.

Can you feel its fingers on your skin? Know its touch and hear its voice? I'm singing to you, Light of my Life; can you hear me? Can you hear my song? Do you remember the tune?

He felt and he heard, he listened and he knew. Her song was an old one, and he found himself humming along.

There's a power in music which everyone knows, Jare, you most of all. Remember the times you took your strings and made beautiful music, serenading me under the same moon that flows past the darkness and into this room.

He tried to turn his head more but felt the leather straps restraining him. At this suggestion of pain, the shadows giggled and chittered all the louder. A wave of distress formed and spread throughout his body, tightening ruined tendons and straining pierced ligaments. What had the joker-faced demon done to him?

The song, Jareth, the song...breathe deep with your ears and take my forgiveness to your heart..

The moonlight grew dim but the dazzle of light from Candace's face burned brighter as she bent her face down toward his. The melody flooded further, flowing from her mouth in waves he could almost see. His eyes traced the contours of her face, touching the rounded cheekbones and velvet lips as they neared. As she lowered herself and kissed him, he drowned in her eyes before closing his own. He felt himself inhaling her into the depths of his soul, placing memory and touch where it once used to be.

Jareth was infused with her very air, with her light, and especially with her song. The verses resonated and like the moon outside, it burst into a million stars inside him, radiating outward until his body could no longer contain their shards of love. Of love, because this was surely the wings upon which her song flew.

For one fleeting moment, song lived again, and he weeped.

Chapter 54

Distance

It was more than an hour and Jareth was still missing. Beryl fidgeted with her fingers, trying to catch the writhing black ink. It was mindless, and something she'd done since she was young, but it helped contain her anxiety. Surely Jareth hadn't left her alone, had he?

Another thought occurred as she restrung her guitar; where was Piper? Had he left her too?

She glanced up again, hoping no one noticed as glasses and mugs were refilled. Nothing but empty shadow. If the animal was still perched on the far beam, she'd have seen his eyes. She hadn't realized how comforting the man and his cat had been for her. Now, the prospect of being alone caused skin to wrinkle, itch and tremble. She'd never been alone, not until mother had been taken. And that day was so bad, she forced the memory to keep its distance.

Beryl's song shifted into melancholy as her thoughts battled a growing fear. One song led into the next with ever more tension. Gone were the syrupy love ballads, those which evolved from older tunes reminiscent of Grimm's fairy tales, where the moral was clear and the means anything but. Her heart directed her mind now and she struggled to continue; all she wanted was to see the hooded minstrel with the goatee, tipping back in his chair once again, feet on the table and looking anything but attentive.

She'd noticed this about Jareth, that he paid attention but it wasn't obvious. Most of the time, he surprised her. Especially when he'd taken the ink from her face. She'd heard of such miracles, but as a singer, she also knew how much was fabricated promise. Though she tried to ignore her own growing knowledge of the field, it was more than true that singers and musicians were dreamers, and very often fools. This code of 'going with the flow' wasn't the most reliable witness for responsibility.

Responsibility was something she could use right now, and this thought colored her repertoire, even more as she segued into a battle hymn. The crowd seemed invested, and as she continued to dredge her mind for similar songs, she understood just a little bit what Jareth had been telling her earlier, before they'd found the run-down bar in the first place...

"There's a part of you that is given to the audience—any audience, be it a parent, sibling, friend or lover—whenever you bare your feelings. The song draws you in with both melody and lyric; the two are not interchangeable though. A melody can begin the spell, can even weave one of its own—I've seen it, sometimes even done it—but it's more a table-setter. When you bring something to say to a tune, well, then you begin to understand what real magic is like."

They'd passed several corner markets and even though she'd frowned in disapproval when Jareth handed her what looked like a yellow pear, she didn't refuse; her hunger was growing. Between bites, she noticed he was continually shifting his gaze, looking for something.

"Are you watching for her?"

Somehow, she knew he'd know who she was talking about.

He cast her a thoughtful glance then continued scanning the crowds they passed. When streetlights needed changing, he gave more attention to where they'd been.

"She can take care of herself."

And Beryl wondered how he could be so sure, although she'd seen the way the muse could use a sword; maybe Jareth was right...

"Besides, if they could be here, they would; something is holding them out."

Holding them out? Beryl wondered what he meant.

"This isn't your world, and yet, it is, at least, one incarnation. Much of this looks different than anything you've ever seen, right?

She nodded, having already told him this.

"And yet, you're not so disturbed that running blindly into it stops you, either."

Which was true; but she'd been comforted by the fact that other than their strange dress, the people here spoke a language she understood, and looked similar.

"It's a world with a lot of problems, girl; there's an undercurrent here that is troubled. The very stone beneath our feet hurts, and the same pain radiates from the shops and buildings around us. They tremble, much as you might before a first audience. Like that moment, a choice has to be made."

"A choice?"

Jareth nodded, his long hair having been swept back into his red hood so that he might blend better. Though, she still wondered where he'd hidden his sword.

"The choice of whether you're going to let go. To embrace the beauty and power of song, one has to give in to whatever demands it makes; one must surrender to really receive its full effect."

Beryl continued to follow the man, waving every now and then at the cat peeking between the backpack and mandolin. Piper merely blinked in response, utterly quiet, as if not calling attention was paramount.

"I know that; if a song doesn't reach an audience, it's probably because the singer is no good in the first place."

"Well..." the man paused at another red light, watching as the traffic coursed in front of them, his demeanor surprisingly engaged. The aloofness which she'd come to associate with him apparently wasn't total. He could be something akin to human after all.

"...there's a song that tells of a man who's lost the word, that he could always play the melody. But if nothing was said—if it had no meaning, what lasting effect could it have? Nothing but the moment could pass and when it was over? We all go about our business as if nothing happened."

She thought she knew this song and lost track of his voice as he continued, while she set about trying to recapture the title. It was an old tune, something her mother may have taught her. Or had it been her father?

"Anyway, just be careful who you sing to...and *what* you sing, for that matter."

When she pressed him to explain the latter, he waved her off, shrugging his shoulders, as if the explanation wasn't tangible yet still real.

"Getting lost in a song is possibly the worst thing you can ever do, girl; don't forget that."

And so she began to understand how her songs could move more than she'd thought; she saw how between the melody and the verse, that a man could go from hating his woman to loving her, all because of strings being strummed inside. But the confidence she'd grown into while on stage was crumbling, now that she felt alone...again.

At last numbed by the music and time, her voice began to crack, and despite a fair number of encouragers still present, she begged off and left the small stage. As she passed between the tables, winding her way toward the man Jareth mysteriously called 'Hollywood', she was nonplussed to find many of the patrons were stuffing pieces of paper into her hand, or if she'd let them, into her pockets. The fact the latter were drunk and possessed of an evil eye made her cringe further. Though a different world, perhaps not so different at all. Were people all the same?

Hollywood was working with myriad bottles, all of which contained the 'liquors of dream', as her father used to say, while Beryl waited patiently. It was a testament to her singing skills that he still heard the notes and hadn't even realized she'd stopped. She heard the echo of words and yet, was lost in an incongruent moment; why was she thinking so much about her father lately?

"Your voice is sweet, honey."

The man's good looks were offset by the strangeness lurking behind his gaze. Beryl braced herself, just in case. He too was someone she'd met many times.

"You know, it seems we could do this again tomorrow, if you'd like. I can guarantee an even larger turnout, it being Friday and all. What do you say?"

But she hadn't even thought of anything beyond the moment, trusting fully in Jareth. Still, she had to say something or he might get belligerent. He might get that way anyhow.

"I'm offering you a job, Beautiful; ain't right to keep a man waiting."

And there it was, the tone she was dreading.

"Did you see where Jareth went?"

It was a blurt born of a choking rising in her throat, but she was at least glad she'd gotten it out. The sudden change in subject was like an intersection crash, causing new attention and different possibilities. Which was something she desperately needed right then.

"He your manager or something?"

Hollywood's face darkened, a scowl forming at the corners of his mouth as he considered the man named Jareth. He remembered the weird silver blue eyes; perhaps this chick wasn't for him after all. Glancing at the other women in his place, he knew there was far easier prey.

"My manager...ah, yeah. Said he'd be back in a minute; have you seen him?"

Trying not to show her nervousness, she needed to dissuade this man from the evil thoughts so obviously running behind his eyes.

"Not much of a manager, if you ask me. Left you to do your gig and not even pick up the take when you'd finished." He shoved a pretzel bowl full of more green paper toward her.

"Not too bad for a first time, either. You should seriously reconsider my offer." He held a full bottle of clear liquid in his hands, silver-tipped and poised above a short, empty glass. "Both of them."

Confusion wanted desperately to claim her but she wouldn't let it. Fear crawled at the back of her mind as images created from his innuendo cascaded. They threatened to overwhelm and she rushed her words still more, along with her hands. Reaching for the bowl, more because the man waited expectantly, her arm slipped from its long sleeve and exposed the staggering pattern of her tattoos.

The bartender's eyes opened and he couldn't help but gasp in surprise; he'd never seen such an intricate pattern—and he'd had more than a few of the young crowd through the years, all with a cock-sure arrogance. This girl's arm was crisscrossed with not just images but words, text flowing and wrapping in what looked like a confusion of lines. But the more he looked, the more it began to make sense and worse, he could swear the lines moved, dodging the symbols and solitary marks which functioned like signposts. It was this that caused him to recoil, not the fact she was all tatted up.

"Where'd you get all that?"

And as he forced his gaze into hers, demanding she explain herself, he realized the girl was terrified. Of what? He'd hit on too many women to think that tattoos weren't billboards of their desire for outside attention.

Beryl felt rising shame, feelings of not being good enough, and the desperate urge to flee, fearing that even more marks might come. Even though Jareth had told her this world worked otherwise—it was more like him; unconcerned about giving disparagement in a different way. His people spread rumor and innuendo when the other was not present.

Hardly the same though, she thought.

She grabbed the paper and turned, heading toward the door, a gauntlet of patrons turned warrior sentinels in her way.

"Don't you want to know where your manager went?"

That stopped her, though it was difficult; the windowless door was almost within reach. She turned, bracing herself because she knew she had to.

"He took off with a bunch of bikers, and a pasty-faced clown who looked like the Joker from Batman. Didn't say he'd be back though, not to me."

Much of the bartender's words made no sense, but she did understand that Jareth was gone. And though the man seemed concerned about only himself, she didn't want to believe he could do this to her. He could have left her anytime he wanted, whether in this world or their own, and many times. The fact he'd stayed wasn't something she could doubt right now. If he'd left of his own volition, it would not have been without a word. Still...

She turned and reached the door, turning the burnished brass knob and stepping out into the street. With one foot out and one still in though, she heard Hollywood's trailing words.

"You might want to reconsider who pimps you girl, when you find him."

She looked at him for longer than either wanted, she full of growing doubt and sickening decision, and he with a growing lust revolving around her tattoos.

But his look changed as he remembered Jareth's face while the girl sang. This woman was trouble waiting to happen, he just knew it, and let her go.

She felt a softness on her leg as it bared itself to the night and sinking air. It was a warm feeling too, a reaching out that dissolved the bartender's comments. There, winding himself between her legs and arching a tail to be scratched, was the cat. Piper lifted his head, full of glowing amber eyes, and held her gaze. She heard the door shut behind her.

"We have to find him, Piper, we just have to; there isn't any place in this world for us without him."

The wind struck cooly off the pavement, painted a wan blue by the single moon above and rasping at the skin of her cheek. Beryl reached down and attempted to pick the cat up but she was far too slow and it bounded out of her grasp. Stopping three yards away, he waited, head cocked to listen.

"Oh, okay; I'll follow."

She had a sudden thought.

"You know where he is, don't you?"

It was then she cocked her head to listen too.

As shadows descended on them both and night merged their forms with that of the street, a single clear note rode the wind, creating purpose where before, there had been none.

Chapter 55

Aha!

He had two problems, both vying to be most important. Throwing down a fist, he was surprised the pain radiated as it did; wasn't *he* writing this? Couldn't *he* allocate such emotions and feelings as he wished? Obviously, he couldn't, though there was still some measure of control. His mind raced, searching for memories of all the text that had come before. Problem was, he couldn't recall it all, and was sure certain details were hiding. Hindsight was always twenty-twenty, as they say.

Rhey scrutinized his hand, noting his skin was bruised from the outburst. This too wasn't normal—it was infinitely more human than anything. What was happening to him, here in Martin's world? Something was amiss.

Actually, there were two missing parts to this puzzle, beyond the obvious hidden location of the DNA chain; if he was able to manipulate the story now, why wasn't he effective? It should have been a simple matter of mental manipulation over the man's material-corporeal body, and that lay in the room inside.

But no, the man still held out, even here where his defenses were intimately more exposed. Was this a result of all the chemicals still dripping into the scientist's veins, in the white sterile lab room of real time?

A suspicion that perhaps this was true dogged him, making his steps hesitant. The pavement outside was glass smooth in the moonlight as he paced. He needed to clear his head, as if the torture scene had affected him too—which shouldn't be happening! And yet it was. Strange.

He looked around, curiosity creeping on the periphery of his thoughts because he'd never really seen this scene, only recreated it from archived video. In the beginning, he and his kind had been too involved wiping out the major military installations to give a shit about how this race lived everyday life. Shit? Now, that too was another human attribute of speech that seemed to have wormed its way into his vocabulary. Something was wrong indeed.

The cars still passed, a mesmerizing panorama of neon and halogen light strung out like unbalanced lines to the horizon. Which actually was the interior of the city. All streets and paths led there and Rhey wondered if this was typical of human settlements. All the pictures seemed to indicate this, except for those clusters furthest away from the conglomerate mess; those tended to be just the opposite, and it was there that any opposition still remained.

Rhey's forehead creased and he ran a hand over it, working to sooth the wrinkles. He was working to fit all the data into recognizable patterns. It was always the key, a logical denouement of the situation that brilliantly solved problems. All except now, when his mind was being pressured from text flowing all around. Once, he'd tried to actually step into it, nearly falling victim to its endless flow, nearly drowning as it were, but he'd pulled back just in time.

Was the secret sunken at its depths? Is that where Martin was keeping it hidden? Certainly from the pain already inflicted, the only logical answer was that Martin's character Jareth didn't tangibly possess it. Had the human been more clever than he had any right to be?

Rhey paced outside the medical clinic, the prop he'd chosen for his retrieval attempt scene. It made sense; everything he'd need to force the man to give him the viral weapon's coding would be available, even chemicals if it came to that. But that too was now in doubt; could chemicals be plied overtop more chemicals, those which had driven Martin into his story in the first place? Somewhere, mad laughter lingered, threatening to actually become audible. Rhey shut his senses to outside stimuli, even if he *was* the one creating each.

There had to be a clue somewhere...and yet, the man inside showed no knowledge that he was anything but a shadow reflection of his human creator. There wasn't a lot of similarity, Rhey had to admit. At least, not physically. Whereas Martin was almost geeky plain and dull, the one called Jareth Rhylan had an inner core of strength that was quite evident in his physical features alone. Still, there were connections, even if some seemed too obvious. But wasn't that part of his problem? The shades of lies between obvious and vague were baffling. Jareth was a singer, a lover of music, and played an instrument—Martin Hennessy did not, though the sounds which had come from the anteroom's small black box could have been inspiration for this attribute. But a lot of humans had music and most did not sing. Or at least, not well. They thought they did, but...

Jareth Rhylan had tattoos, apparently meaningful ones, and Martin did not. He'd had more than enough time to examine the scientist's body, looking for enticing nerve bundles to pinch, to extricate and exhort. The Earthling was clean shaven, Jareth wore his goatee like a badge. Martin's hair was receding, evincing a growing bald spot on top, whereas Jareth was long-haired and swashbuckling. Which brought memory of the sword...

In Martin's anteroom, there'd been no weapons, no affectations of martial arts nor any displays of aggression at all. The only possible connection came from the type of books the man liked to read; science fantasy novels that often included primitives such as swords and bows, and this genre had been well represented on the shelves. Is this where Martin got the attributes for his main character? In thinking over some of the titles—he'd never actually found time to read between the covers as the damned virus wouldn't give it to him—this had to be at least partially true.

The sword...was it a clue or a key? Certainly when he'd had the bikers peel the man's clothes off, the short side sword was found. It didn't seem the type of weapon a 'hero' would have used however, and this fact bothered him. All he'd read of other human idol personas indicated that the lead character leaned toward having talismans that were important.

Holding the blade to the flickering fluorescent light hadn't revealed anything special about it at all. It was not plain per se, but neither was it ostentatious. Workman-like would be the best way of describing it.

So, what about the man's instrument? A six-string variety called a mandolin, something from a much earlier era in human development. Surely there were many more suitable choices for a man of the twenty-first century, and yet Martin had chosen the mandolin. The instrument however, did sound very well when its strings were plucked. But another dead end as there was nothing efficacious about it. No string of molecules, or math representations, spewed forth upon his touching it. Special, perhaps, but more a personal deceit than anything else?

The night was growling along the edge of the horizon and even now, the moon was beginning to receive outriggers of a swelling storm. Rhey looked hard at the lines of his sky, still able to see the vertices and latticework of the crystal dome he'd had to erect in order to maintain such a scene, especially in Martin's world. Once that secret had been found, inserting himself in a more material way had been a bit easier. The effects of the virus did however, make maintaining this facade indefinitely, impossible. No matter here or there, created or real time, he knew he didn't have moments to waste.

Which is why the torture should have garnered results. And still the man lay bound inside, passed out for the third time and withstanding the damage done to nerves and body parts. When he'd taken a saw to Jareth's leg, nothing changed, absolutely nothing.

Or had it? There was always contextual nuances in the inflections of sound emanating from one being tortured; always. Had Jareth exposed himself in that moment of horror? What was his tone? Had he said anything which might have given a clue as to where the DNA chain lay hidden?

Still, he knew he was close; this time, Jareth could not run. There was no story within a story—he'd set up electronic interference in case Martin tried while engaged on a prosaic level, with his antagonist.

Such an irritating trait of humanity, this feeble drive toward survival. Though, some might say it was anything but, and point out how long the man Martin and his reflection, Jareth, had already held out.

Curse humanity altogether; crawling, sniveling, worming creatures which hadn't even the sense to take care of their own planet. So many resources and all hoarded or doled out in the name of profit. This highest of lifeforms here didn't deserve the mercies it received...

Mercies? Now, how had that thought been incorporated into his psyche? Surely he was spending too much of his time trying to understand Martin Hennessy. Turning again, the sidewalk glistened beneath him. How strange; now, that wasn't something he'd read in any archived human treatise...was it important?

The weather was surely building, though he hoped his domes would keep it out. So far, here seemed impervious to the world outside the spheres, where Martin's two sidekicks were held helpless.

And even in that, he'd been as lucky as he was smart; devising a feedback loop to erase any text mentioning either the Cervine or the muse, he'd almost netted another victory. How Martin could

503

have understood and altered that next part of the story was puzzling, but he was not overly concerned. As with the guardians, all Martin's efforts had produced while inside *his* world had come to naught; capture had been almost too easy when Jareth fell limp within his own dreamscape sequence. Fool.

Surprise was Rhey's because he quickly realized he'd had nothing to do with Jareth's malady, almost as if the writing had been altered to fit what *he* needed, not the man. The place Jareth had chosen to hole up required characters that could both quietly intimidate as well as be accepted, hence the neanderthal characterization of the bikers. The rules Martin had erected to run his literary world were merely being used against him.

Rhey grinned and a chuckle of grim irony escaped but no one was paying attention to such an odd character. At first, he hadn't understood why his face and body had been so characterized—certainly some of his needs had been fulfilled, but if this is what the computer did with his desire to be whole again, well, there was an oddness to it. Perhaps his real world physical deformities had to be incorporated into a character that matched, in some way, what he was striving to resist. The view of himself in a basin's mirror hadn't been unflattering and yet, had not given him comfort either. The dark shadow around his eyes and the elongated crimson paint of his lips certainly gave him the look of a mad clown. What bothered him was the human definition of a clown; it didn't sit well at all.

He glanced at the approaching storm again, thinking of passages involving the muse; hadn't she been able to manipulate those elements? This couldn't be her doing, could it? Though held at bay, Rhey still wasn't able to work out how either protector had been fabricated or why. Certainly for protection, but there had to be more...where had they come from in the first place? There was no one in the scientist's circle that even faintly resembled these two...

The muse...her image and visage were pressure points at his temple, pounding continually even as he strove to maintain his purpose here. She was a variable just like the creature called the Cervine. Both inhabited part of the man's psyche in a way that was hard to fathom. On an emotional level, the woman was certainly a fantasy, a form of self-deceit for sure, whereas the Cervine was less tangible, was harder to both understand and circumvent. If the muse was a river current, the Cervine was the undertow of the ocean, relentlessly pulling, pulling...

The muse possessed a sword too...Jareth's sword, she asserted, though Martin's character was loath to readily accept this. Where did the truth lay? Did Martin hide the prop's true purpose from the text, from the unraveling story? Why did it appear to have importance and yet the chosen main character not use it? Could there be clues inside this story arc? What had she called it again?

The Cervine was another matter; called the archer, he was a creature so strange as to defy imagination. And certainly, he'd come across Earthen texts which described this character, all the way from the Horned Lord Cernunnos to the White Hart. But as with all myths, the truth was hardly ever obvious. Superstition played a large part in human history, or at least so he'd read. Where did fact meet fiction in this case?

The muse was the same. Actually, the story calls her the Dark Muse, and researching found her to be a vampiric force of inestimable power, but solitary and without a human ego large enough to even contemplate large scale conquest. Apparently, this character was so self-absorbed that often, there was only her world in which to be consumed, and this she did well, too well; the names of the Dark Muse's lovers read like a presidential inauguration party list, the prominence of each never in doubt.

Rhey considered the past lovers and wondered; could they have come to their share of immortality because of their muse, *this* muse, this Dark Muse called Leanan Sidhe? Or was it they who made her famous when their lives took an unenviable turn?

But the one fact which was obvious by its absence was this; the Dark Muse was never mentioned as ever bearing a sword...could this be where Martin had hidden the code?

The edges of his sky were coruscate hues of velvet purple and pale blue, as if the inner lining of night was being lifted, offering a hint of day's true persona. Not that the colors stopped the build of clouds and released the tension in the air. The wind was still merely a breeze, not out of spec at all, fully within Rhey's parameters. Was this merely a last ditch attempt by the man on the metal table in the real world to circumvent the discovery of his secret?

Why hadn't physical means worked on the man? What source of resistance existed that could withstand such alien-aided technology? Surely this race wasn't advanced, nor did it seem inherently that lucky—as if Chance had much of a mathematical opportunity to affect the cosmos anyhow—and yet, still here he was, running out of time while a simple but effective virus was wrecking the same sort of havoc on his material body as was being brought on the Earth itself. It was as if the two instances were working separate lines that differentiated toward the same point...

If it had been only two or three events, his advanced alien intellect could have handled it, but when more of the matrix broke, he was overwhelmed and froze, the fake smile painted on his face searing in its heat of denial, while his eyes widened and the wrinkles in his forehead disappeared. Aha!

Chapter 56

Death of a Thousand

It began with a rise of sound, but it was not the wind. It continued until the howl could be heard, as if there were wolves hunting in the distance. Like their mournful bay, this sound pierced hearts and minds and went one step further; it touched souls.

But Rhey had no soul and the sound affected him differently, instantly. He pinpointed the source; inside the clinic, from the very room where Martin's character lay in his own blood, one leg missing, along with fingers and teeth. Rhey had no doubt even if the pitch was incongruous. It also meant Jareth was conscious.

At the same time, lightning struck and the sky was illuminated briefly, insanely, followed by street-trembling thunder. The second sound rolled as an undercurrent to the original before the two interwove. The thunder provided the bass compliment and caromed off the city's dome of glass, resonating beneath his feet, and adding yet another associative sensation to the moment.

But it was not the intricate and unearthly sound that captured his attention, nor was it the lightning which had not struck the surrounding towers but higher, hitting the lattice of his encapsulating dome, the merest chip splintering off and birthing a fracture.

It also wasn't the sudden movement of his bikers as they clustered unsure, the glow of a bucket fire casting the alley in shades of orange and yellow. Nor was it their ominous stare for direction, an indication that an alert had gone off in the lab. It wasn't the flickering street lamps nor the sweeping domino crash of shop glass hitting the ground, and it wasn't the low growl he couldn't place as it joined the recession of the crystal sound from within the clinic.

No, it was the emergence of a face, a young face, that of a girl, dark featured with long hair and high cheekbones, that literally glowed beneath the fluttering light of the moon. The clouds which had been horizon-bound, raced in shreds across the moon's face, changing what light there was into scattered lines, like prison bars. And each was moving to capture everything in its way.

Then a shadow moved and it was the last event in a cascade of senses-filling nightmare that triggered the memory, and it was one he knew bridged worlds of text and script, of story lines nearing their climax. The shadow that moved was a cat, a black motion from which twin pools of flame stirred, staring at him as if looks could truly kill.

The memory spun forth, a whirlwind of images wrapping themselves in fluent coherency, showing monitors of colored light, showing red alerts and allowing for the sound of beeping to permeate his psyche. He saw the small screen, one of those that monitored the halls and Martin's anteroom. It was a slim figure, a young human crossing from one dark end of the hall and beneath the lens, oblivious that it was now exposed. It hadn't been hard to conceal this lens within the fluorescent fixture...

It was a girl, probably in her teens but it was hard to tell as the pixels were unaccountably being drained of their color, and even as Rhey saw the image, the edges began to dilate.

He sharpened his focus, ignoring the other events, intent on not missing anything further.

The girl paused, looking back, obviously afraid. What was she holding? Something dark, something black, something that moved...

The rush of sky burned purple and its canvas was a sea of moving streaks, some blue, some blacker than the star field whose visage they blocked. Streaks of wicked light surged forth, striking the dome again and again, their illumination tracking in the channels of growing fissures. Splitting against themselves, the fractures intensified and literally reached for the earth.

From within the clinic, the crystal sound of a single chord burst loose once again, this time sustaining itself to rise above the onslaught of thunder. The pitch rose electric, stabbing out in an endeavor to break Rhey's matrix.

The image on the monitor was breaking up, the frames fluctuating, sometimes clear, other times not, too often a field of snow and noise. Still, he waited, knowing he was so close...

He stared at the girl frozen in the alley's entrance, the cat in her arms an immolation of fiery black. The girl's eyes were wide but she was moving her lips, talking to someone...herself? No. It couldn't be...the cat?

His vision merged the girl in the hallway of the sterile building housing his lab, and the one at the alley's portal. Their features aligned and all noise was swept away. The round eyes of brown, the long dark hair and flush of youth, the look of terror...*this* girl was *that* girl.

Rhey focussed on the monitor's image, willing—writing—in the necessary passages that would fully expose what he was seeing. The girl in the hallway moved and glanced up, for no reason other than wariness, but as she did, he confirmed the two girls were the same, and each carried in their arms a black cat, a black cat with eyes burning like the fires of Hell.

*

I never meant to leave you alone...

But you did.

Jareth was dying at her words, understanding now how the truth could cut more than just skin.

I came back to save you...

But it was too late; he got there first.

I wanted to tell him, but I couldn't...

It wouldn't have mattered, mercy doesn't belong to the enemy.

So I couldn't have saved you?

No. There was only a choice of which pain to receive.

For you?

For you.

The silence was impenetrable, despite the clash of thunder and lightning outside the building.

I don't want to choose.

But you must.

I didn't choose then, did I?

No, you didn't; you ran instead.

The fire of his tears raked trails down his cheeks no matter how hard he tried to turn his head and shake them loose. It was as if he was being branded by their reign.

Is that how I lost you?

No, we were already separated by the distance brought on by taking one another for granted. The enemy just ended any further chances.

I could have made a difference, couldn't I?

It was a hope he couldn't run from, could not keep in its bottle on the shelf. Oh how he wished he could cry himself to sleep, as he once did as a child.

You still can make a difference.

No, I can't; you're dead...murdered; I remember now. He cut you until you couldn't scream anymore. He made me watch...he killed me too.

No, he didn't. You didn't die, Jare, you fled. And in doing so, you kept alive one last hope.

I did?

Yes, you did. There's another.

And the image of a girl, hiding among boxes of books in crawlspaces too small for an adult, superimposed itself on the burgeoning self-pity he was allowing to escape.

Confusion swirled and he grasped at a flood of more memories that tried to evade him still. Why? Why couldn't he catch them? Why did he still try to deny them?

And Candace's crystal voice rose higher toward a single note, her song fracturing the glass of the windows, reaching toward the highest heights with fervent resolve.

He knew then, he remembered; he wasn't denying them at all, he was hiding from them. Or, was it that he was hiding them instead?

Sing, Jare, sing; remember that there is still one who needs you, more than you ever knew. Give her now what you chose not to before. Find her and save her, Jare, for she is your daughter!

The world crashed with song so loud he thought he'd go deaf, the echoes bursting forth from beyond his heart and mind, they soared from his soul on wings of pain and joy.

Pain and joy; so fine is the line between, Jare; remember that.

Jareth heard himself then, not just in his head, but as a resonance issuing forth from between dried and cracked lips. The wind of his exhalation floored him with its strength, and only grew the stronger as his notes chased Candace's. He pulled the joy from his pain and strafed the air with a melody that could only be understood by a bard.

*

The dome was collapsing and no amount of effort was going to stop it. Rhey shot a swift meaningful glance at the bikers and as they got on their bikes, engines roaring as loud as thunder, he saw their forms morph.

Turning back, the girl was still in the alleyway, confusion and fear locking her to the scene's firmament. He heard his voice crack in jubilation.

"You're too late Martin, I have it now."

And so saying, he sprang forward, his painted lips set in a mocking grin, and reached out his hand toward the girl. As he did, he saw she had one hand at her neck, cradling a softly glowing red gem which looked like it was leaking light through her fingers. Surety rocketed through him and he touched her skin, whose surface was a writhing tangle of black lines.

The black cat hissed and raked at Rhey's pasty skin, drawing lines of blackness that might have been blood but there was no proof.

The girl cried out when the clown-faced man grabbed her wrist, not only because of him but because the cat had dug in its claws and sprung from her embrace. Dark dots welled like more ink on her skin and she despaired in the failure of knowing she'd never save Jareth now.

All around him, despite his attempts otherwise, shards of glass were falling, breaking and scattering into the death of thousands. He knew Martin was trying to destroy the sanctuary of his presence, to in essence fight back. Whereas before, the main characters had been in flight, Rhey knew now that he was the one who had to flee. And he would; he had what he'd come for, even if not in the form he'd expected.

Grabbing the girl severely by the wrist, he dashed across the breaking street and past the frenzied supporting characters as they witnessed their sky falling. Past overturned cars and bent street lamps, he vanished into the roar of the storm's destruction, unaffected by the girl's mass of ink stains trying to infiltrate his own decaying skin.

Great paws, with claws extended, metastasized before juxtaposing themselves into feathered tips, serrated and oiled along dark pinions. A cavernous mouth full of yellowed incisors meshed and folded, their form changing too until a bird's beak split the midnight sky. The snarl of anger turned into a strident cark while yellow-irised wide open tiger eyes blinked and became orbs of obsidian, glassy depths into which few would dare look.

With a flourish of melting black stripes on a white field, the large predator never hit the ground, never touched paw or mighty sinew to the alley's broken blacktop. Instead, with a single snap of wings, a large crow shot toward the sky, its pointed aim as alarming as its speed.

On its heels, Leanan and the Cervine stepped through the dome, the glass fracturing where they touched. The single chord of crystal sound wove past them, caressing Leanan's skin as if investigating, before it shot past and began to echo in the land beyond.

The Cervine flared his nostrils and swept his ears wide, his need to learn what the world could tell him acute.

"This way—he's been hurt."

Leanan's eyes narrowed and her brows arched dangerously. She started and then stopped, pausing as the wind finally reached her. A film overcame her pupils then and she looked into a vision that came from somewhere else.

"You go ahead; I have a storm to manage. And be careful to find him fast—I'm going to bring the Hunter's creation down on top of us all. He's made the mistake of creating Jareth's real world—Martin's world—and I'm going to make him pay. Whereas Jareth withheld some of my power in his world, here I am unbound again. Go, he needs you."

The Cervine paused, unsure he wanted to be within the scope of the muse's planned devastation, fully understanding the enemy's mistake. But unlike her, he worried only for Jareth and the girl.

"Don't wait for me..."

A quick turn of his muzzle showed questing eyes, understanding that there was another problem.

"...the Hunter knows..."

Damn. He didn't need to ask.

"...and he's got the girl."

With a swift leap that cleared an overturned truck, the sound of the Cervine's hooves on breaking concrete went unnoticed beneath the maelstrom of the storm.

Chapter 57

Beauty from Pain, The Summoning

Rhey tucked his discovery away without giving further thought; at the moment, he was exercising what little control he still had to maintain the dome's structural integrity. And he was losing.

He knew intuitively that the storm compressing the dome was external—and surely the work of the muse; he was aware of her ability to summon the elementals. With this knowledge lurking, he'd inserted counter measures but for some reason, their effect was being damped. With difficulty, he wove between alleys and wavering buildings, careful not to get too close. Still, it might be worth the risk, if only he didn't have the girl.

He'd put a trigger in place, as he had on his previous incursion, a mechanism that would pull his conscience from the digital world to which Martin had run. Despite being mauled by the tiger last time, the escape trigger had brought him properly back into the lab to witness the after effects of what such a withdrawal could do. All the readings had been within specifications, the parameters all in place and for the most part, had worked. Tweaking one connection and increasing the dosage of blue fluid that seeped into his corporeal body was meant to give more protection.

But something was amiss and without the proper use of his lab equipment, he had to run before the story's stuttering background. He hoped it wasn't from a broken timeline, though.

As mortar spewed from between courses of brick in his fabricated walls, he navigated toward the far northern edge, the origin of his portal. Like a backdoor in computer parlance, it had been the safest place, and ultimately, the last point where his matrix would break.

Rhey was sure the muse was behind the weather but he sensed another force was forming, a backbone beneath the witch's assault, which he could not decipher—not yet. At least he had the grim satisfaction that his bikers, morphed into Bone Warriors, could still do damage. What Martin took away from him, only defaulted into the man's own fears running loose. When he felt the ground begin to grind, Rhey had no doubt the Cervine too, was on his way.

Night was a flood of fury, both figuratively and literally. As the dome cracked and began to shower the world beneath it, the pent up anger of the muse began bending more than elements to her will, it twisted and tangled every pattern having the Hunter's imprint. The Cervine frowned, even if his face was incapable of showing it. The sheer power bound within the Dark Muse's myth was tied solely to her emotional core. Currently, her rage was as gigantic as her fear. But he felt that latter as well, knowing that whatever had been wrought was for protective reasons, for the safekeeping of a secret, necessary if any more stories were ever to be written again.

It had been an admirable attempt, creativity taken to a new high, but ultimately, Jareth hadn't been able to move fast enough. Or was it because his own foibles had finally come to bear? The man ran the gamut of possibilities and always tried to steer away from its fulcrum. Not this time; as the Cervine knew, there had to eventually be a reckoning. With the added pressure of trying to keep the sequence code safe, the man could not hold his own personal demons away at the same time. From the sound of the ringing song that underlay the muse's efforts, he knew Candace was the catalyst. But there was still the edge of balance to walk, the single mote of time where Jareth contemplated which path to choose.

Until that was decided, there was only oaths to be upheld. And understanding this, he rushed toward the spot which spoke strongest of Jareth's presence. Though Leanan was a master of windsong, he too had some affinity for deciphering its fragile weave. That, and the fact he followed the flight of the crow as it fought against the rising hurricane.

And then, as if all the storm had vanished, a new chord reached out and spread like a ray of light, and as it did, song followed in a way that portended change.

It felt so good, the freeing of emotion and surrender to a deeper need; Leanan rose to titanic heights, her persona drawing all the power she needed from the world around her, one which the alien Rhey had mistakenly modeled after the real world. Every whisper of breeze and hush of falling sky heard her call, listened to her verse, embraced her song of summoning. And when they came, they brought devastating force. Arching her arms high, she smote the dome above with complete immersion, her anger directed at the being who threatened her love. When the hail began, she knew the enemy was weakening. What he'd wrought would come to naught, this she promised!

Jareth wanted to curse and cry at the same time. Beneath the churning volcanic flow of immense anger was agony, and something struggling to stay alive; hope, as brittle as he'd ever felt it. Beside him though, the haunting ghost of his dead wife still remained, even as she felt his soul stabbed by the bitter realization his daughter was still alive but in great danger. A danger into which he'd placed her, a trauma he'd found inexplicably necessary. But why? Couldn't he have chosen someone else?

Beryl

He knew without ever knowing why, that the mad clown had seized the girl, Beryl...his daughter reincarnated through his story. Reincarnated was the wrong word choice though, and he frowned.

Not now, Jareth, there isn't time. The writer must give way to the singer—to the bard and poet! The enemy has set the trap and found the key! Even now, he's attempting to escape back to the real world and when he does, surely he'll find where she's hiding!

Candace's words were like pouring gasoline on a fire and Jareth felt the burn rise through every fiber of his being. His heart bled and his mind suffocated while the huge crushing pressure on his soul intensified. A thought tip-toed past his pain and with a clear mind, he knew what to do.

It was there, locked and braced, just as Rhey had outlined it. But the distance was still great and so he began to run, dragging the girl behind him. And it was as much the additional burden as the fact he hadn't counted on Jareth's ability to adapt so quickly that threatened escape. Still, though the storyline he'd created was being erased, as if someone were taking a cursor and highlighting his words, there was an opportunity to withstand imminent deletion. Just a bit more time, that's all he needed...

They wore different armor this time, but Jareth would have recognized them for what they were; Bone Warriors. And as if acts and scenes were now tangled, characters representing minions of alien technology morphed into demons which the author could understand and more importantly, fear. Their chrome and black Harley chariots of metal and rubber turned into the real thing, complete with straining bears in leather harness. But something was interfering as well with Rhey's ability to maintain perception, and this time, with thoughts of the north in his head and the bitter weather outside the lab, polar bears were the metamorphosis of choice, their growls sounding eerily like a tiger's.

As the energy became focussed and side characters were allowed to blend themselves into the scene, the strangeness got stranger. As the Cervine broached the street where he knew he'd find Jareth, the rumble clatter of iron wheels sped like molten rumor down the veins of the earth. The fact he could feel them, could hear their voice, was undeniable proof the Hunter was abandoning this world, or attempting to. That couldn't be allowed to happen, and even though he knew evil minions approached, all he could think about was how to give Jareth more time.

They came dressed in copper scale and horned helmets, looking more like vikings than skeletal beings this time. The Cervine didn't even stop as he yanked his great bow from his back, quickly nocking not one arrow but two. When he was sure the attacking force could not easily escape, he planted his hooves and took aim.

The first bear pitched forward, throwing his rider as the great chariot overran its body, causing the rider and bear nearest to swerve viciously to also avoid crashing. But when they did that, the ever bulging walls of brick leaned out, fusing the rider and half his chariot solid. As the wall contracted, only one arm and leg remained to be seen.

So that's what happens when two story lines overlap, the Cervine thought, not taking his eye off the next rushing chariot.

The second arrow had taken out the center driver and even though there was nothing to kill, it still broke enough bones in the neck to completely sever the head, which meant one chariot was now mindless. It surged straight but the bear didn't have a mandate anymore and gradually slowed. Which caused the one behind to crash and tangle itself.

The next two arrows were away. And they'd be the last; there were too many coming too fast, so the Cervine jumped forward, catapulting over another dying bear and pinned rider, until he landed on the next rushing beast.

519

A smash of his fist caved in the animal's spine and though muscles continued to fire, they did so on the animal's belly as night-wasted blacktop took the brunt of its dying force. Hitting the ground on one hoof, the Cervine thrust his bow at the Bone Warrior still working to command his bear-less chariot. The sound of splintering wood added to the joyful howl of furious song with which the muse smote the air. It didn't last long as the Cervine swept the pile of disintegrating bones out of his way, vaulting over the chariot as he did. And just like that, he was past.

There was no time to finish off the Hunter's monstrosities—a window was closing even as Leanan was fighting to open it wider. He needed to get to the girl...

Jareth sang a song of rotting, of cancerous fibers and pulpous wood, and fed the verse that stripped all vitality from the hides of animals. One wrist was free, then the other.

He sang of verdigris and rust, of salt and relentless ocean waves as they swallowed the iron sinew of ships. He sang of how time could not preserve steel integrity until finally, the pits eroded into holes and dark metal became red dust. His lower shackles were broken but he had another problem.

Trying to roll off the table, he immediately fell to the tile floor, the sick trail of blood and ichor left on the bedsheets all the evidence he needed to tell him that his left leg ended in a bloody stump. His song stalled and then stopped, firmly entrenched in silence. He first cursed then cried, pounding a fist missing two fingers against the floor.

No time for self pity—take my hand!

The glowing light that was his wife simmered like wildfire, anxious to be let loose and yet controlled, and contained, as confident as a new born sun.

Don't think, just do it, Jare!

He reached up and she hauled him upright, set his arm over her shoulder and let her lead him toward the door.

The pain in his leg was immense and he bit his lip trying to keep from being overwhelmed. Limping, he made it to the door. He waited for her to open it and when she didn't he looked anxiously at her.

I only exist because the link of our love still exists, Jare; I am not here, but here.

And she placed her hand on his chest, above the heart, merging her fingers in the grooves of scarred flesh that formed a desolate tattoo. He understood.

Reaching out with his maimed hand, he closed on the knob, willing muscles to move, forcing the pain to wait, holding his breath for fear breathing would overwhelm him too. Nothing.

Sing, Jareth; it's locked.

The words issued forth and immediately he felt a surge of strength, felt muscles and fibers of his body trying to heal.

No time for it all; just get the door open.

Jareth focussed his efforts on metal again, on rust and fire, then on lava and acid. That did it. The whole mechanism fell to the floor, dripping and forming a foaming puddle.

They're coming.

Who? Leanan? The Cervine?

Yes, they come. They heard you call, but so did he.

The Hunter?

Candace nodded, the light framing her face beginning to flicker.

He looked at her full of confusion.

I can't go with you, Jareth, not outside; he created this world beneath the dome. It is not of your choosing and he put safeguards to keep me outside.

But you're here with me.

Because he can't create scenes containing you; that domain belongs only to the author. He'd have written your death too easily otherwise.

Beryl

I don't want to leave you...not again.

No time, Jare; Beryl will be lost...

The galvanizing effect of her words was like having a hot piece of steel rammed up his spine and he lurched forward without even a backwards glance. The door burst open and he hopped out, almost falling.

It was a wild scene with pieces of sky tumbling down like broken shards of glass, curiously dull along their edges. The sound almost deafened him and he fought to filter out which was good and which was evil. He heard the storm and immediately felt Leanan's presence. Like an electric charge, her touch was a lover's caress along the most sensitive part of his body. He buckled again and would have fallen if not for the sword. He didn't even remember picking it up. But in place of his disembodied wife, the stalwart blade kept him upright. Glancing at his leg, the ooze and bleeding remains nearly sickened him to falling a third time.

He picked his head up, the tears merging with blood, matting hair to face. He couldn't even sweep his gaze clear, so clotted had it become. The street was a shattering broken frame whose canvas has been doused with mineral spirits; colors were bleeding into other colors, shapes were becoming unfamiliar. The street was cracking, or rather, re-structuring; the original story's scenery was trying to reassert itself. *He* was trying to reassert it.

The wind wrapped itself around him so he would not fall and he knew it was Leanan's doing. He listened to his heart and heard her words, heard her song as she bullied the creative intellect of the Hunter, wresting away more and more control. And in her touch was the echo of thanks, of relief. Why?

I couldn't have done this by myself, my Love; he is much stronger because he is alien. He controls the wires, he controls the chemicals. But you control the story. When you lent your voice to mine, it was then he stopped fighting and fled.

Jareth scanned deeply into the miasma of falling stages, of collapsing dream frameworks; surely that's what this had to be...a dream.

Stay with me, Jare; it's not over yet—he's got the girl.

Jareth felt the hammer of guilt slam into him again but the wind's grip was firm, and the sword kept him pinned tight.

I know.

He's trying to get out.

He's not already gone?

Not yet; the girl must be yours—she's as stubborn as you.

Jareth wiped his eyes.

What do I have to do?

What you always should have, Jareth; fight for her.

The howl of wind lashed both at his ears and soul, as damning as the truth.

Sing Jareth, sing; sing so she hears you...

The melody was tangled, bubbling from too many emotional wounds, from memories he didn't have because he hadn't been there. Too much time spent at work had robbed him of something he should have had a right to. It was something only the boy Word would be able to define, though.

Sing, Jare—nothing fancy, we don't need that now. We need blunt force. He may have gotten inside your head and learned to work the story's program, but you're the one that understands it because it is you. Hit him hard, where it will hurt the most...

The spike of pure power that lanced from where he stood on the unsure pavement was intense, as if lightning could be defined in terms of sound. He gave his emotions full access and the song he sang was both hard and painful, but inside the hurt, he lashed out at his persecutor. And like a post coital robe being slipped on, he felt his muse rise up behind him, her voice adding blue fire to his.

The street was chaos in the making and more; when the Cervine arrived, he saw the solitary form of Jareth, barely standing, bleeding, maimed and weaker than he'd ever seen him. But the Lord of the Forest knew that what he was seeing was a physical weakness, not an emotional one, one not even close to spiritual tragedy. The man was alive, but barely. Still, alive was good.

And that's when he noticed the shapes that constituted buildings all around Jareth were doing more than heaving, more than exhaling and inhaling; they were beginning to split at the top. This was an urban representation and like all such, there were more high-rises than not. This street was no exception and as the Cervine watched, he saw a pattern to the chaos.

With a barking grunt, he picked up speed and ran toward the man who had no idea of the impending disaster. As the first stone lintels from the tower's summit slipped loose, a new shower of death began.

It had to be enough, there was no more of his mind to use. The city was lost, the dome fracturing and allowing Martin's creation to swallow his. But before that happened, he'd begun a chain of retaliation all his own. It would at least keep the author busy trying to stave off this latest development. And by that time, Rhey hoped to be rid of this incessant fantasy, the one which claimed humans were more than they were.

There were docks here, something he hadn't placed but now accepted. Already his version was being corrupted, though he could not follow the arc's reasoning. A boat lay tethered to a metal dock, with more beyond. The glisten of light off waves showed him nothing else was afloat; there was no one to stop him. His ruse was working.

"On the boat, girl; we'll see to any secrets you carry in due time. I should have known there'd be rats crawling in the rot.

How you eluded my attention before isn't material anymore, even though it is curious. On the boat, now!"

He whipped her forward, causing her to fall face first on the deck before sliding toward the wheelhouse. The boat was a twenty-footer, and speedy too. This would do fine.

Thank you, Martin. But then, very soon, I'll be able to thank you personally! Won't be long now. And before it's your turn, you'll see what I do to your precious secret!

The air was literally melting as the storm's fury slaked its hunger among the warehouses and restaurants lining the wharf. Rhey focussed his mind and thought of the lab in its sterile white enclosure, recalled the various monitors, screens, the table where his victim still lay manacled and pumped with drugs. Where was it? Where was the trigger mechanism to pull him out of the story, as he'd done before? It should be a switch on a panel, a light of red or blue, possibly a toggle...But he didn't see the panel he was looking for and cast his gaze away from his semi-comatose body. In his mind's eye, he could see another strip of muscle peel away from a forearm when he raised it. He began searching the room.

With an ache, he felt the very breath of the storm all around him, something he'd been easily able to shrug off, up until now.

Touching his hand to the ground, the Cervine could only hope the Hunter's matrix infrastructure was sufficiently porous to allow him to find earth, real earth, not that which had been pasted as a floor to the dome. He needed to feel the ground upon which he'd walked, that which Jareth had created, because if he could, then those voices which sung to him could be reached with song of his own. And as he scrambled, prying chunks of cracking cement out of their lattice, he reached down, beyond the dome's influence. At last, he touched soil, the kind upon which his beloved trees grew...

A surge of power ripped through Jareth's body and exited with as much display as Leanan's maelstrom, but much more focussed. It narrowed and arced, aiming for the northern part of the city. He sagged, grateful for the blade. His voice never stopped though, adding fluid fire to the trail his words were taking. It was then he looked up.

From between two barrels of oil, a black shadow leapt, eyes closed until the last minute, giving it an invisibility it never would have had otherwise. The face of the character resembling the Joker had been looking the cat's way all the time and yet had seen nothing. It was as if he stared but was intent on seeing something else, something his mind was conjuring. The bolt of black hit him with malice, claws narrowly missing Joker eyes but tearing flesh nonetheless. Rhey swept his arms toward the monstrosity on his chest, only then realizing that what he was seeing had been real, just in a different way. The animal bounded away hissing and sped into the shadows of the pier.

Beryl watched stunned, not at her captor but at the sky; the clouds were running rampant now. An eddy had turned into a whirling vortex of ripped sky, the colors streaked with shreds of moonlight, barely visible as a backdrop. She saw how the lightning bent and vaporized the remaining shards of the dome before launching themselves downward. Whole buildings were mutated and melted, and in their place saplings unfurled their leaves and sent trunks impossibly fast toward the sky. The earth was reclaiming itself, and with it, time.

And above it all, she saw a black bird, hurtling with a burning sky right for them.

Jareth looked up. A shower of debris was falling toward him and he hadn't the energy to shift his focus, nor did he have the song. Like a murderous deluge of hail, the tops of both buildings above were coming down.   His mouth opened, muted, with nothing but a knowing sense of doom come to claim him.

The sound was like a rifle going off; a sharp crack and then an invisible whoosh of air. The ground surrounding split and spread, allowing spears of branches to arc up, their speed astounding as a canopy unfolded, diverting the stone and metal shower.   The sounds of pieces landing all around reminded him of rain falling on a bog; a steady thunk and then a spongey resonance as each was absorbed by the ground.

And there on the periphery, Jareth found a familiar shape, that of the Cervine, looking as unmoved as the oldest oak tree, both his hands flat on the ground.

He stared back, no words needed. Then, there came just the slightest tip of his many-antlered head. Jareth tried to nod back but felt his energy draining. He must still be losing a lot of blood.

Chapter 58

Pictures

She squelched the urge to howl and quickly brought her arm up to her mouth, the bare beginnings of blood quickly sucked between her lips. It hurt, but she would not cry, would not give her position away; she'd been hiding too long now to let the cat's stupidity betray her. Why she'd had this notion to look at the ceiling baffled her. Had she heard something coming from the air conditioning vent?

She slipped along the wall, watching for shadows and light, knowing that between these, she would be safe. Oh mother, I miss you so much...

The young girl was skinny from lack of food and dirty from hiding in the dust. It had been a long time since she'd been clean but it didn't matter; she'd never be clean again, not after seeing her mom tortured. But what hurt more was the guilt, the shame she'd embraced the day mother had been taken from her. While it was only days, for her, the torture had gone on forever until one day, she'd crept out and found the second table empty. There wasn't any explanation, she was just gone.

In her heart, she knew her mother wasn't coming back. And now, she was so alone. Everyone had long deserted the government building where her father worked, leaving her as the last human being alive. Or at least it felt that way. In truth though, she knew she wasn't the only one; her father still lay on the first table, but he might as well be dead too. There were so many tubes and wires attached to his body, she doubted anyone could survive.

The alien had tortured him as well, but she'd been too afraid to come out during that time. It was all she could do to stay quiet and invisible when the invasion had finally come to her family. It was the day nightmares took her dream away, it was the moment she understood what it was to die by living.

The aliens had taken them both from the house on Kinnick St, on the west end of Philadelphia. The government thought they were so smart, housing one of their secret laboratories in a quaint town called St. David. But the invasion force had caught them all by surprise and almost too quickly, their defenses were destroyed. Mass panic ensued and most of the rest of civilization got caught. The few who didn't follow the herd sought hiding places.

She had a hiding place too, but hers was forced. When the alien had taken them, she'd been locked in a cage, the type used for lab animals. She'd cried until the tears were gone and then rocked into silence, arms and legs so restricted that even the cramps were welcome after awhile.

It had been the last time she'd seen her mom, the day courage and desperation reared up and fought back. Lunging for the cage, her mom had knocked it to the floor, bending the wires, and with a frenzied kick, she'd been able to get free. But the alien wasn't as slow as he looked and mom never got as far as the door. All she could remember was hearing her scream "Run! Run and don't look back!"

She'd run, but the building was huge, the rooms and halls vast and complicated. She began to fear going toward any outside door when dogs could be heard outside. The aliens were rounding up any survivors and the dogs got what was left. Fearful, she instead dug herself into the bowels of the lab, using the ventilation shafts as she'd seen in almost every chase movie. It wasn't long before she found her dad's secret room.

It wasn't really a secret other than to say neither she nor her mom had ever known of its existence. She supposed it was where he went all those times he never came home. Working, he'd say, working on top secret defense projects. After awhile though, it seemed like the house on Kinnick Street was the secret. He came home so infrequently that in time, she did not feel like she had a father.

Her mom had tried to make excuses, but being a teenager didn't mean she was stupid. After all, she was almost fifteen now, wasn't she? Didn't matter, she'd still had mom.

But not anymore. The day she snuck back like she always did and found only the empty table, that was the day she knew life must have ended. It was probably just luck that the alien was absent the day she visited for surely her ability to escape would have been compromised by too many tears. She didn't want to live, not anymore.

Still, the will for survival isn't a trait taken lightly and after she'd grieved in her hideaway, she finally came to realize her mother would want her to live. It was why she'd given her life up in the first place.

Now, time was spent in her dad's secret stowaway room, working through all the books he had on dusty shelves, hoarding the precious food he kept for overnights. Must have meant to spend a lot of time there because she had a whole closet full of canned chili and Hostess treats. She could still drink from the tap—thank God the aliens had not destroyed the plumbing system. But from what she'd gathered, it was for the water that they'd come.

Still, it was the water that had almost given her away. She'd not turned the handle fully off one time, causing a persistent if quiet trail of water to form in the sink. It was the same day the alien had come and entered her dad's room for the first time. Since then, he'd come often, sometimes spending hours reading the same books she read, the same books her dad had read, and other times turning the stereo on to sample dad's music. Which quite surprised her; the books *might* mean something, but the music?

Not that it didn't mean something to her—it did, because it was about the only connection she'd ever had with her dad. It was he that had taught her to play guitar, though it was now so long ago the memory was rusty.

She often put the earbuds in her ears and listened to her dad's songs on his old ipod. Sometimes, she even smiled at songs he'd tried to sing to her.

She looked at her arm, noting the punctures had stopped bleeding. Darn cat; now what had gotten into her? She dared not go looking though—a cat wasn't a threat to the alien so she let it go, confident Hershey would return. They'd had enough time to create a narrow pathway in and out of her dad's room, one by which they could not be seen or heard.

It was time to get back though; too many hours now with too much silence. It meant the alien was gone; where, she did not know. And with that doubt, she grew more afraid. Hershey was gone too but when she came back, there would be a scolding!

Threading her way through the myriad hallways leading down to the lab, she at last wormed her way back into the space between two walls where she then curled up and hugged the picture of her mom tightly, remembering with tears. Behind her was a stack of books where one of her dad's favorites lay with a worn bookmark. She was almost halfway through and this was her third time experiencing the story. The first had been when she was young, when she'd been snuggled between her parents while her father's voice rose and fell as the different characters played their part. She'd always liked Legolas the best...

And behind that stack of books, were two other pictures, one which was as dusty as everything else in her hideaway. It was a picture she'd never seen before the tragedy, one of her dad while opening a box of books. She supposed it was when he'd finally gotten a manuscript published. At least that's what the inscription and date stamp on the back said. It was a part of him she hadn't known, and it was with curiosity only that she read now. Not the same book in the picture—she hadn't found any copies of that—but words that had once brought them together as a family.

Reaching back, she grabbed the Two Towers and slipped the marker out, spreading the book on bent knees, forming images in her mind's eye by flashlight while her other hand fidgeted about her neck. As the words of Tolkien came to life, she was hardly aware that she twisted the small gemstone on its chain, twisting and feeling its smooth, red skin. She'd remember if asked, but it had been so long that only memory now gave it any importance. It was a rather rare stone, something her dad had given for her tenth birthday, a stone he used to say made up one of Heaven's gates. A beryl he called it. It was, coincidentally, also her name.

The electronic beeping had increased its frequency, flashing alternately red then blue. The monitors were dutifully graphing every change, every alteration, whether it be physical or digital, and doing so precisely.

On a table, a man was bound with metal retainers, skin and flesh showing signs of emaciation and atrophy. Eyes were closed and breathing steady, with an occasional long inhalation. His face showed an unkempt beard, the man's occasional drooling fits having dried numerous times without regard. The many electrodes attached to his skin showed red beneath their touch, and the multitude of wires reminded one of an old science fiction movie.

On a chair nearby, another reclined, held in place by a canvas strap, as if without it, the body would slip forward to the floor. His form was much further into decay, with recent evidence spoiling the white tile floor on either side of his chair. And yet, it was he that still showed obvious signs of life.

He too had wires and tubes poking from his body, many containing the same color liquid as those connected to the man on the table. A thin strap of what looked like circuit board tape ran around his forehead like a crown, and from it, two wires led to a portable computer by his side.

The laptop's screen was lit and motion could be seen, mostly in the form of text as it scrawled from one side to the other and then down again, scrolling as needed. The fluorescent lighting cast an unhealthy green glow about both faces. All but one bulb, which flickered to show its age.

And there on the table next to the computer, a black form sat, furry black tail dangling, the tip flicking back and forth nervously. Large green eyes reflected the whole scene, glassy orbs that showed the other two occupants of the room. The animal turned its head toward the table and when nothing moved, gave a single plaintive mew, as if wondering when dinner would be served.

But nothing moved except for its tail, and that never stopped. The black cat turned its head back and meowed at the chair-sitter, still wondering when it would get fed. Again, nothing moved and only the constant beeping sound gave any indication that the world had not stopped.

Flicking her tail vigorously once, the black cat named Hershey got to her feet, and slipping on the smooth surface of the table, leaped to the floor. In her effort however, the cat managed to catch her paws on one of the two wires attached to the laptop, pulling loose a connection. The wire swung carelessly toward the floor, no longer able to perform its mechanical duty.

Hershey lifted her tail and strode out the door and into the hall with the notion that the girl would give her food.

Chapter 59

Memories Within Temptation

"Keep his arms from moving all about, won't you?"

The Cervine's tone was unflappable yet pointed. Leanan, who didn't like being talked to in that way, glared but acquiesced nonetheless. After all, time wasn't on their side and this healing couldn't take as long as it should. Already, the Hunter had a substantial lead.

"We'll be able to track him now."

Leanan indicated her familiar, perched on one of the low hanging branches of the Cervine's rapid tree growth experiment.

But even though his concentration focussed once again on Jareth's leg, he shook his antlers slowly, the same emotionless expression on his face. Which annoyed the muse no end simply because as an emotional creature, she leaned on her ability to read others easily. And the Cervine was anything but easy.

"No, I think you'll find once we leave this area, that any residual effects of the enemy's creation will fade, turning your feathered friend...into something else. We can only hope it's the snow tiger—I think we're going to need him."

Leanan's brow arched and her lips pursed tighter as she considered the Cervine's words. Did that mean her own powers would change back as well?

He lapsed again into silence, hands deftly working the man's skin, from thigh to remnants of the knee; Jareth's right leg was a mess and already the man had passed out twice from blood loss.

The healing was taking longer than expected. With a stirring of molten green in his eyes to reflect his thoughts, the Cervine wondered what the man had gone through during his ordeal with the Hunter.

"Why aren't we calling him by his alien name?"

The muse was trying to make conversation, trying to take her mind off the only artist who'd ever broken the ancient pattern. She liked to tell him that they'd chosen each other, but that wasn't how it typically happened; usually, it was her choice alone, the artist seduced by what she could give. Trouble only started later when mortal confines lapped into self-immolation due to pride. Jareth was the only one who'd found a way to survive.

Leanan eyed the deep ruts on Jareth's chest, shivering unconsciously as she remembered that day. All her pleading in the world hadn't been able to change his mind, and though she could often manipulate his emotional center, she would never admit to not owning him fully. There was just too much to the Bard to contain. Time had taught her that.

"Because it is just another reflection of the same evil, and to say its name as Jareth has written would give evil an advantage. It is only through understanding the all encompassing spectrum with which the enemy fights us that we can keep it from outflanking our efforts. If Jareth was awake, I think he would agree. That is, if he remembered. Though he seems to be coming around, there's still odd lapses that do shake one's confidence. Maybe we need to look more carefully at the interstices of the story's weaving, maybe there we'd be better able to judge how this is to end."

But Leanan wasn't listening anymore as Jareth tried yet again to flail his arms in his semi-conscious state, the words issuing from his mouth twisted and corrupted, their sense totally lost. Only a few were coherent and those caused more anxiety than comfort. Besides, when the creature's soliloquies tangented off into deeper realms, her connection waned.

The leg was severed in such a way that the Cervine had to alter his approach to the mend.

"What are you doing now?"

The concern in the muse's voice was only too obvious. To her, it looked like the Cervine was melding living wood to Jareth's thigh. High above, the crow carked in echo.

"I'm having to tie veins and arteries to the different phelioderm. If I don't get enough of his postsynaptic membranes attached to the vascular cambium, the synaptic vesicles will die and he'll be left with just a prosthetic. Though he'd survive, he'd be too limited to do what he has to do."

Much of what he was describing went over her head. That wasn't what mattered to her. She realized her guess was accurate.

"I mean, is he going to be whole again?"

With his fingers delicately binding fibers of root core and human capillaries, he shook his head.

"No, he'll be better—he'll have even more affinity to the earth, and he'll be able to draw from it more easily."

She considered this, noticing that her long nails had drawn blood from Jareth's wrists. Where it oozed and mingled with the scars of past cuts on one wrist, she frowned. What would it feel like in the future to run her fingers along Jare's leg? She loosened her grip.

"You mean like he drew voice from the trees in the woods?"

The Cervine nodded.

"Exactly like that and more; he could merely hear them then; now, he'll be able to sing his song directly to living roots binding the soil. For all intents and purposes, he'll be more grounded."

Leanan breathed a whisper of the words the Cervine had stopped short from saying.

"Like that's ever helped him in the past..."

As Jareth's muscles relaxed again, she took a chance to place her left hand on his chest and stroked the skin where his tattoo lay emblazoned.

"Do you know why he did this?"

"Of course, and so do you."

"I didn't mean that, I meant why he didn't feel like he couldn't *not* do it."

The Cervine paused only a second, the line of the muse's thoughts touching too closely to his own. Then he resumed, relieved to see the skin pinking as well as the wood greening at the same time; it meant his efforts were not in vain.

"You know, Sidhe, there's something to be learned from a mortal's heart—and that's something in which you excel—while a broad portion of a human's reasoning also can teach you much. That's an area an observer can witness once they're close to the person in question. Both of us know Jareth well this way. Then there's the soul, something which I know intimately, though you often dismiss as of secondary importance. Though few humans draw from this source, it doesn't mean there's a dearth of power there."

He stopped, realizing he was entering worlds of philosophic discussion that usually bored the muse; he'd watched bemused when Jareth had made such attempts with her in the past. But the woman was persistent, maybe because the man's health might depend on her understanding him better. She didn't actually care about many mortals but when she did, she made her concern symbiotic. Which gave the word devotion new meaning.

"But consider what would happen if a mortal could harness emotion, thought, *and* spirit; that is, heart, mind, and soul—what then might happen to humanity's aspirations?"

Leanan was silent because she wouldn't admit to anything. But, she realized this prospect would make mortals mightier than gods, even her own.

"That's never happened."

Her voice was a rasp of sound.

The Cervine nodded slowly, his fingers layering the epidermis of the wood into seven sections, one for each layer of human skin.

"The bards are said to have achieved this."

His voice was barely above a whisper.

Leanan snorted, too quickly. She choked back any further outburst and regained her composure. She massaged Jareth's skin, thinking she was working her own magic without the Cervine being aware, her fingertips pulsing sublimely with blue flame, annealing the skin about his tattoo, but especially in the area of his heart. She realized that maybe there was more to what the Cervine was saying.

"If not for a mortal's predilection toward the enemy, neither of us might be needed."

The Cervine stepped back from the twist of branches and vines that formed his table, looking at the troubled features of the man as he lay supine.

Leanan didn't want to speculate, or had indeed become bored with the Cervine's abstract revelations, preferring instead to retreat into a cocoon of familiar sensations, those that often could not be quantified by anything like an IQ test. She knew the vast expanse that could be emotionally tapped, just as she knew Jareth was similarly aware. And this, she felt sure, was an area the Cervine had little real knowledge.

"That's all I can do; the rest is up to him. He still has to want to live; that's not something any other force can dictate. Without this choice, life wouldn't mean anything anyhow."

Leanan nodded, understanding his declaration, completely agreeing with the creature for once.

"Should I lay the sword near him?"

She hadn't meant the short side version, either.

The Cervine shook his head without hesitation.

"No, he's not ready and though it might help him, I don't think he needs to have his mind pulled in too many directions. I'm hoping Candace's words are still resonating—that will help."

The muse frowned, annoyed, and the Cervine chuckled.

"Jealousy is surely a womanly trait; however did you think to acquire it so intimately, so humanly?"

Leanan Sidhe, the Dark Muse, folded the expression of her face into silence and attempted to do the same for the mocking Cervine, but failed; it was too clear to both that whatever connection they both shared with Jareth, it was as deeply wound as the wood of his new leg.

"Besides, I thought you'd learned to co-exist with Candace, no?"

But she turned her glare away and concentrated on Jareth's bruised and beaten form, caressing the lines of his face with her long fingers. She stroked back the long hair and smoothed the hardness of his lips. Lightly placing her fingertips on his eyelids, she held them steady for a moment, almost as if she could hear his heartbeat that way.

"Oh, I have; I just don't see why he needs her anymore in the first place; he has me."

The Cervine stepped back and cleaned his hands in the spring which newly bubbled at the base of a towering sycamore. It's cool water was refreshing and he thought to cup a small amount in his hands and gently wash the man's face as well as the wound. With the blood and grime dissolved, paleness began to palpitate with color—good color, something that held the promise of life.

The muse stepped back as he did this, understanding that the Cervine was the one necessary for Jareth's physical health right now, though she knew her administrations on his far flung emotional core were also valuable. But those, as was often the case, were never really loose but just misplaced. It was she that helped Jareth re-order how he was feeling into something laced with purpose. And when that happened, there was a depthless well of power from which they both could draw.

"Because she is from him, metaphorically. Therefore, he will know her and she him. It is the wisdom or folly of humanity; depends upon whose perspective you take."

"Makes him weaker than he needs to be..."

"Makes him stronger than you'll ever know, Sidhe..."

The wind sprang up, looking for ears upon which to leave their news, the stirrings of the world having never stopped.

"He's taken to the ocean, to the earth's womb."

The Cervine nodded, already aware of this fact, knowing whom she meant.

"He'll reach the Final Causeway soon; shouldn't we be going? He may not be able to leave this world as it is now, but I wouldn't put it past him to find a way to alter the parameters again to serve his needs. The girl isn't going to hold up long. Too bad the crow didn't get there in time."

The wind swept up, lifting the pin feathers of the crow, its beak pointed and closed, its eyes half-lidded and reflective. It saw how the Hunter's efforts were dissolving into fragments which continued to contort and conform to the re-emerging original scene's intent. Buildings and street corners had collapsed, auxiliary characters had become rocks or lumps of misshapen clay, spent entities of an alien mind. Jareth had had no purpose for these, and as he'd lashed back at the enemy's mind, at the physical being tormenting him from afar, some of the change was transitional and some a combination of description. So it wasn't surprising that the crow saw trees whose bark looked like brick veneer, or skeletal remains of cars that looked like tree stumps. The aftermath though, did not portend good things to come. They'd need to be alert.

"This is Jareth's fight, not yours, muse."

Leanan glared more fiercely but the Cervine continued, ignoring the woman.

"I think the Hunter will be more concerned about isolating her first; he definitely understands fear now, more so than before. There is no more clear distinction between torturer and victim, hunter and prey; Jareth has found his song again and the alien knows what he can do. No doubt he'll be trying to put as much distance between us and build as many defenses as he can. To get past Jareth's encryption is going to be harder than just locating its hiding place. The enemy has won the first skirmish but in the process, has woken the very source of strength we need; Jareth Rhylan, the Bard. He is beginning to really remember."

And Leanan nodded, a small sneer traversing her blood-red lips. Indeed, he is.

"But whereas in the real world the Hunter could not physically break Jareth, here he has wounded him deeply. I am counting on the Unnamed's arrogance to continue, that though he flees, he'll not see the integral connections of Jareth's story lines, not as he should. Therein lies our hope. That, and time. The longer Beryl holds out, the weaker the Hunter becomes. I only fear he'll sense this before we reach him and do something drastic, dooming us to a never-ending war in a place where Jareth's song might die due to a lack of importance."

Leanan started, pulling her hand back, worried she might have accelerated this possibility.

"Can that happen?"

"Some have died trying to achieve their dream, and some have died losing one; to die inside one though, well, it might relegate us all to a limbo we can't alter. If he dies, do we die with him? Or, are we to haunt the scenes with what ifs until another takes up the pen? This is new territory, Sidhe; I'm not sure even your elves could fathom implications of failure here."

Mannanan!

And then there was a scalding howl of angered annoyance behind her. Turning, she was surprised then chagrined; with feathers still molting, her familiar was morphing back into a great black and white snow tiger, its second snarl one of impatience and begrudged acceptance.

Lyr! The Cervine was proving right. They'd not have any eyes in the air after all.

"Not to worry; he's taken to the water, to which your powers are more attuned. And you still will have the wind—maybe more so now that my forests won't be blocking them."

She nodded; he was right again as even then the breeze was rallying to her summons, bringing the enemy's exact location.

"We're going to need a boat too."

The Cervine nodded, already gathering up his weapons and slinging Jareth's over his shoulder.

"Why don't you and the big cat go find us one while I see about waking him."

The Cervine nodded toward the man whose injured leg was still mottled with color, though the union of tree root and thigh was progressing swiftly.

"Can we move him so soon?"

The Cervine shrugged.

"We'll have to; whether Jareth returns to us whole or not doesn't depend on where he is physically, only mentally. There's the living sap of the earth now coursing with his blood, and through the vine's contact, he is being washed anew. It shouldn't be long before we know."

She gave Jareth a long look and then threw one at the Cervine, realizing there wasn't much choice. It wasn't exactly distaste on her face as she watched the vine of the table receding from the man's wounded leg. Turning to grab the longsword and affirming that her dagger was where it should be, she hoisted Beryl's belongings.

Whistling for the tiger, she set off in search of a ship. The black cat watched her go.

The Cervine watched her go too, understanding that once on the water, much would fall to the muse. He hoped Jareth could contain her then, when emotions were stretched thin, as they undoubtedly would be. Jareth's mind was stirring, remembering that once, he'd lost his wife. Could the man handle the fact he faced the same prospect with his daughter, too?

Chapter 60

The Howling, Ice Queen

The bay held a plethora of ships, all abandoned and left waiting. As if for a purpose. Though, Jareth couldn't imagine how, despite an eerie feeling he should. It was much like the remnants of the fallen city bordering the domes—scraps of war that just wouldn't go away despite no obvious reason for the destruction. But it didn't matter now and curiosity would have to be satisfied later; finally, they'd become the pursuers.

It was an old tanker ship, used to haul cargo from the Eastern world to the West, with holds that looked like they'd never been cleaned. By mutual consent, they agreed to keep the hatches shut and stay on the bridge. And truth to tell, other than the relative warmth, they had no reason to go below anyhow.

The air had turned colder, the temperature dropping the further north they went. Already, Leanan could see ice forming on the hull, and mist that rose high enough to cling to braids of steel cable limning the ship's outline. A ghost ship it was and a ghost ship it looked. But at least Jareth had recovered consciousness.

He sat with his leg on a chair, bundled under the few blankets they could find from the Captain's quarters. Leanan supposed she should be grateful they'd been able to get the old tanker moving though it hadn't been her first choice, but the Cervine convinced her that anything with sails in this world would not fare as well the further north they went. And north was the direction the Hunter had taken.

Still, the smell of brine was invigorating, reminding her of the old days, of moments spent at sea with another incarnation of Jareth. Then too, he'd been heavily versed in the music of words. But she didn't have time to reminisce very long; taking control of the navigation and keeping the one hundred and forty foot ship afloat took all her concentration. She needed to find seams in the frigid sea and make up time; that was the challenge. It wasn't like she had a full crew so much of her effort was spent singing to the ocean for assistance. Though the Cervine was still invaluable with physical demands, he couldn't make up for a proper ship's complement of sailors. And, the weather wasn't helping.

"This isn't normal; there shouldn't be any ice this far south."

The Cervine nodded.

"I know; I fear this is the Hunter's doing, that and what happened when Jareth's song smashed the matrix of the dome. I think whatever this world was supposed to be has been warped. We're bound to see other unusual corruptions because I think they're both still trying to wrest control over the words. The enemy might be crippled, but he's not defeated."

The Pacific Heron's paint was peeling, as if the destruction of the dome had also had an effect on the ancillary props. She was primarily blue and white and as the day grew more gray, was trying to take on that color too.

"She was designed to carry nuclear waste."

The voice of the Cervine was a monotone as he read from a ship's description he'd found as part of the captain's private journal. The ship's *last* captain. It was mostly technical jargon and he skipped much of it, preferring to highlight only what might be relevant to navigating northward.

"How appropriate."

It was the first time since they'd left the bay that she really engaged in conversation. Like her tiger, she was ill at ease, as if being at sea wasn't exactly as she'd pictured. But then, the last time she'd done so, there'd been masts and sail to give the situation familiarity.

Unlike the tiger though, she didn't feel the freedom of roaming the deck, preferring to do her pacing inside. She found that unlike the real world, here she could be affected by the weather. It had been necessary to scrounge around and further layer her garments beneath the leather armor. Stubborn, she would not relinquish it.

"Did you find instructions on how to use the forward guns?"

At least this ship had some sort of military arsenal, and what it had was not morphing into something she couldn't fathom. She'd mentioned this anomaly to the Cervine, who'd merely shrugged.

"I suppose it's because Jareth is here and his will is stronger on scenes he's in. I suspect the same will be true of any territory the Hunter inhabits; it could explain why we are entering icy seas, while he seems able to keep his distance. Where he is, the ocean is probably still open."

Leanan thought about the Cervine's words. Open water, but she also knew what the winds told her; where the enemy was, cold was pressing in as well. Perhaps Jareth did have greater subconscious control of the surroundings than he let on. She gave him a glance and increased her level of worry.

Jareth felt weak; more than just physically, he felt the strain on his soul. And this was despite the Cervine's ministrations. The rent inside him ran deep and he was unable to stem the direction of the currents upon which his psyche battled. It was hard enough to accept he'd lost a leg. Bringing his left hand up to his face to scratch at scabbing skin, he was reminded that his hand would never be the same either; two fingers on his sword hand had been taken. Rhey had done this.

Rhey; aye, his persecutor had a name, at last. Within the dome, the unfamiliar became more so, as if outside of the created world, he'd pushed such memories away. No. Rather, he'd hidden them. Still, he wasn't sure why.

He frowned, understanding that unlike the Cervine or muse, he freely admitted the alien's name and let it run loose, as if having a name made the enemy more clear. And maybe that's what he needed. No longer was he running though, and this was a hot poker touching his soul. There was one more reason; Rhey had Beryl—his daughter—and it was only this realization that kept him from falling into abject depravity at his situation.

The words of the others did not placate, they only firmed his resolve, and something inside ate at his misery with delicious anticipation. Was it revenge? Is that why he was denying his leg and fingers? Did his disfigurement really matter though, with Beryl's life now on the line? When *he'd* been the target, the implications hadn't changed his purpose, hadn't altered the trajectory of a path he couldn't remember choosing and yet found himself upon. There was too much still unknown to make his drive for vengeance anything but a subterfuge. That would change though, when they caught up with the alien.

He glanced through the large windows, their edges frosted with a growing creep of intricate pattern. He was glad he had the blankets. Grimly, even through the strange sensation of metal fingers—the Cervine had been unable to graft wood to his hand, the digits too long dead and with less viable reticules—he felt the comforting touch of his sword, waiting to unleash an anger built upon blind ignorance. If ignorance could ever be said to have any sight at all. He liked to think though that at least now his path had a goal, something he could understand, and for the first time in a long time, something by which he could be consumed. The singer in him paced to release a building tension, while the minstrel portion was working out exactly how he'd do it.

If he was honest with himself, he'd have seen it was the merging of his concern for a girl he should have known but hadn't, and the growing promise of an opportunity to do what he should have done in the first place. But such feelings and words would come later; there was still much about him that needed healing.

The Cervine watched him during moments the ship didn't require his attention, which came more frequently as the muse began to familiarize herself with the freighter. But he too saw the build of ice and wondered if Jareth would be ready when their situation worsened. At least upon waking, the man had not sunk into abject despair, or reeled into the vortices of remorse and regret. The will to live was now coupled with the burning wick of retaliation. Which wasn't exactly normal for the man. And when this high wore off? If the Hunter could keep them at bay long enough to find a loophole in Jareth's story—or a flaw in his character's weave—what state would the Bard be in then?

The Pacific Heron lifted her rusting prow higher, cleaving into the embrace of the great northern sea, her propellers grasping fervently at the waves. The wind was building and he certainly hoped it was the Dark Muse's doing and not the Hunter's. He watched her steer as if she were born to it. He shivered, feeling the cold press tighter and thankfully pointed out Jareth's fragile state when she attempted to open a bridge window. It was as if she thought of herself upon a seventeenth century schooner. It didn't take much observation to see she was much more at home, though. The sea was calling and between crashes of waves on their port side, she hummed a tune he knew belonged to antiquity.

Jareth put his head against the back of the pilot house, feeling the surge of diesel engines. What Leanan knew didn't surprise him anymore. Nor the Cervine either. He knew without both, he'd never have survived the dome's destruction. He was tired, very tired.

As if behind him, he felt the muse's touch and closed his eyes, letting smooth hands encapsulate his skin. Memories burst a dam and he remembered when her touch once sought deeper divides of time.

But she was only slipping a wad of musty overalls behind his head as a cushion. He mumbled something that sounded like gratitude and continued to keep his eyes closed, trying to understand what had happened outside the clinic.

With a drawing of air, as if the sea were inhaling, Leanan left the bridge and he could hear her hard soled heels on each rung of the ladder. Where was she going?

"I think she's going to the bow, as if from there she can locate the Hunter easier. Says she doesn't really need the wheel either, that she could guide the ship with ocean currents alone. As if..."

The Cervine stopped, his sentence unfinished but connoting the fact he knew its end.

"As if?"

Jareth heard his voice and all its fatigue.

The Cervine turned toward him and if he could have raised an eyebrow, he would have. As it was, his large ears perked forward and like sonar, homed in on the man's voice.

"Is your memory firming or is that reflex? I wonder..."

Jareth opened his eyes, not sure if he was confused or hadn't heard correctly.

"Reflex? To what?"

But the Cervine shook his head slowly, shrugging off his second query.

"She said she could guide the ship as she could a man between her legs, that the motion was much the same."

Jareth let the image have its moment. He was learning more about Leanan than perhaps he wanted to.

"I think it was her way of trying to see if I could blush."

"Blush? How odd..."

"Aye, I thought so too, but if your memory would serve, it would tell you she's insouciant like no other Siren. I think she likes it here on the water."

Jareth tried to nod but was afraid of loosing his pillow.

"I think so too. But I want to ask; what happened to her familiar? I thought I saw a crow, an image which resonated, that's for sure."

The Cervine tried to smile, not knowing if he succeeded. Secretly, he was glad Jareth was recovering so well. Did that mean their chances had risen?

"It's all because of you, Jareth; when your song punched against the Hunter's efforts to sustain the scene as he'd written it, something got twisted. For the good though, I think. See, he can't escape, at least not yet."

Jareth looked into the great dark eyes of the Cervine. And wondered how it was to get around with antlers; didn't the human-sized doorways limit movement? Ships weren't renowned for their comfort but for their economy.

The Cervine felt a sudden spasm, wondering if Jareth *was* remembering...there had been a time when the man knew intimately what it was like to have horns on his head.

"What's Rhey want with the girl?"

The question had been near and dear to his heart ever since learning who she really was. The Cervine winced at mention of the enemy's name.

"I think you know, Jareth Rhylan, but don't want to admit anything, as if you can continue the subterfuge. I think it's only a matter of time though before your secret's discovered."

"My secret?"

The Cervine nodded, stepping forward to turn the ship's wheel, having seen a motion through the glass from the muse, who even now was straddled at the very prow, the cold wind icing her hair, making pale skin seem frost-imbued. With the stark contrast of her black scale armor, she looked bound by ghost-light. The very thought made the large beast shudder as he thought of Leanan and Jareth together.

"I thought it was *Beryl* who held a secret. What do you mean?"

The Cervine felt the lash of cold air and reaching out, grabbed the door, slamming it shut once again; the seas were getting rougher while turning the color of slate. If it weren't for the sky, he'd have thought another tempest was drawing nigh.

"She holds it, but the secret is yours, Jareth. But I can't say more, it's not my part to do so."

"Not your part?"

"Aye, we all have one, even you. Actually, we've all been playing ours—it's you who's been remiss up until now."

"Until now?"

Again, a slow nod of antler to indicate the affirmative.

"As I said; it was your song that stopped the Hunter from escaping."

"Rhey."

The Cervine continued not to speak the name and just nodded.

Jareth could see he was entering territory that would not produce good fruit, judging by the lapse into silence that followed, and so changed the subject—tangentially.

"I don't even know *what* I did, let alone how."

"Sure you do, but you think denial still serves best. I'll play along for a while, but you're going to have to accept who you are ere this journey is ended."

The man brought the hand with the two steel fingers to his face, forgetting their nature for a moment. He scratched at his chin, the metal as alien as some of his memories.

"So this journey is mine, not Beryl's?"

The Cervine turned to him again, working out what lay behind the man's words.

"You know this too, and it's not one the Hunter has pushed upon you."

"No?"

The antlers shook this time and Jareth wondered if the creature ever dropped his horn, like an elk or deer.

"And where am I going?"

Seemed like an idle question and not something that really could be defined, but he asked it anyway.

"You're going home, Jareth Rhylan, you're going home."

He let the Cervine's words resonate with a vibrance all their own, feelings stirring and thoughts kicked into a panic. Home? Wasn't he already? But the Cervine chose not to intrude upon his mind this time, just when he'd actually have welcomed the interloper's presence, especially if some answers were forthcoming. Straining to catch the form of Leanan from between wave crests, he too noticed the way the sea was becoming turgid and foamy, as if only their speed was keeping the sea in a tumult. Ice was growing, he felt it in his soul.

"Has Leanan always been with me?"

Jareth wasn't at all sure the Cervine would tell him much about the muse but he innately felt he'd get nearer the truth than if he asked Leanan herself. A shadow cut off the light of day as the snow tiger roamed past, its coat looking peculiar; every strand of fur was iced. A growl followed his passage and Jareth knew the big cat wasn't happy either. Suddenly, he wondered where Piper was.

"He's right there above you, on top of the chart case and next to the poor excuse for a heat duct; seems he has your sense of propriety."

Did the Cervine chuckle then? Jareth checked to see that the black cat was indeed curled into a solid ball of shadow near the ceiling, and slung a sideways glance to catch the Cervine's expression. Nothing, just nothing; the buck-headed manling was impervious to outward expression, especially those that would actually say something.

"So? Has she?"

The color inside the Cervine's eyes swirled slowly.

"You're persistent today. That's a good sign; means you're trying to engage. Nice change of attitude, I think. But no, she hasn't been with you long, though even if you do regain that memory, you'll swear to me you've known her forever. That's the way it is with her."

Jareth opened his eyes wider, too many questions rushing their hands up in an attempt to be the first answered.

"She says she's my muse."

"Are you telling or asking?"

Jareth realized he was hoping maybe he was wrong, but didn't want to admit it.

"I'm telling."

"And so she is."

"She says she chose me."

The Cervine nodded again.

"And I didn't have any say about it?"

"Jareth, you're a bard—*the* Bard; do you think she could happen without one? Can you name even one famous artist who hasn't made that claim? The world is littered with talented people—it's part of the way you're all made, and too, a reflection of your maker. But there's a difference between the talent and skill of crafters, and that of true artists; it was you yourself who learned that, and is part of your hold over the Sidhe. If you hadn't, your days would have been counted long ago."

"What's that supposed to mean?"

"It means my dear child, that the stories of the Dark Muse are not just to scare those around a midsummer night's fire, it means she's as voracious in her vengeance as she is in her passion. The very life within her is the death one brings to the table."

Damn, the beast was riddling so thick it was hard to wrestle one thread from another, hard to know where to begin asking the next question.

"Only if living for oneself, I think..."

Did he hear a whimsical, deep dark laugh pervade his soul? Why was he suddenly wary?

The Cervine, seeing the man's sudden devolvement into trepidation chuckled again.

"That's why you're a wise bard, perhaps why you own a title and even she acknowledges it. You have enough sense to understand just how dangerous the Dark Muse really is. Maybe you're recovering after all. Here, let me see beneath those bandages."

The creature's large fur-covered hands moved expertly over his injured leg, feeling beneath bandages that looked more like wet leaves than gauze and tape.

"And they are; leaves of the Tree of Life. If not for their healing sap, I could never have joined fleshy blood molecules to woody cellulose. Turn to your side, let me see the back. The graft there is more complicated..."

The Cervine's voice trailed off as Jareth moved awkwardly and painfully, understanding he was far from healed no matter what the creature said. The injury he'd suffered at Rhey's hands went beyond physical.

"Still some residual blood but even that is being absorbed; you'll have a nice layer of bark before you're done..."

His words hung even as Jareth started, realizing too late that the Cervine was joking.

"Ah, well okay, maybe not; still—it might serve you better the next time someone comes at you with a knife."

"I don't want a damn tree for a leg..."

"You'd have been a cripple without my intervention, Jareth."

"I don't want to know..."

"And really, once I convinced the wood to shrink near the ankle, getting your boot on was easy. You'll never know the difference the further time recedes."

Jareth scowled, the thought of what his leg must look like causing him to shudder.

The Cervine was empathetic, realizing that only with acceptance could man normalize trauma. He'd seen others recoil at the prospect of sharing body parts, even if it meant death to refuse. And Jareth didn't look like a man refusing anything.

"I'm not going to be able to feel anything, am I...I mean, it feels dead to me right now—I can't even tell I have a boot on."

"It won't always be that way, Jareth; wait for the healing to finish."

The man raised an eyebrow.

"Right now, your body is mending physically; when the transplant is complete that way, the life stream of living wood will both transform as well as transmute as your blood cells begin traveling through woody microfibrils. But, no need to be bothered by that yet."

Hell, his wooden limb wasn't like he thought it was at all; the Cervine had not just made it possible for him to stump around and look halfway human, he'd made it possible for him to actually feel in that leg again. Or so he said would happen.

"No phantom pains for you, Bard; you'll have more feeling than you want, but sometimes, wounds and pain can be wonderful lessons."

More riddles. His mind tired with the effort of trying to conceive the Cervine's handiwork. He wanted to welcome silence, urge it to come between them and immerse himself in the rhythmic roll and swell of the great freighter. But it was absent.

"Did you have to choose such an awkward ship? Surely there was a luxury yacht or even a swift cutter we could have found?"

"As with everything of significance this world has to offer, Jareth, we're on the exact vessel we need to be on. If you haven't noticed, the sea is turning—no doubt further ramifications of trapping the enemy here with us. We're going to need this ship's bulk and more importantly, it's double-walled hull to keep the ice from stopping us."

"Ice? I thought you were only kidding, making a play on the cold outside."

"Nay, I think before long, you're going to see why you've called this body of water the Sea of Ice."

Hell, I didn't call this body of water any such thing...

But Jareth's thoughts weren't holding much conviction with himself anymore either; too much of what both Leanan and the Cervine had said had proven true. Maybe it was time he started to listen and not be so adamantly against what he was seeing with his very own eyes. Of course, it meant he'd have to seriously begin to wonder why song was so vital. Apparently, it wasn't just something that could give relief and comfort, it was an entity that was more alive than he'd ever imagined...

The ice was forming, even if it stayed further out from their wake. Still, he saw the first ridges where waves had washed back on themselves and frozen like a crust. No telling though how deep it went. Looking aft, Leanan glittered in iced armor.

"She really makes a striking sight, doesn't she?"

He heard his voice as it scratched at the closed door and iced windows, unable to get out; for which he was thankful.

"She always has, Jareth. It's not fair to say there'd be no Bard without her, but one can't deny how deep her emotional ties go. What you're seeing is in no small part that from which you're hiding. It would be wise not to forget that."

Beryl

And seeing her arms lift, as if trying to embrace each breaking wave against the bow, Jareth couldn't help thinking she was like the figurehead of an ancient sailing vessel, adorning with audacious grace, one that once flew the jolly roger.

"I'll try not to."

Chapter 61

Any Other Name

They were still making twenty knots despite fractures of the sea which reared up on both sides. How the muse kept the ocean solvent in front when all around was nothing but slabs of crystalline brine, boggled Jareth's mind. He'd asked the Cervine, but his answer of 'with the will of her song' didn't seem capable of accomplishing such a feat.

As the sea froze and formed alien creatures out of ice, he saw that in the distance, icebergs raised like purple menace, daring the cerulean sky to get too near.

"That's my doing."

Leanan leaned beside him on the rail, her visage northward as they set course straight for the flotilla of ice.

"I won't let him take control of that part of the scene, even if he has managed to thwart the sea except where we ship. But the sky will stay open to stars and the black velvet of night!"

There was a glee in her voice Jareth found disturbing, as if she were readying for battle, oiling up greaves and gauntlets. He wondered how sharp her sword really was, though.

"Oh, it's plenty sharp, Jare; you should know—you're the one who forged its edge. I only apply a bit of Fae whetstone to it once in a while, just to remind you you're alive!"

Everything about her spoke of consummate passion, whether in her words, her swordsmanship, or song.

"Don't forget in my walk too; don't deny it! I don't need eyes in the back of my head to know what you're looking at when I leave."

He'd have snickered if she wasn't right. But as it were, he scowled and tried not to let her haughtiness get to him.

"Do you know where he's going?"

"The Hunter?"

He clucked his tongue, feeling the cold air slip in and slap him in reproach.

"Who else?"

"Well, you might have meant the thorny brute on the bridge."

Jareth twisted and looked hard through the darkened panes of the pilot house above, knowing the Cervine was holding the wheel steady, more to give the muse a break than anything else. He saw no movement though he could feel the creature's aura even down on the deck; it was always that way, as if roots were still delving deep, infiltrating even the metal of the Pacific Heron. Jareth couldn't help feeling that through their all inclusive touch, that the Cervine could wind into the very fiber of his being. Or maybe he had a newfound sensitivity to the Lord of the Forest because of his new leg...

Leanan interrupted his thoughts.

"You once told me that all paths lead to one last road...I have this feeling, that's where the enemy is making."

"I see no roads, not with all this ice; what path do you speak of?"

And he didn't; to his eye, there was nothing but vast fields of frozen water, ice floes whose layers were building. Only the bergs in the distance offered any distraction from the norm.

"Ah, but there is one; you told me so, once."

"I did, huh?"

He fervently wished to admonish the muse, to let her know how often both she and the Cervine liked to couch their answers in riddles. But somehow, he knew she'd just laugh. And probably kiss him on the cheek at his ignorance.

"On the lips, Love; never waste a kiss..."

Dammit; how was it she could so easily infiltrate his thoughts? But then, the Cervine seemed able to do the same, so...

"What do you think of the Cervine?"

She turned to him, her pale face and hair frost-rimmed, giving her the look of a proper ice queen, though any story he'd ever heard involving one always painted a crystal dress. The muse *did* have the countenance of hoarfrost down pat.

"I think he's dangerous."

Now, that hadn't been the answer he'd been expecting.

"But then, aren't we all?"

Her laughter rang and he swore several yards of ice on the hull broke to plunge loudly into the sea.

"He seems both unfathomable and unflappable."

She eyed him, taking in his words, wondering where her lover was at the moment.

"And so he is, Jareth, so he is. Not all of us can tune into the emotional side we possess; perhaps the Cervine doesn't have one."

But considering this, Jareth dismissed the idea; to him, it was more like the Cervine understood emotion too well. He could manipulate the strings of a mandolin, but the Cervine seemed able to strum strings fabricating the heart.

"He calls himself the Lord of the Forest but doesn't seem to have a name. You'll remember he didn't claim Cernunnos."

Jareth *had* wanted to ask but wondered if a name might be too confining for such a creature.

"You're right; he seems to be more like fluid light holding a vessel, not the other way around."

"You mean like you..."

She laughed, and the sound was something that warmed his heart.

Beryl

"Nice of you to say; yes, like me."

She turned to face him, taking his hands in hers, gripping tighter as she made contact with the two metal fingers, the cold of her flesh flushing with the warmth of his mortal body.

"Oh, how I miss that."

She breathed the whisper, her mind tangential to what she really wanted to say.

"I can't say much about him, Jare, but it does seem obvious that like me, he has a vast well of love for you. That you've chosen two characters so opposite in their corporeal makeup but so stunningly similar in purpose, is not something you should dismiss so easily."

His eyes widened as he lost himself in hers, golden rings of iris out of place in this winter of a world.

"You once mentioned a Horned Lord; is that who he is?"

Leanan, her thoughts still working to melt the air with seduction, shrugged off her reverie and once again was hearing his words, as opposed to feeling them through his touch.

"There are tales telling of such a being, but too many suggest he is an agent of a devil, if not *the* Devil himself."

Jareth glanced up again at the wheelhouse. It didn't seem possible for one whose eyes could lay bare a foundation of fertile earth.

"That would make him an ally of the Hunter, and if I'm sure about anything, he's anything but."

Leanan's hair wound about her shoulder, the gusts of wind lifting and breaking fast forming icicles. The sound went unnoticed though. From atop the bridge, wedged tightly between the twin radar antennae, the tiger gave a short raspy growl, impatience mixed with annoyance because of the weather. The drool which usually lined pink fleshy jowls, iced into strange and beautiful spicules of ice, like miniature menacing spears. As if the beast needed any more intimidating features, Jareth thought.

562

"He is an enigma at most, Jareth, but I don't feel anything but surety when he's around. It's unnerving, truth be told, but I gather, necessary. If all you needed was me, he wouldn't be here now, would he?"

And as she turned the subject back toward him, he had nothing to say. If he knew why he needed such an imposing being like the Cervine, it was baffling that he'd imbue him also with a vast reservoir of compassion. The two attributes seemed to clash.

"It's like he's the most loving creature there ever was and at the same time, I sense he's capable of great wrath."

She paused, staring hard at Jareth.

"The Horned Lord is also known as the god of Fertility and Wealth, did you know that? When I contemplate him though, I am inescapably drawn to look for the comparison within you, Jare."

Her words nearly took the breath out of him and he began coughing harshly, the cold having found a deeper point of egress. Leanan tightened her grip on his arm to keep him from falling over the side. When he was able to sustain himself again, she was loath to release her hold and he was acutely aware of this.

He'd asked the Cervine, now he wanted to know if the muse would answer him.

"Is Beryl going to be all right?"

The muse straightened, not wishing to leave Jareth's strange personal cocoon of need. She knew he was still fragile.

"We've still got our quest, don't we?"

Her words threw him into confusion.

"Our quest?"

"Aye; to get her to Eli; she's searching for something, isn't she?"

But Jareth thought maybe he knew more about that than did the muse, having taken from the girl every last tattoo on her face. Remembering how he'd felt, he was loath to repeat the story though.

"Maybe," is all he could say.

"More than maybe, Jare, she has to find a truth that will set her free. As you, she too is seeking."

"Me? What am I seeking?"

Jareth was afraid to admit he might know the answer, that he was seeking a daughter he hadn't remembered. But his search would take him deep into emotions he knew had been sealed in bottles and placed out of sight.

Leanan nodded, reading his thoughts but not wishing to intrude this time while he was so vulnerable. Fragile wasn't something to be handled with heavy hands.

"In a way, you're both seeking the way home, Jare; but maybe you realize that now?"

And as the muse reiterated the Cervine's words, he knew they had to be true. He played them back and realized it was just an echo, one he'd heard before.

"But you didn't answer my question."

She looked at him and let a morning smile creep over her lips, pressed tight though they were.

"Jare, if she'd really wanted to be lost, do you think she'd have stayed?"

Leanan's words made him dizzy, not because they were nonsensical relative to the moment, but because he felt flashes of memory wash up so swiftly that he could hardly stand. He was on Rhey's table again, instruments of torture lying about and his body prone. The alien was gone, for the moment, and out of the periphery of flickering shadows that wasn't electronic or mechanical, he thought he saw the face of a young girl, a girl he knew, someone linked to his past, moving furtively as if not wishing to be found. But in her posture, there existed the real yearning to end the charade, to indeed be exposed. To be realized. The juxtaposition of who she was and who she is, made his head spin. For a moment, he found his thoughts circling, drifting on the eddies of his mind, trying to make a decision. What decision?

He leaned heavily into the muse, her chilled flesh igniting with his own fleeting warmth. Surprised, she then amplified what he was giving her and returned it tenfold, filling him with a compassion that battled guilt pouring from wounds exemplified by marks on his chest and wrist.

Leanan, for her part, just let his tears fall, looking out at the ice fields, daring the unseen scripts of text ordaining their predicament to attempt a strike. As her blue halo of light deepened, it spread to encompass both of them, melting the ice beneath their feet.

Chapter 62

Protectors of the Earth

It had been too quiet, and he should have known better, but the sea of ice and grate of hull smashing forward had numbed him half-solid, as if he'd become just another crystalline entity for the world of ice to claim. Luckily, he was on the bridge again, stroking Piper with his good hand, still afraid the cat would reject him if he used his metal fingers. Lurching from the makeshift chair, the animal spilled to the ground and with claws slipping on metal, slewed around and under the great legs of the Cervine, who was himself thrown into the wheel. Two great welts were left on the coarse fur of his chest as he straightened. They'd been struck.

Leanan shot out the door, her heels striking like match flints on the metal. Pressing against the rail, she could just see a tail fin receding beneath the edge of the polar pack ice.

With Gaelic curses surrounding her, she moved to get to the deck before the Cervine's call could stop her.

"It's not the enemy..."

Her long black hair flying, she continued hurriedly, gaining the main deck as expertly as an old world sailor, those who routinely slipped down from rigging high atop the mainmast. Her voice came flying back at them.

"I know."

Jareth massaged his leg and fingered the pommel of his sword with the other hand, a reflex because he suspected that blades would not solve this problem.

The Cervine paused a moment and turned toward the man, his eyes appraising. As certainty came, he pulled Jareth toward the wheel while scooping the cat out from under his hooves. Setting the fluff-tailed Piper atop Jareth's shoulders, he pointed toward the flashing blue glow in the distance.

"Just aim for that."

Jareth squinted and shook the hair from his eyes.

"It marks the Last Causeway and our destination; the bridge should still be standing, if I've come to understand this saga at all."

"Where are you going?"

Jareth could see the Cervine was prepping as if for war. Against whom?

"Well lad, as once famously proclaimed; out thar, thar be sea monsters!"

But the cryptic look in the Cervine's eyes belied the humorous remark. And this fact chilled Jareth more than the words' familiarity.

"There's more at work in this world of yours than what the Hunter can plot and plan—he's been using fears at the base level because he knows they can be manipulated. But that isn't the case this time; there isn't any ventriloquist-doll-turned psycho-killer theme to this one. This one, unfortunately, is self-induced."

Self-induced? What was the strange antlered-creature talking about?

But he was gone before Jareth could push his question. Both hands on the tiller, he leaned back and tried to calm the cat, small rumbling growls still emanating. Ahead, it looked like nothing but ice fields occasionally flecked with bergs. And of course, now that he'd been made aware, also a faintly pulsing blue light. His leg ached and his heart constricted even as the next blow vibrated through the hull.

Out at the very edge, the muse was running along the rail, looking to catch sight of their attacker, needing to put an image to the sudden threat. The ship rocked dangerously, threatening to take her over the side and into the near freezing water. Though clear around the ship, masses of pulp churned in the wake of a second monster fin disappearing off to port. The Cervine joined her, his hooves slipping.

"You shouldn't be out here, Fur-face; the deck'll kill you."

He ignored her greeting.

"He isn't going to be of any use this time."

Momentarily, she thought to castigate but then realized the Cervine was probably right. She nodded her head, already solidifying on which song to try. Neither she nor the Cervine had been able to resurrect the ship's guns.

"I know—he isn't ready to fight his own demons yet, just those outside. Taking time to get him to understand that these monsters are his creation would doom us. Already we're beginning to list— see?"

She pointed behind her, noting how one side of the ship was lower than the other.

"We're taking on water already?"

She nodded.

"They can pierce the walls of the double hull?" The Cervine's voice rose a notch, incredulous.

"Jareth wields some fierce fears inside, and with his psyche so sensitive, is magnifying them. I don't know if I can contain more than one at a time, though. When the Hunter attacked before, it was only with Jareth's help I was able to destroy what had been artificially created."

The Cervine's face was implacable, reading the tone of her voice more than listening to her explanation. He knew she was only brushing the surface...

"There! See it? It's coming again."

Emerging from just beneath the jumble of icy slush, a tall blue-black fin arced high, aiming for the ship. The muse raised her voice, no time to warn of her intent.

The song slashed outward like a lance, touching the waves and flattening them. The water changed color from leaden gray to electric veins of blue. Like a sudden underwater depth charge, the surge exploded, sending a shockwave in all directions. The ship halted its progress momentarily as it absorbed the force but so too did it affect the approaching ocean leviathan. Huge, the beast measured more than eighty feet long. A giant crocodile with fins and a scissor tail, the beast plunged low and only grazed the keel as it passed, momentarily affected by the change of water pressure.

Leanan began then to enrich her song, to find notes and chords which ramped both frequency and vibrance. She was singing to her roots, to ancestors of her past, bringing myth and magic to bear in her name.

But as the last sea monster disappeared beneath the lead-colored water, another hit the ship and spilled them both to the deck. Reaching out with her hand, blue flame infused the metal and the ice sizzled, allowing them both to find handholds that stopped their precipitous slide toward the edge. And still she did not stop singing.

The Cervine heard her call on Celtic deities, urging them to come to her aid. There was Dylan and Fand of the sea, and Amemetia of the water. The ship was starting to slow as she brought more of her attention to bear on their attackers.

Still on his belly, the Cervine felt the cold metal beneath him and yet it wasn't, as if the muse's passion was emanating like her mystery, in shades of blue. He lifted to his hands and knees, looking starboard. Out over the lower rail, another deadly fin lanced the winter sea.

Leanan's song rose still higher and shimmered the air as unseen elementals postured, poised to strike, if she could sing them alive. Nuada and Noden, she sang of those who controlled their streams far, far away, looking for rising currents with which to build a wall. Adsullata and Condatis, Siannon and Sabrina. The Cervine heard her call on those as well as Verbela and the twins—Dea Matrona and Dea Sequana.

When the next creature hit, the beast's whole head lay above deck level, a maw of crooked but sharp teeth bristling. With a huge slop of its jaws, the far rail no longer existed when a huge chunk of the ship was ripped away. Bending, the creature dug deep, trying to drag the ship with it.

But thin frozen metal ripped instead and the ship dipped but did not open itself to the sea. The Cervine folded his ears back, anxiety rising. This had to stop before it was too late.

"Try to pull them down, not block them! They're built too formidable to face head on, but maybe we can drag them back into the dark from which they came!"

The muse heard the Cervine's words and altered her tone, deepening her call and furthering her need. For this, the deep ones would have to become concerned.

"Dark seas, loath and loathing,
furrow currents stronger than time
raise an ocean's withering holding
sung to soul and bound with rhyme
Hear the need, swift on rudders
combing sail and clinging anchors
claim the oath the sea gods utter
and lay in blame what pirates hang for!"

Her voice rang out but now two fins were headed right at them. The Cervine froze then, feeling time stall as his gaze picked up another movement.

Against the far rail, a figure stumbled clumsily, unable to find a purchase on the icy deck. It was Jareth, and as he fell he slid toward the open rail where the last sea monster had taken its toll.

His antlers striking metal, the Cervine grunted and rose quickly, hooves smashing down and fracturing the icy surface, sending cracks in all directions. It was as if Thor's sledgehammer had fallen. Jareth realized too late that there was no railing where he was sliding. He heard the tremor in his voice threaten to overwhelm and strangle his fledgling tune but he fought it, forgetting the approaching edge for the moment. He had to lift his voice higher, it had to be heard...

Leanan had already seen Jareth's plight, even before he'd slipped. Damn the man—couldn't he ever follow directions? She eyed the approaching sea monsters and gaged Jareth's egress accordingly, then reached down and with one finger pointed his way, lay her palm hard and sure to the deck.

There were sudden cracks and fissures racing beneath him, and almost as quickly, blue fire, searing the ice and creating great hissing eruptions. As his voice continued to build, he was unaware of tendrils unwrapping from his wooden leg. They bit deep and fed into the fissures in the metal, limned as well with blue light. He concentrated on the verse, on putting coherency into his need, and wrapped it in music.

The leading sea monster's jaw dropped but all three combatants on the deck could see it struggled as it did, the will not on the same page with the way. The other never did open its mouth and both rammed the freighter hard, shivering the metal and cracking whole slabs of ice off the deck. Which rained down on rigid sails of flesh as the monsters dove deep yet again. The Pacific Heron rocked and Leanan and the Cervine dropped to the deck again, her song momentarily suspended.

Even from where they sprawled though, both heard the frailty in the man's voice as he attempted to forestall the next attack.

"Valiant try."

The muse nodded without saying anything, her own voice regaining its rhythm and timber. The Cervine turned to her but she had her eyes closed now, completely shutting out the external world and reaching for something else.

The Cervine heard her ply the refrain and coax the chorus, heard her claim the power of Shoney and then her father, Manannan mac Lyr, before even shaping the image of Lyr himself within her verse. The sea around them began to churn and the Cervine wasn't sure if this meant more sea monsters or that another force had arrived. He didn't have long to wait.

The icy sludge liquified and the ice retreated with hissing vents of water, the edges sloughing off and into the warming currents. Leanan's voice rose higher as the ship stabilized and she could stand again. Slate turned to gray-green and then to green-blue as processes normally slower were enhanced. Algae cells were stimulated by the glaring sun and the warming water. But through this, though from a further distance, three more fins broke the surface and once more set their aim on the Pacific Heron.

Jareth couldn't understand why his song didn't seem effective; surely he was doing it right, wasn't he? If he understood any of what the muse and cervine continually hinted, his voice should be able to quell the sea, to create a barrier between the attackers and themselves. When he'd seen Leanan fall, he knew then he had to do something. And though his leg still ached and he felt doubt in every joint, he grit his teeth and forced himself to go down. Tying the wheel so it couldn't move, and setting Piper atop the chart cabinet again, he girded his sword and let his fingers glide momentarily across the strings of his mandolin. The warmth of the sound was enough to tip the balance between trust and belief.

But now, that decision seemed ill-fated because the sea monsters bearing down on them were unaffected. Was he singing the right words? Was there something wrong with his melody? He heard the muse's voice; was he counteracting her efforts? And with that, doubt took over and his voice cracked.

The leviathans' broad backs were open to the brilliant sun and tossing sky, whose clouds were rifts being torn as if they too were icy flakes seeking to stop the world. Scars and welts from earlier battles rippled throughout their skin, some deeper than others. Above the waterline this time, the Cervine could see their baleful eyes, a place where it was easy to be deceived. Like most seas, they were calm on the surface but harbored great depths where few could survive. He looked on them without surprise though because he'd seen them before. As a mirror of the man's mortal coil, this was nothing unknown. The enormity of their size though, made him wonder if they hadn't grown, or worse, were still doing so. If he was right, these three were at least a hundred feet long and laced with wounds that still bled.

The Cervine grunted and his nostrils flared. From behind the three, long inky black arms were emerging from the water, rising up from both sides. Had Jareth turned his fears into something worse? Wasn't slashing teeth and great size enough? Had they now sprouted fingers from their fin-like appendages? He braced, wondering if the ship would survive.

But he soon saw that the two entities were separate. Behind him, he heard the muse cry out the name of Tethra, god of the old sea and worse, a god of the underworld. Why did the muse choose to call on him?

The arms soon reconciled into suckered limbs, like those possessed by the giant octopus. Each arm reared up and out, and with more speed, dropped down, attaching to the tail of each sea monster. And their grip was as tight as death.

Jareth stopped singing, his nerve failing in the wash of self-pity. Failure was overcoming his efforts; Rhey would destroy his daughter, too. His head dropped without ever seeing the rising tentacled arms.

Water struggled between hissing vents of muse-created heat and the inescapable clutch of ocean cold. As the unseen maw of the submerged giant rasped, its great arms began pulling the struggling three down. And as their struggles intensified, as their will to overcome and overwhelm grew tragic, their scissor tails would break free and smack the ocean's surface while more suckered arms would weave around mighty girths, slowly containing the attackers. As first one sea monster and then the other were dragged beneath, the last lashed out, lifting its staggering girth out of the water and falling toward the Pacific Heron.

The mighty head hit the edge of the freighter with the worst blow yet, crushing in metal and tipping the vessel almost over. As it cantilevered, the ship's keep was exposed to the surface and everything not tied down began to move toward the last sea monster. It opened its mouth and showed a frenzy of broken teeth. In slow motion, the ship tilted and so too did the immense beak-like maw.

Leanan and the Cervine slid until they encountered the handles of the cargo holds. And as they did, the last note of Leanan's song hung like a campfire spark; lasting for a glistening minute until burned up, the shard was gone.

Jareth hung precariously, the grip of the vine winding from his leg having weakened when doubt and misery consumed him. No part of a man is not subject to what lays on his heart. In that moment, Jareth was losing the battle of survival. Having failed again, he wasn't sure he wanted to live to face yet another memory, and so the vining grew confused and loosened their grip until he was sliding toward the opening maw of the last sea monster.

But the Pacific Heron wasn't about to die this way, and with the sea quickly reclaiming its frozen touch, the keel bit deep and refused to completely leave the water. Inertia and buoyancy returned and as it began a slow roll back, Jareth's slide slowed too. The edge of the ship came up and slid along the monster's jaw, shearing teeth and nudging it back with its momentum, not allowing one last victim. With a baleful eye, the last of calamities glided back to shadowy depths of the sea. The monster's mouth closed and its head slipped beneath the surface as the ship's roll quickened.

But it was too late to keep Jareth from sliding overboard, the air chilling all the way down until the impact of hitting the icy water burst the breath in his lungs. Without a sound, he disappeared into the churning sea.

Leanan cried out too late as she and the Cervine let go of their grip on the cargo handle, trying to alter their own slide. It was then a blur of black stripes on white flicked before their eyes. The tiger had been quicker still and before they knew it, there were two in the water.

Reacting the moment he felt the rail's edge, and bracing for the inevitable pendulum backlash of the ship, the Cervine planted his hooves solidly and gripped the railing tightly, hoping the muse had enough sense to hold on to something as well. But his attention was too focussed on where Jareth had gone down to give her much more than a thought. Winding his legs through the rail's piping, he ripped a long arrow from its quiver while slinging the bow in the same motion.

"What are you doing?"

The muse screamed in his ear; evidently, she had indeed found a purchase.

"The Kraken belongs to me!"

The Cervine nodded, understanding they'd been saved. He didn't even shift focus before loosing an arrow as he saw one of the tentacles emerge from the water, not content to merely feed on the sea monsters.

A line had been attached to the shaft, and the moment it found its mark, the Cervine whipped his bow up and over the line, now taut between ship's rail and rising tentacle.

"I know, but at its heart, it belongs first to Jareth."

As his words trailed behind him, the Cervine rode the line down, his yew bow balancing his weight. The water wasn't approaching as fast as he was rising away from it and sliding a hand to his waist, there was a quick flash of a knife and the line went slack. The Cervine fell toward the water.

Leanan cursed the stag-man yet realized her error; she might be able to summon the greater forces inside Jareth, but needed the Bard to control it, not her. At least she'd bought him time.

The water closed in and the shock of its cold actually firmed the ideas in his head. Jareth began to sink, a single lungful of air the only thing keeping him still attached to the world. Or was it? Were his words then so ineffectual that all hope had gone? Did it still remain as long as he did?

The voice of Candace came to him like the sweet light in which she danced, but this time, he knew he saw her in his head.

I'll always be with you, Jareth, especially when it's darkest.

He nodded at her, still feeling a numbness spreading.

But you still have something to do. Beryl still needs you.

He tried to mouth the words but his lips wouldn't move.

I can hear you, no need to make the sound.

He nodded again, remembering.

"I saw her...she didn't even look to where I lay; just where you'd been."

Candace's voice was soft, her face reflecting the same. He wanted to reach out and touch her, to confirm she wasn't trying to fool him.

Then you also saw the picture she keeps of you, there where she hides.

And it was true; but how did he know this?

They say truth is stranger than fiction, Jare; for you, it has too often been the opposite.

He felt a tug on his lungs, the air there beginning to metabolize into his bloodstream, unsure if it was needed.

Sometimes need precedes want, Jareth. Trust me, she needs you more than you can fathom.

Even with the cold pressing, he felt the warmth of tears begin, unsure if his heart could survive.

Your mind is strong, your soul protected; while she lives, your heart still has hope. So live.

A giant tug on his collar nearly burst the breath he precariously held, and he felt his downward spiral stop. Strangely, it reversed and the cold's touch began to recede as well. The air in his lungs burned as he fought to keep it there. Turning water into wine would have been easier.

The Cervine reached out and grabbed the nape of the struggling tiger, pulling himself closer. Quickly, as the chill of the water was affecting even him, he looped the line beneath the giant cat and pulled the knot tight. Raising his arm, he pointed toward the muse who stood ready on the listing deck above. The line grew tight and slowly, with ice forming on exposed portions of the animal's skin, the tiger was hauled from the rapidly icing sea. Treading water and feeling cold's deathly grip, he could at least find warmth and relief in the fact that along with the tiger, clutched tightly in its massive jaws, Jareth's limp but living body lifted skyward as well.

The winch whined and gears grated; his reason still alive, Jareth only had to hold on...

Chapter 63

Canvas

The freighter lay on its side, still alive but without any surety it would remain that way. The pumps which the Cervine had resurrected were trying but appeared to be losing the battle. Here at the end, the Final Causeway loomed, its crystalline foundation invisible beneath the icy sea. Though there was now open water between them and the listing ship, the ice fields had not gone away. Leanan surmised it was because the Hunter's influence was being sequestered, that attention was shifting to a new battlefield. What they saw was more transitional elements between two writers. Each strove to make this world in their image but neither seemed able to dominate. The great antlers of the Cervine pierced the ice-line as he surveyed the path laid out before them.

"Not yet, at least."

Leanan, securing the skiff, paused to respond.

"Perhaps never again, either. Still, I'll put my money on Jareth."

The man though, stood on an ice floe with his head down, staring at his reflection in the lapping water at his feet. Behind him loomed the great suspension bridge called the Final Causeway. The wind rattled its icy cables and filtered through blasted holes in the enormous stanchions holding up the great lengths of road.

Leanan finished securing the skiff which had brought them from the Pacific Heron. If the freighter sank, the skiff would be their only means of escape because the causeway's southern end lay beneath the cold water. Only to the north did a path still lay.

"Why did he have to cloak the world in so much cold, though?"

The Cervine cast a quick glance and snorted quietly.

"You of all people should know him well enough by now to understand how he likens his world of words to his emotional state. Human authors have long used the metaphors of winter and death, summer and life. He's just grappling with the fact that the one who killed his wife now has his daughter."

She nodded, annoyed he was patronizing her, more than she filtered his words for Jareth's feelings.

"I know, but still..."

"You like to think of him as different, but he's more like them than not, Sidhe."

They stood on the broken remnants of the causeway, holding the crystal cables to keep from slipping; the initial length was canted at a very steep angle. She eyed Jareth, watching as he poked at his reflection with the tip of his sword.

"I wish he'd take the other one up."

The Cervine followed her gaze and noted the man's stirring melancholy, mixed no doubt with plenty of what ifs.

"You'll know the right time to return it, Leanan, but don't push. No one does well facing that many demons all at the same time."

She threw him a look, hoping her eyes spoke louder than her gaze. Maybe he was right.

They went and stood beside him, their hands on weapons as if whatever drove Jareth was infectious. That the man feared what lay at the bridge's end was not in question; it was more how he'd fare meeting the enemy again. They'd almost lost him the first time. As it should have been, they waited until Jareth spoke.

"Guess we should be going."

Piper flicked his tail as he stood near Jareth's legs, watching for flashes of silver that might indicate more of the ice fish they'd found upon beaching the skiff.

To Jareth's left, the muse hefted the longsword and let it lie on her shoulder, not fearing its sharp bite. Her other hand bared a knife; she was ready.

Beside her, the tiger looked bored, as if contemplating a nap. Still, it had recovered well from its icy dip in the sea. But whether Jareth had, was still in question. The last two days trying to outrun the resurgence of ice had been wroth with agony, laced with worry while the man struggled through a coma. Even Leanan found graciousness for the Cervine when the creature found a way past the man's defenses. And she was more than grudgingly impressed when both had returned from that world of insanity. Perhaps it had helped after all that only Jareth's mind had been frozen. It would have been a lot more difficult if all three parts had been affected. She knew that most humans thought a person could live if only deprived of oxygen for less than six minutes, but Jareth had been without for infinitely longer. Still, that had been the least of their worries. Being mortal meant far more than the sum of physical properties.

"Guess we should."

She hoped her voice was light even if she felt trepidatious.

"We must be nearing the end, Jareth."

The Cervine hoped stating the obvious would pull the man out of his funk. He'd been like this since emerging from coma. As if another memory was interfering and causing confusion. Is that what it was? Change wasn't easy and growth hurt.

The man nodded, understanding. But what kind of end would it be?

Without another word, they strode through the ankle deep water that separated the risen part of the floe from the cracked end of the bridge. Jareth looked uneasily at it, understanding that this section had never been the first, that they were approaching from the midsection, one which had lost a stanchion. Stretching his gaze beyond, at least it looked like the path went unbroken. This may be their beginning point, but it certainly wasn't the story's start. Much had already happened.

"And many others that had to play their part, too."

Jareth heard the Cervine, understanding his mind was being read again.

"This bridge is not your creation, Jareth, though we're to use it. Where you have to go, the scenes will be both familiar and unrecognizable, with the former trying to placate your needs while the latter will attempt to defy your wants."

Jareth started to unravel the Cervine's words but stopped, replacing his frown with a small grin.

The depths of the Cervine's eyes stirred, recognizing a moment.

"I'll leave the riddles to you two, if you don't mind."

Leanan snorted at his side, startling the tiger momentarily from its lethargy, then laughed merrily, squeezing the man's hand and drawing blood with her nails.

He winced and cast her a look of mock hurt.

"If everything was so clear, would you not grow bored, Jare?"

Her laughter echoed and his heart felt a light touch. Sometimes, it was nice to have her near.

Oh, ho—now, can I repeat that aloud?

He shook his mind as he might his head, immediately aware of his faux pas.

Gaining the slick surface of the broken bridge was easier than actually scrambling up it, but at last, they all stood on its faceted surface. Higher than he'd imagined, a great blue crystal light slowly pulsed. After a bit, Jareth realized it was doing so in concert with the beating of his heart. Strange he hadn't noticed this while the light was still in the distance.

Beyond, the road seemed empty of anything but more stanchions and ice-coated cables. Not every section though had a blue light and he wondered why.

They moved forward breast to breast, with the Cervine on Jareth's left and Leanan Sidhe on his right. The tiger flanked her while Piper had eschewed the cold surface and sought a warm place on his shoulders, beneath the cloak's hood. Memories of the cat perched on his shoulders rippled like the water beneath them, but with infinitely more warmth.

As he looked down, he thought he saw the dim shadow of something large glide past, its tail slowly swinging side to side. A shudder rose.

"It's been awhile since we heard you play for the pleasure of it, Jareth; would you oblige?"

The first stanchion just passed, Jareth glanced up at the Cervine's face, wondering if the creature was toying with him.

"You know, Dear, that sounds like a marvelous suggestion— could you do one of those ditties that includes me?"

Leanan leaned into him, nearly getting scratched by the cat for her effort. The muse's eyes were wide and luminous, nearly all black except for a thin ring of gold which pulsed on its own. Her lips formed a full pout and she batted her eyelashes notoriously. To her right, the snow tiger gave a soft rumble. Jareth wondered if the animal wasn't just clearing its throat. Or was it still annoyed at being unable to fly? He took a deep breath and began his protest...

"Isn't it you who once told me that the music is inside the musician, that melodies and chords line up and flow from the lips of a true troubadour?"

The Cervine's muzzle pointed toward him, as did his ears. They always seemed over-large to Jareth, though not disproportionate. But deer did not reach fourteen feet tall, and none stood on their hind legs, either. Jareth tried again...

"Oh come on, Jare; just something to lighten the heart. The gods know we could use it. Perhaps a walking song, something to make the journey shorter? The bridge looks like it goes on a ways, probably to that ice fortress hanging from the blue cliffs ahead; it's going to be a while before we get there."

He looked to where the muse pointed and for the first time, suspected where the endgame was to be played. He was surprised he hadn't seen it earlier. Maybe he didn't want to lose his state of denial...

He tried counting the blue crystals that traced their way, each set high atop an icy stanchion header, glittering brilliantly in the clear blue sky. But even as he thought that, clouds began to skid down from the north and he wondered if they portended a winter storm. Glancing then back at Leanan, he saw an enthusiastic impatience as she waited for him to sing something. Maybe he could divert their attention...didn't they know he was loath to touch the six-string?

"I think you'll find that just because you lost some sensitivity in your fingers, that the rest of your hand will remember what to do, Jareth."

The Cervine looked long, and then winked at him before facing the looming heights of the icebergs. The water on either side of the bridge was in constant flux, but at the moment, it was liquid cold and showed dark reflections. It was as if the northern ocean was so deep that the brilliance of day could not penetrate. In the distance, the ice reared in layered ridges, like frozen waves dragging at the stanchion, or trying to reach the causeway to pull it down. Much of what Jareth felt as murmurs in his heart were echoed in his head. It was a struggle to keep a lingering despair contained.

"Here, let me help you."

The muse wasn't taking no for an answer and without disturbing Piper, slipped the sunburst colored instrument off the man's shoulder, letting her long nails lightly strum across the strings as she did. The sound seemed out of place but this only helped Jareth's mood, not hurt it. It *had* been a while...

So while columns of ice-coated cables marched past and the powdery snow blew lightly across the fractures of the roadway, he carefully placed his fingers on the fret board, stroking the ancient wood with his other hand, welcoming the music back.

It's never gone away, Jareth.

The Cervine's low resonation seeped into his head.

The music, like water, never sleeps, Jareth.

Leanan liked that metaphor. He observed the muse when her own thoughts followed right on the Cervine's heels.

Touching the strings with the two metal fingers last, it was a stranger sensation than he'd ever experienced. And yet, the sound came true, just as the Cervine had foretold. He played for a while before the music of his verse pounded out a slow, unearthly beat that they all could feel beneath their feet. After awhile, it appeared the song resonated along the length of each cable they passed. He wanted to reach out and pluck them all, like a giant ice harp...

He gave the muse and cervine a look that said he didn't want to be 'told you so.' The music was enough and they agreed.

Though the sky was awhirl with clouds, the stratus streams were too high to bring any precipitation. With the wind stiffening from the west, any fallen snow would swirl and eddy like fog being waved aside.

One day passed into the next and it wasn't until the third that their luck ran out. The Ice Citadel was now so close Jareth could see individual towers, and count the steps of circling stairways, whose outside edge was a drop to the ice below. Less than an hour earlier, the Cervine reported movement in the shadows of the windows and it was obvious that the Hunter knew they were coming.

They felt the change before ever seeing it, as the whoosh of sound built. Leanan confirmed it was not the weather and they loosened their weapons. The tempo increased, causing the tiger to snarl. There was movement in the distant shadows; three stanchions distant from the fortress, they made their plans.

"There'll be more Bone Warriors—it's all the Hunter has to work with now. Trapped here, he has only the memories of what's come before. He knows only what previous pages has shown him. And it has ever been his wont to twist the truth into something it's not. We'll seek to make that his undoing."

The Cervine seemed sure but still Jareth braced.

"Just remember; aim for the base of the neck. A headless emotion will continue to twitch for a while but without concentrated focus, is hardly the threat it starts out to be."

Jareth wasn't sure if Leanan was being reassuring or just blatantly upfront. Reaching back, he fumbled until he found Piper's ears. The animal was still curled tightly inside his pack, but now was tensed. He scratched and gently held the cat's head. It was risky whenever he had to fight this way. Often, Piper had little patience for all the moves that ensued and would burst free to find a safe, quiet place in which to wait out the melee. But this time, there was nowhere to go. No time now for worry or wonder, regarding the cat. Not now, so near last pages...what must Beryl be going through, even at this very moment?

He choked and brought his hand to his mouth, the metal fingers bruising his lips. He doubted he'd ever get used to their touch. Glancing down at his thigh, he bit his lip; the woven mass of tendrils were writhing...as if alive!

He lifted his sword, looking intently at the blade. He could smell the salty tang of the sea infiltrate his senses as it battled the scent of impending conflict. Each had a gritty feel, just as they should.

The Cervine ordered a stop, and sweeping his bow before him, sent a great arrow into the frigid air, speeding between two polished cables and out over the water. Jareth watched as it took the shortest path, cutting off the long curve of the bridge in front of them. At this distance, they could only see its effect. But Jareth wondered if bones collapsing would make much noise anyway.

The sortie was made of more chariots, this time on ski runners, and the source of power was again great white bears, their hulking bodies rubbing against each other, only their dark eyes and nose separating them from their surroundings. Like the Bone Warriors driving the chariots, they were as quiet as a lake freezing, with the only sound being that of skis on snow. It was enough.

Jareth wondered if the Warriors cared that their position was compromised. It wasn't like either side had anywhere to go. And surely no one would be turning around...

The smell of bear reached them, then the stench of something too long dead. Jareth blanched nonetheless; there were at least twenty Warriors, and each held a cat o'nine tails whose eerie whine augmented the sound of the skis. Damn, this was going to get messy.

As the first row bore down on them, the Cervine went forward and kept dropping riders with his arrows until they were spent. By the time the sortie got so close they could all see empty eye sockets and exposed rib cages beneath tattered mail, only ten still remained.

The leading chariot bore down on the stag-man, its driver's weapon licking the air, the speed of its revolutions increasing. When within striking distance, a flurry of braided steel lines surged forth, carrying shiny black claws of pain.

Jareth had an insight; was this Rhey's purpose? To inflict pain more than destruction? Though he knew they all could die, the

Bone Warriors were playing the part of torturers more so than slayers. Could they use this weakness to their advantage?

"They're trying to maim and wound—work your way inside and slash high!"

His voice sounded like a growl, as if he had become the crouching tiger by Leanan's side. And that's when they struck back.

Jareth got inside the first Warrior's guard, letting the flailing steel whip sweep high and wide as he ducked and struck all in one motion. The bears driving the chariot kept going, unaware their rider was headless. The minstrel warrior's blade had gone clean through the vertebrae and hung, poised to parry the next attacker. Steel shards flew around his blade as he held it high, momentum causing the ends to wrap. But Jareth expected this and instead of pulling back and losing his sword, he lunged forward and ripped down, dragging the weapon from the rider's grasp. Leaping aside, he was almost run down by the chariot as it churned past and into Leanan's waiting riposte. Another skull hit the hard ice of the causeway and bounced twice before soundlessly pitching over the edge.

The Cervine took out two by first ramming his bow left and then right, knocking one rider off his chariot altogether while the other collapsed, the arms and head still attached but somewhere in the middle, missing its back. The Cervine had no time though to finish off the fallen as the next Warrior crashed hard into him, the bears swatting with great claws.

The Cervine caught the paw and twisting, broke it before his other hand tore out the second bear's neck. Pushing both aside with a mighty heave, the one carcass and the remaining maimed bear split to either side Then the chariot and a flurry of steel hooks struck him.

Leanan was a dervish with a sword, her cuts and thrusts a flurry of steel as the longsword bit again and again; whether bear or rider, she didn't care. Dancing agilely, she eluded the dead and dying as they careered past her. When one cat o'nine tails touched her, ripping a huge rent in her black leather armor, she hissed and cursed the ruined sleeve even as she dispatched the one who'd done the damage.

Jareth bolted toward the crystalized cables, hoping there was still some flexibility and was rewarded with just enough to launch himself sideways into the next passing chariot. The edge of his sword sheared clean through the Bone Warrior's skull, almost becoming lost as the body pitched out of the chariot. Ripping his sword back, he slashed quickly and severed the spine before looking up in time to catch sight of the Cervine as the bears split and the chariot struck.

Then to his amazement, the chariot was lifting—the Cervine's arms bulged with cords of muscle and nostrils flared wide. With ears flattened back, the great stag-man hoisted the chariot up and over. Still, the wicked whip sliced down and caught his back, tearing furrows in fur covered skin until it caught on the scaled hauberk where the whip then was stripped loose. As the chariot tumbled past, the Cervine reached behind and pulled, grunting as he felt both metal plating and his own hide ripping.

Jareth stopped in awe as the Cervine withstood the mutilation. He saw lines of blood welling and skin oozing. With a cry, he brandished his sword and leaped forward. The wave of bears and Bone Warriors had passed but some still crawled or turned to finish what they'd started. Leanan's voice lashed at him.

"I can hold them—get to Buck-face!"

But Jareth was already on his way, his sword slashing down on the struggling Bone Warrior who continued fighting despite being legless. Once past, he then rushed to the Cervine, his hands ripping off gauntlets, flinching as he saw the two metal fingers of his sword hand.

"Dammit—I don't know if I can do this!"

The Cervine seemed to be in a fog as it rubbed his own blood between matted fingers.

Jareth took his hands and placed them on the Cervine's wounds, forcing himself to ignore the blood and gore, nervous attention distracted by his alien fingers; he knew he would need both of his hands to do this...

And he began to sing, in a voice that cut through the pathos he was feeling, surging past the enormity of the damage, and into the Cervine's fractured flesh. It was the first song his grandfather had ever taught him, saying that the magic of song should at least be good for something.

Then he stopped, startled because as he began, he knew it was not necessary. Looking up into the deep eyes of the Cervine, he saw it was the truth.

"The enemy cannot hurt me, Jareth; but you already know that. It has been ordained that his battle is against you and your race alone."

And then a large deer eye winked, followed by a semblance of a grin spreading across buck lips.

"But it's nice to know you still remember how to heal. And your grandfather was right—music should at least be good for that. It's a lesson you taught your daughter, remember?"

And as the sounds of battle muted, dimming as if the tide was receding, Jareth felt he could take a breath again, knowing he'd survived to fight another day. The chill of the air dropped him to his knees however. With Leanan's help, the Cervine lifted him while the muse returned his sword to its sheath. He looked around them at the carnage; the bears that had survived had dragged their riderless chariots down the causeway, clueless now as to what to do.

There were piles of bones, as well as pieces of Bone Warrior, scattered so far that it would be days trying to piece them back together.

"It should keep the Hunter busy until we get there. He must be running out of material for his armies, I'm thinking."

Jareth turned toward the Cervine, his eyes running over the creature's back, noting how each furrowed wound was closing before his eyes, until not even a scar could be seen.

"There were scars only once, and that time was long ago. Now, there is only the time of patience until the end."

Jareth wasn't sure of what the Cervine spoke but it didn't matter. He was just then remembering...

It had been a sunny day and he'd been with Beryl, picking berries and singing the small 'catch-all' songs that allowed them to find every ripe berry on the bush. When they'd stumbled across the supine form of a rabbit, the girl had immediately poured out her sorrow, reaching down to caress the poor animal, full of empathy.

Reaching her side at the sound of tears, he touched the animal's back and when he did, a brief flicker crossed dead eyes.

Taking the body, he had Beryl stretch out her hands to receive it, but she recoiled, her compassion transformed into uneasiness at touching death.

'Receive its spirit, Beryl; if you're ever to be a real songstress, you need to understand the true beauty of what you sing. Listen to my words and then repeat them, but with the melody of life. Try it, it's not so hard...'

He'd watched as she bravely let him place the animal in her hands, her eyes switching from the rabbit to him and back.

It had been a learning moment for her. When the rabbit's chest began to move faintly, to lift and press against her palm, bringing with it a new warmth, she began to understand. Like his grandfather had taught him, so he'd passed on a basic truth—not that song magic could heal but that one should have compassion for innocence.

Beryl

It was with some surprise that the memory stirred so strongly, but more, he suddenly had an inkling of what the Cervine and muse had been telling him about his song...

He walked past the carnage without a word, feeling a hand taken on each side, one by the Cervine, and one by the muse. But it was a long time before they got any words out of him...the memory of Beryl and the young rabbit had reminded him once again of how he'd failed to live up to his own words.

Chapter 64

Little Lion Man

The walls were as white as he remembered and the interior was definitely just as cold, but that's where the similarity ended. He'd gone over entire sequences of text, having an almost perfect memory, but still Rhey was beginning to feel the constraints of Martin Hennessy's storybook world. Whatever had happened there on the edge of his domed city, on that last pier just prior to his escape, an alteration had occurred that he was still having trouble reconciling. The failsafe trigger really should have worked...

The girl had been giving him fits, too. If he had his usual tools and chemicals to play with, he'd already have uncovered the viral DNA sequence. At least that would have accomplished what he'd come here to do. But while he thought he understood what drove the scientist, it seems he didn't know the man well enough. Or at least, that's what he was forcing himself to accept. It couldn't be that he was at a disadvantage, not when it came to intellectual conflict. His species traveled the stars, for damn sake!

Bringing a pale hand to his lips, he tried to stop the words from following the thought, bothered more than a little that he was falling into more and more human deceits. This wasn't like him, and that oddity preyed more than it should. Fleeing north had been impulse based on intuition—which begged the question of how he'd known to do that. More human frailty directing his actions, as if someone else was in control of his character...

No, that was impossible; he still had the ability to move pieces—hadn't the sortie of Bone Warriors proven that?

Rhey pursed his lips, his fingers still near, and he felt his breath warm on his flesh. The great fortress he'd found at the end of the bridge wasn't as cold inside as it looked from the outside. Though made of ice, he found a freeze even he was loath to trespass against. And yet, the air wasn't frigid, certainly not enough to threaten him. Somewhere, a heat pump must be running; he'd have to investigate. Perhaps he could twist the same power for his own purposes and get back to the lab.

He turned his darkened eyes toward the girl who sat miserably near one of the windows, the idea of escape so utterly ridiculous as to be laughable; where was she going to go? The sides were sheer except for the narrow ice stairs which climbed the outer ramparts and eventually dead-ended in front of great ice slabs for doors. Moving one had almost overcome him as it were, so certainly the girl was in no danger of leaving just yet.

He stared at her as he had for much of the frenzied trip over the frozen sea. At first, the ice followed and closed in upon their wake, surely hindering any pursuit. But they hadn't been long on the bridge before noticing another ship—a large ungainly and listing one at that—break the line of the icy horizon. It didn't bode well that there should be anyone at all, but to ignore this coincidence would put him at Martin's mercy should a quirk of fate be proved true. Again; quirk of fate? He didn't believe in the concept. And the ironic echo that reached out to him was, he doubted that Martin did either.

He surely thought there would be time to work out the human's little ploy, but the girl was absolutely useless on the journey north, and he was kept busy avoiding random floes of ice. For the most part, she rocked with her knees up to her chin, her head buried and her voice alternating between bouts of tears and an odd melody that hardly carried beyond her own space. Still, he heard, listened, analyzed, and finally dismissed. The tune seemed familiar enough for some reason, but the lyrics were just nonsense, as if she sang in a different language. If only he had access to his lab and computer—he had myriad data bases he could cross reference—but alas, he had to use his memory. Which seemed inconveniently incomplete the further north he traveled.

The bridge hadn't been much better, with the girl lagging so much, he'd threatened her. There was no going back though, not after sinking the boat and leaving no evidence of their passage. If there *was* pursuit, he wasn't going to make it easy.

But that was before he realized that the bridge was a last road of sorts; it led directly to a large mass of icebergs with only the frozen rays of the sun to illuminate them. He saw the ice castle early on, and already decided that if there were to be an end to this, that this is where it would be. And *that* decision came after trying to forcibly take the gemstone from the girl. Even now, the tingling in his fingers reminded him of his error. He would have to find another way, or find its secret. That the data he needed was held within, was no longer in doubt; the way the stone pulsed, especially when the girl fingered it in her misery, was just too coincidental. There was a pattern, if he could get all his brain cells to fire at the same time long enough to find it...

He considered another way even as he watched her, waiting for his servants to return, bearing good news or bad. With the way events were shaping up, he was banking on the latter, but hoped to at least slow pursuit. So even though he was in Martin's world and the escape path was still not revealed, time was the one element that remained constant. He was running out of it in two worlds now.

The Bone Warriors had been waiting, as if summoned from a previous moment, or chapter. But had *he* placed them in the ice castle as another failsafe? They certainly responded when he began to order them out, to work their way down the glacier and storm the bridge. The fact their mode of travel again involved bears—albeit white ones this time—was another convenient coincidence he didn't miss. Bound in silence, they were all standing in line, in a hall illuminated by small windows cut in the ice. But the outside light never reached where they stood. Rows of skeletal beings were clothed in ancient tattered armor, with racks of rusty weapons spaced evenly between the groups. Where the chariots were kept, he didn't know, but as he first heard their strange sliding-slashing sound on the ice road below, he felt more secure seeing the tandems move toward the bridge.

The sound of ice cracking was also a constant, without any defined pattern. Mostly, it came from the sea, still liquid but surely near freezing, as it rolled into the glacier. Much of the water returned as ice pellets and sheets that broke as they struck water again, but some actually froze solid, adding to the ice beach. And these new layers would sometimes crack themselves, splitting off. The dark bay outside the window held a split that slowly worked it's way back, as if called home.

That was what was driving the story though, the idea of going home. The man Jareth Rhylan, was being told to go home, the girl was looking for someone called Eli in an effort to get home herself, and well, he too was only looking for the same access. Maybe he should make another attempt to take the gem by force...

His eyes watched, waiting and analyzing, doing what his great intellect did best—find patterns from even the most chaotic of theories. He kept thinking that with such an emphasis on the sung word, that perhaps that's where the secret lay?

Too, there were strange markings, which he knew from studying human culture, were called tattoos. The girl had an inordinate quantity of them, their spidery scrawl mixed punctuated marks that looked somehow symbolic, and covered all but her face. Which surprised him—human conceit generally didn't omit a prime portal of vanity. Still, he understood that many were reserved for secret places.

But not this girl—her entire body seemed an equal opportunity for ink. He observed the gemstone about her neck, gauging the frequency of how often she covered it, wondering at the residual rosy glow that pulsed along with the girl's heartbeat. Even from here, his senses could pick up rhythmic beats, whether heart, lung or song. She seemed fixed on either the stone or the guitar, running her fingers over each string, adding her voice only as an afterthought. Her patterns weren't something he was imagining because the more he watched, the more he could catalog these rhythms. Was the secret held within this emerging pattern? He'd have to monitor one with another to find a correlation. But there was no doubt that the jewel held the whole matrix together...

A thought permeated and broke his concentration; shouldn't the Warriors have returned by now? Glancing outside, his eyes narrowed, working out probable causes for what he was seeing, as well as formulating a strategic response. There, mirrored by the sea, the sky was rushing toward the castle, its advance decidedly unnatural. Whatever had happened to his sortie might never be known. For the first time, he noticed the strange glowing blue lights that marked various sections of the bridge; they were changing intensity. First one than the next started to flare much brighter, the light strangely intense.

Rhey was reminded of an exploding nebula. But then, he'd been light years from any danger. Perhaps not so this time, and he left the great room which he'd fortified to use as headquarters, and heading toward what he'd labeled Warrior Hall, made up his mind that if the girl had to lose a limb or head, the gemstone would come free.

The sound of skeletal movement reached his ears, causing him to smile; he still had control of these, and it was only a matter of time before nothing of this world would ever matter again.

Passing by the narrow windows, he caught movement; it was the tiger, the one so indelibly pressed upon his memory. And behind, the Cervine character trudged. No, rather, it stalked. Rhey felt the wind bite at his bones.

Martin, Martin, Martin; bringing the fight to me? Tired of running? Well, let your bodyguards come; I still have more than a few Warriors gathered in the hall...

And yet, he had to admit a mild curiosity, wondering where the man himself and the woman might have gone...

Pausing, he slipped a gleaming length of sharpened steel from a sheath. Noting the inert Warrior also held an an ancient Chinese wind-and-fire wheel, its cutting edges untouched by rust, he took that too. He'd always found human culture's cleverness at dealing death to be admirable, fascinating to the point he'd absorbed much of the archived knowledge about primitive weapons. Perhaps some of his time spent on this planet would actually come to good use after all...

Sweeping his wrist out as he doubled his speed back to the great room, he was gratified by the deep scoring tear he created with the weapon. It was still sharp...

Chapter 65

Strength of a Thousand Men

Jareth felt a chill working its way inside him as he strove to scale the glacier's side. He had begun to second guess his decision; it didn't seem so imposing a task now, to fight past the unknown number of Bone Warriors guarding the main entrance. He'd found that the cold had its own deadly stabbing weapons, too.

"I don't think you'd want to be where BuckFace is right now."

Leanan's words rasped against the frigid air, her voice floating up, as if the rules of acoustics were being bent. But then, maybe he was hearing her in his mind again.

"You wish."

Her retort made him shut down his idle thoughts and concentrate on the task at hand; Beryl's life depended on it. Each lift brought them closer to the lowermost stair. And hopefully, to an unguarded door. An unguarded door; now, there was a novel idea.

"That's how all this started; how ironic, aye?"

Sometimes her gibes and cuts made more sense than others. This was one of the latter. Her voice was an echoed response.

"You wanted to write a story...well, you got one, that's for sure."

He paused and shook his head; if this was his idea of a story, he had to seriously reconsider his plot planning. Then again, it sounded like he was doing this to himself—all of this; the ice and cold, the near impossibility of his task, the tenuous chance of reuniting with a daughter he'd tried to forget...

"Not tried, did; it was necessary."

He hung, his steel-shod hand firmly gripped about a short stabbing knife securely biting purple shadows in the ice wall. His balance depended on ledges that seemed entirely too narrow. Below him, the muse followed. She'd offered to lead, but when he imagined that scenario, his cheeks flushed and she'd laughed so wickedly that he quickly volunteered, moving upwards before she could fully enjoy her little game.

"Why was it necessary?"

Below, he heard Leanan strike the sheer surface with her blade, establishing another fix-point for their rope. Not that they had much, but with the Cervine's help, they'd loosened one great iced cable from the bridge, and woven a thinner, more pliable version for the ascent. Jareth was doubtful, even after the muse had sung an arcane Celtic song that made the frozen steel almost as pliable as hemp. He shook his head; had this really been his idea?

"You still don't know? Hmm, that might be significant."

And her voice trailed off, leaving him frustrated.

"Not the first time, Dear, nor probably the last, knowing you!"

He began to wonder before catching on to her innuendo, and squelched the thought before she could find further mirth at his expense. He was learning that with the muse, it was wise to be preemptive.

"Are you going to explain?"

But Leanan changed subjects, ignoring his query.

"I don't know how long he'll be able to keep them busy."

Jareth considered the Cervine's distraction that would allow he and the muse to find a way into the fortress. It might be too much to hope that Rhey would personally be at the main gate, but it wasn't much of a leap to assume he would at least monitor their assault. After all, according to the Cervine, Rhey was running low on resources. If they struck quickly, it might be enough to thwart the alien's plan altogether. But what then?

"Then, Jareth Rhylan, then you live. Not as easy as it sounds but much better than you like to make it. Most of your issues are self-induced, a trait to which most mortal's are prone."

Then to live...to life. What the hell then was he doing now?

The woman laughed deeply, the sound of her voice ranging far up the glacier, loud and powerful enough that the man feared she'd given away their position. But the god-awful din in the distance did not relent, and Jareth resumed his grip on both knife and hope.

Damn; what was one person with a bow going to do against dead skeletons in chariots? And for how long? Even if this person did stand over fourteen feet tall and wielded antlers as if they were swords.

"Don't worry, my baby is there with him; the Horned Lord has a lot more help where he is than we have here."

Jareth wondered about the white tiger, understanding it was indeed a formidable foe, even as a petulant hiss swatted at the muse's trailing words. He was glad the woman could not see his small smile then as he considered Piper's annoyance; might be the Cervine didn't have lesser resources after all...

He kept his focus on the bears, realizing that even if the rickety framework of bones earnestly thrusting sharp pointy things at him didn't care, the animals did. Once he wounded a few, the others grew more wary, which kept their charges at safer distances. Slowly but surely, he moved the Warriors out of the way. Once past, it would then be much easier to hold the gate without so much open space all around him. Beside him, almost back to back now, the roar of the great snow tiger was a savage reminder to the thicker-witted bears pulling the chariots. The huge cat wasted energy berating the drivers as well.

Beryl

So far, they'd been able to withstand the first sally, forcing the thrust of the attack toward the icy bay, where fantastic crystalline fragments of ice reared and sparkled. Like frozen jewels, they littered the beachhead.

He and the tiger reached the last segment of the causeway only minutes before the Hunter unleashed more emotional nightmare. Convincing Jareth that time wasn't on their side—it had never been—quickly lead to the fact that finding the girl was paramount. The Hunter had her. And since the story's end still remained unwritten, there was no surety that it would be a happy one. Quite the opposite in fact, because there was no doubt that what Beryl kept hidden was the key to everything.

Jareth had fought the reasoning but there was no answer except to say that which minstrels—and especially bards—liked to repeat; a story isn't good because it's told by a storyteller, it's good because it *is* the storyteller. Of course the man then accused him of being eternally obtuse. The muse's confident nod hadn't helped either.

Their plan in place, despite some haranguing as to who should do what, the attacking Bone Warriors never saw the man and his muse strike off toward the fortress' sheer side. Staying low beneath ice sheets and lifting ridges, they furtively aimed for the lowest stair. A delay would be necessary and for the tiger's help, the Cervine was thankful.

Another Warrior was hauled out of his chariot by his cat o'nine tails when the tiger's paw lashed out swiftly. The bears trampled over their rider before the Cervine turned its pocked skull into powder with a massive hoof. The chariot and its bears curled aimlessly until they stopped. If only he had more arrows...

Retrieving as many as he could from the previous attack, he found only those which had penetrated the polar bears had been unnecessarily messy. Most of his shots, which had severed the Warriors' spine, had landed in the bay on either side of the bridge.

These were the shafts he missed most, and there'd been no time to make more.

Because of this though, he'd appropriated a cat o'nine tails and with his reach, brought the ripping ends to good use. Though the Bone Warriors did not have flesh, the grab and clutch of many steel claws still broke rib cases and separated arms from their sockets. If a Warrior was too slow, the Cervine could also decapitate and that was a good thing too.

Urging the tiger further up the road, he surged past two limbless attackers, threading between them almost as sinuously as the feline. Turning, he caught the Warrior's next slash on his antlers. Twisting, the lash was wrenched away, suddenly bringing the Bone Warrior inside the Cervine's deadly reach. The bow crushed the right side of its face and only one eye socket remained to glare emotionlessly. The irony did not escape; for creatures representing and reincarnating emotions, their true power lay solely without, not within. But this made their weaknesses all the easier to access, and both he and the tiger raked ruthlessly at every opportunity. It was something he'd tried to teach the man, a long time ago. It was a lesson Jareth found hard to retain, though.

From the gate there came a grinding, grating noise and glancing up, he saw more Bone Warriors spilling, many carrying hand-to-hand weapons; this meant the fighting was going to get intense. They would seek to use their greater number to physically crush both he and the tiger. Aye, that's what they all were, actually—seekers. Without searching his mind, he could still feel Jareth's whereabouts, and braced himself for the next onslaught, knowing the man and muse were seeking something far more valuable than what he and the tiger sought. A grunt of impatience left his lips; the man and woman had gained entry and were looking for the girl even now...find her quickly, Jareth, the Hunter has more access to you than you know. Time is short.

Beryl

Like the swell of drums in his head, the air inside the ice fortress vibrated, hitting notes that threatened to divide his purpose. Jareth dropped his sword and covered his ears, the pain not as visceral as the pressure within. He dropped to his knees, the prosthetic making a quieter thump than the flesh of his good leg.

Beside him, Leanan did not drop, did not feel the inner agony which Jareth was battling, but she did understand the situation. The Hunter was aware they'd gained the lowermost door; he knew they'd had breached the icy halls of Frostmoor. So it was called in her language, in her land. The man would know nothing of it, even if he *could* replicate the conditions with amazing accuracy. But replication of something read is not the same as experiencing the real thing; this she knew. The Hunter was trying to use Jareth's idiosyncrasies against him, and by the look of it, had found a chink in mortal armor. And though she clucked her tongue at the ramifications, it was obvious that the man's innermost desires were still not understood, were not clear in such a way to explain her presence in the first place. Well, she'd make the enemy pay for what he was doing to her man, as well as her pride.

"I'll keep him busy while the Cervine detains his Warriors, Jare; you just find Beryl. Don't ask questions; once you're released, take up your sword and go to her. I can't see much from here and I sense the Hunter can't either, whatever that means. It's for you to figure out though, as it has always been."

So saying, she took up Jareth's dropped sword and smashed at a leaded glass window, the force carrying most of the shards outside to drop as crystalline knives into the snow. The force of her blow swept like the sound of a small thunderclap and it echoed below, reaching the alert ears of both cervine and tiger. They would understand its implication.

Standing dead center in the hall, she then raised the short sword high, her voice rising like the tide, but more sonorous, as if she were reaching for notes that founded the tides but did not drive them. Not yet.

Dropping the blade like a staff, a blue arc of light surged from her body and split the floor where a deep crevasse began to form. Beginning from where she stood and stretching in both directions, its speed increased though the gap was still able to be straddled.

"Go Jareth Rhylan; take up your sword and find Beryl!"

Jareth's senses flooded back, the sound cut off as if by two hands over his ears. At first he thought it was gone completely and turned to face the muse, confusion and anxiety rampant, but then he felt its pressure, compressed as it was. She was providing a shield with her Fae magic, with her song, which even now rolled down the ice hallways like an epic theme. The beat of drums increased and deepened, as if a phalanx of timpani were unleashed. Did he also hear scores of violins searing at the deadly cold trying to assail them?

But the muse had no time to shiver his mind and answer his queries, pregnant and honest though they might be; she was bringing to bear everything her kind could muster. Jareth began to see, began to understand then—she was seeking to create a storm within the fortress itself. Could such devastation be manifested if contained by such walls? Wasn't that why walls were created in the first place? To keep the outside from getting in?

Walls can also provide a prison, Love; you have to remember, this fortress does not belong to the Hunter...

Jareth heard her voice even as he unconsciously picked up the sword lying within reach, slinging it over his shoulders, aware Piper had begun howling. Was the animal emulating the muse? Was it pulling on an archaic and mythological source of magic which found its well-soul in song?

...it belongs to you!

Beryl

Leanan Sidhe, Dark Muse of Celtic lore, eternal vampiric spirit unleashed upon a world of mortals, finished her claim, let her words rock the walls inside his head. For the first time, Jareth noticed how alike they were to those walls on either side; cold, smooth, and utterly crystalized into a lattice of solitude.

Piper wriggled from the pack, his claws digging in and slashing at the fretboard of his mandolin to get some leverage. Its tail was twice its normal width and the cat's ears were pinned back, as if the threat was personal.

"Piper!"

It was only a weak attempt to get the animal's attention as he'd seen this posture before; it typically alluded to immediate flight. He didn't need this distraction, not just then...

Too late, the black bundle of fury leaped and with claws sliding on the floor, jumped the still growing fissure.

Cursing, Jareth stretched over the gap and raced after the cat, his breath coming in gasps.

He rounded the corner and soon realized the cat wasn't running away from something, it was running to; Piper was searching for the girl! Of course! Hadn't the animal done the same when Rhey had captured him in the bar?

Jareth knew the cat, had nurtured it since a kitten, and the bond formed was like a parent and child. With a bitter tear forming, he realized it was a feeling he should have had for a daughter—his daughter. For Beryl.

The fortress was beginning to fracture and he noticed branching, one which was following behind him. Up he raced, following the cat, noting that now, there were scratches and gouges from the animal's claws; Piper wasn't slipping anymore. He could only hope that *he* wasn't either.

The Bone Warriors were suddenly rudderless. If they'd possessed eyes, a new wariness would have been evident but they

606

didn't, and it was only by their sudden erratic aim that the Cervine deduced what was happening. The Hunter's mind was being diverted. Was it toward Jareth and the muse?

Biting his lip, feeling flat teeth compressing his tongue, he fervently hoped it was not toward Beryl.

This way! The gate isn't being watched anymore.

The tiger heard his mindsong and broke off its death embrace with a polar bear, dark blood staining white jaws. As the Cervine swept up his bow and forced the gate open, the tiger was right on his heels.

The cracks were forming everywhere but still he was able to think fast enough to forestall their progress beyond the lower three levels. For how long though, Rhey wasn't sure; the magic Martin possessed—nay, this was all Jareth—split the seams of every boundary he'd written into place. Hell, the man was bursting loose from his very own creation...now, where had the girl gotten off to...?

Leanan's body pulsed with blue fire, the sky outside funneling in through the broken window, whirling around her, caressing, before screaming off down the halls to add their fury to the fray. The enemy may have found a way to forestall her breaking the foundation, but he'd have to go up against the nightmare called muse! Oh the lovely darkness of it all if Jareth should add his voice...not if, though, but when! A delicious feeling of seductive guilt wove into her lyrics as she sang anew, the lust adding strength to her fury. Now, what was that mortal saying...Hell hath no fury like a woman scorned?

Shutting the gates hadn't been hard but keeping them so would be problematic; the Cervine knew that from the inside, Jareth could keep just about any door closed, but once it was open, there was no way to hold the doors anymore. So it was with this gate, a fictional representation of the man's inner psyche. It wasn't like the Cervine hadn't been here before, it was only that in the past, Jareth had not been compromised. It had been a self-imprisonment, something he'd created and for which only he held the key. The fact that the enemy had gotten inside was both worrisome as well as instrumental. On a very basic level, the man was being assaulted like never before and if redemption was not at hand, then eternal damnation was. Only time would tell which ending had been chosen.

The tiger was already inside, leaping fissures in the floor and skittering on the smooth glass surface, searching for a way up. And that could be the only way; up. Even the great predator knew as much about Jareth.

The Cervine tried to brace the doors with an armful of rusty pikes lying near the entry, crisscrossing their lengths until the portal was at least going to be hard to break. It wouldn't last, but if the Hunter won, if Jareth chose wrongly, it wouldn't matter; the end of this story would become just another slab of fractured ice in a sea of floes.

He grabbed his bow and leapt after the tiger, ignoring the cold's touch on his hooves, forcing the buried earth beneath to hear his passage. Beneath every foundation of ice, there once was fertile soil. Even beneath an edifice erected by the Bard.

The whiteness of the walls seemed familiar, and yet the coldness is what called most loudly to her. Beryl crouched behind a large bust of a mythical deity she did not know, its visage looking down on her with icy cold eyes. She felt alone, so alone.

The urge to escape, to flee, was familiar too, and this comfort allowed her to go far before she succumbed to a feeling of helplessness and despair. As if running too far would hurt her more than staying captive. But that was absurd, wasn't it? She had to escape the mad-eyed clown whose chalky skin leaked to the floor each time she inadvertently touched him. Even on the ship, she'd known her captor by heart if not by sight. As if she'd seen him from a distance and had thus far eluded him. Like a nightmare from which one couldn't awake.

The writings on her skin had begun to move again, once she'd separated herself from her captor. She wasn't sure it was a good thing though; a great sense of guilt and failure rocked her slim frame, humbling and castigating her at the same time. Panicked, she touched her face, looking hard into the wall, canting her head in a way that the stray light would show her face in the mirror, afraid of what she'd once again see.

But there was no hint that any of the tattoos had returned. And in that moment, she felt a trickle of warmth, even with the chill air hovering so close. It was a good memory for her, something which had affected her more than she realized. That someone would take on her pain spoke volumes...

She had to keep moving, there was no time for self-pity, not anymore. As if that time were over, or there simply was no practical application for her disillusionment, she forced the thoughts aside. As Leanan had once hinted for her to do. And at which Jareth seemed only too skilled. At least once, that is. She wondered at the changes she'd seen, from the very beginning of the journey. Small steps, but she saw them. Leanan had seen them too, even if caution persisted. The Cervine....hmm, now he hadn't said anything at all. Did he see but keep his thoughts hidden? Unlike the muse, the Cervine put more distance between heart and mind. In that way, Jareth and he were alike.

She moved when she felt the floor beneath her tremble, shuddering as if suffering from the massive aftershock of a bludgeoning. She cast one quick glance outside and inhaled sharply; the sky was darkening, was coming straight at the castle. Lightning and thunder were marching upon them. The lead of the glass window began to blister, as if heat were being generated somewhere, somehow. The frame rattled before her eyes, the latch straining to remain locked.

Beryl clutched the stone about her neck, knowing it would give momentary comfort. Then she fled up another flight of carved steps, their dappled blue shadows flickering throughout. Lighting as she placed a footstep, they dimmed just as quickly as she passed. The castle's air felt like an exhalation, of lungs forced to concede their need to breathe. The floor was afire in lines of blue radiation, flaring out as if searching for a grip.

Overhead, the ceilings were becoming slick, and moisture rolled to a low point before falling a single drop at a time, pooling. But they did not re-ice as she expected. Sprinting forward, she caught the next stair, secretly thrilled because the blue light reminded her of Leanan; could she be close? Had the others come for her? It was a hope of which she was most afraid because what if she were wrong and no one cared at all?

The walls were moving now, bending and shifting, causing hallways and doorways to narrow. She barely got past, scraping her guitar on the breeching walls. Where she stumbled and placed her hand in an effort to catch herself, a print remained, melted into the ice. Looking back, she saw it did not disappear; the surrounding ice locked in her passage as surely as time did. She turned and fled up the stairs.

Chapter 66

Never Forget, Two Steps from Hell

The higher Jareth climbed, the less he felt the structural vibrations coursing through the floor where Leanan was now the focal point of their counter-attack. Leanan Sidhe, the Dark Muse. It was a title he really hadn't considered. Why did it strike him now as so maleficent? Then again, hadn't he seen signs that the woman was far removed from humanity, was an entity easily explained by the dark dreams of men?

And yet, he didn't find a desire to distance himself, even reconsidering the ramifications of what 'dark' could mean. Despite the Cervine's warning about the muse—his muse—he didn't relish being without her. Which of course made him question himself. Who then was Jareth Rhylan? He liked to see himself as an itinerant musician with the ability to use a sword. In this world, it worked for him. After all, what else did he need but food and song and a way to keep others from taking either from him?

Then again, it was always only material gain he'd acquired. Those that understood the magic of his music already knew they could never possess it. Who was he to think then that *he* could? Was it all a matter of perspective, or was there a truth behind it all? It wasn't that he was deaf to what the muse and cervine said about magic, it was just the sense of responsibility they inferred. *His* magic of song he readily accepted even if its form was different to him. They called him a bard—nay, *the* Bard—which was a hard thing for him to swallow; he didn't think of himself like that, surely not in the way he had those traveling musicians of his youth. Now, *they* were bards, *they* had something he rabidly chased. Had he actually caught and passed them? It didn't seem possible...

Piper yowled to get his attention. The cracks emanating from below were spreading and as he rounded corner after corner, leaping steps two at a time, he noticed the micro-fractures everywhere. Yet, when he touched the walls, they still seemed so strong and durable...and cold. He hoped the muse wasn't actually trying to bring the fortress down, but he wouldn't put it past her; seems when she became obsessed, there were few limits.

The walls had been moving since the last level, sometimes bending inward, narrowing his path, and other times bowing back, as if the citadel of ice was breathing. Was it only trying to draw enough breath to stay alive? Was it sentient enough to withstand Sidhe magics?

Jareth followed the black cat into rooms of pure snow, with furniture carved from blocks of ice, their hospitality utterly serene and sterile. And though the air was warming, he didn't see any signs of melting, as if what kept everything frozen was powered by a colder core. He searched each room but found no clues, found neither alien captor nor terrified girl. The higher he went, the more anxious he became. A truism echoed at the periphery of his conscious, reminding him; don't forget, you're never more than two steps from Hell.

Like a digital paper trail, Rhey limped through the halls, moving from one room to the next, unsure where the girl thought she could go. He knew the fortress well, had been studying the man called Martin Hennessy for a while. He knew that the upper heights would only be colder, airless and completely frozen. There was no deliverance there, and there was no hope. And since authors liked to pattern their main character after themselves, he knew Jareth too would never commit to the higher paths; they existed simply to keep the man grounded. Without such, insanity would have already claimed him—as it would any human being. Humans used only about a third of their intellectual capacity—many far less—and that gave him a distinct advantage. Whatever barriers kept a human mind and heart whole would not stop him; he could actually breathe air that such as Martin would find toxic. His race had evolved further, longer, better. It was only a matter of time.

He recognized the lattice of Jareth's building, and when it had been altered. Sometimes, it was only a hand print, other times it was the scent of fear, held by the icy fingers of a step or wall cornice. Clues, subtle yet clear. The girl *was* working her way up, as though she didn't know the danger of doing so. Curious, because he'd suspected that what drove the young human character was another part of the author, perhaps a younger version. A new thought occurred to him. Maybe it was a family member instead?

Memories of images on the screen surfaced, prickling at his mind, demanding attention. Obviously, he had an intruder, even if it wasn't unexpected; the human rats had had to hide somewhere after his race had sent the missiles. How she'd kept her presence secret for so long, was the mystery. Still, there had to be a connection between what Martin was writing and the story by which he was now bound.

Of course, that would all change once he had the data sequence. The virus could only be stopped in time if he unraveled the DNA chain. The stone was the only place Martin could possibly have hidden it because once the small anteroom had been found—and thoroughly searched—the reason for what appeared on the scientist's laptop was obvious. What he could not extract physically with drugs, he had been forced to remove by 'playing the game'. And it had been a grand game, to be sure.

Rhey frowned, slowing, allowing his hand to linger just a little too long on the near wall. The one Martin called his muse would just love it if he left it there The fact he continually resorted to human renditions of sentience had bothered him for too long now. What was happening to him? Could it be another effect of the virus, as if disintegrating his skin from bone wasn't enough?

The girl had passed this way, the clues all said so. He could see she wasn't stopping her upward spiral. How ironic; humans often denoted that when a person was losing their abilities, it was a *downward* spiral. For him though, the only thing ironic about it was that he thought so.

He moved his hand off the wall, seeing his skin color smear across the icy plane. He made a clucking sound, to mark his annoyance; was the virus affecting him here too, in the same way now? But no, so far, it was only color; his skin was still hale and pure, albeit snowy white. He looked for the faint outline of his face in a passing window, saw the black painted eyes and elongated, dark red lips; it was a face he liked, actually.

A sound reached his ears and he lifted his head from the mirror. Curiously, his clown lips didn't curl into a smile of satisfaction when he identified the noise as belonging to the girl, crying out as she slipped above. If he *had* smiled, that would have been too human.

In the great entry hall of the ice citadel, the Cervine braced more sheaves of metal against the door, hearing and feeling the Warriors' continued efforts to break past. His hope that all were outside and none left in, was beginning to prove out, and for this he was glad. It meant he could send the muse's familiar to Jareth's aid. He bent his back against the door. Great cords of muscle grew and stiffened while his hooves dug in savagely, their cutting edge carving two great gouges in the floor. Bending his neck, he brought his head back and felt antlers touch the vibrating door.

With a last telling glance at the white tiger, he then lowered his lids and concentrated. He knew it was only one component he was protecting, but that's why the man had the muse in the first place—to protect the other. While he held the soul of the Bard intact, it was up to Leanan to breathe life into Jareth's heart, to fill him up with what mortals called 'evidence of life'. But he knew it was here at the gates where the hardest blow would fall; if Jareth was to face the demons of his soul by himself, it wouldn't matter if he lost his mind—or heart; he'd be lost just the same.

The thunder of the sky rolled about him, stalling, as if Leanan's fae had too much time on their hands; what *was* she doing? Another harsh blow rippled through his frame and he let it work itself into his legs and out his hooves, channeling the power into the ground where beneath any facade, he knew the foundation of everything lay. His song seemed alien here because it was the sound of roots digging through soil and clay, moving aside stones and infiltrating cracks in the bedrock. *His* song was sung in octaves too low for ordinary ears to hear.

Her verse floated upon a sea of rising waves, each cresting until their tops were silvery white in the light. But these waves were formed from air, liquid flowing currents that pulsed shades of purple and blue, surging and plunging at her bidding, assaulting the walls and filling the channels of the fissure she was creating. As she sang, she stretched her mind and heart, not allowing the fortress to assert any will of its own. Though she could feel the elements which alien hands had twisted, she wasn't fooled; this whole structure was imbued with the very essence of her man, Jareth Rhylan, the artist lover of whom she'd never met an equal. The fact he was the only one to ever have survived her didn't matter, the fact he was the only one to have withstood her fury only added to her glee as she began to rip the citadel apart. Oh, she was not mad enough to not understand what she was doing, because she was tearing down Jareth's own, but for her, this was something that had needed doing for a long time. In a seduction-laced, lust-filled moment of time in another world, she'd fought to get Jareth so free, to make him let go of the walls in his head.

And yet, she was also aware, albeit subconsciously, that he'd mortared the blocks of ice with more than his mind; as fractures tried to grow and resisted her intensified thrusts, she knew he'd imbued this place with his passion. And fear, too. Innately, it's how she knew there'd be more Bone Warriors; all mortals had their skeletons in the closet, didn't they?

The light surrounding her was dimmed by raging purple clouds and supplied by scatter shot lightning. Her face was a mask of pale demonic fury though, and if her eyes could be said to have been darkened before, then there was now no shade of black dark enough to do justice. Her hair extended behind her with the white shock sizzling. Her eyes were all pupil now, great glowing predator eyes with a thin ring of obsidian to contain them. Her arms were slung first one way than the other, much like a dark maestro conducting an infamous black concerto. She lifted her head and bared her fangs, the blood of her lips darkening like her eye shadow. A dark trickle fell to her chin. Over and over she smote the floor, driving all her song into it, all her magic and fury.

As the white tiger bounded past, she was only dimly aware of its presence. And yet, it was enough; with the pause, *her* thoughts were the cat's and in that instant, the blue emulsion of her light engulfed the great animal, transforming its fur. It was but for a moment and as a primal scream echoed, the predator leaped away, sure now of its prey. A liquid line of blue fire burned the ice where it passed.

Beryl began to cry; it wasn't fair, she'd been able to hide for so long...and yet, as Joker-face gripped her wrists, she knew she was no match. If only she hadn't fallen and hurt her leg...

Rhey didn't have time for finesse—the fractures were spreading and beginning to widen; the walls to either side were trembling and shifting, as if unsure how long they wanted to remain stable. It was one thing to understand the mind of a man, even dissect the desires of his heart, but when one toyed with the inner workings of a human soul, the consequences were not always predictable.

Martin had surprised him, had proved that he knew more about the elements of a story than was portrayed. How could a scientific mind understand the intricacies of something he didn't even believe in? Magic and science were mutually exclusive; the first being fictitious and insubstantial—ineffectual once you showed how the trick was done—and the latter what made up the cosmos. *His* cosmos, the worlds and planets, galaxies and nebulae through which his kind had already traveled. That a minor species of debatable intellect could house such a surprise, well—that was the surprise.

Beryl felt the stone in her palm warming, knowing its peculiar red glow was flaring. The light would spill if she let go though, so she held tight, no matter that the alien's strength was vastly superior. Something urged her to sustain, to deny. If she lost her light, she knew she was dead; it was as if what lay within kept her alive. As the tears streamed and she struggled in Rhey's grasp, she felt every mark of ink on her body spasm in unison; her fear was their glee.

The girl was stronger than he thought—or was *he* beginning to weaken? No time for idle thoughts now—he knew it was probably another ploy by Martin, something to distract and stall. Surely the man must understand that if he held on long enough, that his and mankind's hope would triumph. The virus, which one man had released, would take down the last of the alien conquerers. That was the hope, that was the aim.

That Rhey knew he was the last of the invading force was only a dim fact he tried to ignore; it had been a while since any of his kind had been in contact. The assumption was that the virus had finished its work. All except on him. And even now, the scientist named Martin Hennessy, as he lay strapped to a chilled metal table, was holding out against an impossible array of drugs his body had no right being able to withstand. The virus was making its presence known, both there and here, in a fictitious fortress made within a man's mind. A place where ice and snow marked winter in ways any alien could understand, but never fully appreciate. It took mankind's type of unique weaving to fully get the gist of mind, heart, and soul.

A wailing cry erupted from the girl as the alien broke her fingers and thrust them aside, ripping the burning red stone from her neck, the filigree silver chain snapping as if a tendon. He pulled the gemstone to his face, opening his palm to the glowing, pulsing light. It reminded him of a human heart...

The room began to pulse with the beryl stone, but its hue was darker, hinging on shades of mauve and purple. The cracks in the floor were reaching inward for each other, extending from one wall to the next. The wrought iron holding glowing globules of flickering fire flared, their source of fuel dripping from the walls themselves. The windows of the room rattled with a growing tension as reverberations made their way up from the lower floors.

From the doorway, Rhey spied a movement, something small, which surprised him because any other element of the scene should have been made inconsequential. At least enough for him to not notice, let alone care. He had the key to his survival, finally, in his hand; what else was there? It would surely be a matter of moments before the lines of the white sterile lab were brought into sharp focus, when white ice was replaced with white paint. The windows would melt down or tear away—he didn't know; how did human authors typically transform their dream sequences? Did it happen with a bang and a whoosh, or was it something less dramatic like waking up? Yes, that was surely how to end *this* story...

And yet, the movement had jarred him out of his reverie, out of his contemplation of what having the DNA sequence would mean. He blinked, and this time, really looked.

It was a black cat.

Chapter 67

Black Blade

A shadow is a curious thing, it can be something easily observed, something normal and natural, but in all aspects, it needs light to survive. This shadow didn't seem to have been born from anything like that, it was as if instead of being born, it had been bourn, carried into a great confluence of conflict in which impossibly, it rose from a primordial vestige his race would never have given credit. But there it was, darker than it should be, more intact than it had a right, hovering, clinging, waiting...for what?

The fact the cat hadn't moved was also discomfiting. Rhey raised his arm as if to throw a projectile at it but the little animal remained stolid, its round luminous amber eyes fixed on him, and only him. That should never have seemed as unnerving as it was. The animal sat upright, its tail curled around it, the tip barely twitching, keeping subtle backbeat to the pulsing of the room, of the light oozing from between his now closed fingers where the gemstone lay, burning his hand.

The shadow grew until details could be delineated, could be thought of as persistent, though his alien senses were analyzing at a formidable rate. By all rights, the scene should be dissipating like mist after quenching a newly forged sword. Now, why had that metaphor been first to his thought?

The shadow fluctuated, tried to materialize, but still seemed temporaneous, as if it wanted to come into the light but feared doing so might destroy it. There was the soft radiance of a red hood about a darkened face, the glint of silver keys—eight of them—from behind the shape's back. There was soft pastels that looked anything but passive now in the blossoming storm-light entering the room from between closed windows. Even the lead holding the glass was darkening, looking more and more like ink.

From the fog of unsurety, the form of a man was taking shape, a man whose chest blazed with black fire, in letters he could not decipher, though they looked familiar enough. It wasn't until Rhey let his eyes drift to the rising arm of the man that he saw more glittering silver, steel silver emanating from fingers which were drawing high and back, reaching, reaching, reaching for something...

"It's too late, Martin—you lost; I got it. Nothing you can do now but end the story. And since you wrote with a specific aim, there is no more purpose to continue; I know it and you know it. There's only another story where the hero fails in the end. Isn't that the way of all your modern books? Such idealism as you were raised upon though, perhaps you never did get the memo? While other writers were evolving, changing, following—and in some cases leading—what the audience preferred, you lay stuck in the mire of such arcane and misconstrued stories like Lord of the Rings and The Lion, The Witch, and the Wardrobe."

The shadow's movement halted, arm halfway to its destination, its face becoming clearer. Tired skin, tired eyes, worn paunches for cheeks, and scars that looked like they'd been recently drawn.

"Oh yeah, Martin, I found the room—and as you can see, I found *her*, too!"

There was a curious glitter of light in the shadow's eyes as it traveled over the two forms, one a pasty fleshed individual whose whole countenance looked fragile and decrepit, while the other was like a molten flow of light. It lay in a puddle, in the form of a sobbing girl, in the outline and trace of a thousand tears. It was there that the glittering gaze lingered, contemplating, pushing around thoughts like words, assessing.

"There's nothing left for this story; see? I hold the key!"

And Rhey unfolded his burnt fingers, allowing the red light to flood the room, still pulsing like a human heart.

"It's the heart of the whole scene, Martin, the baseline of the chapter and blood of the book. *This* is why you wrote the story, this is all there is!"

The shadow reached out with a good hand, still fully fleshed and though pale, still pink. Striding past the black cat, Jareth finished reaching over his shoulder and when he let its motion end, the bright tip of a blade pointed toward the floor, not in defeat, but in abject posture of submission. It was waiting too.

Rhey scanned the face of Jareth Rhylan, Martin's incarnation, and realized that something was wrong; the human was not showing any fear, was not exhibiting any form of denial *or* acceptance. In fact, he was looking right past, as if only one other existed in the moment.

Suddenly filled with a dreadful insight, the alien watched the advancing shadow through the gemstone's pulsing light.

"No!"

Rhey's voice arced up, rearing itself against the ceiling, as if its own shadow could devour the one approaching. Swiftly reaching into the folds of his pocket, he worked his hand until it came free. Then he turned to face the girl.

In the moment it takes the wind to flicker a single flame, Rhey's arm swept around.

Beryl had picked her head up as she too sensed something within Jareth's gaze; she'd heard a voice like never before, and it sang to her in a way it hadn't since she was young. Very young, during a time when it wasn't her mother singing her to sleep, but someone else

Jareth almost missed the flash of steel, but the moment was long enough. He rushed forward, bringing his own arm up and then down again, severing the chalky white wrist halfway through its sweep. The knife in the alien's hand though, creased the skin of Beryl's throat anyway, drawing another line of darkness on her skin. But this line was living and it flowed not like text, but like blood. The girl never even uttered a sound as her body floated to the icy floor.

The trombones surged, sending dangerous notes to smote the air, having fattened themselves on the building tension. Prelude to a symphonic overture of immense proportions, the timpani returned as well, and with the addition of a parrying bass, the choral denouement commenced.

The flaccid white hand hung in midair, the ancient blade it possessed still a glittering arc. Time had not sped up.

A silent pendulum, the joker's body continued turning while his other hand freed an ancient Katsura from the fold of his cloak. Rhey drove the blade up toward revelation with invincible force.

Revelation's veil of shadow dispersed and a man stood where once there was none. Time was like the delicate tuning of a mandolin, each turn of the screw slowing time impractically.

The burgundy pulse of the gemstone hung between bursts, not exhaling as much as drawing breath, feeling abandoned. For icy caricatures, time was suspended.

Three floors down, a snarl of deepest hate mirrored the raging amber pulse of tiger eyes, razed the air and sent a song of revenge before it.

In a hallway, head lowering to hands, wickedly seductive eyes full of fury blanched as a blue nimbus spat sparks and hissed maniacally against the virulent walls. Moments were reversing uncontrollably.

Against the gate wall, the combined might of twenty war hammers cracked, and with them, a song of bones; many, many bones. For them, time didn't mean a thing.

Head bowed, back to the gate, mighty antlers threatened to touch the icy earth; earth now because beneath the Lord Protector, the thaw had begun in earnest.

It was then the black cat burst loose, propelled as if deiced.

The Japanese sword should have found perfect aim, it should have impaled the one human who had single-handedly forestalled alien conquest. Rhey had studied all the manuals, fascinated himself with countless videos and even sparred with the few prisoners his kind had taken in the earliest stages of the invasion. To call this a war then would have been ludicrous. Now, it defined itself by the very nature of their combat. He didn't see the cat jump but when it hit his arm, he knew then why the last page hadn't turned; the story wasn't over yet.

Martin's character flashed past, the Katsura glancing harmlessly off a hardened pauldron. And before the alien could recover from the distraction, Jareth was at Beryl's side, his hands rushing to her throat in a futile attempt to stay the blood.

Rhey whirled around, looking as much for the cat as for the man.

"I should have known."

But if the alien expected further dialog he was mistaken. Jareth began to weep, the choking sound no longer inhibited; he was free to mourn, at last. When Rhey spoke, his voice bludgeoned the walls.

"It was never in the stone at all—you put it in the girl!"

The room baited time, daring it to go in any direction.

"This was all a ruse."

His brow furrowed and his eyes darkened. Biting his lip, he advanced upon the still stooping human, the obvious sounds of despair soiling the perfect crystalline floor.

Off to one side the cat hissed, drawing the alien's attention. But it was momentary as the more obvious threat was now clear. A threat yes, but perhaps a solution as well; if Martin's character died so too might the man on the table, and then whatever force still held him inside this unfinished story would be broken. It was worth a shot. He drew his arm back for a thrust.

She came day after day, Jareth, even though I was gone.

He didn't really want to hear this, he just wanted to die.

I tried to come to her, as to you, but there was something inside that told me she still needed her father. You were still alive on the table, and that was enough.

He tried feverishly to stem the dark tide as pulsing flows of light leaked from his daughter's throat. But the light looked too much like blood.

She still needs you.

She's dying, can't you understand that?

He lashed back at Candace's voice, aware of how much he should be pitied at the moment.

So are you. Can't you see? Did you think you could keep her alive in your book? Did you think you were so clever that only you could know what you did?

I want her to live, I want to tell her I love her...

So tell her, Jare...tell her...

The words rang as loud as any song he'd ever heard; the crystal notes of a harp could not have come close. Candace's face was full of dancing light, just like the very first time they'd met.

The textural contact he felt himself falling into was swallowing him whole, and he wasn't sure he wanted to stop it. It would be so deserved, so justified.

Like a rumble of thunder, it was not Candace who spoke in his head next, it was the Cervine.

Justice isn't something you're to measure, Jareth Rhylan; you have another purpose; do it!

Like a jab of pain, he recoiled, almost letting Beryl's head fall back. He cried harder seeing this and hugged her close to him, feeling as if he was caught in a vortex of time.

The feeling was there, he just hadn't acknowledged it. It lay eddying at first, then swirling as if in time to a lengthy, slow introductory piece, fidgeting while the wind section rosined their bows. But as the music began to join in on itself, the insouciance that was the Dark Muse burst forth, unable to contain itself any longer. It cried at him in a fell voice, in a wrath of dark, enduring words.

He killed them both, Jare; are you going to let Candace and Beryl die for nothing?

The lash of her voice was galvanizing and he fluidly laid his child down one last time, ripping the sword from the icy floor, just then noticing that it was not his short sword. It was the blade he'd made the muse carry the whole journey. The basket weave of intricate steel cloistered his sword hand in a cunning way. He swept it up behind him, satisfaction rearing its prideful head as he felt his blade encounter the steel of another. Rolling he put himself between the dying girl and his attacker.

Rhey felt something suffuse him then, a raw nerve being ripped, surging with both surprise and emotion. Emotion? How could this be?

"You wanted to *know* me, demon incarnate, now you will."

Jareth's first lunge tore through the Joker-faced man's robe before encountering sinewy flesh. Turning his blade, Jareth tore loose the man's left arm, the sound of it hitting the far wall a dull knell of time.

Rhey quickly pulled back, aghast that the man had even been aware of his attack in the first place. But this was not a battle of wills, it was of intellect, and on that score, he would emerge victorious. Getting out of this hellish story depended on it.

The Katsura clove the air succinctly, slipping down Jareth's blade and if not for the basket hilt, would have shorn the man's hand clean off. Withdrawing in time, Jareth maneuvered so he could bring himself into the enemy's ring of reach. This would not be a fight that would see any honor and he knew it. He actually preferred that it didn't.

"You can't win this, Martin; there's already too many endings to choose from, and certainly the death of your daughter wasn't one of them. You're left with only stringless threads now..."

Rhey sliced down and felt his blade begin to bite into Jareth's, knowing that the metal from which the Katsura was made was infinitely better, harder, stronger...

Yet the man managed to shove him off, the two blades intertwining at each intersection of their dancing forms. As the orchestra heightened octaves in the background, they parried and danced as if on the same stage.

Sing, Jareth, use the sword!

He felt the pressure, but resisted; it was a familiar refrain Leanan wanted him to sing, but something he would not choose.

Jareth thrust and scored another hit on the agile alien, his sword burying itself into the ice wall with a hiss of white heat. Yanking it free in time, he moved to parry Rhey's next assault.

Sing, Bard; use the magic!

The Cervine's voice rolled like leaves budding, their reach for the sky unparalleled. Rhey's double cut and slice came dangerously close to his eyes and Jareth arced backward, afraid his leg muscles would break from the extreme speed and angle. But even as he did, the feeling of wound cord, of twisted roots knotting and unknotting, flooded his mind. He dared not glance down at his leg; Rhey was just waiting for his concentration to wander.

Sing, my beloved, bind fire to ice!

He felt tears fill his voice as he heard Candace's plea, both from rage and despair, and the grip on his longsword tightened impossibly. Filled with purpose, he was one with the steel. And he remembered then why it was called Sword of Pain. In that moment though, it was nothing but a black blade.

His voice ripped like a start, like an impatient storm cloud, releasing its bolt too soon. He heard the misery in his own words as he eschewed lyrics and went straight to verse. It was language of a different type, something very alien to the modern world; it was full of imagery so steeped in passion that bridges were erected instantaneously. No more was he separate parts; mind and heart and soul came together and fused in his need. As he came to face his past pain with the one he now chose to embrace, the liquid fire of his anger met the frozen depth of his guilt. In that moment, he knew exactly which song to sing...

The Katsura came in low, obliquely, looking to strike like a snake with Rhey's body twisting to comply. Once fully targeted, there now was nothing but empty air as Jareth once again had resumed being the shadow. Veils were strung and there was no longer a room of ice and snow, there was no longer locked and barricaded windows that never showed the light of day. Instead, there was grass beneath his feet and a wind in his ear. In the sky, twin suns were colliding, sending rays of intense heat to sear his body, to melt his bones. All about him, trees were springing up, forced branches unfurling, their leaves to surgically follow. The battleground was set and Rhey realized he did not know within which scene he was caught.

The longsword ripped laterally, its tip spinning alien fingertips in its wake. Jareth did not let his stroke end though, forcing the blade to continue back, sweeping lower this time and as it did, the alien's legs were cut loose at the knee and Rhey dropped, the look on his face more incredulous than fearful. Still, Jareth did not stop the blade, weaving it in an arc that cut through Rhey's guard and down, forcing his opponent's weapon to scatter across the grass.

Then did Jareth try to slow the black blade, *then* did he try to suppress the feelings that drove his fury. As if willing Leanan out of his head for just a moment, he sucked in air at a frightful pace, knowing he needed more than he was getting. The tears on his face had not stopped, nor would they, not for a long time.

Rhey held his one arm out, an earlier gash on his forehead spilling drops of blood down one cheek. For the first time, he tasted his own blood. The very thought was repulsing and that's when he knew how human he'd become.

"I just want to get home, Martin, that's all. Can't you understand that?"

The wind swept the man's long hair onto his shoulders and into his eyes, momentarily obscuring sight of his foe. Why was this so familiar? The ink stain on his chest blazed darkly, there was a pain in his wrist; and *then* he remembered.

Earthen roots toiled, sending their great vibrato voice into his head, in words that could only come from the Lord Protector.

Because that's what the enemy does, Jareth, he lies and alters your sight.

The man opened his mouth, the words unbidden, the song ordained. He seared the alien with his stare, not seeing Rhey reaching into his belt.

"The name's Jareth, damn you..."

He held his blade in the same hand whose wrist was still deeply scarred. He held his blade with two fingers missing and replaced by soulless metal substitutes. He held his blade with the certainty that he would forever pay for his guilt.

His longsword moved as if of its own accord, sweeping up and catching the dagger in mid flight. Stepping forward, he swung his sword with every ounce of strength he had, his song a rattle of dry bones at a funeral march, but deadly just the same.

The head of the alien hung where it always had for a precious second longer before the wind at Jareth's back toppled it backward and chased after it as it rolled down the hill.

The body of the Hunter took a lot longer to fall, but it eventually did.

A great rending was taking place as the fortress walls were threatening to cave in on themselves, especially now that all restrictions had been removed. And along with the resurgence of the storm inside the walls, the great fissures were free to work past the lower levels and they did so with astonishing speed.

Jareth opened his eyes, a dull haze trying to overcome his heart, a searing pain across his temple and worse, a bleeding, broken part of him that could only be his soul. He opened his eyes and fell to his knees, oblivious to the headless husk of a man lying before him. He didn't even see how the decay was surging as fast as the fissures and storm, trying to take what was finally theirs.

There's still time, Jareth.

And he knew what Candace meant. And this time, he did not hesitate nor wallow in his own pitifulness. Instead, he crawled over to where his child lay in a darkening pool. It was as if all the fractures and fissures working to break down the citadel had decided to ignore this one piece of ice.

Maybe they have, Jareth thought, because it's my ice. Maybe they've decided to let me grieve after all.

He reached out to take Beryl in his arms, the daughter for which he'd named his character, not because he'd wanted to hide from her, but because he hadn't.

"I love you Beryl, I love you forever, my baby girl."

It was a memory from another time, from another place, but it was theirs.

As he closed his eyes, he saw Piper. The animal looked up at him while a single teardrop glistened and fell, falling onto the hand of his most precious jewel.

Chapter 68

Peacekeeper

The walls strove to withstand the backlash of pressure created by the breaking citadel. They bled blue and purple, laced themselves with crystalline forms that stung like a dream just out of reach. They survived because their maker would not relent.

But out of the destruction of fissures and fractures, the cavalry came, though Jareth was hardly aware at first. He held Beryl's still warm body to his, the idea her heart could ever stop a concept he just would not accept. Even as the wind spoke, urging him to let her go, he fiercely rebuked it, calling it callous. He didn't want to let go, ever again...

After awhile, he was aware he wasn't alone. The soft music of predators both large and small came to him, and the song being sung was not one he wanted to recognize.

The tiger sat on its haunches, tongue lolling over black and pink lips. The large cat's eyes were half open, its malevolent yellow stare like a sunset following a storm. It was a horizon for which he didn't have time.

Next to the tiger, Leanan stood, leaning on the short sword, its blade darkened at the edge, as if it had come through lightning and was yet a coal. Her face looked haggard but whole, and she managed to smile softly, eschewing her usual seductive manner.

But it was the Cervine's touch which finally got him to accept what had happened, and to let go. He looked up with unabashed tears and beseeched the large antlered creature, willing his deepest desire on another because he could not contain it by himself.

You can, Jareth, and you will. There's more to life than pain, though you've done your best to run from it. In time, when the grieving is over, you'll learn to live again. But for now, your tears are righteous.

He heard the words in his head but felt that the Cervine spoke for them all.

He brushed his face quickly, bringing icy dirt to his cheeks. He didn't want to give her up and didn't know how.

Give her to me, Jareth, as she was mine before ever she was yours. All the children of the world belong to me, including you. Do not fear, Jareth Rhylan, the time for that has passed.

Through his tears, Jareth forced the words to be.

As the man's arms went limp, the Cervine reached under and took the girl in his arms and truly, she looked like a baby being cradled.

"I failed her again, didn't I?"

The silence which followed though, was not tainted with any hint of shame.

"You did not; she needed you and you came. You did not fail her."

"But she's gone, just like before, just like it was before the story started."

The words sounded strange but they also rang true, as any real song can attest.

"And who said the story was over?"

Jareth didn't understand.

"I was supposed to get her to Eli, the one that would make her whole again."

He said the words, remembering his daughter in another's guise, as one that felt like she was a complete failure, like everyone could put a mark on her and condemn her for even trying.

"But you did, Jareth. The tattoos attributed to others were actually placed there by you. Did you not sacrifice yourself once to take away her pain? Wasn't that what she wanted?"

Jareth remembered entering the dome, recalled touching Beryl's face—his daughter's face—and consuming the blemishes that she felt so shamed her. Yes, he remembered.

And now, it is time to finish it.

Jareth looked up into the dark eyes of the Cervine, his heart aching to break no more.

But then you'd not know you're alive, Jareth. Be at peace, her life is gone but her love secured.

And so saying, Jareth watched as the ink scripts and odd symbols idly lazing on his daughter's skin, now began to move faster, as if being prodded.

"What's happening?"

"Watch; like you, like the marks on her skin, she's being called home.

Jareth watched as the Cervine extended one hand and took Jareth's within his, before placing it in Beryl's. The man's eyes widened in awe as first one string then the next swirled and curled before moving toward her hand, the hand that lay in his. And they did not stop when they reached her fingertips. Flowing like lines in a book, the shapes and text mixed with symbols that only now looked familiar. Like a never ending line of verse, or a passage in a book, the script receded from Beryl's body and entered Jareth through their connection. And when it was done, he understood.

The symbols were encryptions of a sequence of data, the DNA string describing a virus which had turned out to be mankind's last hope. It was only coincidental that it also showed him how much she was like him.

"Will she be okay?"

The absurdity of his question stunned him.

The Cervine nodded though, solemnly.

"She learned that it didn't matter what the others thought of her, it only mattered what Eli thought. As your father loves you, you loved her. She found her Eli, as you must find yours. In the end, no mark of mankind can ever stick, not when the truth of love is realized."

The Cervine lifted the girl higher, motioning for Jareth and the others to follow. Last to leave the room was the cat, and he did so with tail lifted.

The citadel was broken but not destroyed and their way down was treacherous. But with the sure footed Cervine leading, they made it to the broken tundra before the main gate, a barrier whose hinges lay twisted amidst old bones.

*

The muse left her tiger with Jareth and went to walk side by side with the Cervine.

"He didn't let me destroy it."

"I know, he may never."

"But he has to, doesn't he?"

The Cervine nodded.

Leanan looked back at the man, his face still handsome even beneath the pain. She tightened her eyes though as she noted the grim purse of his mouth.

"I didn't want to give him back the sword, not then."

"I know. But obviously, he was able to handle it. Still, it might be best if you continue looking after it for the foreseeable future."

"There's a future?"

"Aye, Sidhe, there is. Like the Hunter said; this story isn't over."

She frowned, a thought traipsing through her head.

"Is any story ever really over?"

"Just one, and that time is not yet come."

She eyed the rack of antlers above the creature's head, snorting.

"You really should pay more attention to the boy."

But already she was re-evaluating the ramifications of his words.

"Will he fully heal?"

The Cervine knew she wasn't referring to anyone but Jareth; it was her greatest strength, and her greatest weakness.

"He's already been hurt so much, and by his own hand."

The Cervine nodded.

"Aye, that's why he wouldn't let you dismantle his fortress of ice; he still feels he needs it."

Leanan cast a long dark look at the receding form of the ice citadel as they moved beyond the broken walls and toward the Last Causeway. It was going to be a hard walk home.

"We're going home, right?"

She didn't really have the same hope hinted by her words.

"Eventually, we all go home."

A Celtic curse birthed itself with her next breath, calling down a pox on shaggy pelted behemoths that spoke in anything but riddles.

"A penchant you share, don't you?" the Cervine reminded.

"With the girl gone, what is to drive him out of this place? I think even you know he's no longer in control of this world; the Hunter made certain of that. This is no longer a place that's friendly to his ways, to his reasons."

The Cervine looked back at Jareth, watching the tiger nudge him when he wanted to dawdle. Even the black cat wasn't getting through to him. Perhaps he'd underestimated how the girl's passing was affecting the man.

"He still created it, and his rules still apply. He may not be in control anymore, but there's still no reason to think he can't find his own way home."

Leanan sighed, her straggly black hair strewn over her face, obscuring vision. She looked comical but no way was he going to tell her that.

"The girl's skin is clear again."

The Cervine was surprised the muse hadn't noticed before this, but nodded just the same.

"Where are we taking her?"

With antlers looking suspiciously like a crown of thorns, the Cervine looked down fondly at the still form, the gash in her neck already disappearing.

"I'm taking her home."

"You can do that?"

Leanan looked skeptical, but realized after seeing some of the other things the Cervine had done, it was probably not as far fetched an idea as she thought.

"The journey won't be the same with her passing."

Which caused the Cervine to look harder at the muse, assessing with new eyes.

"And who says she's passed?"

Which made the muse look even harder at the Cervine, one brow lifting. He chided her.

"You really should pay more attention to the cat!"

The muse turned and skewered the trailing animal with her gaze, willing the creature's eyes to meet hers. Not budging, Piper continued walking behind Jareth, the tip of his tail twitching as if shooing her away. The insolence!

"He's not going to like what happens next, is he?"

The Cervine looked toward the muse, catching her gaze with his, with eyes where the earth's wild magic lived in a morass of green.

"Well, he didn't exactly like this chapter either but look how it turned out. He's free of a great enemy, one which still lurks in his nightmares. If he can free himself of the others and find his way home, he should do okay."

The muse sucked in her lower lip, exposing the sharpness of her teeth. She did this absently, lost in thought.

"There's still himself to conquer...and that damned ice castle."

The Cervine ruffled his lips, a vain attempt to actually laugh.

"We've got enough to worry about without bothering with Jareth's bane. He's felt the fire again, he met the ice; somehow, he's found a way to balance life once again."

"Oh? You think so? I don't know about that."

The edge of the great bridge was almost upon them as Leanan realized they'd been walking and speaking a lot longer than she first imagined. Damn, that meant fixing that leaky tub beached in the distance. Oh but for the true feel of a wooden clipper and three masts of sail...now, there was a proper way to ride the sea!

"Trust me, he'll find a way. He found a way to write himself out of this latest dilemma, didn't he?"

"You mean sing himself out..."

She was still grumbling, thinking about the rusty bucket called the Pacific Heron.

"Semantics. Don't tell him Beryl is still alive. He doesn't need to know that yet."

"No? And why doesn't he?"

He could hear the mothering lover-protectiveness surging in the muse's voice.

"That's the way of mourning; everyone needs to find their own way home. Eventually, he'll come to see that everyone here has been created for a purpose; his daughter was created to bring him home, wasn't she?"

Leanan looked hard at the Cervine, her tongue barely held in check. She realized though, of course he was right.

"You're a death-hard master sometimes, Lord Protector, you know that?"

The Cervine's expression didn't change.

"Hope is like that; it's only in hope's absence that death has any meaning, though."

Beryl

She shook her head, girding her loins, as a writer might say, knowing this was just the beginning and there was nothing any of them could do about it.

Epilogue

Say You Will

The last hinge gave and the door slowly fell to the tile floor, its echo a crescendo of sound that went on for longer than those entering the room were comfortable with. With half the floor already searched, they were nearing a considerable level of fatigue. It hadn't helped that the alien had cannibalized all the loose plumbing for his insidious experiments. Entering the room, it looked like they'd stumbled on another one.

The room still had electricity, which was as large of a surprise as the missing pipes. The rest of the building had been abandoned much earlier. With some growing confidence, they began to think maybe they'd stumbled on an alien headquarters, or at least something equally as important.

So the last remnants of a small town reclaimed the government building too few had been aware of during peacetime. It was ironic, but perhaps this one white room could tell them how Earth had stumbled to victory. There were reports, probably rumor, of other clusters of human survivors. The fact no evidence of the alien invasion still existed, was good news enough for most. They were alive, barely, left with a world which would take unimaginable effort to rebuild. But rebuild they would because well, that's what humans did; survive.

The two leading this expedition were from science departments in a former life, and it was good that they were there or else much evidence might have been destroyed through negligence. But as it was, their expertise understood immediately that the machines blinking beneath the fluorescent light were still functioning, and even more amazingly, they found a man shackled to the lab's lone ongoing experiment. Still alive. Barely.

In another stroke of luck, they found possibly the last alien too, at least what remained of its rotted carcass, as dried bits of skin and bone littered a seat near the table, wires and electrode contacts tangled from femurs and shin bones. It looked like the alien had been trying to keep himself alive with his own concoctions. At least they could now relax and not worry if any of the enemy was still on the loose. It had been at least two months since any activity had been noticed coming from this building, and a good few had even advised against checking. The leader of the search squad was glad he'd put his lot with the former; the poor sod they found on the table was reward alone for taking the risk; there'd been enough dying to last an eternity. If they could save just one more, it was worth it.

The science leader scanned the room; if the monitors could be trusted, and the physical overview of the long-bearded man could be believed, the man's lungs and heart still pumped, blood still flowed and nerves still functioned. But what about his mind?

There was talk and then more talk before any decision was made. It was too risky to just unplug the alien's test vials and strip the electrodes from the man's head, that permanent brain damage would occur if it hadn't already. The readings clearly indicated that though running down, the unknown man still had a chance. They might need time, but eventually, they'd figure out a way to wean him off the devil's concoctions still dripping slowly into his bloodstream. A guard was eventually posted and the man's identity was eventually found. Martin Hennessy; genetic scientist for the government, and perhaps the one responsible for setting loose the virus which in turn destroyed the invaders. The guard was doubled and those with suitable medical ability brought to the sterile white laboratory where a patriot lay. As lives rose from the dust of destruction, it was good to have a symbol of something for which to fight. In time, as a sort of holy revival, candles were lit, candles that signified that at the heart of any vigil lay hope.

They eventually found a young girl too, one with ratty dark hair and emaciated features, her eyes wide and her fear desperate. Even when they found her sneaking between hallways and ducking back into an impossibly narrow vent-way, she'd screamed her pain and anguish, clutching at their hands, trying to tear away her rescuer's grip, when all they wanted to do was welcome her home. For her, it would take a lot longer than most to get past post traumatic stress disorder; it would take time to heal wounds that went beyond alien colonization. For her though, the prognosis looked good.

The only continuing problem they had with her was an insistence that she'd lost her cat. No matter how much they tried to comfort her with stuffed animals made from shreds of discarded clothing, she still insisted the other remained alive. In time, they just shook their head and left her alone to her two obsessions, both of which had been found clutched tightly in her arms; an old, bent paged book which she would not put down, and a broken frame housing a faded picture. Each was precious to her but they did not know why. Being kind, there was little thought to take them away, but it soon became apparent that these two items were all she cared about. It worried the nurses but they'd been through worse; she wouldn't be abandoned because of some childish quirk.

The book was an old one, a novel many considered trite and archaic, having passed beyond any reasonable modern literary standard. Unapproachable, they said, and certainly would never have been published today. It was titled The Lord of the Rings volume two; the Two Towers.

The picture in the frame was damaged and time had wrinkled its canvas. If the girl could tell them her name, they might be able to find out who it was in the picture. But she'd suffered a lot and it was hoped that with time, she might remember.

Inside the broken frame was a picture of a mid-thirties aged man, and he was standing next to a young girl who looked to be eight years old. In one hand, she held an acoustic guitar.

And hugged within the embrace of the other arm, was a black cat.

The End

Outside the Envelope

Gypsy

The gurgle suffuses his ears and he can't know if it's his breath or his blood sounding off to the incoming tides. Night is come again and with it, the need to hold breath. To all good things comes an end, that's what they say...

Staked out in the sand, there's an insidious way to know time slips; it lies in particles of sand, drifting between two halves of an hourglass; filling, falling, forming a hill that is impossible to climb. How can one scale to such heights when the ocean of life is drowning you? How do you ride one wave without touching the crest of the next? It is impossible, and so the story goes. And goes and goes...

A hand reaches down, and taking the hourglass, turns it over, the top having emptied. But then, *is* it the top? Once turned over, does top not become bottom and vice versa? At least with tides, one knows when it's time to hold their breath or not.

Novel trivia #1: Each chapter is titled after a real song. Writing with music looping in the background helps me to keep a consistent 'tone', so know that this book is developed with that aspect in mind. You might even try listening to the same songs while reading.

Novel trivia #2: I typically like to have visuals for my characters so I maintain a further consistency. Some authors will pattern their characters 'characteristics' after people they know—which I've done as well in the past—but for this one, I've used characters about whom I've already written. So, the only change was the visual.

For this novel, I saw Martin Hennessy/Jareth Rhylan played by Johnny Depp.

Leanan Sidhe the Dark Muse is a character created in my first novel, Dark Muse, so I used her likeness even if I massaged the artwork (cover) online before I began (but my wife suggests young Angelina Jolie).

The Cervine is also from an earlier depiction, though I used a painting from the web to get a different 'look' for this novel, but basically it's the character created by Charles De Lint in his book *GreenMantle* (might cast Ron Perlman if just for his voice!).

For Beryl, I chose the singer Priscilla Ahn.

For the antagonist Rhey, I had two images in mind, one more alien than the other and hardly needing a picture, but for the human reincarnation, Heath Ledger's brilliant characterization of the Batman foe 'Joker' was perfect.

For Candace, I had a dark-haired version of Cameron Diaz in mind simply because one head shot showed beautiful eyes that I thought translated well for what I had in mind.

And lastly, for the black cat Piper/Hershey, I used a picture of one of my current pets, a black cat named...Hershey (Piper was the name of my first black cat, long ago since passed but not forgotten).

Dean Michael Christian started as a poet, learning about rhyme while a freshman in high school. From there, a love of words began and during his twenties, he penned his first novel. Well, half-finished novel, of which many authors and would-be authors quite understand. At age 43, life changed and with it came close encounters with emotions he hadn't before experienced. Poetry became a savior and a catharsis (per poet-speak), and he delved heavily into public (and not so public) poetry forums, learning to write in terms of showing and not telling. Once purged of this need, prose beckoned and he laid his heart bare to pen a first complete novel, something based on the year of turmoil that included divorce from a 19 year marriage. The novel redefined 'catharsis' but also brought a hunger for more stories. From this moment, the poet transformed into an author.

Dean has published three novels with Beryl being the fourth. Along with the prose, he's compiled three volumes of poetry, one of which highlights his best. Once the written word took hold, he even dusted off a children's book, one he'd written and illustrated for his then young son Erik.

On a dead-end road in an upscale Michigan suburban neighborhood, he lives with his new wife Traci, grown up son Erik, and three cats. In a ranch home he built himself, relishing moments with family and playing cards in the pondhouse out back, Dean is trying to fulfill his purpose. Like his name, his faith is vital toward forging an identity, with hours spent listening to the Word. It's his hope that he'll grow along with his stories.

Immersed in both photography and computer graphics, he's also an avid gardener and winter weekend warrior on the ice. When summer wanes and words call to be heard though, that's when he takes up the quill, cracks his knuckles, and begins filling the screen with words, describing images which will fulfill his earliest bio:

I am a spirit spilled from the age of Shakespeare and flowing into Frost. Dylan holds my banner, Aragorn my broken blade, and EvenStar my heart. I drown in iambic, look for the golden light, and feel the sand pass between my fingers...

In the beginning there was a poet; now, author Dean Michael Christian speaks in metaphorical tones, not bereft of verse, but rather, filled to the full.

He brings you the magic inherent in words, and hopes you'll lose yourself in their bliss.

Other works available by Dean Michael Christian

On the L: paranormal literary relational fantasy

The Chicago L train was supposed to be empty at 1 a.m. but it wasn't. Instead, Matt finds himself surrounded by those that usually ride with him during his day trips to the city. Some know him, some don't care, some have motives he can't understand, especially the 12 year old boy who continually bounces a blue rubber ball in the back.

They know he had an abusive father, they know he was shunned after the divorce, but worst of all, they know the hurt that came when his eldest daughter left. They were there when he turned to writing because the feelings would not be contained, and each is aware of the growing stack of rejection letters on his desk. They know almost everything about him.

But what they don't know is, he's brought a gun onto the L.

Michelle just wants to be left alone and can't understand why it's she who gets the late night call informing her that her father lies in a coma in the ICU, a Chicago L train crash victim.

At the hospital, when she sees her name in a story her father is writing on his laptop, she can't help but wonder if within his words is the key to why the L train crashed. The more she reads, the more real the characters become until finally, she can reach out and touch those that were there, including her father!

Michelle reads and is forced to face feelings she's buried deep while Matt must confront his own demons before he can carry out his plan. Will she be able to overcome the past and change the future? Does she even want to?

Will the story of the L be Matt's final words in his attempt to stop the pain?

Will the story of the L find Michelle's heart and allow her to stop the tragedy?

What Matt imagines is only the worst...what Michelle imagines, can only happen On the L.

the DeerHunter: paranormal literary adventure fantasy

The hunter Liam Michaels lies wounded, bleeding in the forests of the Canaan mountains. For him, the world is a bloody sky of red beneath which he can't move.

The shooter Ian Lambert stands above him, persecuted by his past. For him, there's only thoughts of how long he must now track the crippled buck.

Sarah Michaels, disillusioned with her marriage, has decided to cross the line. For her, taking off the ring means giving up the fairy tale.

Watching over all, the Lord of the Forest and keeper of the paths is witness and protector.

With brutal force, the truth of Liam's nature is thrust on him in the form of a buck's head, bleeding, dripping, and hollow. What he does with a second chance will redefine love and life.

With the guile of wolves, the war has come to claim him but Lambert takes what he wants and he wants the girl. But wanting her will bring only death.

As the long winter bends and folds into the spring of day, Sarah makes a discovery that questions second chances. Fearing hope has fled through the gap in the fence and into the Forest beyond, she is unaware of what follows.

The Wild Hunt is coming, savage enough to sweep mortals into the Otherworld. Liam, Lambert, and Sarah are prey for the riders of the storm, and stand in their path. As whispers of Cernunnos gather in the name of Herne the hunter, The Cervine is speaking like the sound of roots breaking soil, bringing the message that it is faith to love.

He chose love, finding passion in verse...
She chose him, and bent his passion...

***

the Dark Muse will come to find
there's more to mortal love than words...
Within a quill's ink, the story of Jason will bleed muses and
myths,
romance, seduction and betrayal.

*

Jason, a miller from 18th Century Carolina, seeks to escape a loveless marriage while on an Atlantic voyage to Italy, aboard a ship whose captain hides a pirate past. As he watches his wedding ring disappear beneath the waves, he's chosen to alter his path. Within his yearning to find true love, is a hidden passion for rhyme and verse. Taking strength from his words, he builds relationships with others onboard who share his passionate nature, including a supernatural muse who shapes his words and ideas, and ultimately, the truths he finds within himself.

*

When his poetry becomes more than a connection between himself and his emotions, Jason finds the opportunity for love that he seeks. But another has already claimed him. Exotic and erotic, the Dark Muse clings to his senses, forming the kiss on his lips.

Immortal, Leanan Sidhe is a Queen of the Fae, and daughter of Sea Gods. As Jason holds a hand out to the love he's been seeking, as lust crashes like Atlantic waves on the rock of his soul, his experiences with both will be defined in terms of betrayal...

So, what do you do when your son wants an alligator for a pet? What could possibly happen if you considered the possibility? Complete with illustrations, this is a seriously fun romp that tells the tale of Erik and his desire to own an alligator. A story for all kids, even the big ones!

Moments: poetry best of Dean Michael Christian

268 pages of an eclectic collection of over 180 formal and free verse poems that play on both the heartstrings and mind. A richness of language such as the masters used to use and unique to what is published today. Each poem has commentary about why or how it was written, sometimes giving a glimpse of the poet BrokenSword, aka Dean Michael Christian. These poems bring together reality and fantasy in a delicious way. Moments has something to savor for everyone, from love sonnets to witty Halloween ditties, from epic recreations of mythology to child-like innocence put down on paper.